Elizabeth's chest constricted, her hands grew damp. "I don't like it here," she said. "It's cold and dark, I want to go back!" She turned and made to run down the path, but Harry seized her and held her tight against him.

"Nay . . . you do me wrong. I am not a harlot. . . . Let me be—" she whispered, pushing against him. "Harry, let me go!"

He shook his head and kissed her with all the provocative ardor of experience and with the fierce new passion she had aroused in him. Elizabeth shrank back though her breathing quickened. "Wait—" she stammered. "Please—I'm frightened, let me think—"

He laughed at this; softly. Her mind swam.

He drew her down beside him. As he turned she felt the hard thudding of his heart and the hotness of his mouth. And when he put his hand on her breasts, she did not draw away. . . .

"A ZENITH OF ACCOMPLISHMENT . . . SUPERB AND VIVID."—*Boston Herald*

The
Winthrop
Woman

Anya Seton

FAWCETT CREST • NEW YORK

THE WINTHROP WOMAN

THIS BOOK CONTAINS THE COMPLETE TEXT OF THE
ORIGINAL HARDCOVER EDITION.

Published by Fawcett Crest Books, a unit of CBS Publications,
the Consumer Publishing Division of CBS Inc., by arrangement
with Houghton Mifflin Company.

ISBN: 0-449-23529-7

Printed in the United States of America

10   9   8   7   6   5   4   3   2

CONTENTS

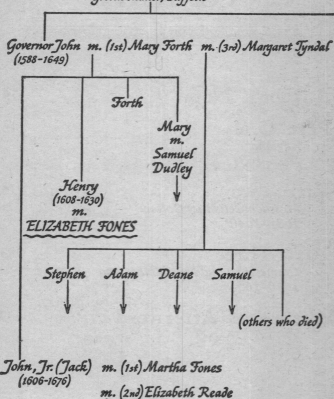

Adam Winthrop (1548-1623) *m.* Anne Browne
Groton Manor, Suffolk

Governor John *m.* (1st) Mary Forth *m.* (3rd) Margaret Tyndal
(1588-1649)

Forth

Mary
m.
Samuel
Dudley

Henry
(1608-1630)
m.
ELIZABETH FONES

Stephen   Adam   Deane   Samuel

(others who died)

John, Jr. (Jack)   *m.* (1st) Martha Fones
(1606-1676)
                    m. (2nd) Elizabeth Reade

Jane m. Thomas Gostlin
(1592-   )

Lucy   m.   Emmanuel
(1601-1679)   Downing

Many children, including Sir George Downing

Anne   m. Thomas Fones
(1586-1619)

Martha   m. John Winthrop, Jr.   Samuel
(1611-1634)

ELIZABETH   m. (1st) Henry   m. (2nd) Robert   m. (3rd) William
(1610-   )   Winthrop   Feake   Hallet

Winthrop Coat of Arms

Sir

my cosin being put back by weather
desireth vs, to goe with him now; for if
the winde be faire : as he cometh back
he shall be loath to put in : also J
am willing to see that place being moued
therto by sumthing which J heard from
a woman in this towne J intreat you to
pardon me that J ~~have bin~~ haue not
come to you to manifest my thankefulnes
and tender my ~~best~~ seruice to your selfe
and my sister the speedie going of my
cosen preuented me therin yet of this.

ouer remaine yours in all
vnfained loue and seruice
Elisabeth Slater

from abord.
the vessell

J pray you remember my best respects
to mr Lake we haue left your table bord
and frame and bellowes bords vppon the
cowhowse and the racke in the yeard.

1649.

*Facsimile letter to John Winthrop, Jr., from Elizabeth,
written under stress "from abord the vessell" at Pequot
(New London), Connecticut, 1649. It occurs in the text
on pages 580 and 581.*

AUTHOR'S NOTE

THIS book is built on a solid framework of facts; from these facts I have never knowingly deviated, nor changed a date or circumstance.

I have hoped that readers would be interested in following the story as it emerged for me in the original documents, and I have included excerpts from some of these documents, *verbatim,* except that for clarity I have occasionally modernized the spelling a bit.

I have also incorporated my characters' own written words into the dialogue whenever possible. All these characters are real; even Peyto and Telaka (though nameless in the references) are based on fact.

My determination to present authentic history has necessitated a scrupulous adherence to the findings of research. And I felt that this woman, with her passionate loves, dangers, tragedies, and courage, lived a life sufficiently dramatic without fortuitous inventions. Mine has been a job of re-creation and interpretation, "putting the flesh on the bones."

Elizabeth has thousands of descendants today; many of these—guided by Victorian genealogists and a biased presentation—have a vague feeling that they should be ashamed of her. A member of the Winthrop family, a hundred years ago, even went so far as to mutilate references to her in the original manuscripts. I believe that her life was significant and praiseworthy.

True, she was a rebel against the Puritan code, as exemplified by Governor John Winthrop the elder, who was her uncle, guardian, and father-in-law. She was also a woman who suffered the handicaps peculiar to her sex and her time, but she had the remarkable endurance which characterized all the first settlers—those who managed to survive.

This is one reason I have spent nearly four years in research and in writing about Elizabeth. Another reason was the attempt to vivify the founding of New England, and New Netherland days, in terms of a particular family—the Winthrops—and of Elizabeth, whose own history is commingled with national affairs. And I particularly wished to allot a proper proportion to the English background.

Almost a third of this book is given to Elizabeth's English life. It has startled me that our early emigrant ancestors are so often treated as though they arrived full-blown from a mysterious "across the sea," and suddenly turned into "Yankees." Lack of research and documentation explains this blank in many cases. I have been fortunate in tracing the English part of this story, since we have old Adam Winthrop's Diary to consult, John Winthrop's "Experiencia" and innumerable family letters; also I made two special and rewarding journeys across the ocean to see for myself. Groton Manor no longer exists as a building, but the topography is unchanged, even the mulberry tree still grows!

Here, among credit due to so many English friends, I wish particularly to thank the Reverend A. Brian Bird, the present vicar of Edwardstone and Groton in Suffolk. He has made intensive study of the seventeenth century Winthrop family—most of whom were born, and some of whom are buried, in his parish. During the course of my visits Mr. Bird and I became friends and he has been tirelessly helpful and enthusiastic about my project.

I also wish to thank present members of the English Winthrop line; and the Reverend G. H. Salter, Rector of St. Sepulchre's Church in London.

The English journeys enabled me to unravel many puzzling discrepancies, and uncover some bits of new data, such as where the *Lyon* sailed from in 1631, and other facts which I incorporated—though their details here would interest only genealogists.

William Hallet's association with the Earl of Bristol is not yet proven. It rests on Dorsetshire legend, but there is enough evidence to confirm the probability.

When we reach Massachusetts in the story, there is Governor Winthrop's Journal *The History of New England* as one guide, and I have preferred James Savage's edition of 1853, since is is not expurgated like the Hosmer edition of 1908, and is enriched by the most lavish and provocative notes.

Like every researcher into early New England families I also owe an enormous debt to the indefatigable Mr. Savage for his *Genealogical Dictionary of the First Settlers of New England* (Boston, 1860).

There is Lawrence Shaw Mayo's valuable *The Winthrop Family in America* (Boston, 1948). Also Robert C. Winthrop's *Life and Letters of John Winthrop* (1864) which is charming, but naturally partisan, and incomplete, since many manuscripts were found later.

The prime—the superlative—source for all this book is of course *The Winthrop Papers* published by the Massachusetts Historical Society, five volumes of them, dating from 1498 to 1649. And these I am fortunate enough to own, for I constantly needed to check with the sources. Much of the story is in the published *Winthrop Papers* for the delving, but does not, as yet, go far enough. So I have spent many an exciting hour in the Massachusetts Historical Society in Boston, deciphering as best I could the original, and so far unpublished, manuscripts and having many of them photostated. Some of my character interpretations are based on my examination of these people's handwritings. As one instance among many, little Martha Fones's childish scrawl as she tried to write to "Jack" Winthrop in their rather pathetic cipher, indicates, I think, Martha's temperament.

My devoted thanks to the entire staff of the Massachusetts Historical Society for their kindly patience with me on many occasions.

Several Boston friends have helped with Boston, Watertown and Ipswich sections of the book, and my particular gratitude goes to Mr. Kenneth Murdock and Mrs. Lovell Thompson.

Professor George E. McCracken of Drake University, Iowa, has helped greatly in disentangling the Feake family, both in person and by his articles on the Feakes in *The New York Genealogical and Biographical Record*.

The Connecticut section is thoroughly documented, by Indian deeds of sale, by Dutch journals (contained in the

Narratives of New Netherland edited by Dr. J. Franklin Jameson), by English translations in the exhaustive *Documents Relative to the Colonial History of the State of New York*, ed. by E. B. O'Callaghan (Albany, 1856); by the late Hendrik van Loon's private translation from the Dutch of one all-important paper relating to Elizabeth's troubled matrimonial affairs.

For the latter, and for permission to make use of her own extensive research on Elizabeth, especially in the Connecticut portion of her life, my fervent thanks are due to Mrs. Lydia Holland of Old Greenwich, to whom indeed I owe my first knowledge of Elizabeth nearly ten years ago, long before I thought of writing about her.

The Huntington History of Stamford and the two Mead Histories of Greenwich were useful (though not always accurate) for this section, and so has been my access to private papers, since Greenwich is my own home town, and I live on what was once Elizabeth's land. I wish to say here that the virtually unknown "Strickland Plains" massacre of the Siwanoy Indians by white men at what is now Cos Cob, Connecticut, seems to have been as shameful and devastating as any massacre—on either side—in our entire American history.

Seventeenth century spelling was a matter of individual choice, or momentary whim. "Feake" is spelled eleven different ways in the records. I have chosen to spell each name in the way its owner *usually* did.

The date discrepancy is always a nuisance when dealing with periods prior to 1752, when England finally adopted the Gregorian calendar. I have followed "New Style" for the years, and contemporary dating for days, but perhaps I should remind ardent naturalists that the day dates given would be eleven days later now, and that therefore seasons were more advanced than they seem.

The seventeenth century use of "Thee" is baffling: it seems only to have been used privately, and connotes strong emotion except in the case of parents to young children—and it was inconsistent. In Shakespeare when Petruchio speaks to Katherine he often uses both "thee" and "you" to her in the same speech. Margaret Winthrop in her sweet letters to John the elder, does the same. I have used the second person singular sparingly.

Rivulets of ink have been expended on the subject of Elizabeth's third marriage. It has fascinated genealogists. It is this personal and international imbroglio (and the astonishing amount of documents we have relating to it) which is responsible for Elizabeth's disrepute. I have weighed all the pros and cons, correlated many neglected clues, followed the chronology minutely and presented what I believe to be the truth.

I have tried to consult all source books, histories, and biographies for the period, both English and American. Also contemporary maps. I wish there was space enough to name each helpful person, but of the latter, besides those mentioned above, I do want to give special thanks to the following. To Brigadier-General John Ross Delafield of New York for his constant interest and illuminating letters to me; to Mr. Robert Winthrop of Old Westbury, Long Island, for his cordiality and the gift of *The Lion and the Hare;* to Colonel and Mrs. Francis Stoddard of New York for help with research; to the American Antiquarian Society at Worcester; to Mr. Robert C. Suggs, archeologist, for permission to "dig" with him on the Indian village sites in Greenwich and for the use of invaluable material relative to the Siwanoy Indians; to Mrs. John H. Tennent at the Bowne House Historical Society in Flushing, New York.

Some of these gracious people are Elizabeth's own descendants, and I hope that they will be pleased by this reconstruction of her life.

Out of the hundreds of source books I have used—and besides those specially mentioned above—I wish to acknowledge my particular indebtedness to *John Winthrop the Younger,* Thos. Franklin Waters; *Builders of the Bay Colony,* Samuel Eliot Morison; the colonial works of Perry Miller; *Three Episodes of Massachusetts History,* Charles Francis Adams; *The Winthrop Fleet of 1630,* Charles Edward Banks; *Genealogies and Histories of Watertown,* Henry Bond; all of Alice Morse Earle's books on colonial customs; *Every Day Life in the Massachusetts Bay Colony,* J. Francis Dow; *History of the State of New York,* John Romeyn Brodhead; *Dutch New York,* Esther Singleton.

PART ONE

England

1617–1631

1

ELIZABETH saw the hedge shadows lengthening across the dusty lane as the Fones family jogged north towards Groton. And yet, only a few minutes ago the church at Boxford had been full of light.

When the Foneses' hired cart had stopped at the "Fleece" in Boxford so that the horse might be watered at the inn-yard trough, across the village street in St. Mary's tower the great passing bell was ponderously tolling. Someone very old was dead, thought Elizabeth on the wagon seat, counting the strokes while admiring the deep melancholy bong, bong, bong. Perhaps the sexton would let her pull on the bell rope. The sexton at St. Sepulchre's in London never would, though she had begged.

Profiting by her mother's inattention, Elizabeth jumped off the wagon and darted over into the church. The little church was empty and smelled of the lilies which decorated the High Altar. There were candles and a silver cross too, the child saw with surprise. High overhead the great brazen voice clanged on, but Elizabeth forgot the invisible sexton; she was awed by the luminous quiet in the church and aston-ished by a feeling of delight. She stood in the center aisle staring about her until she realized that the focus of her pleasure was a great leaded window in the Lady Chapel. This window tinted in jeweled greens, blues, golds, deepened here and there by spots of translucent crimson, looked like a meadow of dream flowers. Elizabeth crept nearer and saw that all the glistening bits made a picture of a lady who was smiling, carried a rose in her hand and wore a shining crown. The whole lady shone with light, and Elizabeth longed to touch the glowing petal-smooth hem of the azure robe. Elizabeth's impulses usually resulted in action, and she had managed to clamber up onto the edge of the small altar and was reaching towards the lady when her father rushed into the church, crying, "So *there* you are, you naughty minx! Come here at once! Hasten!"

Elizabeth descended reluctantly, and pouting murmured that she had been looking at the beautiful colored window.

Thomas Fones gave the window an impatient glance. "Bah! An idolatrous Roman bauble left from the old days. Hurry up, Bess!"

His daughter obeyed, feeling dismay. "Roman" and "idolatrous" were both bad things, she had been told that often enough while learning her catechism. She climbed onto the cart seat beside her mother and soon forgot the window in the excitements of the journey.

The vanishing sun deepened the low Suffolk hills to violet, but the afterglow would last a long time yet, for it was May. Under a great oak beyond the blossoming hedge, a brown-smocked shepherd began to pipe a little homing tune to his flock. Elizabeth heard the tune and the obedient answering tinkle of the bellwether, then the admonitory barks of the sheep dog. The wagon trundled and bumped onward, but Elizabeth gazed eagerly back towards the shepherd, loving his strange little tune. And soon we'll be at Groton, she thought. Jack would be waiting for them, and Harry too. There'd be custard tarts and sage honey for supper, her mother had promised it.

Elizabeth looked up into her mother's face and was puzzled to see sadness in the gray eyes; puzzled and faintly resentful because her mother did not share her own anticipation—and it was seldom that communion between them failed. "When will we be there, Mama, tell when?" She plucked at her mother's velvet cloak.

"Soon," said Anne Fones. "You must have patience, Bess."

Elizabeth sighed and turned to her sister Martha for response. But Martha sat very straight on the other side of their mother, clenching the bunch of primroses they had picked earlier. She looked frightened, her eyes were fixed on the carter's broad sweaty back, she was chewing her lips. But then Martha was only six and frightened more often than not. Sammy, of course, did not count, he was nothing but a swaddled lump on their mother's lap, sucking greedily at the breast beneath the concealing cloak. And Father? She peered around the carter on the front seat to look at Thomas Fones. He was jogging on ahead and having some difficulty managing the horse they had picked up in Chelmsford. Father hardly ever rode and didn't like it. He was a Londoner and hated the country; besides he had pains in his joints. Pains were part of Father. Elizabeth was used to running upstairs from the kitchen with fresh coals for the warming pan, or up from their apothecary shop with a jar of leeches to suck blood from an aching knee or gouty toe.

"Ah, there's something flying by. I *want* it!" cried Elizabeth, distracted by a swift rush of desire for a tiny yellow shape that danced above the hawthorn hedge like a fairy. "Perhaps it *is* a fairy!" she added, catching her breath. Elizabeth's nurse had come from this part of Suffolk, and had seen many fairies.

Anne Fones put a firm hand on her child's shoulder as Elizabeth started to jump from the wagon. "Sit still, Bess," said the mother quietly. " 'Tis only a common brimstone butterfly. You'll see many more in the country."

Elizabeth subsided while she watched the ruby-spotted golden wings flitting off so free and airy into the gloaming, then some disturbing echo from her mother's voice reached her. She looked up and said with wonder, "Are you weeping? There's tears on your cheeks?"

Anne Fones bent her head quickly. "My heart is full because I'm coming home, Bess. These are Winthrop fields, and that wood there is where I used to play when I was seven years old like you. In a moment you'll see the pinnacles on Groton church, and behind them the chimneys of the Manor."

"Where?" cried Elizabeth. "Where?" She peered towards the skyline of elms. "Oh, *why* does this old nag walk so slow!"

But Martha shrank against her mother, and whispered, "I don't want to get there—I'm afraid . . ."

"Afraid of what?" cried Elizabeth impatiently. "It'll be rare sport with all our cousins to play with, and the ponies, calves, lambs, and dogs. Isn't it so, Mother?"

"No doubt," said Anne gently, feeling Martha stiffen. Martha ever shrank from new experience as much as Elizabeth exulted in it. *May God bless and guide both of them in the years to come, since I think I shall not be here to help them.* Anne felt the baby tugging angrily at her breast. The milk was lessening each day, though Sammy was but three months old. That might be because of the cough that wracked her at night, and the distaste for food which had come upon her of late. But it might be—aye. There was no use hiding from or rebelling against the Will of God which had certainly sent into her womb yet another tiny soul. *Was it sin to exhort God that this new baby might live, as three had not? Dorothy,* she thought—her first. Born right here at Groton, she had been found dead in her cradle after their return to London. *And little John and Anne—God had taken them back too, almost at once. His Will was inscrutable, and must not be questioned.* There came into her mind a blasphemous comparison. *A husband's will was inscrutable too, and obedience to it was dreary hard at times.* She glanced at the meager figure plodding ahead on the Chelmsford horse, at the wide beaver hat flopping over the hunched shoulders. *A sickly man in middle life who loved her in his fashion, and yet would not contain his lust and forbear a few weeks longer—as she had implored.*

"Mother, is it Groton Manor there?" cried Elizabeth, grabbing Anne's arm. Anne looked towards the four high chimneys twisted like barley sugar, saw the many gables, the oak beams of the half-timbering stoutly brown amidst the cream plaster walls. "Yes, dear."

"It's large," cried Elizabeth. "And grand, fine as the Lord Mayor of London's Manse!"

"No," Anne shook her head, ever watchful to curb Bess's exaggerations, "but it is a fair manor house." It had been built way back in 1558, the first year of the good old Queen's reign. It was partially constructed with bricks and stones from a little priory which had belonged to Bury St. Edmunds and once flourished here, before King Harry had seen the wickedness of papacy and decreed the Dissolution. Anne's grandfather, Adam Winthrop, had been a wealthy Suffolk clothier at Lavenham but he had by no means confined his talents to the country since he had risen to be Master of the Clothworkers' Guild in London. And like many another he had felt the need to celebrate his successes by joining the gentry. This was easily accomplished by means of a coat of arms awarded by the Royal College of Heralds and a manor grant bought from the King. The Winthrops were henceforth esquires and Lords of Groton Manor. To this position Anne had been born, and had not escaped pangs when she exchanged it for that of a London apothecary's wife, and had gone to live in a cramped town house above the shop in the Old Bailey. But Thomas Fones had been handsome enough eleven years ago, and he was well educated and prosperous; moreover, the eldest of three daughters must not be laggard in accepting her father's arrangement for any suitable marriage.

They entered the drive between two stone gateposts bearing the Winthrop arms. The carter's whip flicked the horse, Thomas Fones's mare whinnied greeting towards the stables and jumped forward, nearly unseating him. At once a half-dozen dogs rushed towards them barking furiously, the great front door swung open, and two boys tumbled through, calling welcome.

"Lord, Lord, what a hurly-burly!" cried Elizabeth with satisfaction.

"Bess!" said her mother nervously. "You MUST guard your tongue, we've taught you not to take the name of God in vain, and especially not here. Your grandmother and your Uncle John would be angry."

Bess, waving with abandon to her cousins, scarcely heeded the rebuke, though one part of it penetrated. She was afraid of Uncle John, who had stayed with them in London and once given her a severe lecture on her sins.

At her mother's nod of permission she jumped off the wagon and ran towards the boys. Jack rushed to meet her and the cousins exchanged a hearty kiss. She would have kissed Harry too but he ducked and said, "Let me be, your face is dirty—hug *him* instead"—and thrust a woolly ball of mastiff puppy at her. Elizabeth willingly complied. Harry was always teasing, his two visits to London had taught her that, and she preferred kissing the puppy. She loved Jack better anyway, he was merry and kind and always seemed to like her. They went into the huge firelit hall to be greeted by the rest of the family and there was a lot more kissing; an irksome interlude for Elizabeth and a terrifying ordeal for Martha, who clung to her mother and choked back tears.

Kisses of welcome and departure were ritual. The men kissed each other gravely on the cheek, the women were nearly as ceremonious, the Winthrops each said solemnly as they kissed, "God be praised for your safe journey here," to which Anne and Thomas Fones replied, "God be praised that we find you all in health."

"Except Forth and Mary," said Mistress Winthrop, the grandmother. "They are sorely ill with the measles, but will no doubt mend in God's own time. Anne, cleanse yourself and your children, you have your old room, then descend for prayers before we sup."

"Yes, Mother," said Anne Fones, curtseying, and the years she had been away melted to nothing. Her mother was as erect, assured and sharp-eyed as ever. Her pointed chin rested upon a ruff so starched and glossy white that it dazzled. Her cap and apron were edged with the finest pillow lace. Her gown of dove-gray silk rustled as it always had from the brisk motions of her body. In her father too there was little change, thought Anne, deeply comforted. Adam was stouter perhaps, his cheeks and nose redder from the tiny broken veins, his vigorous curls grayer, but as he stood by the fire, legs wide-spread, warming his back and beaming at her, he looked as he always had—the contented English squire and patriarch.

Anne's two sisters were present too. Jane Gostlin with her new husband had driven over from their home for the welcoming, and sixteen-year-old Lucy; but having greeted them, Anne lost no time in obeying her mother, which meant retrieving Elizabeth who had already run out to the entrancing dog- and horse-filled courtyard with the boys. As Anne passed again through the hall with the mutinous Elizabeth in tow, she asked of Mistress Winthrop the question which had been fretting her.

"Where is Brother John, my mother? Does he not mean to greet us too?"

Mistress Winthrop frowned down at Elizabeth. "You are too lax with that child, Anne, I can see she wants chastisement." The old woman added in a lower voice, "John is in his closet, wrestling with his soul and the weakness of the flesh. He fasts much and groans and prays. He has been thus since the affliction God sent him in December."

Anne nodded slowly, then motioned Elizabeth to pick up a candle. With Sam in her arms, she led her two little daughters upstairs. Elizabeth, carefully holding the lighted candle, said nothing as they went down a dark twisting passage to another wing and entered a richly furnished bedroom, where a little maid in a mobcap was poking at the fire. The child even, with unusual restraint, waited until the maid had gone, and Anne had put the sleeping baby on the great four-poster bed, before saying, "Why does Uncle John groan and pray, Mother? What affliction did God send him?"

Anne did not answer, while she poured hot water from the copper kettle the maid had left by the fire and began to wash Martha's pallid face.

At last she said, "Your Uncle John's young wife died in childbed, Bess, last winter."

Elizabeth frowned. "I thought my cousin's mother went to heaven *long* ago."

"That was the first one," said Anne, startled as she often was when her feather-brained child showed awareness of mature concerns. "The mother of young John and Harry and Forth and Mary died two years back, not"—she added in spite of herself—"so *very* long ago."

Two wives dead, Anne thought—Mary and Thomasine, and John himself just twenty-nine. Soon there will be another wife, no matter how much he is groaning and praying now. How soon? And when my own time comes—she looked at her two little girls and the baby on the bed. How soon will Thomas find a new mother for these? She shut her eyes, then walked to the window. Martha curled up on the brocaded counterpane with the baby and fell instantly asleep. But Elizabeth followed her mother and pressed in beside her at the leaded casement. "There's the moon," said the child softly. "It looks nearer than in London. I can see the man in it with his lantern and his dog."

"Can you, Bess?" Anne put her arm around Elizabeth. "So could I, once, and from this very window."

"Sing the 'Man in the Moon,' Mother—sing it, I pray you."

Anne smiled and sang in a low breathy voice:

"The man in the moon came down too soon and
    asked the way to Norwich,
He went by the south and burnt his mouth
    with eating of cold pease porridge."

Elizabeth gurgled. "Such a silly man, but perhaps on the moon—" She stopped because her mother had gone into a paroxysm of coughing. Elizabeth was not disturbed, Mother always coughed a lot, but she did hope it would not wake Martha or the baby; it was seldom she had her mother all to herself. The younger children did not wake, but Elizabeth's moment passed anyway, for Thomas Fones flung open the door saying, "Come, come wife, what's keeping you, your family waits below." His scraggy eyebrows drew together and he added with a blend of irritation and concern, "Where's the hoarhound potion I made you for that cough, why don't you take it?"

Anne sank onto the bed and motioned towards the traveling coffer. Thomas took out a flask, poured some drops into a cup and gave it to her. "There's damp in this house," he said peevishly. "I feel it. See that these maids warm the bed properly. I dislike very much sleeping away from home, I shall suffer for it. Had it not been that you implored me—"

"The country may do you good, Thomas," said Anne faintly, "and it does give me pleasure—to be here once more . . ."

"Well," he said with an anxious smile, not devoid of tenderness, "since we *are* here—but hurry. The Winthrops do not like to be kept waiting, especially your brother, John. He has come down and will lead the evening prayers."

Is Father afraid of Uncle John too? thought Elizabeth startled.

The Winthrop family were gathered in the low-ceilinged parlor next the Hall. It was a room they used for the normal routine of living, and it was beautiful; richly paneled with linen-fold, and a great fire crackling beneath the carved plaster mantel. Elizabeth, kneeling beside her mother and father, and trying hard to keep awake, stared around the room while Uncle John's voice went on and on. He had been intoning a psalm when the Fones family crept in. He had turned his long haggard face towards them and given them a grave bow, and paused until they were kneeling on the bright Turkey rug with the others, and then he had continued. He was dressed in mourning black for his wife, of course, with a small prickly-looking ruff around his neck. His wavy hair fell down to the ruff; it was the color of a chestnut, so were his mustache and small pointed beard. His eyes were light and not really unkind, Elizabeth thought, but they didn't look as though there'd ever be a twinkle in them; though Grandfather's did, and Jack's. Her own gaze blurred, while Uncle John's voice droned on. She began to nod and felt her mother's hand give a warning shake.

Elizabeth blushed, anxious not to show herself a sleepy baby before Jack and Harry who knelt perfectly still on the other side of the room near the servants. But there were never long prayers and psalms like this at home. They had to be endured only in church on Sundays, and there in London at their parish church of St. Sepulchre's the service was all read out of the prayer book. You knew when it would end.

Elizabeth's knees began to throb, her empty stomach growled. All at once her nose tickled unmercifully. She made no effort to restrain the result—a vociferous and lusty sneeze. This pleasing sensation repeated itself at once and more loudly. Young Lucy Winthrop knelt in front of Elizabeth and the sneeze sprayed her bare neck. She turned and glared at her niece, while Uncle John stopped in the middle of an "And furthermore, Dear Lord, we beseech . . ." to rest his somber gaze on Elizabeth.

"No child is too young to observe proper decorum and reverence in the Presence of the Lord," he said and shifted his eyes towards Harry who had dissolved into hiccupping giggles. "Henry, you will leave the room—Anne and Thomas, you must take measures as to the conduct of your own child."

"Oh, well-a-day, my son," interrupted Adam Winthrop suddenly from his chair of privilege by the fire. "Be not so harsh, a sneeze or two is no great matter, and in the truth though you pray eloquently—'pie et eloquenter orabis'—" The old man paused, suddenly smiling, to savor the little Latin tag. "None the less, to everything there is a season and a time for every purpose. Now our visitors are weary, and it is time for food."

Elizabeth looked at her grandfather with gratitude, marveling that even *he* dared rebuke his awesome son, who had flushed, and drawn his breath in. She was the more amazed that after a moment her Uncle John answered humbly, "Aye, sir—you are right. The devil ever lures me by new guises, and it may be now by unworthy pride in my own eloquence." He bowed his head and clasping his hands again added, "We will now say all together—'Lighten our darkness, we beseech thee, O Lord; and by thy great mercy defend us from all perils and dangers of this night; for the love of thine only Son, our Saviour, Jesus Christ. AMEN."

The ordeal was over; Elizabeth escaped further scolding, though when they did go to the supper table she was too tired to enjoy the custards for which she had longed. The candles danced before Elizabeth's heavy eyes. In her heart was a confused rebellion, but even through this and her weariness, her natural optimism remained. Though the joys of Groton Manor were dampened tonight by a disapproving atmosphere to which she was unaccustomed, and by the boredom of those interminable prayers, surely everything would be all right tomorrow. She would be very, very good, and besides there was always Jack. She looked at him where he sat across the table—a stocky dark boy of eleven, quietly munching his rabbit pasty, silent as children were expected to be. Still, from the alert cock to his head you could tell he was listening to the conversation between his father and grandfather. Jack did not talk much but he always knew what was going on around him. He proved it now, as he felt Elizabeth's stare. He met her eyes across the table, smiled and gave her a small heartening wink.

Elizabeth's optimism was justified by reason of two unexpected circumstances, and the ensuing summer weeks flowed along happily. The children romped together in pasture and farmyard, they raced on shaggy ponies, they sailed chips amidst protesting ducks on the pond, they wandered the nearby woods and stuffed themselves with wild strawberries. They explored all the fascinating features of the Manor lands; the mill with its big slowly turning sails, the little heath where Harry had once found some Roman coins, the ruins of a castle haunted by a headless lady in gray. The miller's children said so, and that you could hear the lady moaning on nights of the new moon. Elizabeth was eager to creep out of the Manor House and try to hear the moans, but Jack said no. It would not be a seemly thing to do.

It was not only because his elders trusted Jack to care for the younger children that they all had so much freedom in those early summer weeks of 1617, but that the day after the Foneses' arrival John Winthrop had been summoned to London on business connected with his first wife's estate, and he took Thomas Fones back with him, to the apothecary's flattered relief. And as it happened, the morning after the departure of the two men, Mistress Winthrop slipped on the stairs and went to bed with a cracked ankle. Groton, freed from the pious restraint of mother and son and the atmosphere of discontented ill health diffused by Thomas, burst forth into gaiety. Prayers were short and sometimes forgotten, a good deal more wine than usual was consumed. After supper, of nights, Adam would take out his recorder and, tootling merrily, urge all the young people to sing the jolly catches and rounds of his Elizabethan boyhood. One day

he sent word to the village that he would require musicians.
He summoned Betts the thatcher who played the fiddle, and
told him to bring others with him, a piper and a drummer at
least. Groton Manor would have dancing that night. At
dinner Adam added an extra flagon of stout to his usual
cups of wine, his brown eyes sparkled as bright as his
grandsons', his cheeks and nose turned mulberry, his white
curls quivered, his barrel body shook with joviality as it
strained the seams of his old-fashioned bottle-green doublet.
The doublet had slashed red sleeves, and was trimmed with
ribbons.

"Aye, daughter," he said to Anne in response to her
startled look when he appeared in this gay garment. "A pox
on long faces and I'll not wear mourning today. 'Tis over a
half-year gone since John's poor wife died, God rest her
soul—and what's more, daughter, we must celebrate today
our King Jamie's birthday, like all loyal Englishmen."

Anne smiled, looking at her father with affection. This
was the way life used to be at Groton in her girlhood. "Yes,"
she said, "I remember how merrily we did celebrate Queen
Bess's birthday long ago—and May Day and Christmastide
so blithely—though Thomas does not hold with that . . . I
cannot think it wrong."

"Nor I, my dear," said the old squire. " 'Tis your mother
and brother John who have come to think so here, but I'll
stick to the old customs long as I live."

"Father—Father!" cried Lucy Winthrop, stamping hard
on the treadle of her spinning wheel. "You would not still
have us follow Papist superstitions, I hope!" Lucy was a thin
brown girl of sixteen, stoop-shouldered and high-nosed. She
was her mother's pet, and knew it, and she had listened with
pressed lips to the conversation between her father and sister.

They were sitting in the small paneled parlor, Anne and
her father ensconced in the great court chairs on either side
of a small crackling fire, for though it was June 19 a chill
east wind blew from the sea that linked their Suffolk coast
with Holland. The boys had ridden off, as usual in summer,
for two hours of Latin tutoring with Mr. Nicholson, the
rector. The youngest Winthrops, Forth and Mary, had recovered from the measles and were with their grandmother
in the great bedchamber upstairs, reciting the alphabet to
her from their hornbooks. Though Mistress Winthrop was
still in great pain from her ankle, she yet managed to supervise the education of the motherless young Winthrops. The

Fones children already knew their hornbooks, indeed Elizabeth read and wrote quite well, but the grandmother had allotted tasks to the Fones girls too since Anne seemed to have no ability for systematic discipline.

Martha had been told to sort wool near her Aunt Lucy, who sat on the window seat spinning. Elizabeth had been presented with a canvas sampler, needle and silk and commanded to embroider her name and then the alphabet upon it—an occupation she detested. The silk snarled, and broke when she yanked at it, the needle pricked her fingers, the E.L.I.Z. were lumpy little botches. She had almost completely managed to avoid working on the sampler, by crouching over it so that her long dark curls made a shield, and by the further duplicity of hiding the result from inquirers, saying she was going to surprise them with her remarkable progress later. That there would inevitably be a day of exposure did not bother her, something would take care of it, the sampler would get finished—maybe even by Puck, she thought —if she put bread and cream out for him in the kitchen. There were several hobgoblins that did good deeds in the night.

Elizabeth was often puzzled by her elders' remarks and she now lifted her head from the sampler and addressed her grandfather. "Why are Papists so wicked, sir? Our King's mother was a Papist, was she not? The 'fair and feckless Marie—Queen o' Scots,' " said Elizabeth, quoting a phrase she had heard used in London.

"Damme, if little pitchers haven't big ears!" Adam chuckled, and tapped the warm bowl of his clay pipe against his knee. "The Papists are wicked, my dear, because our good Queen, for whom ye're named, said they were, 'tis not to be questioned . . . forbye I can remember how it was when I was a wee lad in the time o' Bloody Mary—the screams and the agonies, and the burnings of us Protestants. 'Twas dreadful!"

Elizabeth considered this with interest. Uncle John owned a Foxe's *Book of Martyrs* and she with all the other children had pored over the shivery woodcuts of tortures and burnings. So there were Papists who were bad, and Protestants like her family who were good, only, thought Elizabeth frowning, there seemed to be two kinds of Protestants. There was a kind who had candles and a cross like in the Boxford church and who bowed at the name of Jesus and who kept Saint's Days and Christmas, as Grandfather did and Mother too. But then there was another kind who hated all those things. Uncle John and Grandmother and Aunt Lucy seemed to be that kind. They had a name that also began with P. "Puh, Puh, Puh—" chanted Elizabeth experimentally under her breath, "Puh, Puh, Papist, Puh, Puh, Protestant, Puh, Puh, Puritan. . . ."

"What's that you're saying, you naughty child!" cried Lucy, scowling at the culprit. "Anne, did you hear what she said?"

Anne sighed, and eased to the other arm the heavy baby who had finished suckling. "Bess is forever making up little songs, it does no harm."

"That word she used, 'Puritan,'" snapped Lucy. "What do you mean by it, Elizabeth?"

The child stared at her aunt, startled at this vehemence. "Old Giles, the Thetford tinker, last week when he was here at the Manor, he was laughing with the maids, and I heard him say . . ." Elizabeth paused, then went on in a deep voice that passably imitated a thick Norfolk accent, "'The Winthrops has altered o' late, that they have! Turned Puritan I hear, leastwise *young* squire has, there's a mort o' them canting, psalm-whining Puritans about these parts nowadays!'"

"Bess!" cried Anne shocked. "You mustn't listen to or repeat things you don't understand!" She bit her lips, wondering suddenly if she herself quite understood. "Puritan" was a insulting epithet, never used kindly, and yet was that not precisely what John and so many others in the eastern counties were trying to do? "Purify" their beloved church of its more venal bishops and of the Roman idolatries, so as to rely only on the Word of God for all their worship—as put forth in the Bible, and in no other place.

Lucy twitched her shoulders and returned to her spinning. "You see," she said, "what comes of letting children roam about unhindered, to learn foul words . . . and if you will permit me, Father," she glanced at Adam who was watching his two daughters quizzically, "my conscience bids me say that all this winebibbing, and talk of dancing and romping much disturbs my mother on her bed of pain, and will certainly displease my brother when he returns home."

"Indeed," said Adam, puffing Virginia tobacco smoke through his nostrils. He crossed his plump black velvet thighs. "Well, my conscience bids ME say, miss—that I am still master here at Groton, that I understand my son quite as

well as you do, and that no chit of sixteen has leave to censure her elders!"

Lucy flushed crimson, Elizabeth's eyes sparkled, but Martha,
frightened as always by any sort of adult anger, let fall the
piles of wool and ran to hide her face on her mother's lap.

Anne smoothed the silky brown head. What a fuss about
nothing, she thought; surely it is the Will of God that we
should all be happy, and knew at once what a
foolish spineless thought that was. John, and Mr. Nicholson,
the Groton rector, said that was not the Will of God at all.
He wanted them to mortify the flesh, and earn salvation. If
I were not so weary, Anne thought, I could worry more about
my own and the babies' souls. And the new one . . . dear
God, don't let it die—or me—when it is born . . .

Adam held his revelry that night in honor of the King and
it was to be—by reason of a guest who came to Groton—an
occasion which affected all their lives. The old squire had
sent his undergroom with invitations to several of the neighboring big houses, and was particularly gratified by the unexpected acceptance of Lord and Lady deVere who were
temporarily in residence at their country seat near Hadleigh,
and were kin to the Earl of Oxford. No one so exalted had
ever honored Groton Manor before. Even Mistress Winthrop
was pleased when she heard of this, and made arrangements
to have herself carried downstairs. Although Lord deVere was
a worldly peer, and spent much time at court where it was
well known that matters of strict decorum and religious reform were not as important as they should be, still he was
a Baron, and it was impossible not to feel flattered by his
graciousness. True, Adam was a generation removed from the
Suffolk clothier who had become first squire of Groton
Manor, yet Mistress Winthrop herself could claim no aristocratic tinge at all. She had been plain Anne Browne of
Edwardstone, a yeoman's daughter. She ordered her best dress
of black brocaded velvet to be brought from its chest and
pressed, and by six o'clock she was downstairs and installed
in the Great Hall with her injured ankle propped on a
footstool. She wore her four gold rings, and even carried a
small painted fan that had some French writing on it,
"L'amour se trouve aux fleurs, dans la beauté de ses coeurs."

Anne, waiting as they all were for the first guests to arrive,
watched her mother with amusement, knowing that when the
deVeres came, the old lady would find opportunity to read

out the motto on the fan. She was proud of her French, which she had learned from a Belgian lacemaker who had settled in the village of Edwardstone.

"Now ye look like yourself again, daughter," said Adam, coming up to Anne and pinching her cheek. "Like my pretty lass that was the fairest bride in Suffolk when she wed . . ." He lowered his voice. "I didn't give ye to a bad husband, did I, darling?" he said anxiously. "Thomas Fones is good to you?"

"Oh yes, Father . . . He's a fine man . . ."

Adam nodded, satisfied at once, unwilling to have any disquiet spoil the satisfaction of his party. His family, dressed as richly as any gentry in the land, affirmed his prosperity, as did this great room glowing with tapestries, lit by a hundred candles, and the carved oak table with its bulbous legs, its beeswaxed board loaded already with punch bowls and cold pasties and flagons of nut-brown ale, while the servants scurried back and forth to the kitchen for fresh supplies. Four musicians were waiting too by the screen that led to the parlor—the fiddler, a gittern player, a piper and a little drummer. Lucy was even prepared to play on the virginals, if the deVeres were inclined for singing. Nobody could deem the entertainment niggardly.

"That's a fair little wench you've got there, Anne," said the old man, his complacent eye suddenly caught by Elizabeth, who was sitting sedately as near the fascinating drummer as she could get, and whispering to Jack. The younger children had been put to bed, and Elizabeth was very conscious of privilege and of her rustling green taffeta dress, edged with silver lace exactly like her mother's. " 'Tis a pity she has the Winthrop nose," the grandfather added, "a mite long for a girl—my old grandame always used to say the devil tweaked the first Winthrop's nose in passing one black night—but wi' that mass o' hair and those big eyes and cheeks like a blaze o' poppies, she'll win many a lad's heart someday."

Anne smiled. "Bess loves Jack, child though she is." She broke off. "Look at Harry!"

Young Henry had been taking copious samples from the punch bowl, and was quite tipsy. He was also intoxicated by the occasion, and by a desire to impress Bess who was being dignified and as priggish as Aunt Lucy. Acting on wild impulse Harry had seized a handful of walnuts from the table, and swarming up the fireplace like a monkey, perched on the mantel, six feet above the hearth. There he crouched, teetering on the narrow ledge, his long bright curls too near the candles, and began to pelt his brother and Elizabeth with the nuts.

"Come down, sir—" shouted Adam, striding down the Hall. "Come down at once!" Harry, whose hair was beginning to singe, and who had begun to feel giddy, would have obeyed but the drop looked formidable from the top, and he swayed uncertainly.

"He'll fall . . . !" Lucy shrilled. But he did not. Jack acted with the speed and instant comprehension which were to be his all his life, and before their grandfather got there, he had pulled a stool to the hearth, got up on it and scooped his younger brother down. "You dunce," he said good-humoredly, yet with an exasperation which was nearly adult. "Why do you always have to play the fool!"

Harry flushed, muttered something and glared at Elizabeth whom he obscurely blamed for all this. Adam strode up and dealt his grandson a resounding box on the ear, and there would have been other punishment except for the pounding of the great bronze door knocker. The Waldegraves had arrived. Adam immediately forgot his grandson, who vanished to spend the next hour in the pantry sulkily filching comfits from the pastry table whenever the cook's back was turned.

Fortunately—since the food and wine could not be touched nor the musicians play until they came—Lord and Lady deVere were not tardy. They arrived in one of the new German coaches drawn by four horses, and their entrance into Groton park was announced by a bugle strain from the outrider.

The noble couple swept into the hall on a wave of musk and magnificence, dispensing gracious smiles and nods. Mistress Winthrop murmured apology for her condition while Anne and Lucy curtseyed low. Elizabeth, though nobody saw her, curtseyed too, and stared in admiration. She had seen fine folk pass on the London streets, but never near like this. The deVeres were a blaze of lace and gold and jewels. The Baron's doublet was brocaded with roses, his hose were blue, there were red rosettes on his silver shoes, his long curled hair and pointed beard glistened above the wired Valenciennes collar. The Baroness wore one of the enormous new-style farthingales Queen Anne had introduced; it stood out around her hips like a silk tent. Her greased hair was swept up high over pads and studded with sham jewels. The neck of her pointed bodice was cut so low you could see a little bit of her

stomach between her breasts. Elizabeth thought that interesting, and she noted too that the lady did not seem very
clean. There were shadows in the creases of her neck, a large
stain of what looked like wine on the embroidered skirt; a
strong smell of sweat mingled with the musk, and the heavily
beringed hand had black fingernails. It must be that she was
so rich and grand she did not have to wash, thought Elizabeth
enviously.

So entranced was Elizabeth by the deVeres that for a
while she did not notice they had brought people with them,
two ladies and a gentleman. These weren't nearly as impressive. The younger lady wore red silk edged with gold lace,
and had some little pearls around her neck, yet she was
somewhat dowdy. She was dark and plump and had a
motherly air, like the Winthrops' little spaniel bitch, Trudy.

Jack, as the elder grandson and eventual heir to Groton
Manor, had been taken around and introduced to all these
people, but being now dismissed, he came back to Elizabeth,
who greeted him eagerly. "Who's *them?*" she whispered,
"that came with the lord . . . I like the red one, she looks
like Trudy."

Jack's brown eyes crinkled. "Mayhap she does! 'Tis a
Mistress Margaret Tyndal, and her brother, Arthur, and
their mother, Lady Tyndal. They've come with the deVeres
from Essex near Castle Hedingham where the Earl of Oxford lives."

"Are these Tyndals noble too?" asked Elizabeth, thinking
how gloriously she could boast to her friend the goldsmith's
daughter when she got back to London.

"No," said Jack. "Lady Tyndal's husband was a knight,
a Master of Chancery . . . He was murdered last year by a
madman."

"Oh," breathed Elizabeth, staring with all her eyes at
Margaret Tyndal, who didn't look at all like someone whose
father had been murdered.

Healths were drunk to King James and his Queen, and
to their children: Charles, the Prince of Wales, and Elizabeth,
the Queen of Bohemia. The Baron praised the Winthrop
malmsey, and after several cupfuls proceeded to tell an exceedingly coarse story. It was about his sovereign, and two
pretty Scottish lads. Mistress Winthrop did not hear the anecdote; Lucy, the children and most of the neighbors did not
understand it, but Anne who lived in London, blushed, while
Adam roared out between dismay and laughter, "Damme,

my lord—d'ye mean our King must have his catamites? . . .
I'd thought him a roystering full-blooded *wencher!*"

"Ah, that's as may be," answered the Baron smiling, but
with a shade of reserve to indicate that this country squire
could scarcely be supposed to know what occurred at Court.
"What of the dancing now?" went on deVere. "Let's see how
Groton music sounds . . ." His pale eyes roved over the assembled women and lit on Anne. "Mistress Fones shall
dance with me. I'll teach her the latest galliard."

Anne's heart sank. The wine she had drunk no longer sus-
tained her, an aching tiredness flowed through her bones, but
there could be no refusal. She accepted the Baron's moist
hand, followed his high prancing steps as best she could
and tried to avoid both his foul breath and the amorous looks
he bestowed on her. Adam danced with the Baroness, the
rest of the company paired off; the fiddler squeaked, the
gittern plinked, the piper tootled, and the village drummer,
much awed by the grandeur of the occasion, timidly thumped
his tabour when he thought of it.

Nobody noticed the great door open, nor saw the tall man
in black who stopped in astonishment to stare at the gyrating
couples. He watched them for a moment, then walked across
the end of the room to Mistress Winthrop's chair. "For the
love of heaven, my mother—what is the meaning of this?"
he said in her ear as he kissed her cheek.

The old lady had been dozing. "Mercy, what a startle!
Why, John, son, your letter said—we didn't look for you till
Thursday . . . 'tis the King's birthday we celebrate, your
father did wish it . . . and imagine, the deVeres have actually
honored us!"

"So I see," said John Winthrop. "And I have a very good
notion as to why." He had been hearing of deVere in London.
The Baron was out of favor at court, had run up huge gam-
bling debts, there was talk of bankruptcy. The favor and in-
ded more tangible help of a prosperous neighbor might well
be useful. Still it was agreeable to be on equal footing with a
nobleman. John withdrew behind his mother's big chair and
gazed thoughtfully at the dancers.

On all this trip to London John had been wrestling with his
soul, endeavoring to follow the rigid course of discipline he
had laid out for himself. He had avoided all drink but water,
he had eschewed smoking of which he had been overly
fond. He had read nothing but the Scriptures, spoken no ungodly word. He had kept the Sabbaths with careful piety and

found a nonconformist church where the minister bravely ignored the ceremonies ordained by the bishops. Above all John had resisted the lewdness of the flesh which had bedeviled him since his wife's death, and there had been a moment of hideous temptation one night on the Chepe—a beautiful Spanish whore. God had rewarded him. Every business matter had been decided in his favor, the final settlement of his first wife's estate had been made. He had returned home with his money-bag far heavier than when he started. But his mood was lighter. A month ago this frivolous scene would have disgusted him, he would have felt it his duty to remonstrate with his father. But now as he watched the bright couples change from the galliard to a livelier hay and listened to the cheerful music he began to wonder if extreme asceticism were not another of the Devil's guises for Pride, for somewhere on the journey home the certainty of righteousness had vanished. And it is true, he thought, that David saw no harm in dancing, and that Our Blessed Lord smiled on the feast at Cana. "Who is that young gentlewoman in red?" he suddenly asked his mother. "The one dancing with Edward Waldegrave."

Mrs. Winthrop squinted towards a group near the door, and said, "Oh, 'tis Margaret Tyndal, a spinster. Her brother, Arthur, is yonder by the stairs, and there is her mother, Lady Tyndal, dancing—and at her age I find it unbecoming—with your father."

"Indeed," said John, "not the family of Sir John Tyndal who was cut off in London by the mad assassin last year?"

"The very one," said his mother. "They have large property at Much Maplested in Essex. I hear that the young gentlewoman is well dowered."

John said nothing for a moment, as he watched Margaret. He thought her somewhat short and dumpy and saw that she was unskilled at dancing, but the round face between the bobbing round ringlets was comely enough, and as she answered something said to her by young Waldegrave she showed a singularly sweet smile. "She seems not far from thirty," he remarked. "Strange that she has not married . . . perhaps some physical weakness we see not . . ."

His mother shot him a shrewd look. "I believe it's nothing of the kind. I had some converse earlier with Lady Tyndal. Mistress Margaret has been betrothed but the man died, and then this tragedy to her father, and besides I believe the brother is most proud, wishes a great match for his sister."

John listened with the grave attention which was characteristic of him but said no more except, "She has rather a sensible air, though I cannot say as much for her scarlet and gold dress, uncommon garish for a God-fearing maiden." The music and dancing stopped suddenly. John walked to the center of the Hall and greeted his father, who let out a roar of delight and embraced him heartily. "Welcome, welcome, my son! A splendid surprise! We have company, you see, to honor the King's birthday. My Lord and Lady deVere are here, and with them the Tyndals. Let me present you at once."

"It will give me much pleasure," said John and he smiled.

His sisters watched him with astonishment. Lucy, whom John had often urged to beware of the world, had been ready to deny all pleasure in this festivity, and point out that she was but obeying their father's regrettable orders, but she saw that this denial would not be necessary. John showed no signs of disapproval and was chatting easily with the deVeres and Tyndals. He fetched a cup of wine and presented it to Mistress Margaret, and he even drank some himself, which further amazed Lucy since he had been for some months denouncing wine as the devil's spittle. Anne saw deeper into her brother. From childhood he had been prone to sudden variations of mood, but it was the time he had spent at Trinity College in Cambridge and met many gentlemen under Puritan influence which had given these moods so strong a religious tinge. That and the deaths of his two wives, of course, thought Anne sighing. Suddenly she looked at her brother and Mistress Tyndal with sharp attention.

Margaret and John had seated themselves on a cushioned bench, and they were talking gravely. The gravity did not preclude another element no discerning woman could have missed. John's long rather harsh face showed an unmistakable desire to please, while about Margaret there was a suggestion of coquetry. Her plump cheeks were pink, her fingers twisted a little scented pomander she wore at her girdle and her round bosom beneath the scarlet taffeta rose and fell more rapidly than recovery from the dancing would explain.

"Is it possible?" Anne murmured . . . "so soon and so quickly . . . ?" And knew that it was. John had not loved Mary Forth, his first wife whom he had married at seventeen, and who had been some years older, but for little Thomasine Clopton, his second, he had shown affection and grief. Had felt them too, she knew—John was no hypocrite. It is simply the practical way of men, she thought bitterly. A wife is needed—as house directress, as mother to the children, as purveyor of yet more land and property, as . . . ah yes, as the fulfiller of one role above all. She looked at the sensual red curves of John's mouth between the russet mustache and beard, at the thin flare of his nostrils. It is better to marry than to burn, she thought, and how willingly John would again follow that woman-despising apostle's advice.

"Mistress Fones," said a thick voice beside her. "Will you pledge me in a cup of wine?" She started and looked up at Lord deVere, who stood in front of her swaying a little. "Come, sweetheart, why so dismal?" he added, putting his thick sweating hand on her neck. "Will you show me the Manor gallery? I've heard you have a portrait by King Harry's painter fellow, Holbein."

"I beg you will forgive me, my lord," said Anne, moving back. "I've not been well. I'm mortal weary."

DeVere's eyes narrowed, a glint came into them. "Mealy-mouthed little rustic," he said below his breath. He turned on his silver heel and stalked away to Adam whom he approached with a smile. "Well, sir, what say you to the gaming table? At court now they are hot for 'Trump.' Have you the cards? If not, my lackey will have brought a deck."

Adam's ruddy face puckered with dismay; hospitable and merry he might be, and also desirous of pleasing his noble guest, but he could not countenance gaming in his home. A wager now and then perhaps, or even a throw of the dice, but not cards which were a dissolute foreign invention. He was saved from refusing by the Baroness, who called imperiously, " 'Tis late, my lord, and we have far to drive, we must take our leave."

The Baron was not easy to persuade, for he had planned upon recouping some of his London losses from these simple folk, but his wife had grasped the situation and knew that future favors were dependent on tact at present. The deVeres and Tyndals began the round of ceremonious farewells. When Margaret gave her hand to John Winthrop, he pressed it slowly, and said, "Since you stay some days at Hadleigh, may I give myself the pleasure of waiting on you there . . . tomorrow. . . ?"

Margaret looked up into the intent eyes, then lowered her own. A pulse began to beat in her full throat, she withdrew her hand. "Why, I don't know sir—it seems hardly—"

"I beg of you, Mistress Margaret. I have found it so agreeable to converse with you, a pleasure I dared hope you

shared." He had a warm vibrant voice and Margaret was
quite experienced enough to recognize sincerity in it, but she
was embarrassed that this country squire, this twice-made
widower whom she had just met, should give her a sense
of excitement. "It is a long ride to Hadleigh . . ." she began,
and stopped, for her brother came up to them impatiently.
"Margaret! His Lordship is waiting. Good night to you, sir!"
He looked at John coldly. Arthur Tyndal was a great bull of
a man with an air of importance, and his manner clearly
showed that he found John Winthrop negligible.

Margaret flushed; gentle though she was by nature, a
spark of revolt against her brother's arrogance made her
murmur to John as she curtseyed. "As you like, sir," and
her brown eyes smiled a little. She turned abruptly, and
nearly fell over Elizabeth whose curiosity about these grand
people neither a surfeit of food, nor the lateness of the hour
had yet sated. "Bless you child!" cried Margaret, "I didn't see
you, did I tread on your toe?"

Elizabeth nodded solemnly. "It doesn't matter. I—I wanted
to sniff that little ball on your girdle, it smells so sweet."

"And so you shall," said Margaret, holding out her pomander. The child inhaled the odor of sandalwood and violets
ecstatically.

"Bess! You presume!" said her Uncle John, but there was
a gratified light in his eye as he watched Margaret give his
niece a swift kiss. He had not been wrong in seeing a moth-
erliness in Margaret. She would be kind to stepchildren, and
with those broad hips and full breasts she was doubtless a
good breeder herself. After the noble party had finally left
and the tired Winthrops were all in bed, John stayed up in
his private closet, thinking. He glanced at his journal, the
"Experiencia," which he had been writing before he left for
London. Phrases here and there caught his attention.

> *I purpose by God's grace to meditate more often upon
> the certainty and excellency of my everlasting happinesse
> through Christ, and of the vanitye and perill of all worldly
> felicity . . . O Lord crucifie the world unto me, that
> though I can not avoid to live among the baits and snares
> of it, yet it may be truely dead unto me and I unto it . . .*

There were a dozen pages of renunciation and repentance covered with his cramped strongly characterized writing, but he
pushed the pile of manuscript slowly aside.

"It is no sin before God," he said aloud, "to long for a suitable and faithful bedfellow, and if this woman be somewhat frivolous and inclined towards the world, I'll yet vow she is submissive and will be guided by me." He smiled, thinking of Margaret's confusion, her plump cosiness, her soft eyes. I believe I love her already, he thought pleasurably. His first two wives had been well dowered, but they had not also been knight's daughters. This brought him to a less pleasing thought. Margaret's family would make objections, Arthur Tyndal's bearing had been unmistakeable.

But the opposition would be surmounted, he was sure of it. Confidence surged back, as it ever did after a period of heartsmart and misery. God will help me, he thought, if, to be sure, it be His Will. And went to bed.

For Elizabeth, in after years, those summer months at Groton merged into a vivid memory of two days. One was the glorious feasting and dancing with which they had celebrated King James's birthday, and the other was the August day of her own great wickedness.

Elizabeth's troubles began as soon as she opened her eyes and heard rain hissing down the latticed panes. She crept out of the trundle bed she shared with Martha, now that Thomas Fones had returned from London and occupied the big bed with his wife and the baby. Elizabeth went to the window and cast one despairing look at the gray teeming sky. Jack had promised to take her to the Fair at Boxford today. He and Harry had already slipped over there themselves after lessons with Mr. Nicholson, and Elizabeth's ardent heart had thumped over descriptions of the Fair's attractions. There was a dancing bear, and a juggler who could balance a sword on his nose, there were mummers and cockfights, there were booths that sold gingerbread toys and pink pigs made from marchpane. Jack had said he would give her a penny to buy some. Her mouth watered when she thought of the melting sweet almond taste of those little pigs. She had dreamed of them last night, had seen herself sharing one with Jack while they made a wish. And now it poured. "Rain before seven, clear by eleven," old Lem, the reeve, had said the other day when the Manor folk were still bringing in the harvest, but it hadn't cleared then. And it wouldn't today. She felt it. Elizabeth looked miserably at Martha who still slept, and at the drawn brocade curtains around her parents' bed. Her father inside there was snoring rhythmically. If he were not there she would have crept in to her mother for comfort.

Elizabeth mournfully yanked her little linen shift from the stool where she had flung it last night; she pulled it over her head and then her thin blue wool gown. She bothered neither to wash her face, nor comb the tangled masses of dark curls. She had an urgent errand in the kitchen, and no idea just how late it was. She slipped out of the bedchamber and down the crooked stone back stairs into the buttery. It was empty; on the oak counter fresh-baked loaves of bread were neatly ranged for serving, a keg of ale was already dripping at the spigot where someone had drawn off a mug for breakfast, but through the open door into the great kitchen she could see Nannie Podd, the head cook, stirring a pot over the fire. This was bad luck. Podd was a cantankerous old woman who disliked children and resented intrusion in her domain. Elizabeth edged through the buttery door, holding her breath and praying that the cook would not notice her while she tried to see the spot where she had hidden the sampler and dish last night. She had put them behind the broom by the hearth because that was where the goblin would look, and she had said the charm three times. But the broom had been moved. On the bricks there was no sign of the rolled up sampler, or of the dish of bread and cream.

Perhaps Puck had taken them away to finish the work? . . . She gave a jump, for she felt a sharp pain in her right ear while fingers jerked the lobe, and Lucy's voice said crossly behind her, "What mischief are you up to now, Bess? What do you here at this hour?"

"N-nothing," said Elizabeth squirming. The cook turned around, her under lip thrust out, her fat cheeks glistening beneath the mobcap. "Good morrow, Mistress Lucy. Oi've the sage ready steeped as ye ordered—ah—" she added with malice catching sight of Elizabeth. "Miss Goody-body! And dew ye be arter that mucky ould bit o' stitchery Oi found hidden wi' a bowl of slops behoind me besom Oi wonder!"

"What's that!" cried Lucy, staring at Elizabeth's scarlet face. "What are you talking about, Cook?" The woman reached up to a cupboard, brought down the crumpled dirty sampler and held it out. Lucy gasped as she looked at the straggling ELIZ and saw the rest blank. "Oh . . ." she breathed. "You wicked lying child! You said it was *finished*, that you would give it to my mother today!" The girl was genuinely shocked; not even Harry had ever exhibited deceit and disobedience of this magnitude.

Elizabeth said nothing. She felt some guilt, but stronger yet was despair. She had been so sure that the goblin would help her, and he had not; so sure that she would get to the Fair with Jack and she could not. She had prayed the Lord Jesus for fine weather too. Prayers were not answered, charms failed. There was nothing.

"Come with me," said Lucy, breathing hard and grabbing the ear lobe again. "I shall take this straight to your father, and then to my mother, and may God forgive you."

A frenzy like the fireworks on Guy Fawkes Day suddenly exploded in Elizabeth's chest. "I don't care if He does. I *hate* God!" she shouted.

She ducked so violently that Lucy lost hold of the ear. The child turned and ran through the buttery slamming its door in her astounded aunt's face. She flew through the scullery where a sleepy boy was peeling onions, and past the pantry, which Lucy had that moment unlocked on her way to the kitchen. On the shelf by the door there was a silver dish full of rare dates imported from the Levant, which were Adam's favorite delicacy. He had once given Elizabeth a taste, and she had liked it almost as well as marchpane. She did not know that she saw the dish as she ran past, or how it came to be clutched in her arms, she had no plan but frantic flight as she darted out into the dripping courtyard across the slippery flags to the stable. She wedged herself between a water barrel and the stable wall as Lucy peered out the door across the courtyard. The girl was young and active but she had been impeded in the chase by her full silk skirts, and now seeing no sign of Elizabeth through the sheets of rain, she shut the door and went to rouse the household.

In the stable a groom whistled as he curried one of the horses. Elizabeth dared not go there for refuge. She peeked gingerly around the side of the barrel and spied the bakehouse. There was a small disused door that led from its loft to the garrets of the main house. The boys had shown it to her though their elders had long forgotten its existence. She acted again without thought, streaked back across the courtyard and into the bakehouse which was still warm from the ovens and smelled of recently baked bread. Clutching her dish of dates Elizabeth climbed the ladder to the loft, opened the low door and entered the great shadowy attic. There were but two tiny cobwebby windows, high up in the gables; near to one was an old black chest carved in the Gothic manner of long ago. Elizabeth sat down on it, shivered, and began to cry.

She cried for a long time before wiping her eyes on the bedraggled damp skirt of her blue gown. It was then that she consciously saw the dates. Fear trickled down her spine like the drip from her hair. I can't ever go back, she thought, they'd never forgive me, never. Even Mama. She began to cry again, thinking that one day years from now they would come up here and find her bones heaped on the chest. "Moldering bones," the sexton at St. Sepulchre's always said. She glanced fearfully into the shadows. There was a rusty suit of armor hanging from a peg and a queer helmet a hundred years old that had belonged to a Winthrop. There were piles of dusty chests and a broken spinning wheel, and the looming brick bulk of the great kitchen chimney. The rain pattered on the tiles above her head. I'm so hungry, she thought. Her hand went out of itself and took a date. The sweetness was cloying, she bit down, and her teeth were jarred by the unexpected pit. She spat it out. I wish I was dead already, she thought.

An eternity dragged by. Then she heard a noise behind her and started in terror. Rats?—or ghosts? She huddled on the chest, her heart thundering in her ears.

"Bess?" whispered a voice. "Are you there?" A boy came through from the bakehouse loft.

"Jack!" She gulped and ran to him, flinging herself against him, clinging.

"Hush," he said awkwardly patting her shoulder. "I guessed you might be here. They're hunting everywhere. Oh, Bessie, what a coil you've got yourself into." His eyes fell on the dates. "So you did take them, Aunt Lucy said you had."

"I didn't mean to. I only ate one, it was nasty. Oh, Jack, we were going to the Fair and it rained—and the charm didn't work for the sampler, Puck nor Robin Goodfellow nor any goblin came at all."

"What a baby you are!" The boy shook his head. "Elves do *good* deeds sometimes, they don't help people who should have helped themselves."

Elizabeth gave a little whimper and sank back on the chest. Jack had always taken her side before, and now his grave voice sounded like his father; he even looked just like Uncle John with the twinkle all gone from the round eyes under high arched brows.

"You must come down now, Bess," said the boy more gently. "It's best to face it and be done with it."

"I can't! I can't! They'll kill me!"

"Fiddle! They'll but give you a flogging. That's naught to be very much feared of, I've had plenty. Haven't you?"

She shook her head. She had been spanked once or twice, and her father had boxed her ears, but Thomas was too sickly and indolent for the corporal punishment of his eldest, and Anne was too gentle. Elizabeth looked at him piteously, wanting always to do as Jack said, and yet afraid. The dark lashes stuck out in spikes around her tear-drenched eyes, eyes called hazel, that were changeable in color as a brook, gold-flecked brown, mossy green, or black pools as now. Her pink mouth trembled. The vivid rose had drained from her cheeks.

Jack felt something peculiar stir in his chest as he looked down at the wan, big-eyed child. He had never been embarrassed by the affection between them, he had never thought of it particularly, nor realized that of the many womenfolk of all ages who surrounded him, he was perhaps fondest of this one. He bent suddenly and put his arm around her. "Come, little coz. I've always known you brave. D'you remember the day Black Brutus ran away with you? You kept your stirrups and sawed his mouth as well as any horseman in the land."

Aye, she had mastered Black Brutus that day, nor known fear, only a wild exultation, but that had been very different. "For you want me to, Jack," she whispered, and taking his stubby callused hand, she stood up slowly.

Elizabeth's punishment was worse than anything she had imagined, and the whole family was assembled in the Great Hall to witness it. From the moment of her reappearance downstairs with Jack, she had been received with head shakings and cold stern looks. Some of these looks, like her mother's, were sorrowful too, but even Anne Fones accepted the family verdict that Satan had somehow got possession of her daughter and must be beaten out of her.

"It is for your own sake, Bess," said Anne sadly. "For the sake of your soul, my poor child. Your Uncle John will conduct your chastisement. He has had more experience than your father in such matters, and also your father has a fit of his ague today." She steeled herself against the fear in Elizabeth's eyes, and being now in her fifth month of pregnancy, sank heavily to a seat in the circle of benches and chairs which had been arranged in the Hall. It was her mother's exhortations which had brought Anne to such cool detached speech, but there was no doubt that her own lax discipline had been culpable, and the list of Elizabeth's crimes truly appalling.

The prolonged deceit and lies about the sampler, not to speak of the laziness involved—these were bad, but the subsequent blasphemy against God, and then theft, were beyond any condoning as childish naughtiness.

John Winthrop stood behind the lectern on which lay Adam's great new King James Bible open at the thirtieth chapter of Ecclesiasticus. John's brooding gaze slowly circled the assembled family. His father and mother sat in tall-backed carved chairs, Lucy next to them, Thomas Fones on a cushioned bench, shivering from his ague, rubbing his gouty fingers nervously, but grim-mouthed above the sparse beard. Thomas did not look at his daughter who had disgraced the Foneses, he stared at the thyme-strewed rushes at the base of the high stool where Elizabeth had been perched in the center of the circle. He heard Anne beside him begin to cry and murmured, "Now, now, wife." All the children were there in the Hall too, and the younger servants, huddled near the kitchen door. So regrettable a circumstance as this would nonetheless yield profit as an example, and prevent others from wrongdoing. Little Martha crouched beside Anne, and stared with horrified eyes at her sister, but John's own children were ranged at his right, below the lectern—Jack, Harry, Forth, and Mary who was but five years old and the only one who did not understand what was taking place.

John Winthrop cleared his throat, and held up his hand. "We are gathered here in sorrow this morning, for the performance of a distasteful duty. It is one from which I shrink, and I pray the Dear Lord to strengthen me." His voice faltered a moment. It was true that only a clear sense of duty upheld him, and the necessity for correcting wickedness within his own family. John could be angry under direct provocation, his temper was hot, but the deliberate infliction of pain on a girl child distressed him. Moreover, this interruption to his morning's plans was extremely inconvenient. He had been engaged in writing a decisive love letter to Margaret Tyndal for which the Essex carrier was waiting, he was also due by noon at the Manor Court next the church where his services were required as magistrate. But the salvation of a child through whom ran Winthrop blood must take precedence over all other matters. "Elizabeth," he said leaning on the lectern and looking sadly at the huddled little bunch on the stool. "Raise your head and tell us the deadly sins of which you have been guilty."

Elizabeth swallowed hard. There was an enormous choking

lump in her throat, but a numbness had come on her, and a bewilderment. She couldn't seem to remember exactly what had happened this morning, it had gone misty like a dream. She stared at her uncle and said nothing. There was a long silence.

"Very well, since you wish to add obduracy to the rest," said John at last. "I will enumerate for you. You have been disobedient and slothful, first, then you have been mired in deceit and lies. This is wicked enough, *but* when your deceit was exposed, you most horribly blasphemed against God, you fled from just retribution, and on top of all this—you turned *thief!* Do you understand that, Elizabeth? Were you older and of the lower classes you would have been put in the stocks, and a letter T branded with a blazing iron on your face."

The child gasped. "I only ate one," she said. "I didn't mean to take them."

John sighed. "I'm glad to see some glimmer of repentance, but you must be brought to the full of it. Listen to God's express word." He bent his head and began to read from Ecclesiasticus. *"He that loveth his son causeth him oft to feel the rod, that he may have joy of him in the end."* He read on, intoning each verse, *"An horse not broken becometh headstrong . . . Cocker thy child and he shall make thee afraid . . . Give him no liberty in his youth . . . wink not at his follies . . . bow down his neck while he is young, and beat him on the sides while he is a child lest he wax stubborn and disobedient . . . and so bring sorrow to thine heart."*

Elizabeth heard nothing, and nothing of the long prayer that followed. I won't cry out, she thought, I won't, no matter what he does, not in front of Jack. But she hadn't guessed where her uncle was going to beat her.

"Now, Elizabeth, you have heard the word of God and our prayer to Him. Lift your skirts and bend yourself over this bench." John drew a limber hazel stick from behind the lectern.

"No!" cried the child. "I can't!" She would have run to her mother, but John seized her and held her pinioned. "It is meet and just that you be shamed. Come, come Elizabeth—is it necessary to *bind* you?" He yanked up her gown to expose the small naked buttocks and turned her over the bench. The child suddenly went limp. "There will be one stroke for each of your sins," said John and slowly raised his arm. The hazel stick swished in the silent room. A fine scarlet line appeared across the pink skin. Anne Fones made a choked sound, and jumping up, quitted the hall, while Martha ran with her. Jack turned his head and looked out the window. Six times the hazel whip flashed through the air and snapped on the flesh. Elizabeth made no sound, no one in the circle made a sound until the last stroke. Then Adam leaned forward and said in a low voice, "I fear the little maid has swooned."

John lifted the child's head. "Not quite," he said. "Bring wine and a feather. She *must* finish the chastisement properly that her soul will profit by her correction."

They wet the child's lips with wine. Lucy burned the feather beneath Elizabeth's nose until she sneezed, and opened her eyes to become conscious of a fierce smarting pain. "Is it over?" she whispered.

"Yes, child," said John gently enough. "Except one thing. You must now kneel and kiss the rod which has saved you from damnation." He held out the reddened hazel switch. She obeyed mindlessly and brushed her mouth across the stick, but when John said, "Now affirm to us your full contrition and repentance, your determination never again to offend our most loving God," Elizabeth clapped her hands to her mouth, sweat broke out on her forehead, and leaning over she began to vomit on the rushes.

"Let her be, my son," said Adam. "She'll carry scars from your hazel wand. She'll repent better now if ye do not force her."

" 'Tis not what the Bible says, Father," answered John frowning. "She must now bear witness to a broken and a contrite heart. This foolish retching is surely but the Devil's doing."

"And I say let her be!" thundered Adam, suddenly angry. "You've become overhard and canting of late years. Before God I liked the old ways best when there was more talk of love and merriment and less of the Devil and groanings of sin."

The men looked at each other. They had forgotten Elizabeth. A seldom realized conflict had flared between them. The old man rose and walked over to the lectern, beneath his bushy gray brows his eyes snapped. "Since ye hanker so to quote Scripture, ye might mind ye of the Fifth Commandment!"

John's skin darkened and a tremor ran through him. He moistened his lips and spoke with difficulty. "Aye, my father,

I do. I wish in nothing to offend you, it is but my zeal to . . ."

"*Zeal*, forsooth! Ye've plenty of that!" cried Adam. It cost him something to combat his son whom he deeply admired, and truth to say was sometimes a bit in awe of. The old man reached down and lifted up Elizabeth. "There, there, poppet," he said stroking her curls. "Ye'll be good now, I vow, and ye'll never forget your correction."

Elizabeth looked up at him dully. "I'll never forget it," she whispered, and only her grandfather thought that there was something strange, and woefully unchildlike in her manner.

2

It snowed softly on Christmas Eve in the year of our Lord 1628, which was the fourth year of King Charles the First's reign, and on Christmas morning a fleece as white and soft as a Cotswold lamb lay over London town. It hid the wooden gables and the red roof tiles, it hid the piles of filth dumped into the narrow cobbled streets. It muffled the rumble of carts, the clop-clop of hooves, the acrid cries of the street venders, but the church bells clanged out clear as ever above the stilled city. And while Elizabeth in the Fones apothecary shop impatiently pounded snail shells in a mortar, she heard rowdy singing directly outside the shop door on Old Bailey Street.

"Is it mummers?" she cried, throwing her pestle down on the counter top and rushing to the twinkling-paned, bow-fronted window. It was a group of mummers, disguised merrymakers, standing under the swinging apothecary sign of three fawns painted gold, in apt allusion to the Fones name.

"Lewd roisterers! I must bid them begone!" said Richard Fitch the apprentice sourly, in the nasal twang of Lincolnshire. "They'll disturb the master." He raised his eyes to the smoky dark-beamed ceiling. Thomas Fones lay above in his chamber, suffering from a violent attack of rheumatics.

"Mummers are a bawdy godless crew," went on Richard, pulling down the corners of his mouth as he peered through the window beside Elizabeth.

Elizabeth paid no attention to him. She was laughing at the cavortings on the snowy street. There was a boy dressed as a hobbyhorse, and a "green man" with bits of ivy and holly stuck all over him, and another in a shaggy skin who lumbered and shuffled like a dancing bear on a leash held by the Lord of Misrule—a striped jester with cap and bells. "God rest ye merry—" bawled the mummers, "God rest ye merry, all good folk. Let nothing you dismay, for Christ our Saviour is born to us this Christmas Day."

" 'Tis wanton, God has naught to do wi' merriment," said Richard Fitch drawing back. "Roman blasphemies. They're all drunk too and in broad daylight—that one," he pointed with his thumb, "mumming as a bear—'tis Sim Perkins, 'prentice to Mr. Thurlby, the grocer in Ludgate, what a beating *he'll* get when 's master cotches him!" Richard nodded with satisfaction. He was a thin pimply boy of twenty who had nearly served his time with Thomas Fones, and would soon set up for apothecary on his own. He was much given to psalm singing, and the reading of his Geneva Bible, and his behavior was so impeccable that in the five years he had been here, he had never been beaten once. "Come, mistress," he said to Elizabeth, as he returned to the tobacco leaves he had been grading and chopping, "you'd best get on wi' your task or the mithridate'll never be ready in time for her Ladyship of Carlisle."

"Oh Dickon!" cried Elizabeth. "This is *Christmas* Day! Most London folk don't work today!"

" 'Tis not the Sabbath—'tis a Thursday," said Richard sternly. "The Bible says naught anywhere about Christ masses —that's the Pope's doing. The Scripture commandment says, 'Six days shalt thou labor and do all—' "

"I *know* what it says—" cut in Elizabeth, "but even King Charles himself keeps Christmas, and there'll be a royal masque today at Whitehall."

The apprentice sniffed. "The King has a Papist queen to his bed, and women be like serpents to sting poison in a man unawares."

"Oh fiddle-faddle!" snapped Elizabeth, returning to the counter and picking up the pestle. "How would *you* know? I'll vow you've never had a woman in your bed, be she serpent, dove, or even Bankside harlot." She peered at the battered calfskin book which contained her father's secret prescription for the famous mithridate remedy. Many apothecaries made "mithridates" of their own concocting, but this one was particularly efficacious. It contained forty ingredients: herbs like rue, and more exotic materials, powdered snails, dried mummy, fresh-water pearls, and a piece of lung from a hanged felon.

Elizabeth read her father's cramped Latin with ease and duly added a dram of camphor to the mixture in a beaker.

The apprentice had reddened at her accurate taunt, and he now watched her from the corners of his eyes with resentment and unwilling admiration. A provoking lass, she was, and considered by most men to be a beauty, for all that her nose was something long, her cleft chin too square, and her profusion of curly hair, black as a wicked Spaniard's. There was a bursting carnal femaleness about her, though she was but eighteen; it showed in the full mouth and small square teeth, the vivid red of her round cheeks, the heavy-lidded hazel eyes, the creamy column of her neck above the white fichu—and more. Richard Fitch glanced lower at the firm outline of her breasts, the supple waist, the shape of thigh not quite concealed by the thin wool folds of her maroon skirt, and he remembered a shameful dream he had had of her last night. Satan sent these lewd thoughts . . . He turned angrily to sweep the pile of minced tobacco into a box as Mistress Priscilla Fones waddled into the shop from the inside passage. "Oh dear, oh dear," said Elizabeth's stepmother unhappily. "Bess, have you made up the mithridate yet for my Lady Carlisle, and I'm sure I wish her ladyship would pay her bill before we send her more of these chargeable drugs—your father is quite distracted—and 'tis the first time he ever failed to mix the potion himself, he says you must bring the bottle upstairs for his inspection as soon as you've finished . . . and did you steep the betony with Ach—Ach—"

"*Achilles millefolium*," said Elizabeth smiling. "I did. Is my father worse then?" She looked at her stepmother with mild affection and some amusement. Priscilla Fones was fat and good-tempered and ineffectual. Life constantly presented her with discomforts she had no notion how to ease except by a flow of gently fretful speech. She had however done her best to rear her three stepchildren, Elizabeth, Martha and Samuel; and to recover from her own frequent miscarriages and the birth of her little Mary, now eight, who ailed as mysteriously and continuously as did her father, Thomas.

"I don't know," said Priscilla vaguely. "It's still his gout, I believe, but of course there's so much sickness about—another case of plague near Newgate, I hear . . . and then all this worry about your Uncle Winthrop, though Mistress Margaret—thanks be to God that she came up here from Suffolk to nurse him—when I saw her yesterday she felt the ague was lessening . . . if it *is* the ague; your father's been wondering if your uncle had maybe one of the purulent fevers . . . Oh, Richard—" said Priscilla suddenly turning to the apprentice, "I'd forgot. You're to go at once to the conduit and fetch us another barrel of cooking water . . . the conduit on the *Chepe*, mind you, your master feels 'tis the purest at present."

"Aye, mistress." The apprentice began to stack the long brown tobacco leaves on a shelf.

"Is this the tobacco Mr. Harry sent from Barbadoes?" asked Pricilla, her harried mind lighting on a new topic.

"No fear, ma'am," answered Richard scornfully, "That was foul stuff, that was, stinking and full o' stalks. Master he wouldn't touch it, not for *our* quality trade. We sent it to the grocers."

"Oh yes, I remember now," said Priscilla to Elizabeth. "I fear Harry's a wild young man, costing so much money to set him up as a planter on that island wherever it is, and I know your Uncle Winthrop has near beggared himself paying Harry's debts, and the tobacco he sends no good at all . . . he was a most handsome lad though when he passed through London two years agone . . ."

"Was he?" said Elizabeth, stirring her mixture in the thick glass beaker. Two years ago when she had last seen Harry she had hardly noticed him at all, beause his brother Jack had also been in London practicing law at the Inner Temple, and her every thought had been for Jack; praying for their meetings, planning what she would say to him, and then too shy to say it when the time came. And Jack had treated her like a little girl, oh most kindly—gently teasing her, as he did Martha—but no more than that . . . until last summer . . . three nights before he sailed for Constantinople. Her fingers tightened on the wooden spoon, and she heard again Priscilla's voice which had not ceased.

". . . and then young John is so different in other ways too, such a credit to the Winthrops, he did so well those years at the University in Ireland and then fighting for Rochelle with the poor Duke of Buckingham . . . what a fearful

thing it must have been for Jack to hear of the Duke's wicked
assassination, after serving under him that is, though there
were many who were glad the Duke was murdered—if
Jack *has* heard way off there among the heathen Turks . . ."

"You know Jack has heard," said Elizabeth sharply. "That
my Uncle John and Aunt Margaret have several letters from
him." But I have none, she thought, though he promised.
And in Jack's letters to his family there had been no mention
of her except the formal "remember me to all my cousins."

"The mithridate is finished, I think," said Elizabeth. "I'll
take it up to Father."

"Send Martha down to tend shop, or I'll stay here until
Richard gets back, or perhaps one of the maids—but they're
so busy in the kitchen . . . oh dear . . . I wish we could afford
another servant, two is little enough for a family like this,
but these London wenches want so much in wages now, and
the times so unsettled . . . one never knows just . . ."

Elizabeth quietly escaped, but as she reached the narrow
stairs which led to the great bedchamber, depression seized
her, and a stifling sensation, so that on impulse she put the
little flask of mithridate on the bench in the passage, seized
a cloak left there on a peg by one of the maids, and went
out into the garden. On the hidden paths the snow crunched
beneath her soft leather soles. The orderly herb plots were
obliterated now, though here and there in sheltered spots,
snowdrops pushed green spikes through the whiteness. Little
icicles dripped from the trellis of the rose arbor, and from
bare branches of fruit trees; but it was of last June that she
thought. Of the summer dusk when she and Jack had stood
here together by the old old wall. London Wall. The Fones
home halfway up Old Bailey Street was immediately outside
the ancient fortification built by the Romans, and their half
acre of garden was backed by it. London had long since
grown beyond the Wall, it had crept in this westerly direction
across the Fleet and along the Strand nearly to the King's
Palace at Whitehall. The Wall had no meaning now, in
places it was crumbling, one could no longer easily circle the
old City along its broad top. Ivy grew all over the Wall and
it showed the mellow pathos of desuetude and ruin. Elizabeth
had been born almost in its shadow and was fond of it. She
had gone to it instinctively on the June night when she had
last seen young John Winthrop.

He had come to say farewell to his Fones relatives, having
suddenly decided to embark on an extended tour of the Adri-

atic and the Levant. At supper he had entertained them in
his own vivid way with tales of the wonders he expected
to see on his travels, the water streets of Venice where people had black and gold boats tethered at their doors instead
of horses—the ferocious Sultan of Turkey with his seraglio
of a thousand wives.

"Oh, Cousin Jack, what marvels!" little Martha had
breathed. "And will you not see dragons and mermaids too?"

"Very likely. Shall I bring you back one to play with?"
Jack had said with the twinkle in his dark eyes. For all that
she was past sixteen, Martha was still so small and ingenuous
that they all treated her as a child. But the old easy relationship between Jack and Elizabeth had vanished. On this
evening there had been a new constraint. When they rose
from supper she announced that she must see to the herbs,
and he followed her to the garden.

At once at his nearness, Elizabeth was seized with quivering embarrassment. Without looking at him she was yet op-
pressively conscious of him—of his body; not very tall, but
strong and well muscled, of his quizzical brown eyes set beneath arched brows—of the long thick Winthrop nose and
cleft chin, the full-lipped mouth indented at the corners like
her own. "I must trim my herbs before the dew falls heavy,"
she said making great play with her knife and the herb basket,
though tonight, skilled as she was, she could scarce tell
rosemary from verbena.

"Bess—" said Jack smiling. "You've changed of late, little
coz. You've grown into a woman." As she continued to stoop
over the plants, he took the knife and basket from her, and
putting his hand under her chin, raised her face. He looked
long at her, while her color deepened, and she strove to
stop the quivering of her lips. "A Winthrop face, but fairer
than the rest of our women," he said musingly.

"You think me so?" she whispered, smiling in a way she
had learned would soften most men, looking up at him
through her lashes with all the force of her yearning. But he
came no closer, though he was troubled and removed his
gaze with difficulty from her red mouth. "I have always been
so fond of you, my dear," he said. His hand dropped from
her chin. "Fonder than of my own sister . . . Before I leave
on this long journey I'd like to know that you have prospects
of happiness . . . my Uncle Fones mentioned that you've
several suitors . . ."

She stiffened and turned from him. "I think not of marriage yet!" she cried. "Do *you?*"

"N-no." He was discomfited by her question but he answered it with his usual consideration. "I've thought once or twice to change my state, there was a lady in Dublin while I was there at Trinity, and last year the daughter of Sir Henry—"

"Yes, I know," she cut in. The whole family had known of Jack's transient courtship, and it had cost Elizabeth many an hour of anguish, crying by stealth in the night so that she would not wake Martha. "And why did you not marry her, Jack?"

"I'm scarcely sure," he said, puzzled by her vehemence. "We both cooled, I think, at least I found myself grow tepid—then her father had a better offer for her. I'm restless, Bess—I wish to see something of the world before I settle to a squire's life at Groton like my father . . . nor do I wish to go on with the law, as he has—though I will always try to do his bidding."

"Aye," she said softly, anger leaving her. She moved from him and rested her hand on the wall, plucking and twisting at a clump of orange wallflower that grew in a cranny. It was *that* which kept him from seeing and perhaps returning the love she felt for him. Not the nearness of their blood, an impediment which could be surmounted by special license or indeed without it, by going to one of the dissenting ministers who found nothing in Scripture to forbid the marriage of cousins. It was his father's influence, the authority of John Winthrop who was ambitious for his favorite son and heir, and who had never truly liked or approved of Elizabeth since the day he flogged her in Groton Manor eleven years ago.

"Bess," said Jack coming slowly up to her with a diffidence unlike him, "How is it that of late we seem to jangle when we talk together? I feel you out of temper with me . . . all I wished to say was that my friend Edward Howes, if you have set your heart on no one else—he loves you very much, and . . ."

"Edward Howes . . ." she repeated bleakly. "My Uncle Downing's clerk. A dabbler in alchemy. A pettifogging lawyer. Is that what you'd have me marry?"

"Indeed you do him wrong, Bess. He has a brilliant mind, and property in Essex. I thought you liked him."

"I like him well enough—" She tossed the shredded flowers on the ground. "But—oh—I too am restless, Jack, I too yearn for freedom and far places and adventure . . . but I yearn more for something else . . . something that's in my bones and blood . . ." She held her breath, looking up at him through the dusk. Her long hazel eyes were dark with tears, the white kerchief which bound her hair had loosened and her black curls fell on her shoulders.

"What is it you want so much, little coz?" he whispered.

"You don't know?"

He shook his head. "But I pray that God will give it to you, and perhaps it is *God* that you want . . . I think you've never yet found Him."

After a moment she managed to laugh. "So farewell, Jack. Farewell on your journey to the far Levant."

"The Lord be with you, sweet, I'll pray for your happiness." He bent and kissed her on the lips, as he had a hundred times, unthinking, but now he felt the lips part beneath his own and warmth as from a draught of strongest mead rushed through his body. He drew back, dismayed, and unbelieving.

"I'll write to you, Bess," he said quickly. "Aye, I'll write to you, as soon as I'm aboard the ship." And he walked from the garden.

She had hoped that he might have tried to see her again before he set off for Gravesend, where his ship, the "London of London" would sail, but he did not. She lived then for the letter he had promised, thinking that surely in it there would be some recognition of the moment when their lips had met in a different way. But there was no letter—and I am a fool, thought Elizabeth, standing by London Wall in the snow, nearly seven months later. What greater folly for a woman than to love without requital.

Love. So it was to be a lean diet of that for her. Those who had truly loved her were dead, long ago. She thought with a forgotten ache of her mother, but she could remember nothing clearly except that once they had stood together at a window and looked at the moon. She thought of Adam, her grandfather; he had not died until five years ago, and always with him there had been a feeling of safety, and cherishing . . . but he had stayed in Suffolk and she had seen him so seldom. What of your father? said conscience. Surely you love your father, and family? Her mind slid past them all rapidly, without acquiescence or denial, then checked itself on Martha. Yes, for that little sister there was love.

Even as she thought of Martha the house door opened and

the girl appeared calling anxiously, "Bess! Bess! Where are you? Are you out there?"

Elizabeth answered and started down the path, her feet numb with cold. Martha came running towards her, a small gray figure in her workaday homespun gown, her baby-soft brown hair bound tight by the linen kerchief. "Bess—Lady Carlisle's come herself for the mithridate! At least she's waiting in her coach. We couldn't find you. Father's so upset!"

"Oh Lud!—I'm sorry," said Elizabeth. "I but went out for a breath of Christmas air. Don't look so worried, poppet, the mithridate's ready."

She ran into the hall, retrieved the flask and rushed upstairs to her father's bedroom to show him the potion. "I followed the prescription precisely, Father, I'm sure it'll do." She held out the flask of brownish liquid. "Aye, to be sure— I'm sorry," she added to Thomas Fones's burst of querulous reproaches. He sat in his dressing gown huddled in a large court chair by the fire, his nightcap pulled down over his ears. He took the flask in his gouty fingers, sniffed and tasted the potion. "It must do," he said dolefully. "Hasten, Bess, her ladyship'll be angered by waiting."

"And if she is!" retorted his daughter. "What loss? Since she's paid nothing in years and already owes you nine pounds! She'll at least pay for this, if I can make her."

"No—no. Bess!" the apothecary cried, knowing his child's headstrong ways. "I forbid it. Say nothing. We can't afford to lose her patronage. Why, she is close to the Queen, we may yet have a royal purveyorship!"

"Ha!" said Elizabeth shrugging. "Can't eat that! If the Queen pays no better than her lords. I know what the shop book says—'Desperate' next to the accounts of the Earl of Ormonde, and Lady deVere, and Lady Carlisle . . ."

"*Elizabeth!*" Thomas pounded the floor with his blackthorn cane, the moisture of helpless anger in his sunken eyes.

"Never mind, Papa," she said in some contrition, patting his shoulder. "Trust me—pray don't fret." She ran downstairs to the shop, where a supercilious footman in the Carlisle livery was bullying Martha.

"*So,* Mistress—" he greeted Elizabeth, "'ave ye brought it at last? 'Tis 'alf an hour gone, by St. 'Pulchre's bell thet 'er lidyship's been waiting," but his face softened as he stared at Elizabeth. "Naw then—ye couldn't 'elp it, no doubt, sweet-'eart."

She pushed past him and opening the shop door stepped

outside. The magnificent Carlisle coach and four restive black horses blocked the street. A baker's cart was drawn up patiently behind the coach, a crowd of urchins and beggars surrounded it. A postilion stood at the horses' heads, soothing them. Elizabeth glanced at the gilded coach with its glass windows, at the coat of arms emblazoned on the door. Lucy, the Countess's, own arms—Percy impaling Carlisle, for she was the daughter of the great Earl of Northumberland. For a moment Elizabeth's courage failed her, then she tapped resolutely on the windowpane while the coachman looked around in astonishment, and the footman came hurrying out of the apothecary shop.

A dim figure moved inside, a face covered by a fashionable black velvet mask peered through the window. Then the door was opened. "What is it, young woman?" asked a cool pretty voice, tinged with the Border accent.

"I am Elizabeth Fones, the apothecary's daughter, m'lady," said the girl, curtseying. "I've brought you the mithridate, my father being ill, and we crave pardon for the delay. There is one new secret direction for the taking of it that your ladyship should know."

"Indeed?" said the voice. The moment the coach door opened the beggars had rushed forward, and were now whining in chorus, with outstretched hands. "Alms, your noble ladyship, Christmas alms for the love o' God . . ."

"Come in here, mistress," said the Countess to Elizabeth, motioning with an ermine muff; as the girl obeyed and entered the coach, the Countess called impatiently to her footman, "Throw that rabble some farthings and be rid of them!"

Elizabeth sank nervously onto the purple velvet cushions beside the Countess, for there was no other place to sit. There was warmth in the coach, from a foot warmer of live coals, and it was deliciously perfumed by the jasmine which exuded from the great lady's furs and from her ringlets of gilded hair half concealed by a rose satin hood. Elizabeth sniffed appreciatively, knowing from experience in the stillroom the difficulty of extracting scent like this, and she kept respectfully silent, bearing as best she could the scrutiny of unseen eyes.

She knew that all court ladies wore masks when they went abroad, but she found the nearness of one slightly disturbing, and wondered if it hid any ravages of the smallpox from which Lady Carlisle had suffered some months before, when the apothecary had filled prescriptions frantically sent in for the Countess by the Queen's own physician. At least the pouting rouge mouth and white chin below the mask were flawless.

"Give me the mithridate," said the Countess, stretching out a gloved hand on which sparkled three diamond rings. "It has great efficacy as your father makes it, and I wish to take some now for plague preventive since I am driving into the City."

"It is a powerful preventive, madam," said Elizabeth, while her heart beat fast, "but only under certain conditions . . . if they are not fulfilled it may prove quite useless." And she held the flask tight on her lap.

"Ah . . . ?" said the Countess. "And what condition makes the potion sure of success?"

"That before it is taken, it is first *paid* for, my lady."

The Countess started. "Why, you brazen baggage," she cried, the sparkling hand raised to box Elizabeth's ear.

The girl moved back quickly. "It is not from brazenness I speak, but from justice. My father is ill, times go badly with us, the mithridate is very costly to make, and so were all the other remedies we've sent you these past three years. Were we wealthy folk we would deem it honor to serve your ladyship for nothing, but we are not."

The Countess's anger ebbed, and the lightness of spirit which so endeared her to Charles's little French Queen now bubbled up. She began to laugh. "My dear lass, do you think I occupy myself with petty tradesman's accounts? My steward attends to those."

"But he hasn't, my lady," said Elizabeth.

"Belle sainte vierge!" cried the Countess, using the Queen's favorite expletive. "Here's a wee terrier that'll worry a bone till Doomsday. How much do I owe you?"

"Ten pounds, your ladyship—including this." She touched the flask.

"So much?" said the Countess faintly surprised. "Well, child, I'll instruct my steward to pay you after Twelfth Night. You may send your account again." As Elizabeth made a sound of disappointment, she added, "Come you don't think I go abroad with a pocketful of sovereigns like a money changer, do you?—Look, my dear, here's a Christmas handsel for you, as earnest of my intent." She drew from her muff a small scented handkerchief, embroidered with a coronet and edged with Mechlin lace. "Now give me the flask."

Elizabeth murmured thanks for the handkerchief and

surrendered the flask, for there was nothing else to do, but there was a hot baffled feeling in her breast. The Countess had been kind enough; no doubt she meant to speak to her steward, but this would be the end of it, Elizabeth was sure. Elizabeth revered King Charles, and was fascinated by the few glimpses she had had of Queen Henrietta Marie, who was exactly her own age; she would, indeed, have described herself as a passionate royalist. And yet, the discontent in London, the feeling of oppression and injustice in the air, had affected Elizabeth too, and this encounter with Lady Carlisle seemed smothering and inconclusive. It was like trying to make a permanent dent on a swan's-down cushion.

St. Paul's bells began to peal for noon service, while Lady Carlisle tilted the flask and swallowed some of its contents. Though the great cathedral stood on the other side of London Wall, they heard the melodious clangor through the coach windows.

"I must hasten," said the Countess. "I wish to hear our good Dean, Master John Donne, preach—the King is so fond of him. If you go to the service, mistress, you may ride in my coach as far as Paul's."

"Oh, no thank you, my lady, we don't attend church on Christmas."

"Indeed?" Elizabeth felt the sharpened attention behind the velvet mask. "Why not? Are you dissenters, then? *Puritans?*"

Elizabeth winced at the term, though of recent years it had been so often applied to anyone who opposed Bishop Laud's Papist tendencies that the Winthrops and many others no longer resented it.

"In a way, perhaps, madam," she answered uncomfortably.

"But that is very wrong!" cried the Countess with anger. "Wrong-headed and disloyal to the King who knows what's best for all of us. Do you *dare* to question the Established Episcopal Faith of England?"

"Oh, I do not—" protested Elizabeth a little frightened. "I was raised partly in the old ways, at least our Parish Church, St. Sepulchre's, I think conforms to what the Bishop says."

The Countess was not listening. "That's enough, mistress," she said coldly. "Had I known the Three Fauns Apothecary Shop was owned by Puritans, I'd never have granted it my patronage. Good day. No," she added as Elizabeth unhappily made to give back the handkerchief, "you may keep that because it's Christmas, no matter how you stubborn fools deny the spirit of Our Lord's Day of Birth."

So Elizabeth descended from the coach. She watched the postilion mount the off leader and sound his trumpet, while the footman climbed behind on the box. The coachman flicked at the four horses, and the huge gilded vehicle lumbered off down the Old Bailey towards Ludgate. The traffic penned up behind gradually began to move. Elizabeth re-entered the shop where Martha had been crammed against the window, watching.

"What happened, Bess? What took so long? I thought you'd never come out of the coach. Fancy talking all that time to the Countess of Carlisle!"

"Far better if I hadn't," said Elizabeth mournfully. "She'll not use *us* again for her remedies. Father will be . . . will be . . ." she sighed, sinking down on a stool. "Though 'twas not because I tried to get the account paid, 'twas because we're Puritans. Oh Lud—" she sighed again, and put the little handkerchief on the counter. "At least, I got this . . . as a Christmas gift. And the beggars got a few farthings too," she added with bitterness.

Martha did not understand. She gave a cry of delight and pounced on the handkerchief. "Oh, 'tis so beautiful, how can thread be wove so fine . . . and the lace; like frost flowers!"

Elizabeth looked at her sister. "Take it, Matt, dear, if you like it. 'Tis yours, a Christmas gift."

"Oh, Bessie, you're good to me!" Martha kissed her sister. "How Madge and Dolly will envy when I show them this. I'll put a mask on my face and wave this handkerchief and pretend *I* am a Countess!"

Elizabeth smiled, thinking how easy it was to please Martha, whose chief happiness still lay in pretending . . . and in playing with the waxen doll baby her stepmother had bought for her at Bartholomew's Fair years ago.

The door opened and Richard Fitch stamped in bearing a wooden keg. "Whew, it's cold!" he said to the two girls. "Water's near froze in the conduit . . . Mistress Bess, your lover's a-coming up the street, I saw him turn the corner." He gave Elizabeth a malicious look.

"I've told you not to speak of Mr. Howes like that!" she snapped. "I *presume* you mean Mr. Howes since he's coming here for dinner."

"Well, he'd like to be your lover," said the apprentice, "and from what I hear, the Master's going to give you to him, lessen ye can quick snare yourself something better like a knight or baronet."

Elizabeth bit her lips and turned away. She was accustomed to Richard's baiting, which she knew sprang partly from his resistance to the attraction she had for him, but his words now gave her a shock, for they exposed something she had avoided facing.

Thomas Fones was inclined to accept the offer Edward Howes had made for her hand two days ago, and unless she could muster a more convincing reason against the match than her disinclination, she was like to become Mistress Howes before long. And live at Aunt Lucy's! she thought with increased gloom. Lucy Winthrop had long been married to the prosperous attorney Emmanuel Downing, and Edward was his law clerk. But it was not her father's command that Elizabeth dreaded; though he was stubborn enough, she knew how to manage him. This marriage proposal was backed by John Winthrop as well. Which was a very different matter. Since old Adam's death nobody in the family had ever questioned her Uncle Winthrop's decisions, and least of all Thomas Fones.

The shop bell jangled as the street door opened and Edward Howes walked in. He was in his early twenties, tall, and stoop-shouldered, rather like a heron, even to the untidy crest of drab hair on his narrow head. His gray doublet and breeches hung limply on his lean frame and were well spotted with ink and sealing wax. His eyes were vaguely blue, the eyes of a sensitive dreamer, and indeed of late he dabbled secretly in alchemy and mysticism. He had attended Oxford, and excelled in mathematics, he was thoroughly versed in law and the classics. In moments of embarrassment he often became pedantic, and he was never easy with Elizabeth whom he desired to the point of anguish at times, and who treated him with alternations of tolerance and boredom.

His long eager face lit up as he saw her behind the counter, he walked boldly towards her with hands outstretched. "How do you, Bess? Nay, leave your pills and potions be—for as John Lyly had said, 'Where is that precious Panacea which cureth all diseases . . . or that herb Nepenthe that procureth my delight?' Not on the shelves, Bess—but in your own heart—I hope?"

She smiled faintly and let him take her hand. "I fear my heart will dispense no merry medicine today, Edward, and that it lacks the wish to."

He swallowed, dropping her hand. "Cruel heart then, O Cor Crudelis! Why does it lack the wish?"

"For I am in a sorry mood."

"On Christmas?"

She shrugged. "And what is Christmas to us, Edward? You know well what my Uncle Winthrop and my Aunt Downing think of Christmas. No matter, they aren't here, and we have for dinner a Christmas pie thick with plums. Come and eat it with us."

They dined at the long table in the hall, all the Foneses except Thomas. Priscilla sat at the head in his place, with Edward on her riight. She chattered at him and he was content to be silent and watch Elizabeth, whose discontent with life gradually lessened under the delectable influence of suckling pig and roast goose, of marrow puddings and herb tarts, and especially of the strong ale she had herself made last year.

And when they had finished they sang madrigals together, softly so as not to disturb the ailing father upstairs, though he did not disapprove of singing which was part of the English inheritance back to the days of the wild Norsemen's invasion and the minstrels. Even John Winthrop had not yet come to frown on secular music, if it were seemly, for knowledge of part-singing and some instrument were signs of gentle birth.

Elizabeth had enough skill with the lute to strike a few chords, and she dearly loved to sing, especially the silver harmonies of Thomas Campion. Martha had a sweet little voice to follow the air, the children Sam and Mary piped off and on tune, while Priscilla wheezed in an adequate contralto, but at the discovery that Edward had a true baritone, Elizabeth looked at him with startled, if momentary, pleasure.

They sang "Now winter nights enlarge the number of their hours . . . now yellow waxen lights shall wait on honey love," and as the young man caught her eye, she felt a quiver of sensual excitement, born of the song, though she tried to attach it to Edward. They sang "The Silver Swan" and they sang Christmas songs, "Wassail, wassail all over the town," and "The Holly and the Ivy."

They might have sung all afternoon, except that Thomas sent word down by one of the maids that he wished to see Elizabeth. At once her gaiety was extinguished and her heart sank. He was going to ask her about Lady Carlisle! But he did not, for his thoughts were full of another matter.

"Bess," he said, as she came in still flushed from the singing. "Edward Howes is here, is he not?" As she nodded, he went on, "He has asked for you in marriage, has he spoken to you yet?"

She shook her head. "Not in so many words. I haven't permitted him."

"T'cha," said her father irritably. "Well, permit him then, for it's settled. 'Tis a good match for you, sober, steady young man, will go far in the law, and inherit fine Essex lands when his grandfather dies. Also Mr. Howes is quite satisfied with the dowry I can give you, the four hundred pounds left you by your mother, would have been satisfied with less, for he seems to have an immoderate attachment to you."

Elizabeth glanced at her father, then at the small coal fire. "I don't want to marry him. I don't want to go and live with him in two rooms of Aunt Lucy's house, and I don't love him at all."

Thomas's foot began to tap the floor beneath the blanket; he poured himself a draught of calming poppy broth from a pitcher at his elbow, and spoke with tense control. "Love will *follow* duty. I have been an indulgent father, I refused that offer for you from Master Thurlby last spring, because you said he was too old, but this is different. Mr. Howes is close to your Uncle Downing, near one of the family already, and your Uncle Winthrop feels it an excellent match for you."

As she said nothing but gazed frowning into the fire, he said, "Come, come, Elizabeth, what is this stubborn silence? I feel death near, my days are numbered, and I wish to see you, at least, settled, before Merciful God terminates my sufferings."

This plea did not affect her; for as long as she could remember, her father had been 'prophesying his imminent death; but her mind seemed stupefied, she could think of nothing to say except a plaintive "I love somebody else" and regretted it, as her father naturally asked "Who? Why have you not told me? Who is it?"

"No matter—" she said on a long breath. "I've not seen him in months and he doesn't love *me*."

Something in the droop of her head reminded Thomas of her mother, Anne. This and the sadness in her voice pierced the wall of his own discomforts.

"Bessie—" he said gently. "Come here."

She obeyed, and sank to the stool he indicated beside his chair. He put his gnarled hand on her dark shining hair. "I would not be harsh with you, my child, nor force you to obey, except that I have prayed on it and know what is best

for you, and your wayward heart, which has learned as yet
nor discretion nor moderation."

She sighed, grateful for the touch of his hand on her head,
moved by the rare softness of his voice, but suddenly twisting
and looking up at him, she cried, "No, I am *not* moderate,
Father! Or tame, or sober of thought—God forgive me—
sometimes I feel torn in two—by the strength of passion in
me, by a longing for wildness and freedom . . ." She checked
herself. "This I know you cannot understand."

Thomas Fones felt sharp apprehension as he stared at the
flare of her nostrils, the lush curves of her mouth.

It was not Anne Winthrop whom she resembled now, but
Thomas's own grandmother, the passionate Cornish woman,
with the long lewd eyes of a gypsy. And he remembered that
there had been sorry stories about her in the Fones family, stories that many men had desired her, while she had loved too
well a Spanish sailor cast up from the Armada on the Cornish
coast near her home. Wanton blood, he thought with shame,
and for the girl's own safety she must be bled of it quickly.
"So, Bess," he said, "you are condemned out of your own
mouth, my dear. You admit fierceness of passion and need
for guidance, and Our All-seeing Lord has given you through
me the means to subdue the one and find the other. You
know your duty to your father, indeed you've proved it, and
I am mindful of how well you've learned the arts of the
apothecary and stillroom, and of the help you've given me
in the shop."

She turned quickly to him, delighted at the compliment,
but he, fearing to incite her to vainglory, hastily went on, " 'Tis
a pity you've not the *same* skill in ordinary female tasks
as well, your mother tells me you have scant interest in
stitchery or spinning . . . but let that be. You will *have*
to learn those skills when you are a wife—the wife of Edward
Howes."

His voice ended on a much sharper note, for still he was
not sure of her obedience, and his knee had begun to throb
again. There was a swimming in his head that always came
with anger. "Enough of this!" he cried, pounding his fist on
the chair arm. "Have you no regard for *me*? Do you not
care that I am ill and weak, and that your obduracy increases
my sufferings?"

"Yes, Father," she said dully. "Forgive me." What's the
use? she thought. What else is there for me to do, and Edward's naught so bad, he loves me . . . and Jack himself

wanted me to marry him. "But one thing I ask, Father . . . give me a few more months . . . let not the marriage be till summer."

Thomas slumped back in his chair. "There, there, Bess. I knew you'd be a good lass. No doubt the wedding may wait a bit. Now I want you to go to the Downings and inquire for your Uncle Winthrop's health. Mr. Howes can escort you. Take your uncle the Purple Electuary. It may cure him. And send your mother to me. And ask cook for a warming pan well filled with coals, the bed was damp yesterday."

"Yes, Father." Elizabeth lingered a moment, wondering if he would offer to kiss her in reward for her submission, longing for more of the affection he had shown her so briefly. But she saw that he had sunk back into his own preoccupations.

Elizabeth and Edward walked down the Old Bailey, turned west up Ludgate Hill, then mounted the Fleet Bridge. She walked very fast, wishing to ward off her capitulation and ignoring Edward's tentative clearings of the throat as he shambled beside her. But on the bridge, the mud-spattering passage of a nobleman's coach forced them into one of the jutting safety nooks for pedestrians, and Edward seized her arm.

"Wait, Bess! I never see you alone, and I must know. Did your father speak to you of me?" His urgent clutch hurt her arm; she moved away from him, pulling her fur-lined cloak tight around her. She leaned on the stone parapet, so that her hood concealed her face, and gazing on the frozen canal below, she said, "Aye. He told me of your offer. He is in favor of it."

"And you, Bess—are you in favor? Will you not look at me?" She had raised her eyes and was staring at the huge gloomy pile of the Fleet prison, where there was a man's hand clenched from inside on one of the thick iron window bars.

She turned slowly but did not look at the anxious face beside her. "I will marry you, Edward, because you wish it, and my father and uncles wish it, but I do not love you."

"You will, my sweet," he cried. "In time you will. 'Amor gignit amorem.' Plutarch has said it, and Seneca too, 'Ut amaris, ama,' Love begets love."

"Let us hope so," said Elizabeth with a small laugh. She was suddenly sorry for him with his long storklike body, his myopic eyes, and the stock of quotations with which he bolstered his speech, fearful that it would not stand alone.

"Will you please to kiss me, Bess?" he begged. "I'll not hurry you or do anything you don't like, I vow it."

Dear Lord, what a wooing, she thought, with a contempt she could not help. Tentative, humble, fearful of rebuff . . . there *might* be women would be won by this approach, but—She raised her face and offered him her cheek; as he kissed it furtively she felt him tremble, and her eyes went back to that clutching prisoner's hand on the window bar.

"So," she said briskly. " 'Tis getting cold now the sun's gone, let's hurry to the Downings." They walked off the bridge.

"We'll tell them, Bess? Tell them our news?" He was discouraged by the coolness she showed him, and yet so inexperienced with women that he wondered if she were simply being modest. "We'll tell them now?" he asked again, hoping that public affirmation would bring the triumph he had hoped to feel.

"If you like," she said . . . "Oh, look, Edward, here comes Lady Carlisle's coach returning from the City!" They flattened themselves against the house wall as the four black horses came trotting up Fleet Street, the postilion blowing blasts on his trumpet, the coachman shouting, "Make way! Make way for her Ladyship of Carlisle!" The masked face flashed by in profile.

"They say she is a meddling woman, an intriguante," observed Edward as they regained the cobbles, "and has far too much influence with the Queen and thus the King."

"She is certainly no friend to our form of worship. 'Puritans' she calls us, of course."

"How do you know?" asked Edward astonished, and Elizabeth, willing enough to talk of impersonal matters, told him of the morning's episode with the Countess.

"That was perhaps unfortunate," he said gravely, as she finished. "She might make trouble."

"How could she?" said Elizabeth frowning. "Neither a great noblewoman nor certainly Their *Majesties* will bother over the conformity of a little apothecary!"

"No, I think not, though the King has lately concerned himself with a great many strange things when it comes to suppressing our forms of worship and foisting the old Roman ceremonies on the Church of England. And now with Laud become Bishop of London . . . we may soon be forced to bow at the Name of Jesus, kneel to painted images, say no prayers that aren't in the prayer book, and profane the Sabbath with sports and games!"

"Why not?" she said without thinking. "All these things my grandfather believed in, and kept Christmas too. I vow I like it better."

Edward turned and looked down at her. "Never talk that way before your uncles, Bess—Mr. Winthrop especially would be appalled."

"I know it," she said quickly, but she had noticed a faint reserve in his voice, and she added, "Are you truly a Puritan, Edward?"

He was startled by a question he had sometimes put to himself, and he laughed. "Nay, I don't know. I fear I'm not overgodly. At least I think everyone should worship as they like. Religion has not my interest as it should." He thought of the things which did hold his interest—the search for the philosophers' stone, study of the new logarithms, and of the law.

Elizabeth suddenly laughed too. When he was not trying to make love to her, he had directness and some humor. "I'm not godly either," she said. "Nor do I worry enough over the salvation of my soul . . ."

"And yet," he went on still following his thoughts, "the man I love best in the world, Jack Winthrop, has a true piety I can admire, it sits on him well and quietly, not like some ranters. Bess," he added reaching for her hand, "how pleased your cousin Jack will be when he knows we're betrothed."

Though candlelights were pricking through the windows of all the huddled houses, Fleet Street darkened for Elizabeth. The mention of that name combined with Edward's pleading touch gave her a sick pang that was physical. She said nothing, and withdrew her hand.

Near the Fleet Street conduit, a weathered old sign of a Bishop's Head swung at the corner of an alley. They silently turned up the alley which was virtually a tunnel since the lattice windows of the upper floors projected within two feet of each other. At the end of the alley was Peterborough Court and the imposing Downing mansion which occupied three sides of it.

Elizabeth and Edward were admitted by a liveried man-servant—the Downings lived elegantly—and received by Emmanuel Downing himself beside a roaring oak fire in the elaborate Hall. He was a stout, rather pompous man of forty, dressed in a plum velvet doublet, on which he had loosened the buttons for greater ease during his after-dinner doze. He was shrewd about finance and the law, and had last summer entered the Inner Temple as an attorney of the Court of Wards and Liveries, a remunerative position which his brother-in-law, John Winthrop, had already enjoyed for a year. Downing had been born in Suffolk and rejoiced in the acquaintance of several prominent Puritan lords as well, so that his religious views coincided with John Winthrop's. But in Emmanuel these were more a matter of custom and expediency than conscience. It was not fear of the King's possible papacy that worried him, it was the need for resistance to the King's shocking unconstitutional raids on citizens' rights and purses.

Today he awoke from his nap and greeted his niece and clerk hospitably if somewhat absent-mindedly. "Well, well, youngsters—where have *you* been, Edward? I thought you were working on the Hankin petition, or is it the Stewart wardship?"

"You gave me the half day off, sir, to dine with the Foneses."

"Ah, to be sure—so I did." Downing yawned, belching slightly, reached to the mantel for his long clay pipe, stuffed it with tobacco from a cannister and motioned to Edward to light a spill at the fire. When the clerk obeyed, Downing took a deep pull, voluptuously emitted a cloud of smoke, and said, "Bess, you look most pretty, lass, is't the walk in the cold, or perchance something else?" He gave a broad wink.

"I don't know, Uncle," she said, and hesitated, so that Edward threw her an anxious glance, then gulped out, "Elizabeth and I are to wed, sir."

"Excellent! Excellent!" cried Downing heartily. "Though scarcely a surprise. We must drink on it, eh?—my best malmsey put down in '19! *Lucy*—" he bawled suddenly, "Wife, come! Here's a joyful occasion!"

Lucy Downing was in the nurseries, supervising the swaddling of Joshua, the latest baby, and scolding the nurse. She did not hear her husband's bellow, but one of the servants went to summon her, and she presently came down to the Hall. "What's ado, what's ado?" she said with irritation as she entered and saw only their clerk and her niece.

Lucy, now twenty-eight, had been married seven years to Emmanuel, had duly presented him with three children and was six months pregnant with the fourth. Maternity, position, and a sojourn amongst the wild Irish in Dublin had

mellowed some of her tartness, but in brisk angularity of face
and manner she increasingly resembled her mother, Mistress
Winthrop, who still presided at Groton Manor.

" 'Tis these two . . . " said Emmanuel, "who are now
betrothed this Christmas Day. We must have up the butt of
malmsey on 't."

"Is it so?" said Lucy smiling thinly. "Felicitations." She
motioned to Elizabeth who came up and curtseyed. Her aunt
kissed her on the cheek and turned to Edward. "Well, young
man, you've got yourself a balk-mare. Bess Fones has ever
had a will of her own, but since you'll be bringing her under
my roof for a bit, I'll lend you a hand with the bridling of
her!"

"Thank you, ma'am," said Edward flushing, and though he
was in awe of Mrs. Downing he went on to quote Chaucer
in a reproachful tone. "*I* feel that Bess will ever be 'her
husband's help and his confort, his paradise terrestre and his
disport.' "

"Ah, my lad, we all feel that in the beginning," cried Emmanuel laughing. "Eh, Lucy, my dear, don't glare at me like
that! Have up the malmsey!"

Lucy turned to the bell rope and rang for the servant, but
her lips were tight. No reason to waste their most costly wine
on an occasion of small importance, but Emmanuel was generous, and besides like most men he tended to spoil Bess, who
was even now looking at her uncle with the soft seductive
smile which infuriated her aunt. Lucy knew that the smile
owed more to nature's fortuitous arrangement of the girl's
features than to deliberate intent, but found its dithering effect
on men nonetheless tiresome.

Actually Elizabeth was smiling because her uncle was being
kind, but she was not thinking of him, or her new betrothed.
She was weary, and longing to be home. Before there was
any hope of this she must discharge her errand.

"Aunt—" she said. "I have drugs for my Uncle Winthrop,
sent by Father, and wish to inquire how he does today."

"Better, it seems," said Lucy. "You may go up to the
chamber."

"And come down soon," cried Emmanuel, "that we may
drink to you! . . . Poor brother John, he's had no wine in
weeks, he even eschews tobacco, though there is naught so
good for the health."

Elizabeth mounted the graceful flight of stairs, went down

a passage past several shut rooms, then tapped at the door of a chamber that overlooked the garden.

A gentle voice bade her come in, and as she opened the door Margaret Winthrop held her finger to her lips and pointed towards the great curtained bed at the other end of the room.

Elizabeth curtseyed, and tiptoed towards her aunt who sat by the fire hemming one of her husband's night shirts. "Asleep?" whispered the girl, hoping it were so, for always she found converse with John Winthrop an ordeal.

"I think so. Sit down, dear. I'm glad of company. I must stay by him, since he'll let nobody else nurse him." Margaret smiled proudly, her soft brown eyes examining the girl.

Elizabeth seated herself on the cushioned bench near her aunt, savoring the kindly warmth that seemed to flow from the placid face, and the plump little body—far plumper now than when Elizabeth had first seen her on the night of King James's birthday celebration at Groton Manor eleven years ago. Since then Margaret had borne four living children, and despite her husband's obduracies, found affectionate contentment in her marriage.

"How you've changed of late, Bessie," she said with her sweet smile, "become a woman."

"Jack said that . . . last time I saw him . . . before he left for the Levant," Elizabeth blurted out, stabbed by painful memory, and knowing that with Margaret one need not be on guard.

Her aunt studied her quietly. "You've become a most *fair* woman, Bess. Did Jack also say that?"

The girl nodded, the rose on her cheekbones deepened. She looked away and said quickly, "Auntie, I am today betrothed to Edward Howes. Jack said that too, that I'd do well to marry Edward."

Margaret sighed with relief. "Ah, yes. I believe you'll do very well to marry him, dear." She was not accounted a clever woman, she read nothing except her Geneva Bible when John reminded her to, she knew no Latin, her household accounts were always muddled, but she had an intelligent heart. She grasped from the girl's manner a nearly exact view of the situation, and was sorry for Elizabeth, but very glad of the outcome. She knew her John, and how bitter a blow it would have been to him, had his son entangled himself with his little cousin, though she doubted that John had sensed the danger. He neither expected nor received any disquiet from his eldest. It was always Harry whose behavior gave him concern.

Elizabeth turned sadly away. Had she really been so foolish as to expect that Margaret would give her sympathy; or that she might even, from her knowledge of the beloved stepson she had raised, hint at some hope?

The girl fumbled in the pocket of her skirt and brought out the flask of medicine. "Father sent this for my uncle," she said.

As Margaret took it there was a stirring behind the bed curtains, and a muffled voice called, "Who's there, wife?"

Margaret hurried across the room and drawing the curtains said cheerfully, "Why, it's your niece, dearest—Bess Fones, come to inquire for you."

John Winthrop was not wholly awake, and his comprehension was dimmed by recent worries as well as by the weeks of fever. His fretful answer was quite audible to Elizabeth. "What has that wretched girl been doing *now* to plague her father? Some new disobedience, no doubt."

Elizabeth gasped, while Margaret said, "No, no John! Bess is right here, and has done nothing but obey her father's wishes and betroth herself to Mr. Howes."

"Oh, well enough, then," said John, still unaware that the girl could hear him. "But let her marry soon, before she brings disgrace upon the Winthrops with her carnality. I've heard that she makes lewd sheep's eyes even at their 'prentice."

"Dear husband, you talk too harsh!" cried Margaret, and she sent Elizabeth a look of apology, while forming with her lips, "He still wanders a bit."

The girl had gone very white, her hands were clenched. Her heart pounded and, mixed with fury at the injustice of her uncle's words, was a bleak despair.

She looked towards the bed where the big-nosed profile above the pillows was something like Jack's as the cruel voice too had been a travesty of his son's. I hate him, hate him—she thought.

She put back her shoulders, lifted her chin and without another word, walked out of the room.

Margaret, somewhat troubled, watched her go. Poor child, it was a pity that she should have heard such wounding criticism, but John had not meant to hurt her, and when he saw faults either in himself or others, his need to circumvent evil wherever found made him at times seem harsh. But

Margaret knew him in many tender moments; he had given her a devotion and sometimes astonishing passion that she had little expected during their betrothal. They had built together a satisfying married love, for which she thanked God daily in simple gratitude. No doubt Bess would find the same, in time, with Edward Howes, when she had learned to conquer daft desires such as that for Jack Winthrop.

Margaret instantly forgot Elizabeth as John stirred again. She felt his forehead, and found cool sweat there. "I praise God, love," she cried. "The fever's broken, and sooner than last time. We'll have you on your feet in a day or two!"

"Aye." He smiled a little and his fingers closed around hers. "I had not wanted to bring you up from Groton, but, my sweet wife, I am so glad you came. I pray that Our Merciful Lord has chastised me enough for my own good and will suffer me to return to my chambers for Hilary Term . . . I'm in dire need of the fees."

He sighed and while Margaret mixed with water the Purple Electuary, he thought glumly of his mounting debts. He had financed young John's trip to the Levant, and Henry's plantation venture in Barbadoes by selling the Essex property left him by his first wife, Mary Forth. But that was insufficient. Henry not only sent abominable tobacco home, as sole return on the venture, but kept demanding money and servants as well. Moreover there was the next son, Forth, to be educated at Cambridge, a dowry to be found for little Mary, and Margaret's sons to be provided for in a few years. I scarcely know how, he thought, tugging unhappily at his small pointed beard and frowning at the brocaded tester above his head.

Margaret proffered him the pewter mug of medicine, and he drank it absently. "I must soon answer that distressing letter from Henry," he said. "The boy's vain overreaching mind will be his downfall. I marvel that he dares to ask me for more money; he knows I have none without sale of our manor lands, and I am already much in debt to my brother Downing."

"Think not of those things now, love," she said. "The Lord will provide."

"Sometimes I think the Lord has turned His face from England," John said slowly. "How can it be that He permits the King to so oppress us with false loans and taxes imposed without consent of Parliament! How can it be that He per-

mits popery and Arminianism to seep like plague throughout
our land?"

"Now, dear, pray, don't heat your blood with such thoughts
. . ." coaxed Margaret, and she added timidly, for she knew
little of such matters, "Will there not be a Parliament soon
that can show the King where he does wrong?"

"Aye," said John. He struggled up from his pillows, his
eyes stared from their hollow sockets at the Bible on his
table. "And we must pray that the King will listen . . .
otherwise there will be a scourge and judgment come upon
us from these evil times, a heavy dreadful scourge."

"But what should we do then?" she asked, a little frightened, for John's voice had risen to its full resonance as it
did when he read them a psalm.

He did not answer at once, and when he did it was as
though he were speaking from afar off to himself. *"It may be
that if the Lord seeth fit, he will provide a shelter and a
hiding place for us, as God sent Lot to refuge in the place
called Zoar."* He shut his eyes and sank back on the pillows.

She looked at him in dismay. He cannot mean that we
should go to Holland like those dreadful Separatists from
Nottinghamshire, she thought—he could not mean that. For
he had often said that he loved Groton above all earthly
places, and that the Lord would sustain them so that they
might live on the Manor till death, and then Jack and his
children after them. No, she thought, this talk is nothing but
speech born of fever. No more than that.

As the days went by till his complete recovery, and he
made no further dark allusions, all uneasy wonder slipped
from her mind.

3

ON FEBRUARY 14 Elizabeth awoke to hear a thrush caroling in the garden while warm air seeped through the heavy green brocade curtains which enclosed her with Martha in the girls' carved, four-posted bed. Through every nerve she felt the thrill of coming spring and with it an excited sense of release for which there was no other basis at all. Except that Hilary Term had ended in the courts and John Winthrop had yesterday quit London and returned to his home at Groton. Her hurt fury at his speech on Christmas Day had gradually subsided into the usual dullness of impotent rebellion. He had been pleasant enough the few times she had seen him, and had even offered her a brief apology for the words she had overheard. This apology she knew came partly from Margaret's suggestion, and partly from his own formal sense of justice. He had however indicated to Thomas Fones that he saw no reason whatever to postpone Elizabeth's wedding beyond late April, whein he would again come up to London for the Easter Term, and be pleased to attend the marriage ceremony. Thomas had at once agreed.

But I've still weeks and weeks, Elizabeth thought, I'll not fret today. She pushed the curtains aside and saw pale streaks of dawn through the diamond panes of the garden window.

She swung her bare legs over the edge of the bed, and as the thrush trilled again she sang too:

> *"Good morrow! 'Tis St. Valentine's Day,*
> *All in the morning betime*
> *And the very first lad that I shall see*
> *In* spite *of fortune will my true-love be!"*

Martha whose face had been buried in the down pillow, jerked her head up and gave a little moan. "Bess—Hush I pray thee! You know very well your valentine must be Edward, and anyway don't SING!"

At this unusual peevishness, Elizabeth examined her sister, saw the right cheek swollen, the pain-dark hollows beneath the eyes and said, "Is it the toothache again, Matt?"

The younger girl nodded, putting her hand to her jaw. " 'Tis getting worse, throbs so I scarce can stand it."

"Best have it out, dear," said Elizabeth gently. "I'll send Dickon for a tooth-puller, I hear there's a good one lives near St. Bart's Hospital."

"No, I can't! I can't! I'd rather die!" Martha covered her face with her hands and burst into terrified sobs. Elizabeth was silent. She had once herself been through the agony of tooth-pulling; the gagging from the clumsy iron forceps as they fastened on the tortured molar, the grinding splintering shocks of pain as the tooth-puller sweated and jerked with one hand, while forcing his patient's head back with the other. But she had set herself to stand it without screaming, and she had stood it, until the ecstasy of relief, when the tooth-puller waved the bloody tooth in the air and demanded sixpence in payment. But to Martha pain of all kinds meant fear and disintegration so piteous that one had not the heart to force it on her.

"Well, lie quiet then," said Elizabeth. "I'll bring some laudanum and ground cloves to put in the hole." She jumped out of bed and pulled her linen night shift off. For the first time since October the air in the room was not chilling, and she opened the garden window and stood naked in front of it, breathing deeply. The air smelt of coal smoke from London's kitchen fires, of low tide from the river and of the night-soil which was even now being dumped from windows into the streets in hope that an ordure cart would come by eventually and remove it. But Elizabeth's nose was used to these city smells, and picked up with joy the unaccustomed ones of rich brown earth steaming in the dew, and of the hyacinths that had opened overnight in the garden. Suddenly she stretched and lifted her arms high above her head. Lowering them slowly she ran her hands over her large firm breasts, her flat stomach, her flanks and hips, rejoicing that her skin was smooth as ivory. She took her wooden comb from the chest, and began to comb the curling strands of dark hair so long and thick that they fell like a cloak and covered her body in all modesty nearly to the knees. She breathed deep again and shut her eyes while rich words chanted in her mind: *The hair of thine head is like purple; the king is held in the galleries . . . How fair and pleasant art thou, O love, for delights! This thy stature is like to a palm tree, and thy breasts to clusters of grapes . . . like two young roes that are twins . . . O I am my beloved's, and his desire is towards me . . .* She opened her eyes and stared unseeing at the high gray mass of London Wall, until Martha made a whimpering sound in the bed. Elizabeth shivered and her shoulders sagged. She put down the comb, and took a clean day shift from the chest. Dull shame oppressed her. It was the Church and Christ that those troubling, beautiful words referred to, not man and woman. Uncle John had made that clear when she had heard him read the Song of Solomon at a family service. Later she had looked it up in the Fones Bible and seen that it was so. Though the thrush still warbled in the cherry tree, her exhilaration vanished.

Elizabeth dressed herself in her maroon serge workaday gown, tied a white fichu around her shoulders and a white apron around her waist. She braided her hair and bound it with a linen kerchief, then she went to the kitchen to get a mug of breakfast beer on the way to fetching Martha's palliatives from the shop.

She found a scene of confusion and snivelings in the kitchen, where Priscilla was halfheartedly beating Tib, the youngest maidservant, with a small cane reserved for this purpose; though Priscilla's good temper and lethargy prevented her from chastising either her children or servants as often as her gossips did theirs. The cook, who had got her underling into trouble in the first place, was virtuously stirring a potful of eel stew and egging on the punishment. "And a fearful liar she is too, ma'am, said she'd swept the stairs when she 'asn't touched 'em in donkey's age, said she wasn't a-kissing the sweep be'ind t' scullery door, when I see 'er face wi' me own eyes all smooched wi' soot—"

"I never! I never!" wailed Tib, sniveling harder, and wriggling expertly so that Priscilla's blows hardly reached her. "Ow, ma'am, ow! You're a-killing me!"

Priscilla's fat arm dropped, and she sank onto a stool, mopping her face. "Well, see that you be good in future, Tib —go to the stillroom and fetch me some fresh vinegar, I'm quite faint . . ." As the girl scuttled out of sight, Priscilla said to Elizabeth, "Ah—good morrow, Bess, you're down late, where's Martha? . . . these wenches . . . it wearies me so to wield the cane . . . but when I found she'd eaten up a whole crock of butter, and in truth she is of late so greedy, I pray the little slut's not breeding, 'twould be most inconvenient . . . Sammy—" she turned to Elizabeth's twelve-year-old brother who was perched on a stool munching toast and scowling into his Latin Grammar, "You'll be late for school again."

Samuel Fones shut his grammar with a bang and flung it in a bag with the abacus he used for arithmetic. He was dressed in the yellow stockings and blue coat worn by Christ's Hospital scholars, and he had been quite oblivious to Tib's punishment, canings being of daily occurrence at school. Moreover he was at the age when his home interested him little and he lived entirely in those moments when he escaped with his comrades to investigate the London docks, or play football at Smithfield. He gave Elizabeth, of whom he was rather fond, an absent-minded wink; bowed to his stepmother, saying "I gi'e-you-good-day, ma'am, may-God-keep-you-in-health," and pelted out the door.

I wish *I* was going to school, or rather I wish I was going out *somewhere*, thought Elizabeth while she explained to Priscilla about Martha's toothache. She finished her beer and walked along the passage to the apothecary shop, where her father was already rolling pills on a marble slab by the light of a candle. He had recovered from his last bout of illness, but it seemed to have shrunk him, and the tremor had not left his knotted hands. He greeted Elizabeth, and told her to continue making up the pills when she had attended to Martha. Elizabeth enjoyed much of her work in the apothecary shop, but pill-rolling was dull, and this morning she protested. "Oh, Father, can't Richard do it? I wanted to—" She thought rapidly and amended, "That is, my mother badly needs new needles so that we may sew on my bride sheets, I could just run out to the tailors and buy some . . ."

"You know well I won't have you running the streets alone

like a beggar wench," snapped her father. "If Edward comes over later, he may take you, and Richard has gone 'cross river to Southwark with the Unicorn's Horn for Mrs. Elwick's babe. If that doesn't bring the little one out of its fits, nothing will."

Elizabeth sighed and resigned herself. At least the Elwicks paid quite promptly, and for the use of the marvelous Unicorn's Horn—which was a spiraled white bone—one could charge as much as a guinea, so later Thomas might be in a good enough mood to give her a few pence pocket money.

The morning passed like a hundred other mornings. A few customers sent in their servants with prescriptions to be filled or simple requests for plasters, and physic. Thomas left the shop to Elizabeth and remained in the stillroom behind, while compounding the most complicated of his mixtures, but he emerged twice to greet clients of importance. One was the assistant to the eminent Dr. William Harvey who lived a few blocks north at St. Bartholomew's Hospital, and was famous for his discovery of the blood's circulation. Thomas was flattered that this physician relied on him for many remedies, and eagerly questioned the young assistant about present conditions at the hospital.

The other customer was a stranger, and obviously a gentleman, for he was dressed in taupe velvet with a sword at his hip, and wore a large plumed hat above curling lovelocks glistening with pomade. He strode into the shop demanding with some arrogance to know whether they carried the best Verina tobacco, and upon Thomas's bowing low and assuring him that they did, the young man leaned against the counter and requested to try its merits then and there, while he stared boldly at Elizabeth. She was used to that type of stare, which she calmly returned before lowering her lashes and fetching one of the little clay pipes they kept ready. She filled the pipe with their best minced tobacco, then lit it for him, smiling faintly, pleased with so interesting a break in the day's routine.

"Ah—splendid . . ." drawled the young man on a deep breath, letting the smoke drift out of his nostrils. "Fine tobacco . . . and I should know. . . . since I have recently been growing it in Barbadoes." It seemed to Elizabeth that he spoke with meaning, and that his eyes moved watchfully from her to her father. This puzzled her, but Thomas noticed nothing, and said without enthusiasm, "Indeed, sir? We have a young kinsman who is there now, but this is none of his tobacco, I assure you. *It* was most inferior."

"Ah so?" said the young man . . . "sad, sad." He seemed about to add something else, but did not. He looked at Elizabeth instead. "Well, this is excellent," he said, "I vow I shall return later and buy a pound of it, for the moment I've not my purse with me . . . unless, perchance . . ." he paused delicately and looked at the apothecary, "My name is Robert Seaton, esquire, I have lodgings at the Sign of the Bell in Aldersgate, near in fact to my good friend the Earl of Thanet's mansion."

Thomas hesitated only a moment. "But of course you shall take the tobacco now, sir, and settle the account at your leisure, and I trust that in the future you'll be pleased to patronize The Three Fauns again!"

"Why, to be sure—" said Seaton smiling, "and since you *are* so kind, I've a touch of the ague, perhaps you have some electuary that might help . . . ?"

As Seaton had hoped, Thomas nodded and turned in to his stillroom. The young gallant leaned close to Elizabeth and whispered, "Slip out into your garden quick as you can . . . over to the Wall behind the rose trellis!" As she looked both startled and indignant, he added urgently, "There's a valentine awaiting you!"

"Sir—" she said tartly though she kept her voice low, "I assure you I've no interest in your valentines, find yourself another."

He shook his head violently, in denial of exactly what she was not sure, because Thomas came back with a flask of betony water. The young man thanked him, took the pound of tobacco, and went out, but his lips formed "the garden" to Elizabeth behind her father's back.

Such effrontery! I certainly shall *not* go, she thought as she dusted the tobacco crumbs off the counter, nor did she find him particularly attractive. Yet how did this Robert Seaton know there was a rose trellis in the garden, how did he expect to get into the locked garden, and how was it that he had a valentine all ready for her? It could do no harm to find out, she decided suddenly. It was even perhaps her duty to investigate so peculiar an invasion herself, since Richard was out and her father virtually crippled.

She murmured a quick excuse to Thomas and slipped past him into the house. As she walked down the passage to the garden door, she wiped her hands on her apron, and loosened her kerchief so that several dark curls escaped to frame her forehead and cheeks in the becoming way the Queen had made fashionable. The garden appeared quite deserted. She walked a trifle nervously up the brick path around the sundial whose brass pointer shadowed XI, past a bed of sweet marjoram and yellow violets to the trellis. Between the trellis and the wall there was an ancient spreading yew, and she saw a flicker of motion behind it.

"Who's there?" she called resolutely. "Is it you, Mr. Seaton? I only came to inquire by what means you intrude on our——" She stopped with a gasp, as a tall figure in brown emerged laughing from behind the yew, grabbed her roughly and stifled the scream in her throat with a kiss. Her response was a violent resounding slap. She was instantly released while a voice between mirth and anger cried, "God's bloody wounds! What a greeting?" She stared and her jaw dropped. "Harry . . . ?" she whispered uncertainly. "But you're in Barbadoes . . ." So astonished was she and so unlike her memory of him did he look that she felt a quiver of fear. There were ghosts that appeared like this, there was witchcraft—whereby the devil took on human form to tempt maidens who were not discreet.

"Aye, I'm Harry, in truth," he said ruefully rubbing his cheek where the marks of her fingers sprang red against the tanned skin. "As you, Bess, have turned a vixen, in truth . . . but let be—I'm pleased to find my cousin so virtuous. Did you think it was Seaton?"

She nodded, still staring at him. His blond hair was bleached with flaxen streaks from the sun, his skin was browner than any she had ever seen. There were small gold hoops in his ear lobes; he wore a cutlass and a pistol at his belt. There was a careless swagger about him even though his leather jerkin was sweat- and sea-stained, and one seam was ripped open. He was tall, taller than the other Winthrop men, and far handsomer than they. His eyes were blue, heavy-lidded and bold, yet in their mirthful light and the deep set beneath arched brows there was something of Jack. And seeing this she felt the familiar pang, and consequently a melting towards Harry whom she had always thought of as a nuisance and a scamp.

"Tell me," she said slowly. "How is it that you're in England . . . and why this stealth . . . and *how*——" she said frowning and still perplexed, "did you get into the garden?"

He laughed and jerked his chin. "Over the Wall, my lass, how else? 'Tis simple enough though I tore my jerkin on the iron spikes atop. No matter, I shall now order me a new scarlet suit at Seaton's tailor. This is hardly garb for a gentleman o' London—where by the way I arrived this morning."

"Why?" she said. "I mean, why didn't you come to us openly, since you are back?"

He spoke slower than he used to, almost in a lazy drawl which now had a mocking edge. "Because, I have some reason to doubt my welcome in certain quarters. My father's and Uncle Downing's letters have been scarce admiring of late, . . . so, my sweet coz, I thought I'd see you first, mayhap learn from which quarter the wind doth blow." He gave her a lopsided smile of considerable charm, and leaned towards her touching her bare arm. "You've not turned long-mouthed and decorous while I've been gone, have you, Bess? As I remember our childhood you were nearly as black a sheep as I!"

She tried to look rebuking, and she tried to still a quickening of her pulses, but she could neither. Instead his touch pleased her as had no man's but Jack's. *It is because it's his brother,* she thought—*their kinship that I feel.* And she said, "But why did you come back, Harry, and what is it you want now?"

"'Tis a dry tale, sweetheart," he said shrugging. "So let's wet our whistles and sit there, for the telling of it." He pointed to a wooden bench beneath the trellis.

She cast an anxious look towards the house, knowing she would soon be missed when the family gathered for dinner, but she sat down beside him. A leather flask hung from his belt. He unbuckled it and took a long drink. "Now *you*—" he insisted. She sputtered and coughed as the burning pungent liquor ran down her throat. "What *is* it?"

"Rum," said Harry laughing at her. "The joy and solace of the Indies. 'Tis a drink of almighty Mars's own blood to fighters, of Venus's enchanted milk to lovers!" He took another pull from the bottle.

"Harry—what is this talk!" Surely these were pagan gods he named in the same chanting voice his father used for public prayer! "You sound nothing like you used to."

"Nay, and why should I? I was a raw lad of eighteen when I left, and now I'm twenty-one. I've learned hunger and danger, and the gut-shaking peril of the sea. I've learned the sweetness of a moonlight beach where the water laps like warm velvet, and it matters not that the woman in your arms is black." At her in-gasp of breath, he turned to her, his eye-

brows raised and he drawled even slower. "I've learned what it
is to have an enemy, and walk ever watchful in fear of murder, and then . . . to *kill* that enemy before he cuts *me* off."
He tilted his eyebrows, watching her shocked face sardonically.

"Harry—" she whispered, after a moment. "This man you
killed . . . he was a black?"

"Nay, sweet. He was an Englishman, even as I. And until
last September we settled our quarrels amongst us on Barbadoes, each man as he saw fit. But then alas a governor was
sent us, one Wolferstone, a narrow man—and before he
pried his long nose too deep into my matter, I thought it best
to leave."

She looked at him in wonder and excitement, aching to
know more and yet afraid to question.

"Might the Governor send after you to London?" she
asked at last.

Harry shook his head. "Far too busy with the Spaniards
who are assaulting the Islands again; moreover who's to
carry the word to London? Since the two captains of the only
ships that touch Barbadoes are friends of mine!" He grinned
at her. "Bess, it would be wise to forget what I've just told
you. In tame and peaceful little England they take crotchety
views of bloodshed."

"Yes," she said, gazing at his handsome face. "I will forget . . . yet, Harry, I think England is not so tame and peaceful as when you left. There be bitter things take place in
Parliament these days, and fierce murmurings against the
King and Bishop Laud."

"Pah!" said Harry, raising the flask. "So Robert Seaton
told me when I went to him this morning from the ship.
This pother about religious practice! It irks me—" He
clamped his mouth shut, aware that he was talking very
freely, and that it was not only the rum had loosened his
tongue. It was the girl and her wide-eyed interest, the admiring looks she gave him from her beautiful heavy-lashed
eyes. There had been a lord's younger son on Barbadoes, more
scholar than planter, though in truth none of the sixty
planters gave much thought to the plantations where the
indentured servants from England, the slaves, both African
Negro and Carib Indian, all labored fitfully at the soil while
their masters lazed or fought the days away beneath the
tropic sun. The lord's son had brought vellum-bound and
entertaining books from home. Harry for the first time discovered that there was pleasure in reading and that not all books

were pious. There had been a folio of plays by some actor
at the Globe that had many good stories in it, including that
of an adventurous Moor who boasted of his exploits to a
lady who listened much as Bess did. The Moor had fallen
madly in love with her and she with him . . . Harry checked
himself. That was a foolish thought in regard to his little
cousin, Bess. London was full of fair women, and with Seaton
he hoped to sample some of them tonight. Let him not grow
maudlin over the first pretty white wench he had talked to
in years. He had moved away from her on the bench and
said abruptly, "Where is my father, Bess—at Uncle Downing's?"

She shook her head. "Back at Groton, since Hilary Term
has ended."

He nodded with relief. "I've no wish to see him yet, *nor*
be packed off to rusticate in Suffolk. On the other hand, well,"
he cocked his head and gave her the lopsided smile, "not to
beat the devil round the bush, I've landed without a farthing
in my purse. I can't lodge with Seaton who already owes a
quarter's rent, nor do I care to beg for shelter under our
estimable Aunt Lucy's thumb, so—"

"So you'll come here, of course!" she said, trying to hide
a rush of joy.

"Will he receive me?"

"Aye," she said, thinking fast and summoning all her
knowledge of her father. "But best not like this. You must
seem prosperous, assured. Borrow fine clothes from your
friend Seaton, talk big of your prospects, show condescension,
yet flatter him—you must know what I mean."

"I do," said Harry laughing. "And I thank heaven I've so
clever a little coz. I'll be back later at the front door, but
first a kiss before I go, sweetheart, one that doesn't end in a
slap!" He started to pull her into his arms, but she twisted and
jumped up from the bench.

"No, no, I beg—" she stammered, "Listen, you hear it's
very late," for Paul's bell began to clang out the noon strokes,
and then St. Sepulchre chimed in with its lighter peal. "Go,
please, hurry!"

Harry shrugged, amused at her panic, yet touched by it
too. "Till later then!"

She watched anxiously while he scaled the twenty-odd feet
of wall, finding hand and toeholds where she could see none.
She held her breath as he edged himself around the ridge of
overhanging sharp iron spikes, until he finally stood on top and

waved down at her. Then she ran through the garden into the house, just as the family were gathering for dinner. Fortunately Thomas had been so pleasantly occupied in concocting a special strong physic for a new customer, Lady Deborah Moody, that he had not noticed the length of her absence.

Harry returned at five that afternoon and rapped boldly on the front door. Elizabeth watching her father's startled greetings had much ado to hide her mirth, for Harry had followed all her instructions. Though he was taller than Seaton, that young man's second-best clothing fitted him well enough. The slashed green doublet and falling ruff, the high leather boots, embroidered gauntlets, and large black felt hat were those of an elegant cavalier. He had even borrowed Seaton's ivory cane—the height of fashion—though the fine sword and engraved scabbard were his own, and the only thing of value he had been able to bring with him in his hurried escape; except a squat young man carrying a sea chest, whom Harry beckoned through the door, before the startled apothecary had had time to think.

"My servant—" said Harry carelessly, pointing to the man. "Name's Peyto, very devoted to me. Can no doubt make himself useful in the kitchen, by your leave, Aunt?" He smiled charmingly at Priscilla, who fluttered and murmured, "To be sure, indeed. For certain . . ." while staring as they all were at Harry's companion. Peyto was short and swarthy with alert black eyes and a scar on his cheek which was shaped something like the letter T though he had done his best, by means of a sharp knife, to reduce the resemblance. And Peyto wore his hair longer than befitted a proper servant, since this covered the cropping of both his ears. He was, however, correctly garbed in frogged tunic, gray knee breeches and white cotton stockings; a livery he had that afternoon appropriated without the knowledge of its owner, a servant employed in the house next to Seaton's lodgings. Nor had Harry inquired too closely into the providential appearance of these clothes, knowing that Peyto never answered questions he did not wish to. But the man was devoted to Harry, and grateful in his own way that in the guise of Harry's servant he had been able to slip back into England. Peyto Smith was a gypsy from a tribe that wandered the North, in Cumberland and the Scottish Border. Six years ago, his inherited talents for horse-stealing had brought unfortunate results, which culminated in branding, and ear-cropping, and then deportation to Virginia with a shipload of other young felons. Peyto was immediately bored with Virginia and home-sick for his own people, so he set his considerable wits to work, and stowed away on the first likely ship that touched at Jamestown. This took him to Barbadoes, where he soon discovered Harry and attached himself to him, while Harry for his part found Peyto far more congenial than the three plodding Suffolk servants his father had sent him, and whom he had left behind to shift for themselves.

"It is a surprise, a great surprise, my dear Henry," said Thomas Fones, still recovering from the sweeping entrance of his nephew. "A pleasure, of course—'twould seem you've been prospering . . . though the tobacco you sent . . ."

"Ah yes, shocking—poor stuff," interrupted Harry, shaking his head. "Entirely the fault of my stupid slaves, but now the crop is vastly improved, vastly! I brought you a sample." Harry smiled and pulled from his pocket the pound of to-bacco which Seaton had that morning taken from the apothe-cary, though it had been transferred to a pouch. "Please to accept it, it's yours," he added graciously. "And when my goods arrive, I hope that you—and my dear aunt—will do me the favor to accept some other trifles."

"Very kind, I'm sure," said Thomas sniffing at the tobacco. "Aye, *this* is fine—the best Verina, I judge . . . my lad, I'm glad you're doing well. 'Twill delight your father, and Mr. Downing . . . have you seen him yet?"

"Oh, no," said Harry. "I've come first to you. Perhaps I shouldn't confess it, but of all places in London the Three Fauns has ever seemed more homelike than any other and its occupants more dear to me."

Elizabeth turned to the window to hide laughter. The graceless rogue! she thought. Not only for magnificently pre-senting the apothecary with his own tobacco, but for knowing that Thomas Fones was in awe of Emmanuel Downing and faintly jealous of him because of his closer intimacy with the Winthrops. Harry had surely struck the most expedient note, and the apothecary smiled. "Well, well, nephew, I scarce think my simple home deserves much praise, but such as it is, pray consider it yours, for as long as you will honor it. Come, join me in a drink to celebrate your homecoming, while the women prepare the guest chamber."

Thus to Elizabeth's delight, and her father's initial gratifi-cation, was Harry installed at the Foneses'. Thomas presently dispatched to John Winthrop a reassuring letter which enlarged on Harry's remarkable improvement, and prosperity. Harry himself, though he loathed writing and spelled worse than any of the family, judged it wise to send his father an accompanying note. It was full of filial affection and vague though confident reference to plantation affairs, urgent need to stay in London near influential friends, and impressive plans about to ripen. It closed with a tactful request for money to cover a temporary embarrassment until the next ship arrived from Barbadoes.

On an afternoon three days later at Groton Manor, John Winthrop received these letters from the London carrier and read them with astonishment and disquiet. Then he went in search of Margaret who was still in the washhouse with her two-year-old Sammy clinging to her skirts. She was superintending the laundry maids, and starching the family's delicate lace collars and pleated ruffs herself. "Come out here, my dear," said John, sniffing distastefully at the steamy air in the washhouse. "There's news."

She wiped her hands and followed John into the sunny courtyard where chickens scratched at piles of manure and two blooded hounds basked by the stables. "Is it bad?" she asked anxiously. "Not the King again!"

John frowned. "Aye, there's trouble in that quarter. Though Parliament still sits, he tries to dissolve it; but 'twas not that I meant. Son Henry is back. In London, stopping with Thomas Fones."

Margaret uttered an exclamation and read the letters he handed her. "Ah, 'tis not bad news, after all," she said, her face clearing. "It would seem he scarce deserves the last angry letter you sent him."

"And which he was obviously not there to receive," said John dryly. "I pray that the Lord has truly touched his wayward heart, and these are signs of reformation—but I mistrust." He sighed heavily, and glanced up at a window in the Manor House where old Mistress Winthrop lay moaning with pain from a cancer in her breast. "If 'twere not for my mother's grievous illness, I'd feel it my duty to go up to London forthwith, and confront my son."

"No, dear, no," pleaded Margaret, taking his hand. "There's no need for you to so disturb yourself. He's well off at the Foneses'." She hesitated, then went on lower, "Dear husband, be not vexed with me, but always it has seemed you show this one child less trust and affection than the others."

So rarely did she criticize anything that his spurt of annoyance was extinguished by self-questioning. He thought of John, the much-loved heir, and of Forth, the earnest Cambridge scholar who was now home and dutifully acting as secretary for his father. He thought of his one daughter, Mary, a quiet docile girl of sixteen who was at this moment tending her suffering grandmother. He thought of Margaret's quartet of little boys, Stephen who was ten, the younger ones Adam, Deane, and this little Sammy, clutching at his mother's apron. Was it true that for each of these he felt more warmth than he did for Henry? "And if it's so," he said sharply aloud, "what wonder, since he has been so oft reckless, improvident, a very rakeshame to disgrace me!"

"But if he's changed—" Margaret said softly, wondering at herself that she dared question John, and yet suspecting that his father's antipathy and excessive sternness had always augmented Henry's worst traits. "Think of the Prodigal Son, dear," she said, coaxingly.

John bit his lips, then gave her a wintry smile. "Aye, the lad has ever had keen advocates amongst women! Well, I'll direct Brother Fones to advance him five pounds for the nonce, as it's certain I have no spare money myself until the rents come in on Lady Day." He looked down into her flushed, earnest face and suddenly bending kissed her on the cheek. "Ah, Margaret sweet—thou art indeed above rubies, and all my children have cause to bless thee as I do." They stood contentedly arm in arm for a minute, looking out past four splendid walnuts to the rolling fields of their own land, where the dark earth was ploughed and ready for the spring sowing. The ducks quacked on the pond below the crowded pigsty; three fine mounts and two draft horses stamped in the stable while the ostlers curried them. The granary was filled, the cellars were stocked with good wine as well as ale; even though winter had depleted the stores, there was plenty of pickled meat and bacon left in the larder. There were new calves in the cow byre—and the ewes would soon be lambing. These broad acres, this beautiful old manor house, this plenty and graciousness were home, and John felt them as solidly interwoven with his own fiber as the warp is with the weft. And yet there came to him again the new foreboding and restlessness. Of what use these dear homelands if the spirit were stifled, if the air of even these sweet Suffolk meadows were poisoned by oppression and sin? And of what use were these lands if they were too cramped, and despite their bounty could not amply support eight children,

or launch them into lives commensurate with Winthrop birth
and gentility? It had been different in old Adam's day, in the
reign of the wise and tolerant Elizabeth. Nor had England
been so crowded then.

He forgot both Henry and Margaret as his thoughts followed the worn fretful paths which they, of late, so often
trod. There seemed no solution as yet, none that a gentleman
could stomach. If the King granted Parliament's requests to
cease from exacting forced loans, and above all to cease from
encouraging Bishop Laud in his devilish persecution of true
believers in the Gospel, then there might yet be hope for
easing of the lot and conscience of a loyal Englishman. John
clasped his hands behind his back and strode towards the
house. In his private chamber he gloomily perused the disquieting secret newsletter Downing had sent him and which
contained details of new Protestant disasters on the Conti-
nent. In Germany both Calvinists and Lutherans were being
smothered by the Roman Catholics; in France, Richelieu had
seized La Rochelle and crushed the Huguenots. *"God help us*
in these evil and declining times," John murmured as he
locked the newsletter in his private coffer. He bent his head
and prayed.

Margaret returned to the washhouse, warmed by her
husband's praise, and pleased that he had taken her advice
about Harry. She enjoyed starching the exquisite lace and
worked deftly until a foreboding struck her too, though
of a different nature from her husband's. All the same, she
thought suddenly, I wish Harry were lodged at the Downings'
instead of the Three Fauns, while a picture of Bessie's lovely
unhappy face formed itself on the glossy starch water. Yet
how foolish, Margaret chided herself. The girl had been in
love with *Jack,* but had now sensibly settled into her betrothal
with Edward Howes. There could be no possible danger
from Harry. She reasoned herself out of that fanciful worry,
and continued to cope serenely with the normal cares of a
household, children, and a dying mother-in-law. But her
fancy, no matter how foolish, had by the end of March become an incontestable fact.

Elizabeth, both by temperament and destiny, was to experience many overwhelming emotions in her life, but never one
so gaily reckless, yet compelling as the physical passion
which awakened in that London spring. Though for some
time, neither she nor Harry recognized the strength of their

attraction for each other. He plunged at once into the plea-
sures of London, and found Robert Seaton a resourceful guide,
nor did lack of money particularly embarrass the young men.
Shopkeepers were willing to extend credit to such dashing
gallants and moreover Seaton's boast of friendship with the
Earl of Thanet happened to be true. They were soon caught
up by that young nobleman's set, and found ready entertainment not only at Thanet House in Aldersgate Street, but in
various other fashionable houses. There came, however, a
day when Seaton's long-suffering landlady turned him out of
his lodgings for nonpayment of rent, and rather than confess
this to their aristocratic friends, Harry airily invited Robert
to share his room at the Foneses'. When Thomas was informed that he had a new guest, he demurred feebly, but
there was little he could do, since the young man had already
moved in, and also Thomas's health had failed again.

He was attacked by bronchitis, and when the fever receded
he suffered from joint pains so violent that for some days
he could not even feed himself with his throbbing swollen
hands. The dreary and familiar sickroom routine recom-
menced. But Elizabeth was scarely aware of it, except that it
gave them complete freedom below stairs, where Harry and
Robert took to inviting their friends in for drinks, or even
meals, and the house rang with the sounds of young male
laughter. Elizabeth moved in a daze through the sickroom
and apothecary duties she could not avoid, but all her
thoughts were of Harry and his merry companions who
treated her with flattering warmth.

It was on Lady Day, March 25, that the new year of 1629
officially began and it was four days later on Palm Sunday
that Elizabeth's maidenhood ended. It had rained all morning,
but by noon the blue sky was studded with puffy white clouds,
while the wet red roofs and gray cobblestones, the garden
flowers and the great rushing Thames all sparkled under a
warm sun. To non-Puritan Londoners it was a day of festivity, and after church the streets were full of strollers in
spring finery. The tavern doors stood open, and from the
more raffish ones drifted lute-accompanied voices of Singing Girls wooing customers with bawdy music.

Edward Howes, stalking along the Fleet towards Elizabeth's home, was not one of the merrymakers. His long head
drooped, his shortsighted eyes peered down at the cobbles;
there was no spring in his heart. He had for some time been
trying to deny a painful realization. Bess had not grown to

love him during the three months of their betrothal, she did not even hate him, which might have been encouraging. She simply, and increasingly of late, acted as though he did not exist at all. She forgot when he was coming and was often out with her cousin Harry when he arrived, having left no apology; or if she received him, it was with the glazed look of boredom, before she turned her long glowing eyes on the young cavaliers who were now always lounging about the apothecary shop. And especially she turned those eyes on Harry Winthrop. Edward had not seen her alone in weeks, and his patience had finally fractured.

"Her conduct is insupportable!" he muttered as he rounded the corner onto the Old Bailey and collided head-on with a muffin man. The muffins flew in all directions, the man shrilled with anger, but Edward strode on. On Easter the very next Sunday the first banns were to be cried in St. Sepulchre's, as had been long ago agreed. And yet she behaved as though he had no more right to her company than a butcher boy. Thrice cursed be Harry Winthrop, for so unsettling her with his rowdy ways, and his gallantries, and his new scarlet suit, and his mincing high-born friends. To be sure, these might unsettle any silly lass, Edward thought, at once excusing her; maybe all she needed was a stern talking to, and he as her betrothed had set out today with that purpose.

He clamped his jaw and knocked on the shop door. Richard was inside reading the Bible; he unbarred the door and let Edward in, then surveyed him with some sympathy. "If you're looking for Mistress Elizabeth she's not here, Mr. Howes, she's gone off junketing wi' Master Harry, My Lord Thanet and that there Seaton—and on the Sabbath too."

"Where have they gone?" said Edward grimly.

The apprentice shrugged. "I heard talk o' St. James's Park, an' summat about a bear-baiting, an' they was wondering would there be a masque shown anywhere, but Seaton he said No, because it's still Lent."

Edward drew in his breath sharply. "They wouldn't take her to a bear-baiting, or a theater!"

"Little ye know!" answered Richard. "Master Harry he does as he pleases and Mistress Bess *she* does as he pleases too, and who's to stop 'em!"

"They must be stopped!" Edward banged his hand on the counter. "I'll talk to Mr. Fones now, myself. He can't know what's going on."

"No more he does, the mistress says he's that fidgety and ailing, she don't want him vexed; properly cozened and hoodwinked *she* is by Master Harry too. It's Harry this and Harry that, till you'd think he was the King himself . . . or more likely the Devil!"

Edward frowned, much perturbed, and yet unwilling that the apprentice should forget respect for his betters. "Guard your tongue, Fitch, that's no way to speak!"

The apprentice jerked his head defiantly. "Well, ye needna be so high and mighty, Mister Howes. For there's devilish things a-going on. Wot about that man o' his—Peyto? He's an Egyptian, for all they try to hide it, and he's fair bewitched the maidservants wi' his fortunetelling and his greasy blandishments. That's by days—nights he spends in Tib's bed, or sometimes Cook's. A fine godly home this'll be wi' a gaggle o' gypsy bastards underfoot i' the kitchen."

"That's unfortunate," said Edward stiffly, "but the morals of the Foneses' servants are scarcely my concern."

"Aye—" said Richard, " 'tis your betrothed you think on, and I'll say naught to fret ye there—though I might—except how do ye like that your sweetheart should consort wi' a scarlet Papist?"

Edward startled and glared at the apprentice. "You're mad!" he cried. "Henry Winthrop is no Papist!"

"Nay, nay—not Master Henry. 'Tis that Robert Seaton. I've had suspicion, an' this morn I followed him when he sneaked out at dawn. D'ye know where he went? To Newgate gaol where they've lodged those viperish Jesuitical priests the Queen brought over. I saw that Seaton a-kneeling in the gaol courtyard, an' the priest signing crosses over him, and muttering the filthy prayers o' Rome. And they say there's a cell inside wi' candles and crosses and all manner o' idols for the saying of MASS!"

Edward bit his lips. "You must keep quiet about this," he said sternly after a moment. "I'll tell Mr. Fones. This whole matter is far worse than I thought."

"That it is," agreed the apprentice with gloomy relish. "And danger on all sides, now the King's to rule the country by hisself, and no one to gainsay him."

Though there was scarcely room amongst Edward's personal worries for national affairs to affect him at present, he knew that most of London was gravely disturbed by the King's furious action a fortnight ago, when His Majesty had forcibly dissolved Parliament without granting any of its requests. There had been a shocking scene when Black Rod knocked upon the great Commons door at Westminster, thus notifying the Speaker that the King commanded them to adjourn. The frantic members who saw their last hopes vanishing had wept and shouted, they had locked the doors and forcibly held the Speaker in his chair, while they hysterically passed their resolutions anyway, regardless of His Majesty's pleasure. And Sir John Eliot had cried out in a great voice, "None have gone about to break Parliaments, but in the end Parliaments have broken *them!*" Now Sir John Eliot and several other members were imprisioned in the Tower, and the King was about to make a proclamation signifying his intention of ruling without any Parliaments in future. The citizens saw their precious liberties threatened and the power of Rome returning, the Puritans saw themselves in imminent danger of active persecution for their beliefs, and all of middle-class England quailed at the menace to its purses, from which the King might now extract what he wished without hindrance.

A dismal world this one is becoming, Edward thought as he climbed the stairs to knock on Thomas Fones's chamber door. Nor were his spirits lightened by a distressing interview with a peevish and harassed invalid.

For Elizabeth it was not a dismal world. It had the glitter and sparkle of the diamond brooch which fastened the ostrich plume to Lord Thanet's upturned hatbrim, and it had the rich softness of Harry's new scarlet velvet suit. They rode in Thanet's coach towards a bear garden near Blackfriars, and the coach stopped along the way to pick up two pretty masked ladies, thus rounding out the party. The ladies were painted and scented and fashionable. They were introduced only as Chloe and Sylvia, and it soon appeared that they had taken these pseudonyms from a court masque they had recently attended. It also appeared from Thanet's jests that they had husbands someplace, but wherever or whoever these were, the absent husbands in no way affected the damsels' complaisance.

The coach, large as it was, seemed cramped for six, so Chloe, giggling, presently established herself on Lord Thanet's lap.

"An excellent idea!" cried Harry, and Elizabeth's heart paused while she saw him glance at Sylvia who had clusters of yellow curls, and what seemed through the mask to be a languishing glance. Elizabeth knew that she herself looked her best. Powerful incentive had overcome her distaste for sewing, and under little Martha's awed gaze she had been working secretly at night to refurbish her most becoming gown of saffron silk until it approximated the style of court ladies. She had cut the neck down to show the top of her breasts, she had ransacked the coffer of laces left by her mother and pieced together some strips of Venice needle-point for a falling collar and cuffs. She had made herself a black silk mask, and she had dusted herself with powdered orris root. Fortunately her cheeks and lips were highly colored by nature, for there was no rouge in the shop; Thomas refused to stock it though many other apothecaries did a brisk business in cosmetics. She had finished her toilet with lavish application of gillyflower essence she had herself distilled, and she had felt satisfied with her efforts until she examined Chloe's and Sylvia's voluptuous elegance. Now she was not so sure. And her relief was tremendous when Harry suddenly turned and carelessly scooped her up onto his knees.

"Mistress Sylvia shall be for Seaton!" Harry said grinning. "I'll make shift with my little cousin," and he added some ribald words in a Carib patois she did not understand but which caused the other men to roar with laughter. Though the Earl of Thanet had not, like Seaton, lived on Barbadoes he knew much about it, being a friend of Lord Carlisle who claimed it, and brother to Sir William Tufton whom the King was appointing as the Island's new governor; a prospect gratifying to Harry who saw therein the means of special privilege when and if he should return to Barbadoes.

But at that moment in the coach Harry had no thought of his nebulous future, for he was startled by his sensations as he held Elizabeth in his arms. They had had no close contact since his impulsive kiss in the garden. He had enjoyed her company, and seeing that the other men admired her had good-naturedly included her in some of their more suitable festivities, but he had given her little personal attention, while he amused himself in other quarters. And besides, though Harry was neither introspective nor unconscientious he had paid heed to the bars between them—their relationship so close that it was almost fraternal, and her betrothal to that gangling lawyer's clerk of his Uncle Downing's.

Now he felt Elizabeth tremble and yield her soft weight against his chest. He smelled the flowery clove perfume from the dark curls on his shoulder; and he plunged with the suddenness of drowning into love. Or at least into desire of a kind he had never felt before, since beneath its physical urgency there was tenderness, and uncertainty of his own attraction for her—a type of doubt which had never troubled him with other women. Yet he could not doubt long, for she fell as silent as he did. The amorous skirmishes and jests of the other four washed unnoticed around them. They were afraid to speak or move lest they shatter the drugged sweetness which overpowered them.

"Come, come, you both!" cried Seaton as the coach stopped by an alley which led to the Bear Ring. "By our Lady, you've not gone to sleep, have you? Hasten or we'll miss the famed Norway bear that's already killed twenty dogs!"

Elizabeth roused herself and slowly slid from Harry's knees to the step of the coach, where Seaton gallantly helped her to the ground. She drew her thin brown wool cloak tight around her and pulled the concealing hood over her head, feeling as giddy and unreal as though she had drunk a flagon of madeira. Harry came up behind and silently offered her his arm. She took it with a sensuous shiver, and they walked together up the alley to the Bear Ring behind the other laughing couples. Neither of them spoke.

Lord Thanet had reserved a box in the covered galleries which surrounded the bear pit; a bowing attendant ensconced them in cushioned chairs, and at the Earl's command brought them sweetmeats, and ale. Elizabeth tasted nothing. She had never seen a bear-baiting, and normally, being fond of animals, she might have been revolted by the anguished howls of the mangled dogs and the ferocity of the chained bear. As it was, the gruesome shambles of ripped guts and spouting blood was tiny and far off, as though she saw it through the wrong end of her father's spyglass.

The crowd roared and stamped, applauding now the bear, now some more valorous dog who managed to get a grip near the bear's jugular vein before the murderous claws tore him to ribbons. Thanet and Seaton laid bets, Sylvia and Chloe shrieked and shuddered and beat their fans on the chair backs. Harry tried to join in the furore, but the sport of which he was a connoisseur did not interest him today. He looked at Elizabeth's full slightly parted lips, at the cleft in her round chin, at the curves of her breasts, and could not stop staring.

"Bess——" he said at last almost timidly in her ear. "Bess—
let's go from here."

Lord Thanet heard him and cried, "Aye, let us! 'Tis dull
sport today. The dogs are poor." He stood up and flung some
shillings into the pit where the bear wards scrambled for
them. "We shall go on the river!" he cried. Elizabeth at once
acquiesced. Though she longed for it she was afraid to be
alone with Harry.

They went down to the wharf at Baynard's Castle where
Lord Thanet's own barge was kept and the Earl's four oarsmen rowed them upstream, expertly threading a way amongst
the busy traffic of barges laden with farm produce or lumber;
of ferries whisking across to Southwark, of pleasure boats
like their own.

The water lapped, the spring air grew softer and more
golden as the sun dipped towards the leafing oaks and elms
beyond Westminster. They were young and happy, all of
them that afternoon, and not the less so because each had a
secret distraction to be surmounted. Seaton's had to do with the
religion which he dared not publicly avow, Thanet's with his
state marriage to Lady Margaret Sackville which would take
place next month and mean the curtailment of such diversions
as this, while the young ladies' enjoyment was spiced by the
simple fear of discovery. Elizabeth and Harry too had their
preoccupation, but it was so immediate that they both shrank
from the next step, and were content for the present to drift
and wait. She had removed her mask, when the other girls
did, and looked up once into Harry's face. The long meeting
of their eyes was as intimate and frightening to her as the
ultimate caress, and she moved from him a little, crying
wildly, "Oh see, what is that barge down there? Aren't they
the royal arms?"

"By God, it is!" cried Thanet, peering ahead over the
water. "It's Their Majesties. Ladies, your masks!"

Chloe and Sylvia did not have to be told. Both were known
to the King, who unlike his father, James, was extremely
straightlaced, and endeavored to regulate his court with the
strictness of a Papist convent or a Puritan minister's household—much as either of these comparisons would have outraged his dedicated Anglicanism.

Elizabeth also replaced her mask though there was not the
slightest danger of recognition by the King, and she almost
forgot Harry in her fascinated curiosity.

The royal barge, bound for the Palace at Greenwich, where

Their Majesties proposed to sojourn, was elaborately carved and gilded, pennants fluttered from the corners of its striped silk awning, England's shield was mounted on the prow. The King and Queen sat in twin armchairs, making the very picture of marital felicity, for they were holding hands and the little French Queen, in her seventh month of pregnancy, had proudly made no attempt to conceal it. She was smiling and pointing out something on the bank to her husband, who inclined his head gravely and nodded.

How *small* they are! thought Elizabeth amazed. And how much like anybody else. The Queen looked no bigger than Martha, and in fact she slightly resembled Martha. The King's plumed hat hardly reached to the top of his chair. But as the royal barge came abreast of them Elizabeth saw that the King was not just like anyone else. He had a cool majestic stare, a palpable aura of authority. He raised his hand upon recognizing Lord Thanet, and both barges paused while the oarsmen's skillful feathering kept them stationary.

"Oh Christ—" whispered Chloe, curtseying, and pulling her head deep into her hood like a turtle. "Pray that he passes on quickly!" But Charles was in an amiable mood, enjoying the spring with his wife of whom since the death of his favorite Buckingham he had at last become very fond.

"Well, Thanet," called the King graciously, his stammer hardly noticeable today. "'Tis a pleasant afternoon for the river, you have a charming p-party I see." His eyes roamed benevolently over the young people. "Isn't that the Lady M-Margaret with you?" he asked, referring to Thanet's affianced.

Chloe and Sylvia quaked, and it took them all a minute to realize that it was Elizabeth the King was indicating with his thin white hand.

"No, sire," said Thanet quickly. "Lady Margaret is out of town. This is a friend—a cousin of this young gentleman, who has lately come from Barbadoes," he added hoping to distract the King from awkward questions.

"Ah, yes, that troublesome colony," said the King indifferently. "Strange, she resembles the Lady M-Margaret somewhat. Who are these young people? You may p-present them."

Thanet hissed "Unmask" to Elizabeth, who obeyed while she curtseyed, and Harry bowed low as best he could in the cramped space, while Thanet spoke fast. "This, Your Grace, is Henry Winthrop, Esquire, second son to John Winthrop, Lord of Groton Manor in Suffolk, and also attorney at the Court of Wards and Liveries—and this is his cousin, Mistress Elizabeth Fones, daughter to an apothecary on Old Bailey Street."

The King nodded graciously, but was obviously not interested in this undistinguished lineage. "Ah yes, I see now that there is no real resemblance between M-Mistress Fones and the Lady M-Margaret." His eyes started to roam towards the other occupants of the barge, as if he were going to demand their identity, but the frightened girls were saved by the Queen, who leaned forward with sudden interest to examine Elizabeth. "Fones?" she said in her strong French accent. "Fones—mais c'était surement le nom de la petite impudente—"

The King turned towards Henrietta Marie with his habitual grave courtesy, but he frowned, for he disliked her to talk French. "What do you mean, Madam?"

"Lady Carlisle, she 'as told me of a—very, how you say—*bold* apothecary's daughter called Fones, it was an amusing story—as dear Lucie tell it—except, now I remember, the girl would not go to church on Christmas, zey are Puritans, sans doute." The Queen laughed, for her friend had made a witty anecdote of her encounter with Elizabeth, and used it to ridicule the bigotry and money-madness of nonconformists in general. The Queen who took nothing seriously was diverted by this coincidence, but the King was not. He inspected Elizabeth again and said, "Does your apothecary shop serve the C-Countess of Carlisle?"

"It did, sire," answered the girl, scarlet-cheeked. The King moved his head until his cool stare rested on Thanet.

"I find your choice of friends a trifle singular, my lord. I d-did not know that you were of the same rebellious stamp as the Earls of Warwick and Lincoln."

"I'm not, Your Grace, I assure you," cried Thanet sincerely. "You *can*not doubt my proven wholehearted loyalty to your Majesty's belief and wishes." The King remained somber for some moments while he searched the young earl's frank eyes, then the royal face was illumined by its rare sweet smile. "Aye, I believe you," the King said sighing. "I've had m-many vexations of late, and become harsher by them, I fear." He waved his hand and settled back in his chair. "Enjoy your outing, my g-good Thanet." The royal barge proceeded downstream.

"Whew—" said Robert Seaton on a long whistle. "I'm glad that's passed over. I feared we might all be hauled off

to the Star Chamber!" Though he tried to jest, his voice was
unsteady, and they were all shaken. Chloe and Sylvia emerg-
ing from their hoods burst into nervous titters mixed with
tears.

"Nay," said Thanet, answering Seaton. "The King is just,
and gracious, no matter what the Commons think of him.
He has cause to detest some of the more fanatic of the Dissenters—not of your ilk, to be sure," he added kindly to
Elizabeth.

"I'm sorry," she murmured, subsiding on the bench. "Sorry
to be the cause of—of your embarrassment. I was that moon-
struck I didn't know what to do—but fancy being presented to
the *King!*"

"Aye, that'll be something to tell!" said Harry. "What *did*
you do to the Lady Carlisle, sweetheart?" he added chuckling,
and looking at her with even deeper admiration. They had
been jarred out of their enchanted quietude, but this whole
episode had increased her attraction for him. She had been
specially noticed by royalty, had been mistaken for one of
the most aristocratic ladies in the land, and now he was
charmed with her reluctant account of her pertness to Lady
Carlisle, though Elizabeth did not share his amusement. It
was far more upsetting than flattering to find that she had
been the subject of unfavorable comment in the highest cir-
cles, and she was shrewd enough to fear any conspicuousness
at present when one's family held views that Charles detested.
But we are such small fry, she thought, and the King was not
really angry. Soon Harry put his arm around her, and she
forthwith ceased thinking and only felt the honeyed closeness
of their bodies.

The Abbey bells were ringing for vespers when the barge
reached Whitehall and they all disembarked at the Palace
landing. Led by Thanet they took a short cut through the
Palace courtyards and emerged in St. James's Park which,
though not open to the general public, was nonetheless
thronged today by pleasure-minded aristocrats and all those
who had been able to bribe their way past the gatekeepers.

There were many distractions in St. James's Park; bowling
greens, ornamental water jets, a cockfighting pit, the remnants of the menagerie King James had established, several
taverns and oyster booths, but at none of these did the young
people linger.

"Where are we going?" Elizabeth asked dreamily, as

Thanet continued to walk rapidly up a path, while Chloe clung to his arm.

"Mulberry Gardens," said the Earl, trailing his fingers over Chloe's bare shoulder. "Where there are pleasant bosks of privacy."

"Amorous seclusion," affirmed Seaton, tightening his arm around Sylvia's waist. He glanced at Harry and Elizabeth. "Of which we *all* stand in need, it seems."

Sylvia giggled and tossed her yellow curls. "Oh la, sir! What could you mean?"

Harry laughed, a little off key. He leaned over and kissed the top of Elizabeth's head. "It will be good to be alone, sweetheart," he whispered, "For that we've never truly been."

Nor should be now, she thought in panic. I must go back. Dear Jesus Lord, give me strength to run away. But her feet continued walking on the brick path which led to the Mulberry Gardens.

The grove of mulberries was thickly grown and nearly in full leaf; though the trees had been unsuccessful in nurturing the silk worms for which King James had planted them some twenty years ago, they gave a delicious shade, and formed green tunnels, while dotted here and there amongst the trees were rustic ivy-shielded arbors furnished with benches. Some of these arbors were already occupied, murmurs and low laughter floated from them, and in one a man sang slowly the most poignant and voluptuous of tunes, "Greensleeves."

Elizabeth's chest constricted, her hands grew damp, "Let us stay with the others, Harry!" she cried and looked around anxiously. But her friends had disappeared. "I don't like it in here," she said, her words tumbling on each other. "It's cold and dark, I want to go back!" She turned and made to run down the path, but Harry seized her and held her tight against him. He looked down into her averted face and sang in tune with the unseen voice from the arbor near them:

"*Alas my love, you do me wrong, to cast me out discourteously. . . .*
Greensleeves is all my joy, Greensleeves is my delight;
Greensleeves is my heart of flame, and who but my Lady Greensleeves?"

"Nay," she whispered, her voice trembling. "You do me

wrong to sing that. Greensleeves was a harlot, and I am not one!"

"No, Bess," he said hoarsely. "You are my love, though never did I know it till today. Raise your head and look at me!"

She obeyed slowly, her eyes black in the shadow of the leaves. As he kissed her a sobbing laugh rose in her throat. Yet far off a tiny little voice piped like a farthing whistle: What are you doing, you fool?

"Let me be—" she whispered, pushing against him. "Harry, let me go."

He shook his head and kissed her again with all the provocative ardor of experience, and with the fierce new passion she had aroused in him. "I love thee, Bess." He put his hand on her breasts and pulled her against him. She shrank back though her breathing quickened. The tiny whistle voice had stopped. "Wait—" she stammered. "Please—I'm frightened, let me think—"

He laughed at this; softly. He glanced towards the arbor where the man had ceased to sing. "Come then, my love, we will walk a bit. I would not force thee, Bess."

He encircled her with his arm, and she walked beside him blindly. Her mind swam.

They came to the beginning of the wilderness or maze, where the close-cropped yews encircled a bank of moss. Harry spread out his scarlet cloak, sat down on it and pulled her beside him. He flung his plumed hat and sword on the ground, and smiled at her. "Since you will not kiss me, then drink, sweetheart," he said. From his belt he detached the same leather flask she had seen in the garden. He offered it to her, and when she hesitated he tilted her head against his chest, and laughing held the flask to her lips. She drank, nor this time felt the burning of her throat, or anything but warmth and greater ease. She drank again, and then Harry finished the flask. "You see, Bess—" he said quietly. "You have no need to fear me." He lay back on the moss bank and looked up at her. It was nearly dark now by the yew hedge, and very still. She heard the sound of her own quick breathing, mingled with his, but neither sound seemed real.

He lifted his arms and reaching for her drew her down beside him. As he turned she felt the hard thudding of his heart and the hotness of his mouth. And now when he put his hand on her breast, she did not draw away.

They lay on the moss bank together until a vaporous little sickle moon glimmered through the leaves, and somewhere towards Knightsbridge an owl hooted, when Harry started and sat up. " 'Tis late, Bess. I must get you home."

She sighed a little and smiling drowsily into the darkness touched his cheek with her hand. "Aye, I suppose we must go, dear." She rearranged her dress, smoothed her hair, and wrapped herself in her cloak, for the night had grown chill. "How strange it is," she said with wonder, "that I feel no shame." Why do I not? she thought. Is it that I am by nature lewd and depraved? Was my uncle then right? John Winthrop's condemning eyes seemed to stare at her, but had no power to reach her yet.

"You need feel no shame, Bess," said Harry, roughly. "For I love thee more than before." At this, he too was amazed. When he had had his will with other women, he had been sated at once and contemptuous. "We must be married, Bess," he said, and was dismayed to hear these words which had spoken themselves. He had not thought to say them for years, and least of all to her.

"Marriage," she whispered dreamily, as though he spoke of something as remote as Antilles or Cathay.

"Aye!" he cried with sudden anger. "I'll want you in my bed and often. But you're a Winthrop and my cousin. I cannot tumble you in the hedgerows again; besides, you little dolt, d'you not know there may be fruit of this night's work?"

"Oh—" she said faintly. "I had not thought . . ." These past hours she had ceased to think. There had been nothing but new feeling, turgid, exquisite. She started to speak, but he turning sharply said, "Hist!" and reached for his sword that lay on the bank beside them.

There was a rustling and sound of footsteps on the path. They both listened tensely. No part of London was safe at night, and least of all the parks where rogues and cutpurses often hid until dark.

Harry drew his sword and stood poised as the footsteps neared, until they saw the wavering yellow light of a lantern, and a man's voice called, "Harry! Harry Winthrop!"

"Here!" answered Harry on a long breath, and to Elizabeth he said, " 'Tis Seaton." He stepped forward on the path, and his friend ran up to him.

"By God, Winthrop! What sort of games are these!" Seaton cried. "I've been hunting you this past hour. Could you not at least do dalliance in an arbor like the rest? Jesu, man, there's danger in lurking here so late. Thanet and the wenches left long ago!"

He continued to scold until the two stepped into the light of his lantern, then he examined them and suddenly laughed. "By Corpus Venus, I believe you're both bewitched! Come now, hasten!"

The two young men put Elizabeth between them, and held their swords ready as they hurried down the path and out of the Mulberry Gardens. Thanet had left orders at the Palace Gate and the gate ward let them through. They had not money enough to hire a wherry to take them home by river, so there was yet a long and risky walk from Whitehall, through the village of Charing Cross and along the Strand to Fleet Street. They had no trouble until they had passed the Temple and reached the warren of tenements and vice called Alsatia. Then four filthy beggars darted at them from an alley, and demanded alms in menacing whines.

"Be off with you, you clapperdudgeons," cried Harry jerking his sword. "We've nothing for you!" But the beggars barred the way, and two more glided from the alley to join them. The latter were furnished with long knives. On all their naked legs and arms were running sores made with lye, which were for the daytime arousing of compassion. But now they abandoned their plea for alms and moved stealthily nearer to the edge of the lanternlight. Harry shoved Elizabeth behind him against a door, and the two young men backed against the wall.

"Your purse, gi'e us your purse, me young cocks—" growled one with a knife, watching the swords warily. "Or ye'll see 'ow far me little comforter c'n fly!" He swung the knife by its hilt.

"There's naught in our purses," cried Harry, and when they answered this with an evil jeering cackle, he reached down and yanked the leather bottle from his belt and threw it amongst them. "Very well, here it is!" They fell upon the bottle, scrambling and cursing, and before they discovered what it was, the young men had scooped up Elizabeth and begun to run. Fortunately at Fleet Bridge they met the Watch ambling towards them with his rattle and his bludgeon, and two stout armed lads with torches behind him. "Ye're late out, citizens," cried the Watch suspiciously. "Where be ye going?"

"We've been reveling at the Palace," said Harry. "Aye—"

chimed in Seaton, "and our coach has met with an accident, so we must walk."

The Watch examined them by the light of the torches, then he nodded, convinced by their clothes and gentlemen's voices.

"Bad luck, sirs," he said. "I'll see ye safe 'ome."

He turned and accompanied them up the Old Bailey, pausing at the corner to cry out ," 'Tis past two o'clock of a chill spring night, and all is well."

At the Three Fauns every window showed light, while Richard Fitch and Peyto, for once in agreement, were standing by the open door, peering anxiously up and down the street. They let out a shout when they saw the advancing party. The gypsy ran and kissed Harry's hand, muttering thanksgivings in his own language, but the apprentice hunched his shoulders and pulled down the corners of his mouth as he said, "So ye've come back from your lewd roisterings. We made sure ye'd all been murdered, but it seems the Devil keeps his own."

"We had an accident," began Seaton. "We could not help—"

Before he could finish, the apprentice was shoved aside, Thomas Fones stamped onto the doorstep in his nightcap and dressing gown; he brandished his blackthorn stick and shouted, "You knaves and ribauds, you lying bawdriminy dogs, where have you taken my daughter?"

"Father, Father!" cried Elizabeth running to him. "I'm here. There's no trouble, *Father!*" Her voice ended in a gasp, for he brought the stick down furiously across her shoulders, and she staggered. Harry rushed to her, and turning on the enraged Thomas cried, "Indeed, Uncle, you must not hit Bess, and we are sorry to cause you concern—but—"

"Must not!" screamed the apothecary. *"You* say 'must not' to *me?"* He trembled violently, his pinched face had gone purple, and he choked, tottering backwards to a chair in the hall. Priscilla was there. huddled near the peeping titillated maids. She gaped at her husband whom she had never thought strong enough for such rage, and ran to him with a cup of posset, but he pushed her off with his stick, still choking. Martha had crept down at the uproar and stood timidly on the stairs staring with fear at her father, and with wonder at Elizabeth who looked beautiful, untidy and not at all repentant.

"Look you, sir—" said Seaton coming forward with a conciliatory smile. "When you hear the true tale of our day's adventures, you'll be mollified. Why sir, what say you to the knowledge that your daughter has now met *Their Majesties!*"

At Seaton's voice Thomas had stopped choking, but he listened to not one word as he drew himself shakily up from the chair. "Get out of my house!" he cried, pointing to the door with his quivering stick. He no longer shrilled, his shrunken little figure had a sudden dignity.

"Why s-sir—" stammered Seaton. "I don't understand."

"I am sick unto death," said the apothecary, "but I am still master in mine own house, and you—filthy skuldugging Papist—will leave here NOW!"

Seaton whitened, and stepped back. So that was it! He saw the apprentice's malicious smirk and guessed that he had been followed that morning to the priest at Newgate. He saw Harry's startled frown. Matters of religion had never been discussed between them. Seaton drew a hard breath before he said quickly to Harry, "Aye, it is true. I belong to the Holy Catholic Faith, the one true church of Rome."

Priscilla gave a moan. The harboring of a Romanist in their home seemed to her more horrifying than anything Harry or Bess might conceivably have done. She began to weep, snuffling noisily and murmuring, "Oh dear, oh dear."

"Where will you go, Robert?" asked Harry, himself shocked at this revelation, and though troubled for his friend, aware it was not possible to keep Seaton here.

"To Father Christopher at Newgate. The *gaol* at least will take me in." Seaton attempted a jaunty smile, waved his hand and strode out the door. Thomas Fones slumped in his chair, but straightened at once, turning on Harry. "I give you credit that you did not know the full duplicity of this knave you foisted on me, but you have much else to answer for."

The apothecary stopped while a spasm of pain knotted itself in his left breast, ran down his arm and ebbed. He had been about to confront his nephew with all the misdemeanors Edward Howes had brought to his attention that day, and also with the sheaf of unpaid bills he himself had discovered in Harry's room. But he had not sufficient strength. He gestured to Priscilla for the posset, gulped down a few swallows, then said grimly, "Were you not so near allied to me, and the son of him I so respect, I could not bear such oppositions in mine own house, but this I do command. From now on you will not see my daughter, Elizabeth, nor be able to include her in your bawdry."

Elizabeth stiffened, She and Harry looked at each other. "Not now," she whispered, consious of great weariness, and of faint pity for her father too.

But Harry had never been one to wait, and the threat of coercion in regard to Elizabeth determined him at once.

"This command I cannot obey, my good uncle," he said briskly. "For I mean to marry your daughter Bess—at once."

There was a dead silence. Martha sank upon the steps twisting her hands with excitement. Richard's and Peyto's jaws dropped. The maids began to giggle, and Priscilla to weep louder.

"What?" whispered the apothecary. "What did you say . . . ?"

"That Bess and I love each other, and mean to marry." Harry put his arm around the girl, and she leaned against him. "It is so, Father," she said.

"But you are mad," said Thomas Fones in a small voice. "Bess is already betrothed. You are cousins. 'Tis no fit match for—for either of you. She is not of age. You've gone mad . . . mad." His head waggled, and his sparse little beard sank forward on his chest. "I want to go to bed," he said thickly. "Wife, help me! I can bear no more."

4

IN AFTER YEARS Elizabeth never could clearly remember the events of that month, which was hazed by turmoil of all kinds. On April 2 Thomas Fones wrote to John Winthrop a distracted letter, telling of Harry's behavior, and the efforts which had been made to put up with his

> much expense and rioutous company . . . but will you know the Issue and requitall of my kindness—your son hath wooed and won my daughter Besse for a wyfe and they both pretend to have proceeded so far that there is no recalling of it at least promise of Marriage, and all without my knowledge or consent, what grief this is to me I leave it to your consideration . . .

and later he added:

> I cannot write you the many troubles of my mind what to do, for my nephew says plainly if he can not have my good will to have my daughter he will have her without . . . I am weak and cannot, I see now, be master in mine owne house, and tis hard meddling between the bark and the tree . . . he so near allied to me and son of

*him I respect . . . I am overwhelmed with troubles and
afflictiones on all sides . . .*

John Winthrop was accustomed to discounting much of
the apothecary's nervous agitations, but there was no mini-
mizing this letter. As he read it, John's face fell to its stern-
est grooves, his eyes went stone-gray. He handed the letter
silently to Margaret, and at the same time beckoned to
Bluet, his manservant, and ordered horses saddled for the
journey to London.

"This is shocking news—" said Margaret slowly as she
put the letter on the table. "Oh, what is to be done, John?"

"Done?" he said through his teeth. "How can I tell until
I get there? What needs to be done shall be, before the Winthrop name and blood is further disgraced. The Lord sees
fit to humble me through my son. That Henry is profligate
and dissolute," he pointed to a paragraph in Thomas's letter,
"even that he has been 'consorting with Papists' scarce aston-
ishes me . . . no wonder then that he should add the seduc-
tion of his cousin to his sins. No doubt they are birds of a
feather, those two, and shall be roasted in the same hell fire."

"Yet—" said Margaret anxiously, after a moment, "you will
not be overharsh, dearest, will you? He wants her in lawful
marriage, they may have true love for each other which con-
dones much."

"Ha!" said Winthrop. "You prate the silly woman, Margaret. I shall act as is just and fitting—with the Lord's direction."

And in this mood he rode off to London. But when he arrived there, Harry and Elizabeth's behavior was not of
paramount importance, for Thomas Fones lay on his death-
bed.

The family were gathered in the parlor at the Three Fauns.
Emmanuel and Lucy Downing sat a little apart conversing in
hushed tones. Henry and Elizabeth stood without speaking
by the window. Martha, twisting and untwisting a corner of
her apron, crouched near her stepmother, Priscilla, who wept
without restraint, while clasping her own little Mary to her
breast. Sammy, subdued for once, huddled by the fire and
gaped at his elders.

The great Doctor Harvey from St. Bartholomew's had
been summoned to examine the patient, and he now ponderously descended the stairs, shaking his head. "There is no

hope, my good people," he said. "None at all. You'd best say farewell to him."

Priscilla uttered a shriek, and the others clustered around the physician to ask frightened questions, but Elizabeth stiffened and ran frantically up the stairs. It can't be true, she thought, always he has talked of dying, but it couldn't really happen. She entered the sickroom and knelt by her father's bed. Already Thomas had drifted into a peaceful world where the tempests of this one seemed remote. But he opened his eyes as she took his hand and laid it against her wet cheek. "Bessie . . . " he whispered, "Poor Bessie."

"Dear Father, forgive me, I know I've been such a trouble to you, I'll obey now, anything you wish, I swear it."

He shook his head feebly. "No matter, child—let be . . . seems long ago . . . Trust in God." He sighed and made a further effort. "Is John Winthrop . . . ?"

"Aye," she said. "He's below. Shall I fetch him?"

"All of them," he panted.

So it came about that as anger had dropped away from the dying man, John Winthrop could not hold on to his, and when Thomas Fones asked it, John gave a stifled consent to the marriage.

"They have . . . done wrong," whispered the apothecary. "They must not postpone the righting of it even for my death . . . Forgive my daughter, Brother John . . . as I do your son. Anne would have wished it so."

"Aye," said John, and at the memory of his sister tears came to his eyes. He glanced once at Elizabeth, seeing there briefly the image of her mother and not the flaunting carnal beauty which always infuriated him. "God's will be done," he murmured.

Thomas Fones died at dawn. All the windows were shuttered, black wreaths were nailed to the door, the sound of weeping filled the house. There was the funeral and burial at St. Sepulchre's, then almost at once the news of another death. The carrier brought a letter from Margaret saying that old Mistress Winthrop had finally succumbed to her sufferings on April 19, four days after Thomas Fones.

The old lady's death gave nobody great sorrow, but certainly added no lightness to Elizabeth's pre-bridal days. She and Harry were to be married April 25. John Winthrop— having made up his mind to this date, coldly furnished money for the special license, and apprised the Rector at St. Sepulchre's—would not swerve from the decision.

"I do not," Winthrop said to Harry with distaste, "wish to know what the probabilities are for disgraceful evidence of your sin with Elizabeth, but the marriage will take place as I have arranged. You will then both proceed to Groton, and stay there in seclusion until I have fully acquainted myself with your deplorable financial affairs here in London, *and* decided when you return to Barbadoes."

Harry gulped and reddened. "Yes, sir." Always his father reduced him to the status of a discomfited child, try as he would to assert his manhood and own opinions. Also it was true that there seemed to be a startling amount of debts to be paid, and the usual dearth of money with which to do it. His father was being fair, and even spared him reproaches, for the present. But he was also inflexible—and in charge. Harry had not seen Elizabeth alone since Thomas Fones's death; she seemed sad and remote when he did see her. He still yearned for her but the glamour of those first hours of their love had been dimmed. Harry, who now lodged at the Downings', stole out of their house that night, found Seaton and Thanet in one of their favorite taverns near Smithfield and got prodigiously drunk.

On a rainy Saturday morning, April 25, 1629, Elizabeth and Harry Winthrop were married at St. Sepulchre's in the briefest of ceremonies. They stood and then knelt by the altar rail, swathed both of them in black, as were the handful of family crowded behind them in the bare aisle. There were no candles, no flowers—and Elizabeth, at John Winthrop's decree, received no ring from Harry. The wedding ring was a superstition to be abolished like all the other Roman follies which tarnished God's revealed word.

Marriage was an earthly necessity permitted by Scriptures but the Lord Jesus had also explicitly said that in heaven there was no marriage or giving in marriage, and some Puritans now considered that a civil contract was sufficient. John Winthrop did not yet subscribe to so sharp a break with tradition, but he insisted on the minimum of ritual, and Elizabeth found herself married before the frightened mist had cleared from her eyes or she had had time to look from the rector's grave face to that of Harry which had flushed a deep red. He smelled strongly of the brandy he had been swigging since dawn, and seemed to her an utter stranger in the tight black suit and plain white falling collar his father had provided.

As the rector said, "I now pronounce you man and wife" Harry bent to kiss her, but she scarcely responded for she heard Martha weeping behind her, and John Winthrop's voice saying, "Very good. So that's done. We will leave at once for my brother Downing's." And they filed silently out of the church.

The wedding breakfast was to be held at Peterborough Court since the Fones family was in deepest mourning, and Emmanuel Downing had generously hired two coaches to convey them all to his home. He had also overridden Lucy's objections and ordered a lavish feast with capons, wine and bride cake. "How can you so countenance this disgraceful marriage!" Lucy had repeatedly cried. "The behavior of those two has been the death of Thomas Fones, and is like to be the death of your poor clerk Edward to whom that little trollop had given her solemn promise!"

"The egg is burst, m'dear," rejoined her husband. "As for Edward he's not the first man to be jilted, nor will he be the last. He'll recover, and there's plenty o' pretty faces in Essex to help him."

Edward Howes had been sent to his home on a holiday, as soon as Elizabeth and Harry's intent had become known.

It was Emmanuel who instigated what jollity there was at the wedding breakfast. He circulated flagons of sack, he proposed toasts to the young couple. Gradually the atmosphere thawed, and after John Winthrop yielded to his brother-in-law's urgings and drank some of the strong sweet bride-ale, he rose to his feet and held up his pewter mug, smiling stiffly. "I drink to the good health of the new Mistress Winthrop," he said looking at Elizabeth. He paused and went on, "I propose to let bygones be bygones. You are now wholly a Winthrop, my dear—and have become my daughter. I am sure that with God's direction you will do credit to your new state and be a true helpmeet to your husband." His glance flickered over Harry, who was nervously chewing his lips, having downed his mugful of ale at one draught. "And Henry, on this your wedding day I give you my blessing, with the prayer that our Gracious Lord will make the light of His countenance shine in your heart, from henceforward."

Lucy said, "Amen," and Harry mumbled, "Thank you, sir," while Elizabeth managed to smile back at her new father-in-law. Indeed, through her continuing daze she was grateful for his speech. It was rather like God relenting. Elizabeth was not wholly aware that when she thought of God, she always saw him with John Winthrop's face.

"And now," continued John, his eyes softening and his voice rising to genuine warmth, "I wish to propose the healths of two absent ones who are dear to us all. My sweet and good wife, Margaret." He sipped while they drank, then he added, "And to my beloved son, John."

At the mention of this name Elizabeth's numbness shattered. Her cheeks flushed red as Harry's and then paled. Oh, what have I done! she thought. I never meant it to be Harry —how did it happen—I've been mad! But Jack didn't care for me, he never wrote. Yet now I'll have to see him all the time when he comes back, and I'll be his *sister*! IF he comes back . . . her thoughts raced like started hares. She tried to hide her face in the mug and choked on a mouthful of ale. Nobody noticed except Martha who sat across the table, for Emmanuel had risen to propose other toasts. Elizabeth saw the girl's sympathetic but bewildered eyes watching her. "What is it, Bess?" the little mouth silently formed the words, and they steadied Elizabeth's panic. "Nothing, darling," she signaled back, with a rush of love for this sister who never failed in natural sensitivity though her childishness sometimes precluded understanding. Soon I shall take Martha to live with me at Groton, Elizabeth thought. And with the realization that she had the power now to do this, that she had become a Winthrop of Groton Manor, faint new pride stirred in her.

"Well, Bess—" said a rough voice at her side. "You've not spoke to me since we left the church. I never thought you'd prove so modest a bride!" Harry grabbed her around the waist and kissed her lustily on the mouth. Emmanuel roared, the others all smiled. John Winthrop said tolerantly, "The time has come for the young couple to have privacy, no doubt. You may retire to your chamber when you like."

"Aye—indeed—" cried Emmanuel slapping his thighs. "We'll all see ye to the marriage bed—as we did in the old days—there's a song I've a mind to sing that'll fit the occasion.

> *"O lay her 'twixt the fair white sheets,*
> *Come my bully boy!*
> *Uncover then her fair white t—"*

"Husband!" screamed Lucy, drowning him out. "Before

God in His mercy, I don't know what's got into you!"

"A mort of fine bride-ale and sack's got into me," said Emmanuel somewhat sheepishly. "But I see no harm at a wedding. Well, let be—no song then, but I shall insist on one old custom. I'll kiss the bride."

And he did, a wet-mouthed smack that Elizabeth endured gladly. She liked her Uncle Emmanuel. Everyone followed suit, Winthrop kissed her on the forehead, Lucy gave a peck at her cheek. Priscilla and the children kissed her heartily, and Martha clung to her a moment, whispering, "Bess dear, I'm sure you'll be happy, Harry's so handsome!"

So Elizabeth and Harry went up to the garden chamber at the Downings'. Later they found again some of the rapture they had known in St. James's Park, and by morning they were sure that the violence of their passion was proof of unique and undying love. And yet it was not quite the same as on that golden Palm Sunday a month ago. By Tuesday, when Elizabeth and Harry mounted the Winthrop saddle horses to set out for Suffolk, she had already learned that while Harry was an accomplished lover, he had not the slightest interest in being a husband, and that routine, economy or forethought bored him to exasperation which he drowned in drink whenever he could escape his father's eye.

"You will stay at Groton until I summon you," said Winthrop from the steps as the young couple left the Downings'. "Henry, I shall occupy myself with the preliminaries of your return to Barbadoes—and" he added dryly, "settle those of your debts for which I can possibly eke out the money."

"Thank you, sir," said Harry, while he smoothed his horse's mane. "It's very good of you."

There were a great many aspects of the return to Barbadoes which he had not mentioned to his father, but with Thanet's brother, Sir William Tufton, as Governor, life there might after all be pleasant enough, and it would be fun to show Elizabeth off to the other planters. He had described the Island in terms that dazzled her—lazing in the sun on long white beaches, blue skies, and bluer waters warm as milk to bathe in, rum mixed with the juice of a huge nut to drink, and no work that one need ever do—the slaves and servants did it all.

"It would seem heavenly," she agreed. "But, Harry, what of the tobacco plantation? Surely it must be overseen, and the crops tended, garnered, and then sent back to England—accounts kept too?"

"Oh . . ." said Harry shrugging. "Don't trouble yourself about that, sweetheart; it all gets done somehow."

Elizabeth remembered the poor wisps of tobacco Harry had sent home, but she was still far too much in love to question.

They rode happily together into the City at Ludgate, then up past St. Paul's to the broad Chepe, where despite the little market stalls there was more room for traffic than on bustling streets nearer the Thames. They passed the beautiful block of fifteenth century buildings called Goldsmiths' Row and Harry glanced at them but it was not here that the goldsmith he sought resided, though here still lived the more fashionable ones. Emmanuel Downing had given him the name of a man in Lombard Street, when Harry had consulted his uncle privately, this being a matter not to be called to John Winthrop's attention.

Elizabeth looked up in surprise when Harry suddenly dismounted before an imposing shop in Lombard Street. She had been giving all her mind to the management of her horse, which shied at dogs and running children. She had had no chance to ride except at Groton, but she was fearless, and loved animals, so that her horse had begun to obey her. "What's ado here?" she asked Harry, smiling as he gave her his hand to help her dismount. "Why, it's a goldsmith's!" she cried as she saw the characteristic arms over the door.

"It is, my love," said Harry twinkling, and looking very pleased with himself. "I'm going to buy you a gift."

"How kind, but darling, we've no money."

Harry laughing swept her in through an elegantly carved door to a spacious dark room lined with padlocked coffers. Behind a velvet-covered counter a sleepy apprentice was spitting on and polishing a large silver spoon. Harry addressed him grandly. "Send for Mr. Robert Feake, your master. Say it is Henry Winthrop, Esquire, nephew to Mr. Emmanuel Downing, who wishes him!"

The apprentice grunted and disappeared, while Harry turned triumphantly to Elizabeth. "Ah, but I HAVE money, my love. Look at this!"

He opened a little belt purse and showed her a gold sovereign. "Thanet gave it to me on our bridal eve, he said we should spend it as we pleased."

Elizabeth was delighted, yet during the last days she had learned new prudence, and though she gave Harry a grateful kiss, she said, "But only spend a little on my gift, we'll save some, won't we—'tis all we have for pocket money, you know!" John Winthrop had seen that they were provided with the exact sum necessary to secure one night's lodging en route, but burdened as he was with Harry's debts had given nothing else, nor did he wish Harry to have the wherewithal for visits to the taverns at Hadleigh. His written instructions to Margaret had specified that she should labor to keep Harry close on the Manor at all times.

When Robert Feake, the goldsmith, came into the shop bowing and smiling a tight mirthless smile, they had decided to use but a crown for the gift. Harry, though generous, had at once seen the force of her argument. He then proceeded to ask the impossible of Mr. Feake, demanding for this sum a brooch of gold and diamonds. "You are an excellent man, sir—" added Harry with his most charming smile. "A pillar of our reformed Faith, Mr. Downing tells me, you will not I'm sure strike too hard a bargain as our enemies, who call us Puritans, say some do."

Robert Feake bowed again; his right eyelid twitched almost as though he were winking. "I will do what I can, sir." He coughed and opening a coffer which stood under the counter brought up a velvet-lined tray of cheap brooches.

Elizabeth had stared in momentary surprise when the eyelid began to twitch, and she saw a thin young man of medium height. His pale eyebrows were drawn to a habitual nervous frown. His flaxen strands of hair were so scanty that the scalp showed through. He was dressed in sober gray, and she thought him insignificant, except for the long delicate white fingers, almost womanish, which looked as though they would be skilled in the intricacies of his craft. Harry and Elizabeth leaned together over the tray, and both ignoring the well-fashioned silver pieces, pounced on a gaudy mixture of twisted yellow metal and rock crystals. "There!" cried Harry. "Almost exactly what I wanted. How much do you ask?"

Robert Feake coughed again. "You may have it for a crown," he said slowly, "but it is not real gold, you know, and those are but Scottish diamonds—Edinburgh pebbles we call them. In fact, sir, I'm bound to tell you the whole brooch is of inferior workmanship, and none of *my* craft I assure you."

"Oh, but I like it!" cried Elizabeth, thinking what a fuss-budget the man was, longing to possess such a showy piece of jewelry and delighted that they could afford it.

Her voice had been warm, vibrant and subtly caressing as it always was when things pleased her, and it was then that the goldsmith really looked at her; at the rosy face, the beautiful hazel eyes, the dark curls thick beneath the black hood. She gave him the feeling of abounding health and vigor. He felt a curious flutter beneath his gray doublet, glanced quickly at Harry's jaunty good looks, and said carefully, "If I might suggest, miss—"

"Madam," interrupted Elizabeth, laughing with pride. "Mr. Henry Winthrop is my husband."

"Ah, yes, forgive me—Madam—" said Robert, conscious of dismay that went far deeper than this trivial encounter. Was she laughing at him? Jeering covertly? Yes, both these people were. The recent depression, laced with formless fears, settled over him again. He had been about to suggest other brooches of sound workmanship, had for a moment even thought of sacrificing all profit on a delicate silver and moonstone brooch which would suit her. But now he wished only to be rid of them. "This, then, is what you want," he said plucking out their choice from the case. Harry pinned the brooch to the girl's white collar and flung the crown on the counter, since the goldsmith made no move to take it. The young people went out laughing.

Robert Feake sank down on the great carved chair, which had belonged to his father—Master-Goldsmith James Feake—and Robert rested his head on his hands. The happy echo of Elizabeth's laughter rippled afar off through a mist of futility and hopelessness. A state that had bedeviled him at times since his parents died. I must get away, he thought vaguely, London air is unhealthy for me. He thought of Wighton, his boyhood home in Norfolk but there was nobody close to him there now. They all had died. The old house stank of death. Of death and madness, for it was at Wighton they now kept the old, old woman, his Aunt Mary, who had been a lunatic since long before he was born. He would never return to Norfolk. He glanced at his Bible which lay on the shelf near the coffers. His long delicate hand groped out towards it, then dropped flaccid on the chair arm. His chin sank on his chest.

No customers came in and Robert sat on silently in the shop while the morning passed. Ralph, the apprentice, came back and, throwing his master an uneasy glance, began the vigorous polishing of a silver tankard. Master was in the dumps again; it had been like this before two years agone,

and worse, when Master took to talking to himself, and
staring into corners like the devil was hiding there.

And sleepwalking! Give you the creeps, Master would,
during that time; in especial one night when Ralph had
awakened in the loft to find Master bending over his pallet
with his eyes closed and jabbering and weeping. Ralph had
shoved, yelled and run out of the house the whole length
of Lombard Street before he found the courage to go back,
and there was Master quiet again and in his own bed.

But this behavior had passed, and since then you couldn't
call Mr. Feake a bad master. Hardly one at all, thought the
apprentice with contempt. Soft, and wouldn't say "Bo" to a
goose, most of the time never noticing what a lad was up to,
or what hours he kept, never on his toes to snatch an order
for plate or a jewel from that sly thieving goldsmith next door.
And never a bit o' fun or lollygagging with the lasses, not
Master, for all he was only twenty-seven. It's dull here,
thought Ralph, whistling "The Merry Month of May" between his teeth. I'll be glad when my time's up.

And still Robert sat on staring at the floor until two panting messengers arrived at once bearing letters. One letter had
been sent from Germany, and the boy brought it from a newly
docked ship. It was from Robert's sister, Alice Dixon, whose
husband had moved to Germany on business. Robert glanced
through it listlessly, skipping Alice's accounts of little Judith
and Tobias Feake, orphaned children of Robert's brother
James, whom the childless Dixons had adopted as their own.
Robert was not now interested in his small niece and nephew,
though at times he sent them gifts. He let Alice's pages slide
to the floor and opened the letter delivered by the other messenger. It was from John Winthrop and Emmanuel Downing.
As he gathered its purport, his apathy lifted. He carried the
letter to the shop window, reading the cautious phrases again
with full attention. "Nay, nay—" he said aloud, while the apprentice looked up nervously. " 'Tis too fantastic, too risky—at
least *I* will never be party to such a plan." But after a while
he put the letter in his doublet and began to pace the floor.
The recurrent image of Elizabeth rescued him at last from an
agony of indecision.

She would not dare laugh at a man whom her uncle and
father-in-law consulted, whom they had actually sent for.
He put on his wide black hat and cloak, said to the apprentice,
"I have an errand off Fleet Street," and walked out the door,

thinking of Elizabeth, and amazed at his own audacity in wondering if he would ever see her again.

Harry and Elizabeth had no thoughts at all for the goldsmith, as they rode merrily on through the heart of the City to Aldgate and the Colchester Road. Just outside the walls, Harry suddenly stopped before a tavern. "Oh, love," protested Elizabeth, really disconcerted, "surely not more ale already, my head's still buzzing from Uncle Downing's stirrup cup!"

"I'll drink when I please," Harry retorted, though quite amiably. "You needn't. But I've another reason for stopping here." He raised his voice and shouted, "Peyto!"

At once the little gypsy trotted from the tavern courtyard and laid his forehead on Harry's hand. "Here I be, Master!"

"Well, bring me out a tankard, then come on. You've some kind of mount?"

"To be sure, Master." Peyto's eyelids drooped over his black eyes, he grinned slyly, and led from the courtyard a plump, dark, well-saddled donkey. Harry laughed. "I know better than to ask where it came from! But what would you tell me?"

"That I found the poor little beastie a-straying and a-starving on the heath, Master, and I knew at once 'twas meant for Peyto, as shown in my tarot cards."

Harry shrugged again, chuckling. "I've missed you, you Egyptian jackanapes." Peyto had been dismissed as soon as John Winthrop took over direction of the Fones household after Thomas's death. Winthrop had said that Harry could do without a manservant until his debts were paid, and that in any case this particular servant was impossible.

"He'll liven up the Manor," said Harry, grinning at Elizabeth over his tankard. She did not doubt that, but she knew another moment of disquiet. Should Harry so flout his father's wishes? Would not the introduction of this unprincipled little knave at Groton end by distressing Margaret? But she said nothing, for she was fond of Peyto and knew now that he had virtually saved Harry's life in Barbadoes. Soon the three of them were trotting between the flowery hedgerows of enclosures. Cuckoos called from thickets, the air was warm and scented, and presently they all sang a rollicking catch in imitation of the cuckoos. They laughed a great deal, Peyto contributing his queer throaty chuckle, and Elizabeth put aside her qualms. She entirely forgot them that night in Harry's arms at a Witham inn.

On the morning that the bridal couple set out for Suffolk, a solemn group of five men were gathered around a table in Emmanuel Downing's private parlor in his mansion off Fleet Street. They had had wine and pasties earlier but now the servants had cleared up and gone and the men sat tensely waiting, while they eyed a long silk-wrapped roll in Matthew Cradock's hand. Emmanuel Downing and John Winthrop, Sir Richard Saltonstall and Matthew Cradock were all men in their forties, but their fifth member, Isaac Johnson, was a fresh-faced eager young man of twenty-eight who looked younger. And it was he who burst out at Cradock, "You've really brought it, sir? That is the charter, isn't it? Oh, how I long to see it."

Cradock smiled, "And so you shall, sir. Not only see it . . . but—" He paused, his shrewd little eyes slid over the faces of those around the table while he weighed each expression carefully. Downing, he was sure of—a hearty man who would give backing without question, up to a point. Sir Richard, plump, blond and elegant, would be moved by both his sympathies and self-interest—and it was gratifying to have secured a well-to-do knight to head the company list. Mr. Isaac Johnson, a very wealthy man, was already heart and soul in the project, as was his wife Arbella's Lincolnshire family, and especially her brother, the Puritan Theophilus, Earl of Lincoln.

But this Mr. Winthrop, thought Matthew Cradock, was still something of an enigma. Winthrop sat a trifle apart from the others, spoke little, and appeared to brood, though his eyes also were fixed on the silk covered roll from which Cradock with a flourish extracted a large parchment embellished by the King's seal. He spread the parchment on the table.

"Here!" he cried. "The King's own patent for the Massachusetts Bay Company. And I might say, gentlemen, that few know it to be in my possession."

"But you're Governor of the Company!" cried Johnson. "Have you not the right to it?"

"To be sure," said Cradock, shrugging. "I dare say—but in any case 'twere better that His Majesty forget its whereabouts at present, and indeed forgot its very existence. It was miracle enough that we got it."

They all nodded, while Winthrop said quietly, "The hand

of God." In the same week, scarcely over a month ago, in which the King had permanently dissolved Parliament he had also signed a charter incorporating the Company of the Massachusetts Bay in New England and granting it all territory between the Piscataqua River and Plymouth colony, and westward to the Pacific Ocean. Nobody was at all sure why Charles had thus favored the Puritan sect he detested, and Emmanuel spoke thoughtfully after a moment.

"He meant then to get rid of those who do not think as he does, lure them to drowning or death in the wilderness? Or mayhap 'twas but one of his whims."

"I think not," said Cradock, shaking his head. "I fear he means to keep that grasping lustful hand of his on New England should any prosper there, and milk us of all that comes from it, as he is milking us at home."

There was a silence, then John Winthrop stirred, raised his eyebrows and said in his low vibrant voice, "It would seem providential that the charter is so accessible." He touched it with his thin blunt forefinger. "It might even seem desirable that it were *not* accessible in England later."

The others did not at once grasp Winthrop's meaning, but Cradock looked at him with hearty approval. "I see that you're a man of my own kidney, sir! This very thought was mine too."

Isaac jumped up, his blue eyes shining. "You mean to take it with us! Then indeed we'd be safe from His Majesty and the Lord Bishops. We could rule ourselves as we please, our lives, our lands, our spiritual welfare!"

"Soft, soft, young sir—" said Winthrop, with a faint smile. "Except for the struggling little toehold at Naumkeag, there is no real plantation yet on Massachusetts Bay, nor means of making one. And if there were such a plantation it could not—as I see it—be ruled by *anyone's* pleasure. Only by God's word in the Scriptures, and by the terms of this patent, and by English common law."

"To be sure," answered Isaac blushing and nodding. "I meant nothing else, sir."

Cradock had scarcely listened to this, but he increasingly approved of Winthrop and interjected quickly, "Aye, the law. It would be of great help to our company, Mr. Winthrop, did it include an attorney of your standing amongst the leaders." He looked at him hopefully and waited.

Winthrop's mouth pulled to a thin groove; he glanced at his brother-in-law, to whom this would be a shock, and he said without emphasis, "My office at the Court of Wards is gone. I am nearly certain of it."

"Good God, John!" Emmanuel started back, staring. "What does that mean?"

Winthrop's thin shoulders sketched a shrug. "Doubtless that in some mysterious way I have come under unfavorable notice from—" He lifted his hand in the direction of Whitehall, then let it drop.

" 'Tis yet another straw in the wind," said Sir Richard Saltonstall heavily. "My dear sir, my deepest sympathies. You will then retire to your estates in Suffolk, I suppose?"

"My estates are much impoverished—my three elder sons must be provided for, and one of them—" He stopped. "But my family afflictions have no bearing on the matter in hand."

"We must move fast," said Cradock, leaning forward and speaking low. "Everything points to that. Fast and—and cautiously. Or we may be hindered."

"Come to Lincolnshire!" burst out Isaac Johnson. "My noble brother has authorized me to ask you. There at Sempringham we may all confer in utmost secrecy. Lord Lincoln yearns to be of help in establishing a new kingdom to God's glory and the Church's good!"

Again Cradock glanced at the faces around the table, until his eyes rested on Winthrop, noting that the others unconsciously did the same. The man had strength and a powerful attraction, for all his brooding gravity. "*You* will go to Lincolnshire, Mr. Winthrop?"

John exchanged a look with Emmanuel, and slowly nodded. "Mr. Downing and I will be pleased to confer with the Earl of Lincoln and the others . . ."

"Ah, but you'll go over *there* too—to the new land with us, sir, won't you?" cried Isaac. "I saw your eye kindle when I spoke of it!"

"I've given the matter insufficient thought," said Winthrop after a moment. "It seems unlikely, but it is a decision only God can make."

They all bowed their heads, and Sir Richard said, "Amen." For the ensuing hour, they arranged matters preliminary to the Lincolnshire conference. They made lists of possible financial backers, and lists of the few men amongst these whom they felt it safe to sound out at this time. Robert Feake was one, and a message was dispatched to him. It was Emmanuel Downing and Cradock, both shrewd merchants and men of substance themselves, who led in this discussion, and though Winthrop listened and contributed at times, he also fell into long abstractions. In his heart was a great question, and his thoughts—despondent and elated by turns—could neither be marshaled nor quieted.

At Groton Manor during May and June, despite lovely weather, an unhappy restlessness prevailed. Margaret and Elizabeth were drawn close by their mutual cares, for neither was sure of her own husband's intention, and each letter from London added to the uncertainties. Harry too was in London, though out of touch with his father, and all Margaret's dutiful efforts to keep her stepson on the Manor had failed. So had Elizabeth's.

In the long June evening of the 29th, the women sat together in the walled garden by the mulberry tree and watched the Manor road for Bluet, the servant, who had been sent as usual to meet the London carrier in case there should be letters. For some days he had brought none. Margaret's little boys were in bed, Forth, Harry's younger brother, had ridden to Cambridge to give up his chambers there, for he was no longer inclined towards the ministry. Mary Winthrop was visiting her Aunt Gostlin in the next village. The two Winthrop wives were alone, and this rarity moved them both to more frankness than usual.

Margaret sat on a bench sewing a pair of linen drawers for her youngest, but Elizabeth sprawled on the grass idly combing the thick turf for four-leaf clovers. The last rays of mellow sunlight gilded her rich dark hair and pretty downcast face. The older woman said gently, "Will you read us a psalm while we wait, Bess? 'Tis always better not to mope in idleness."

The girl sat up and cried passionately, "I can understand that he has merry times in London, with Thanet and Seaton no doubt and with—" she bit her lips thinking of all the Chloes and Sylvias with which London abounded, "but he does love me in his way. I know that! Why does he not write!"

Margaret sighed thinking of a sentence in her John's last letter.

> *Henry is in London, but I have seen him but twice, I know not what he doth nor what he intendeth, I mourn for his sins and the misery that he will soone bring upon himself and his wife.*

Yet she tried to comfort.

"Harry was never one for letters, dear, and is naturally busy arranging your voyage to Barbadoes." Her own voice faltered, and the girl said with quick bitter sympathy, "Aye, Mother—'tis of a different voyage you think, isn't it!"

Margaret put down her sewing. "I cannot think John means to go . . ." she said half to herself. "Not to that wilderness of wild beasts and savages where so many have perished. To leave me and the children behind—to leave this—" She opened her eyes and looked at the rosy gables behind them, at the great sheltering roof, the smoking chimneys of the Manor House. She looked at the little walled garden with its sweet trim roses, gillyflowers and lilies she tended herself. Both women were silent while the church bell chimed the hour gently across the meadows, and the doves cooing in their cote seemed to answer the bell.

"But I'm weak," Margaret whispered. "This shrinking savors too much of the flesh. John has said so. He told me that it would be a great service to the Church to carry Gospel to that other land and raise a bulwark against the kingdom of anti-Christ which the Jesuits labor to rear in all parts of the world. He told me that the land here in England groaneth under her inhabitants, and there is so much deceit and unrighteousness that it is almost impossible for a good man to maintain his estates and live comfortably in his profession. He is right, ever right, and I will always submit to his wishes." She bent her head.

Elizabeth had not been listening; her thoughts had flown to Harry, praying that he were indeed hastening their own voyage to Barbadoes or anywhere that he would stay with her, yet something in Margaret's speech caught her laggard attention and she said slowly, "Do you know why Father Winthrop lost his office at the Court of Wards when Uncle Downing is still secure in his?"

Margaret shook her head. "John knows not how it was, but somehow the Winthrop name would seem to have vexed the King himself. These are dreadful times."

Elizabeth thought of that far-off happy day on the Thames, of their meeting with the royal barge and the King's questions, and was stricken with guilt. But of what use to mention it? The damage was done, if indeed it were her fault, and the memory of that day was filled with nostalgic pain. She touched the gaudy gilt and crystal brooch Harry had given her, as though it were a talisman. He *does* love me, she thought. I must be patient, but while she thought this, deep down a hot rebellion stirred. She grabbed up a handful of grass and threw it violently at the mulberry trunk. "Why was I not born a man?" she cried. "Why can't I enjoy myself in London too? Why must I sit here waiting, wondering—it's too humbling—and dull—dull!"

"Hush, dear," cried Margaret, momentarily dismayed. "You mustn't question God's provision for you, or your lot as a wife. You will settle to it better, when the babes start coming."

"Ah . . ." said Elizabeth glumly. There had been no shameful result from that night in St. James's Park. Had I known for sure of that, she thought—would I—? And at once chided herself. It was not because of that she had married Harry; they loved each other, and also John Winthrop had made them marry. That there was some contradiction in these thoughts she saw dimly, and suddenly began to cry.

"Poor child," said Margaret patting her on the shoulder. "Oh, look, Bess, there's Bluet coming and he has letters in his hand!"

The girl dashed her apron across her eyes and sprang down the lane. There was a note from Harry, terse and misspelled, but it supplemented the letter from John Winthrop to his wife. They would all be arriving at Groton next week, and Winthrop said he was bringing Priscilla Fones, Sammy and Martha too. "Harry *is* coming, and oh, how glad I am that Martha comes too at last!" Elizabeth cried, laughing huskily when they had read the letters.

Margaret nodded. "You see, Bess, how God is good and kind, always, if we be patient."

5

In August John Winthrop and Emmanuel Downing rode to Lincolnshire and visited Theophilus Fiennes Clinton, the young Earl of Lincoln, at Sempringham. There in the great mansion which had been recently erected on the site of the once famous Gilbertine Priory, John Winthrop definitely made up his mind for the adventure overseas. He found himself in the company of an earnest charming family, all of whom were dedicated to the glorious enterprise and had thought of little else for two years. The Earl, because of his responsibilities and vast estates, could not emigrate, nor of course could his Countess, Bridget, though she was the daughter of the Puritan Lord Say, and as enthusiastic as her husband in furthering the new plantation. The Earl's three sisters had each married men to whom the colonization of a new and freer England was of paramount importance. The Lady Frances and her husband, John Gorges, were not present at this meeting in Sempringham, but the Lady Susan, with her husband, John Humphrey, and the fair Lady Arbella were anxiously awaiting discussion of the great project. Arbella's husband, Isaac Johnson, was even more fervent than he had been in London and—it soon developed—he was prepared

124

to invest a very large sum in the Massachusetts Bay Colony as well.

On the second night after his arrival John Winthrop sat well up the board at the Earl's huge dining table, and having eaten superbly and drunk three silver gobletfuls of excellent claret, he leaned back in his chair content as he had ever been in his life. Amongst the score of diners there had been much inspiring talk, after a beautiful prayer offered by John Cotton, the nonconformist rector of St. Botolph's Church in nearby Boston. Long ago Cotton had been at Trinity College when John himself was there and he found that the lanky young Cotton had developed into a man of magnetic power, whose long fluffy white hair, flashing dark eyes and bell-like voice combined to move his hearers mightily. An Ezekiel himself, Cotton seemed, when he had quoted that prophet in heartbroken tones:

> *Son of man thou dwellest in the midst of a rebellious house, which have eyes to see and see not . . . therefore thou son of man prepare thee stuff for removing, and remove by day in their sight . . .*

When he finished his prayer, tears had flowed from Lady Arbella's eyes, and John himself swallowed a lump in his throat.

There were two other clergymen at Sempringham that night; Roger Williams, a young firebrand with ginger hair, pronounced liberal opinions on everything, and a quick pleasing smile. Also Thomas Hooker, a placid middle-aged vicar from Chelmsford, who spoke very little but watched the others, particularly the Reverend Mr. Cotton, and the disciples Cotton had brought with him from Boston. There were a couple called Hutchinson, a weedy little merchant of obvious means, and his tall vibrant wife, whose brilliant gray eyes rested admiringly now on the Earl, now on the Reverend Cotton. No doubt she was in awe of the people she found herself amongst, Winthrop thought quite wrongly, not hearing her occasional decisive remarks, nor knowing that Mistress Anne Hutchinson was in awe of nobody.

But John, beneath his polite smile, was intent on his own problems.

For weeks he had been uncertain of his course. He had written page after page of argument pro and con the new plantation in endeavor to clarify his own mind, and he had waited on God's sure direction, aware of the pitfall of vanity. For it had been most agreeable to feel that his participation in the infant company was so much wanted and by such exalted men. Nor was this for the money he might invest in the venture; he had made clear his financial embarrassments. They wanted him for himself, for the qualities of leadership, administration and integrity they so flatteringly imputed to him, and during this dinner his uncertainty ceased. The Earl suddenly leaned down the table and said earnestly, "Well, Mr. Winthrop, may we hope that you are definitely joining the company and will go to New England?"

John bowed his head and answered solemnly, "Aye, my lord, I will."

The Lady Arbella clapped her slender hands, Isaac, her husband, laughed with relief, Sir Richard Saltonstall cried, "Splendid!" and was echoed by most of the others around the table except Downing who gave a dismayed grunt, for he had decided that though he would venture an investment, he would not himself emigrate at present.

"It'll be hard, John," he said below his breath. "You're forty-one, used to gentle living, and not so hale—"

John did not hear him, for the Earl was speaking again. "And to what, Mr. Winthrop, do we owe your most gratifying decision?" Lincoln asked with the warm shining smile which was like Arbella's.

John hesitated; he might have referred to Cotton's prayer, or to the glow of fellowship and dedication he had found at Sempringham, but he instinctively substituted a Sign. "On my way here, my lord, as we crossed the fens, my horse fell in a bog, and I in the water. I'd have been drowned, had not God preserved me for a manifest purpose, and thus made known to me His Will."

They all nodded understanding and Cotton said resonantly, "Praised be His Mercy!"

The Earl glanced down his great candlelit dining table, at his sisters and their husbands, at the three ministers, at Cotton's forceful follower—Mrs. Hutchinson. He looked at William Coddington, a substantial Boston merchant who was anxious to emigrate, perhaps not entirely for religious reasons, the Earl thought. There would be self-interest, the acquisition of land, particularly, to influence many of the venturers, or even the hope of ruling. His eyes grew troubled as they rested on his old steward, Thomas Dudley. Dudley was a red-faced truculent man of fifty-three who intended to emigrate, as did his seventeen-year-old daughter, the dreamy Anne, who sat beside her husband, young Simon Bradstreet. Both Dudley and Bradstreet were members of Lincoln's own household and eminently efficient men. The Earl glanced at Sir Richard Saltonstall. He then thought of the other directors of the Company who were known to him and not present; and particularly of the Governor, Matthew Cradock, who had remained in London but had sent the Earl certain advisements by letter, "in case Mr. Winthrop should find himself persuaded . . ."

This will go hard with Dudley, thought the Earl, but I had better give some warning. He motioned the footmen to refill the goblets and rose to propose a toast "To John Winthrop, Esquire, who has joined our great enterprise," he paused, "and whom I believe we may see become the temporal leader of it in the New World!"

John barely smothered a gasp, while dull red flushed his thin cheeks. Now what does he mean by that? he thought in confusion. Surely not the governorship! A leap of excitement was balanced by dismay. As he made some vague mechanical response, he received impressions from the faces at the table. Some looked surprised or uncertain, some like Isaac Johnson looked pleased, but there was no mistaking Thomas Dudley's reaction. His big hairy hand clenched on the goblet, while he choked on a mouthful of wine. His jowls quivered, and though he said nothing, Dudley sent Lord Lincoln a glare of indignation.

Surely there was no doubt that *I'd* be made Governor! Dudley thought, since Cradock won't emigrate. He stared down trembling at his dish of sugared figs, while blood drummed in his head. Who was this new-come pettifogging attorney anyway! An attorney who had lost his job, and admittedly most of his lands as well. A country squire whose grandfather had been a clothier. While I—thought Dudley burning with injustice—well born, of the great Dudley blood, raised with noblemen—Lord Northampton, Lord Say—and my long services to this ingrate, the Earl of Lincoln!

The Earl had been bankrupt when Dudley took over the stewardship of the estates, and in twenty years had managed them so well that now the Earl was solvent. Who better qualified than Dudley to administer a new colony? And besides there were the rights of birth and seniority. I'd not have agreed to go if I'd had wind of this, he thought, which brought an unpleasant corollary. For the Earl had urged his going, and Dudley's work at Sempringham, Tattershall, Folkingham, Lincoln, and a dozen smaller properties was done. The Earl had no further need of him, nor even of his son-in-law, Simon Bradstreet. Dudley looked up suddenly to see that his daughter Anne was staring at him. In her lightly pock-marked face the big eyes shone with concealed anxiety. At once he softened. Never mind, darling, he thought, your old father'll be Governor yet, and in the new land we'll bow to no Earls, or Bishops, or—his wrinkled lids raised to stare at Winthrop's flushed uncomfortable face. What do they SEE in him? thought Dudley. They *can't* make this Suffolk squire-let Governor!

Yet John Winthrop was elected Governor of the Massachu-setts Company in London on October 20, 1629, and after long delay Dudley was named Deputy. Like it or not he must go second to the new land. Dudley did not like it but by then he had cooled off, and also been won to grudging acceptance of Winthrop's indisputable sincerity and energy—so he bided his time.

Dudley had seen Winthrop's qualities best exhibited on the 26th of August, when they had all left Sempringham and foregathered in Cambridge, with the other members of the Company who were going to emigrate. There Winthrop had behaved himself with intelligence and foresight, collaborating so wholeheartedly with Dudley in the draft of the "Agreement" proclaiming the venturers' right to take their charter with them that Dudley could find no fault with the clear and earnest document, nor for the moment with Winthrop.

It was while his father was in Cambridge, signing the historic agreement, that John Winthrop, Junior, came home to Groton, thereby greatly disturbing Elizabeth's hard-won peace of mind. He had arrived in London from Venice via Amsterdam on August 13, he had exchanged letters with his father and with Margaret, he had announced himself as de-lighted with the Massachusetts project, and ready to co-operate in all things with his father's wishes. So Elizabeth had been prepared, and thought herself fortified, yet when he dismounted at the door of the Manor on that late August afternoon she discovered that she was not.

Led by Margaret, the whole family rushed out to meet him except Harry who had profited by his father's absence to pelt off to London, but when Elizabeth saw the sturdy green-cloaked figure, the long-nosed merry face tanned by sea voyaging, the brown hair, the alert eyes misted now by the emotion of homecoming—she drew back behind Martha, and clung to the door frame. It was Martha who rushed up to him with a cry of welcome, and flinging her arms around his neck, burst into tears. "Jack, Jack—we thought you'd never come!" cried the girl, clinging to him, "and *I* thought you'd been gobbled up by monsters!"

"Not a single monster did I see, Mattie," Jack answered, laughing and kissing her on the top of her head, "But I'm glad to be home." He gently disengaged the girl and kissed all his relatives—Margaret; his quiet plain sister Mary, who was also weeping; his brother Forth, "So you've grown into a man, youngster! Are you still for the ministry?" Forth shook his head, and Jack with a nod said, "You must tell me of it later, d'you know I've not had one letter these fourteen months since I left home until I got back to London!" He embraced his four wriggling little half-brothers, Stephen, Adam, Deane and Samuel, then looked beyond them to Elizabeth who still stood in the shadow of the doorway. "Ah, there you are, Bess," he said, his voice changing slightly. "I was indeed astonished to return and find that you had become my sister!"

"Yes," she said through a tight throat. "It was—was sudden." She forced herself to walk towards him, and offered him her cheek, but she could not smile. Nor did he. His eyes had grown stern as his father's and he turned away from her abruptly to enter the Hall, where Margaret and Martha and Mary fluttered over him, stuffing him with all the delicacies they had been saving for this occasion.

Elizabeth sat silent in a corner while Jack ate and answered questions and told them some of his adventures, though "Truly," he said smiling, "I've become sated with such diversity of countries, and find little difference when it comes to journey's end."

Elizabeth thought, That doesn't sound like him, as he *was* —all afire for new sights. And Margaret said with hesitance, for the subject upset her, "Yet, dear Jack, I know you've told your father that you would go with him to that dreadful —to that new plantation on the other side of the world." Her voice dropped. "He was much heartened."

Jack looked at her with sympathy, and answered gently, "I had much time for thought on my voyage, and I know that I'll always call *that* my country where I can best glorify God and enjoy the presence of those I love. I've read my

father's Conclusions for the departure, and I think them un-
answerable, and that it can't but be a prosperous action.
You'll come to feel so too, my mother."

Margaret sighed and put her arms around his shoulders.
"I pray so," she whispered, thinking with a fearing pang of
the new life which had started in her womb. John did not
know yet. But nothing would deter him from his purpose,
nor should, of course.

"You saw Harry in town?" she asked quickly, glancing at
Elizabeth who looked both unusually lovely and very somber
as she sat turned from them, staring out the window, though
she lifted her head at Margaret's question.

"No," answered Jack shortly. "Though I heard he was
there, staying with friends." That was not all he had heard
from his Aunt Lucy. There had been a detailed account of
Harry's misbehavior in general, and of Elizabeth's. And for
some reason not quite clear to him, Jack had made no effort
to find his brother and tell him he was home.

Elizabeth spoke defensively. "Harry will be here on Tuesday or Wednesday, he has written me so. He had much to do
about our voyage to Barbadoes." She glanced at Jack and
then away.

"Oh, and Harry has such grand friends in town," cried
Martha. "The Earl of Thanet and—and others."

"Indeed," said Jack. He smiled at Martha who was looking
up at him with open admiration in her large brown eyes. Her
cheeks were flushed and her babyish mouth was parted, for
the short upper lip seldom covered her rather prominent
front teeth. She was a small girl, but in the time he had been
gone her figure had rounded and her soft chestnut hair was
neatly coiled at the back of her head instead of loosely flowing as it had been. "You've grown up, little one," said Jack,
"and become very pretty, upon my word!"

Martha blushed and her eyes sparkled. "I'm eighteen,"
she said proudly, but a knife turned in Elizabeth's chest.
Does he know he said that to ME, scarce over a year ago, she
thought, while reason battled with the pain. It was Jack's way
to speak pleasantly, and he was devoted to all his family,
and in any case what difference did it make if he admired
Martha!

"Jack—" cried the girl, still red from her compliment, "the
mulberries are ripe, the old tree's loaded with them. D'you
remember how you used to love them? Do come and see!"
Martha put her hand shyly on his arm, then dropped it in

confusion. "I mean if you want to."

"Of course I do! You shall show me every single thing on the Manor." He stood up, the little boys prancing ahead of him to the door.

"You come too, Bess," cried Martha.

Elizabeth shook her head. "I've work to do." She glanced at Mary and Margaret who were supervising the servants as they cleared the table which had been set with earthenware and some silver in Jack's honor. She saw that the kind-hearted Margaret was about to send her off with the others and said stiffly, "I've much linen to sort."

Margaret sent her a troubled appraising look, while Martha, Jack and the boys went out into the garden. Elizabeth stood a moment by the open window, watching. She saw Martha pop a mulberry into Jack's mouth and heard the girl's soft timid laugh, which held for the first time a note of coquetry that Elizabeth knew to be unconscious. She quitted the Hall, and walked across the inner court to the other side of the great house, but she did not go to the linen room; she went to a small chamber near the dairy, that Margaret had allotted to her. It was a combination stillroom and surgery. Elizabeth had herself fitted it for the brewing of simples and cordials, and for the treatment of small injuries amongst the servants and tenants, or ailments for which it seemed foolish to summon the doctor at Boxford. Elizabeth found this work congenial, as many household duties were not; it filled the days that Harry was away, and she took pride in her knowledge of drugs, and in the trust which Groton inhabitants were beginning to have in her remedies and diagnoses. This afternoon she glanced at the crocks where herb vinegars were infusing, at the tray of sun-dried fennel waiting to be powdered, but she touched neither. She sat down on a stool and stared at the scrubbed brick floor until the light died and the cows in the byre across the meadow bawled to be milked.

It was in the same place, the following afternoon, that Jack found her. One of the kitchen maids had burned herself on the soup kettle. Elizabeth was binding a poultice of yellow calendula salve over the blisters and did not at first see Jack who stood in the open doorway watching. And thinking how beautiful she was in her black silk morning robes and white apron, they gave added transparency to her vivid coloring and luster to her long, intent hazel eyes. When the kitchen maid had departed with bobbing curtseys, he walked into the surgery and said, "Bess, we've been avoiding each other, it's best to have it out."

She started, and stiffened. "There's naught to have out," she said faintly, stacking the pile of old linen rags she used for bandages; then adding charcoal to the little brazier which fired the still where she was preparing her father's mithridate. "I'm wed to Harry. I love him passionately. There's no more to say . . . nor," she added in spite of herself, "did I ever receive any word from you, though you promised."

Jack glanced at her averted face. Mechanically he fingered a bunch of drying thyme which hung with other herbs from a pole. "I myself received no letters from home all the time I was gone, so I might tell you that I had written you and it miscarried. But I did not write. Yet I thought of you often and I thought that you would——" He stopped sharply. What nonsense, that he had been about to add the word "wait." Had he thought any such thing at all? Had he not in fact nearly succeeded by use of his strong emotional control in forgetting that disturbing scene in the apothecary's garden before he sailed? There was no excuse for the dangerous implications which had suddenly arisen. He went on with considerable coldness, "Bess, you behaved abominably to my friend Edward Howes. I fear he still loves you. I have just seen much of him at the Downings' and he is very bitter—— justifiably so."

"Ah," she said turning around at last, with a green spark in her eyes. "I'm sorry for that. Aye, you urged me to marry him, did you not!"

His hand clenched on the thyme which floated in powdery shreds to the floor. "I thought you'd make each other happy, I—Harry's my brother but—I doubt that he—I never thought that you——"

"The milk is shed," said Elizabeth tartly. " 'Tis useless now to water it."

They stood and stared at each other, both in varying degrees, now aware what their anger hid. Bubblings in the retort over the fire, and the hiss of the burning charcoal alone broke the silence. Then John mastered himself and said, "Aye, you're right. I yammer like a weanling. But, Bess, we've become brother and sister, can we not also be friends as we used to be?" His face broke into its warm smile.

I doubt it, she thought, but she bowed her head and murmured acquiescence, while conjuring up with all her strength the image of Harry. His handsome blond head that would have grazed the ceiling, his swagger and grace, his knowing hands and lips for which her body yearned each night. And she thought of something else, which would seal the barrier between herself and Jack for all time. She added a handful of rue to the simmering mithridate and said, "I have but lately known that I am with child."

Jack hid from himself a twist of distaste, and said lightly, "What excellent news! The first Winthrop grandchild. Now surely that will steady Harry's character!"

And mine, I hope, she thought. They talked then of nothing but her medical activities in which Jack was much interested. He examined her father's book of receipts and Gerard's invaluable *Herbal*. He had a quick scientific mind and made several suggestions for improving her equipment—a different shape retort—new steel lancets for bloodletting such as he had seen in Holland. He helped her untwist and clean the coils in her still, and their hands touched by accident once. They both drew back quickly but as he continued refitting the still he could not help glancing at her hands. They were not small, the palms were square and capable, but the long fingers ended in polished rosy nails and the skin looked like white velvet. Elizabeth took great care of her hands because Harry admired them. Indeed he often expressed pleasure in all her bodily charms, which did not, however, suffice to keep him from London, she thought bitterly—and when I am swollen with child . . .

Jack saw her face set, and the cloud in her expressive eyes. Once he would have tried to cheer her, but now he felt a painful constraint so alien to his nature that it brought annoyance.

This is ridiculous, he thought, and will surely pass. I'll not allow this—this chimera to cloud my homecoming. "How glad I shall be to see my father," he said brightly, "and to learn more of this tremendous move, on which if it be God's will we shall embark."

"Aye," she said, removing her apron and hanging it on a peg, "And I'll be glad when we leave for Barbadoes. Harry has told me of its beauties." And glad to be away from here. Alone with Harry there would be no memories, and no Jack.

"Do you pray sometimes when you're alone, Bess?" he said suddenly. "Oh, I've not the piety of my good parents, I fear, nor am I sure of my salvation as I might be—yet I know that God listens when we beseech His love and kindness, and He helps us to bear the unhappiness He sometimes sends for our own good."

She looked up at him and smiled a little, but she did not answer. Even to Jack she dared not admit how prayers and sermons bored her, and that in the fastness of her heart there was a void of disbelief, or rather a secret certainty that there was nothing in the world or out of it to sustain her but herself. It had been thus since the day her uncle flogged her here at Groton Manor.

The autumn passed quickly in a constant bustle of prepara-tions, letter writings, interviews with prospective emigrants, and strange visitors at all hours. From the moment of John Winthrop's return and even when he made quick trips to London, the entire manor was imbued by his fervor and his three older sons were all pressed into service. Jack was his father's able lieutenant and coped with much of the business matters besides acting as magistrate in the local court at Groton Hall. Forth transcribed dozens of letters at Winthrop's dictation, and Harry's wanderings were summarily curtailed. Since his father and brothers were so immersed in matters relative to the Great Migration, he was allotted the super-vision of the manor work. This at least gave him fresh air and the enjoyment of riding and shooting with his grey-hounds, while he visited the various tenants, collected Michael-mas rents, inspected winter pasturage, and the condition of the stock, oversaw the threshers, the garnering of fruit and nut crops, and the cutting of wood logs for winter fuel.

Harry was subdued and compliant during those months; Jack's presence always had a sobering effect on him, and there had been a painful scene with his father and brother combined, when he had had to confess the inadequacies of his arrangements for return to Barbadoes, which was more-over being bombarded by the Spaniards.

"That settles the matter," said Winthrop with exasperated finality. "We will efface the whole Barbadoes venture, where you were apparently swayed by vicious company, and I shall endeavor not to remind you how disappointing and costly it has been. You will come to New England with me where I can keep an eye on you, and where you will have ample op-portunity to serve God and your family."

"What about Bess, sir?" said Harry glumly, accepting the decision as inevitable. And in truth his London life had ceased to be amusing. Thanet was married, Seaton had gone to

Papist Ireland, other acquaintances were cool towards a youth without money.

"Elizabeth—" said Winthrop, sighing. Since learning of her pregnancy he had come to feel more kindly towards her, and sorrow for his second son's obvious deficiencies as a responsible husband. He picked up his pen and addressed a letter to "The Rev. Mr. George Phillips, Boxted, Essex" before he went on. "Elizabeth will wait here at the Manor with my wife, until it is sold. Since they are both with child, it is better thus anyway. John will look after them, and see to the Manor sale. When that is concluded he will bring them over, but *you* will come with me." He sighed again, not looking at Harry, who stalked out, and he returned to his letter which was an urgent invitation for Mr. Phillips, vicar of Boxted, to join the Massachusetts Company and sail with them in March. "I pray that this Phillips will be moved to come with us, and that the good reports I've heard of him are true," Winthrop said to Jack who was copying lists of necessities to give the prospective Planters. "It would be unthinkable to sail without a Man of God amongst us."

"I thought Mr. Wilson had consented to go," observed Jack, who had found the scene with Harry painful though he entirely agreed with his father.

"Aye, I believe Mr. Wilson will go, but not as soon as we. His wife holds back and his parish is loath to part with him."

I wonder at that! Jack thought with an inward laugh. He did not share his father's admiration for John Wilson, the rector of Sudbury, who was a fat pompous man without a gleam of lightness, and whose splayed toadlike nose was famous for its ability to smell out the slightest want of zeal in his flock. Jack was aware that he was thinking of Mr. Wilson so as not to think of Bess, and the dismay she would feel when she heard the new plan for Harry. There were many times when he avoided thinking of Bess. Still, now that Harry was home it was usually easier. Martha too made it easier. He had become fond of her trusting innocence, her dependence on him, and one could not help but be flattered by the adoration in her eyes.

When Harry told Elizabeth of his father's ultimatum, she was indeed dismayed. She had been lying in their great carved four-poster listlessly watching the bare elm branches writhing against the dun December sky, while the sleet hissed on the windowpanes. Her condition bothered her very little, but she had moments of queasiness. Harry burst into their room, kicked angrily at the log fire, and went to fish in the cupboard for a jug of brandy he kept hidden there. He took a long pull, then going over to the bed, said, "We're not going to Barbadoes. We're going to Massachusetts instead."

She made a quivering sound and stared up at him. He told her what his father had said, and when he finished she turned her face into the pillows and began to cry.

"Don't Bess—don't, love—" cried Harry, much moved. He had never seen her cry before, except at her father's funeral. "I don't like it either, or leaving you at such a time. But I have no say, you know that. It can't be so long until you come with our babe, and Brother John'll look after you."

At this she cried harder, and he lifted her up in his arms, kissed her wet cheeks and her mouth, and settled her head on his shoulder. "Here, have a swig." He held the jug to her lips and she swallowed. "Breeding ever makes women upset," he said tenderly. He was very proud of having begotten a child, the first of the new generation, and certain it would be a son. Once in Massachusetts he could get a land grant far larger than on Barbadoes, and no plaguey tobacco to struggle with either. There'd be game to hunt, forests, Indians, adventure and freedom. He had no doubt that he could avoid his father's watchfulness after landing. "You'll like the New England, darling, I know you will." He kissed her again with enthusiasm.

"Must we *always* do as HE says?" Elizabeth cried, yet yielding to his arms. "You're of age, Harry."

"But I've no money, or property left," he answered cheerfully. "You know that. There'll be a fine chance to get both in a new land."

You didn't in Barbadoes, she thought. "There's my four-hundred-pound dowry," she faltered. Both she and Martha had inherited this sum from Thomas Fones's estate. "Couldn't we use that?"

Harry shook his head with regret. "Father has it, nor will he let me touch it." He did not add that his father had been forced to spend much of this sum in settling Harry's debts. "He feels that he provides for all your needs here, and will for mine if I do as he says. There's no help for it, sweetheart." He slipped his hand on her breast beneath her bodice, and began to kiss her neck. "No more tears," he said. "There are far better things to do." He unpinned the brooch he had given her, and untied the lacings at her waist. She started to push him away, but her hand instead began to stroke his thick blond hair, drawing his head close against her breasts. "Harry, Harry—" she whispered falling back on the pillows. "When we are like this, together, I forget everything but you—" He laughed low in his throat, and she shut her eyes, abandoning herself to pleasure so keen that it was indistinguishable from love.

They were aroused some time later by a timid knock on the door. Harry cursed and shouted out a sleepy "Who's there!" to be answered by an indistinct murmur.

" 'Tis Sally," sighed Elizabeth. She pulled herself from the bed and wrapped the satin coverlet around her nakedness. She unbolted the door, knowing that her little maid would never disturb them except for real cause. "What is it, Sal?" she asked through the crack.

Sally was a buxom Suffolk lass of sixteen with squint-eyes and pimples. She bobbed a curtsey and said, "Beg pardon, ma'am, but Marster Winthrop he's a-waiting to star-rt the prayings, an' he sent me tew fetch ye."

"Oh, to be sure—" said Elizabeth blushing. She noted that Sally held a candle. It had grown late while they dallied together and dozed. "We'll be down directly," she said to Sally, but the girl still lingered. "Oi've a message fur Marster Harry special. It come from Boxford some hours agone, from the Fleece, it dew."

"What's that?" cried Harry sitting up. "Bring me the message, Bess!"

" 'Tis not wrote, sir—" said Sally, she twisted one red chilblained hand in her apron, and glanced nervously over her shoulder down the long shadowy corridor. "A wee lad come privily to me to say thot the Egyptian's in bad trouble, will ye tew the Fleece and help him, sir!"

"Blast and damnation—" muttered Harry below his breath, while Elizabeth thought, Can it be Peyto? though Harry said he'd left him in London. "What sort of trouble, Sally, do you know?" she asked the girl who nodded and shivered.

"They be saying in Boxfor-rd, that he's a *witch!*" She gasped, putting her hand over her mouth, and scuttled away towards the servants' quarters.

Elizabeth lit the candles in their bedroom and said, "Is it Peyto, Harry?" He grunted, and she went on, frowning, "But I thought you got rid of him long ago. You promised your father—"

"Can I help it if the scamp is devoted to me? If he got a job in the stables at the Fleece to be near me! Good Lord,

Bess, he risked his life for me in Barbadoes."

"You've been seeing him then?"

He shrugged. "Now and then. He's done me some good turns."

Ah, she thought, sighing—that's where the brandy comes from. "What will you do, Harry?"

"Go to the Fleece and see what this all means. Hurry up, sweet, there'll be enough trouble without our being late to prayers!"

They dressed hastily and went to the parlor. John Winthrop absently accepted their excuses and did not give the prayers and psalms his usual impressive emphasis. As soon as he had implored God's blessing for the night he dismissed the servants and younger children and addressed the others. "There's been called to my attention a matter of such grave concern, that occupied though I am with preparations for departure, I feel it must be dealt with."

They all looked at him anxiously except Jack who had been with his father when the angry delegation of townsfolk from Boxford stamped through the sleet into the Manor. Winthrop continued frowning. "The Landlord of the Fleece, Constable Cole, Mr. Doggett and Goodman Biggs, all waited on me here this afternoon to prefer a charge of witchcraft against—" he paused and looked at Harry, "a fellow recently hired as ostler at the Fleece."

"Witchcraft!" cried Margaret, her round face paling. "Oh, John, how terrible!"

"I don't understand, sir," said Forth in his rather pedantic way. "Why did they come to you if the alleged witch or warlock is at Boxford? Why did they not take their charge to Mr. Brand at Coddenham Hall, is he not their squire?"

"They came here," answered his father, "because this knave is known to have been in the service of a member of my family. He is, in fact, Peyto, that disreputable gypsy churl I repeatedly told you to dismiss, Henry, and whom you assured me you had."

"I did, sir," said Harry quickly.

"Had you any knowledge of his presence now so near us at Boxford?" Winthrop's eyes flashed with anger born of distress. There had been no witchcraft, no such hint of the Devil's presence in this part of Suffolk for years, and the delegation had heatedly assured him that it was being taken as a sign of God's wrath and divine opposition to Winthrop's plans for leaving home. Mr. Doggett had even said that local men who had signed agreement for New England and guaranteed passage money were withdrawing their names.

"Answer me, Henry!" cried Winthrop in a thunderous voice. "Do you know aught of this man's being at Boxford?"

"No, sir," said Harry looking his father straight in the eye. His lie sprang not entirely from cowardice though he was afraid, but from loyalty to Peyto whom he thought he might help more easily if their recent connection was unknown. Jack raised his eyebrows to give his brother a sad speculative glance, but Winthrop accepted the statement with relief.

"What do they say Peyto has done, sir?" asked Harry in a small voice.

Winthrop pulled a sheet of paper from his pocket, and scanned the arraignment Doggett had written for the aroused townsfolk to make their marks on. He then read the gist of it aloud.

"1. He is admittedly an Egyptian, and all such are known for evil practices, the landlord hired him unaware, thought him Welsh or Cornish, having never seen natives of those places.

2. He is given to secret sorcery and divination by means of Satan's own tool, some strange-pictured playing cards.

3. He has a familiar, a nearly black donkey to whom he often talks in a strange language, and the donkey has been heard to answer him.

4. Since he came, there have been many marvelous disasters. Six cows died along Stone Street where he was seen to ride his donkey, then Robert Reynolds, the cordwainer's entire shoe shop was burned last Sabbath day. At the Fleece, they have heard strange noises in the night, particularly the ringing of the chamber bells in the courtyard, from rooms known to be vacant. This has so frightened travelers, that the Landlord is losing his custom. Worst of all, when Goody Biggs began to suspect him by reason of her horse running away out of the Inn courtyard after this man had watered the beast, and came to accuse him of malicious mischief, he denied it with a foul oath and the next day Goody Biggs' young daughter fell into fits. Upon her mother asking her if they were caused by the foreign ostler at the

> *Fleece, the girl said they were, and that she had been bewitched.*
>
> 5. *The man was accordingly seized, stripped and searched. His ears had been cropped, the scar of an apparent brand burn on his cheek had been tampered with so its letter was uncertain, and many thought Satan might have made it. There was found also a large mole on his arse shaped like a cloven hoof. There is thus no possible doubt that this man who gave his name as Guy Smith, alias Peyto, has formed a covenant with the devil. And we demand that he be burned at once without trial."*

Winthrop folded the paper and put it back in his pocket. There was a long shocked silence, during which Martha began to weep. Finally Margaret said in a trembling voice, "This is fearful, my husband, surely they won't *burn* him—if these, these horrors be indeed true, yet surely he may but hang."

"They can neither burn nor hang him without a trial," said Jack sternly. "My father told them that. But they were very angry and Doggett quoted Moses' own law as given by God. 'A man also or woman that hath a familiar spirit, or that is a wizard shall surely be put to death.' "

"What have they done with Peyto?" asked Harry roughly. He believed in witchcraft, of course, and it was true that his servant had uncanny skill at reading his peculiar cards, but for the rest the charges were ridiculous; he knew Peyto as well as he did his brothers.

"He *was* chained in the cellar of the Fleece," said Winthrop, "but just before prayers Doggett sent word to me that he has escaped. They think he bewitched the cook's little lad, who helped him."

Fortunately nobody but Elizabeth was looking at Harry, for he could not hide his relief, while Jack said, "I did not know that. He'll get away then, out of the country, and perhaps the trouble will be over!"

Winthrop shook his head. "He'll not get far in this weather; he fled naked as a frog, and Cole has the whole of Boxford out searching for him. We must at once rouse all our Manor folk to help."

He'll come here to me, Harry thought. Even now Peyto might be hiding in the abandoned mill on the Box they had used for their meetings these past weeks. "Aye—" he cried jumping up. "The Manor must be aroused. I'll set about it now. It horrifies me inexpressibly to hear that Peyto has lost his soul. How right you were, Father, to forbid me his foul company, and what a deluded fool I was!"

The harrassed Winthrop heard nothing but proper sentiment in this speech; the women were exclaiming and shuddering, except Elizabeth who guessed her husband's motives well enough, and was frightened, while she rushed after him whispering, "Oh, my dear, be careful!" He nodded, grabbed his cloak from a peg, and ran out to the stables, shouting for his horse.

When she returned to the group, she caught Jack looking at her. He shook his head imperceptibly, but he said nothing, and she noted that he made delays in joining Forth who had already gone to alert the servants. Pray God Sally holds her tongue about the message, thought Elizabeth, her heart thudding. She ran to the offices and found Sally alone crouched by a candle in the brewery, clumsily mending one of Elizabeth's plain lawn collars.

"Would you like that collar for your own, Sal?" she whispered.

The girl goggled at her and finally said, "Yus, thot I would, ma'am."

"Then say nothing of the message to Master Harry. You haven't, have you?"

Sally shook her head. "Oi'd be afeared. Oi'm feared of going tew bed even—Oh, ma'am!"

"No, no—" said Elizabeth urgently. "There's no need for fear. Peyto's no witch. Why you *liked* him when he was here! It's just those Boxford folk have gone mad!" This was a shrewd touch since Sally came from Edwardstone which had a constant rivalry with Boxford.

The girl nodded slowly. "Oi won't say naught. Oi'd never make tr-rouble fur Marster Harry."

"Good lass." Elizabeth smiled at her. "And wear the collar on Sunday!"

She walked slowly back to the parlor, conscious now of the fluttering burden she carried, though her waist had thickened but little. The men had disappeared; Margaret was sitting by the fire, idle for once, her hands clasped on her belly where a dull pain mingled with the movements of her own child which had also lately quickened. Margaret was forty, had borne five children and buried one, Nathaniel, and she suffered many discomforts this time though she never complained.

"Sit down, Bess," she said gently. "You look white. You must not let this horrible business upset you, it might mark the babe. Let us talk of other matters—or Mary, read aloud to us, dear. What have you there?"

Mary's sober young face was bent close to her book, for she was short-sighted. She looked up and said, " 'Tis a description of New England by a Captain John Smith, a great warrior it seems. Brother John gave it to me, it tells of the very land we're going to."

Margaret had long since resigned herself to the move her husband so delighted in and she said, "That will be most interesting."

Martha who had been huddled nervously on a stool by the fire, brightened. She never found pleasure in reading herself, but she loved hearing stories. She took silks, needle and a half-finished purse from her pocket and continued its embroidery. The purse was for Jack's birthday gift in February, but she had told this to nobody.

"Captain Smith is writing—" said Mary, "about the country of the Massachusetts—is that not where my father will go?" Margaret nodded, and the girl went on, "He says it

is the Paradise of all those parts. For, heere are many Iles planted with corne; groves, mulberries, salvage gardens, and good harbours—"

She stopped, for they heard a sinister clamor outside, the hallooing of men, the barking of hounds, the thump of horses, all mingled with the long drawn wailing of a horn.

The women looked towards the windows. "The hue and cry," said Margaret faintly. "They've not caught him yet, then."

"I pray they don't," said Elizabeth. It sounded like the howling stampede of great bloodthirsty beasts out there, and the beautiful firelit parlor suddenly seemed full of fear-stench.

"I know," said Margaret. She reached to the table and poured cups of mead. "But Scriptures also say "Thou shalt not suffer a witch to live.' We *must* keep God's Law. Perhaps some mead will strengthen us . . ." She gestured towards the cups. "And go on reading, Mary."

The young girls obeyed, but Elizabeth stood up. "I'm sorry, my mother, I am too disquieted to stay. I'll go to bed."

She was in a fever of worry for Harry, and suddenly it occurred to her that if he needed her help she had best be alone in their bedroom. The hue and cry passed on towards Castling's Heath, and dwindled away while she sat waiting.

It was near midnight when Harry came stamping into their room; the sleet had changed to snow, and he shook flakes off his shoulders, crying loudly, "No, Bess—alack, we haven't found the skulking bastard yet! But no doubt will, as soon as it's light!"

She saw that this was for the benefit of his brothers in the passage, and when Harry had shut and bolted their door, he held his raw hands to the fire murmuring, "I've got him safe. 'Twas a near thing. The hue and cry went by us, but I had him on the saddle with me, covered by my cloak. They never saw."

"Where is he now?" she whispered helping to pull off the sodden boots.

"D'you remember the old attic we used to climb to from the bakehouse?"

"To be sure, and the hours I lurked there the day your father flogged me—Oh, Harry—you've never put him *there!* In this very house!" She sank down on the hearth settle and began to laugh hysterically.

"Hush!" he said. "There's naught for merriment. He's half froze, starved, he's hurt his foot, and I know not how to free him either. I must fetch him food tonight, since all day the bakehouse is in use."

"There was a little door bolted, behind that suit of armor, I remember—" she said. "It must lead to the other attics. Let's try and get it open now."

Harry bent to hug her. "That's my plucky girl. I told Peyto you'd be with us. He's—he's much afraid of burning, poor little wag."

During the days that they managed to tend Peyto, Harry and Elizabeth were nearer in spirit than they had ever been, or were to be again, and both of them enjoyed the perils of their adventure, though well aware of the gypsy's pathos and continuing danger.

The hidden door was warped, cobwebbed, and the bolt rusted so fast that it had to be shattered, but Harry nonetheless managed to open it and then it was easier to visit Peyto. The servants who slept in the far attic chambers complained of noises and footsteps in the night. Upon hearing of this from Sally, Elizabeth said anxiously, "Oh, I *hope* it is not old Adam Winthrop the first, who is 'walking' again. 'Tis supposed to be bad luck to those who see him!" That disposed of all nosiness on the part of the servants, and as for the family, Margaret, and the younger members had never heard of that particular attic, while John Winthrop had long forgotten its existence, nor had reason to remember it now.

Boxford and Groton folk, having beat over every foot of ground for miles, came to the reasonable conclusion that the Devil had again saved his own. In fact Goody Biggs's young daughter said she had seen Peyto flying past her window on a broomstick before dissolving into a ball of fire, so there could be little doubt how he got away.

There remained only one thing the uneasy townsfolk could do to insure themselves against further malignant sorcery. On the third day after Peyto's disappearance they gathered around a pyre of burning faggots in the marketplace and solemnly burned Peyto's familiar, the little black donkey. There were several who were enraged when they found the donkey already dead in the stable before the burning because someone had stabbed it to the heart, but more were secretly relieved. Many folk who did not mind a bull- or bear-baiting, because it was sport, were squeamish about the agonies of fire. The minister, Mr. Grant, read the old form of exorcism over the donkey's ashes, and said a very fine prayer of his own. The landlord of the Fleece invited all to open house, and it was generally admitted that the whole grievous matter were best forgotten now. In a day or so Reynolds, Biggs, and others of the erstwhile emigrants sheepishly returned to Groton Manor and asked Governor Winthrop to reinstate their names for the Plantation, whereat he was much pleased and relieved.

But in the meantime Peyto still lay hidden in the attic by the bakehouse. Besides injuring his foot he had caught a fearful cold the night of his escape, and spent the time shivering and coughing with his face muffled by the velvet robes of a long-dead Winthrop, so that no untoward sound might be heard.

Elizabeth smuggled to him flaxseed poultices and infusions of camomile, along with all the food she or Harry dared sneak from the pantries. Peyto gradually improved and might soon escape to the North where he wanted to go, but there were difficulties. His wrenched or broken foot—Elizabeth was not sure which—would not permit of his walking far yet, and neither she nor Harry had any money to give him, let alone the means of getting him some sort of mount.

It was on Christmas Eve, and Peyto had been there a week, when Elizabeth retired very early and requested that supper be sent up to her room. Sally brought her a jug of wine, half a cold duck, and a large plum pasty garnished with holly, at which Elizabeth stared with astonished pleasure.

"It was Cook, ma'am, what made thot little ould Christmas pie," said Sally defensively. "Being new to the Manor ways, and more'n half Papist if you arsk me."

"It's all right, Sal. I'm glad to have it!"

Elizabeth ate moderately, then dumped the remains in a basket. She made sure that everyone was busy with supper below, including Harry whose rather tipsy laugh she heard. She sneaked along the passages and up the little stairs that twisted around the kitchen chimney. She groped her way to the concealed door and crept in to Peyto who was crouched by the old chest, mournfully flexing his injured foot. There was light from a lantern Harry had brought him, and in consequence they had shrouded the small gable window with some Winthrop wife's moth-eaten green cloak. Peyto had also made use of the chest's contents to cover his nakedness, but the Elizabethan crimson doublet and breeches engulfed the little man. They had cut all his hair off when they searched him for witch marks, so that now with his round head, cropped ears and sad dark eyes he looked like a costumed monkey Elizabeth had once seen at the Bartholomew Fair in London.

"Cheer up, Peyto—" she said. "Look what I brought you!" She gave him the food, stuck a branch of holly in her hair, and another in the slash of his doublet. " 'Tis Christmas Eve!"

"Well I know it, Mistress—and I think I'm not like to see another."

"Nonsense! We'll get you safe away from here!"

Tears glittered in his eyes as he looked up at her. "Ye've been good, Mistress . . . and my dear master." To her dismay, he suddenly crumpled with his face on his arm and his shoulders heaved. "Would that I had my cards—" he moaned. "My tarot that they took from me and burned up like my poor donkey. But I must've read the cards wrong on All Hallow's Eve. Could I cast them again on Christmas Eve I'd know surer."

"What do you mean?" she cried. "Oh, Peyto, did the cards show you this dreadful trouble for you?"

He shook his head. "Never can I read them for me. It was for *him*."

"For Harry?" she asked sharply. "What did you see?"

Again he shook his head. "Naught, naught." He spoke with almost sullen misery.

She looked at him frowning, while foreboding gripped her.

"Wait!" he cried, suddenly grabbing her left hand. "Mayhap I can tell something from this!" He turned her palm over and stared at it by lantern light. "My mother taught me this way too, though for long I've not used it." He stared at her palm, took the right one, and peered at them both, muttering, while she waited uneasily. He let her hands drop. "It was true what I saw before."

"What—?" she whispered shrinking.

"Death," said Peyto, staring into the shadows of the attic. "Oh, not yours—death around ye, by water—by sickness—by madness—by bullets—by fire!"

"I'll not believe it!" she cried angrily. "Before God, Peyto, I believe you are in league with the devil. We should have let you burn!"

"Nay, nay, Mistress—" said the little man sadly. " 'Tis not the devil gives my people a look at the future, 'tis the ancient art we've never lost . . . But there's more than death and violence in your hands, Mistress—there's love and far places and strivings—ever striving for something ye cannot have. Freedom. Ye'll hanker after freedom, like my own people who cannot *live* cribbed and cabined." He reached out and took her right hand again, staring at the pink palm and its mesh of lines. "Ye'll get what ye want in the end," he whispered, "but ye won't know it at first—for it'll not be what ye thought to be seeking all the long years—all the long years . . ." he repeated, running his dirty brown fingers down her life line.

The door swung open and Harry stuck his head in. "What's ado here?" he cried laughing. "You graceless knave, you hold my wife's hand behind my back?"

"Oh, hush!" Elizabeth said, for Harry's voice was loud and thickened by drink. He stumbled a little as he stooped to get through the door. "Peyto has been telling my fortune, and a most horrid one it is too."

"But ye'll be happy in the end," said the gypsy earnestly.

"And I?" Harry stuck his big hand under Peyto's nose. "Read me money and land, my boy! And plenty of merriment, children too—a round dozen of 'em—eh, Bess, my beauty?"

But Peyto turned away. "I'm weary, Master," he said. He

rested his chin on his knees and closed his eyes. Harry felt irritation. Peyto had lost all his gaiety and impudence, had become limp as a snared rabbit, and what was to be done with him anyway?

The problem was solved almost at once. "Hist!" whispered Elizabeth. As Harry started to speak she put her hand over his mouth. They all heard approaching footsteps. Peyto sucked in his breath, and hobbled frantically to an angle behind the chimney where he hid. The other two waited, until the little door opened and Jack walked in carrying a candle. "So—" he said looking calmly at Harry and Elizabeth, at the disordered robes on the floor, at the remains of food. "I might have guessed this sooner, but I fear my childhood play is long behind me. Where is he?"

"I don't know what you mean," began Harry, jutting his chin, but Elizabeth acted from surer instinct. "Oh, Jack—help us, help poor Peyto! He's still ill, and we can't go on like this. How did you find us?"

"Followed Harry's noisy and by no means difficult trail," said Jack with a faint smile, "though I've suspected you had the gypsy hidden somewhere all along."

"Does Father?" asked Harry quickly.

"No. Nor do I think it wise to disturb him, *unless*," he added sternly, "the man be indeed involved in witchcraft. I wish to question him, and inspect the mole alleged to be a witch mark."

"Come out, Peyto!" Harry called, and the gypsy obeyed, looking at once so forlorn and funny in his vast old-fashioned clothes, hopping on and off the bandaged foot, that Harry chuckled.

Jack's questions relative to the death of the six cows, the firing of Reynolds's shoe shop, the fits of Goody Biggs's daughter, did not take long to answer. Peyto denied knowledge of all the accusations and Jack, who was intuitive, shrewd and almost free from superstition, knew that he heard the truth. Then Peyto pulled down his crimson breeches and presented the mole on his buttock for Jack's examination, who was soon satisfied. "An ordinary round mole," he said, "and I see no more likeness to a cloven hoof than to a skillet or a peppercorn."

"So you'll help him get away?" cried Elizabeth anxiously, thinking that it was a good thing Jack had not walked in on the fortunetelling.

"Aye—" said Jack, looking at the gypsy with pitying eyes

as the man was racked with a spasm of coughing so violent that blood flecked his mouth and chin.

Peyto got away next evening, properly clothed, with ten shillings in his pocket and his fare paid to London. Harry drove him, hidden in a farm cart, as far as Witham, then put Peyto on the Ipswich coach. Jack had made all easy, and provided the money. At the moment of parting the gypsy kissed Harry's hands, wet them with his tears, whispering, "I'll ne'er see ye more," and made a long speech in his own language. Harry clapped him on the back, and said "Farewell" with affection, but he was impatient to try the ale at Witham's White Hart, and anyway the adventure was over.

The White Hart's charms proved alluring, and it was three days later before Harry came back to Groton with the cart, but Jack covered this from his father by saying that he had sent Harry on an errand, and John Winthrop was far too busy with the ever increasing details and problems of the Migration to question his eldest son.

"I suppose you gave him extra money beyond that needed by Peyto?" said Elizabeth with gloomy resignation to Jack one noon while they were still waiting for Harry's return. "You might know he'd drink it—or worse." She and Harry had been so close for weeks, she had thought he would never leave her until he must.

Jack said, "Aye, I'm sorry, Bess," looking at her discouraged face. "I should have known better." His arm itched to hold her against him, and comfort her, but instead he swung on his heel, stalked out the door into the courtyard and ran smack into Martha who was hurrying from the wash-house with a pile of freshly ironed linen. Their collision was so violent that two of John Winthrop's elaborate white ruffs fell in the mud, and Martha's dismay at this was so great that presently Jack found his arm around her shoulders, and that he was comforting Martha instead. The girl, still clutching her linen, nestled against him, and before he knew it Jack had kissed her several times and found it very pleasant.

6

IMMEDIATELY after Christmas, John Winthrop went to London, and used for headquarters either the Downings' home or Isaac Johnson's house in Soper Lane. Despite inevitable annoyances and hindrances, the affairs of the Massachusetts Bay Company were prospering incredibly. God was smiling on the project. The Cambridge Agreement had stipulated that they sail in March, and they would be ready to sail in March—the ten chartered ships and also the splendid converted privateer of 350 tons which the Company had managed to buy for 750 pounds. This great ship once called the *Eagle* had been rechristened the *Arbella*. That gentle lady herself would sail on her, as well as the other principal passengers.

Some seven hundred folk of all ages signed up for the Migration to New England, and by February the fleet could accommodate no more. Winthrop most regretfully had to turn down applicants. It disappointed him that only two ministers had agreed to sail at this time—George Phillips and John Wilson. Still, from those he had met at Sempringham—Thomas Hooker, Roger Williams, and the redoubtable John Cotton of Boston—he had received constant backing and the hope that they might come later. In fact most of

149

the nonconformist ministers throughout England had miraculously heard of the brave new colony which was to be founded to the glory of God, and had subtly encouraged their various flocks to consider removal.

On Valentine's Day, Emmanuel Downing returned to his home from a busy session at the Inner Temple and found Winthrop huddled over a table in the small parlor. The table was littered with passenger lists, bills of lading, agreements for provisions and a sheaf of letters from backers and persons of quality which John felt he must answer himself. He looked up as his brother-in-law entered and said jubilantly, "They come from a score of counties. See how the Lord's hand has quickened seed in half this realm!"

Downing glanced at the passenger lists and remarked, " 'Tis true, but more from your Suffolk and Essex than the rest. It shows what faith in you they have who know you. And never did I think this work could be done so fast . . . You sail from Southampton then, the last week in March?"

John nodded. "If God sends us fair winds."

Downing yanked at the bell pull. "I've a fancy for mulled sack, and 'twill do *you* good, you work too much. You've grown haggard as a hound. The company has a deputy and assistants besides you. Why don't you go home to Groton a while?"

"I shall this week," said Winthrop. He picked up his goose quill and made a note. His hand quivered suddenly. "For the last time," he added very low.

Emmanuel loosened his doublet and settled his bulk in a chair. "Aye—" he said with sympathy. " 'Tis hard to leave the place ye were born, harder still to leave the others—especially Margaret in her state. She's a fine wife to you, John, loves you true."

Winthrop dropped his head, and said with an emotion that embarrassed the bluff Downing, "She is my heart's comfort, my other self, and I sorrow to think how little of my time I've given her of late."

"Well-a-day," said Downing, hastily accepting a mug of hot sack from the servant. "I expect I'd be sorry to part from my Lucy. Her prickles are wearing softer with the years, and she's an able breeder like your Margaret."

Winthrop smiled, and took a sip of sack. "I've good children—save Henry, I fear, though I believe he mends."

"Ah, in clutches large as ours, we must expect to hatch one goshawk," said Downing, belching pleasurably. "My little

George will prove a handful, I've no doubt, unless I can beat it out of him. How is the beauteous Bess?"

"Tamer, it seems, as I hoped she would be in a truly God-fearing household. My wife is fond of her, and says she proves dutiful as—" he added with complacence, "does my son John, always!"

Downing laughed. "I vow you dote like a lover on that lad."

"Since the days when I had to whip some childish mischief out of him, never has he displeased me." Winthrop began to gather up his papers thinking with tender pride of young John. The scene in the fields with Jack on the morning after Winthrop's return to Groton Manor was therefore a severe shock.

The Manor had not yet sold, though there were negotiations, but they were gradually selling off furnishings and stock, and a buyer had been found for one of the saddle horses. Winthrop went to the stables to conclude the transaction, while Jack as a matter of course accompanied him. When the farmer had trotted off on the horse, Winthrop turned towards the house, but Jack stopped him. "Could I speak with you privily, sir? Might we walk a bit?"

It was a soft misty morning with the promise of sun, and the smell of fresh earth where the mole-catcher and his terrier were rooting through the new-turned fields. Winthrop, though a trifle startled and also suffering pangs at viewing the dear lands he was so shortly to leave, gladly acquiesced. They walked past the dove-cote and the pond, and up the manor rise where they could see their sheep-filled pastures, and the nearby pinnacles on Groton Church. Far to the south soared the graceful tower of the church at Stoke-by-Nayland.

They came to the hedge and stile near the highway, and Winthrop stopped. "Well, what is it, John? I've much ado at the house." He examined his son's embarrassed face, and said with faint humor, "You've not fallen in love, have you?"

Jack took a deep breath, glanced at his father, then down at the blackthorn hedge. "Yes sir . . . that is I think . . . I think it wise to change my state, I mean it would be helpful here and even more so when I finally join you in New England."

"But, of course, son—'tis most natural." Winthrop smiled and put his hand on Jack's shoulder. "Why, you've just turned twenty-four, have you not? I can scarce credit it.

Who is the lady, not—" he said eagerly, "Mary Waldegrave, or one of the Alabasters?"

"No, sir," said Jack, still staring at the tangled blackthorns. "'Tis little Mattie—my cousin Martha."

There was a sharp and painful silence. Winthrop's hand dropped from Jack's shoulder. The mole-catcher's dog streaked by barking frantically, and Winthrop called out with irritation, "Tom! Quiet that cur! Take him away!"

The mole-catcher looked frightened. Squire seldom spoke harsh like that. He pulled his forelock and grabbed his dog.

"I'm sorry, sir," said Jack. "I didn't think you'd be so displeased. She's a sweet gentle girl and I—I've grown fond of her."

Winthrop clenched his hands and rage flamed through him. "Is there nobody for my sons to wed but those Fones wenches!" he shouted. "If you must marry your cousins are there not plenty of others to pick from! Or is this like Henry's, a case of 'needs-MUST-wed'?"

Jack stiffened and stared angrily back to his father. "It is NOT! And naturally I shall not go on if you forbid the match, though I did not expect your violent opposition and have applied for special license."

"Without consulting me!"

"It will not be used until you give consent, sir, but I may remind you that I am of full age and that you have entrusted my judgment in all *other* matters!"

Winthrop turned away, biting his lips. "God forbid that there should be anger between us," he said at last in a trembling voice. "But, John, you and Martha are so near akin—that couldn't be helped with Henry—and she has no lands, no portions—"

"She has four hundred pounds, sir, and a tender docile heart."

Winthrop was silent trying to master his disappointment. Always he had thought that Jack would marry well, even grandly, and of late he had hoped that in the new land the boy might choose from one of the aristocratic planters' families. A Saltonstall perhaps, or even some kin to the Earl of Lincoln . . . that is if there were no previous match with a fine Suffolk family like the Waldegraves. And all these hopes to be dissolved by little Matt Fones! Yet he loved his son and could not bear the cloud between them. Also he felt that there was about Jack's choice some strange motivation that he could not fathom.

He sighed deeply and put his hand again on Jack's shoulder. "I cannot pretend this is not a blow. It may be the Lord wishes to chastise me that I may not take for granted all the success and benefits He has reaped upon my Company. I do not forbid the match, my son, but I ask that you will wait before you wed, wait and pray, as I shall, that God will show you His *true* will."

Jack seized his father's hand and grasped it warmly. "Thank you, sir. We'll wait, and I'll try to pray on it." I'm glad to wait, he thought ruefully. The sudden application for special license had been an impulse designed to hide from himself his own lukewarmness. Yet—Martha—so gentle, so trusting—and so joyful. She had misunderstood his kisses and gratitude on his birthday, February 12, when she had given him the embroidered purse. He had found himself betrothed to her without quite knowing how it came about.

Elizabeth had been in her bedroom with Harry that afternoon when Martha rushed in with the news. The girl was so excited that she didn't notice that Harry clad only in his breeches was shaving his golden beard at the washbasin. "Bess, Bess!" cried Martha, her small face transfigured. "Fancy what's happened!"

"I fancy you might knock, child!" Elizabeth snapped. Lately she had found Martha exasperating for a very good reason which she was too honest to deny to herself. Also she had just discovered that she could no longer fit into her favorite velvet dress no matter how she loosened the waist.

"But listen!" cried Martha, flinging her arms around her sister's neck. "Jack and I are to be wed! He's writing the Archbishop for a license. Oh, Bess, I'm so happy!"

Elizabeth swayed and her bright cheeks went gray. Her silence penetrated even Martha's rapture. "What's the matter?" cried the little sister, anxious at once. "You look queer!"

"A belly qualm . . ." Elizabeth murmured. "I think the herring was tainted." She could not embrace Martha. She sank instead on the bed, fighting a churning jealousy.

"What's that?" cried Harry striding over from the washbasin, his strong chest naked and damp. "What was that you told Bess, Matt?"

"That Jack and I are to be wed," answered the girl less surely. "He—he asked me not an hour ago."

Harry stared,—then he flung his razor to the floor and threw back his head with a roar of laughter. "By God and

all the little devils! This is beyond all! Oh, this is a jape!"
He laughed so hard he choked.

"Why do you laugh, Harry . . ." Martha whispered, and
her underlip began to tremble.

"I laugh for what my father will say!" cried Harry between
gasps. "He that's been angling for a Waldegrave, or higher.
Oh glee, oh rapture that I should see the day when *Jack* has
fallen out of favor!"

"Harry! You're cruel!" Elizabeth cried, starting from the
bed. "There, there Matkin—'tis not bad as all that!" She
put her arm around her sister, forgetting everything but the
terrified stricken look in the brown eyes that had been so
joyous a moment before.

"You mean Uncle John will forbid us?" the girl murmured
shrinking into herself. "He won't want me for Jack? Aye, of
course, he won't! How could he? What a dolt I was. And no
doubt Jack didn't really mean to wed me, he was but being
gallant." All her hard-won confidence had vanished. She
turned away from Elizabeth, and dragged over to the window,
where she rested her forehead against the panes.

"Oh, come now, Matt!" Harry cried with some contrition.
Martha was far too small, pale and wambly for his personal
taste, but he was fond enough of her, when he noticed her.
"You needn't sag like a punctured pig's bladder! Jack'll talk
Father 'round in time, I shouldn't wonder, if need be the
same way I got Bess."

"If he really wants to," Martha whispered, scarcely listening. "But I am not Bess." She turned and looked at her
sister, dimly hearing as she spoke that her words held deeper
meaning than she had known, and she felt an added thrust
of bewildered pain. She looked quickly away from Elizabeth
—the elder one, the strong one, the beautiful one, who had
surely never known defeat.

Elizabeth saw the stiffening, and knew the miserable barrier that had risen between them. " 'Twill be all right, darling,"
she said with effort. "You'll be very happy, Mattie, you'll
see," and she kissed her.

Martha responded a little, but there was still a shrunken
look about her as she walked out the door. Harry returned to
his shaving and began to sing:

> *"Troll the bowl, the nut-brown bowl,*
> *And here's kind mate to thee!*

> *Let's sing a dirge for St. Hugh's soul,*
> *And down it merrily.*
>
> *Down-a-down, hey, down-a-down*
> *Hey derry derry down-a-down!*
> *Ho! Well done, to me let come,*
> *Ring compass, gentle joy!"*

"You're in high fettle," observed Elizabeth bleakly as he sluiced his face and head, emerged with yellow curls dripping, and his face ruddy.

"Why not, my sweet? Jack's love affair amuses me. Life amuses me. I'm strong and I'm young. I've a fair wife—" he blew her a kiss, "who is plumped as a plum by my fair son—and I'm off to the Fox for a whet of March beer!" This afternoon visit to the local tavern near Groton Church had become invariable since Peyto was no longer there to provide strong spirits. And the landlord extended willing credit to a Winthrop.

"Wait," she said, putting her hand on his wrist. Harry, who had been adjusting his sword belt over his black satin doublet, looked at her with surprise. "For what, my pet?"

"Harry—" she said, her hand tightening on his wrist. "How soon will you be leaving with your father and the little boys? Leaving for good, I mean."

"Oh," he put his arm around her, " 'twill be soon, dear heart. Ten days at most. The *Arbella*'s ready now at Hampton, you know. But think not on that—we'll have merry times yet together."

"Don't go!" she cried in sudden anguish. "Harry, don't leave me here! Make some excuse. Don't leave me here with *them!*"

"With them?" he repeated, stroking her hair and frowning. He had never heard her so desperate and wild.

"Jack and Martha." She buried her head on his breast and clung to him frantically. "I couldn't bear it."

Harry took her by the shoulders and pushed her away from him. He lifted her convulsed face and stared at her. "WHAT couldn't you bear?" he said sharply. "What am I to understand by that?" His blue eyes had gone hard as turquoises and they held an ugly light she had never seen.

"Nothing," she faltered, while an inner voice whispered: You fool! What havoc are you trying to make? She drew a harsh breath, and said more calmly, "I mean nothing,

Harry, except that bereft of *my* husband I am weak enough
to flinch from the sight of other happy lovers. What else
could you think?"

His grip on her loosened, the glint faded slowly from his
eyes as he relinquished the extraordinary suspicions which
had suddenly assailed him. "Aye, I see," he said at last, and
in the saying convinced himself. All the more so because he
could not imagine a woman to whom he had taught the arts
of love preferring Jack or indeed any other man. "But I
cannot stay here, my poor sweet," he said. "Be reasonable,
we've had this all before. I'm for New England with my
father. As for those two—whether they wed or not, you'll
ne'er notice them, once you've our babe to dandle!" He
flicked his lace-edged cuffs and seized his black plumed hat.
"Come—no more moping! Smile for me, Bess . . ."

She moistened her lips and lifted their corners a trifle. He
kissed her lightly on the mouth and went out the door singing, "O, troll the bowl, the nut-brown bowl."

John Winthrop could stay but a few days at Groton, and
on the 26th of February there came the last farewells. At eight
of a cold gray morning, the entire family assembled in the
Manor courtyard where three horses awaited, and two farm
carts piled high with chests and last-minute provisions. The
bulk of the Governor's goods and servants had been sent on
their way days ago.

While the women, Winthrop, and Jack himself, still observed the full year's mourning for Thomas Fones and old
Mistress Winthrop, the rule had been relaxed for Harry and
the small boys, Stephen and Adam. These latter all had new
clothes for the journey.

Harry was handsome as a hawfinch in his long ruddy-
brown jacket, his slate-blue cape and broad-plumed hat. His
new Cordovan leather boots had been made by Reynolds,
the Boxford cordwainer, and were cut with swagger. Winthrop
had not begrudged the money for this finery, so long as it
was practical—the gentry must dress according to their rank
—and he himself had a store of elaborate lace-edged ruffs and
shoe buckles of glittering silver and steel. Stephen and
Adam were both gay in Lincoln green and Margaret could
not bear to look at them as they cavorted around the horses,
squealing with excitement. She had wept last night in John's
arms, and he had been supremely tender. His own tears had
flowed as he tried to comfort her with the words and promises

of God. I'll not break down again now, Margaret thought—
but dear Lord they are so young, my little lads—if I should
never see them more—and John. He came up to her then
as she stood on the steps between Elizabeth and Mary.
Martha had withdrawn to a corner by the mounting post.

"It is time, my own dear heart," said Winthrop softly, kissing Margaret on the cheek. "If we meet not here on earth
again, we shall do so in heaven. Remember Mondays and
Fridays at five, as I shall."

"Yes—yes—" said Margaret, trying to smile, and thinking
how little people knew her John who thought him severe,
for they had made a pact to commune with each other in
spirit at these hours, no matter the distance that separated
them. "Farewell," she whispered, "I can't say more."

He squeezed her hand, and kissed each member of his
family; the seven-year-old Deane, the baby Samuel, Forth
and Mary, Elizabeth, and after the slightest hesitation—
Martha, who responded with a muffled "God be with you,
sir." At no time had her uncle mentioned her betrothal to
Jack, but Jack had told her of his promise to wait and
soothed her with evidences of affection, so that she had
been reassured. Jack too was leaving now to accompany his
father as far as London, and though this separation could not
compare with that of Elizabeth and Harry, or the elder Winthrops, she was much downcast, for Jack seemed to have
forgotten her while he and Harry greeted the relatives and
neighbors and tenants who were flocking into the courtyard for
the good speedings.

A watery sun blinked over the Manor's mossy roof tiles
when Winthrop having shaken all the well-wishing hands, gave
the signal to mount.

Harry dashed up to Elizabeth and enfolded her in a hug.
"Be good and patient, sweetheart!" he cried gaily. "I'll send
for you before you know it, and mind you give me a fine
bouncing son!"

He chucked her under the chin and strode off to his horse.
She watched him with dull misery. They had made love last
night, and she had wept then. Now she was dry-eyed, but as
the little cavalcade and carts started from the courtyard,
she hurried down the steps and called, *"Harry! Harry!"*

In the din and confusion he did not hear her. She drew
back against the house wall. What had she meant by that
cry? Not to keep him here, for that would be impossible,
not a plea for one last word, they had said all there was to

say between them, and never had that been much. The cry
had come from some unplumbed depths, and she knew there
had been fear in it.

The others ran out on the road watching and waving
until Harry's tall blue-caped figure disappeared last of all
around the bend to Boxford, but Elizabeth returned to Margaret, and found her crumpled on the great chest in the entry.
She sat down heavily beside Margaret and put her arm around
her. The two women leaned against each other a long time
without speaking.

On Saturday, April the tenth, of that year 1630, Governor
John Winthrop stood with several others on the swaying
poop deck of the *Arbella* and looked his last at England.
Far to the north, Cornwall faded on the dipping horizon,
and the great dark cliffs of "The Lizard" merged into an
increasingly foggy sky.

"We are truly on the way at last—" said Winthrop solemnly. He turned with his air of command to the lean earnest
minister who stood beside him. "Mr. Phillips, be good
enough to pray for us!"

"Yes," agreed the Lady Arbella sighing. She sat on a
small walnut armchair which was nailed to the deck and had
been carved with her family coat of arms. From her ermine
hood her pale face strained back towards England.

Young Anne Bradstreet who sat beside Arbella on a stool
could not hide her tears. They ran down the faintly pitted
skin. In Anne's mind verses began to form themselves as
always when she sought comfort. "Be still thou unregenerate
part. Disturb no more my settled heart"—and she thought of
her husband whom she loved, and wished he had come on
deck. But Simon Bradstreet had disappeared with William
Coddington and Isaac Johnson to quell some fight amongst the
servants in the fo'castle. Anne's father, Thomas Dudley, was
confined to his cabin with a sharp attack of gout, while many
of the other passengers like Sir Richard Saltonstall, and most
of the women, lay in their bunks retching with seasickness.
Though they had been near a fortnight on board, contrary
winds and minor mishaps had so delayed them near the
Isle of Wight that until now they had always been in sight
of land, and even had opportunity to disembark at times.

A few minutes ago Captain Peter Milbourne had summoned to the poop deck those of his top-ranking passengers
who were able. " 'Tis farewell for sartin, this time, my lady,

and Sir Governor . . ." he boomed cheerfully, squinting his
keen salt-bleached eyes towards the vanishing shore, then
quickly up at his taut sails. "We'll soon be past the Scillies.
After there's naught 'twixt us and your Promised Land but
three thousand mile o' water, and—if God be willing—" he
interpolated this in deference to these Puritan folk, though he
was none himself, "a run o' codfish off the Banks. We'll have
need o' them beasties, I'll warrant!" He bowed and stamped
off to his quarters, for a noggin of rum and another glance
at his chart and cross-staff.

The minister, George Phillops, did not at once respond to
Winthrop's request for prayer. He was a gaunt little man like
a whippet with eyes grown myopic from much learned reading. As he stood watching the blur of England slide below the
waves, he knew a bleak misgiving. I'll not be at the Governor's beck and call, he thought, and I shall hold him to
the spirit of "The Humble Request" we wrote at Yarmouth.
"Aye—" he said, at length, smiling faintly at Lady Arbella.
"I *will* pray that God guide our perilous journey, but now
that our last link with that dear land of our birth is gone,
I would first remind us that we go not like those invidious
Separatists who wrangle and rant at Plymouth Colony in the
New World. For we will never forget the Church of England,
our dear Mother, from whence we rise, and we go forth but for
the enlargement of her bounds in the Kingdom of Christ
Jesus, and I will pray in the exact words of our prayer book.
'O Eternal God, who alone spreadest out the heavens, and
rulest the raging of the Sea, we commend to Thy almighty
protection . . .' "

When he had finished, Winthrop said "Amen" with the
others, though annoyed that the only minister on board the
Arbella should be laggard in extempore praying, and at once
more independent and yet hidebound by the old forms than
had appeared before sailing. Still there was no help for it
now, and John's heart was oppressed by other matters. Not
only the poignant visions of home they were all having—he
thought of Margaret, seeing her in the Manor garden near
the mulberry tree, wondering if the babe were delivered yet—
but he had another carking worry. They were two passengers
short on the *Arbella*.

While the fleet had yet lingered at the Isle of Wight, John
had sent Harry ashore with a young man called William Pelham to locate some missing cattle which should have been
delivered to the ship. In due course the cattle arrived but

neither Harry nor Pelham did. And a servant later reported
that the young men, thinking there was plenty of time before
sailing, had gone back to Southampton. Each day John had
waited, but there was no sign of Harry, and the *Arbella* had
finally left without him.

"You look dejected, sir," said Lady Arbella gently, gazing
at the black-caped Governor, whose firm mouth was drooping
between the small chestnut mustache and pointed beard,
and whose heavy lids veiled his eyes. "You've left so many
dear to you at home—nay I mean in England—for we must
call the *new* land home now—'tis hard to be resolute—but
think as I do of the wondrous farewell sermon Master John
Cotton preached at us at Southampton. We will be heartened
by God like the children of Israel."

Winthrop started, and took the stool Anne Bradstreet had
just vacated. "And indeed you hearten us all, my lady," John
said fervently. "I fear I was thinking of my son Henry—what
has become of him—though well I suspect." His lips tightened.

She also suspected what had become of Henry, as did all
on the ship, but was far too courteous to say anything. While
she strove for a comforting word, John added flatly, "There
are many taverns in Hampton."

"He will come by another ship," she said quickly. "He
would not have returned to Suffolk!"

John shook his head. "No. He was anxious to emigrate.
But I wished him with ME. I was a fool to trust him on shore
again. Sometimes, my lady, I am very foolish, and over-
confident. Arrogant in mine own opinions."

"No, no," she said, laying her delicate white hand on
Winthrop's knee. "You do yourself injustice!" She, like her
husband Isaac, was of those who thoroughly admired the
Governor, nor thought him arrogant, as did her old steward
Thomas Dudley. Though, to be sure, Winthrop never showed
Arbella aught but deference and warm subtle recognition of
her beauty as well as rank. She thought him a charming man.
"And look—" she said smiling. "Take comfort that your two
younger sons are frisky as pups!" She pointed through the
carved wooden rail to the deck beneath where Stephen and
Adam with many of the other children on board were engaged
in an uproarious tug-of-war, made more exciting when their
hands slipped from the tarry rope each time the ship lurched
down a wave. "And look there!" she said, pointing to two
ships whose flags and sails were faintly discernible through the

increasing mist. "Aren't those of our fleet? Perhaps your son Henry is on one of them!"

Winthrop peered out to sea, and shook his head. "No, my lady, those are still the *Ambrose* and the *Jewel* which have stayed near us since Yarmouth. But we've lost the *Talbot*, long ago. I hope," he said with sudden anger, "Henry is safe AND repentant on the *Talbot*."

Harry was indeed on the *Talbot*, but he was not in the least repentant. He was enjoying himself mightily; showing off his seamanship, dicing with the boon companions he had found, prodigally ordering casks of spirits opened at will, and commanding obedience because he was the Governor's son. He had not deliberately set out to miss the *Arbella*'s sailing, but the Mariner's Ordinary on the quay at Southampton had seemed a comfortable place to wait for the tardy winds to blow; moreover Will Pelham who was cousin to the Earl of Lincoln was well provided with pounds, and willing to spend them.

Then Harry's normally strong head was vanquished by some innocent-looking Dutch liquor two soldiers provided, and it was several days before he awakened one morning in a shabby room at the Dolphin, cold sober at last, to find a giggling Flemish whore in his bed. "God damn you, get out!" he cried, kicking her, and such was the glare of his bloodshot eyes that she scuttled from the sour room. Harry poured a jugful of water over his head, pulled on his clothes which nobody seemed to have stolen, staggered from the Dolphin and down to the Ordinary on the quay. Here, where he demanded meat and ale, he found two military men who seemed mistily familiar. A big red-haired one, and a dapper dark one, breakfasting by the fire which glinted on their engraved steel cuirasses and the muskets and scarlet-plumed helmets they had placed on a bench.

"So ho!" cried the dark one chuckling, as Harry entered. "Here's our bully boy, at last! Have you guzzled and wenched your fill, lad? Then come breakfast with us."

Harry grinned ruefully as he joined them. "I'd no notion I was so cup-shot! We've met, gentlemen?"

"Now there's gratitude for ye," said the red-haired one mournfully. "When we've been your chums this past three days, sharing our precious genever and loving ye like a brother!"

"Oh," said Harry. "That was it. My apologies, sirs, but—"

"Ye don't recall—well 'tis no crime. Me—" said the red-haired one, "I'm Daniel Patrick, and him—" he pointed across the table, "is John Underhill, and you'd best mind us, me gossoon—since we're both captains in your father's company, and sworn to keep law 'n' order!" He burst out in a guffaw, and slapped Harry on the back.

Harry choked on a gobbet of meat, then drank his ale with avid thirst. So these were the two men John Winthrop had hired to protect the colonists, and give them military training. He had heard Jack discuss them with his father. Both captains had seen much service in the Netherlands, and had married Dutch wives. They were both in the early thirties, and stalwart men by the look of them. Underhill he remembered had spent his early years at Kenilworth Castle, where his father had been steward to the great Earl of Leicester, Queen Elizabeth's favorite, but of Patrick he knew nothing, and was curious about the lilt and intonation in his voice. "Would you be from the north country, Captain Patrick?" he asked.

Patrick responded with a twinkle. "That I would, young sir—but not the north of *this* one! The saints forbid—ooh—" he said clapping his hand over his mouth. "I forgot saints is a word I must NOT use. Don't ye be telling your father on me!"

"You're Irish?" exclaimed Harry, beginning to laugh. "And a PAPIST!"

"Papist no more! I've recanted long ago. And why wouldn't I, when the good monks who raised me kicked me out o' the monastery on me bum, one fine day—not but what I'm grateful to 'em. A devilish poor monk I'd a made, but I'm a fair soldier!" He chuckled and wiped his mouth on the sleeve of his buff coat. Harry laughed again, not sure how much of this was serious, but perfectly certain his father had no inkling of any Papist tinge infiltering his company, and at this thought Harry started and said, "My God! The *Arbella* must have sailed!"

"She has—" said Underhill, shrugging. "You gave the Governor the slip, eh? Your friend Mr. Pelham got on the *Mayflower* yesterday, much distressed he couldn't find you. But I said we'd do our best if you turned up, and now you *have*, we'd best be off to the *Talbot*. She's riding down Hampton water and the wind's shifting!"

Before they left, Harry scrawled a note to Elizabeth, moved by compunction for the way he had spent these last

nights, and he ended it with all his love and a row of crosses
for kisses. He told Daniel Patrick about her too during the
long evenings at sea, but this did not prevent him from flirting
with the lasses on board, nor with Patrick's pretty Dutch wife
Anneke who spoke little English but was plump and rosy
as an apple. John Underhill's wife Helena was also on board,
but she was fat and chiefly concerned with hopeless efforts to
eradicate the *Talbot*'s vermin and filth.

Elizabeth received the note at Groton on the day after
Margaret had been painfully delivered of a puny baby girl,
who was baptized Ann on April 29. Despite Goody Hawes,
the skilled London midwife, Margaret and the baby remained in danger for some days, and Elizabeth had her
hands full helping the midwife with the nursing; and though
she cried a little over the note, she had few thoughts for
Harry, and it was impossible not to feel exasperated too.

"You might know he'd manage to miss the ship," she said
to Martha, shoving the note into her bosom. "Lord, I hope
they've no taverns yet in Massachusetts, not that Harry
couldn't find spirits in a howling wilderness, or the bottom
of the sea, if he wanted to. The Devil must guide him."

"Don't say that, Bess," cried Martha sharply. "You talk
sometimes, as though—as though you didn't love Harry—
not the way I love Jack!"

There was no answer to this, and Elizabeth, now that Jack
was in London, had recovered her protective fondness for her
sister. She merely smiled and went to her surgery where she
was steeping a poultice for Margaret's caked breasts. Martha
followed her uneasily and tried to help, but her fingers were
clumsy and her mind elsewhere. Suddenly she said, "Bess,
don't be vexed with me, but are you sure you're right in
letting our folk celebrate May Day tomorrow? Our Uncle
Winthrop would never permit it . . ."

"No more he wouldn't," said Elizabeth dryly, crushing row-
anberries to put in the bubbling flaxseed. "But our grandfather
did, and I see no harm in it. 'Twill sweeten the malcontents on
the Manor, and besides 'tis time we had some merriment. I'm
sick of long faces."

Martha brightened for a moment, looking trustfully at
Elizabeth, then she shook her head. "But how can you want
merriment, when your time is so near?" said Martha dolefully. She had been much frightened by Margaret's recent
agonies and danger, and Elizabeth's own baby was due soon.

"Oh, I wish Jack was here to tell us what to do."

I'm very glad he isn't, Elizabeth thought. Nor was Forth at the Manor, he had gone on a long visit to Exeter. Thus it was—Margaret being too ill for consultation—that a delegation of Groton villagers had waited on Elizabeth as sole authority and requested permission to have dancing and May games on the Manor lawn as it was in old Squire Adam's day.

Pond, the miller, was spokesman, and he had added, "Oi'll not conceal it from ye, Mistress—there be surliness an' grudgings in some quarters 'gainst Wintrups—they know ye mean to sell, 'n they don't fancy their homes 'n loivelihoods bandied about loike sacks o' corn. Thass the truth." There were murmurs of assent from the other men.

Old Kembold, the thatcher, stepped forward and said angrily, "The Squoire've unsettled us, he hev—luring off our young men overseas to be ate by salvages—deserr-rting us ye maught say; when toimes is bad enough here, there be *some* o' us who don't hould wi' all this sarmonizing 'n stinting the good ould ways—" His voice which had risen, stopped with a grunt because Pond had trodden on his foot.

The miller said apologetically, "We don't mean fur to berate you, Mistress, it was just if we maught have a little ould May Fair, 'n a bit o' sport, loike we used to, them as grumbles 'd forget . . ."

"I don't see why not!" said Elizabeth hardily. "Do as you please." And she smiled at them. They shuffled out in a cloud of gratitude and compliments. "A foine young 'oman" "even though breeding she's a comely poppet"—"Now if Marster *Harry* were squoire matters'ld stand different."

Elizabeth heard some of this and was naturally elated. It was agreeable to be head of the Manor, even temporarily, and she was not worried about Jack's feelings when he found out. She could surely handle Jack, and as for Margaret, that poor lady was too miserable with milk-leg, sore breasts, and worry about the much-longed-for baby girl to give heed to Elizabeth's offhand information about "some Saturday games for the village."

Elizabeth had not however envisioned quite what ensued. May Day dawned warm and shimmering. A steadfast sun drew up perfume from dew-spangled carnations and honeysuckle. It gilded the field of daffodils by the garden wall. Song thrushes warbled in the flowering hedgerows, robins chirped on the lawns amongst tiny pink daisies, and from the copse near the church a cuckoo called twelve times, which was good luck, thought Elizabeth as she woke and counted. She turned and kissed Martha who slept with her, now that Harry was gone. "Wake up, sleepyhead—Listen, someone's singing!"

The door flew open and disclosed Sally with a great branch of hawthorn.

> *"Good morrow, Good morrow, good mistress*
> *I wish you a happy day*
> *Please to smell my garland*
> *Because 'tis the first of May"*

sang Sally in a shrill tuneless voice, thrusting the white and rosy blossoms under Elizabeth's nose. Sally set down the mugs of morning ale and pulled the bed curtains.

"They making ready for the fair?" asked Elizabeth, drinking her ale. She felt extraordinarily well this morning, full of restless energy. I wish I could dance, she thought, but I *can* wash my face in the May dew, and she motioned for her red woolen chamber gown.

"Thass roight," answered Sally, her squint-eyes sparkling. "Wat Vintener arst me to go with him, thot means he's to be me boy—Oh but we'll have a toime!" The girl giggled, but suddenly remembered something. "Oh ma'am—Vicar's below in the Hall, been waiting fur ye. He *is* in a taking!"

Elizabeth muttered one of Harry's best oaths. She had forgotten their rector, Mr. Leigh, chiefly because between Sundays everyone did forget him. He was a pallid wispy man who had pleased John Winthrop with interminable and learned sermons, but otherwise kept to his parsonage. Elizabeth dressed and went to the Hall, where Mr. Leigh was pacing up and down the tiles, his black gown flapping, the falling bands of his white collar all askew.

"Mistress Elizabeth!" he cried when he saw her. "Did you permit this monstrous ribaldry—do you know what they're DOING?"

"I said they could have a May Fair."

"My dear young lady, they've put up a MAYPOLE!" The word shuddered from his lips as though he announced that the flaming pits of hell had opened on the Manor lawn.

"Oh——" said Elizabeth weakly. Of all heathenish rites Puritans considered Maypole dancing the worst, and Winthrop had once gravely explained to his family the lewd symbol involved.

"Well, I can't stop them now," she said. "I'm sorry."

"I forbid it," cried Mr. Leigh in a high quavering voice.
"I won't have orgies in my parish, why they've got tons of
strong ale, and mummers, and I think they're building a
stage for—play-acting. They've gone mad, all of them
except a few of my godly folk. You'd think us back in Papist
days. Mr. Winthrop would—would—" He choked, and beat
one hand against the other. "I forbid it!"

Elizabeth was faintly sorry for him. "I wouldn't try, sir.
They wouldn't heed you, and besides it might make real trouble. They're discontented as it is."

The rector knew that this was true. Church attendance had
fallen off sharply since Winthrop left, and Mr. Leigh's exhortations had met with taunts and insult. He threw her a look of
thwarted anger, cried, "Surely God won't permit this outrage
in my parish," and scurried out across the fields for the
parsonage to muster what forces he could.

Oh dear, thought Elizabeth, but she was determined to
let nothing cloud the exciting day. And it was a day long
remembered in Groton. A day of constant music from pipes,
drums, gitterns and singers. A day of dancing. Goody Vintener
had unearthed the gilded crown and long colored streamers
for the Maypole—they had lain hidden in her attic for nearly
thirty years—and everyone danced around the great painted
oaken shaft, weaving and skipping the ribbons. They had
morris dancers too, all fitted out with jingling bells; and the
ballads of Robin Hood. There were booths with simple
fairings, sweetmeats, buckles and rosettes. On the little stage
a wandering juggler who had been found starving in Hadleigh
gave a puppet show that had the Devil himself in it doing
obscene and shocking things, but everyone roared and asked
for it again—even Martha and the sedate Mary, who at first
had tried to hide her eyes. Both girls had crept nervously out
from the Manor House as the music started, and both had
been too fascinated to leave.

Something came over them all that day, something from
the ancient soil which had known scenes like this before the
Romans came, and through the centuries thereafter. Something burst through which had long been flattened. They
were no longer sober godly folk who yearned for salvation,
they grew wild as their ancestors before them with the spring-
magic of the May. All but the rector, his wife and five of his
faithful flock who huddled in the parsonage, shuddering at the
debauched sounds they heard across the fields, and praying

the Lord to strengthen them for righteous battle.

Afternoon came and the glee grew louder. Elizabeth donated a butt of sack from the Manor. And the young swains brought a chair all decked with greens and flowering cherry, which they set upon the stage. "Now the Queen!" shouted old Kembold, hoarsely. He was well flown with ale and acted as master of ceremonies because he best remembered how it used to be. "We maun have a Queen o' the May!"

This was greeted with huzzahs, and a babble of nominations. "Wait, men!" shouted Pond the miller exuberantly, leaping to the stage. "Who best fur Queen but our own Bess? Bess Wintrup—the fairest wench in Groton!"

"Moind your manners, Pond!" cried the Manor baker, shocked at this boozy disrespect, but Elizabeth was touched.

"I thank you, goodman—" she called from her place near the Maypole, "But I could not. You all know why I cannot." Indeed, for some time she had been aware of a dull backache and nausea, which she ignored.

They all cheered her, and God-blessed her, while other voices rose in favor of Peggy, or Thomasine, or Doll. Wat Vintener even yelled for Sally, who gobbled and blushed with pride.

But Pond had his own ideas which sprang from confused gratitude and feudal loyalty. "If not Mistress Bess—" he shouted over the hubbub, "then her sister Martha—she's fair enough, lads. Oi say we'll have little Mattie Fones!"

"Oh no!" cried Martha in a panic, but the crowd roared approval. Two husky young farmers rushed forward and seized her; they carried her to the flowery throne and sat her on it. They put a crown of daisies on her head and loosened her hair until it flowed in a rippling chestnut mass down to her waist. And they kissed her, crying, "She's our queen, our nut-brown maiden! We will love her for aye!"

Martha gasped and protested, but as they circled around and drank to her, gradually a look of shining wonder came into her eyes, and a smile to her lips. She glanced instinctively at Elizabeth who was laughing and clapping her hands, then at poor Mary Winthrop whom nobody had thought to choose. "Thank you—" she said breathlessly. "Thank you all. I'm so happy to be your queen."

"Then dance with us, Your Majesty!" cried Pond, his moon face beaming. He raised his hand to help her off the stage. And Martha danced, danced with all of them whirling and floating like a wood sprite, her small face aglow under the daisy wreath.

Elizabeth watched her in proud affection. This was the way Matt should always be, freed to a childlike gaiety. I have crushed out that miserable jealousy forever, Elizabeth thought with a resolution that seemed easy—I'll never feel it more. She accepted a mug of sack from old Kembold, drank a little and regretted it, for it sat uneasily on her stomach. She longed to lie down but could not bear to go.

The shadows were lengthening on the lawn, and the light grew more green and golden. While Martha and many of the young people still danced, some couples slipped away to the shielding hedgerows, or behind the dovecote and stables. Two lads began wrestling under a walnut tree, others ringed themselves around two fighting cocks, and Kembold suddenly bethought him of a pastime of his youth. "A duel, a duel!" he shrilled happily, his grizzled locks flying. "Lad, fetch me little ould quarterstaff—" he commanded a grandson who rushed off. "Now who'll go me a round wi' the staves again?"

"Oi will, ye ould whinnier," cried John Rice, the master shepherd, "and break thy pate as I ever did!"

Kembold responded with a jeer. The stout oaken poles were brought. The thatcher and the shepherd fortified themselves with draughts of sack, the dancing stopped and the cockfighters joined the circle around the two old men, who began warily crashing and feinting with their long staves, until with increasing tempo they began to flail wildly.

It was this moment that Mr. Leigh chose to come stalking around the edge of a booth shouting, "Halt! Halt! I command it! Stop this disgrace!" The rector had stumbled over an intertwined couple in the fields which added to the indignation some drinks of claret had finally spurred to action. His followers lurked nervously behind him. As the duelers did not hear him, he rushed up to Kemhold and grabbed his arm. "Cease! 'Tis the Sabbath Eve!"

The old thatcher turned with a roar of rage. "Ye dommed fule!" he screamed. "Oi was winning!" And he fetched the rector a great clout on the head with the quarterstaff. Mr. Leigh fell backwards on the turf, and was still.

Dear God—thought Elizabeth as she hurried forward. WHY did he interfere—there was nothing wrong until he made it. She tried to bend down and examine the rector, but the Boxford barber forestalled her. "He'll be all roight, ma'am . . ."

he said, feeling Leigh's head, "leastways he's not dead. See his lids flicker."

The crowd, which had drawn around murmuring, heaved a long sigh. Kembold, wagging his head, muttered feebly, "He shouldna've touched me, he shouldna've—"

"Ye're in trouble, ould man," said Pond very low. Of the five men who had accompanied the vicar, two were missing. "They've gone for the constable."

The thatcher gasped and his dirty face paled. "They'll hang me . . ." he whispered. He slumped on the lawn not far from his victim.

"Naw, naw—" said the shepherd. "Vicar's opened his eyes."

The rector stirred, put his hand to his head and stammered "What happened?"

"An accident," said Elizabeth firmly. "Lie there, while we get bandages from my surgery. Look after him, Mary and Martha—" she said to the girls. "And remember—" Elizabeth added in a carrying voice, "if anyone asks, it was an unfortunate accident."

"God bless ye," said Kembold looking up at her with tears in his bleary eyes.

"I must go in now," said Elizabeth aside to Martha. "I feel ill. But I think we should have a last song," she cried to Pond. "Can you all sing 'The Maytime Carol'?" For she couldn't bear the lovely day to end like this in fear and confusion.

They obeyed her, softly and tentatively at first, the youngest ones following those who knew the plaintive ancient melody.

"How beautiful May and its morning came in!
The songs of the maidens we heard them begin
To sing the old ballads while cowslips they pull
While the dew of the morning fills many pipes full . . ."

When the constable came from Boxford, they were still singing and he found it hard to believe the horrified accounts he had been given of debauchery and murder, especially as the vicar was sitting up, and not dead at all, though somewhat addled in his wits.

As for Elizabeth she hauled herself up the stairs in the Manor and went to Margaret's room, where Goody Hawes was rocking the whimpering baby. The midwife put up a warning finger and went to forestall Elizabeth at the door. "Mistress Winthrop sleeps—" she whispered, "Though 'tis a wonder with the racket there's been outside all day—Ah—?" She put the infant in its cradle and peered hard through the dimming light. "So, 'tis your turn now, is it, my dear? We'd best get ye to bed."

" 'Tis naught so bad," said Elizabeth faintly. "Only I think my back will break in two. I expect it'll be over soon."

"Ha!" said Goody Hawes without the least conviction. "We'll hope so, you're *built* for a good breeder." But she had sensed trouble as soon as she arrived at the Manor and examined the younger woman. Her fat sensitive little hands had assisted at a thousand births, and they could guess many things from the shape and feel of the belly. That little one in there's a-coming bottom side up, or I'm a Welshman, she said to herself, we're in for a bit of work, we are. And so it proved.

All that night and the next day and half the next night, Elizabeth labored. The pains came in whirlpools—blood-red, streaked with black, they came as grinding knives, as fire, they came like the tortures of the rack. She heard herself scream and wondered what the noise was; exhausted at times she fell into stupor. Frightened faces swam past her bed, Martha's, Mary's, Sally's, and at one time Mr. Leigh with a bandage on his head, who said, "My poor child, I fear you must prepare for death, have you made your peace with your Maker?"

"Go away—you fool!" she screamed through bared teeth. "Always you interfere!" Then Goody Hawes came with a cup of poppy juice and she slept a little before it began again. She did not think of Harry. She did not think of Jack. She was alone with this monstrous thing that clutched and rent and would destroy her. But once as the second evening advanced towards midnght, she whimpered for her mother. Soon after that, she felt a gentle hand on her clammy forehead, and a voice full of pitying tenderness said, "Bess dear—my poor Bess. Be brave a little longer, the physician's coming from Hadleigh." And she opened her eyes to see Margaret's woeful haggard face looking down at her.

"You shouldn't be from bed," Elizabeth whispered.

"Nay—think not of that," said Margaret smoothing the damp hair. "But pray, darling. Pray with me."

Elizabeth couldn't pray but she followed the sound of Margaret's voice and knew a moment of surcease. I will not die, I'll not give up, she thought in some far-off realm where the pain did not reach. At midnight the physician arrived from Hadleigh, consulted hastily with Goody Hawes, ripped off his cuffs, rolled up his sleeves and took a small iron instrument from his pouch.

Monday morning at one o'clock Elizabeth was delivered of a baby girl.

When Jack arrived from London on the Friday, Elizabeth's strong twenty-year-old body had nearly recovered and when he came in with Martha to see her, Elizabeth was sitting up in bed nursing her baby, a dreamy smile on her red lips. She wore a crimson chamber gown, and her black curls tumbled loose down to the brocaded coverlet. "Greetings, Jack—" she said from the remote fastness of a blissful preoccupation. Suckling was to her a sensual joy from the first. "See my babe? She's still a mite puffy and askew from the fearful time she had a-birthing, but Goody Hawes says she's sound as a trivet."

Jack swallowed, discomfited by her almost ethereal beauty, as well as by the fullness and whiteness of the blue-veined breast as which the baby tugged avidly. He had been deeply shocked at the accounts of her danger, shocked also though in different degree by the rector whose head was still lumped and who met Jack in Boxford with a lurid relation of the scandalous happenings on May Day, climaxed by Elizabeth's insufferable rudeness and virtual blasphemy when the rector, exercising Christian forgiveness, had gone to prepare her for death. Elizabeth was certainly too headstrong and irreligious, Jack thought, and meant to tax her, as his father would have done. But when he saw her he forgot her misbehavior and was stricken with confusion.

He inspected the baby, which seemed to him remarkably ugly though its abundance of light fuzz prompted the only remark he could think of. "Twill be like Harry, no doubt."

"Aye," she said kissing a tiny wrinkled fist. "Poor Harry, he was sure a boy . . . but next time. . ."

"Oh, Bess—" cried Martha, staring at her sister. "How *can* you speak of that—so—so calmly?" Still Martha heard in nightmares the echoes of Elizabeth's screams, still saw how she had looked with face like a clay death's head—and the disgusting smell of blood.

" 'Tis over and forgot," said Elizabeth smiling. She shifted the replete baby and covered her breast, then looked at Jack and Martha. "She'll be baptized Sunday of course? Will Mr. Leigh do it or is he too angry with me?" The green twinkle of mirth shone in her long hazel eyes.

"Of course he'll officiate. I'll tell him to," answered Jack.

"I wish you two to be godparents, please." Elizabeth gave them both a look of purest affection from which all baseness had been purged by agony, and now the bliss, of motherhood.

Jack suddenly realized that Martha was there, clinging to his arm. He patted the childish hand and said quickly, "We'll be honored, won't we, Matt dear?" The girl nodded looking up into his lean brown face, and Elizabeth thought, They are alike these two in feature, I never saw it before because Martha's so small.

"I wish the baby christened Martha Johanna for you both," she said.

Martha reddened with pleasure. "Oh Bess, TWO names for such a wee scrap!"

Elizabeth nodded. Her eyes met Jack's in a fleeting glance that said, And thus we will always be reminded by my babe of the barrier between us.

"We'll soon need Mr. Leigh to officiate at something besides a baptism, eh, Mattie?" he said, putting his arm around the girl. "As soon as we hear of my father's safe arrival in Massachusetts I'll write to him and tell him we've waited long enough."

On Saturday, the 12th of June, the *Arbella* having been nine stormy weeks at sea slid along the southern coast of Cape Ann and sighted journey's end at last; the collection of bark huts and sod-roof dugouts which the Indians called Naumkeag, but the settlement's temporary governor, John Endecott, had rechristened Salem.

The air was fresh and sparkling with a whitish light unlike the golden mists of England, a land breeze brought the eager passengers the fragrance of pines and wild strawberries. They were crowded on the decks, exclaiming, cheering, and some weeping, as the *Arbella* ran up the Royal Ensign and shot off two salutes to alert those on shore.

John Winthrop stood with the gentry on the poop deck. They had all donned their finest clothes, just unpacked by their servants. John Winthrop wore a new black silk doublet trimmed with gold braid. His ruff was edged two inches deep with Mechlin lace. His hat though unplumed was garnished with gilt band and buckle. Across his chest a baldric of red, silver and blue, the royal colors, supported an impressive sword of state. On a stool beside him in an elaborate padlocked box, reposed the precious charter. John saw a shallop put out from the flimsy-looking dock on shore and knew it contained Endecott, because Captain Peirce of the *Lyon* had gone to fetch the supplanted governor.

"How happy they'll be to see us!" cried the Lady Arbella, leaning against the rail in her rustling blue taffeta dress, "and to know we've brought the *Charter!*"

Winthrop bowed to her and smiled. His heart swelled with pride and thanksgiving. "Praise God that we have come here safe!" he cried impulsively, "and that it seems such a fair goodly country."

They all assented: Lady Arbella, Isaac Johnson, and Thomas Dudley who stood slightly apart with his wife and children. George Phillips and the Boston merchant, William Coddington, stood together with the other Company assistants, Sir Richard Saltonstall, and Increase Nowell, all gazing with excitement at the shore.

"O Give thanks unto the Lord, for He hath led his children to the Land of Canaan, where milk and honey flow," said Phillips solemnly.

But it very soon developed that neither milk nor honey flowed at Salem. When Endecott and his minister, Mr. Skelton, had boarded the *Arbella* they were sparing of their welcome speeches, nor had Endecott bothered to change a stained leather jerkin and frayed shirt. He made slight obeisance to the new governor who ousted him, and seemed preoccupied as he invited Winthrop and the principal gentlemen on shore. As soon as they had landed, Endecott led the way up a muddy path to a one-and-a-half-room timber house floored with packed earth, which was the largest Salem afforded. " 'Tis the best we have," he said in answer to Dudley's look of dismay.

Endecott was a big pompous man of Winthrop's own age. He had a forked grizzled beard and a grim fanatical eye which never softened. He was a man who did his duty and had a horror of episcopacy so intense that even Winthrop was startled. Conference with Endecott, and Salem's two ministers, Skelton and Higginson, soon showed John that Salem's religious views had in two years grown far closer to those of the Separatists at Plymouth than to the reforming Anglican spirit Winthrop and his company professed. But there were more critical matters even than religion to be dealt with.

Endecott fed Winthrop and his assistants a good venison

pasty and some beer, and when they expressed their thanks, said "Aye 'tis a change from sea fare, but not to mince matters, Sir Governor, that's the end of it. We're well nigh starving here, and you mustn't think to stay. We can't feed our own, and now you tell me you've scant provision left. You must find some other part of the Massachusetts to plant in with the great company you're bringing."

"I intended to," said Winthrop stiffly after a moment. "We'll set off down the coast at once. I see you've no room here."

"We've sickness too," said Endecott. "There's not three sound folk in my town; if they're not coughing and sweating, they're puking and purging, and a fair lot of 'em want to go back to England when your ships leave."

"You're something gloomy, Mr. Endecott," said Isaac Johnson, his fresh boyish face darkening. "I trust you're not of those who would leave."

Endecott shrugged his massive shoulders. "I've no love for England. I'll do my best here, if I'm spared. But you'll find it naught so easy to settle in this devil-scourged wilderness."

"Nevertheless—" said Winthrop rising, and putting on his hat, "I intend to do so." He bowed and walked with the others down the muddy track to the dock and the *Arbella*.

On the 6th of July, John Winthrop sat in his private bark wigwam at Charlestown on the Mystic River, writing homebound letters for which Captain Peirce, Master of the *Lyon*, was waiting.

It was hot in the hastily built wigwam, but hotter yet outside, where the sun glared down as it had for days, and never did in England. John wiped his face on a small linen towel, and tried to marshal his thoughts. There was a crowd of people milling as usual outside, desirous of interviews; some were discontented settlers who were tired of existing on mussels, wild berries and Indian corn, and many had constant belly gripes which Charlestown's brackish water augmented.

There were also four Indians whose frame of mind was not yet apparent except that they felt they owned the land hereabouts, and wished to know how long the English intended to camp here in their Mishawam. Two of these Indians were called John and James Sagamore, and with them was the chief of the Neponsetts, Chickatabot. They were tall smelly bucks who wore nothing but red or yellow paint, turkey feathers in their scalplocks, and deerskin breechclouts.

The fourth Indian was oddly enough a forceful woman, known as Squaw Sachem. She had a string of the valuable purple wampum around her thick neck, owned considerable land, and gave herself airs. All four squatted outside the wigwam, peering curiously at the scowling English, and greedily guzzling the precious beer Winthrop had ordered his servants to give them.

John dipped his pen and wrote on. Just within the canvas door Captain William Peirce, ablest of all the master mariners, stood gazing out to sea while he smoked his pipe and wished the Governor would hurry with the letters. The *Lyon* must set forth at once if she were to fetch the provisions from England so urgently needed, and return before the winter storms began.

And I know not what the poor gawks'll do whilst I'm gone, Peirce thought, looking at the Governor with pity. The English did not seem to be able to live off the land as the Indians did and most of the farmers and artisans in the fleet were poor huntsmen too. Many of Winthrop's company were sick of the scurvy and flux, the water supply at Charlestown was poor. It was obvious, as the ships straggled in, that so many people could not exist on this barren peninsula. Already Sir Richard Saltonstall and the minister, George Phillips, had gone up the Charles and found a new location which Sir Richard called Watertown. While Isaac Johnson had rowed across the river to explore the queer three-hilled peninsula called Shawmut, where lived—they said—a mad or eccentric Englishman who was probably bewitched.

In truth I believe they're all bewitched, Peirce thought, to leave their good homes and risk their lives in this heathen wilderness. But that was none of his business—his was to ferry them across in his staunch little *Lyon*, a job which he had done excellently for seven years now. He straightened, suddenly peering over the heads of the squatting Indians.

"Ship's just 'ove in sight, sir!"

"Oh?" said Winthrop raising his head. Each day since arrival at Charlestown the ships had been coming, after touching at Salem for directions. The *Mayflower*, the *Whale*, the *Hopewell*, the *Trial*, the *Success*, the *William and Francis*, and at each landing Winthrop had questioned the passengers about Harry. Will Pelham from the *Mayflower* told where he'd last seen him in Southampton, but that was all.

" 'Tis the *Talbot*, sir!" said Captain Peirce triumphantly, knowing how eagerly Winthrop awaited this particular ship which was long overdue. Winthrop jumped up and stood in the doorway beside Peirce. " 'Er flag also is at half-mast," Peirce added sadly. There had been deaths on nearly all the ships, not only human deaths but what had come to seem almost as bad since it imperiled those who survived—heavy loss of cattle, the precious cows, sheep and goats which were to start the new stock, and supply food through the winter.

Winthrop returned to his letters. "When they land send them here." He had checked his first impulse to rush down to the shore. If Harry were indeed on board he was not to be forgiven so easily.

Captain Peirce went off followed by the Indians, who were still fascinated by those monstrous white-winged floating birds, and soon joined by the Winthrop lads, Stephen and Adam, who were equally attracted by the Indians.

Winthrop wrote on to Margaret:

> *Blessed be the Lord, our good God and mercifull father, that hath yet preserved me in life and health to salute thee, and to comfort thy longing heart, with the joyful news of my wellfare, and the wellfare of thy beloved children . . ."*

when he heard a low, shocked murmur of voices outside, and the heavy tread of measured footsteps.

He put his pen down and waited, while his heartbeats slowed. A black-haired soldier in a cuirass stepped through the doorway, saying, "By your leave, Your Worship." He held his helmet against his chest and bowed. "I am Captain John Underhill from the Netherlands reporting for your service according to the agreement."

"Ah, yes, Captain, welcome. You came on the *Talbot?* And Captain Daniel Patrick? And your wives?"

"They are all here." Underhill usually had a handsome mobile face quick to laugh or frown, and was something of a dandy with small clipped mustache and pomaded hair. But now he was unshaven, his hair unkempt, and his dark eyes held only a painful reluctance.

"Your Worship, I have bad news—" he said staring at the earthen floor.

Winthrop's hand tightened on the pen. "You lost many on the *Talbot?*"

"Fourteen at sea, sir—and—and one other."

"One other—" repeated Winthrop in a whisper. The pen

dropped and rolled off the table. "You mean something, Captain," he said steadily. "Who was this other?"

The Captain glanced at his governor, and back to the floor. "Your son Henry—sir. And it is near the greatest grief I've known that I must say so. We were fond of him, Patrick and I. He was a fine lad."

Winthrop drew a sharp breath, and bowed his head on his clenched fists. Underhill heard the low sounds of stifled prayer, and though he was no man for religion his eyes misted. Harry's death had been so sudden and so senseless; they had stood like stones, he and Patrick, on the riverbank, helpless as it happened, though both had rushed in later for the grappling.

"How was it?" asked the Governor in a wooden voice.

"Four days ago, sir, when we touched at Salem, it was mortal hot. We went for a bit of stroll along the North River, and across it saw one of these Indian canoes. Master Harry, he was merry at being on land, and he laughed and said 'twas like some the Caribs had at Barbadoes. 'I'll get it for us!' he cried, 'and show you rare sport!' He was the only one of us to swim, having learned in the Indies. He wouldn't listen to us. He plunged in as he was, except for his boots, and we thought he'd make it—but the water was cold, and he overhot." Underhill paused.

"Overhot with brandy too . . ." murmured Winthrop closing his eyes. "Oh, my son Henry, my son Henry—poor child—" His voice broke.

Underhill turned away. "He sank like a plummet, sir, in the middle of the river . . . but later—too late—we found him."

"You've brought him here then . . . ?"

The Captain nodded slowly and gestured towards the outside. Winthrop lifted the canvas flap and saw the raw pine box resting on the ground beside a sandy bank of scrub oak.

"Thank you, Captain," asid Winthrop. "I know you did what you could . . . find and bring to me Mr. Wilson, the minister, if you please,—and tell—tell the Indians I will receive them presently."

John Winthrop did not finish his letter to his wife. He wrote instead to Emmanuel Downing by the *Lyon,* and held Margaret's letter for another ship.

It was on Michaelmas Day, September 29, that Emmanuel Downing and his manservant trotted through Boxford, noting despite the melancholy of their journey that the church was being decorated for the Harvest Festival. Lads and lasses were nailing sheaves of grains upon the door, a cartful of garden stuff and fruit was drawn up by the lych gate, awaiting ornamental distribution along the nave and through the chancel. As Downing pursued the road to Groton, he encountered a procession of tenants plodding towards the Manor with their rents—many of them in kind; lambs, fat geese, barrels of apples or sacks of barley.

At least the harvest's been good he thought, no matter the other trials,—which included Winthrop's mounting debts. And the Manor, through some legal oversight in Winthrop's method of conveyance, had not yet sold. A bungling matter, thought his brother-in-law sighing and reining in his horse, for all John's training he had scant head for business. And yet a stubborn man of vision who let naught daunt him.

Downing turned his horse through the Manor gates and saw a happy party on the lawn. Everyone in the house was nutting, as was the custom on this day. The manservants flailed and shook the four magnificent walnut trees that stood near the garden well, while the children and maids capered beneath, gathering the crop in sacks, cracking and eating as many as they gathered. Martha, Mary and Elizabeth were also nutting, and Emmanuel paused to admire. The three girls made a charming picture of youth in their bright-colored clothes—especially Elizabeth in a new saffron gown, girdled tight around a waist even slenderer than it used to be, though her bosom was fuller, and her skirt kilted up like a milkmaid's showed off her pretty ankles. Downing stared at her appreciatively, seeing the vivid rose of her cheeks, the glossiness of her black ringlets. Poor lass, he thought, mindful of his tragic errand—ah well—she'll have no trouble finding the next one.

He dismounted heavily, having grown stouter of late, and walked to the bench by the garden well where Margaret was placidly mending linen while she kept an eye on the two babies in their cradles. She rose to meet him with a cry of delighted astonishment.

"Why, Brother Downing, what brings you here from London to our great pleasure?" She had no thought of trouble, because Forth, still in Exeter, had written that a ship at Bristol had brought news of the Governor's safe landing with all his party. The whole family had held Thanksgiving in Groton Church. "You've brought letters, at last?" she cried, her plump face glowing. "We so long for them!"

"A letter—" said Downing slowly, and at her sudden look of alarm, added, "Oh, Brother John is well, and your little boys, fear not, but—" he glanced at the nutting party which had not yet noticed him—"where's Jack?" he asked, shrinking from his task and knowing that his nephew's notable tact might make it easier.

"Receiving rents in the Hall, I believe, or physicking one of the horses—he has so much to do—and I don't know how we'd manage without him—but what *is* it, Brother?"

"A heavy blow," said Emmanuel, sitting down beside her, and resigning himself. " 'Tis Harry."

Margaret flinched and put down her linen. "He's disappeared?" she said, "Or is it disgrace . . . ?"

"Drowned," he stated flatly. He fumbled in his pocket and brought out his pipe, stuffed it with tobacco, made a great play with the flint until he got it lit, while she stared at him, and her gentle eyes filled with scalding tears. "God be merciful . . ." she whispered. "Oh, my poor Bess." She looked at the girl's laughing face as she played a game of catch with the walnuts, tossing them to the enraptured little Deane.

"You'd best read the letter," said Emmanuel giving it to her.

"John is so brave," Margaret murmured, wiping her eyes as she finished. "You see how staunchly he takes this—" She quoted from the letter:

"Let us join in praising our mercifull God that howso-ever he hath Afflicted us, both generally and particularly mine own family in his stroke upon my son Henry, yet my selfe and the rest of our children and familye are safe and in health, and that he upholds our heartes that we faint not in all our troubles, but can yet wait for a good issue . . . Besides in this, that God begins with us thus in Affliction, it is the greater argument to us of his love . . ."

"Aye—" agreed Emmanuel somewhat dryly, thinking that if it had been one of John's other sons, particularly Jack, God's personal affliction might not have been so well borne.

"He speaks, too, so tenderly of Bess," continued Margaret, "saying it grieves him so much for her. 'The Lord strengthen and comfort her heart to beare this cross pa-

tiently—' It *will* comfort her, I know, that John is so pitiful
of her, and has come, I believe, to see her worth as I have."

"No doubt." Emmanuel puffed on his pipe and shook his
head. "All the same I'd not like to be the one to tell her."

It was Jack who told her that evening. They kept the secret
until Elizabeth had eaten the traditional Michaelmas dinner
with its great roast geese stuffed with apples and walnuts. She
noted that her uncle plied her with wine, and looked at her
with special tenderness, but then she knew she had always
been a favorite of his. They waited until she had nursed the
two infants, lest the shock turn her milk. Margaret's milk had
given out long since, and Elizabeth, having an abundance,
offered to suckle the puny little Ann as well as her own,
whereupon Ann began to thrive though never as big and
healthy as Martha Johanna, whom Elizabeth called Joan.

From sure instinct Jack called Elizabeth outside into the
garden, knowing that the flowers and the old mulberry tree
she loved might help sustain her, as would the concealment
provided by the evening shadows, for she was proud—and
for all the strength of her passions, tried to conceal them.

He told her very gently, holding her hand in his, while his
voice thickened, and moisture stung his lids.

She was quiet a long time after he had finished, clinging
hard to his hand and leaning against the gnarled old mulberry
trunk. Then she whispered, "Peyto knew it was coming—he
saw it." Jack did not understand and thought her dazed.
"Perhaps I knew too," she went on. "The day he left here—
so bravely—in the blue cloak—I felt—I remembered Peyto—"

"Bess, dear," he interrupted softly. "I've not the faith my
father has, but we must believe, we *do* believe that you two
will meet hereafter."

"Harry died as he lived . . ." she said in a thin remote
voice. "Merry, confident and strong in his own whims—'tis
not so bad a way."

Jack was silent. Perhaps it was not so bad a way. He
thought of his brother, who would now be forever young
and golden-haired, whose faults would be forgotten—while
otherwise—what unhappiness might there not have been
for Bess? But she's free now, he thought with a blinding flash
of pain and dismay. She's free, and I am not. The marriage
to Martha was arranged for next week, though now would
be postponed of course since the Manor would be plunged
into mourning. Yet even were he free, it was impossible to
wed his brother's widow in the face of scriptural law. Jack's

hand trembled on Elizabeth's and he checked these riotous
thoughts with shame.

"Shall I leave you now, dear," he said quickly. "You'll like
to be alone perhaps."

"Aye . . ." she answered after a while. "Perhaps." Her
hand went to the gaudy brooch Harry had given her; she
unfastened it and held it, staring at the crystals and false
gold. "'Tis all I have of Harry, now—" she said with a
strained wonder, "except my Joan." And the memory of one
completely happy day—long ago in London.

7

THE AFFLICTIONS suffered by the Winthrops did not cease with Harry's death. In November, Forth came home to Groton after his long visit at Exeter, where he had fallen in love. He was full of plans for his marriage, and the whole family's eventual voyage to New England.

Somehow on the journey between Devonshire and Suffolk, Forth caught a virulent cold which developed into lung fever. He took to his bed with an excruciating pain behind the ribs and a barking cough that distressed them all, but did not alarm them until the 25th of November when he suddenly grew delirious and the sound of his agonized breathing seemed to fill the house. Elizabeth searched frantically through her father's receipt book for new concoctions which might help, they sent a groom galloping for the Hadleigh physician, they got the barber to bleed him, the women rushed to and fro with warming pans for his clammy feet, or steaming cloths for his chest. All to no avail.

Forth died that night, within five weeks of his twenty-first birthday.

"It is the Lord's Will, the Lord's Will . . ." moaned Margaret. "God give us grace to make use of this new stroke He has visited on us! But I know not how to write of it to John!"

She gathered her own little Sammy fearingly in her arms, and broke down completely for some hours. Elizabeth wept too, but she felt something stony grow around her heart. God's purposes were doubtless inscrutable to humans, and Death might be only a Dark Angel, but she found no comfort in this. She felt instead a great resentment against God, and a blasphemous wonder whether He indeed concerned Himself so closely with mortals unless it was to mock and punish. And after Forth's funeral she kept much to herself, finding pleasure only in the baby, as it had been since she heard of Harry's death.

And yet through the winter as Margaret read her parts of John Winthrop's letters, Elizabeth felt grudging admiration and some envy for the unvarying fortitude he showed in bearing not only his family losses but the continual tragedies which were occurring in Massachusetts. He stated these baldly enough, and without comment.

In the three months since the landing of the fleet, nearly a third of his company had died. The Lady Arbella survived but a month and died in Salem, her husband Isaac Johnson lost heart without her, and by October he had been buried amongst the straggling collection of shacks which he had himself named Boston. Salem's minister, Francis Higginson, died. Mrs. George Phillips died in Watertown. Mrs. William Coddington died. Mr. Rossiter died, and Mr. Gager, their only physician, died. Winthrop lost twelve from amongst his own servants' families.

There was smallpox, sweating sickness and sudden fevers. Too, almost everyone had scurvy, and it was noted that those who yearned "and lingered after England," bemoaning their folly in having come, died fastest of all. And yet Winthrop wrote staunchly to Margaret:

> *Thou maiest see the goodnesse of the Lord towards me, that when so many have dyed, and many yet languishe, my selfe and my children are yet living and in health . . . we conceive that this disease grewe from ill diet at sea and proved infectious. I write not this to discourage thee, but to warne thee and others to provide well for the sea and by Godes helpe the passage wilbe safe and easy . . .*

And he sent detailed directions for the voyage.

In the face of all these disasters Margaret had often nourished the craven hope that John might yet give up and return home. Sometimes she would even talk to the little round miniature of him he had given her. It had been painted in London and was an excellent likeness. Margaret weeping over the ivory disk would implore John to come home, though she never did in her letters. And she could not help but be grievously affected by dark whisperings amongst Groton's Manor folk who interpreted all these deaths as showing God's curse upon the move.

Pond, the miller, one spring day received a letter from his son in Massachusetts, and being unable to decipher it, carried it to Margaret whom he found in the courtyard hurrying from the bakehouse. Pond, agog over his letter, had come straight from the mill and was powdered with flour from his wool cap to his huge boots. "Would ye be so koind, Mistress?" he said tendering the letter anxiously. Young Pond's year at the Boxford grammar school had not made him a scholar and Margaret stumbled aloud through the missive with growing dismay at its contents.

> *I knowe, Lovinge father . . . I wase an unduteyfull Cheilld unto you. I trust in God that you will forgive me for it . . . Peple her have deyeid . . . two hundred and ode, beside maney lyeth lame and all Sudbery men are ded but three . . . here is no bever and here is no cloth to be had . . . we do not know how long we may subssiste for we can not live here without provisseyones from ould England . . . The cuntrey is not so as we did expecte it . . . I thinck that in the end if I live it must be my leavinge for we do not know how long this plantacyon will stand . . . I purpose to com home at Myckellmas . . . we were wondurfule sick as we cam at sea withe the small poxe, no man thought that I and my littell chilld woolld a livid and my boye is lame and my gurll too, and thar dyeid in the ship that I came in xiiij persones.*

There was a silence when Margaret had finished. Then Pond spoke heavily.

"So he's coming home—is he! And would a saved me a purseful had he listened in the first place. But Oi'm glad he's aloive as yet, there's plenty went from here who aren't."

"I know—" said Margaret turning away. "I know. Why did your son go, Pond?" she said after a moment. "It would seem not for spiritual reasons."

"No more it was," said the miller, shrugging. "He went tew better hisself, the dom chucklehead, he'd dreams o' free land an' lazy living, of setting up as squoire, no doubt. Thass why he went, but glad enough now tew come home and help me wi' the mill. The young fule."

Margaret sighed, and handed back the letter, which the miller tucked under his floury blue smock.

"Write the Governor, Mistress!" he cried, seeing her dejected face. "Tell him ye feel 'tis a sign he's mistaken God's bidding—all the troubles there's been—and his own two sons dead so fast loike a judgment . . . all of us here mourn Master Harry and Master Forth as our own!"

"He does not see it so," she replied with difficulty. She pulled John's latest letter from her bosom. "Listen what he writes—

> *I prayse God, that the Lord will abundantly recompence for all the trouble we have endured . . . we heer enjoye God and Jesus Christ, is not this enough? I thanke God I like so well to be heer as I do not repent my coming: and if I were to come again I would not have altered my course, though I had foreseen all these Afflictions . . .*

"Always he writes thus and urges my going to him quickly with my family."

"Ah—" said the miller shaking his head. "A stubborn gentleman—if you'll forgive me, Mistress. Won't owe he's wrong."

"He's NEVER wrong!" said Margaret sharply. "And I'm hastening to do as he wishes. The Manor is sold, Pond—to a Mr. Waring of London. Everyone will know it soon. And we will sail for New England in August."

The miller's round face fell into disconsolate lines. "So it's come . . ." he muttered twisting his hands in his smock. "It's come. Will ye all be going?"

She nodded with a firmness she did not feel.

"Mistress Bess?" he questioned wistfully. His admiration for Elizabeth had grown even greater since last May Day because she had recently healed a sore on his wife's breast.

"She too, I believe," said Margaret. "At least she must leave Groton, of course."

"Aye," said the miller. "There'll be naught but strangers at the Manor now. And the land don't *loike* it, I tell ye, Mistress—there's a two-headed calf been born at Gosling's, and the gray lady's walking o' noights i' the ruined castle again!"

"I'm sorry—Pond," said Margaret unhappily as he bobbed his head and walked sadly off.

She went in search of Elizabeth who was the only person she could share her fears with. Jack was in London immersed in a hundred activities relative to Bay Company business and their own departure; besides, since his marriage to Martha on February 8 he had grown extremely restless, impatient of delays and would talk of nothing but New England and its development.

Jack's marriage had partaken of this restless impatience too, since he had suddenly decided on it and given them all scant time for preparation. Though in truth there was little to prepare, with the family in deep mourning. Groton Church had however been decorated with pine boughs and holly over Mr. Leigh's protests. Martha wore a white gown she had made herself, and the wedding feast in the Hall had been lavish. They had summoned the village musicians for dancing, of which Jack was as fond as Martha, and both bride and groom had seemed very happy on that afternoon. Margaret had rejoiced at that, and tried to ignore some doubts later. The new-wedded pair spent their honeymoon at Groton, and except that a large four-poster had been moved into Jack's room, and Martha shared this with him, it was hard to believe they were married, so little had their usual attitudes towards each other changed.

Jack continued to treat his little wife with a somewhat absent-minded consideration, Martha seemed as adoring, shy and childish as ever, though in her case there was an added stress of embarrassment, and constraint. This would have disturbed Margaret had she not had troubles enough of her own without seeking to analyze subtleties.

After the miller's disturbing visit, Margaret found both sisters in the small wainscoted parlor beside a crackling fire. Elizabeth was lying on the Turkey hearth rug playing with Joan, who now at a year walked a little, investigated everything and actually knew three words, "Ma-ma," "milk," and "no." She was a plump baby with rosy cheeks, and was gurgling happily while her mother played "This little piggy to market" with her toes. Margaret suppressed the customary pang that her own baby Ann still showed no interest in anything, but lay quietly in her cradle, gazing upward with wide, vacant eyes.

"Bess," said Margaret, advancing to the fire, "Pond the miller's been here, had a letter from that great hobble-de-hoy son of his, who is—is coming home. He told of yet more deaths out there—it was distressing . . ."

"Oh?" said Elizabeth sympathetically while rescuing her crystal brooch from Joan's clutch. "Still you must not *let* it distress you, my mother—since there's nothing for it—but to go."

They both heard the involuntary sound that Martha made. The girl was perched on a stool by old Adam's desk box, laboriously writing to Jack. He had taught her a simple cipher for their private use, partly to amuse her, and partly because his eager mind was interested in ciphers, as it was in alchemy and medicine and all branches of physical science.

Martha had the key to the cipher beside her, but was proud of having nearly learned the numerical symbols, each one of which stood for a letter, and she tried to make her sprawling unformed writing neat. She had been, as she did repeatedly, assuring him of her love, quite unable to explain the dark resistance and fears which had clouded their wedding night and thereafter. *That's* it—she thought—as she heard her sister speak. 'Tis the prospect of this fearful journey that makes me act so strange with Jack. She dipped her pen, and a great blot of ink slipped off on the paper. She stared at it through hot tears.

It would be shame to send him a blotted letter, as so many things were shameful. Shameful as her behavior to him their wedding night when they had been alone in the great bed upstairs. Screaming, fighting, sobbing, until as last he turned from her saying in a voice of sad aloofness, "My poor Martha, you need not struggle with me, nor ever fear me." He had not touched her again except to kiss her lightly now and then as he had always done.

She pulled another piece of paper from the box, and started once more in cipher, "Deare husband."

The other women had gone on talking and Margaret said, "Pond asked me if you sailed with us—I said I thought so—yet Bess dear—how I hope that you will make the match with William Coddington—John wishes it—and it would settle you so well over there!" Winthrop had twice mentioned William Coddington's projected visit to the Manor, and a groom had gone to fetch Coddington from Sudbury this very afternoon.

Elizabeth sat up, pushing back her hair which the baby

had tumbled. "I won't know until I see the man!" she said briskly. "But I mislike what I've heard about him—writing the vicar to inquire about my virtues! Writing you the same! And I've little fancy for a widower, no matter how Uncle John thinks to get me ably off his hands!"

"Bess!" cried Margaret, noting sadly that Elizabeth had returned of late to the rebellious bravado of her girlhood, but Margaret was staunchly fond of her, and had come to depend on her too. "You speak most unreasonably. *You* are a widow, and since Mr. Coddington has most unfortunately buried his wife in New England . . ."

"And is looking for another as fast as possible, and is rich, and is willing to consider me on Uncle John's recommendation, I should be thanking God for my good fortune?" Elizabeth burst out in one of her rare laughs at Margaret's rueful face. "Never mind, dearest Mother. I promise to charm Mr. Coddington if I possibly can. I suppose I must marry, if only to get a man in my bed. I find the nights lonely, and I want more babies."

Margaret shook her head. "I grieve to hear you so flippant—did I not know your warm true heart . . ."

"Warm true hearts profit little," said Elizabeth gathering up Joan. "I will go now and make myself beautiful for Mr. Coddington!" She spoke pertly, but as she passed the desk where Martha was hunched, she gave her sister an anxious look, knowing well that something was wrong between the new couple, and sorry for them, even though she could not help relief that she had not had to witness raptures.

William Coddington duly arrived in time for supper, and Elizabeth had made herself as lovely as the black silk dress and plain mourning collar allowed. She wickedly left off her starched widow's cap, and twisted her hair into little tendrils around her face. She rubbed some red salve Harry had given her on her lips. She doused herself with rosewater and patted orris-root powder over her neck and arms.

Sally was in ecstasies as she helped her mistress, crying, "Oh, ma'am, ye dew smell good n' thass the truth. The gentleman'll never leave wi'out declaring hisself!"

Elizabeth's hazel eyes sparkled as she descended the stairs, and her heart beat with an anticipation she had not admitted to Margaret. It would be pleasant to be wooed again, to feel desirable and female. It would be delightful to be kissed, and if Mr. Coddington pleased her, she had little doubt that she could kindle passion in him. Fifteen months had passed since she had said farewell to poor Harry, and his image had faded. Recently she had even enjoyed correspondence with Edward Howes, who apparently still wanted her and was making overtures by letter, though she had no intention of allowing him to get serious again. Her awakened body yearned for lovemaking after the long abstinence; she wished for new romance that would release her once and for all from any forbidden preoccupation with Jack.

But William Coddington, despite Sally's prophecy, did leave Groton without declaring himself, for after one horrified look at him as she entered the Hall, Elibabeth behaved outrageously.

Coddington was no more than thirty but his head was nearly bald, and fringed with straggling locks. He was pock-marked, much shorter than she and very fat. He was stuffed like a sausage into an elegant brocaded doublet and velvet breeches. There were several gold rings on his puffy hands. Bowing, he greeted Elizabeth in tones of measured condescension.

"Good evening, Mistress Winthrop, this is a pleasure long desired, I have heard interesting reports of you, and am gratified to see that those of your comeliness at least were not exaggerated—" He gave her a smug appraising smile and she noted that his breath was foul from rotted teeth.

"And I've heard of you," she answered, furious with disappointment. "And I observe that perhaps reports of famine in New England *are* much exaggerated." She glanced from his plump cheeks to his paunch, but her voice was so soft, and Coddington so sure of his own worth, that he merely smiled again in a startled way and said, "I believe they are, at least it is largely the lower sort of folk who complain."

"I see—" she said. "How foolish of them." Her smile became more brilliant, gliding away from Coddington to rest on young Leigh, the vicar's eighteen-year-old son, who had just come down from Cambridge. The Leigh family had been asked to supper to meet Mr. Coddington.

"Is it not foolish of the lower sort to complain of scanty food—Mr. Leigh?" she said to the young man looking at him through her lashes. He was immediately dazzled, and stammered some fatuous reply.

Throughout the supper, Elizabeth flirted with young Leigh, she drank too much claret, she laughed too high, she interrupted Coddington whenever he tried to deliver an opinion. Martha and Mary stared at her in amazement. Had Margaret been there, she might have controlled this madness, but Margaret had excused herself from the supper party because her baby had again developed fever and convulsions.

Mr. Coddington grew very quiet, and pursed his little mouth uncertainly as he watched Elizabeth. He knew himself to be a man of consequence both in Old Boston and the New—a most eligible husband. He had however been prepared to overlook the fact that Elizabeth was a mere apothecary's daughter, prepared even to forget somewhat damaging gossip he had heard about her impetuous marriage to Harry, since her double relationship to Governor Winthrop mitigated these. So undoubtedly did her beauty. He felt himself as powerfully attracted by it, as he was shocked by her hoydenish behavior, which grew worse. After supper Elizabeth, sweetly enquiring if she could entertain them, picked up a lute and sang in her true husky voice a ribald tavern song she had learned from Harry. She was presently joined in the chorus by young Leigh despite the rector's glares.

"You do not like my song?" she asked anxiously in the silence that followed. "Oh, Mr. Coddington, I am so disappointed, for I wished so much to please you. Perhaps *this* one will, I think it charming." And she launched into "Cuckolds all in a Row."

Before she had finished, Mr. Leigh rose, signaled his wife and grabbed his son by the arm. "We must be going," he said in outraged tones, throwing Coddington a look of commiseration and apology.

Elizabeth too looked at Coddington, and was dismayed to see a lustful glint in his small eyes which kept roaming over her neck and bosom. She poured herself more wine to offset a fear—the lifelong buried fear of John Winthrop and his wishes. She had defied these once, and dared not do so again by explicitly refusing her uncle's choice for her. The opportunity must not arise. "Wait," she cried wildly to the Leighs. "It is yet early, let us play a game of names—to see what images they present!"

The Leighs paused, compelled by her vibrancy and force.

"My maiden name—" she cried, "was Fones—that's easy, since it makes us think of fawns. But yours, Mr. Coddington—why what a wondrous suggestive name it is! We think of a great fish, do we not? We think of little pods, and bags —aye, and can we help—when viewing so handsome, so virile an owner of the name," she paused, went on with silken malice, "Can we *help* think of a codpiece?"

Coddington drew in a hissing breath. His pride of name was as great as his physical deficiency in the area to which Elizabeth so monstrously referred. He threw her a look of fury, and said with considerable dignity, "Your game is a poor one, Mistress Winthrop, and I perceive that you have drunk to excess. I shall return to Sudbury if you will kindly have the horses brought."

It was some days before her baby recovered and Margaret heard of that evening from the rector. She went straight in search of Elizabeth who was working in her surgery looking pale and drawn.

"Oh, Bess, how COULD you?" Margaret cried, sinking down on the stool and gazing woefully at the girl. "What Mr. Coddington must think—and will tell John!"

"He'll not tell much," said Elizabeth slowly pounding cardamon seeds in her mortar. "Except that he found me unsuitable, 'tis better that way. You scarce saw him—he was—was—" she shuddered, "like a bloated toad, and yet Uncle John would have had me marry him."

"Men think not of the looks of other men," said Margaret helplessly. "And my John is best judge of what's good for you and all of us. Bess, he is your guardian, your uncle and your father, you MUST obey him."

Aye, thought Elizabeth, and he has my dowry too, my four hundred pounds which he said he would repay but has not yet. Dear God, that I were born a man, and could strike out alone—with Joan.

"And, in your behavior you most dreadfully breached the laws of hospitality," said Margaret fastening on another unhappy aspect of the rector's account.

"For that I'm sorry," said Elizabeth dully. "I was highflown with wine."

"May God correct and guide you, my poor child," sighed Margaret rising with difficulty for she had remained heavy after Ann's birth, and her leg veins were swollen. "I pray all the time that you will be touched with His sure grace."

Elizabeth put down her pestle. She bent and kissed the older woman. "I would be like you if I could, my mother, but I cannot."

On August 15 of that summer, 1631, the Winthrops arrived at Sandwich in Kent to await Captain Peirce and his ship *Lyon,* which had been laden at Gravesend and was sailing down the Thames and around Kent to pick them up before continuing the voyage to New England.

Mr. John Humphrey, who was married to Arbella's sister, Lady Susan, had kindly placed a house he owned in Sandwich at the Winthrops' disposal while they waited for the *Lyon,* but though it was a goodly Tudor mansion near the Guildhall the Winthrop party was so large that some must stay at the Fleur-de-Lys, which enchanted Elizabeth who insisted on being of that number.

The Inn was small and musty, the beds none too well aired but it was gay, the taproom filled with jovial drinkers, the courtyard always a-bustle with travelers and sailors, and passengers like themselves, who meant to embark from the Downs. And at the Inn one could better smell the sea.

Elizabeth had been bred in London and the gentle countryside, and was fond of both. Yet from her first glimpse of the distant line of breakers on the Sandwich Flats, she felt a compelling new thrill. Let the rest of them, Margaret, Martha and Mary, weep for Groton, as they did that night, Elizabeth could not join them. She suffered nothing but relief and anticipation. The Winthrops had brought four servants, amongst them Sally, who had decided to emigrate with Elizabeth when Wat Vintener proved fickle. Elizabeth nursed Joan, then left her in Sally's charge and escaped into the warm summer twilight, heading through the quaint winding streets for the sea. The sea was retreating from this town that had once been the chiefest of the Cinque-Ports, but a short walk brought her to the wide brown sands, where she stood transfixed, gazing with awe at the crashing breakers, the flying spume, the suck and power of the watery masses, ever striving, pounding, ebbing, indifferent and beautiful.

"Ah—" she breathed, stretching wide her arms into the salt-sweet wind. She walked so near the marge that one wave greater than the rest swirled round her ankles, and she laughed.

"So, Bess—you laugh?" said a quizzical voice behind her. She turned and saw Jack standing on the sand. Some of her own exultance showed in his eyes. "The sea," he said, "pathway to the New World."

"To freedom," she answered, throwing back her head. They looked long at each other and Jack moved closer, then checked himself. "I guessed where to find you, for it's where I would come too. There's news. The *Lyon* was sighted passing Ramsgate earlier. She'll soon be in the Downs with this wind. We may leave tomorrow."

"I'm glad—" she cried. "Glad!"

"Not afraid?"

"Only of your father, I think. Of nothing else."

He started to say that she needn't be, that his father was wise and essentially kind, that in any case she was but an inexperienced girl of twenty-one and must be guided. Instead he said, without wishing to, "Mattie is afraid."

"I know." Elizabeth pulled her gaze from the waves. "She doesn't want to go." She hesitated. "Why can't you reassure her, Jack? What is wrong between you two? She loves you so much."

"Martha is a child," he said roughly. "Nor wishes to be anything else."

They were alone on the beach, and plunged unsuspecting into an intimacy they had never permitted before. The gulls wheeled and mewed, heading inland towards the town. The sky turned violet and the waves flung diamond showers upon the glistening dark sand.

"How can she be afraid with you beside her?" Elizabeth's voice was muted by the waves, but he heard her.

"She is afraid *of* me—of being a wife."

So that is it, Elizabeth thought. She had begun to suspect.

"She fears childbirth," said Jack heavily. He reached down and picked up a cockle shell; frowning, he fingered the delicate flutings. "Fears it more than is natural. She may love me but not enough to—" He flung the shell far from him. "Nor should I talk to you like this." He raised his head and looked at her in her new crimson gown. The strong breasts and shoulders, the proud lovely face silhouetted against the sky.

"You must woo her," said Elizabeth faintly. "Gentle her, persuade her, then maybe force her in the end, a little."

"Aye—" he answered after a moment when her meaning reached him. Then he stiffened. He raised his eyes, staring at her now with what seemed like anger. "But by God, I don't *want* to!"

"Jack—" she whispered. She caught her breath, and the words tumbled over each other. "Jack, we both love her, you do, you know you do, you must have patience, she is so tender, so unaware . . ."

He said nothing. He took a sharp step forward and seized her in his arms. She made a whimpering sound, but she yielded her mouth to his. They stood there interlocked and trembling, while the waves pounded behind them. A fishing boat grated on the shingle nearby. There were voices and the light of a lantern.

Jack's arms dropped, he jerked his mouth from hers, pushing her away. "Unclean," he said through his teeth, "incestuous. May God forgive me." Dim as the light had grown she saw real anger now in the brown eyes that were usually merrily observant. An anger that engulfed the world. "Come, Bess—" he said sharply. "My mother will be wondering where we are."

They walked up the beach far separated from each other. They went silently through the twisted streets of Sandwich until they came to Humphrey's house and were greeted at the door by Martha with a glad cry of welcome.

The next afternoon the entire Winthrop company having driven the six miles to the quay at Deal, embarked in the *Lyon's* longboat. Though Margaret said nothing as she settled herself in the stern, a tear glistened on her cheek, and she clutched her whimpering baby tight in her arms. Her four-year-old Sammy nestled beside her and stared with open mouth at the half-naked sailors, but she had had to leave Deane in London with the Downings. He was a delicate child and a scholarly one. John had written that he thought it best neither to risk the journey for Deane, nor interrupt his schooling. It was a sorry blow. Yet soon I shall see my *oldest* boys and my beloved husband, if God wills it, Margaret thought, seeking acceptance as always. And the rest of her family were here with her, comfort enough for leaving Deane —and England. The sailors began to row and Margaret though herself frightened of the water managed to smile at Martha who sat rigid on the next thwart beside Jack. The boat started to pitch as they moved from shelter. "See our ship!" cried Margaret encouragingly. "Does she not look large and staunch?" She indicated the 250-ton *Lyon* which rode far out at anchor in the middle of the downs, her flags flying, her high poop newly painted in red and blue, the rampant lion on the prow sparkling with new gilt.

Martha did not turn to look, nor answer. She fixed her eyes on the dirty water that sloshed in the bilges, and pressed her pale lips hard to keep from whimpering as did the infant Ann. Jack despised her fears, she knew, and she despised herself. Already the motion of the boat and the vast insecurity of the treacherous sea made her sick and giddy. She sat frozen,

while her muscles tensed as though they could rush her back
to land.

Mary Winthrop crouched on a chest of their household
goods, beyond the four rowing sailors. Her plain freckled
face was composed. Under her serviceable brown wool cape
she held her vellum-bound psalm book; in her personal chest
she had some other books she had bought in London. These
and needlework were all Mary needed to while away the
voyage. She longed to see her father of whom she was quietly
fond. For the rest she was a philosopher, and though only
eighteen was untroubled by youthful turbulence. She appeared indeed older than Elizabeth, who had wedged herself
into the bow with Joan and was eagerly savoring the motion
of the boat, the slapping of waves on the hull, and the flying
spray. Elizabeth had been somber enough through the night
of sleepless worry over those moments on the beach with
Jack. Guilt-ridden because she could not help reliving them
and longing for their repetition. Towards dawn her thoughts
had grown so unmanageable that she had even dug her Bible
out of the bottom of her bride chest and fumbled through
Leviticus until she found the Lord's terrible ordinances in the
twentieth chapter: *The adulterer and the adulteress shall
surely be put to death . . . If a man shall take his brother's
wife, it is an unclean thing: he hath uncovered his brother's
nakedness . . .*

And if a woman should lust for her sister's husband . . . as
well? She had tried to pray for the first time in years. She arose
very weary but calmer. She and Jack greeted each other
coolly, but both plunged into the bustle of departure.

I can manage to avoid him on the ship, Elizabeth thought,
and once over there I shall be free. She had no idea how, but
she vaguely envisioned herself and Joan alone in a pretty little
forest cottage surrounded by a flower garden, far from interference or temptation.

The bo'sun piped them on board and Captain Peirce greeted
them on the *Lyon*'s deck as they climbed the wooden ladder.
"Welcome! Welcome!" he cried bowing. " 'Tis honor to
carry the Gov'nor's family! I've 'ad cabins built for ye next
my quarters in the poop, I 'ope they'll serve."

A wise tough cockney was the famous master mariner,
who had been born in a tenement on London Bridge and
raised on the docks. He had had schooling before he took
to sea, read for pleasure when he could and had shrewd
knowledge of life besides. He was a broad powerful man, just

forty, and sun-squint lines had begun to show, the tiny red veins to burst, in his black-bearded cheeks. He maintained a fierce discipline on his ship, but was not lacking in humor, and after greeting the Winthrops a rueful twinkle appeared in his sharp eyes.

"We've a passenger, ma'am—" he said to Margaret, "I didn't expect, and find a bit awkward, though I couldn't refuse 'er."

"Her?" said Margaret, casting anxious glances at the decks which seemed very small and crowded under some fifty milling passengers, bundles, chests and shouting sailors.

" 'Tis Lady Gardiner," said Peirce. "Leastways *one* of 'em. The French one." Seeing that Margaret did not understand, he turned to Jack. " 'Ave ye not heard, sir, about the rogue in Massachusetts called Sir Christopher Gardiner? A mort o' trouble 'e's made for your honored father!"

"Aye," said Jack, frowning, "I have. Gardiner's conspired against our colony, he plots with Sir Ferdinando Gorges to seize us and destroy our independence. He lives with a wench not his wife and yet has two wives in England."

"Just so," said the Captain. "And this is one of 'em. Coming 'ot-foot to fetch 'im back. She 'ad the passage money, and letters from 'igh places, so I couldn't say 'er nay, but I misdoubt she'll fit well wi' your God-fearing company, sir." He chuckled, then looked apologetic.

"I thought my father had put Gardiner in gaol to await deportation to England," said Jack, still frowning. He too had spent a sleepless night.

The Captain shrugged. " 'E *was* in gaol. No telling where 'e be now."

Elizabeth heard, but was not much interested, being in a fever to explore the ship and see where they would lodge for the voyage. This turned out to be a tiny cabin in the poop, with an upper and lower bunk no larger than coffins, and scarce room enough to stand beside them. This cabin she was to share with Mary, and, of course, Joan. The next cabin contained Margaret, Sammy and the baby; the third Jack and Martha.

Though these cabins were remarkably cramped they represented luxury compared to the rest of the passengers' hammocks or pallets in the hold. Each Winthrop cabin had a minute square porthole and a bucket dangling on a rope beneath it for the disposal of excreta. The common folk had no privacy at all.

"Hush thee, poppet—hush thee—" Elizabeth crooned to Joan as she snuggled the protesting baby down on the straw sacking of their bunk. "This'll be our home for many a long day, we'd best like it!" Elizabeth raised her head sharply listening to strange sounds that were to become as familiar as the noise of London traffic or of cawing rooks at Groton.

She heard the Captain shout, "Heave away-y-yy!" and the clanking of chain, then the squeak of the windlass as the great anchor rose from the water. She heard the straining chant of the sailors and the bo'sun's whistle. She heard the unintelligible orders to "Man the royals" and "the topgallants," the answering hubbub of "Aye, aye, sirs!" followed by the squealing of blocks and swish of unfurling sails. She rushed out eagerly to the quarter-deck, and felt the gentle rocking give way to a thrill and thrust beneath her feet, as though the ship had wakened. The ten square sails and one lateen bellied out taut against a blue-and-mare's-tail sky. The *Lyon* quivered and plunged southward to the Straits of Dover, on a brisk north wind.

Captain Peirce stood by his helmsman watching narrowly till they should be past Goodwin Sands, but he threw Elizabeth a word of reproof. "Ye're not wanted on the steerage, Mistress, ye can take leave o' England from the stern gallery if ye wish—but 'twill be tears wasted, for ye'll 'ave sight o' English coast a long time yet."

"I'm sorry," she said. " 'Twas not to say farewell I trespassed here—it was because—Oh, the ship is so *beautiful*, so splendid!"

The Captain snorted. "I 'ope ye think so a month from now when we get the line storms, 'stead o' puking in your bunk as ye'll surely be!"

"No, I won't," she retorted, and went back through the tiny companionway. Peirce laughed. "A fair saucy wench," he said to the helmsman. "She and that Frenchy Lady Gardiner'll spice this v'yage—'ard over to larboard, ye damn fool!" he added in a bellow.

The north wind held, the Dover Straits were as rough as usual, and the Captain's expectations as to his unseasoned passengers was justified by suppertime, for which nobody appeared in the officer's saloon but Elizabeth, an unknown man and a startling young woman.

The Captain made hurried introductions though he did not stay with them to eat. "Mistress 'enry Winthrop, widow. This is the Reverend John Eliot, boarded at Gravesend. 'Is

Worship the Gov'nor'll be pleased to get another minister."
Elizabeth inclined her head, and the short curly-haired young
man bowed with a peculiarly sweet smile. He doesn't look
like a minister, she thought. He looks almost jolly.

"Lady Gardiner, Mistress Winthrop," went on the Captain,
with a wink at Elizabeth, who curtseyed and stared, seeing
in that first instant only an improbable mass of violet-red hair,
brocaded green taffeta, scarlet lips in a pointed face and
nearly naked bosom with a black beauty patch on the curve
of the right breast.

"Enchantée," said Lady Gardiner in a husky drawl. She
extended her hand, which released a wave of musk. "Charming that you are not seeck like the others, Madame. Oh my
dear love of a capitaine, you must not leave us? Mr. Eliot
will find it hard to entertain two young ladies alone. You
must stay, Monsieur, you promised Mirabelle she would have
a gay voyage!"

"And so no doubt ye will, my lady!" said the Captain
chuckling. "But 'twill be gayer if the *Lyon* stays on course
and above the waves, so I ask ye to excuse me." He bowed
and walked to the door.

"So agreeable a captain!" cried Lady Gardiner in loud
cooing tones. "So virile, how you say? *Manly*. And you
too, sir." She turned to Mr. Eliot. "When I see you embark
at that terrible Gravesend—what macabre names you English
give places!—I say to myself, 'Mirabelle, we shall be dear
friends, thees young minister and I'—You have so sympathetic
a face!"

"You do me too much honor, my lady," said John Eliot,
retreating slightly along the seat, and flushing. "We'll all be
friends before journey's end, I'm sure, and you ladies'll help
me endure the heartache I feel at leaving my betrothed to wait
in England."

"Aha?" cried Mirabelle with warm interest. "So you have
a fiancée? You must tell us about her, mustn't he, Madame?
Do you like to kiss her very much?"

She's incredible, thought Elizabeth, fascinated, while John
Eliot laughed. "I do, my lady, or did rather, and hope to
again before very long." It was impossible to be angry with
Mirabelle, though by the time the *Lyon* had reached the
Isle of Wight, Elizabeth knew that she should disapprove of
her. Mirabelle dyed her hair with henna powder she had
brought from Paris. Mirabelle painted her face, she swung
her hips when she walked. She blandished every man she

saw, not excepting the sailors, and she laughed at all the
virtues Elizabeth had been taught to consider sacred. Particularly chastity.

"That is because I am an aristocrat," Mirabelle explained
to Elizabeth one calm bright day while she sat on a stool in
the open stern gallery carefully plucking her eyebrows. "My
father was a marquis, and considered chastity vulgar. True,
I was born on the wrong side of the blanket, as you say, but
no matter. I inherit the trait. Love-making is agreeable. Why
not enjoy it?"

Elizabeth gulped and laughed. Mirabelle constantly said
things Elizabeth had chided herself for thinking, and had
even voiced in moments of rebellion, though she later repented. But Mirabelle seemed unaware of sin or guilt, and it
was extraordinary that she seemed to have escaped all
righteous punishment. She was gay and charming and titled;
half of the men on the ship were in love with her, while
even the minister John Eliot did not censure her. It was
puzzling.

"You are too serious, ma petite," said Mirabelle squinting
into her hand glass and rouging her wide voluptuous mouth.
"Much too pretty to be so serious. You must please yourself
while you can."

"I'd like to," said Elizabeth slowly. "I did once—" she
thought of the Mulberry Garden and that ecstatic Palm Sunday, "but it was wrong—and I was punished for it."

"Bah!" said Mirabelle, smiling at the girl. "You think that
because you are a Puritan. Always examining conscience."

"But I'm not! I'm not truly religious at all. Not like the
others!"

"You cannot help it, chérie." Mirabelle's small greenish
eyes fixed themselves kindly on Elizabeth. She nodded and
shrugged. "You cannot *help* acting from what you were
taught in childhood, even though you don't want to. Above
all this is true for a woman."

"Have you no religion, my lady?" said Elizabeth, disliking
the other's calm certainty, and finding that an image of a
frowning John Winthrop had risen in her mind.

The Frenchwoman laughed. "I was baptized a catholique.
I shall die one, sans doute. In between I don't concern myself. Time enough to worry about my soul when my body
no longer gives pleasure."

They were silent, Elizabeth gazing back across the water
towards the dim line of the Devon coast, while Mirabelle

affixed a tiny black star beneath her collarbone to emphasize the whiteness of her skin and draw the eye lower towards the charm of her décolletage. Elizabeth watched and said timidly, "Forgive me, but why do you make this voyage to find a man who deserted you?"

"But I desert *heem!*" cried Mirabelle, showing all her beautiful teeth in a hearty laugh. "I disappeared one day to Anjou with a so handsome colonel, you can't imagine! My poor Christophe consoled himself by going to London and marrying a very rich English lady. I did not blame him. But soon I tire of my colonel, and it appears Christophe tires of his new wife—she is quite ugly, poor thing, and thin, it must be like sleeping with a rake—so he goes off to your colonies, and I go to London to find him."

"You found his English wife? But weren't you angry?"

"Ah ça, non," said Mirabelle laughing harder. "*She* was. But I am the first—'la légitime.' I still feel tendresse for Christophe, and say I'll go to fetch him back—if I want him. Or maybe I'll send him back to her, or it may be he's happier with the doxy he has now. How do I know until I see? En fin, I like to voyage, and certain complaisant gentlemen in London made me presents, so I can do as I please."

"I see," said Elizabeth, wondering what such a life could possibly feel like, envying it, even while aware of more shock than she wished to admit. She gazed at Lady Gardiner, thinking that without the paint and powder and hair dye her looks would not be remarkable at all, and yet she gave the impression of assured beauty.

"Chérie," said Mirabelle gently, shaking out her taffeta skirts and standing up. "I've noticed something. I'm older than you—how many years I don't tell—and I like you very much —so you must not mind what I say. You are not happy, your brother-in-law, Monsieur Jack Winthrop, is unhappy, and your little sister—she is sick in her cabin all the time, so she is unhappy too."

"Well?" said Elizabeth sharply, turning away and clenching her hands on the railing. "There's naught to be done about it."

"Quelle folie!" Mirabelle sighed. "When it is so simple. You two desire each other, and pretend you don't, so you suffer. Je suis pratique, moi. Satisfy this desire—oh very discreetly—and soon you won't have it. The little sister will be none the wiser, and you will all be happier!"

Elizabeth drew a rough breath, and her eyes blazed. "That's

wicked! It's disgusting! How dare you say such a thing!"

"Voilà," said Mirabelle sadly shaking her head. "The little Puritan indeed. Why can I not *say* what you have often *thought?* I give you good advice. I am very experienced."

Elizabeth's hands relaxed, and her anger died, quenched by her inherent honesty. She stared at the white board planking with its lines of oozing tar, and said in a low voice, "How did you guess? It frightens me that anyone should have guessed—surely nobody else . . ."

"No. No one else." Mirabelle put her scented hand on the other girl's shoulder. "But *I* can tell by the way you and Monsieur Winthrop avoid each other, by the way you look at him when he does not know. I can tell he is the only man on the ship who has no awareness of *me*. Tiens, chérie, do not be a stupid little provincial. All could arrange itself. My cabin behind the roundhouse is most fortunately placed for privacy, this I have proven. You may use it any time."

Elizabeth felt her cheeks turn hot. She glanced at Mirabelle and saw in the seductive face only sympathy and some amusement. She understood that to Mirabelle this was all a game, that to her the bars of guilt and rigid prohibition actually did not exist.

"I could not," said Elizabeth quietly. "But even if I could —Jack would not, so please never speak like this again. It pains me."

"Pauvre chou," said Mirabelle, tucking her cosmetic box beneath her arm. "As you wish. But then you must find another man soon. A husband you can manage. A husband who adores you blindly. Yes, a man like that would make you happy." She kissed Elizabeth on the cheek and went in through the companionway to her cabin, where she was not surprised to find the second mate—a lusty young Scot— awaiting her impatiently.

The voyage continued. Two days later they passed Land's End on a stiff breeze and the passengers crowded the decks to watch granite cliffs and the lighthouse slide past and fade into the sky behind them. All the passengers were very quiet —the ordinary folk crowded in the waist of the ship, and the privileged ones on the poop. Of the former only Goody Knapp from Suffolk wailed convulsively, and one elderly tanner who was going to join his son in Boston cried out in a high quavering voice, "God Save the King, and God bless Our Old England!"

The Winthrops stood close together. Margaret's eyes were

wet, and there was a lump in Elizabeth's throat, but these Cornish cliffs were not their England and two weeks on shipboard had dulled homesickness.

"I shall be back again someday," said Jack confidently. "I'll not say adieu." He knew that his father would need an emissary to the Old World, and that there would be business for the Colony to transact there. He had no feeling of exile, nor fear of the journey, having spent too long at sea on his trip to the Levant and being at heart a voyager.

"*I* shall never go home again," said Martha in a small wooden voice. "Never." She turned quickly from sight of the water, and leaned her head against Elizabeth's shoulder.

"Nonsense," said Elizabeth, putting her arm around her sister. "If Jack returns, doubtless you will, and anyway the *new* country will soon be 'home'."

Martha said nothing. She had nearly recovered from sea-sickness but had grown very thin; her blue wool dress hung limp as rags, and her little bones jutted through the pallid skin. She looked at Jack, a dark veiled look, but he did not see it. He was talking with John Eliot by the rail. The two young men found each other congenial and were full of eager speculation on what they would find. Eliot was particularly interested in the Indians and made plans for their conversion. He had read everything he could about them, and even memorized the names of some of the tribes. At Jesus College in Cambridge he had become a linguist and exceptional scholar. In the ship's saloon he and Jack passed many an hour together discussing their specialties. Eliot expounded the Bible and the liberal Puritan views of Mr. Thomas Hooker with whom he had studied in Essex, while Jack drew sketches of fortifications, of windmills and saltworks. Jack's mind teemed with ideas for establishing the new country, and making it profitable. While he was occupied with these things he forgot his troubled marriage, and the dark disturbances produced by Elizabeth.

Captain Peirce came out to them in the poop, swept them all with a rather sardonic eye and said, "Well, we're fairly off at last into the open sea. Glad to see ye're not sobbing." Nor praying either, he thought. This shipload was the least canting and psalm-singing of all he'd carried to Massachusetts. Even Eliot, the minister, minded his own business, and only preached on Sundays.

"Where's Lady Gardiner?" Peirce asked, though he suspected the answer.

"Why, she went in some time ago," said Elizabeth. "Said she was tired of staring at the English coast."

"Aha," said the Captain. MacDuff, the second mate, was missing too. Still, the Scot was off duty now, and Peirce was far too canny a Master to concern himself with anything which did not prejudice the ship or passengers' safety.

"How is your babe today, ma'am?" he asked Margaret, who tried to smile and did not answer. Each day little Ann grew more listless, and could scarcely be roused to drink the goat's milk a servant brought up from the hold where the beasts were kept.

"May I go below, Captain?" said Elizabeth quickly. "To wherever my chest of herbs is stored. I've some dried valerian I think would help the baby, and I can best find it myself."

The Captain gave ready consent, though he did not permit female passengers to run about the ship at will, getting in the sailors' way and hurting themselves in heavy weather. "Since ye've knowledge of physick, Mistress, will ye 'ave a look at the Beamsley boy while ye're down below. They tell me 'e sickens." And the Lord grant it's neither measles, plague nor smallpox, thought the Captain grimly. Any of those killers could halve a shipload in a fortnight.

Elizabeth was given a sailor as guide, and followed him down the stairs to the main deck. Several children were crouched by the windlass playing at Hot Cockles, while a large lad of about fifteen sat on the windlass, whittling and good-humoredly umpiring the game. The wind was veering, and the sea roughened. The *Lyon* gave a lurch as Elizabeth passed the group. She caught at the lad's shoulder, and landed almost in his lap. "Forgive me!" she cried laughing. "I thought I'd better sea legs."

The youth laughed too, setting her on her feet. "Do it again!" he said. " 'Tis a fine game with so fair a player."

Elizabeth looked at him with attention, startled by this gallantry. The voice, deep and nearly a man's, had the lilt of the southern counties. He was dressed in the common leather jerkin and red Monmouth cap of the artisan class, but his inflection and words sounded almost like gentry. His rosy, beardless cheeks, freckled nose, and the softness of his lank taffy-colored hair indicated his age, but if he had not yet his growth—he was going to be a huge man, for already he topped Elizabeth by four inches and his shoulders were thick and broad as Captain Peirce's.

Elizabeth's sailor guide was waiting, yet she lingered, curious and attracted by the youth who was looking at her with open admiration. "What are you whittling?" she asked at random. She examined his piece of wood, and cried, "Oh, how skillful!" He was fashioning two intricately carved balls out of a maple burl.

"Well," he said, showing how one ball moved within the other. "I must keep my hand in, I was 'prenticed to a joiner in Dorset."

"But surely you've not finished your 'prenticeship!"

He shook his head and grinned at her. "No, Mistress. Just begun. But I'd no stomach for daily beatings, and naught to eat ever but bowls of slops."

"You ran away . . . ?" she whispered. "How did you dare?" The punishment for escaping 'prentices was rigorous. "And how did you get passage money?"

"I didn't steal it, I assure you," he answered the startled speculation he had seen in her eyes. Years later she was to remember this moment on the *Lyon's* main deck, and the sudden attraction that rose from nowhere between them. Even at the time she wondered at herself for her compelling interest as she said, "What is your name, and where are you bound?"

"William Hallet," he said, sketching a bow, "and I'm bound for where pleases me most. I'm my own master now." He spoke with perfect courtesy, yet she was conscious of reserve and dignity beyond his age.

She recollected herself, said hastily, "Good Luck to you, then," smiled and joined her guide who was picking his teeth and staring gloomily towards the western sky where black clouds were massing. She descended through the hatch by a steep ladder to the 'tween decks, six feet high, where many of the passengers had hammocks slung. It was preferred space since it had portholes but these were battened down at present; the stench was strong, and the light poor. The Beamsley boy was twelve years old and lay doubled up and moaning in a hammock, while his mother who was great with child watched him anxiously. "He've bin so, sence daybreak, Missus," she said to Elizabeth in broadest Lincolnshire. "Writhing 'n' a-clutching his belly till I'm fair beset."

Elizabeth bent over the boy, who seemed slightly feverish, but had no pocks or spots. She poked gently at his rigid abdomen, and he cried out when she touched the right side near the hipbone, but Elizabeth did not think him very ill. "Just some cramp and wind in the bowel," she said reassuringly to the mother. "Has he been purged?"

"Aye-that, Missus. Mr. Atkins, the barber, drenched him good, not two hours a-gone."

"Hot cloths on his belly might ease him."

"There's not room at the fire to heat water, Missus," said the goodwife distractedly. "Cook won't let me near."

"I'll see about that," said Elizabeth, and she went down another ladder to the dark, smoky hold where a small hearth had been built of fire bricks. Over it the ship's cook in a greasy apron was stirring an enormous iron pot. It contained a stew of salt beef and dried peas, for the common folks' and sailors' dinner. The Captain and cabin passengers had a separate galley under the poop.

The cook turned a surly face on her request. His main function was not the preparing of food, which consisted almost entirely of this stew, but the guarding and doling out of provisions. "We've no water to spare," he growled, but seeing from her dress that she came from the privileged class, he added, "Ye can heat beer, if ye must. We've more o' that." Elizabeth looked around for a pannikin, and was rescued by Sally, who came lurching amongst the piled kegs, holding a mug of goat's milk for Ann. "Be ye here, then, ma'am!" she cried in astonishment.

Elizabeth explained her errand, and left the heating of beer for compresses to Sally while she followed the sailor to the compartment near the fo'castle where were stored the Winthrop's private chests and household furnishings. The sailor held a candle while she rummaged. There was less motion down here, but the air was fetid. The goats, pigs and a brood mare were quartered nearby, as she could hear by bleatings and snufflings which rose above the constant creak of wood and slap of water. There was the smell of tar and bilge, and worse ones too, for the common privy bucket stood outside the compartment.

Strong as Elizabeth's stomach was, her nose was sensitive, and she began to get queasy while she searched amongst the kegs of oatmeal, sugar, figs, pepper, saltpeter, suet, tallow, wine vinegar which John Winthrop had bidden them bring. There were three firkins of butter and dry-goods boxes too, containing hats, shoes, stockings and bolts of wool in sad colors and red. Except for the necessary pewter, iron pots and andirons there had been scant room for furniture, though Margaret had brought a bedstead, some Turkey carpets, and a huge carved court cupboard which had belonged to her father. Of personal furniture, Elizabeth had only four well-stuffed chests and the great silver salt cellar which had been given her by Adam Winthrop.

She came at last upon her store of herbs and seeds, and found the packet marked "Valerian." She sniffed the heliotrope odor gratefully, and filled her pockets with other herbs which might prove useful, feeling as she did so an instant of content. Suddenly, in the *Lyon's* stinking, swaying hold she had a moment of acute awareness, seeing that the skill she had acquired in the use of these simples was a pure satisfaction, an island of refreshment amongst the turmoils of love-longing, of grief or even zestful hope which usually tempested her. Then a rat darted out from behind a keg and ran across her feet. She jumped, and hurried from the hold, back up to the deck where she looked for the lad, William Hallet, but he was nowhere to be seen.

The next afternoon at dinner, the Captain announced sadly that the Beamsley boy had just died. A sorry shock for the parents, since the child had taken a turn for the better soon after they put the hot cloths on him. The pain had stopped. But he died all the same.

"Oh, I'm so sorry," breathed Elizabeth, stricken and bewildered.

"It is the Lord's Will," said Eliot kindly to her. "We must not question God's decisions."

"Amen," said Margaret in a trembling voice. "God is all merciful, no matter what afflictions He sends to try us." Her baby seemed no better today, despite the concoction of valerian.

"Tiens, what a pity," said Mirabelle, delicately gnawing on a chicken breast—the Captain's galley still had fresh meat. "But me, I am sceptique. I do not call this boy's death God's Will. It is mauvaise fortune, or destiny, or perhaps man's ignorance—I do not mean yours, chérie," she said to Elizabeth. "You did what you could."

Margaret looked unhappy, feeling that she should wrestle with Lady Gardiner's laxness, but Eliot did it for her. "That is not a Christian view, my lady," he said gravely. "Beware of the Devil's insinuations."

"Oh I do, my friend, I do," said Mirabelle smiling sweetly at him. "And I know I am a foolish woman, in need of guidance." She gave him a soft submissive glance, and the young minister thawed.

Jack watched with detached amusement. He believed that the boy's death was God's Will, or it would not have hap-

pened, but he shared with Elizabeth the urge to heal, and
far surpassed her in scientific interest. If we could have seen
into the boy's belly, he thought, I wonder what we would
have found. There must have been a bodily cause, even
though God instigated it. This speculation led him to Martha, who still looked very ill. She sat as far from the others
as she could in the tiny saloon. She had eaten nothing but
broth, nor spoken a word during dinner. He knew that she
slept badly, for he heard her tossing and sighing in her bunk
beneath his. Once he had seen a wild hunted light in her
eyes, and when he spoke to her she had not answered, nor
recently had seemed to want the reassurances she had always
implored.

"—And so we'd best get on wi' it!" said Captain Peirce
rising and finishing instructions to Eliot. "Ye can pray what
ye like, sir, but on my ship we'll 'ave the burial service as
well."

Eliot asquiesced and read the prayer book over the little
canvas-wrapped bundle on the main deck. He, like all the
nonconformists, had broken with set prayers, as they had
with other forms and rituals of the Church of England, but
he was a reasonable man.

The crew and passengers stood, bareheaded, by the rail
as the weighted bundle slipped into the sea. There was a
shrill scream from the mother, and then silence. The sailors
swarmed up the rigging. The Captain ordered an extra ration
of beer for everyone. The ship's life continued.

A week later in the driving rain, the scene was repeated.
All night they had been tossed and buffeted by an equinoctial
storm, and at the height of it the baby, Ann Winthrop, loosed
her tenuous hold on life. Margaret took it quietly, though
into her soft brown eyes there came an added depth. She
listened gratefully to Eliot's prayers, and she read incessantly
in her Geneva Bible. Elizabeth noted with wonder that Margaret's staunch faith seemed even to strengthen after this
tragedy, and she grieved less than any of them, but applied
herself to helping Elizabeth with Joan, who remained healthy,
in extra cherishing of her own little Sammy, and in trying to
hearten Martha.

There was no doubt that Martha must have some strange
malady. She had ceased to speak at all, except for one sentence when they told her of little Ann's death. "Good," she
whispered, and went on with confused words from the burial
at sea in the prayer book. "We commit her body to the

deep . . . until the sea shall give up her dead . . . and the corruptible bodies of those who sleep there . . . shall be . . . shall be at peace . . . in the Lord." The girl turned her head and wept without sound as she had taken to doing.

Margaret and Elizabeth exchanged a frightened glance. They found that Jack shared their mounting worry, though man-like he tried to make light of it, saying that sea voyages often depressed sensitive organisms. They called Atkins, the ship's barber-surgeon, who examined Martha's mouth and said she had a touch of scurvy. So Jack ordered up from the hold the gallon of infused scurvy grass, saltpeter and lemon water Governor Winthrop had written them to prepare in Groton. Martha drank the medicine when told to, and seemed a little stronger. Sometimes she sat on the poop deck and gazed down at the waves with a listening look as though they spoke to her, but mostly she lay in her bunk and stared at the rough planking above her head.

In the middle of October, they entered their eighth week of the voyage. Lately they had been delayed by contrary winds and fog, interspersed with sudden gales which occasioned the usual accidents. The spritsail had torn off in a heavy sea, some of the shrouds on the mizzen had parted. These had been repaired by the sailmaker and ship's carpenter with help from male passengers. There had been other mishaps which Captain Peirce looked upon as routine. Two of the goats died and the company greedily feasted on them since three casks of provisions had spoiled. A sailor pitched from the rigging of the mainmast and broke his leg on the deck. There had been two vicious fights, one between sailors, and one between two drunken passengers. The sailors had been well flogged by the bo'sun. Jack Winthrop had disciplined the landsmen in an improvised pillory.

Somewhere in mid-Atlantic they had sighted a ship with a strange rig and feared she might be an enemy privateer. They had manned the guns. But she turned out to be a harmless Swedish trader bound home with cod from the Great Banks. One time they narrowly avoided a gigantic waterspout, which whirled and funneled to leeward, another day there was anxiety about a frolicsome school of whales near as big as the ship, which surfaced and blew too close for comfort.

The master mariner remained imperturbable through all these incidents, but there came an afternoon of dead calm when he summoned Jack to his quarters. "Sit ye down, sir," he said, puffing on his pipe and extending a mug of rum. "I wanted a word wi' ye."

"Anything wrong?" Jack asked slowly, smiling thanks for the drink.

"Not yet, but I'm uneasy. There's a queer thick smell to the air, and it's turned too warm. Look at us!" The Captain pointed through the porthole to a yellowish sky and glassy sea which undulated in huge lazy swells that scarce rocked the ship. "Wallowing in doldrums we are, and at *this* latitude!" He placed a stumpy finger on his chart. "I figure we're about crossing forty. We're a couple o' days off the Banks on a stiff breeze, and we should be getting it, or cold fog. *This* feels like the Indies." It felt like the coming of what the Caribs called a "hirracano" such as Peirce had once battled through on a voyage to Barbadoes, but that was ridiculous so far north.

"The bo'sun saw St. Elmo's fire ball skipping up 'n' down the foremast yester e'en," said Peirce heavily. "Mebbe I believe it, mebbe I don't—but the crew's fidgety."

Jack nodded gravely. Not a seaman lived but considered the spectral lights of the "corposant" boded disaster. "What can I do, Captain?"

"Look to the passengers, quiet them if trouble comes. I'll 'ave me 'ands full wi' the ship. And muzzle that Goodwife Knapp in the 'tween decks. She's taken to ranting and prophesying. First she saw a merman, then she saw a sea sarpent. Now she's crying that there's witchcraft aboard, and the Devil's lurking in the sail locker. Oh, there's one or two like 'er on every v'yage, and about this time the landsmen allus get excitable, but I want as little of it as possible. Get Mr. Eliot to 'old a psalm-sing, *that*'ll calm 'em when we begin to strip the decks and batten down the 'atches." He paused and sniffed the heavy air like an old hound. "Aye, there's something bad a-brewing."

Jack went off to obey orders, and tried to do so without alarming anybody. But there was tension and foreboding throughout the ship.

In the poop they all reacted to the unrest. Margaret redoubled her private prayers and helped Elizabeth soothe Joan who had grown fretful. Mary indulged herself in the gripping romance of Sir Philip Sydney's *Arcadia,* and managed to forget her surroundings. Mirabelle decided to profit by the calm and a bucket of rain water gathered in the last gale. She proceeded to wash and dye her hair. To the women's astonishment, Martha got out of her bunk, dressed herself in a gray silk gown hitherto unworn, put on her best lace collar and cuffs and went to the stern gallery where she walked back and forth in an agitated manner, quite unlike her previous torpor.

In an hour a southerly wind began to blow, and the wide oily sea ruffled. There was general relief as the ship moved again—under moderate sail. The familiar creakings and strainings and swishings were welcomed. Soon the sky darkened and fat raindrops began to fall. The wind increased and the Captain furled the topsails, rejoicing that the *Lyon* had always been maneuverable, answering quickly to the helm as he tacked, hoping that they might withstand being blown straight back towards England. But by seven there was a full gale, worsening every minute, and shortly thereafter Peirce knew that all his fears were realized. The wind passed the tempest point into a howling fury with mountainous crashing waves as bad as the "hirracano" near Barbadoes. He had got her turned into the wind, and reefed all but a section of the mainsail before the worst of it. Then he lashed himself to the mizzen, near the grim sweating helmsmen on the tiller.

They could see the black waves towering and crashing over the fo'castle as the *Lyon* continually plunged, shook herself, hesitated and sluggishly recovered. They heard above the din a sickening boom like a cannon shot, and peered through sheets of rain, until there was a lull. "Half the mainmast's gone!" groaned one of the helmsmen, while they saw the tattered mainsail flying off white against the blackness. "If only the rudder'll 'old!" cried Peirce. "By God— if only the rudder'll 'old. Ye might pray, men."

In the poop they were already praying, each in his own way. Eliot was not with them since he had been battened down in the hold with the common passengers, and there they had long ceased to sing psalms while they desperately calked leaks and worked the pumps. The Winthrops, white-faced, were huddled in the saloon, clinging to each other and the fixed center table. Jack helped steady the women and soothe Joan and Sammy who were both wailing as they were all thrown from end to end of the pitching cabin. Mary moaned from time to time and retched into a bucket.

"Lord be merciful, be merciful," Margaret kept murmuring. "Yet if it is Thy will that we drown, take our souls straight to heaven and Thy loving arms."

"I do not wish to drown," cried Mirabelle plaintively. She

had wedged herself on the floor between the table and bench, her damp red hair flowed around her. "It seems I do not wish to die without the last rites. I am not so sceptique as I imagined!"

Nor am I, thought Elizabeth, clutching Joan harder as a thunderous wave crashed over the main deck and deluged them with spray through the portholes. She found that she too was praying; frantically pleading with the Almighty to save them and making Him promises. "I will be good always. I'll have no more sinful worldly lusts. I will obey and worship Thee as I should. Oh, save Joan at least—Dear God!"

After a while there came a sudden stop to the roar outside, the ship steadied a trifle. They looked at each other with fearing wonder. "Can it be over?" whispered Margaret.

"I don't know," said Jack. "We can pray so." He flexed his cramped limbs and stumbled to the brandy keg. "Here," he said dipping out a mugful. "We need it." They all drank, even Martha who seemed in this moment of general terror to have forgotten her own. Her little face was exalted. She looked as though she had some happy secret.

"That Goody Knapp!" said Jack at random, speaking to distract them. "From Silly Suffolk, like us! She sees monsters and goblins and enchanted islands, she prophesied this tempest because she says we've a Jonah aboard."

Martha drew a sharp little breath, and fixed her hollow eyes on her husband.

"How interesting," said Mirabelle, easing herself and shaking out her hair. "Who could the Jonah be? Not me, I hope. Some of the good women below do not like me because their husbands do."

"No, not you," said Jack, smiling faintly. "She's fixed on some wretched sailor her goodman ran foul of."

"Jonah had to be thrown into the sea because he was wicked, didn't he?" asked Martha in a quick breathless voice.

Jack assented, relived that she spoke and looked brighter. Elizabeth was not relieved. She heard a note in Martha's voice that escaped the others, but had no time to think of it, for the lull abruptly ceased. The wind swooped down with a roar more violent than before, and fear returned.

The poundings and crashings and terrifying lurches resumed. Though protected by horn frames, the candles guttered wildly and went out. In darkness and silence now their bodies were rolled or pitched about in the saloon. Sea and rain water deluged them through a dozen leaks. Time blurred and stopped. In Elizabeth's mind ran strange fancies. She thought of her packets of seeds lying patiently in the hold wishful of turning into bright flowers in the new land. She saw them blooming as they would have been, the hollyhocks, the marigolds, the violets and wall-flowers. How sad for them that they must lie forever barren at the bottom of the sea. She thought of Harry, and saw his golden laughing face, his reckless swagger. She saw his finger lift as though he beckoned, and she cried to him, "Nay, Harry, nay. We are not ready yet, your child and I!" Harry dissolved and in her head she heard music. The singing of many voices very pure and low, not as the Puritans twanged through their noses, but as she had once heard St. Paul's choir in London long ago. Yet it *was* a psalm the voices sang. *"If I take the wings of the morning, and dwell in the uttermost parts of the sea; even there shall thy hand lead me, and thy right hand shall hold me . . ."* The voices sang like chiming bells that ended in a jangle, when her outer ears caught a new sound. She started, and stiffened as her mind cleared. It was the sound of shouting outside the door Jack had bolted against the waves.

"Ahoy! Ahoy! Are ye all right in there?"

Jack threw open the door, and the Captain staggered in holding a lantern. His face was glistening and haggard, but he smiled at them. "Thanks be to God, it's passed over," he shouted. "I believe we've weathered it. Can ye leave the women?" he asked Jack. "I need every man on deck. 'Alf the mainmast's gone, the longboat's stove in, and part o' the fo'castle, and the main 'atch is jammed, but we're still afloat!"

"We're all right," cried Elizabeth, and rushed to light their candles at the Captain's lantern. Margaret began to cry softly. Martha was curled in a corner of the benches with her head in her ams and did not look up as Jack went off with the Captain.

The sea dropped rapidly, and the stars came out brilliant in a chilly sky. Presently Jack came back and said they had unjammed the hatch and released those below decks, all of whom had survived. The carpenters were at work and there was no more to be done till daylight. They had better go to bed.

The women obeyed. Elizabeth tumbled into her bunk with Joan, and after one great sob of thanksgiving fell instantly asleep. She was shaken awake an hour later in the dawn light to see Jack standing by the bunk and more fear in his face than there had been through the tempest.

"Bess—" he said, "Bess—Martha's gone. I can't find her. She went while I slept, but her going roused me. I've searched the poop."

Elizabeth gasped and jumped to her feet. They rushed together through the companionway and down to the quarter-deck, where the helmsman stared. They looked down on the main deck and saw figures, two carpenters hammering on the longboat, and near them, also working, Elizabeth recognized the lad William Hallet. She clutched Jack's arm and cried, "Look!"

The saw a little figure, in gray, slip along the deck from behind the broken mainmast. It paused an instant by Hallet who was next the starboard rail, and seemed to speak to him. Then, as Jack shouted "*Martha!*" the girl turned and waved, throwing her arms above her head, and darting through the partly shattered rail, plunged into the sea.

Jack flew down the stairs with Elizabeth after him. He dashed across the deck, but young Hallet was quicker. He dove in almost as Martha hit the water and grabbed her floating hair as she came up. "Throw me a rope—" he yelled. The carpenters came running with the boat hook and its attached line. Jack seized it and heaved it out. The lad caught it, they pulled him in, and Jack, held by the men, clambered down the side until he could grab his wife from the boy's clutch and haul her up and onto the deck, where she lay in a swoon, breathing heavily. Hallet climbed up and vaulted onto the deck. He stood panting and looking down at Martha. "She spoke to me, just before she—she did it," he whispered. "Said she was a Jonah. Everyone'd be happy when she'd gone. Poor little thing."

Jack took the lad's hand and shook it. "Thanks be to God you were there and can swim," he cried. "Get some dry things on."

He picked Martha up and carried her across the deck to the poop stairs. Elizabeth, who was trembling so she could hardly stand, cried, "Jack, shall I change her clothes and heat her some sack?"

"No," he answered grimly. "I will deal with her myself. Don't interfere with me, Bess, and don't leave your cabin, no matter what you hear!" He mounted the stairs and stalked back to the saloon with his burden. He forced brandy through Martha's lips until she sighed and opened her eyes. She gazed up at his grim face with a remote wonder.

"My love—" she said. "My love. I thought never to see you again."

"Why did you do it, Martha? *Why* did you do it?"

"Because you don't love me, and because I am guilty—guilty—"

"Hush!" he said. "I do love you, and we are all guilty. We have each one been saved from death this terrible night. I don't know what for, unless it is to learn the meaning of life." He downed a mugful of brandy, gave her some. He carried her to their cabin, where he ripped off her wet clothes, dried her with the blanket, and lay down with her in her bunk. He pulled her roughly into his arms.

PART TWO

Massachusetts
Bay Colony

1631–1640

8

ON THE LYON, the next morning after the tempest, the sun shone, and a light northerly breeze gave the ship steerage way, but permitted most of the crew to join in the repairs. Mr. Eliot held a solemn Thanksgiving on deck, then went to bed exhausted. Most of the passengers slept all day, including Martha, but when Elizabeth went to her sister's cabin at twilight, the girl was awake, and greeted Elizabeth with a smile.

"Bess," she said softly, "I've been living in black shadows a long time, haven't I? I don't remember much."

"Don't try." Elizabeth kissed the thin cheek, rejoicing that all strain and wildness had left Martha's face.

"I know what I tried to do," said the girl quickly taking Elizabeth's hand, "but now I don't know why, or remember all that happened last night, except the tempest and I had much brandy—and Jack—Jack—" She colored and stopped. "He does love me."

"Yes," said Elizabeth steadily. "I think you are at last truly his wife. I'm very glad. Now why don't you get up and make yourself pretty? We're to sup soon and the Captain's ordered a boiled suet pudding stuffed with raisins to celebrate our safety!" Still she spoke to Martha as a child, for still she so appeared and had always acted.

But Martha gave her a long grave look that was not childish, and said, "You're good to me, Bess. You've all had patience with me. I hope there is not talk about—about what happened on the deck. I wouldn't have you shamed."

"There'll be no talk," said Elizabeth. "Jack's spoken to the carpenters, the helmsman and the young lad who—" She paused, wondering if Martha remembered the boy who had saved her, and knew instinctively that she did not. "A lad who was also there," she continued. "Jack told them you were distracted by the tempest. It was a night of extraordinary happenings which everyone wants to forget."

"Aye," said Martha quickly. She swung her thin legs over the bunk. "Do you suppose Lady Gardiner would help me dress my hair like hers? It's so becoming."

Elizabeth laughed. "I'm sure she'd be delighted. And lend you rouge and beauty patches too if you'd be so brazen."

The supper was festive. The breeze continuing light, and all repairs going forward rapidly, Captain Peirce honored them with his presence. Martha was transformed, not only by Mirabelle's handiwork but by a soft glow as she sat beside Jack, who kept looking at her with open tenderness. Only Elizabeth knew and Margaret guessed that this was the true beginning of their honeymoon, yet all were conscious of manifold dangers passed and the richness of their escape. They drank some of the Captain's excellent sack. Elizabeth longed for her lute, but Jack had a jew's-harp to set the pitch, and they sang together—ballads, love songs and country songs in which the young minister joined heartily.

Elizabeth was deeply grateful for her sister's recovery, and the assuaged look in Jack's eyes, and she went to bed happy. Yet in the middle of the night she awoke to find that she was weeping, and knew that she had been crying in her dreams. "I am a simpleton," she said aloud, but softly so as not to wake Mary who was snoring in the upper bunk. She put her arms around Joan and drew the baby's head onto her breast. Joan snuggled down, and presently they both slept.

Five days later the *Lyon* arrived at the Grand Banks which were swathed in the usual fog, and the Captain hove to so that the sailors might fish for the cod of which they stood in great need. Provisions were growing scanty, and even the Captain's mess was reduced to half rations of salt beef and pease for every meal. There were several cases of scurvy in the hold, and much coughing and sniffles, for the weather had turned bitter, and there was no way to get warm but lie in sour, verminous bedding, or to fight for place near the cooking hearth.

Peirce relaxed rules during the fishing, and Elizabeth profited by this to wander over the ship. She was tired of confinement, anxious to forget hunger pangs, and wishful of finding William Hallet.

The catch was good, and she picked her way amongst fishing lines and a mass of flopping silvery bodies. Finally she spied Hallet near the fo'castle. He was fishing too. He had hooked a large cod, his young face was intent, his big body leaned far out as he dextrously played his fish, and jerked it over the rail to land with a watery smack at her feet. He cried, "Careful, wench! You'll get hooked yourself if you stand so near!" Then he saw who it was, and said, "Pardon, Mistress Winthrop."

"Good day," she said, smiling. "What a big fish . . . I wanted . . . I've been wanting to . . . to thank you . . . for the . . . what you did . . . that night . . ." She knew that she was stammering, and that her constraint came from more than embarrassment at referring to Martha's near tragedy. He was years younger than she, only a common lad, and yet somehow he made her feel like a green girl.

"I don't want thanks, Mistress," he said coolly, while he cut off his fish's head with his knife. "Mr. Winthrop's loaded me with thanks, and five pounds too, which I wouldn't have."

"Why not?" she cried. "You deserve it. And surely five pounds would help you get settled in New England."

"I wouldn't take money for a thing like that." He spoke with anger. "You're like all the gentry, think you can buy a man body and soul for silver. I'll make my own way and work for what I earn."

She was discomfited. The gay intimacy which had sprung between them the first time was gone.

"Will," she said after a moment of watching him bait his hook, "why do you speak so sharp? Isn't it natural that I should thank you for saving my little sister's life?"

He looked at her slowly as she stood beside him in her thick crimson wool cloak, her dark curls wet with fog beneath the hood, her nose red from cold, her long hazel eyes troubled.

"The sharpness wasn't for you," he said casting his line out. His tawny hair, salt-crusted, and uncombed, swung forward to hide his face as he peered down into the water.

"For what then?" she persisted. "Won't you tell me? You're overyoung to be so grim."

"By God, Mistress—" he said suddenly turning on her. "Grimness has naught to do with years. You speak like the sheltered ninny, no doubt you are!"

"And you—" she cried, stiffening, "speak like the boorish rustic, no doubt *you* are!"

At this he laughed suddenly, a boyish peal, not quite steady. "Touché," he said, to her amazement. "A neat thrust. I see I must make amends."

"The best amends you can make is to tell me how you come to speak in fencing terms, and use words like 'amends' which fit strangely with your clothes and general carriage. Are you perchance some young lord in disguise?"

"Far from it!" he snorted. "I'm a yeoman, at least I come of yeoman stock. We Hallets've farmed Dorset lands back to Domesday, and the Devil take me if I'd be anything else!" He peered over the side at his line floating limply on the waves, and said with a mixture of gentleness and impatience, "Look, ma'am. There's no mystery. You'll have my tale in a trice. I spent six years as page in the household of the Earl of Bristol at Sherborne Castle. I lived with his children, the young Digbys. I was tutored by their tutor, and befriended— for a time—by Lord George, the heir."

"Ah. . . ." she said staring at him. "I see now." That explained his speech, and flashes of a manner which had reminded her of the few noblemen she had met. "But was that not an unusual honor for a yeoman?"

"Very." He folded his arms and leaned against the bulwark. His face darkened. "The way it came about was not so unusual. While the Earl of Bristol was in Spain, chaffering for that Infanta King Charles thought he wanted, my father one black day did ride to Sherborne Fair on his blooded bay stallion. A bay stallion just like it was missing from the castle stables. The Earl's steward spied my father, convinced himself and Sherborne town that my father had stolen the Earl's horse. Father was hanged in the marketplace that night."

At her gasp he nodded ironically. "The Earl's stallion was found some days later, peacefully grazing in a pasture whither it had escaped, and the Earl came home, heard the story and was shocked. He dismissed the steward and set out to find my mother and make restitution. My older brother had the farm, and Mother, poor woman, could think of nothing better to ask than that I should be raised a fine gentleman. And so I was, from my eighth to my fourteenth year."

"But then? What then?" Elizabeth cried as he peered over at his fishing line and seemed to have finished. "Surely you're not fourteen now!"

"I'll be sixteen come Christmastide." He paused, and went on reluctantly. "Why, then I overheard the Countess talking to her cousin. My lady said she had enough of me, that I made too free with her daughters—which was a lie—and had forgot my station—which might be true. She said that since I should take up a trade and showed a peasant skill with my hands, she'd 'prentice me to a joiner in Dorchester. I thought in my folly that Lord George would speak for me, he and I'd been good friends, but he was roistering merrily at Magdalen College, and never answered my letter. So I went to be a joiner, as I told you, and I liked it not. After a year I ran from my master to my brother at our homefarm."

"Then your mother helped you?" Elizabeth asked eagerly.

"My mother was frightened, and ashamed of the way things turned out—and my brother told me roundly I'd become neither fish, flesh, nor good red herring, which when I cooled off I saw the sense of. Our farms were prospering, and he gave me a share of my inheritance, forty pounds, and said I'd best be off quietly before my master caught me, then make my way as I liked in the world. And so I am."

Elizabeth was silent. She understood now his truculence and touchy pride. She saw that in the end the noble Bristols had done injustice twice over, not only in killing his father, but in dislocating William's life to no purpose, and wounding his confidence and self-esteem. But he was strong, intelligent and able, he might well find fulfillment in the new country.

"Thank you," she said, "for telling me, Will. I see why it was painful." His big chilblained dirty hand rested on the bulwark, and without thinking she put her gloved hand over his. "I hope to see you again after we land."

He grew scarlet, staring at her hand, and she thought he would snatch his hand away. Instead he turned it and carried her hand to his lips. "I think not, Mistress," he said gruffly. "I'll not tarry in Boston." He tucked her hand inside her cloak, a strangely tender little gesture. "I see we're setting sail. You'd best return to the poop." He gathered up his line and went into the fo'castle. She did not see him to speak to again.

After they left the Banks, northeast gales began to blow, but the passengers were all so accustomed to storms that these gave only satisfaction, for they hastened the interminable voyage. In the tenth week of it, Elizabeth was roused one morning by a pandemonium of shouts and the clear voice of the watch calling above the racket, "Land Ho! Land Ho!"

She threw on her cloak and rushed to the stern gallery where she saw some leagues to the west a dark wooded mound, which the Captain presently explained was an island named Mount Desert by a French explorer.

From then on they were in distant sight of land, and taking soundings every half hour, as the *Lyon* slipped down the coast past places Peirce called Agamenticus and Piscataqua; uncouth Indian names which interested Elizabeth and John Eliot particularly, though there was nothing to be seen but forest. On Halloween they rounded Cape Ann, and Goody Knapp took to prophesying again in honor of the day. She said she saw goblins with fiery heads bouncing amongst the rocks on shore, and heard the shriek of specters on the night wind. This was reported to the Captain who replied that the goblin lights were lanterns on fishing shallops near Gloucester, and as for spectral shrieks, he wished he could hear some himself for they might be a useful warning of reefs.

The next day they sailed past Salem, though too far out to see anything, and Elizabeth thought of Harry's death there. Her heart was heavy, for she found that she could no longer recall his face clearly.

On the following evening, Wednesday, November 2 of that year 1631, the *Lyon* being unable to enter Boston Harbor against a strong west wind dropped anchor in the Nantasket Roads, and lowered the longboat. At dawn of the next day Jack clambered down the rope ladder into the boat and was rowed the six miles to Boston to give news of their arrival.

It was a dazzling blue and gold morning. The air felt crisper and seemed thinner than it did in England. The passengers, all but those too sick with scurvy, were crowded on deck, mostly silent as they stared at the multitude of little islands. Captain Peirce showed the poop passengers a desolate stony beach to the east which he said was a peninsula called Nantasket. He pointed south to the mainland where he said there were villages, Wessagussett or Weymouth, and the deserted remains of Mount Wollaston where the lewd, raffish

Thomas Morton had shocked Plymouth Colony with May Day revels at his home, Merrymount.

"So it was *there* he so naughtily put up his maypole?" asked Mirabelle with lively interest. "I met him in London, where these Puritans had banished him. He was so enraged about it, poor man. He is a friend of my husband's," she added.

"I know, m'lady," said Peirce, chuckling. Mirabelle, dressed in embroidered green velvet, with her flaming hair, décolletage and daring beauty patch, was certain to produce quite an effect on Boston, especially if Sir Christopher were still in gaol. But the young lady could take care of herself; of that the Captain had grown very sure in these weeks.

He looked at the Winthrop women, also dressed in their elegant, brightly colored best, and felt satisfaction. They were thinner than when they sailed, of course, there were some scurvy sores around Mistress Mary's lips, and Mistress Winthrop Senior's plump cheeks had sagged, but none of them looked too peaked.

"Journey's end, ladies!" he cried to them. "Barring that tempest, and considering the time o' year, not so bad a passage—eh? Oh, and your loss, ma'am—" he added hastily to Margaret. "Ye know 'ow sorry I am for that." He had momentarily forgotten the death of two sickly children at sea, so usual were such occurrences, but it was unfortunate that one of them was the Governor's baby.

"I marvel at your skill and excellent care of us, Mr. Peirce," said Margaret gently. "We all thank you from our hearts." Her voice trembled. It was hard in these last moments of suspense to keep from tears. *They* had finally arrived safely, but who knew what might have been happening here in the seven months since John's last letter to them left Boston on this same *Lyon*.

"How far away England seems," whispered Martha, pressing close to Elizabeth, who was leaning on the rail, ecstatically sniffing the pine and earth smell. "It seems so strange to see no houses, and I never expected it, yet I dread to leave this dear old ship . . . Oh, what's that!" she ended with a little shriek.

Elizabeth looked where her sister pointed and saw a birch-bark canoe gliding near them, paddled by two feather-topped figures. "Our first savages, Mattie," Elizabeth cried, peering down.

The canoe grazed the *Lyon*, and the Indians rested their

paddles. The stern paddler was a small young Indian dressed in a blue English doublet and breeches. The doublet was lavishly trimmed with brass buttons sewn on at random. His dark face was tattooed on the cheeks and painted with ocher stripes. His head was shaved except for a long scalp lock which was stiffened with bear's grease and pierced with pheasant feathers. He wore three necklaces of dark blue shell wampum beads and one of wolf claws. His companion was far less splendid, and wore nothing but a skin mantle and breechclout.

"How!" called the first Indian raising his paddle in salute to the row of faces on the poop deck. "Netop. Friend. Call Captain!"

Peirce had gone to his quarters, but now reappeared, and recognized the Indian. "Ahoy there, Chickatabot, ye rascal!" he shouted jovially. "I'm back again, ye see. 'Ave ye beaver for me?" He turned to the gaping English. " 'Tis Sagamore Chickatabot, chief o' these regions on the Bay. Lives by the Neponset River. A good Indian. Damme if 'e 'asn't got a fine mess o' skins too." For Chickatabot was pointing to a gleaming pile of fur in the bottom of his canoe, and crying, "Trade, Trade—" while he beamed up at the Captain.

"Is he a Christian?" asked John Eliot earnestly.

"Bless ye, sir—I shouldn't think so. They believe in a kind o' Great Spirit called Manitoo, and a devil named Obbomock —that's all I know. Say, ye rogue," he called down. "Where'd ye get the English clothes?"

Chickatabot nodded complacently and ran his hands over the gleaming buttons. "Governor give," he said.

Margaret drew a sharp breath. "Ask him if the Governor's well!"

Peirce smiled and invited the Indians aboard, where communication was easier. They soon gathered that the Governor had been well when Chickatabot last saw him several sleeps ago. Margaret murmured a prayer of thanks and went to her cabin, followed by Martha who hated the way the Indians stared at the women.

Elizabeth, though intensely curious, was overpowered by the Indian smell. Not the stink of unwashed bodies, she was used enough to that on shipboard, but a heavy animal scent augmented by the rancid grease in their hair.

Captain Peirce dickered for the beaver, while Eliot fetched his writing materials and listened, occasionally interrupting to ask the meaning of an Indian word, and write it down.

Peirce finally traded three knives and six clay pipes for the skins, having sternly ignored all Chickatabot's plaintive requests for strong water. "That's *one* thing ye'd best take note of," Peirce said, eying the minister's linguistic labors with some amusement. "Spirits sets Indians wild. They've no 'ead for it. And don't give 'em firearms neither. These Massachusetts are friendly knaves, but we must keep the upper 'and."

"I shall endeavor to do that by leading the poor innocents to Christ," said Eliot smiling. "And I fear the early settlers have much wronged them."

Peirce scratched his nose and shrugged. "Mebbe so. Ye talk a'most like a parson I brought over 'ere last winter. Roger Williams 'is name was. Claimed the King 'ad no right to give the land to the English, 'cause it belonged to the Indians. Said the planters should *buy* it! Lot o' contentious ideas 'e 'ad, and Governor Winthrop wasn't pleased. Last I 'eard, Mr. Williams 'ad quitted the Bay Colony."

Elizabeth listened and was chilled. Here was still another man who had disagreed with Uncle John, and gone or been banished elsewhere. I'll *not* be afraid of him, she thought. He can't force me to do anything I don't want to. After all I am a Winthrop, and he's never been overharsh to his own family—nor, she admitted after thought—to anyone else that she knew. Yet Mirabelle had told her of a young man called Philip Ratcliffe, who had been brutally punished in Boston last June for criticizing the colony. He had had both his ears chopped off his head, and been shipped half dead to England. "They are saying in London," Mirabelle had added, "that Governor Winthrop thinks himself a king, takes the law into his own hands, and punishes all who do not see religion as he does. This I find confusing since that was précisément the Puritans' complaint against the established Church in England, when the Star Chamber chopped off *Puritan* ears."

Elizabeth also found it confusing, but thought Mirabelle dangerously outspoken.

"Don't you fear for yourself in Massachusetts?" she had asked, and Mirabelle laughed. "Ah ça, non. The Governor is a *man*, is he not?"

Elizabeth admired this superb confidence, but was unable to apply it personally. During the hours that they waited on the *Lyon*, her apprehensions grew, and were no less uncomfortable because she did not know what she feared ex-

cept her uncle's powerful will. She applied common sense to
these forebodings, telling herself that Margaret and Jack
loved Uncle John, that many of the Groton Manor folk had
too, and reminding herself that on the night of the great
tempest she had promised God—in the likeness of John
Winthrop—to be obedient, and must fulfill her vow. Yet the
unease continued, and the feeling of urgency as though she
must arm herself for battle.

It was nearly dusk before the lookout raised a cry and
they saw a large sailing shallop round the tip of Long Island.
It flew the British ensign and was crowded with men amongst
whom the Governor in black doublet trimmed with silver lace
and wearing the sword of state was easily recognized. The
Lyon set off three cannon in salute, and its passengers began
to cheer.

Margaret snatched little Sammy's hand and hurried down
to the main deck, Elizabeth carried Joan and was followed
by Martha and Mary. Mirabelle tactfully held back with
John Eliot until the family should be reunited.

The sailors and common folk ranged themselves on either
side of the gangway, where the Captain stood with the
Winthrop ladies. The bo'sun piped a patriotic tune as the
Governor was assisted up the ladder, and stepped majestically onto the deck. He shook hands with the Captain, raised
his arm slowly in greeting to all the shipload, then turned
and looked at his wife, saying in a low voice, "God bless you,
my dear. This is a happy moment."

He *has* changed, thought Elizabeth, seeing that he held
back from kissing Margaret as he had always done, and
that consciousness of his position gave him a new rigidity,
but his wife crying out, "John, my dearest—" flew into his
arms. And he did kiss her, though hurriedly, before picking
up Sammy. Their two elder sons, Stephen and Adam, scrambled on board and ran to their mother. There was a babble
of greetings and tears, but Winthrop said, glancing at the
watching crowd, "This is too public a place for reunion. Let
us adjourn to the Great Cabin."

When they were sequestered, Winthrop became more
natural. He kissed Elizabeth, Martha and Mary on the cheek.
He admired Joan, his only grandchild so far. He put Sammy
on his knee and stroked the little boy's hair. He voiced his
joy at their safe arrival, and uttered a long prayer of heart-
felt thanksgiving in an unsteady voice. Yet there was constraint about him, and he had aged. His eyes were tired,

there were deeper wrinkles on his forehead, new gray in his hair and pointed beard. When Jack proposed a toast to their reunion, he shook his head. "No, my son, I no longer drink to anyone. It is frivolous and leads to inebriety. In fact I take no spirits nor tobacco now. I would prefer that my family didn't. Remember we set an example to the entire colony, and there is no sanction in Scriptures for strong waters, or smoking."

Jack put down his mug of weak brandy, and ventured to say, "There is none for beer either, sir, is there?"

"Precisely," answered Winthrop. "So I do not drink it, though I have not yet been able to enforce this view."

I should hope not, thought Jack dismayed. To deprive English folk of beer would be as galling as to forbid them bread.

"Mr. Dudley, my deputy, combats me in this as in other matters," continued Winthrop heavily. "Sometimes I feel he does not heed God's clear directions as he should, yet ever pray that Mr. Dudley and I shall work together in Christian love."

Jack was not at the moment interested in Thomas Dudley, so unpleasant did he find his father's new convictions of the need for total abstinence. "But sir—" he cried, "Our Lord Jesus drank wine, and Paul said 'Use a little wine for thy stomach's sake.' "

"For thy stomach's sake, not for pleasure," answered Winthrop, but he suddenly smiled, the rare sweet smile that few had seen. "Come, my son. This is no time for argument. You will do as conscience bids you. Where is the young minister, John Eliot? We're in sore need of him to preach in Boston, since Mr. Wilson is now in England."

Eliot was brought into the cabin, and conferred some time with Winthrop, and then after some hesitations and throat clearings, Captain Peirce produced Mirabelle. "Lady Gardiner, Your Worship. The first—that is, I mean to say, the *French* wife o' Sir Christopher."

Elizabeth barely suppressed giggles, when she saw Mirabelle who had had ample opportunity on deck to size up the Governor and whose female instincts were infallible. From Elizabeth's cabin she had filched a large demure collar which completely hid all the charms she usually displayed. She had braided her fiery hair and covered most of it with a kerchief. She had removed her lip paint. She walked in with downcast eyes, and curtseying low to Winthrop, seized his hand and kissed it. "Oh, your most honorable Excellency—" she faltered in a melting voice, "Do you know where is my so wicked husband, who has broken my poor heart?"

Margaret looked astonished, not having hitherto received this impression, but she chimed in kindly, "Poor Lady Gardiner."

Winthrop's face darkened at Gardiner's name. Sir Christopher had caused Winthrop and Governor Bradford at Plymouth much anxious embarrassment. Gardiner had been exposed as a Papist and also as a spy for the wicked Sir Ferdinando Gorges who sat comfortably in England and plotted to seize all the country from Virginia to Quebec for himself. Yet Gorges had much noble backing, and Winthrop had not dared punish Sir Christopher as he deserved. Winthrop examined Mirabelle searchingly, and she gave him a lovely tremulous smile. He stood up and raised her from her curtsey. "You've come in search of your husband, my lady?" he said, his voice softening.

As Mirabelle nodded, he went on. "My dear, I sorrow to tell you this, but he has gone, fled north to the country above Piscataqua that Sir Ferdinando Gorges claims—Agamenticus. I had Sir Christopher in detention here for—well; no matter—I would not cause you added pain. But he escaped, with the help of his—h'm—of a young woman who claimed to be his cousin."

"Ah, quelle misère . . ." cried Mirabelle who had listened attentively, and she burst into most becoming tears.

"There, there," said the Governor patting her shoulder, and looking helplessly at Margaret. "Pray don't weep. We'll take care of you here, as long as you'll stay. I'm sure we can find room." He checked himself, for in his unfinished Boston house there was certainly not room in view of all these new arrivals. "I'll place you with some gently bred family who will respect your rank, your beauteous youth and your unhappiness. I shall personally interest myself in your welfare."

"How kind, how good you are!" cried Mirabelle, sending Elizabeth the tiniest flicker from the corner of her eye, that said, You see how easy it is to manage him.

Elizabeth saw, and resolved that she would profit by the lesson. She too if need arose would be all soft pathos and tender submission. She would coax, flatter and weep; her future would be easy, she would gain the freedom for which she yearned; she would find new love, true love, at last and would marry when and as she pleased, but first perhaps she could enjoy herself in the adventurous new land.

Yet not an hour passed before all her resolutions were forgotten. Winthrop was to spend the night on board, but before he retired with Margaret, his respect for both ceremony and family ties prompted him to private interviews with his daughter Mary and his two daughters-in-law. He seated himself in the Captain's chair and summoned the girls one by one, while the rest of the company chatted at the far end of the cabin.

Elizabeth saw Mary's serious face lighten with a contented smile while her father spoke with her. Martha blushed and looked delighted when Winthrop bade her officially welcome as his daughter-in-law, saying that he was sure she would make Jack a loyal wife.

Elizabeth's turn came last. She chided herself for previous anxiety when her uncle took the reluctant Joan from her arms and settled the child on his knee, saying "Nay, nay, poppet. You must not startle at your grandsir," and he bounced Joan up and down and let her play with the silver buttons on his doublet. "She's something like Henry, Bess, is she not?" He said with a sigh, "You will have seen from my letters, how deeply I felt for you in that terrible affliction the Lord sent us all."

"Yes, my uncle," she said softly.

"You do not call me 'Father'?" he asked in faint reproof. "Yet that is what I am to you now, and I've thought long for your future, as a father should."

Elizabeth stiffened, she felt her heart beat, yet remembered enough of Mirabelle's example to lower her lids and say meekly, "Aye, my father, you are ever wise."

The lass had matured, thought Winthrop, gratified. God through affliction had much improved her. She was a trifle pinched and wan from the voyage, but still an exceptionally pretty woman, and her new suitor would certainly not repent of his generosity.

"I was sorry to hear that you displeased Mr. Coddington," he said, but kindly. "I thought the match most suitable."

"He displeased *me*—" she began, then bit her lips. "I'm sorry, sir, that you were disappointed."

"No matter, it was doubtless the Lord's all-seeing providence, for this match will do as well."

Elizabeth's chin jerked up, she looked Winthrop full in the eye. "This WHAT, sir?"

"Why, this match, this marriage I have consented to for you. You must have known I've worried about your situation, and would try to better it. Yet so few men in the colony are eligible. Mr. Robert Feake is—a young bachelor, church member, gentleman, and sufficiently well off to overlook the —the—well—smallness of your marriage portion."

Elizabeth clasped her hands and pressed them hard against her chest. "It matters not that I've never heard of this Mr. Fick, I suppose?"

Winthrop looked genuinely puzzled. "But he knows you. He speaks as though he'd formed a deep attachment for you. I assumed you had been in correspondence."

"You assumed wrong!" she snapped and clenched her hands tighter, for they were trembling.

Her tone was rude and Winthrop's benignity faded. He put Joan on the floor, eying Elizabeth's flushed face coldly. "Whether you know him or not, is immaterial since you soon will. And I'm sure find him to your liking if the Devil does not tempt you into your old stubborn, headstrong ways. The matter has been arranged, and I know what's best for you."

"You don't. You *don't!*" she cried so wildly that the group at the other end of the cabin all turned their heads. Joan stared from her mother to her grandfather and began to wail. Winthrop rose, trying to master the uprush of anger which foolish opposition roused. They looked at each other with the mutual antagonism which had always been latent, and Elizabeth's eyes fell first.

"We'll speak no more of this tonight," Winthrop said harshly. "I pray God will bring you to a better frame of mind, but in any case, the matter is decided." He turned on his heel and walked over to the others.

A flood of bewildered rage and fear choked in her throat as it had fourteen years ago at Groton, but she was twenty-one now and could not scream that she hated God, or run away, or swoon as she had then.

She sat on the bench staring at a crack between the boards, until Martha came over to her. "Bess, dear—what is it? How did you offend our father?"

"Leave me alone, Matt," Elizabeth turned from her sister. "I must think—think what to do."

The next morning the wind had veered to the east and blew them chilly rain, but it also filled the *Lyon's* sails and the ship glided slowly through the islands and dropped anchor in Boston Harbor.

The Captain ordered the longboat launched and handed the entire Winthrop family into it. He embarked himself, while the *Lyon* fired off seven cannon shots to apprise those on shore of the Governor's arrival.

Elizabeth was silent in the boat as she had been all morning before entering it. Through the night she had considered many fantastic plans for defeating Winthrop, but sober dawn had shown her that none were immediately feasible, and she had Joan to consider. There was nothing to do but wait until she understood conditions in Boston, found out exactly what had become of her four hundred pounds, and try at least to control the situation without panic. But the inner turmoil precluded normal excitement over landing at last. She glanced almost indifferently at the misty silhouette of a three-mounded hill, and what seemed to be a cluster of small wooden huts near it, then back to the *Lyon*. The decks were filled with impatient passengers, who would presently be ferried to shore, and as she looked she saw William Hallet, hanging over the rail. He extended his arm in a wave, quickly checked, as though he'd thought better of it. She was too dejected to wave back, but the Governor's sharp eyes had seen, and he turned to the Captain in surprise. "Was that long lad in the Monmouth cap waving at us? It seems very forward."

"I believe 'e was, sir—" said Peirce. " 'Tis a young joiner from Dorset, very popular on board, and 'andy with our repairs after the tempest."

"Indeed. An indentured servant, I presume. We've had trouble with them. They turn lewd and brazen over here."

" 'E's no servant, sir," said Peirce. "Paid 'is own passage money, and talks a'most like a gentleman. Just a lad who wanted a change o' scene."

Winthrop frowned. Footloose youths were not desirable members of the colony, but he dropped the topic, and began to show Margaret various landmarks ahead. The hill to the left where he intended to build a fort, as soon as possible, if Dudley would stop palisading Newtown across the Charles, and belligerently insisting that Newtown should be the capital. He showed her Trimount, the three-mounded hill, where they kept a sentry posted, and would burn a warning bonfire in case of danger, and another hill where he hoped that Jack would help erect a windmill.

"And our house?" asked Margaret faintly, gazing through the drizzle at the bleak, treeless peninsula.

"There," said Winthrop pointing. "On the flat near the meetinghouse. Oh, we've near a score fine wood houses built, as you will see. Mr. Coddington, he's started one of brick too, will finish it when he returns from England." He glanced at Elizabeth's set, withdrawn face, shadowed by the hood, and his lips tightened.

"I'm sure it looks like a sweet town," said Margaret hastily. During the night she had heard of Elizabeth's graceless behavior, and of John's many other worries too. But she had finally managed to soothe him, and he had slept in her arms.

The boat pulled up at a wooden pier, near which were crowded all the Bostonians and many from Newtown, Roxbury and Charlestown as well. The young men of the militia or train bands had drawn up in formation and now fired ceremonious volleys of gunshot into the air. They had organized a fife and drum corps which began to play. Their captains, Underhill and Patrick, in polished armor, and plumed helmets, stood bowing at the head of the ladder. There were cheers and huzzahs and "God Bless You's," as Margaret stepped up behind her husband to the pier. Elizabeth followed with Joan. She did not look at the mass of curious, respectful, welcoming faces. She watched four halberdiers step up to Winthrop and range themselves importantly before him, also a liveried beadle who carried the Charter in a long leather box. Winthrop said a few words to the people. He raised his hand and his procession formed.

The captains and the train bands started marching two by two. After them the halberdiers, the Governor's guard of honor, then James Penn, the beadle, with the Charter which preceded Winthrop on every ceremonial occasion, as a reminder of the authority invested in the Governor. Winthrop drew Margaret's hand through his arm, and indicated to Jack that he and Martha should follow, and the other members of the family—in strict order of precedence. They all fell in and solemnly trudged up the muddy lane. "Journey's end" indeed, Elizabeth thought as she marched. I have now arrived in the free, the glorious new land.

The muddy lane was called King Street, and ended at the temporary church, a small thatched building with clay-daubed walls and no steeple. It stood at the junction with the High Street which led off the neck to Roxbury. But they did not march as far as the church before a portly gentleman on horseback came hurrying to meet them. It was the Deputy

Governor, Thomas Dudley, and the procession halted while he rode up to Winthrop.

"Beg pardon for my tardiness, sir," he said snatching off his black felt hat, "I was delayed at the ferry. Welcome, Madame," he said to Margaret. "I trust the voyage was not too arduous."

She made a polite reply and gave him her usual sweet smile, but having heard from John of the constant friction between them, she decided that the man had a truculent coarse look. His jowled face was red above a grizzled beard. His swollen nose was laced with tiny purple veins. His rumpled brown cloak and mud-spattered boots exhibited none of John's nice elegance.

"Will you dine with me in Newtown, Mistress Winthrop?" Dudley went on brusquely, " 'Tis where you should be anyhow, and will, soon as the Governor's finished his house there. 'Tis the right place for our capital."

"I do not think so, sir," Winthrop snapped. "I prefer it here, and don't intend to settle in Newtown."

"You *agreed* to!" cried Dudley, beginning to breathe hard. His son Samuel, who was an officer in Underhill's train band, seeing that his father was working into a choler, broke ranks and hurried up.

"His Worship's family must be cold standing in the rain, my father," he said quietly. "Shall I help you dismount?"

"No, Sam," said Dudley controlling himself. "If the Governor and Mrs. Winthrop'll excuse me, I have business in Muddy River." He bowed, jerked the bridle and rode to the High Street. Sam Dudley gave Margaret an apologetic smile, and stared at the girls, especially Elizabeth, before he returned to his men.

"Young Dudley seems a courteous personable gentleman," remarked Mary, vaguely astounding Elizabeth who had never heard Mary praise any young man, but she was far too chilly and despondent to answer.

The procession reformed and presently turned left down a cross lane. It stopped before a rush-thatched, clapboarded house two stories high but otherwise about the size and shape of the wash-house at Groton. The windows had shutters but no glass. On the door made of three planks of unseasoned wood, little drops of sap had formed and mingled with the rain drops. The house stood starkly in a sea of mud and trampled weeds.

"Our New England home, my dear," said Winthrop. "I

pray God will bless it, and make it a happy one."

Margaret pressed his arm, touched by his pride, aware of pathos too in the brave little procession, and John's obvious pleasure in the honor the people accorded him, but as she looked at her new home she was appalled. Could he have so soon forgotten Groton that he really thought this ugly cot a fine house! And it seemed that he had forgotten other things too. She had been shocked in the night to find that, after all, the churches here had patterned themselves after the Separatist Colony at Plymouth, and that they allowed no man the franchise unless he first became a church member and publicly attested to his salvation. There had been no plans so radical for the colony when John left England.

Winthrop dismissed his guard and the family filed into the house, which was indeed large for Boston, since it had two twenty-foot rooms in front and behind the central chimney. One was the Hall and the other the kitchen. Upstairs the space had been divided into four. Above that was a dark garret where the unmarried maidservants slept on pallets. The indentured male servants lived in a hut near the house.

The Hall contained a long trestle table piled with offerings sent from all over the colony to greet the Governor's family. There was poultry—partridges and geese, some unplucked, some already cooked; a haunch of venison, apples, and a large cheese. Margaret gave an unfeigned cry of delight when she saw this, and Winthrop smiled complacently. "You see what joyous manifestation of love my people show me!" he said. "It is a great marvel that such store of provisions could be gathered together at so few hours' warning."

To Elizabeth this speech was smug but her mouth watered as she looked at the food, and the gnawing in her stomach became so intense that she forgot her other problems until her uncle said, "We will eat nothing until certain guests have arrived—fasting is one of God's most skillful means to chastise the flesh—Mr. Feake will dine here, Elizabeth, and I command that you treat him agreeably."

"I trust I know my duty to all your guests, sir," she said, and went upstairs to the room she would share with Mary. It was furnished with a crude wooden bedstead, roped for support of the bedding they had brought on the ship. There were two stools and nothing else. Though the servants had strewn a thick man of rushes over the floor, it was very cold. Elizabeth opened the window shutter and saw that the rain had stopped, patches of blue showed amongst the clouds.

She sat down shivering on the stool and nursed Joan, then carried the child next door to Martha and Jack's room, which was warmer, since it and the elder Winthrops' room had a fireplace. "Keep Joanie for me, Matt," she said. She shut the door on Martha's anxious questions and went downstairs to the Hall, where she eyed the lavish display of food, hesitated, and cut herself a slice of cheese. She devoured it avidly, ate an apple, picked up a cold roast partridge and ate that.

She was sucking the last of its bones when John walked in with Margaret. Elizabeth was unable to control a guilty jump, and the childish impulse to hide the partridge leg behind her back, as Winthrop said in an icy voice, "I ordered that no food be eaten until the guests arrive."

Margaret stepped forward quickly. "Indeed, John, you are too harsh. Bess needs strength for suckling her babe, and we have none of us eaten our fill in weeks. I too am famished."

Winthrop looked startled. So accustomed had he become to ruling every detail of his household and the colony that any doubts as to his judgment no longer troubled him. But with Margaret he was never unjust, and he said, "My dear, no doubt you're right. Eat then, since you have such need." He turned to Elizabeth, his eyes hardening again. "Why have you your cloak on? I told you to make yourself ready for our company."

"There is nothing I can do, sir, since my chests have not yet been delivered from the *Lyon*. I wish to go outside and walk a bit, I've been so long confined."

"True," cried Margaret before her husband could speak. "Exercise will benefit you, but be back soon."

As Elizabeth escaped, Margaret said in a low troubled voice, "John, be gentle with her, as you are with the rest of us. She's not of a nature to be forced."

"And why not? Since it is for her own good, and the child must be obedient to the father. You're quick to plead for her, my dear wife, but forget that her immortal soul is imperiled by the faults she shows. Has she talked to you of her salvation? Is she one of the elect? Has the Lord Jesus marked her for Himself?"

Margaret sighed, having often worried over Elizabeth's lack of piety. "I believe not, but she will come to Him in time, for He is a loving God."

"He is a God of Wrath when He is mocked," said Winthrop grimly.

Elizabeth wandered down King Street towards the pier until she could see the *Lyon* rocking at anchor in the harbor. It would sail again in a fortnight. But how could I get on her? Elizabeth thought. Not as a stowaway, concealment was impossible on that ship. As a passenger then? But who would pay her fare? And even were she to get aboard in some way, what awaited her in England? Ignominious shelter by the Downings, the butt of Aunt Lucy's carping. Elizabeth thought seriously of Mirabelle's method of living as she pleased. I'm comely enough, she thought, but how did one get started? How find men who lavished presents on one, and yet were as complaisant as Mirabelle's lovers seemed to have been.

Even as Elizabeth considered this, she grew more discouraged. For she had neither Mirabelle's temperament nor upbringing. Besides there was Joan.

She turned and walked back up the lane, the cold mud squelching under her shoes, but now that her stomach was full, she no longer shivered. She met two young menservants, who started to accost her, when one murmured to the other, "Wintrup!" They touched their foreheads in respect and passed on. A goodwife in homespun cape came hurrying out of a tiny shop, whose bootshaped sign proclaimed a cordwainer. She stared at Elizabeth, and curtseyed, saying, "Good day, Mistress Wintrup, I saw ye land."

Elizabeth nodded. So already everyone knew who she was. On the green before the meetinghouse there was a puny man standing in pillory, his head and arms thrust through the holes between the locked boards. There was a large placard on his back with the letter B on it in red. He was groaning feebly and shuffling his feet to ease his tortured muscles. Elizabeth paused. They had stocks in the churchyard at Groton, but she had never seen them used; petty crimes had been fined, and serious ones sent to Hadleigh for punishment.

"Goodwife—" called the man in pillory, seeing only her skirt and feet because his head was vised downward. "In mercy will ye tell me what o'clock it is?"

"About two, past noon, I think," said Elizabeth gently, and as the man groaned again, muttering "Lord help me," she said with pity, "How much longer have you to stand there, poor soul?"

"Till sundown. The pain's so bad now, I doubt I can bear it."

She saw that as he was a short man and the pillory too

high for him, he was virtually hanging by his neck. She also saw a bit of plank leaning against an unfinished house across the High Street. She went and got the plank and put it under his feet.

"God bless ye—lass," he whispered, with a long sobbing sigh, as some of the strain eased. "I hope nobody saw ye do it."

"No," she said. There was nobody in sight but some children playing ball near the town pump. "Forgive me, but why are you pilloried? What does the B stand for?"

"Not buggery," he said with a bitter laugh, "or they'd 've hanged me. The B's for Blasphemy, you must be strange here not to know."

"I am," she said, "and sad to find Boston stricter than ever Suffolk was."

"That's it!" he cried, trying to twist his head to see her. "That was my blasphemy. D'ye know what I said? I said I'd left England to be rid o' the God damn Bishops' rule, and found myself worse off here under the God damn Brethren's rule, and I say it again."

"Ah—" she murmured after a moment. "Then why do you stay?"

"Ye may be sure I won't if I can help it. But winter's no time to be starving alone in the wilderness, and every place in the Bay's as bad. Come spring, I'll get me up to Piscataqua where they leave a man's soul be, if he's willing to work . . . Ye'd best move on from here, gentle lass—" he added quickly, "The guard'll be making rounds and nobody's allowed to talk to prisoners."

Elizabeth walked slowly down the High Street, past a few new houses, and struck off on a path which led towards Trimount or Sentry Hill and the Common. She paid little attention to her surroundings, for the words of the man in pillory had closed still another imagined avenue of escape. No, winter was no time to be starving along, or with Joan, in the wilderness. She came to the burying ground which was enclosed by a sapling fence. Already there were over thirty headstones in it. She leaned her elbows on the fence and looked at them. The most elaborate one commemorated Isaac Johnson, the next stone was for Mary Coddington, and then an infant, Edward Aspinwall. The rest were wooden slabs, with hasty carving.

"Have you melancholy thoughts, Mistress, so soon after landing?" said a diffident voice beside her. She turned to see a slight young man well dressed in black cape and plum-colored doublet fastened with tiny gold buttons. As she looked at him in surprise, he removed a fine beaver hat, which disclosed short cut flaxen hair, so light it was almost white. His features were neither large nor small, his eyes pale blue set between pale lashes, had a trick of blinking as though the light hurt them. He was smiling in a timid, anxious way as though begging her not to resent his having spoken, and she was quick to put him at his ease.

"I scarcely knew what I was staring at," she said. "But perhaps my thoughts were melancholy."

"I'm—I'm deeply sorry to hear it," he said with so much emotion that for the first time in two days she felt like laughing. "I know what melancholy is, I would never have *you* suffer from it."

"ME?" she said. "La! Sir, do you always flatter ladies so, on first acquaintance?"

His face fell. He moistened his lips and said very low, " 'Tis not first acquaintance, Mistress Winthrop. I sold you that brooch you're wearing."

She looked down at Harry's gilt and crystal gift. "The goldsmith—" she murmured, groping. "The goldsmith—on Lombard Street?"

She remembered their laughter in that shop, the pleasure of finding the gaudy brooch so cheap, the excitement and passion that quivered between her and Harry. She didn't remember the goldsmith at all.

"Aye," he said, in the same anxious tone of apology. "I am Robert Feake, I—I've never forgotten *you*."

Elizabeth took a quick breath and stepped back, staring with more amazement than indignation. When Winthrop first mentioned his plans for her marriage, she had pictured Feake in the likeness of William Coddington, or at any rate as a burly domineering man whose arrogance and self-interest had deceitfully leagued him with the Governor into pretense of affection which he could not possibly feel.

The reality was a startling contrast to her fancy. This was a delicate-appearing man scarcely taller than she, nor could he possibly be out of his twenties, though his pale hair and lack of beard might make him look younger than he was. His clothes were fresh and spotless. She caught from them a whiff of lavender. He had withdrawn one glove and was crumpling and smoothing it as he bore her scrutiny with obvious unease. She saw that the long sensitive hand was white as the Earl of Thanet's had been, and moreover Feake's fingernails were clean. In that first moment of shock, her heightened senses received three strong impressions. He had been hurt at some time, and was afraid of being so again, beyond that she felt a strange quality, eldritch, fey—an echo from the fairy tales of changelings her Suffolk nurse had told her. And the third impression startled her most, for the look in his light blue, occasionally blinking eyes seemed very like pleading tenderness.

"You say nothing . . ." he said at last, with a sigh. "Do you know something to my discredit? Have I offended?"

"Aye," she said, smiling faintly. "You had no right to speak of—to speak intimately about me to Governor Winthrop, nor give him to think that I knew you."

He swallowed; pink stained his fair skin. "I didn't, Mistress, I but said I admired you and grieved to hear of your widowhood. I wouldn't have presumed to say more. It was *he* who mentioned that you must marry again after landing, since women need protectors in this wild place. It was he who hinted subtly, and then as I still dared not think—he asked me straight out if—"

"Aye. No doubt he did," she cut in dryly. "But I believe you will understand my displeasure at being told I had no choice, that my marriage had been arranged."

"I do," he said humbly. "I never meant it like that, nor will I thrust myself on you. I know nothing of women. With none have I aspired to be a husband, nor would have now—much as I've cherished you in memory—except the Governor . . ."

"Yes. Yes. I know," said Elizabeth with exasperation.

He stooped and picked up the glove he had dropped. "I see you can't abide me," he said turning away. "I expected nothing else."

"Oh, fiddle!" cried Elizabeth, half laughing, so harmless had this opponent turned out to be. "How do I know whether I can abide you or not, Mr. Feake? I don't know anything about you, yet admit to some curiosity—but we must hurry back and dine, it's never well to keep the Governor waiting."

"You are even lovelier than I remembered," said Feake in a muffled voice as they began to walk, "and I've thought of you so often." She did not answer, being much perplexed and conscious chiefly of respite.

His compliment and the devotion in his eyes were naturally not unwelcome; more welcome yet was a sense of power, a sweet she had never tasted with Harry—or Jack. The thought of Jack brought its customary miserable pang, and she hastened to efface it by asking questions of Robert Feake.

By the time they reached the Governor's house she had learned the outward facts of his life. He was twenty-nine years old, and had been born in Norfolk, but apprenticed at thirteen to his father, James Feake, who had been a wealthy goldsmith in London. Robert inherited from his father not only the business, but Puritan leanings, which brought him in contact with Emmanuel Downing, and eventually John Winthrop, and eventually bought shares in the Massachusetts Bay Company.

"I marvel, Mr. Feake," she said, "In view of what you tell me, that you left England for this raw, uncomfortable land —was it conscience' sake?" Not a yearning for adventure surely, she thought, nor for gain, nor did he seem the type of man to have been galled by religious oppression.

He was silent so long that she turned to look at him, and saw confusion in his face, almost fear. He glanced sideways at her, and spoke hurriedly, "Conscience, aye—There was some trouble. It—I wasn't well, an ague, I think—yes—that was it, it must have been an ague. My memory is clouded of that time. Forgive me."

"What for?" she said, pitying his confusion. "I didn't mean to pry. And agues with their fevers often haze the memory."

"London air is unhealthy," he said in the same harsh hurried voice. " 'Tis better here. I feel better. I was too confined in London."

As he spoke, they passed the man in pillory, and Elizabeth glancing at the prisoner, shook her head. "I trust Boston'll not grow too confining also."

"Nay," he said eagerly and his face cleared. "If you would, Mistress—if you should *ever* think to join your lot with mine, it need not be in Boston. I have fair land at Watertown. I've started a house by the river, and 'tis freer there in Watertown. The minister, Mr. Phillips, rules with a gentle hand."

"In neither Groton nor London where I've lived, did the ministers rule at all," said Elizabeth, "but I see that you understand certain things about me very well."

They had turned down the lane and were in front of Winthrop's door before he murmured in answer. "I understand, I think, because I love you," he spoke so low that she barely heard, then she stopped and stared at his averted face.

The ensuing dinner was pleasant. Winthrop had favored Elizabeth with one startled approving glance when she came in with Robert Feake, and he placed the two side by side at table. He asked the blessing on their meal, and forgot all domestic matters, in the larger interests of listening to Captain Peirce's news from England, and discussing letters the *Lyon* had brought. Margaret had prevailed upon her John to serve canary wine at least for this reunion, and as their great pewter tankard was passed from hand to hand and the lavish feast was consumed, Winthrop relaxed into geniality. He enjoyed being a host, and his ever-anxious conscience produced no conflict between the ingrained traditions of the English squire and Biblical injunctions—which approved hospitality. His eyes moistened proudly as he glanced at Margaret beside him, and down the long trestle table at his children and his guests. These included besides Captain Peirce and Robert Feake, his colony assistants—Sir Richard Saltonstall who had come down river from Watertown and was returning to England on the *Lyon*, Mr. Increase Nowell, Mr. William Pynchon, and Simon Bradstreet, Dudley's young son-in-law. Mirabelle also contributed to the general glow. She was charming and told tactfully edited anecdotes of her life in London and Paris. She flattered all the men, and got her own way as usual.

Winthrop had decided to board Lady Gardiner with the Aspinwalls, whom he considered the most suitable family in Boston for her reception. Mirabelle had other ideas. She too had been out walking that afternoon and she too had encountered a young man. Hers happened to be Captain Underhill. They had come, as she later told Elizabeth, to an instant understanding. "I like soldiers," Mirabelle said with her throaty chuckle. "I like thees one. He is big and strong, he has a naughty eye. Also he like me. So I decide to board with him while I stay in Boston."

"But he has a wife, hasn't he?" asked Elizabeth, slightly dazed as always by Mirabelle.

"Of course. Or it would not be comme il faut. A fat Dutch cow of a wife, but a good cook. I am comfortable. And I amuse myself."

The two young women had met by chance on the Common where the train bands were drilling to the pleasing tootle and thump of the fife and drum corps. It was Friday, November

11, a week after the *Lyon* had landed, and a holiday, since the Governor had proclaimed it a Day of General Thanksgiving. In the morning Eliot had prayed and lectured in the church, thus much edifying Boston folk, and now relaxation was permitted. The weather was warm and misty; most of the town had taken to strolling around the Common. Aside from the marching train bands there wasn't much to look at but the cattle which had been driven onto the Neck for wintering and a little pond on which children were poking at chip boats with birchbark sails; but Elizabeth was relieved to be outside.

There had been a great deal of work to do this week in the Governor's crowded house. The servants were so few compared to Groton and three of the maids they had brought were sick. Sally had collapsed the day they landed. It was obvious that she had scurvy, her teeth were loose, her breath fetid. She lay on her pallet in the garret and moaned for Suffolk. Elizabeth had brewed scurvy grass for her but she was not yet improved. Mary too was sickly, and on Margaret, Elizabeth, and Martha had devolved much manual labor to which they were unaccustomed. They had had to help the one remaining maid with the work, roasting venison on the spit, steeping porridge made from the unfamiliar and—to the newcomers—extremely unpalatable Indian corn meal. Worst of all they had had to launder the mountains of filthy linen which had accumulated on the passage over.

"I wish *I* could amuse myself," said Elizabeth wistfully, as she and Mirabelle paused to watch a group of lads playing at stool-ball. "And this place is so dreary." She looked around the muddy, treeless Common with the great three-crested hill lowering against a dun sky. "Mirabelle, why do you stay? You don't have to."

Mirabelle glanced at the helmeted figure of Captain Underhill who was cursing his raw recruits in fluent Dutch fortunately not intelligible to the godly spectators. "The Captain makes love very well, for an Englishman," said Mirabelle shrugging, "but I think you are right. I leave soon to find my Christophe. Underhill say I shall find him at Piscataqua, and that he has married off his doxy to someone else; that means he is tired of her."

"But how *can* you go to that wild northland alone?" Elizabeth cried.

"It's only about two days' sail, chérie—and Underhill know of a trading shallop which will take me."

Elizabeth was smitten with envy and a sense of loss. Without the gaudy shameless Mirabelle, Boston would be dreary indeed. "Couldn't you take me too?" she whispered hopelessly.

"Non, non—ma pauvre. One must be practique. You could not bring your baby, and you would be miserable running away from your family like that—the good Margaret, your sister, and Monsieur Jack—ah, but THAT is finished, isn't it? At least the little sister has won, though she never knew she was fighting, and you *would* not. It will be a marriage now for them—comme les autres—not very good, not very bad. And for you too there must be marriage. I see no other way."

Elizabeth drew a sharp breath. "You talk like the Governor!"

"Yes, I know. But you will be out from under his thumb. *Take* this Monsieur Feake who looks at you with the eyes of a faithful dog. I told you on the ship you need a man you can manage, and now here is one, surely."

"I don't love him," said Elizabeth dully, staring at the ground. "Though I don't find him exactly displeasing—but there's something strange about him, so pale and meek—yet sometimes I feel that—"

"Sacré nom!" cried Mirabelle, interrupting with vehemence. "How hard you make everything for yourself, you and all these Puritans! You look behind, you look before, you ask the moon, then think it wicked. Here is a man who is in love with you. And me, I find him interesting—these frail silvery types are sometimes piquant—there was a young Swede in Paris—enfin, no matter. This Feake is rich enough and he also pleases your father-uncle—whatever you call Monsieur Winthrop. You can certainly tolerate the young man, and if he bores you, distract yourself elsewhere, voilà tout."

Elizabeth gave a small bitter laugh, and did not answer. But her resistance to Robert was ebbing. She longer for a place of her own, and to be out of Boston. Nor was she impervious to the joy that she could apparently confer on Robert if she consented. She had seen him twice since the first meeting, and always he was gentle and mutely adoring. Sometimes he attracted her, yet sometimes she felt a subtle shrinking, and heard a warning toll, far off and meaningless as church bells in a distant town. I don't know what to do, she thought, and the lifetime instinct of her heart prompted the only solution. She would consult Jack.

Privacy was nearly as impossible in the Governor's house as it had been on shipboard, and Elizabeth waited several days before she realized her wish. It was not only their tacit avoidance of each other, but also that Jack was constantly riding out on his horse, investigating the other plantations, or surveying the probable sites of the fort and windmill, or conferring with Captain Peirce who was shortly to leave for England via Virginia.

Her chance came at last on the night that Governor Bradford of the Plymouth Colony sailed into the harbor and came ashore to pay his fellow governor a visit.

Winthrop, much pleased, conducted Bradford around Boston that afternoon, and Jack remained in the Hall to write letters at his father's desk.

Elizabeth escaped from the kitchen where the other women were bustling to prepare a special dinner for Bradford and walked resolutely down the other room towards Jack.

"I wanted to speak to you, alone," she said, "To consult you." She saw the stiffening of his dark mobile face, and a veiled look cloud his grown eyes as she came up to the table, and knew that she showed the same constraint.

"But, of course, Bess," he said quickly. "Is it about the sickness? Your maid still ails, I understand. Why not try a laudanum clyster? I have some laudanum in my surgery chest. Has she been bled properly?"

"Aye," said Elizabeth. "And Sally mends, now. 'Tis not that."

"What then?" he asked, as she paused. She disturbed him as she stood there looking her prettiest. All the Winthrops wore their finest clothes in honor of Governor Bradford. She was dressed in a maroon taffeta gown, looped back to show a quilted yellow petticoat. Her sheer lawn collar and cuffs were trimmed with a fine edging of gold lace. Her hair fell in black ringlets on her forehead and shoulders and the rest was pinned into a high glossy knot. She was still thin, but the vivid rose had returned to her cheeks, and the luster to her long hazel eyes. He had not truly looked at her in weeks, and did not wish to now, though the sensations she had used to arouse in him, he believed entirely conquered. He cast sand on the letter he was writing, and jabbed his pen sharply into the little noggin of shot. "Whatever *is* it?" he repeated.

"It's about Robert Feake," she answered at last. "Didn't you guess?"

His restless hand stilled. The sudden pain he felt dismayed him. "You are going to wed him?" he asked in a toneless voice.

"I don't know. Your father orders it. What do *you* think?"

Unwillingly he raised his eyes again and they looked at each other. The thought of the last evening in England on the beach at Sandwich cut down between them like a sword, and they both turned away. She walked to the fire and stood gazing at the crackling pine logs. He sat on at the table staring at his half-written letter.

But there was far more between them than forbidden passion, or even the compelling ties of kinship. Beyond these were the golden memories of their childhood's affectionate trust, and in them both was bred loyalty and decency.

Jack rose and walked over to her. "Do you dislike Mr. Feake, Bess?"

She shook her head. "But I feel some singularity—some mystery about him. Do you know *why* he left England?"

"Why, for the same reasons we all did, no doubt," answered Jack thinking this foolish question an evasion. He went on anxiously. "Is there someone else you wish to marry? Are you unhappy here? Remember Edward Howes still loves you. He told me so in London. Would you go back to him?"

Elizabeth laughed on a weary note. "Oh, Jack—spare me Edward Howes again, I beg. Don't you remember how you urged him on me before you sailed to the Levant?"

"Aye, I remember." He picked up the poker and turned a log. "I was a fool, Bess. If I had thought—if I had spoken then—if I had stayed—or asked you—"

"Hush," she said. "What use is that?"

"None." He put the poker in the great fieldstone hearth. "Yes, my little coz, I think you should marry Robert Feake. My father knows what's best."

She sighed. "So everyone says—Jack, what has happened to my jointure? My four hundred pounds. I know your father had it, but now he says my portion is so small that Mr. Feake is amiable to want me."

Jack started and frowned. "But, my dear, the greatest part went to pay Harry's debts, long ago. Didn't you know?"

"No, though I've wondered. Do I have *nothing?*"

"A little," said Jack uncomfortably. "My father will give you some settlement, I'm sure, he is never ungenerous." Never ungenerous, but often muddleheaded when it came to money. Jack seldom permitted himself criticism of his father, but there was no doubt that financial matters might be better handled. Already Jack had discovered that the Governor had poured his own scanty funds into colony finances, and was considerably embarrassed for cash. Perhaps what remained of Elizabeth's portion had vanished in the same way. But this he would not tell her, and now the four thousand pounds from the sale of Groton Manor would certainly ease the situation.

"I wanted *something* of my own," Elizabeth said bitterly. "Not always to be beholden, a chattel like the maids and kine. Taking board and house room upon sufferance—"

"Bess! Bess!" he cried. "My father doesn't grudge you house room! You know that. You heard how in the starving time last winter here he gave his last handful of meal to a stranger!"

"It is easier to love a stranger," she said, "and your father has never loved me."

Jack was silent, knowing she spoke truth, and sensing from the conflict in himself something of what might lie deep hidden under his father's enmity towards this luscious, forceful woman of his own blood.

Elizabeth answered part of his thoughts as though she had read them. "You all think me strong-willed and rebellious. I've been so at times, I may be so again. But it seems I'm not now. For I will marry Robert Feake, since you desire it too."

"Oh, Bessie, dear—not like that. Not because I ask it. Not unless you feel it is God's Will. Have you asked *Him?*"

"No," she said, "and if I did, and He should hear, I cannot think He would answer in any voice different from your father's."

Jack stood gazing at her sadly before he leaned down and kissed her on the forehead. "If you should ever need me, Bess—my help—no matter where I am—and I shall travel widely—send me as token—" He paused thinking. He had no ring but the gold one his grandfather had given him; a button might be lost, and he wished to give her nothing trivial. He walked over to the chest where lay his hat and sword and gloves. He picked up one of his London-made doeskin gloves. The Winthrop crest had been embroidered on the cuff, "A hare proper, running on a mount vert set upon a helmet."

"Keep this, dear," he said, handing her the glove. "And

swift as this hare which is our crest, I'll answer your need, if you send me the glove. I'll keep the other in memory of what might have—but has never been between us—and God bless you."

She took the glove and put it in the bosom of her dress, beneath the brooch Harry had given her. She pulled her collar down to hide the bulge it made, and ran from the room upstairs to her cold bedroom. She shivered, and crouching by her chest under the window, took the glove and brooch in her hand and stared at them. Tokens from both brothers who had loved her in varying degrees, and she them. And this was the end. This was the turning of a page, the shutting of a door. It is finished, she thought, and soon I shall not even be a Winthrop any more. She put the brooch and glove in a little casket at the bottom of her bride chest, under her piles of linen.

Elizabeth married Robert Feake a month later in the middle of December. It seemed that in the Bay Colony marriage was no longer considered a sacrament or performed by a clergyman. Governor Winthrop, as chief magistrate, married them in the front room of his house. Elizabeth wore her maroon taffeta gown, Robert wore his plum-colored doublet. The Winthrops stood behind the bridal couple, and during the five-minute ceremony Elizabeth heard Martha crying softly, as she had nearly three years ago in St. Sepulchre's Church at the other wedding. Except for Martha there was no sound but Winthrop's measured voice, the murmured answers, and the hiss of burning logs. When the newlyweds had signed the contract, Winthrop smiled and said, "You may now kiss your wife, if you like, nephew Robert."

Robert flushed up to his silvery hair, flattered by his relationship to the Governor, and so awed and confused by his status with Elizabeth that he did not move. She threw him a look of almost maternal pity, and laughed. "Come, come, husband—" she cried in a brittle voice. "You must not be so ungallant!" She brushed his smooth beardless cheek with her lips, noting that he trembled, and also that he smelled pleasantly of lavender. It won't be so bad, she thought. And thank God, I'm quit of this. She saw relief in Winthrop's eyes, and murmured recklessly, "Aye, my uncle. You'll soon be rid of me."

He started, uncertain of what he heard, but the group

dissolved as Margaret rushed up to give Elizabeth a warm hug, and the others followed.

Elizabeth picked up Joan who had been standing owl-eyed through the ceremony, clinging to Martha's hand. "Here is your new father, poppet," she said in the same brittle tone. "Isn't that splendid?"

Robert smiled nervously and touched the baby's hair. Joan stared at him without interest, then began to nuzzle Elizabeth, and pull at her bodice. Everyone laughed a little too loud. Margaret said, "Oh, for shame—'tis time you weaned her completely, Bess . . . Fetch us wine," she called to the servants who had clustered near the kitchen door. "We must drink to the bridal couple!"

"We do not *drink* the health of anyone, my dear," said Winthrop. "You forget. God alone has the power to grant health or contentment. But we may break bread and take a sip or two of wine in simple amity."

Oh lud, thought Elizabeth, and the shell in which she had enclosed herself nearly cracked. At Martha's marriage there had been music and dancing, even at her own to Harry there had been Emmanuel Downing to lend jollity. But now they stood solemnly around the trestle and bowed their heads through Winthrop's extended prayer. Thomas Dudley and his son Samuel had come to the wedding. As soon as the blessing was over, Dudley and Winthrop began heavy frowning converse, which Margaret watched anxiously, knowing that the disagreements between these two were mounting. Samuel Dudley however whispered to Mary, who actually fluttered and looked almost pretty. Poor Mary, Elizabeth thought. If she'd set her heart on young Dudley, she'd have small hope of gaining him in view of their respective fathers' feelings. Yet Winthrop was ever indulgent with *Mary*.

Elizabeth did not know she sighed, but Robert leaned near her and murmured, "You're weary? I too wish we could leave."

"Why can't we!" she said. "I want to go. I will go."

"But Elizabeth—to leave table before the Governor, and the ride is long and cold to Watertown. 'Twill soon be dark, and my home so poor yet, I've been wondering if for tonight you'd not better stay here in comfort . . . and your child . . ."

"Nay, Robert," she said gently, knowing that he feared to be alone with her, and feared that he could not please her. "We will leave Joan until tomorrow, she is weaned enough for that. And we will start now for my new home. The

Governor is no more my master." Nor, she added silently but looking hard at Robert, is *any* man.

He swallowed and pushed back the trencher they had shared. "As you wish, Elizabeth. I will always—if I can—do what you wish."

9

DURING the first months of her marriage to Robert Feake, Elizabeth was content at Watertown. She enjoyed her four-room house, small as these rooms were. She loved her tiny garden and the river that shimmered and curved at the foot of their homestall. At last she was her own mistress, and Watertown, seven miles up the Charles from Boston, was usually far enough from her uncle to give her the independence she craved. Though Winthrop had unexpectedly appeared several times in the town. Once, to discipline the Reverend George Phillips for not banishing Richard Browne, an elder in the Watertown Church, who persisted in voicing the hideous opinion that Papist ceremonies might be valid for some, and that even Roman Catholic Churches were true churches, and not temples of Babylon. Though most of Watertown's congregation sided with the Governor, Mr. Phillips continued remarkably stiff-necked, and refused to admit that Boston had jurisdiction over anything that went on in his church.

Worse followed in February when Phillips and others of the principal Watertown men refused to pay the levy of eight pounds the Governor had ordered for the fortification of Boston. Phillips actually said that he did not think Win-

throp had the power to make laws or raise taxes with
consent of all the people in the Bay, nor did he believe
power granted by the Charter. This disagreement lasted some
time, and ended in Phillips's unwilling submission when
Winthrop demonstrated that the first General Court had given
full powers to the Governor and his assistants, no matter
what the Charter said, and anyway the obstreperous inhabitants of Watertown could air their grievances in a few months
at the next Court.

Elizabeth was amused by these incidents, and delighted that
she lived in a place which dared combat Uncle John. Though
Robert was never of that number. He continued to be in awe
of the Governor, and anxiously adoring of Elizabeth. This
frequently touched, and sometimes exasperated her. If she
had loved him, her bridal nights might have been tragic, but
as it was, Robert's fumbling overeagerness, his total inex-
perience, his peculiar embarrassment all produced in her
no deeper feeling than sympathy. Harry had well taught her
the arts of love-making, and though she was startled to find
herself in the role of teacher, the matter was soon adjusted.

Robert clung to her, he was incoherently grateful for her
soothing kindness when he had nightmares, he derived comfort from her nearness, but as the months went by his never
importunate virility dwindled.

Elizabeth accepted this philosophically. Robert never
seemed quite like a man to her; not that he was actually
effeminate, but their relationship, she realized when she
thought of it, was more that of mother to a rather shadowy
but devoted child. And for the present that sufficed. Especially as Robert had after all given her freedom, of a sort,
and lavished on her every material comfort that he could
afford. She was grateful, and accepted. The ninety pounds'
jointure that Winthrop—urged by Jack—had finally settled on
her she kept locked in her chest with Harry's brooch and
Jack's glove. Nor did Robert ever ask about it.

On the morning of August 24, Elizabeth awakened after
a stifling muggy night, and turning in their big bed saw that
Robert was already up and pulling on his breeches. "Lord help
us," said Elizabeth yawning and twisting her hair off her
sweaty shoulders. "What a night, I'm measled with mosquito
bites, all of an itch. There's much to be said for the old
country."

Robert did not answer, he was carefully washing his ears
at a basin. Always he was very clean. Elizabeth scratched her

arms, stomach and breasts violently, looking at the red splotches with disgust, yawned again and got out of bed. " 'Tis St. Bartholomew's Day," she said, and sighed. "Oh, Rob, d'you remember the Fair? How I loved it. Every year I went, and it so near our home in the Old Bailey, I could hear the music while I lay abed too."

"I never went to the Fair," said Robert with constraint. "Or at least I don't remember it." He began to comb his thin flaxen hair.

"But, of course you'd remember it! And of course you went. All Londoners did." She had spoken without thinking, but now she saw what she thought of as "the strangeness" in his face, a shut, dark look, and it occurred to her that this came whenever there was mention of London.

"Why do you always seem so moon-struck when I speak of home?" she cried in sudden irritation. "Before God I believe you've some shameful secret of the past!"

He winced, and his eyes blinked rapidly as they had almost stopped doing since his marriage. She saw his long fingers clench the comb. "Don't speak to me in such a tone, my dearest wife," he pleaded, walking slowly towards the bed. "I can't endure your anger." He knelt beside her and put his cheek on her knee.

"Oh, pother!" said Elizabeth. "I'm not angry, only hot and uncomfortable. Why must you make such a fuss about naught? If you've a secret, keep it, only *I* like to think of home sometimes."

"Is *this* not yet home, Bess?" he said sadly. "I've tried to make it so."

"Of course it is—you ninny." She patted his shoulder. "I hope Sal's put a keg of beer in the spring, or it'll sour in this thundery weather. That wench gets more careless every day."

"Shall I find you another maid, Bess?" asked Robert quickly, looking up into her face.

"And *where*, I'd like to know? There's scarce a lass over here willing to be a decent servant. I doubt Sally stays after her passage money's paid up, she's none too content now unless she's bawdy-trotting with one of your men." Sally had made it obvious that the only amenities she found in Watertown were the dubious attentions of Robert's two indentured menservants.

"You don't sound content yourself," persisted Robert, increasingly disturbed by Elizabeth's sharp tone. Though he knew she had a temper, she had never lost it with him, nor had he ever known her to grumble.

"I *am* content," she snapped, then shook her head with a half-laugh. "Oh Rob, don't act so downtrodden. You're very good to me. Women have moods, my stomach's queasy, and in truth I think I'm breeding."

"What?" he whispered, drawing back. "What did you say, Bess?"

She laughed outright at his dazed face, thinking that any other husband would have guessed. "I said I'm almost sure I'm with child, and you needn't look shocked, my dear, we've been married eight months, so the court won't have us up for lewd questioning, should the babe come early."

"Do you want it?" he said, swallowing.

"To be sure I want it. I always wanted more babies."

"But the dangers. I can't bear to think of you in pain or danger."

"If I'm not afraid, you needn't be," she said. "The second comes easy. Look at Aunt Margaret, she near died last time, she's way over forty and yet whimpers not at bearing her seventh."

"Aye, that's true," he said, reassured as Elizabeth's decisive strength always reassured him. "I suppose it will be pleasant for us to have a baby. Though I can't imagine it."

"You're good to Joan," she said looking at him kindly. "And will dote on your own. Now, Rob, shouldn't you be hurrying out to the fields? Aren't the men cutting corn today?"

He started and nodded. He finished dressing and went out while Elizabeth thought it was fortunate that his servants had been farm lads in the old country and had enough knowledge to tend the Feake crops, for Robert certainly had not. He was as ignorant of husbandry, cattle care, or land-clearing as she was herself, but she at least understood gardening and the stillroom, and she had been used to the partial supervision of a manor, while he apparently knew no skills but his former craft. Sometimes she wondered why he never seemed to miss that or wish to exercise it. He had given her a fine gold neckchain and an exquisitely chased silver ladle for wedding presents, and both he himself had made in London, so that she knew his ability. There were, of course, no materials in Watertown for him to set up as gold- or silver-smith; also it was clear that he no longer wished to have anything to do with trade, but she thought it odd that the thin sensitive fingers should lie idle of an evening when he might have tinkered with their pewter or made tools as most other men did here.

But her thoughts never dwelt long on Robert when he was not with her. While she dressed herself in her one cool gown of rose tiffany, bundled her hair into a kerchief and tied on a workaday apron, she thought again of Margaret whose babe was due in a fortnight, which meant it has been conceived almost as soon as they landed from the *Lyon*, and inescapably brought to Elizabeth an image of her uncle in a grotesque light. Impossible and revolting for her to imagine him in any act of intimacy, and she felt an irrational anger too on Margaret's account, though the feeling was unjust. Margaret, incredible as it seemed to Elizabeth, truly loved her John and delighted in submission. And she has God too, Elizabeth thought a trifle wistfully, a God whom she believes watches over and loves her.

This meditation was brusquely interrupted by Joan, who had learned to unlatch the door and ran into the bedchamber crying, "Mama! Mama! Injuns!"

There had been rumors of unrest amongst the Indians lately, nothing definite, but the Feakes' neighbor, Captain Patrick, had told them that he and Underhill were on the alert. Elizabeth was not given to worry; moreover she had become friendly with several of the local Indians who lived across the river in their village called Nonantum, so that the note of fear in the child's cry scarcely disquieted her, but she was startled when she hurried down to the kitchen and found two strange Indians standing on the hearthstone smoking English pipes and gazing fixedly at the terrified Sally, who was huddled over the spinning wheel trying with shaking hands to twist a length of broken yarn.

"What are you doing here?" cried Elizabeth to the Indians, pushing Joan behind her and wishing Robert and the men were working the home lot today instead of their fifteen acres by the Common.

The two Indians swiveled their beady black gaze from Sally, and contemplated Elizabeth with the same detachment. She saw by their face tattooings, the quality of their fringed buckskin breeches, their many wampum necklaces, and the amount of red-dyed deer hair and feathers in their roached scalplocks that both must be some sort of chief. One carried an English pike, and the other taller handsomer Indian a stone tomahawk with an elaborately painted wood handle.

This Indian also wore with great dignity a mantle of woven turkey feathers.

"What do you want?" cried Elizabeth again. "How dare you enter my house!" And she made shooing gestures towards the door.

The taller one blew a cloud of tobacco smoke through his nostrils, and said, "Want Mr. Oldham—my friend."

"Well, you won't find him here," said Elizabeth, relieved to hear English. "His house is up the river about a mile."

"He not there," said the Indian. "We look. Oldham where?"

"I haven't the least idea," snapped Elizabeth who barely knew John Oldham, a famous Indian trader, seldom at his house in Watertown. "Who are *you?*" she said, lifting her chin and frowning.

"Me," said the tall one after a moment, "Miantonomo, Big Sachem Narragansetts. This—" he pointed to the other Indian, "English call James Sagamore—live near."

"Oh, to be sure," Elizabeth cried, still uneasy but enlightened. Patrick had told her that a great chief of the Narragansetts had recently been to see Winthrop in Boston, ostensibly to ask for an alliance against the fierce Pequots whose lands adjoined the Narragansetts' to the west. Winthrop had entertained the Sachem, his squaw and twelve braves hospitably, but there was doubt as to the real purpose of the visit. James Sagamore Elizabeth had also heard of, since he and his brother John ruled the Massachusetts tribes from Watertown to Salem. It seemed wise to pacify such prominent chiefs, and Elizabeth decided she had been discourteous. She managed a nervous smile. "I'm sorry I can't help you to find Mr. Oldham. But could I offer you something to drink, it's so warm."

Miantonomo grunted, while the muscles relaxed around his glittering jet eyes. James Sagamore yanked a stool from under the table, settled himself on it, and said, "Beer."

"Get beer, Sally," Elizabeth hissed over her shoulder, not removing her gaze from the Indians. The girl scurried out towards the spring. She came back staggering from the weight of a small wet keg. Behind her through the door waddled a fat, befeathered squaw, wearing a red English petticoat, and nothing above it except strings of wampum which flopped between her pendulous brown breasts. She gave Elizabeth what seemed to be a friendly salute, then seated herself on the bench near James Sagamore and eyed the beer keg expectantly.

"Your woman?" Elizabeth asked, looking from one to the other of the men. Definitely relieved now, she felt inclined to laugh.

"No," said Miantonomo. "She belong no man. She squaw sachem. She *rule* many men."

Oh, thought Elizabeth, a female chief. I'm honored but I hope there aren't more of them. Though the hearth fire was low, yet it made the kitchen sultry, and the Indian smell was overpowering. She pulled the bung from the keg and, letting beer flow into a big pewter tankard, offered it to Miantonomo who drank deeply and passed the tankard to the others. Elizabeth prayed they would go, but James Sagamore put his pipe back in his mouth, while his eyes roamed around the whitewashed walls where the Feake firearms rested on wooden pegs. There were two muskets, a pistol, and a carbine. Powder horns hung beneath each. Robert had taken the fowling piece with which he was an indifferent shot, but he sometimes got wild fowl or small game.

"Guns," said James Sagamore, speaking for the first time. "I want. You sell."

Elizabeth's heart jumped. She did not need the memory of Captain Peirce's advice to Eliot on the *Lyon*, nor the knowledge that selling firearms to the Indians was an offense punishable by flogging and branding, to appreciate the danger of her position. I must keep my head, she thought, and instinctively turned to Miantonomo. "I cannot sell any guns, you know that, Sachem," she said speaking very distinctly. "The white Governor has forbidden it. He would be *angry*."

Miantonomo nodded slightly but said nothing. James Sagamore got up and walking to the nearest musket, ran his stumpy finger down the barrel. "I take," he said, and glanced at the silent sachem, in a wheedling voice he added to Elizabeth, "I give you beaver."

Elizabeth shook her head, while her thoughts jumbled. Were there more of them outside? If she pretended to send Sally to the spring again, would they let the girl go, and where *was* the nearest help? Or would it be better to pretend to bargain?

"The guns are my husband's. My man's" she said, edging towards Sally who had grabbed Joan and was hiding with her behind the spinning wheel. "I can't sell. My man would beat me terribly."

James Sagamore shrugged, unmoved by this plea. He lifted the musket from its pegs. He also reached for the powder horn. "I take," he said, but the watchful Miantonomo spoke in rapid guttural Indian. The Sagamore hesitated. The squaw said something too. Soon all three Indians were obviously arguing, and Elizabeth bent close to Sally, "Are there more savages outside?"

"Aye—" gasped the girl. "By the river."

Elizabeth breathed hard and saw that now having put the musket on his stool, James Sagamore was fingering the carbine. "I take," he said putting the carbine beside the musket. He glanced at the sachem and added reluctantly, "Will pay more beaver."

"Leave him have 'em, mistress," wailed Sally. "Leave him or they'll murder us all!"

"No, they won't!" said Elizabeth, fear suddenly giving way to fury. "You can't take those guns and you know it!" she cried stamping her foot. "This is English land, I won't sell and if you steal you know what'll happen to you! We have many soldiers, right near. I'll call my husband, you can't stop me, I gave you beer, I made you welcome, this is an outrage!" She flew at the astonished Sagamore and jerked the carbine from his hand, while Miantonomo gave a grunt that was very like a laugh.

At the same moment the door swung wide and a loud voice boomed, "Here, here—what's all this!" Captain Daniel Patrick, fully armed and in helmet and breastplate, stepped over the sill. He stared from the shaking Elizabeth to the three Indians. He saw the musket on the stool and the carbine in Elizabeth's hands. "Trying to get firearms?" he asked.

"That one was—" she panted, pointing to James.

"So, James, me greasy slubber, ye're up to your old tricks, are ye? I thought as much. I've been keeping an eye on ye, followed your trail downriver to here. Did they threaten you?" he asked of Elizabeth.

She shook her head. "N-no. Not really, but they wouldn't go, and James kept taking down the arms."

"Buy. Not steal," interrupted Miantonomo quietly.

Patrick turned to the sachem. "I marvel to see *you* in this, Your Highness," he said with deference, eying the chief narrowly. "You Narragansetts protest great friendship for us, at Plymouth they trust ye, as they do your royal uncle

Canonicus, and Governor Winthrop is your netop—your friend."

The sachem bowed. "I *am* English friend. And am friend to Oldham who know our people well. I seek him."

"But ye let James Sagamore try to get firearms, and terrify women!"

Miantonomo opened his hands in a wide gesture. "He not under *my* rule, and we have peace with Massachusetts tribes."

"Aye," said Patrick quickly. "Well, be off with ye. You too, me dark-skinned beauty," he said to the squaw sachem who was curiously twirling the spinning wheel, while Sally glared at her. "And don't try this game with any other planters, d'ye hear?" he added to James Sagamore, who looked sheepish and waggled his head.

The three Indians walked outside while Patrick followed to watch them rejoin a small party of their braves who were squatting on the riverbank. The Indians all boarded waiting canoes, and Patrick came back to Elizabeth who had collapsed on the stool.

"Were ye much 'frighted, sweetheart?" he asked, putting his big freckled hand on her shoulder. "Though from what I heard ye gave 'em a good tongue-lashing." he chuckled, and poured himself some beer.

"Thank God you came," she said. "I *was* frightened, I didn't know what to do." She gave him a trembling smile. She liked the bluff, auburn-haired Patrick, who had a way with women, but she also liked his wife, Anneke van Beyeren, who was placid, and pretty, and the only one of her neighbors Elizabeth found congenial.

"There's no great harm in the Indians, if ye treat 'em right," said Patrick wiping the beer froth from his bushy red mustache. "Some're tricky like that James, some're real gentlemen like Miantonomo—but ye know, Bess, I own to a sly fondness for the rogues. They put me in mind o' the wild Irish tribes I was raised in."

"Do they?" said Elizabeth faintly. Usually she was interested in Patrick's stories of his boyhood, and flattered that he trusted her with many details which would have horrified the Bay Colony, but she was still shaken. She distastefully sipped some beer and nibbled on a corn flatcake.

"Aye," he said, reaching for a flatcake. "*I* know what it is to have the English come stravaging an' strutting, to claim your own rightful lands! I mind me father, when the bloody English Protestants first o'erran Ulster, spat on our churches and called us slaves. Ha! There was good Irish fighting in those days. I mind once when the O'Neills—" He checked himself, and banged his fist on the table. "Whist, Danny, me lad, ye're a blabbermouth fool! Ye're in English pay now, and ye've taken English oaths, Protestant oaths. And ye do what the Governor says!"

Elizabeth laughed. "Oh, Dan, I fear you're a sad hypocrite."

His twinkling blue eyes grew serious. "Nay, lovey, I'm but a damn good soldier and I earn me living by it. And let nothing interfere with that duty. Naught else matters—except—"

"Except?" she questioned.

"Room to breathe in, I suppose. Someday I'll take nobody's pay, I'll be me own master."

"I know," she said with a little sigh. The Captain turned and looked at her. A handsome spirited wench, with wanton eyes and a ready wit, yet there was always something held in, a broodiness and uncertainty. Aye, he thought, but she's a Winthrop after all, I keep forgetting that, and tied to that poor milk-molly of a Feake. Not that he's so bad, but hardly suits *this* woman. Patrick leaned across the table and said suddenly, "I've never told ye, Bess, how fond I was of your Master Harry, God rest his soul, and how mortal sorry I was at the—the ending. All the sorrier since I've known ye—"

She looked up, startled and touched, yet ashamed that Patrick should seem to think her grieving for Harry still, but before she could speak a woman rustled through the kitchen door crying, "Mistress Feake! Mistress Fea—" and stopped by the threshold as she saw Elizabeth and Patrick sitting with their heads close together at the table.

"Oh, beg pardon, I'm sure," said the woman, raising her scanty brows. "I didn't know Captain Patrick went calling of a morning."

"I had some embarrassment with the Indians, Goody Warren," said Elizabeth, resenting the need for explanation. "Captain Patrick rescued me from it."

"Ah—" said Goodwife Warren, her sharp little rodent face turning from one to the other. "The Knapp girl—Judith, it was—come running to me, saying she'd seen a pack o' savages crossing Bank Lane. Thinking you'd be *alone*, Mistress, I come to see how you did."

"That was kind of you," said Elizabeth. "Have you breakfasted?"

She had not been long in Watertown before discovering that her neighbor, Goodwife Peg Warren, was a credulous busybody, whose chief pleasure was reporting any sort of moral dereliction to the Reverend Mr. Phillips, who by no means always listened. Her husband, John Warren, had been a well-to-do yeoman back in Suffolk, and one of Watertown's first settlers two years ago, so that Goody Warren aspired to leadership amongst the Watertown women, and had not been pleased to have Mr. Feake bring in a wife who definitely outranked her.

"Well . . . I could fancy a taste o' beer and a mite o' cheese since you're so kind," she said perching herself primly at the far end of the bench from Patrick, and folding her hands, while her bright mouse eyes darted around the room which she had never been invited to enter. She noted the great silver salt and the array of pewter on the dresser, lots *of* it but none too well polished, and the hearth was covered with grease and tallow stains. Aye, my fine lady, she thought, no doubt you've merrier things to do than housewifery, and her eyes slid over Patrick who was known to be a lusty, profane man.

"I wonder you're not keeping an eye on them heathen, Captain," said the goodwife. "I heard tell there's a whole gaggle of 'em massing at Muddy River."

"You may be sure I know me duty, ma'am," said Patrick, reaching for another flatcake and crossing his thick legs. "What other news've ye been hearing? I'm certain ye'd not miss any."

The goodwife bristled, but Patrick's expression was so bland that she eschewed annoyance. "Have you heard," she said eagerly, "that the Clark lass was taken wi' fits? Goody Knapp and me think the Devil's in it, 'cause young Chadwick saw a black man with horns and a tail flying over the Fresh Pond yester e'en. And then there was that battle against nature last Sabbath Day. I was there. I saw it. The chills ran up an' down my spine."

"You mean that mouse that killed the little snake?" said Elizabeth, resigning herself.

The goodwife nodded. "That was a *sign*, a fearsome portent, and right beside the meetinghouse too! I couldn't sleep nights for worriting as to what it meant, no more could

Goody Knapp. But Mr. Wilson prophesied on Lecture Day and told the meaning."

"Mr. Wilson?" said Elizabeth. She had seen Boston's newly returned minister but once, and thought him a sleek pompous man, who seemed unlikely to concern himself with Watertown fauna.

"Aye," said Goody Warren nodding solemnly. "Mr. Jennison was in Boston Thursday and heard the sermon. It seems the snake was the Devil and the poor contemptible mouse was us, the saints, which God has brought hither, and we shall overcome Satan here, and oust him from his kingdom. That's what it meant, and Mr. Jennison said the Governor was pleased, but said he didn't know why *Watertown* was favored wi' such a godly sign."

What a tarradiddle, Elizabeth thought. Yet why don't I believe it? Uncle John does, and Mr. Wilson has been to Cambridge and is far better educated than I.

"But the Devil's not downed yet," went on the goodwife, her eyes gleaming. "There's more wickedness every day. Did you hear that Mr. Masters' serving wench, Molly, was caught fornicating in the meadows with Thomas Smith? Ah, they'll get a flogging at the cart's tail, they will, come next court day. Branding too, I shouldn't wonder."

"I shouldn't wonder," said Patrick, rising and putting on his helmet. "I'm sure ye'll not be bothered by any more *Indian* chance-comers, ma'am," he said to Elizabeth, "but I'll post one o' me men on Bank Lane till Mr. Feake comes back. I gi' ye good day." He bowed to both women, sent Elizabeth a private twinkle of sympathy, and stalked out.

Elizabeth looked hopefully at her visitor, but the goodwife had no intention of moving until her curiosity was satisfied on several counts. She began on Daniel Patrick. Had Mistress Feake heard of Patrick's quarrel with Mr. Clarke over the setting of the Watertown watch? Didn't the Governor account Patrick a violent, ungodly man? Was it true he often beat that simpering little Dutch wife of his? Not but what she doubtless deserved it. Elizabeth replied briefly that she knew nothing to Captain Patrick's discredit, and was very fond of Anneke Patrick.

Goody Warren, baffled, and somewhat in awe of Mistress Feake's august relationship to the Governor, nevertheless tried to garner information which she could proudly retail to her special gossips, the goodwives Knapp, Bridges and Lockwood. Did Mistress Feake know, asked Goody Warren, that

Mr. Dudley had angrily tendered his resignation as Deputy to Governor Winthrop, and was it true that at the last assembly the two gentlemen were at each other's throats and had to be separated, and all because Mr. Winthrop accused Mr. Dudley of usury and wainscoting his Hall in an extravagant manner? And that then Mr. Dudley raged back because the Governor *would* build his house in Boston instead of Newtown and was running everything his own way?

Elizabeth truthfully replied that she knew nothing about the matter. Goody Warren found her hostess equally unresponsive to the burning question of Elder Browne's continuing stubborn use of the prayer book.

As the morning passed, it grew even hotter; Elizabeth's eyes glazed and she was guilty of a hearty yawn which finally silenced her visitor, whose natural envy of Elizabeth's beauty, possessions and doting husband had now definitely become dislike. Goody Warren took her leave and walked back through the fields to her own homestall, while framing various trenchant criticisms with which to regale her friends.

Elizabeth rambled despondently around the kitchen, noting that the eels they would eat for dinner had not yet been skinned, that the vinegar had developed a disgusting layer of mother, and that their scanty store of wheat flour was weevily. Sally had disappeared to carry a nooning snack to the men in the fields—one task in which she was never laggard. Joan was happy in the shade of their great sugar maple playing with a spaniel puppy Anneke Patrick had given her, and Elizabeth, resolutely ignoring all the waiting chores, picked up her herb knife and went outside to her little garden.

The English marigolds and gentians had done well in the new land; the foxgloves too had scarce finished blooming, though the rose cuttings had not taken hold, nor the poppy seed come up. Still most of the herbs had prospered, though some like the delicate basil were wilting in the heat and should be picked at once for drying. Elizabeth gathered up the corners of her apron and tossed into it cucumbers and purslane to be used as salad, for these were under the dominion of the moon, and cooled the blood. She moved to the next plot and picked a mess of beans, being careful to include a good pinch of summer savory which expelled wind and should always be cooked with legumes. Her most flourishing import of all, Elizabeth saw with satisfaction, were the dandelions. She had a whole bed of them, some in golden flowers the size of shillings, some already turned to thistledown. She dug up a few of the flowering plants which were vulgarly known in Suffolk as "Piss-in-beds," because when steeped they yielded a liquor which quickly opened the urinal passages and thus carried off disease from the entire body.

She was admiring a ruby-throated hummingbird that darted at the melissa, thinking idly what a marvel the tiny creature was, and unknown in the Old World, so that King Charles had demanded to see one; and she was wondering if the hummingbird which had been sent caged on the *Whale* last month could possibly have survived when she heard galloping hoofbeats on Bank Lane.

Horses were so rare in the colony that she ran around to the front of the house with Joan and the puppy at her heels. The horseman drew up at the gate in their sapling fence, jumped off and cried, "Mistress Feake!"

Elizabeth recognized young Tom French, who, with his sister Dorcas, was serving in the Governor's household. "What is it, Tom?" she cried, anxiously hurrying to unlatch the gate.

" 'Tis Mistress Winthrop, ma'am—" he cried, touching his forehead, then mopping his sweaty face with his shirt sleeve. "She's took bad!"

Elizabeth's heart jumped. "Which one? Mistress Margaret or Martha?"

"The old one—Gov'nor's lady, she was brought to bed at cock's crow, but something's wrong. She's crying out for you, ma'am. His Worship sent me."

"Is there no midwife?" said Elizabeth as she picked up Joan and hastened towards the house.

"Only Goody Munt and she's skeered, and none too skilled, the women say."

Elizabeth took no more time for questions. She dumped her load of greens on the kitchen table, and was relieved to see Sally sauntering along the path from the Common. Elizabeth gave the girl quick instructions, and ran upstairs for her summer cloak and a basket in which she threw her scissors, lancet and a flask of mithridate made at Groton and carefully saved for great emergency. As she kissed Joan goodbye she suddenly remembered an herb the London midwife had given Margaret last time when Ann was born; surely it was basil, which gave speedy deliverance to women in travail? She ran back and gathered the cut basil plants from the kitchen table before mounting pillion behind Tom. They started off towards

Boston. On the way she discovered that Jack was absent from Boston at his father's farm "Ten Hills" near Medford, and she was both disappointed and relieved.

When Elizabeth and Tom reached Charlestown they found the ferryman had waited for them by the Governor's express command, and it was scarcely three o'clock when they arrived at Winthrop's house. Martha was standing by the door and she rushed out crying, "Bess, Bess. Thank God you're here! The child was born right after we sent for you, but *she* is going fast." Martha choked and added, "Oh, she looks so horrible!"

John Winthrop was sitting in the Hall, hunched over his Bible. Margaret's three little sons, Stephen, Adam and Sammy, clung together on the settle, gaping at their father. He raised his head as Elizabeth entered, the sunken eyes glaring from a haggard face. "The Lord gave and the Lord hath taken away. Blessed be the name of the Lord," he said, looking at Elizabeth as though he didn't know her. "And yet I can't resign myself, God forgive mine infirmity, for I pray—pray that she'll be spared. And I search my heart to know why God should so afflict me."

"But He hasn't yet—" Elizabeth whispered, seeing that there were tears on his cheeks. "Martha, take this basil, bruise it quickly, then steep it, while I go upstairs." Though if the babe were already born, she did not know if the basil would help.

Winthrop clenched the Bible, and groaned. "Mr. Wilson is with her exhorting her to compose her soul. Ah, I've lost two dear wives, but none so dear as this one—too dear—and that is why the jealous Lord would have me give her up."

Elizabeth tightened her lips, flung her cloak on the chest and ran upstairs. Boston's pastor, a short, stout man in black robes and skullcap, stood beside the great bed on which lay a silent sheeted form. The midwife crouched behind him, a feebly mewling bundle in her arms. Mary and two women servants hovered white-faced by the window. Elizabeth pushed past the minister, and saw with a spasm of fear that what they said was true. Margaret lay in a swoon, yet drew great snoring breaths, and all her muscles jumped constantly. Her face was unrecognizable, swollen to a glistening grayish sphere, her twitching hands likewise were puffed so that the knuckles had vanished.

"She took a shaking fit sudden, this morn," whispered the midwife to Elizabeth, "Just as the babe slipped out easy, but the afterbirth's not come—I dared not pull on it—and she's been like this since."

"Has she been bled?" whispered Elizabeth.

"Nay," said the midwife. "I was afeared. I've ne'er seen 'em like this wi' the dropsy and fits, and she's not passed water since I come here yester morn, neither."

Elizabeth too was afraid. Nor had she seen anyone like this. But she took her lancet, and while the midwife held the pewter bleeding basin she opened a vein in Margaret's arm from which dark blood oozed. Could the trouble be the stoppage of urine? Elizabeth thought, and wished passionately that she had brought the dandelions, and that Jack were here to give advice. Yet if they could only make Margaret sweat, so the watery humors would pass out that way. Elizabeth said to the maids, "Bring hot bricks and blankets!"

"But surely not!" said Mr. Wilson, who had ceased praying and was dubiously watching. "It's so warm in here now."

"I know," she said, "But I think it's right—I feel it—and if I can get *this* down her—" She uncorked the flask of mithridate which she knew was diuretic since it contained quicksilver.

Mr. Wilson shook his bullet head. "I doubt anything'll help, and I've some knowledge of chirurgery. But there was one remedy oft used in Sudbury for extraordinary travail. You must take a lock of virgin's hair, the virgin exactly half the age of the parturient woman, and make a powder of it with twelve ant's eggs, and a quarter pint of Red Cow's milk, then if God be willing—"

Elizabeth had listened with half an ear while she tried to spoon the mithridate between Margaret's flaccid lips. "I know not where we'd find the ingredients here—" she said distractedly, and went on speaking to Margaret in a low urgent voice. "Please, my dearest mother, please try to swallow!" But Margaret could not.

"Too true," said Wilson gravely. "I fear the proper age virgin might be impossible to find, and I know of no red cows in Boston."

The maids ran in with hot bricks wrapped in cloths. They put them next to Margaret and piled blankets on her; her stertorous breathing quickened a little and she moaned. Under the blankets Elizabeth massaged the flabby, still distended belly, and then as though a voice spoke in her head, she thought, A clyster. The anodyne clyster! And saw the instructions clear in her father's crabbed Latin script. She ordered

the astonished Wilson from the room, then sent the maids
for Jack's surgery chest, and the family clyster pipe. In the
chest she found the little glass bottle marked Laudanum. She
emptied half the bottle into a jug with the mithridate and
the basil water Martha had brought. With the midwife's
help they turned Margaret on her side, and Elizabeth, in-
serting the clyster, dribbled the mixture through the pipe.

They waited in the fetid stifling room, and heard the
Governor's wall clock strike four, when Margaret gave a
choking gasp, opened her swollen lids and broke out into a
drenching sweat. "Bess—" she croaked, looking up at Elizabeth. "Where's John? Has God let me live?"

"Yes, dear, *yes!*" cried Elizabeth with a great sob of relief. "You'll live!"

The other women drew around murmuring and not yet
comforted, but Elizabeth was sure. An intuition that had
never failed her when it came to healing told her that Margaret would recover.

By the time John Winthrop came in to kneel and weep
thanksgivings by his wife's bedside, they all knew that Elizabeth was right.

Two days later on August 26 Mr. Wilson baptized the
infant, which was a boy, and the Governor in an excess of
humble gratitude named it William which signified a common man. There were no sponsors, since that Papist custom
too had been abolished, but Winthrop, who was for many
days upset and gentle, said to Elizabeth that if the colony
still observed the old ways, he would have asked her to be
godmother, and he thanked her with deep emotion for her
help. "God has given you this skill, Bess, never forget to
bless Him for it, and use it in His service."

Ah yes, she thought, now I see why some do love him,
when he looks upon them kindly, and she forbore to sadden
him by saying that no skill of any kind could long save the
baby. They found a wet nurse for it, but it had not the
strength to suckle; puny and blue as a newborn kitten to start
with, each day it dwindled, and by the weekend died. John
and Margaret bore this sorrow with fortitude, and if John
ever repined that he had lost four children within two years,
no one knew of it, and after all he had five sons left—and
Mary.

The infant was scarce laid in the burying ground before
the quiet Mary thunder-struck her family and diverted all
the colony by riding off one morning to Roxbury and marry-

ing Samuel Dudley before a magistrate there. Amidst the ensuing uproar, Mary stated calmly that she and Sam loathed a fuss, and knew there would be one since both fathers were at loggerheads and agreed on nothing; that nobody could justly call unsuitable a marriage between the two principal families of the Bay, especially since Mary had her own jointure from her mother, Mary Forth; and anyway the thing was done and could not be annulled since she and Samuel had prudently lain together several times before they announced the marriage.

Reasonable as these views were, they did not placate the two outraged fathers, who were drawn by the unfilial behavior of their offspring into a kind of truce. The young Dudleys, unperturbed, withdrew into a cabin Sam had built on land he owned at Newtown and ignored the storm which soon blew out, for in the meantime there were worse Indian troubles.

Elizabeth remained in Boston for some time, nursing Margaret, and was there on the early September night of the Great Alarm.

In the morning, Governor Winthrop received John Underhill who came in looking gloomy, declined soft cider with a shudder, and stood waiting by Winthrop's desk.

"What is it, Captain?" said Winthrop pushing aside a difficult letter he was writing to Governor Bradford at Plymouth. There seemed no end to little jealousies and misunderstandings between the colonies; perhaps the best way to settle them would be to undertake a return visit and talk to Bradford in person.

"There's been an Englishman murdered by an Indian, up above Piscataqua," said Underhill brusquely. "Jenkins, late of Dorchester. Chopped to bits while he slept in Passaconamy's wigwam, just after the peace pipe had been smoked."

"Treachery, eh?" said Winthrop frowning. "That's bad. But those are Mohawks up there, aren't they?"

Underhill shrugged. An Indian was an Indian and he disliked them all. "I don't fancy these Narragansetts still lurking around us here, they've got our Massachusetts lot excited. Ye can see it, powwows in the forests, canoes darting up and down the rivers then vanishing when ye try to challenge 'em. James Sagamore *says*, and that Miantonomo backs him up, they're planning some kind o' war on the Nipmucks who've pinched their western hunting grounds. But last month it was the *Pequots* they were out to fight."

Winthrop looked anxiously at his captain whom he knew to be able and courageous, though his private morals were suspect. "Miantonomo seems a good man, ate at table with me, and behaved nearly like a Christian."

Underhill brushed this aside impatiently. "There's not been an Indian in Boston for days, which is peculiar. And one of Chickatabot's braves, or sannops, whatever ye call 'em, I gave him an old rusty helmet once and he's that proud of it, he keeps an ear to the ground for me—he says the whole boiling lot of them are plotting to surprise us. They want our victuals and our guns."

Winthrop swallowed. "Well, we'll have to take precautions. Double the guard, alert every household—"

"Nay, sir. Not like that. I've been training and alerting these draggletails ever since we landed, so has Patrick. Lot o' peagoose farmers and tradesmen who still don't know one end of a musket from t'other, and they won't listen neither when I say there's danger. Only thing to do is show 'em for themselves. I want to sound the general alarm tonight, and see how they behave. Captain Patrick agrees."

"I see," said Winthrop after a moment. "It'll frighten many. We'd better privily warn those who are ill if we can, but it's not a bad idea. If the Indians *are* plotting, it'll mystify them."

"Aye," said Underhill, his brown eyes sparkling, for he found Boston very dull, and the sloppy military ignorance of the Bay exasperating. "Tonight then, sir, about nine o' the clock."

Underhill had already laid his plans and he moved fast. He gathered together the few professional guards, and the halberdiers, and he sent horsemen to summon his lieutenants and the most likely of his train band. He pitched a tent on Boston Common and received them all with a long face and dark talk of Indian raids that night.

On the other side of the river Patrick did the same for his territory of Charlestown, Newtown, and Watertown.

At nine o'clock Underhill fired an enormous bonfire on the Sentry crest of Trimount to act as a warning beacon. When the flames were leaping twenty feet in the air, and could certainly be seen by all the villages, he began to set off cannon in series of three blasts, the long-arranged signal for imminent danger, when all settlers in Roxbury and Dorchester were supposed to rush into Boston whose narrow neck could easily be barricaded and defended.

On Patrick's side the same procedure was carried out,

but there the settlers were to go to the palisade at Newtown.

From the two captains' pessimistic point of view the alarm was a great success. The people panicked and most of them forgot their instructions. The few who came into the camps milled around in wild excitement, weeping, wringing their hands and refusing to obey orders. Some dashed off in boats for one of the Bay islands, some fled into the forests, but most stayed cowering in their homes, many cursing their carelessness in not having seen to a low stock of powder, or a jammed matchlock. The rumors flew apparently through the air. It was King Charles's fleet come to punish them for leaving England. It was the French come to claim Massachusetts. It was pirates. It was Spaniards. Very few thought of the Indians, whom they all saw daily and were accustomed to.

"Well, sir," said Underhill triumphantly to Winthrop next day when the Governor walked to the Common to see how things were going. "Was I not right? They scattered like fowl, 'stead o' banding together in strength, and they cackled and fluttered like hens too."

"Aye," Winthrop nodded gravely. "We'll appoint new officers, Captain, strengthen the train bands, and keep watch day and night. I pray the people will profit by this lesson, which God inspired you to teach them."

Elizabeth and Margaret had of course been forewarned of the alarm, and stayed quietly indoors during the excitement, so that when Elizabeth finally left the nearly recovered Margaret two days later, she was startled to find that people outside Boston had not settled down yet. She rode pillion behind Tom French again, and noted as they passed through Charlestown that folk were still gathered in knots anxiously whispering, and that there was a crowd before the Newtown Meetinghouse where those who could read were explaining a reassuring placard put up on the door by Patrick.

She arrived at her home in the late afternoon, and hastened to inquire from Sally how things had gone in her absence.

The girl was evasive, her squint-eyes shifted. Now and then she cast a nervous glance over her shoulder towards the door.

"Was the alarm very scary?" asked Elizabeth sympathetically. "There was no danger, you know, it was sham."

"Aye, ma'am. Oi know." Sally began to pound corn in a mortar, and seemed to be reluctant to say more, while Elizabeth watched her puzzled.

"Joan and Mr. Feake weren't very upset, were they?" she persisted.

Sally shook her head. "Captain Patrick warned us ahead. 'Twasn't that."

"What then, Sally? Something's troubling you."

Sally's hand dropped from the pestle. " 'Tis Marster," she whispered. "He's not been roight since directly after ye went."

"What do you mean, Sally? Surely he hasn't been ill. He could have sent for me."

The girl shook her head. "Not wot ye'd call ill, only he'd shut hisself up i' the chamber, day in day out. Oncet Oi heard him talking as if someone was in there—then he took to straying in the woods all day, our men said they didn't know where . . . Oh, ma'am—" Sally gave a gasp and put her hands to her mouth. "D'ye think he's bewitched?"

"Fiddle!" said Elizabeth with more firmness than she felt. "Where is he now?"

Sally hunched her shoulders. "Oi don't know, ma'am. He went out afore sunrise."

Much disturbed, Elizabeth walked back along the path towards Newtown and the Patrick house. If anyone knew what had been happening, Daniel would, and she prayed he was there. He was. Anneke came to the double door, her rosy face beaming when she saw her visitor, and the women exchanged a kiss. " 'Tis good you're home," said Anneke, hospitably ushering Elizabeth into her shining, scrubbed kitchen. "Ve have missed you."

Patrick too welcomed her warmly, but she wasted no time in greetings. "Sally tells me Robert has been acting strange. Do you know anything about it?"

The Captain's smiling face sobered. "Aye. He was a little odd, wanting to be alone. I kept an eye on him when I could. Some fit o' the bile perhaps, but I wouldn't fret. I think he's out of it. I appointed him me lieutenant, and he acted as though I'd dubbed him a knight."

"He was *pleased?*" she said, trying to imagine Robert in a military role.

Patrick nodded. He had no intention of telling her how very peculiar he had thought Feake's looks and actions for a few days, and that they had culminated on the night of the alarm when he had gone into a kind of frenzy, partly it seemed from fear for Elizabeth, and partly that the booming of the cannons, the bonfires and general panic seemed to touch off some private fear in him, and this even though he had been told that the alarm was not real. Feake had clung to Patrick at that time, following him about, seeming lost and dazed. Patrick had had to speak to him roughly, and order him to shoulder a gun and drill with the others who had come to the Common.

Certainly nobody would think Feake promising material for a lieutenant after that, and yet Patrick, who instinctively understood men's quirks and recognized self-distrust and misery when he saw it, was sorry for the man. Even sorrier for Elizabeth in whom he took a strong protective interest. So he had decided to risk the appointment as a temporary measure. Patrick's hopes were justified. The honor and confidence the Captain bestowed jerked Feake out of his queerness. He was conscientious and pleasant-voiced. The men liked him well enough, and his relationship to the Governor precluded jealousy at the appointment.

"Well, I wish I knew where he was," said Elizabeth disconsolately after a moment. "I don't understand where he's been roaming."

"He's not roaming *now*—" said Patrick, stuffing one of Anneke's Dutch honey cakes in his mouth and washing it down with brown ale, "He's drilling Watertown train band on the Common."

"Ah—" breathed Elizabeth, deeply relieved and proud too. Obviously that foolish Sally had exaggerated her tale. She walked home again in a happy mood, and was further reassured when Robert came running in later and very nearly wept with delight at seeing her back.

In his cuirass, high boots and red sword-sash of office he looked more manly than she had ever seen him, and she responded with warmth to his embrace. She never questioned him about the period of her absence, and he never referred to it.

10

ON WEDNESDAY, May 14, 1634, Boston held a meeting of the General Court and an election by ballot which resulted in shock and humiliation for John Winthrop. He had been under a constant fire of criticism lately. Watertown continued to clamor for a direct voice in the government. The other towns followed suit, particularly Newtown, where Dudley's disapproval of Winthrop now gained backing from the newly arrived minister, Thomas Hooker.

John Winthrop himself had a new partisan in the Reverend John Cotton who had arrived last year from Boston in Old England, to share new Boston's church pulpit with Wilson. Cotton was a dramatic preacher and a striking man with his fresh rosy face and fluffy white hair. He believed as thoroughly as Winthrop did in the Bible Commonwealth and in the divine right of vested authority. And he preached a sermon informing the people that those set over them to rule must never be deprived of power and "turned into private men" except for extraordinary wickedness. The people listened, but fear had been growing. They had fled Old England to avoid the tyranny of kings, and many thought that someone as entrenched and arbitrary as a king was rapidly developing in their midst. Also it was pointed out that sinister meaning might well lurk in the Winthrop family motto "Spes vincit thronum."

Many too pondered uncertainly over Winthrop's pronouncement that "If we should change from a mixt aristocratie to a mere Democratie, first we should have no warrant in Scripture for it—there was no such government in Israel, and a Democratie is, amongst nations, accounted the meanest and worst of all forms of government." On the whole they agreed with him, yet some wondered uneasily whether the Bay Colony was never to be permitted *any* form of government except that used by Hebrews many thousands of years ago.

The unrest grew and in April a delegation of freemen from each town waited on Winthrop and demanding a look at the Charter, crowed with triumph at finding it stating that they should take part in the General Court and all lawmaking. The Governor, who did not so interpret the clause, kept his temper with difficulty, and finally conceded as a favor that he would allow each town to select three men to appear at the court as representatives for the other church members. Those not so sanctified had naturally no hope of legislative voice. The delegation accepted this concession with only temperate enthusiasm, and when John told Margaret about it his voice shook.

"The ingrates," he said. "I gave them all that they could want—and more. They've not the wits to rule, or meddle with the laws. The best part of a community is always the least, and of that best part the wiser ones are fewer yet. As the excellent Mr. Cotton said, 'If the people be Governor who shall be governed?' Consider, Margaret, if Groton Manor had been ruled by tenants, what a sorry botch they would have made!"

Margaret agreed anxiously, not understanding all this very well except that John was harassed, and as usual exhausting himself trying to govern people many of whom were unappreciative, and inexplicably hostile. Besides she was near to term in another pregnancy, and though in better health than last time, had no thought for public worries.

The towns hastened to avail themselves of their new privilege and each chose three deputies to go to Boston and the General Court on May 14. Watertown picked its three largest landowners: Richard Browne, John Oldham, the Indian trader, and Robert Feake.

Thus it was that the whole Feake family was in Boston

on Election Day and that Elizabeth was standing with other women on the sunny green outside the meetinghouse listening to the hum of male voices inside and wondering why there was a sudden hush, then an uproar of shouts, groans, hand-clappings and hisses.

She soon found out, for Jack Winthrop who, as one of the colony assistants, had of course been present, stalked out of the meetinghouse looking grim and seeing her, came over. "They've ousted Father," he said in a low tense voice. "Dudley's in."

"What!" cried Elizabeth staring at him. "You don't mean Dudley's to be *Governor!*" It was impossible to think of her uncle as anything but supreme authority; impossible and dis-concerting too, unnatural.

"Aye," said Jack. "Father's not even deputy. Roger Lud-low is. Those new selectmen did it."

"Not Robert—?" she faltered, frowning and still trying to rearrange her ideas.

"Oh no, not Robert, of course—but most of the others." Jack laughed suddenly on a sharp note. "Ah well, it's an ill wind that blows good to none. Dudley's been hankering after this for years and Father needs a rest. He'll put a good face on it, though 'tis a bitter pill, for now Dudley'll move the capital to Newtown—well entrenched with his cronies, Lud-low, the Reverend Mr. Hooker, and John Haynes."

"I can't believe it," said Elizabeth, astonished to find that she felt sorry for her uncle; and in a few moments, proud of him, as he walked out of the meetinghouse side by side with Dudley who was flushed with victory. Winthrop held his head high, his smile was tight, but it *was* a smile, as he ceremoniously waved to his beadle and halberdiers to take their places before the new governor. He showed none of his inner confusion and dismay while he labored to accept, not the will of the people, for this he considered stupid if not wicked, but what was perhaps the Will of God.

"I must go to him," said Jack, watching his father walk with Dudley while the people cheered uncertainly. "Dudley and Council will dine with us as arranged before this—this reversal. 'Twill not be an easy meal—but Bess—I must ask you something first."

"Yes?" she said wondering. She had seen Jack but seldom since her marriage and not at all since he and Martha had moved thirty miles north to the new settlement at Agawam last autumn.

" 'Tis my poor Martha," he said. "Hasn't she written you that for three months or so she is at last with child?"

"No!" Elizabeth cried. "Jack, how wonderful! But why hasn't she written? I confess it pains me that she hasn't."

"Oh, she's had a cold, and her spirits are mopish," he said with some exasperation. "She has nervous fancies, like all breeding women, I suppose. But she longs for you, Bess. I found her weeping over a fine lace handkerchief she says you gave her once at Christmas in London years ago. 'Tis wild country up there and lonely, so few women yet. Bess—could you?"

"Go to Agawam?" she said slowly, thinking of Robert, Joan, and her own baby of scarce a year, and still unweaned.

"Aye," he said. "If you could go to Agawam, or Ipswich rather, for so we've named it—just for a visit, I know 'twould cheer her. I must be away so much and she frets after me, poor lass, she's so timid."

"To be sure I'll go," Elizabeth said after a moment. She looked up into his steady brown eyes. He clasped her hand, said, "God bless you, we'll arrange later," and strode off down King Street towards the Winthrop home.

Robert came out of the meetinghouse much distressed at the way the election had gone, and fearful that Winthrop might somehow blame him for not having influenced the other two Watertown deputies. Elizabeth reassured him, and forbore mentioning Martha or the trip to Ipswich as yet. This was a holiday, the only one permitted by the colony, and the Feakes, like all the settlers from nearby towns, planned to enjoy it, no matter who was Governor. The Feakes had come downriver by water and brought food in baskets. Before running off to amuse themselves, Sally and the men-servants laid out the provisions on the grassy slope of Tri-mount, in the shadow of apple trees planted around William Blackstone's spring. The center of the Common was still nearly treeless, and very hot on this bright May day, so that other family parties crowded near the Feakes, and there was a temporary awkwardness when members of the Dudley clan ensconced themselves nearby. These were the new governor's daughter—Anne Bradstreet and her children; also Mary and Sam with their baby. Robert, at once embarrassed, wanted to move away, but Joan darted over to play with the little Bradstreets, and Elizabeth, feeling that constraint was un-tenable, called out laughing to Mary, "Aren't *you* the fortunate lass! Since you have a father for governor no matter *what* happens!"

Mary smiled. The tall dreamy Anne Bradstreet, who never seemed quite aware of her surroundings, looked around and smiled too. Soon all the new babies were being compared, and Robert was relieved when he heard his own little Lisbet admired. She was very like him in coloring, a silvery fairylike child, undemanding and quiet. She had given Elizabeth no trouble at her birthing, and she seldom cried now. Robert was wonderingly proud of her and had insisted she be named for his wife, much against Elizabeth's wishes who yearned for something romantic like Celia or Pernelle. But Robert had shown a curious streak of stubbornness until Elizabeth had yielded. And now in its shortened form of Lisbet the name did suit the child.

That Election Day was a merrier gathering than any Elizabeth had seen in New England. Several ships had come in that week; the town was full of newcomers, by no means all of them strict Puritans. On that brilliant spring day, little Boston wore an almost settled and cosmopolitan air. The ships had made quick voyages and had supplies left to sell. John Coggin, a wealthy merchant, had opened the first general shop, and public pressure had finally resulted in a licensed tavern—an ordinary—run by one Samuel Cole. The delighted settlers patronized it lavishly, though Cole's brother, Robert, wandering the streets with a red D for Drunkard sewn on his doublet, also provided a warning which went unheeded as the day advanced. Nobody was very sure how severe Dudley would be on moral laxities, and it seemed reasonable to enjoy oneself in the interregnum. Moreover, Boston's ministers Cotton and Wilson were dining at the Winthrops', so that except for the very godly, who soon withdrew to their homes, there was no curb on the normal English love of sports, drinking and horseplay. It was very like a Fair Day at Boxford.

There were three military leaders in the colony now, by the addition of John Mason who commanded the Dorchester militia, and on the parade ground all the captains held competitive drilling of their train bands, which produced an agreeable background of stamping feet, drums, fifes, and occasional wild musket shots. Soon there was singing too. Some of the new-come lasses and lads began the May songs they had loved in their English villages, and Robert Cole, unabashed by his red badge of shame and half tipsy despite it, started up the ballad "Robin Hood and Little John, They both are gone to the fair, O!"

The sport rapidly grew rougher. A squealing greased pig was brought and set loose for the young men to catch, there was a tug-of-war, and a wild sack race to the ducking pond and back. Near the Feake and Dudley parties somebody started to play the fiddle and a group of youngsters from Essex caught hands and began to dance while the surrounding ring jiggled and clapped hands and cheered when shrieking girls were caught and kisses snatched.

"This is getting very lewd," said Mary drawing her brows together like her father. "Samuel, I think you should stop them. Dear me, isn't that *Stephen*, wrestling with that chandler's boy?"

Elizabeth, who was thoroughly enjoying herself and wishing she dared dance, looked with interest where Mary was pointing. It was indeed Stephen, Margaret's eldest son. He was as panting and yelling and dirty as any of them, and this despite his dramatic conversion two months ago, when as Winthrop had solemnly recorded in his journal the fourteen-year-old Stephen had been

buffeted by Satan, and so broken for his sins that he mourned and languished daily, until at last he confessed his blasphemous and wicked thoughts openly and was freed from temptation and received into the church.

"Aye—His Worship—that is—Mr. Winthrop will be much upset when he sees this revelry—" said Robert nervously, while Samuel went off to reprimand Stephen. "Come, wife, I think we should go."

"Wait," Elizabeth said scarcely listening. She stood up and shielding her eyes peered down the Common where there was a cannon-ball-pitching contest. There was something familiar about the large figure which was whirling and flinging the heavy iron ball.

"I'll be back soon," she said to the astonished Robert. She walked around the dancers and down the strip of trampled rough grass through the crowd until she came to the contest. "Will Hallet," she whispered, and felt a peculiar, not entirely pleasant thrill. He had changed a good deal in three years, grown and broadened so that he was much larger than all the other men except his opponent—Bigelow, the blacksmith. Will's face was still fresh colored though shadowed now by a stubble of beard, his lank hair was darker and cut off below his ears. His sweaty leather doublet hung open and disclosed a chest full of curly hair. As he lifted the cannon ball with two hands and swung it back for the throw, the muscles swelled in his powerful arms and long sturdy thighs. The ball fell on the far side of a stick, beyond that thrown by the blacksmith, and some of the crowd cheered, "Good lad, Will! Go it, Hallet. I've bet all my pence on ye!" Others groaned and encouraged the smith.

Elizabeth waited at the edge of the crowd until the cannon balls were thrown again and Hallet won, when a pretty girl of about sixteen rushed up to him and throwing a garland of green maple leaves around his neck gave him a hearty kiss. Oh, thought Elizabeth. Of course, there'd be a girl with blue eyes and yellow ringlets, maybe there was even a babe at home somewhere.

She turned to leave, chiding herself for the unconsidered impulse which had made her rush over here, when Hallet saw her. The girl was clinging to his arm, but he pushed her aside impatiently, tore off the maple wreath and strode towards Elizabeth. "Mistress Winthrop?" he said with the gently-bred intonation which seemed so incongruous with his rough shabby clothes and workman's haircut.

"Not Winthrop now," she said quickly. "Soon after landing I married a gentleman called Robert Feake. We live at Watertown."

"Ah so?" he looked down at her with courteous interest and something else she couldn't quite fathom, since it seemed to be compounded of admiration and wariness. She noted for the first time that his eyes were gray, and their composed stare had the remembered effect of embarrassing her.

"Where have *you* been, since we left the *Lyon?*" she said, turning away and starting to walk.

"Roving," he answered, falling into step beside her. "North of Piscataqua, even into New France. By-the-bye I saw Lady Gardiner up there last year."

"Mirabelle?" she cried. "Oh, what's happened to her? I still miss her."

Will laughed. "You shouldn't by rights, since she pokes fun at your colony. You should hear the drolleries she tells of Puritans! In Quebec she made de Champlain and the Abbé of the Récollets shake with mirth."

"No doubt," said Elizabeth dryly, knowing nothing of New France except that the English considered it a fearful

Papist menace. "Is she there now?"

"Nay, she returned to England with her husband." Where Sir Christopher, still smarting from his treatment in Massachusetts, had every intention of making trouble, Will thought with amusement. The inborn shrewdness of the English yeoman had, in Will Hallet, through the accident of his aristocratic rearing, ripened to a sophistication which his recent years of total independence had matured. People's foibles and motives often amused him, and for his age he was an acute observer.

They had both unconsciously paused near the pond, and Elizabeth saw the yellow-haired girl hovering behind them and pouting. "Is that your lass?" she asked suddenly, with a casual smile, "or wife, mayhap?"

Hallet looked around. "Good Lord, no! I ne'er saw her until I came back here two days past. D'you think me fool enough to marry at eighteen? I've no wish for shackles."

From this reply Elizabeth derived both satisfaction and a qualm. Eighteen, she thought, not yet a man despite his size, while I am twenty-four and well shackled. She saw that several people who knew her by sight were staring at them curiously, and she drew herself up saying in a brisk condescending voice, "It's been pleasant to meet you again. Always I'll feel grateful for your brave act on the ship. Do you stay long in Boston?"

He shrugged, instantly noting her change of tone, and his became as formal. "I daresay not. I've kin from Dorset now in Plymouth Colony. I may see them, but I've a fancy to go south for a change, maybe Virginia. The ships'll always sign on a good carpenter."

"Ah, would that I were free as you!" Elizabeth cried involuntarily, swept by a familiar ache, and a new pain too which was in some way connected with this huge sweaty lad who stood beside her. She swayed closer to him without knowing it, and his wary gaze softened in response. "But you're a woman," he said. "For a man 'la plus grande chose au monde c'est de savoir estre à soi'—his own master—but a *woman!* A woman, an ass, and a walnut tree, the harder you beat them the better they be!"

"You knave!" she cried, with a spurt of startled laughter. "Was that *French* you spoke?"

"Montaigne," he said grinning. "I told you I'd a most elegant education, and the run of one of the best libraries in England."

"Will, you're—you're fantastical," she said. "Why don't you use that education, why you could be schoolmaster here, I shouldn't wonder, or you could—"

"Elizabeth?" called a querulous voice behind her. "Bess, where have you been? I've been searching the Common!"

It was Robert, his face pinched with annoyance and uncertainty.

Elizabeth flushed and recovered at once. "Oh, Robert, I'm sorry, but this is William Hallet. I haven't seen him since we crossed on the *Lyon* where he gave all the Winthrops cause to be grateful to him."

"Oh indeed," Robert faltered, mollified by her smile and mention of the Winthrop name.

"Forgive me for detaining your lady, Mr. Feake. I was telling her of my travels in New France," said Will quietly, absorbing in one quick glance the slightness of Elizabeth's husband, the white-lashed eyes that watered and blinked nervously in the sunlight, the slender womanish hands, the immaculate lawn falling-bands and cuffs.

Robert, in his turn staring at the young giant who looked like a laborer and spoke like a gentleman, responded to the attraction which strength and masculinity always held for him. "Why, good day, Mr. Hallet," he said, inclining his head. "I didn't mean to speak harsh but I was worried about my wife's absence. Our relatives have been waiting—some members of the Winthrop and Dudley families, that is."

Elizabeth noted Robert's unconscious use of the honorable prefix "Mr." and also that Will ceased to smile when Robert mentioned her exalted relatives. He will never allow himself to be patronized again, she thought, and spoke quickly. "*Do* come to see us in Watertown, please! Any day take the ferry to Charlestown, then follow the riverbank west a few miles until you come to our home lot. The house is quite large, thatched; there's a sapling fence covered with honeysuckle, and an iron door knocker with a lion's head."

"Aye, do come," said Robert dutifully, though he did not understand the urgency in his wife's voice.

Hallet bowed. "You are both very kind." He hesitated a moment, looking at Elizabeth's eager lovely face. A sudden confusion came on him, for he felt his heart beat thick and fast. He reddened, seeming all at once the boy he still was, and he spoke awkwardly in the rougher language of his early childhood. "Shan't have time enough. I mean to ship out —tomorrow. And I must shog off now." He turned briskly and beckoned to the blond girl who had seated herself on the bank of the pond and was sulkily picking apart her rejected maple wreath.

He's nothing but a rude boor, after all, thought Elizabeth. She raised her chin and said, "Well, then some other time perhaps, if amongst *all* your journeyings, you should return to Boston. I give you good day." She managed a quick thin smile, and linked her arm in Robert's. She did not look back as they walked towards Blackstone's spring and the waiting children.

It was not until they reached home that night that she remembered her promise to visit Martha, and realized that if Will Hallet had come to Watertown, she might well have not been there to see him. She put him resolutely from her thoughts, which did not prevent a strange and humiliating dream some nights later in which she lay in Will Hallet's arms, felt his naked hairy chest pressing on her breasts, and kissed him in an abandon so piercing sweet that she awoke; and saw Robert creeping out of bed in the dawn-light bound, she thought, for the privy. She stared at the hunched-over form in the white night shirt while the dream faded. Then she said quietly, "What is it, Rob? The gripes again?"

He started, and turned his head, seeming confused, as sometimes happened at night. "The gripes—?" he repeated, his voice hoarse and dragging. "Pain—in the darkness—like it was then—but not for *him,* not any more—nor can he tell them unless the Devil tells them—"

"Rob!" she cried, jumping out of bed. "You must have fever!" and she felt his forehead which was cool and dank. "Pray God 'tis not smallpox . . ." she whispered. There was a raging epidemic of smallpox amongst the Indians, but it seemed to spare the whites.

"Let me go," said Robert in the same hoarse voice. "I must wash my hands. Wash them in the Blood of the Lamb . . ." He pushed past her and ran to the ewer of water on the table.

"Robert! Wake up, dear," she said shaking him. "Your hands are clean, you needn't wash them!"

He put the ewer down, heeding her voice. "I needn't wash them?"

"No, no," she said. "Come back to bed. Lie down. I'll bring you mint to breathe, 'twill clear you of these vapors."

He obeyed her, and after he had sniffed the crushed mint, fell into a heavy sleep, but she was uneasy until morning when she examined his fair thin skin closely for any sign of the dreaded pocks. There were none, and Robert seemed his normal self, except that he questioned her anxiously as to what he had said in the night.

"Some nonsense about washing your hands," she said. "I was so sleepy I really don't know. As long as it's not small-pox—"

He shook his head. "I had that as a babe in Norfolk, I believe. But you, Bess, on this trip to Ipswich, you will pass through Indian country where they say all are dying of it."

"Oh la. Don't fret," she said smiling. "A London-reared child has taken every sickness by the time it's grown—if it survive. Have no fear for me." She watched to see if mention of London would cause the "strangeness" but it did not. And she wondered too if there would be any repetition of his odd actions the last time she had left him alone. She was taking Sally with her since Martha badly needed servants, and now her usual semi-maternal care for Robert, sharpened by contrition over the shameful dream of Hallet, suggested an idea. Robert should go with Joan to the Patricks'. He always seemed content near the big rough Irishman, while Anneke was the soul of beaming hospitality. And so it was arranged.

The next morning Elizabeth set off at sunrise on the long Indian trail through the wilderness. Her uncle had sent Tom French with the horse. Elizabeth mounted, holding Lisbet in a basket across her lap. The servants, Sally and Tom, walked alongside. Their clothing hung in saddlebags behind the cantle. Elizabeth, as they struck north past Fresh Pond towards the Mystic River, was not pleased to hear from Tom that they must stop at Winthrop's farm "Ten Hills" where His Worship would join them for the journey as far as Saugus. She had wanted to enjoy the silence of the forest and the feeling of adventure, and always found her uncle's company a strain. But there was no help for it.

At eight they reached a well-cleared grassy plateau, with a view of both the Charles and Mystic Rivers. Here fruit trees had been planted, and an experimental crop of barley. Here too was a flock of sheep, and a long low house made of wattle and daub. Winthrop had designed to make "Ten Hills" his country estate, but spent little time here since recently gratifying the perennial English itch for land. He had now acquired many other acres around Boston Harbor and an island called The Governor's Garden which Margaret much preferred for its safety and accessibility.

John Winthrop greeted his niece somewhat absently, offered her cider and hasty pudding, then mounting his own horse hurried them all down the hill to Medford where they were ferried across the Mystic. Winthrop remarked politely that he hoped Elizabeth had left her family in health and would find Martha improved, then lapsed into a dark silence until they reached a collection of wigwams which he said was John Sagamore's chief village.

"It seems deserted," said Elizabeth, staring at the smokeless vents in the round bark shelters. There was no life to be seen except a brindle cur scratching its fleas on the muddy bank where a dozen empty canoes were drawn up. Half a deer carcass, hung on sticks, was oozing putrefaction in the sun, but the nauseating stench of the village did not come from the deer carcass alone. Their horses quivered and shied. Tom had trouble holding the bridles.

"Ho there! Netop! Netop! John Sagamore, are you there?" Winthrop called. There was no answer for a moment and then a faint ghastly wail came from one of the shelters. "Aieah-aieh-ah . . ."

An old woman crawled through a door, inching along on her elbows, her matted gray hair streaming around her. "Aih-eh-yah," she moaned again, lifting a sightless face encrusted so thick with sores running yellow pus that she had no features.

"My God," whispered Elizabeth snatching up the baby and holding her so that she might not see, while Sally with a cry of horror hid behind a rock. Winthrop dismounted and walking carefully around the moaning old woman peered into the wigwams.

"Dead. All of them," he said as he came back. "John Sagamore too. You see how God fights for us in smiting our enemies. The Massachusetts tribes are near wiped out, the Narragansetts also. Ah, the Blessed Lord hath tenderly cleared our title to the land we possess!" He clasped his hands and raised grateful eyes to the sky.

"But these Indians weren't our enemies," said Elizabeth sharply. "The raids we feared never happened, and *we* brought the smallpox to them on our ships."

"What matter the channel God uses, Elizabeth?" said her uncle frowning. "Why must you always be contentious and ignorant? Do you not know that Captain Stone and his men were killed by Indians last winter, and another trader too?"

"Yes, I know," she said. "But that was in Pequot country."

And who knows what provocation the Pequots were given, she added to herself. She had no special fondness for the Indians she had met, but the sight of this gruesome village sickened her, as her uncle's smug certainty of God's intentions always annoyed her. Winthrop mounted and flicked the bridle.

"But she's still alive! We can't leave her like this!" Elizabeth cried pointing to the body on the ground that flopped back and forth gasping like a great fish.

"What could be done for her?" said Winthrop in icy tones. "And she's not a Christian."

Elizabeth bowed her head and suffered Tom to lead her horse along the trail. What indeed could be done? Except, she thought looking angrily at her uncle's back, pay these poor savages at least the tribute of pity, and not glory in their destruction.

They continued for some time silent on the trail that led through a virgin forest of maples, hickory and elm. Here and there Elizabeth noted the strange native wildflowers in bloom, so different from any seen in England, though the settlers had given them English names. The curiously shaped jack-in-the-pulpit, the roots of which the Indians boiled and ate like turnips; the shy beautiful lady's-slipper; and clumps of the white perky little flowers that Plymouth's children fresh from Holland had christened Dutchman's breeches.

As they reached a tiny pond, Lisbet began to whimper. "The babe's hungry, sir," called Elizabeth to Winthrop's back. "I fear I should stop and suckle her."

He reined in his horse at once and dismounted. "Sit there —" he said indicating a fallen tree trunk, at a little distance from the horses. A trifle surprised, Elizabeth obeyed, and began to unfasten her bodice when her uncle walked over and stood beside her in a preoccupied manner. "You think me lacking in pity or lenity," he said abruptly, scowling down at the rich dark earth.

Elizabeth, more astonished, saw that while she had been able to forget their disagreement in gazing at the wildflowers, Winthrop must have been brooding over her unspoken criticism. "I would not presume to judge you, sir," she said covering her breast with her kerchief as the baby began to nurse.

"There were some Indians came to my house for succor last week," he said. "I took them in. They died except for one boy child, whom I've named Know-God and shall keep as servant and raise a Christian."

"Everyone knows you to be charitable," she murmured, amazed that he should bother to explain himself to her.

"I thought so," he said. "I've beggared my own fortune and most of my son John's for the public weal, and yet they *dare* to call me to account as though I had embezzled colony funds!"

"Call you to account?" she repeated, and saw that after all he was not really talking to her; it was but the boiling over of his long-pent wrath.

"I'd not give the purblind knaves their accounting—why should I? When God set me over them to rule them, an honor I had never searched—except that—" His nostrils dilated, his round eyes hardened like agates in their bony sockets.

"This commonwealth is founded by our Blessed Lord," he cried with passion. "It *must* succeed! No enemies within or without, no jealousies, no factions, not even righteous indignation, must be allowed to interfere with God's plan for His Elected Saints!" His voice trembled, and with awe she saw the tears start to his eyes. "We are but four thousand people yet, like the Israelites, and pressed like them from all sides—Sir Ferdinando Gorges' hirelings and New France on the north, across the sea our persecutors in England; to the south beyond the Dutch a Papist place called Maryland has been established. The west has cannibalistic Mohawks. Beset like this from every quarter, what hope have we but to stand close together in ourselves—with amity?"

He has been suffering, she thought astonished; in that nature which she felt to be harsh and bigoted, there was yet a burning ideal, and a desire so great for the welfare of the land he had founded that he would sacrifice his pride to it.

He raised his head and gazed across the little pond towards a distant hill. "Would that like Moses I might hear the direct Voice of God on Sinai . . ." he said beneath his breath. "And yet have I not, like all of the elect amongst us, had sign of God's special favor? If He were not pleased with our inheriting these parts, why does He drive out the natives and diminish them as we increase? Why hath He planted His true Church here, and declared His presence among us by the saving of many souls?—Ah, *this* I shall say to Mr. Williams at Salem tomorrow."

He turned and walked away from her, clasping his hands behind his back. So Roger Williams had been fulminating against the colony again, thought Elizabeth, enlightened as to the particular reason for her uncle's explosion. Even in Watertown they heard often about the firebrand of a preacher who had returned to Salem on sufferance, but would not be stilled. He constantly disturbed the people with his doubts—of their exclusive sainthood, of the infallibility of ministers and magistrates, and of their moral title to Indian lands. And, thought Elizabeth suddenly, I think this Williams is *right!* The conclusion dismayed her for its disloyalty to the Winthrops. She sighed heavily, glimpsing conflicting values which seemed to threaten all the structure of her life.

Then the baby grunted and fell back replete. Elizabeth kissed Lisbet's silvery curls, fastened her bodice, and breathed deep of the soft shimmering air. The sun was warm on her shoulders, but a little breeze quivered through the leaves and made ripples on the blue pond. She saw a scarlet bird streak by and wondered what it was, but a chattering blue jay she recognized. Pale pink flowers like stars were struggling towards the light from under the log she sat on. She leaned over and freed them from grass and choking bark, then without picking it cupped one in her hand. In *these* things are my content, she thought with immediate guilt. Surely content should not come from the beauty of a tiny flower, but from religious conviction, and the certainty of righteousness.

They continued on the trail which widened and became a lane as they approached Saugus. Winthrop, his dark mood relieved, presently fell back beside his niece and spoke of family matters. He said he hoped Elizabeth would return in time for Margaret's confinement, but he was not unduly alarmed about it since there was now an excellent midwife in Boston—Mrs. Hawkins. He told her news of little Deane still at school in England and of the Downings who were at last seriously preparing to come over, though, said Winthrop, his sister Lucy was much afflicted with ague and eye trouble, and dreaded the voyage. When they entered Saugus, he mentioned its nearby deposits of bog-iron ore, adding with the pride in which he always spoke of Jack, "Son John thinks to found an ironworks here, for he understands such things, and it would be a marvel for us to dispense with importing costly English implements."

Elizabeth politely agreed, and they drew up before the largest house in the village which belonged to Nathaniel Turner. Here Winthrop was to spend the night before going on to Salem to see Endecott and the rebellious Roger Williams.

At the Turners' there was a rearrangement. Winthrop retained Tom, since it was unthinkable for the former governor to travel without a manservant, and Mr. Turner lent Elizabeth his stalwart young son for escort. Also another horse, that she might make the remaining miles to Ipswich in safety before dusk.

"God preserve you, my dear," said Winthrop, kissing her gravely on the forehead. "Have no fear of wolves or other wild beasts, they are menacing only at night, and besides you see Mr. Turner's lad is well armed."

Sally unfortunately heard this, and letting out a shriek, plumped herself down on the Turners' floor, and refused to budge. "Oi'll not go further, thot Oi'll not! Ye can do wot ye loike, Oi'll not go on amidst the Indian pox, nor gi' meself fur mincemeat to wolveses!"

"You shall certainly be flogged if you're a disobedient servant," Winthrop said. "Get up and accompany your mistress at once!"

Sally shook her head and drumming her heels on the boards yelped hysterically. Whereupon, Mrs. Turner, brawny ruler of a well-disciplined household, came rushing up and glared at the culprit. "Lack-a-day—" she said to Elizabeth. " 'Tis a snotty-nosed wench ye have there, Mistress Feake! Since ye've the babe in your arms, I'll mend her ways for you." The goodwife boxed Sally hard on the ears, then picking up the hearth broom belabored the girl across the back and shoulders. Elizabeth had slapped Sally once or twice under great provocation, and sometimes spanked Joan, but her own childhood memory prevented her from beating either, and she made a sound of remonstrance now.

The effect on Sally however was certainly salutary. She jumped up, crying, "Oi'll go, Oi'll go—" and running to Elizabeth moaned for forgiveness.

"Ye see?" said Mrs. Turner complacently, "Cut a limber stick when ye're on the way, switch her well wi' it, if she try more tricks."

Sally's revolt was over. Sniveling she mounted pillion behind young Turner and rode off on the Indian trail to the north. They continued without further incident. The sun was low behind the western hills when they saw chimney smoke. The sky darkened and the wind began to blow, whistling through a stand of hemlocks. The air suddenly smelled of storm. As they passed the first cabin of this desolate frontier hamlet a dog somewhere howled mournfully, and Elizabeth shivered. They followed the sharply curving riverbank and the ford. The water looked black and sinister, bordered as it was with great rocks and overhanging pines. In the eerie yellow gloaming the handful of little houses seemed to huddle anxiously, with their backs pressed against the bleak ridge of a stony hill. The wind puffed harder and dust swirled around them, stinging their eyes and making the horses snort.

"Is that the meetinghouse?" Elizabeth asked young Turner, more to hear a voice than because she doubted the identity of the only large building in sight, a great raw boxy structure flanked by stocks and whipping post.

"Aye," said young Turner, "and someone's got wolf bounty, I see." He pointed to three bleeding wolf heads nailed to the church door. "Ten shilling a head they fetch up here!"

They continued, walking slowly, near the river. "Yon—" said the lad, pointing again, "is young Mr. Wintrup's."

It wasn't a bad house considering, thought Elizabeth. And the outhouses looked adequate. It was but the owl-light of coming storm made everything seem to melancholy, and it would be a sorry thing if she gave way to dumpish fancies when Martha needed cheering.

Fat raindrops began to fall as they knocked. There was an uproar of deep barks and growls from three Irish wolf-hounds Jack had imported and kept chained in a shed. The door was flung open by Jack with a hearty "Welcome! Welcome, Bess!" They kissed briefly because it would have looked strange if they hadn't, and entered the front room which was lighted by many rush dips and the fire. Martha sat shivering on a stool by the hearth, a linen kerchief pressed to her mouth. She got up slowly as her sister entered. "I thought you wouldn't come—" she said, holding out her arms. "Oh, Bess, I didn't believe you'd come, way up here."

Elizabeth put down the baby and running caught her sister close to her, feeling with dismay the frailness of the little body; and seeing as Martha's handkerchief dropped to the floor that it was covered with blood stains.

"I told you Bess'd be here today," said Jack, pouring beer for them all. "*Now*, my dearest Matt, you'll have good care and cheer up and be quite well again!"

"I will, I will," said Martha, her large sunken eyes turning trustfully towards her husband. She began to choke. A spasm of coughing racked her and she sank down on the stool, grabbing the handkerchief.

"You'll know some simple that'll cure the cough," said

Jack to Elizabeth with assurance. " 'Tis just a lingering cold she caught in March; the house was chill before we got all the chinks properly daubed."

Chill indeed, Elizabeth thought, for the walls were not yet tight and draughts blew through the room. She turned and looked at Martha, who had stopped coughing and lay back exhausted with her head against the rough fieldstone chimney piece. Elizabeth saw the hectic red spots on the girl's cheekbones, the blue veins showing through transparent skin at the hollow temples. She saw that the little hands had shrunken like birds' claws. She heard the shallow rapid breathing and saw in the dark eyes a look of dumb suffering. There had been someone else like this long ago, a memory which brought sharp, sad fear before it crystallized. Then Elizabeth knew that it was a memory of their mother.

"We must make cheer for you, Bess," said Jack. "I've asked some neighbors. My men caught four great lobsters today, we've wild fowl too, and had a piglet slaughtered. After supper, let's have music! Alack that you've not your old lute, but we can remember a ballad or two, no doubt!" She could not answer, and he went on with pride. "Our child, the new Winthrop, must be a godly little soul, of course, but we would have it merry too at times, wouldn't we, Matt?"

Doesn't he know? Elizabeth thought. Could he really be so blind to Martha's condition—and saw that he was. Though Jack had much medical interest, and more knowledge of chirurgery than she had, yet accustomed as he was to Martha's puniness, and having no sudden shock to face as Elizabeth had, no forebodings yet clouded his optimism. He leaned in fact to the usual masculine assumption that a baby would solve everything, and was happy that Martha was at last fulfilling her proper function.

"By all means, let us make merry—" said Elizabeth at last, trying to smile, "but I think Martha should lie down."

"Oh, don't send me upstairs, Bess," said the girl piteously. "I'm alone so much."

"No, darling," said Elizabeth. "You shall stay here. Surely there's a truckle bed we can set up?"

There was, and Elizabeth made her sister comfortable in the corner of the parlor, propped on pillows and well wrapped in blankets.

Jack had naturally invited the spiritual leader of Ipswich, the Reverend Nathaniel Ward, who arrived promptly, cast a pleased eye at the feast the servants were spreading on the table, and settled himself in Jack's own walnut armchair as a matter of right. He was a quite elderly widower, and a man of the world, having traveled and studied law in England for many years before taking orders. Behind square spectacles he had shrewd eyes, and a sharp tongue when one of his several strong prejudices was aroused, as the company presently discovered.

Beside the Turner lad, the other guests were Mr. William Clarke, a young man who acted as steward for Jack in his absences, and an erstwhile Suffolk yeoman, John Gage, with his goodwife Amy, who was the only woman, except for servants, as yet to join the score or so of men at the new plantation.

Mr. Ward greeted Elizabeth with pleasant courtesy, and drawing his chair over to the truckle bed, expressed concern for Martha's health and quoted comforting verses from the Psalms. But after he had asked the blessing and everyone was happily spooning food from the great pewter platters onto individual wooden trenchers, he turned his ironic gaze on Amy Gage. The goodwife was young and comely, her apple cheeks still retained their English bloom, her hair was glossy as a chestnut, and—overawed by the grandeur of her invitation to the Winthrop home—she had dressed herself in the bridal finery with which her prosperous father had once furnished her. This included silver earrings, a lace head veil, and a yellow gown with enormous slashed sleeves. Also several cherry-colored bows and a green taffeta petticoat of which she was very proud.

Mr. Ward said nothing until the lobsters and the piglet had been all consumed, then he observed to the air in general, "How odd it is to find aping of the courtly goosedom in our simple Agawam!"

Amy Gage, not understanding this, went on eating nervously, watching from the corners of her eyes to see how Mistress Feake managed her spoon and napkin. "I see no objection to the true gentry honoring themselves with brave attire," continued the minister, "so long as they be not 'These whim-crowned shes, these fashion-fancying wits who are empty thin-brained shells and fiddling kits,' but when I see a barnyard fowl tricked out in peacock plumage, I cannot cleanse my fancy of it."

Amy understood now that she was being criticized, turned scarlet and her underlip began to quiver.

"Fie, Mr. Ward!" cried Elizabeth indignantly. "You shall not poke fun at our guest. I think the goodwife very sweetly dressed, a gay sight for this dark stormy evening. Had I brought my best clothes you would have found *me* as fashion-fancying!"

The minister was imperturbable. "You, Mistress, by reason of your station, may wear fine feathers if you must, I'll not say nay, though hoping never to find you amongst the squirrel-brained of your sex," he paused, and added solemnly, *"frisking in frippery."*

"You are hard on us, sir," said Elizabeth, suddenly joining Jack in laughter, to which Goodman Gage added a chuckle before saying to his mortified wife, "There, there, lass. Oi told ye not to deck above yourself, or parson's wit'd slice ye down, but the poor girl's been pining fur a mite o' fun. 'Tis not wot she's been used ter up here, an' thass the truth."

"Aye, it's hard for women," said Jack, glancing at Martha who was lying on the pillows with her eyes closed. "But soon Ipswich'll be a proper town. The Bradstreets are coming and young Richard Saltonstall and many more. By year's end, I hope some will push further on to the Merrimac. We must populate our land lest ill-wishers to the north should try and seize it first."

"Even so," agreed the minister, appreciatively sipping the canary Jack had broached for the occasion. "I have ever detested foreigners dwelling in my country. There is but one thing worse—toleration of divers religions." He paused again, carefully framing his words into one of the aphorisms for which he was famous. "Poly-piety is the greatest im-piety in the world, and *all* mixtures are pernicious."

"No doubt they are—" said Jack hastily, thinking his father would have enjoyed this minister, but himself no more inclined than Elizabeth for religious debate. "You'll not object, sir, if we sing—I confess I alwalys doted on music and hear so little now."

"Not at all, sir," said the minister, finishing his wine. "So it be not bawdy. In fact—" he said with a sudden twinkle, looking at Elizabeth, "I'll start with one I learned myself in Bohemia, for I find it as stuffed with wisdom as a sausage with meat." He leaned back in his chair, pushed his spectacles down his nose, and peering over them, sang in a placid cracked baritone:

"The world is full of care, much like unto a bubble,

*Women and care, and care and women, and women
    and care and trouble . . .*

Shall I go on?"

The men roared. Gage slapped his discomfited wife on the
thigh, crying, "Eh, our parson be a rare one for heckling the
wenches!"

But Elizabeth tossed her head and snapped. "Nay, I'll not
stand for this, Mr. Ward!" and she lifted her pure pretty
voice in a madrigal she had used to sing in London.

> *"Away with these self-loving lads,*
> *Whom Cupid's arrow never glads . . ."*

The minister smiled a little and hummed the tune. Jack
soon joined in, and Martha tried to, but it brought on the
coughing and she lay back again watching her sister.

They sang other songs, and especially the country ballads
that young Clarke and the Gages knew. The servants sang too
in the kitchen, while Ned, the Indian boy Jack had taken
from the Agawam tribe as servant, tried to beat time on the
copper kettle. For an hour they all forgot the pelting rain
and the close-pressing wilderness. Then just as Mr. Ward
said, " 'Tis getting late and that's enough frivolity, I shall
now offer a prayer," Martha started up from the bed crying
in terror, "Dear God—what's *that!*"

They hushed at once and all heard what her keener ears
had caught—a sobbing screaming wail outside, like a woman's
voice, yet inhuman and fiendish.

" 'Tis a ghost—" whispered Amy Gage, grabbing her
husband's arm. "Thot ridge up back's haunted, Oi knew it."

"Forfend 'tisn't ould Satan himself," said Gage, glancing
fearingly at the minister, who did not hide his own unease.

"Where's The Book?" said Mr. Ward. "If it should be
something devilish . . ."

The sobbing scream came again and nearer; they heard
too the frenzied growls of the three chained wolf dogs, and
a commotion in the kitchen. Ned, the Indian lad, came in.
"Lion, Master!" he cried to Jack. "Lion. Gun!"

The young men all jumped at once, and grabbing muskets
from the wall ran out, the minister after them, his long black
robes flapping.

The three women stared at each other. Elizabeth and Amy
both hurried to Martha and crowded beside her on the

truckle bed. How could a lion make such a noise, Elizabeth thought, holding Martha close, and trying to keep the fear from her face. She had heard captive lions roar at the Tower zoo in London, but never a sound like this.

"'Tis a ghost—" sobbed Amy. "An evil Indian sperit, come to witch us off the land."

"Hush!" said Elizabeth sharply, because Martha was trembling. "If 'tis a ghost—Mr. Ward's the one to lay it. Nothing'll hurt you, Matt—don't be frightened—"

The girl gave a moan and hid her face on her sister's shoulder. They heard three shots, a silence, and then the wild barking of the dogs. Jack opened the front door and strode in, his musket still smoking.

"It got the calf," he said angrily. "The doltish cowherd had left it tethered in the lot."

"WHAT did?" cried Elizabeth. "What got the calf?"

"Why, the lion, Bess. I've never seen one close, but they're like yellow panthers here. We shot, but missed. I let loose the dogs, but they themselves are so wild and fierce I know not if they'll return, nor are they trained in Ireland for aught but wolf-hunting."

"'Twas a ghost—" said Amy rocking herself back and forth. "Or a were-lion. Parson can read it out from The Book as he loikes, but Oi'm a-going ter set the charm too."

"What charm?" whispered Martha.

"Ah, 'twas what my grannie did in Polstead, when we had a sperit haunting us. Ye cotch some little ould toad—must be toads here—Oi've seen frogs—and make a cage for him wi' rowan wood—" She hesitated. "Oi've seen no rowan, but hazel'll do Oi think—then drag toad 'round the church three toimes an' bury him next churchyard wall . . ." She hesitated again, frowning. "We've no graves yet, nor burying place, but Oi'll ask parson where 'twill be."

Jack, cleaning his musket and worrying over the loss of the calf, paid no attention, but Elizabeth, now relieved from any supernatural fears, had a moment of amusement for Amy's struggles to adapt a Suffolk charm to the alien land.

"I'm sure there's no need to take such trouble, Goodwife," she said kindly.

Amy shook her head. "Oi'll not rest easy till Oi do it. Ye'll see after—we'll all breathe freer."

Amy's chance words echoed long in Elizabeth's mind. The toad charm worked, perhaps, for they heard no more horrid screams or even wolf howls, and the dogs came back clotted

with blood and led Jack to the killed panther. But there was
one who certainly did not breathe freer in any sense. Martha's
coughing fits increased; she had a constant pain under her
ribs, and of mornings, Elizabeth found her sister's sheets
damp from drenching night sweats. They moved the great
bedstead down to the parlor, so that Martha's care would
be easier, and Elizabeth slept on the truckle beside it with
Lisbet.

Jack, still not seriously disturbed about his wife, went off
the first of June to Cape Ann shore where he was trying to
start a much-needed saltworks for the colony. From there
he went on to Boston to find his father excited over the
arrival of John Humphrey and his wife, the Lady Susan, who
was sister to poor Arbella and the Earl of Lincoln. Winthrop had conquered his chagrin that the aristocratic family
was temporarily housed at Governor Dudley's in Newtown—
after all, Dudley had known Lady Susan from childhood
while he acted as steward for her brother. Moreover, Humphrey had brought news so disquieting that the general
anxiety left no room for personal pride. Laud, the deadly
Puritan-hater, had become Archbishop of Canterbury, and
the King doted on him. The Bay Colony's known enemies,
Sir Ferdinando Gorges, who wished to own New England
himself; Thomas Morton, the ribald exile from Merrymount,
and Philip Ratcliffe with his cropped ears and his grievance,
had now managed to get Laud's attention and represented to
him the schismatic, treasonable behavior in Massachusetts.
The formidable archbishop had flown into a passion, and
vowed he would crop "King" *Winthrop's* ears for him. The
colony's friends in London, Sir Richard Saltonstall, Emmanuel Downing and Matthew Cradock, the erstwhile Company
Governor, labored all they could, and invoked the powerful
Puritan lords to help, but the dangers were mounting. And
Cradock, frightened at last by the uproar and threats, had
written that the Charter must be sent back to England.
"Which we will never do!" cried John Winthrop to his son.
"Dudley and I are at one in *this!* The Council also."

"What will you do, sir?" asked Jack, fully aware of the
menace to their freedom, and dismayed to hear that many
Massachusetts-bound ships had been stayed by royal command, and others searched for fleeing and dissenting ministers.

"We'll answer Cradock courteously, and ignore the request
for the Patent, as though it had not been made," said Winthrop sharply. "If they want it they must come and get it . . .

Son John, while you're here in Boston, I want you to help with the fortifications. We must strengthen ourselves in every way."

So Jack sent a message to Ipswich that his return was delayed, and begged Elizabeth to wait, saying that he had explained to Robert, who was well in Watertown.

On a warm pleasant day in mid-July Martha turned twenty-three, and Elizabeth helped Sally bake a special cake in celebration. This was difficult since their few fowls had all mysteriously died; the one cow was dry; and wheat flour unobtainable in Ipswich. Elizabeth did the best she could with gulls' eggs found by Ned, the Indian; cornmeal, wild honey, and a gill of goat's milk donated by Amy Gage. She decorated the cake with mauve milkweed blossoms and was delighted with Martha's pleasure. The girl seemed stronger this morning; she ate of the cake with more appetite than she had shown in a long time. "Why, you're better, poppet!" cried Elizabeth gaily. "Mayhap 'tis that hyssop and thyme I've been giving you, or could it be that on your birthday your stars have moved into a stronger sign? Edward Howes used to say something like that."

"Edward Howes," repeated Martha slowly. "How far away and long past he seems . . ."

"Well, he still writes to Jack. I believe he sent him those wolf dogs. What are you doing, Matt?"

"I want to get up," said the girl. "I want to get dressed and go outdoors. There's something I must do."

Elizabeth finally gave in to Martha's insistence. She helped Martha into a loose green wool gown, noting that though the little body was alarmingly thin, the belly was about the right size for the sixth month, and reminded herself that the baby had duly quickened some weeks ago, and prayed that her constant foreboding was stupid.

"Now, will you sit in the sun, dear?" Elizabeth asked. "We can put a chair by the door."

"I want to cross the river. There's a hill over there, I must get to the top!" Martha spoke with an almost frenzied urgency, and to Elizabeth's horrified protests, replied only that she was well enough, that they could take two of the lads to carry her. But go she would. Again Elizabeth reluctantly gave in. She summoned their herd from the Common where he was tending their cow and pigs, she took the Indian from his wood-chopping, and the two strong youths had no difficulty in transporting Martha. The river was only a few rods from the Winthrop house and they crossed it in a flat-boat, then at Martha's direction followed a lane which eventually led to some land Jack owned and had christened Argilla Farm though so far the ground was scarcely cleared. The hill that Martha sought was much nearer the river than Argilla, but the trip was long enough, and when the young men, now puffing from their burden, reached the top Martha was exhausted. The men laid her on a blanket, and retired down the hill to wait.

Elizabeth, mystified and perturbed, knelt beside her sister, saying, "Matt—why did you insist on coming here? 'Tis just a hill like any other."

"No," said Martha softly. "Look behind you, Bess."

Elizabeth turned and saw the sea. Dark, shining blue, it stretched calm and limitless to the horizon where it merged with the misty sky. Martha raised herself on her elbow and gazed out, her eyes black with yearning. "Last fall when I was strong I came here often," she said. "I used to look and look and fancy that I saw it."

"Saw what, darling?" Elizabeth took her sister's hand.

"Home," whispered Martha. "It's still there, you know—across all those endless leagues of ocean."

Elizabeth caught her breath and her throat grew tight.

"Once as I watched, a ship went by to the north," continued the soft expressionless voice. "It was bound for England . . . I did a silly thing. D'you remember, Bess—the fern seed? The fairy tales Grandfather used to tell us? There was a clump of fern growing right by this rock. I scraped off the seeds, and put them in my shoes—and I wished—wished. For a trice I thought it worked. The ship seemed to stop, I thought she was turning to come here for me, but she didn't. She sailed on and vanished." Martha sank back on the blanket. "It was foolish, but that's why I called this Heartbreak Hill."

Elizabeth exhaled a long trembling breath, "Oh, Matt—" she whispered, blinded by tears. "Why didn't you tell Jack? He thinks you contented now, and so did I."

"What use?" said Martha in the same remote and patient tone. "I think all my life I've known it would end thus. Bess, don't cry," she said in sudden wonder sitting up and looking at her sister. "Don't you see—you must always be strong. It's such as you who'll go on, and endure, and found this land. To your children it *will* be home."

"And to yours," said Elizabeth violently.

Martha shook her head. "I am made of cobweb that tears at a touch. But you, Bess, have fiber like the great seines that seldom break no matter their burden, yet if they do they can be mended again and again."

They were silent. Elizabeth bent her head, unable to look at the little sister, who now seemed so far away and wise. A squirrel chattered in the elm behind them, the sunlight shifted and dappled the blanket on which Martha lay, and she spoke again. "Bess, I've done much wrong. I knew it long ago and would not see. I made Jack marry me. I've been a drag on him. He always loved you. You and he would have been happy. And now it's too late."

Elizabeth jerked up her head. "It was *always* too late! Martha, you shall not talk nonsense. Come, dear!" she cried, jumping up. "Don't be morbid and fanciful. I'll call the men, and we'll go back for you to rest. Soon you'll have your baby, and be well."

Martha looked up at her sister with a tired smile. "Aye, call the men," she said. Her eyes moved slowly past Elizabeth and rested on the sea.

That night, as she was settling to sleep, Martha had a paroxysm of coughing worse than any before, and at the end blood gushed from her mouth and soaked the pillow. Two days later, Jack came home, and could not help seeing the change in his wife. He grew tight-lipped and silent. He inquired minutely into all the remedies that Elizabeth had used, then took his chest of chirurgery to the barn and compounded stronger medicines from the contents of his vials. He stayed with Martha now, telling her of what had passed in Boston, and of the loving messages that Margaret sent. She had been safely delivered of a little daughter, christened Sarah, and said she longed to see Martha's babe and hers together. "She said how strange it was that once she and Bess had babes at the same time, and now 'tis *you*, Matt, love."

Martha smiled, squeezing his hand feebly.

Four days later, labor pains began. Jack and Elizabeth worked together to ease the tortured body all they could. Amy Gage came to help, and Anne Bradstreet who had lately arrived in Ipswich. At last they called Mr. Ward who stood beside the bed praying, and reciting psalms in a low compassionate voice, which seemed to soothe Martha. The tiny girl was born, and never breathed. Two hours later Martha opened her eyes which had been wild as those of a snared beast, but now she raised herself and looked up at her husband and sister. "I longed to leave—" she said almost with amusement, "But now I know I shall remain in the new land—God wills it so." She gasped. The warm blood gushed up in her throat, and she fell back on the pillow.

They buried Martha and her baby on the hillside near her house, the first burial in Ipswich. Elizabeth and Jack knelt together by the grave. "I did love her, Bess," he whispered, "as much as I could. She is in heaven, and knows it now."

Elizabeth bowed her head. The grave faced to the east, for Elizabeth had so insisted. She too had suggested the epitaph on the wooden slab, which had been hastily carved by the village carpenter. The headstone read:

> Martha Winthrop, b. London 1611, d. Ipswich
> in The Massachusetts, 1634.
> The Lord hath brought me home again.

11

ON JANUARY 19, 1637, Massachusetts proclaimed a day of fasting and humiliation in order to soften God's wrath. The news from the Old World was bad again. Papists in Europe, Episcopalians in England—both viewed by the colony with equal alarm—were forcing their scarlet ceremonies on the True Believers. Dissenting ministers were being persecuted now as well as silenced. Furthermore there was plague in the colony, and a new Indian menace. The Pequots having murdered John Oldham, the trader, whom they were supposed to love, were now attacking the infant settlements on the Connecticut River. Nor were these afflictions the worst threat to the Massachusetts Bay Colony's comfort. A woman was—

A tall, burning-eyed, intractable woman of forty-six named Mistress Anne Hutchinson. "Troublemaker, Jezebel, libertine daughter of Beelzebub"—so John Winthrop thought her, and his opinion was shared by all the ministers in the colony except Mr. Cotton, whom she had so admired in Lincolnshire, and her own brother-in-law, John Wheelwright. But she had much following amongst ordinary folk in Boston, where the women flocked to her afternoon meetings when she expounded the Scriptures in her own way and prophesied at times. They came to her for material help too, domestic and medical, and she gave to them lavishly; of late even men had sought her wisdom and the peculiar comfort her presence evoked. Yet many distrusted and feared her strength. She inspired violent partisanship or violent enmity. She provided the greatest immediate excitement the colony had ever enjoyed and Elizabeth who had led three dull years at Watertown since Martha's death, was elated by the furore; an interest all the more stimulating since it must be hidden from her uncle.

On that January Fast Day, when the schism in the colony became obvious to all, Elizabeth and the two little girls were in Boston visiting Margaret, while Robert was at Dedham, the new settlement on the Charles River, whither the Feakes thought of moving. Watertown was now crowded, and with the exception of the Patricks, Elizabeth found her neighbors uncongenial. Goody Warren's malice—now unrestrained because Elizabeth's uncle was no longer Governor —could usually be ignored, but there were other reasons for moving. Robert had become more moody: feverishly restless at times, depressed and apathetic at others. She had thought a change of scene might be good for him, and welcomed the thought herself. Last year when many from Watertown, and half of Newtown under the leadership of the Reverend Thomas Hooker, had packed up and left the Bay, Elizabeth had wondered if they too shouldn't move to the wild but fertile lands along the Connecticut River. Robert had been briefly enthusiastic, and they had got so far as to write Jack for advice on the matter and send a manservant off to clear land and build some kind of shelter, when Robert suddenly lost interest. He took to reading the Bible daily, and finding there apt verses which he said were clear guidance against the move. She also realized the strength of his attachment to Daniel Patrick, and that Robert dreaded going so far from the Captain. She thought this adoration odd, but also touching.

Anyway the matter dropped, and Elizabeth was ultimately relieved when rumors began to filter back indicating that the new Connecticut settlements were even stricter and more godly than those of Massachusetts. Then Winthrop, himself, ever jealous for the supremacy of the Bay, and therefore anxious to establish as many towns near Boston as possible, suggested to Robert that he might help settle Dedham. Robert was flattered and set off at once to buy land.

The morning of the January Fast Day was exceedingly cold. A raw east wind blew in from the sea, and there was ice in the ewer of washing water when Elizabeth awoke. She was grateful for the comfort of the Winthrop mansion, where the windows now were glazed and tight, and where there were plenty of servants to draw the bed curtains and light a fire in her chamber. In Watertown there was no such luxury. Sally was gone. Coincidentally with the expiration of her bond, she had been caught fornicating with one of the Saltonstall servants and haled before the local court, which duly ordered for both culprits twenty stripes at the whipping post, and the wearing of a red letter V for venery upon their backs. Elizabeth had made Robert plead for mercy, but his speech had been so mumbling and indecisive that the town fathers had ignored it. She had then appealed to Daniel Patrick, and was never told what happened, but Sally unaccountably escaped from the gaol on the night before her punishment, and was seen no more.

When Elizabeth questioned Patrick anxiously he winked and said, "Faith, Bessie, me love, what's the use o' being Captain hereabouts if ye can't juggle a thing or two for your friends? Might be there was a shallop at Medford what would smuggle on a wench as far as Piscataqua where they don't take sich a gloomy view o' love-making as we do here."

So now, though Robert still had his two menservants, there was no female help obtainable except the occasional hire of one of the neighbors' daughters.

Elizabeth let her two little girls sleep. Joan was a sturdy child of seven, as brown and buxom as the four-year-old Lisbet was delicately fair. Had this been the Sabbath, Elizabeth would have had to arouse them for the morning service but towards observance of a Fast Day sermon, Elizabeth knew that Margaret would be lenient. Elizabeth herself avoided church whenever she dared in Watertown, but no such slackness was possible at the Winthrops'.

She dressed hastily in her warmest gown of heavy blue serge and put on her plain collar and cuffs, for the wearing of any lace was now forbidden by law. She went downstairs to breakfast with the family on dry cornbread and water. After a prayer, John Winthrop asked the blessing in an abstracted manner, they spoke sharply to his young sons who had been whispering and scuffling their feet.

"You behave yourselves in the meetinghouse, do you hear? I'll not have it said the tithing man has had to chastize Winthrops, *ever!*" He looked at each one of his boys.

Stephen, now eighteen, was a gravely handsome lad, dark like Jack and their father, and possessing like them the long Winthrop nose. Adam, at seventeen, favored his mother's side, and resembled Margaret in plumpness and a naturally contented nature. Sammy was still but a child of nine and his mother's pet, since the baby, Sarah, had died. He was an exuberant little boy; yet he and his two oldest brothers quieted at once. The fourteen-year-old Deane however looked mutinous, to Elizabeth's secret amusement. The years Deane had stayed behind in England under the genial guardianship of his Uncle Downing had bred in the lad some headstrong opinions which he usually stated, and did so now. "Oh, Father, please, sir, do I HAVE to go to church twice TODAY as well as on Sundays?"

"You *do*, sir!" said Winthrop. He had spent many hours praying for Deane and for guidance in subduing him, being aware that he was the most like Harry of all Margaret's brood. "Also," continued Winthrop, "is it necessary to remind you again that here we say 'meetinghouse,' and 'Sabbath,' not those Popish terms you used?"

"They were saying in London that New Englanders've changed the names of everything to suit themselves—seasons, months, days, churches and taverns—" said Deane not quite pertly. "I don't like calling this good old January 'Eleven month,' and why can't I call today 'Friday'?"

"Deane!" interrupted Margaret. "Stop fretting your father! You've been told why. We don't use pagan names or Papist ones, and anyway 'tis not for you to question. Eat your cornbread!"

"I don't want it," said Deane. "It's like sawdust."

"It might taste better to you after a good thrashing," said his father wearily, "which I should certainly administer now if there were time." He got up and walked out to his study, where his table was littered with notes relative to the dreadful Antinomian behavior of Mistress Anne Hutchinson and her brother-in-law, Wheelwright, and pages of his own agonized religious experience with particular reference to the opposed covenants of Grace and Works which were splitting the colony.

"How can you be so thoughtless as to add to your poor father's grave anxieties?" said Margaret. "He scarce slept last night."

"I don't see why he bothers so," said Deane, unmoved by

the thought of a beating to which he was well accustomed. "'Tisn't as though *he* was Governor, and why doesn't he let Harry Vane do as he pleases, and that Mrs. Hutchinson too? I like her and maybe she does hear the Holy Ghost speaking. How does Father know she doesn't?"

Margaret looked so shocked that her eldest came to her defense. "Oh, stop blabbering, Deane—" said Stephen. "Get up and go wash your hands for the meeting, or I'll give you that thrashing myself."

Deane made a rude noise, indicative of his disbelief in the threat, for he was as big as Stephen, but he got up and shambled out of the room. The other boys followed, and Margaret said sighing to Elizabeth, "I wonder why the Dear Lord wished me to raise only sons. They can be so trying. A daughter would have been a comfort." Her gentle brown eyes filled with the tears that came easily of late. She had grieved much for little Sarah, and was afflicted with melancholy and physical ailments relative to the age she had reached and the certainty that she would never bear another child. "And it seems that I have nothing *but* daughters," said Elizabeth as lightly as she could.

"Oh, you'll bear a son, dear, I'm sure," said Margaret, instantly sympathetic. She thought it strange that four years had passed since Lisbet's birth, and tried not to guess the reason, though she was quite perceptive enough to see Robert's peculiarities and effeminacy. How sad that God had thought it needful to afflict Bess with unfortunate marriages. The women, in silence, exchanged a look of affection, then jumped as the warning horn blew from the meetinghouse steps, and the bell-ringer paused by the corner of School Street jangling his bell and calling, "Hear ye all! Hear ye all! Come to Meeting!"

Most of the morning service was as excessively dull as Elizabeth had feared. Mr. Wilson had the pulpit and prayed for nearly an hour on the general themes of fasting and humiliation. But then came a more stimulating moment as the minister lined out for them the Seventieth Psalm in the Puritan's special old psalm book, and the congregation started off in the nasal drone considered appropriate until at the second verse Wilson suddenly became impassioned. His thick voice rose to a shout, his bullet head stuck forward, and everyone saw that he was glaring from the pulpit at Mrs. Anne Hutchinson and her family, while he sang:

"Confounde *them that apply*
And seek to make my shame
And at my harme do laugh and crye
So there goeth their game."

Elizabeth could not resist turning in her pew to see how
Mrs. Hutchinson took it. The lady, her dark eyes flashing,
stood stiff and straight, and immediately raising her own
voice, sang all the words of the psalm right back at the
minister, who reddened with anger. By this time the whole
colony knew that at her afternoon meetings Mrs. Hutchinson
had called Mr. Wilson unsanctified, a benighted adherent to
the Covenant of Works, like all the other ministers at the
Bay except Mr. Cotton, and her brother-in-law. But the
battle had never come into the open like this and there was
an irrepressible gasp when Mrs. Hutchinson, instead of seating herself for the sermon, walked majestically down the
aisle, followed by her meek little husband and their older
children. The street door shut behind them and Wilson,
turning purple, clenched his fist on the Bible.

How brave Mrs. Hutchinson was! Elizabeth thought. Fancy
defying Mr. Wilson and Uncle John like that, and yet there
was such dignity about her. She had an almost tangible
magnetism and real beauty despite her iron-gray hair and
plain big-boned face; a shining secret look that made Elizabeth long to know her.

The ripple of excitement gradually died down. Mr. Wilson
controlled himself and having apparently decided to avoid
further conflict, fashioned his two-hour sermon around some
obscure text from Deuteronomy to which Elizabeth did not
bother to listen. She clasped her cold gloved hands tight in
her muff and allowed her mind to wander. The women sat on
the hard unpainted benches to the left of the aisle, the men
on the right, and all arranged according to rank. The Winthrop ladies shared the first pew, but the new young Governor
Harry Vane held the corresponding seat of honor across the
aisle.

Elizabeth therefore had a good view of the handsome
aristocrat. His blond hair fell to his shoulders over an elegant
green mantle. He had extremely regular features and a full
sensuous mouth, slightly petulant. A pretty boy, she thought,
and not a very wise one. Winthrop, and indeed all the colony,
had been immensely flattered last year at the arrival of this
newly converted Puritan whose father, Sir Henry Vane, was

actually Secretary of State to King Charles. They had fawned on the young man, despite the fact that he set out at once to reform the colony, and had even taken Winthrop and Dudley to task publicly for their many disagreements. Then he had been elected Governor and horrified Winthrop, who had been elected Deputy, by siding with Anne Hutchinson, and passionately maintaining that he DID have a personal union with the Holy Ghost and believed in the Covenant of Grace. In the ensuing fuss Vane tried to resign, and finally burst into tears before the whole court. They had persuaded him to remain until May, when his term was up, chiefly because Winthrop was afraid of what might be said in London if he went home like that. But Vane looked, Elizabeth thought, like an unhappy lad, and she knew that he and her uncle had ceased to speak to each other in private no matter their public courtesies.

How many mistakes in judgment Uncle John had made, Elizabeth thought, remembering how delighted he had been with Vane at first, and with Mrs. Hutchinson too. Or were they mistakes, exactly, since all his actions sprang from his consuming desire for the colony's survival, and she had not forgotten the respect she had felt for his ideal on the day they had journeyed to Ipswich. If only he weren't so deadly serious always. She glanced back to the next pew behind Governor Vane.

John Winthrop sat there gravely listening to the sermon with his two eldest boys. Deane and Sammy were stuffed in the gallery with other lads where, if they misbehaved, the tithing man could bang them on the head with the knob of his tipstaff.

Jack was in Ipswich, but between Elizabeth and Margaret sat Jack's new wife. "The intruder," as Elizabeth always called her to herself, nor had she been able quite to conquer her shock and resentment when Jack returned from a long voyage to England the year after Martha's death bringing with him a strapping, fair-haired girl of nineteen called Elizabeth, who had been a Miss Reade of Wickford in Essex, and was stepdaughter to Salem's vociferous new minister, Hugh Peter.

There had been a bitter scene with Jack on the October night of the reception in Boston for his new wife. The Feakes, of course, had been invited and Elizabeth had stood stiffly in a corner gazing at the "intruder" when Jack came up, and taking her hand, pulled her out the door into the chilly garden.

"Bess," he said smiling uneasily as she snatched her hand away. "You were staring at my wife as though she were an adder—don't!"

Elizabeth backed against the house wall, and raised her chin. "You lost no time in replacing my poor Matt, did you, Jack!"

"Why—" he said, still smiling into her angry eyes. "You couldn't expect me to remain a widower? A man needs a wife and children."

"Ah, to be sure," she said grimly. "This one looks very healthy too, and I see has already started breeding. She should suit you well."

His smile faded, and he responded in a sharper tone. "Elizabeth suits me very well, and I marvel that you seem so shrewish."

Her eyes blazed green, and she could not stop herself from crying, "And she *would* bear my own name, of course! Not even that is left to me for myself."

It took Jack a moment to understand this speech, yet because of all that had been between them, and which could never entirely die, he finally did. He looked with attention at the flushed face, framed by dark curls, at the red trembling mouth, and said quietly, "She cannot help her name, Bess. There is nothing taken from you, or Martha . . . but what must be . . ." His voice trailed off.

There were leaves burning in the High Street side of the garden near a clump of frost-bitten marigolds. The fragrant blue smoke drifted around them, and they both thought of a London garden where they had stood facing each other like this, nine years ago, before Jack had sailed for the Levant. Then they heard a babel of voices from inside the house, and the high-pitched assured laugh of Jack's new wife.

"I'm off for Saybrook—" he said abruptly, "for the Connecticut country—on the business My Lords Say and Brooke entrusted to me in London."

"Ah . . ." she said with malice, "so even this fair, suitable young wife cannot keep you at her side. She will be desolate."

This time he ignored her tone and looked deep into her eyes, seeing there the desolation she imputed to another, and said, "Bess, I wish to God you were happy—if ever I can—" He dropped his voice and flushed, "You still have my glove?"

"Aye—" she said on a long breath, the jealous hurt dissolving a little. She slowly raised her face to his with an almost soundless murmur of longing, and in return he whispered something while he bent and kissed her on the mouth. A timeless instant that yet included time enough for the door to be flung open, and the other Elizabeth to step out and give a sharp cry "John!"

They sprang apart, and Elizabeth leaned against the house wall, trying to still the pounding of her heart, but Jack, from guilt and confusion, spoke in anger to his wife. "Well, what is it, that you gape like a hooked fish?"

"You were kissing her," gasped the fair-haired girl, her handsome rather bovine face turning pink.

"And if I was!" said Jack. "She is my sister, as you well know. And we had been speaking of Martha."

His wife drew back. Into her calm blue eyes there came a glint. "You wish to pain me with mention of your first wife? To remind me of all your life in which I've had no share? I'd no notion you were so fond of this '*sister*'!" Her large white hand pointed to Elizabeth who had recovered, and was now wavering between pleasure at the intruder's discomfiture and sympathy for Jack who looked as miserable as did all men when caught between two women.

Elizabeth finally spoke quietly. "Cousin," she said, "Jack and I have indeed known each other all our lives. We have the same Winthrop grandparents, he married my sister and I his brother; in view of this, I think you need hardly question our relationship."

The other Elizabeth looked uncertain while she considered this slowly. She had a well-bred, usually complacent nature unsuited for delving into motive. In England she had loved long walks and hunting and dog-breeding, and she loved her husband in the same forthright way. She was willing to be reassured, especially as Jack took her hand and said. "You see, my dear, you are making a pother about naught. Come, we must go in to our guests."

However, since that time there had been constraint between the two Elizabeths, who seldom saw each other since the younger Winthrops had their own house in Boston, and now in the meetinghouse as Mr. Wilson droned on and turned his hourglass yet again, the two women sat far apart, so that their fur-lined capes did not even touch.

It had started to snow outside and it turned bitter cold in the meetinghouse. Margaret had a charcoal foot-warmer but the other women did not. Elizabeth managed to tuck her feet up under her long concealing skirts, while watching her breath float out in vapor. There had been a moment of diversion when Mrs. William Coddington, a buxom matron, fell asleep in the corner of her pew, and the watchful tithing man came down the aisle and tickled her awake with the foxtails on his staff. Mrs. Coddington sneezed violently, and Elizabeth would have giggled as hard as the boys in the gallery had she dared. She did steal a look back at the lady's husband, Elizabeth's erstwhile suitor, who was now the Colony Treasurer. She saw Coddington send his wife an outraged glare and amused herself for some minutes by remembering the night at Groton when she had so thoroughly disenchanted him. Thank God at least for that, she thought. What a husband *he* would have been——and wondered what Robert was doing in Dedham, poor soul. An uncomfortable recognition came to her that some such faintly contemptuous pity always accompanied thoughts of Robert, and she sighed, easing her cramped legs into a new position.

She was stupefied when the service finally ended at noon, and convinced that she could not possibly endure the next one, and yet she was ashamed of her weakness. The rest of the congregation obviously derived enjoyment from sermons and prayers that she never did; even Margaret had been interested in some of Mr. Wilson's points and discussed them at the exceedingly scanty dinner, where nobody mentioned Mrs. Hutchinson's behavior. Elizabeth, eating boiled salt cod in silence, suddenly felt a surge of loneliness and exile. These aren't really my people, she thought——I don't belong to them——even Margaret. At twenty-seven Elizabeth was too old for indulgence in the changeling fancy which came to many children, and yet on that dreary January day, she first consciously felt herself an alien to the thoughts and wishes of all her family, and saw no means of breaking through the suffocating gray veil into any brightness where she might feel at home.

It was in a rare mood of bleak depression that she trailed through the snow with the rest of them to the afternoon service, which was, however, sufficiently lively to startle her out of introspection.

Mr. Cotton, Boston's "Teacher" and co-minister, was now in the pulpit, while his colleague, Wilson, sat in a chair behind the Communion table, chewing his lips and glowering at Mrs. Hutchinson's pew, where she had arrived early and was now reinforced by her brother-in-law, Wheelwright, who had ridden over from his own little parish at Mount Wollaston. In view of the snowstorm Wheelwright's presence here was startling. John Winthrop and Mr. Wilson exchanged a foreboding glance, while Margaret whispered to Elizabeth, "Oh dear, I feel there's going to be some sort of trouble."

Jack's wife had not come to the afternoon service, having sent a message that she had been seized with a sudden chill. And whether it were really a chill, or avoidance of herself, Elizabeth cared not at all, buoyed up like the rest of the congregation by cross currents of tension and expectancy. She found herself really listening to Mr. Cotton.

Even Elizabeth who understood little of the controversy knew that Cotton had jumped into the middle of the fray when he announced his text as verses from the Forty-eighth Chapter of Isaiah, which declaimed the intent of prophecy and was obviously aimed at convincing Mrs. Hutchinson's enemies. The cherubic face, crowned with fluffy white hair, was illumined, the organ-toned voice which had so moved the citizens of old Boston had lost none of its power as he cried out to them, "I have shewed thee new things from this time, even hidden things, and thou didst not know them!"

Before he had spoken many words, Elizabeth heard a stir in the pew behind her and Mrs. Hutchinson's unmistakably exultant voice, "Aye, Aye, HE is sealed with Grace, Mr. Cotton is of God's elect, the spirit hath told me so."

It was a powerful sermon, clothed in poetic language, nor was it inflammatory, since Cotton, using all the force of his golden persuasiveness, endeavored while expounding the Doctrine of Grace to spare the feelings of those ministers who still adhered to the plodding, uninspired Doctrine of Works. But his opponents were not appeased. Wilson's foot soon began to tap on the floorboards, his jowls quivered with indignation as he saw his brilliant colleague sway the meeting as he himself never could.

John Winthrop listened in gloomy quiet. That female has bewitched Cotton, he thought. That virago, that false unwomanly prophetess who had set herself up as judge of salvation and its secrets. He saw that the young governor's face was afire with excitement, and that Vane even forgot all decorum by turning and sharing with Mrs. Hutchinson looks of triumphant delight. And why is Wheelwright here? Winthrop thought. What are they plotting? What new threat is this to our unity? Surely they don't hope to oust Wilson from his own church, and undermine all the other ministers! His worst suspicions were soon confirmed.

Cotton finished his sermon, then instead of lining out the final psalm for them, he held up his hand, and smiling somewhat anxiously in Winthrop's direction, said, "Mr. Wheelwright, our reverend brother from Mount Wollaston is here today. And I have invited him to exercise for you, so you may better understand these matters."

John Wheelwright jumped to his feet and hastening down the aisle, climbed into the pulpit with alacrity, then bowing to Cotton and ignoring the outraged Wilson, he launched into what was ever after known as "*The* Fast Day Sermon."

Wheelwright was a large, powerful man of decided opinions like his friend Oliver Cromwell, with whom he had studied in Cambridge, and who he hoped would shortly join them here in the New World, as England became increasingly dangerous for Puritans. Wheelwright was ambitious and brash, he admired his sister-in-law Anne Hutchinson, and believed in her Covenant of Grace, but he was also profoundly impatient with what he considered the bigoted hidebound form of government he had found in the Bay. He had expected a position of ministerial power fitting his proven talents, and had run headlong into opposition and lost the first skirmish, when he had been shunted off to the tiny distant parish south of the Neponset River. Where he had no intention of remaining. He detested Wilson and Winthrop and considered them negligible, for was not Governor Vane on the Hutchinson side? Also Mr. Cotton, and influential men of the town sitting now below him in the pews and looking up at him with approval—Mr. William Coddington, Mr. Coggeshall, Mr. Aspinwall, Mr. Hough—even Captain John Underhill, and solid tradesmen like William Balston.

So, rejoicing that at last he had opportunity to rally his friends from Boston's own pulpit, he began confidently, "The way we must take, if so be we will not have the Lord Jesus Christ taken from us, is this: We must all prepare for a spiritual combat."

The meetinghouse grew very quiet as Wheelwright's eager voice went on, using over and over again words which lost the unworldly meaning with which he was glossing them, and became by very repetition the primitive war cries which rang truer in their hearts than mystical analogies. "Fight!" "Gird our loins!" Sword in hand—show ourselves courageous!" "When enemies of truth oppose the ways of God—

we must Kill—" "If we do not strive, those under a Covenant of Works will prevail." "*Kill!*"

Mr. Cotton began by looking anxious, then with murmurs tried to stop his protégé, who did not listen but rushed on. Winthrop sat petrified, mastering his initial fury with savage control. This was sedition, this was real danger, and they must be careful. "Careful—" he signaled to Wilson whose eyes were bulging, and whose whole squat body could be seen shaking beneath the black robes. The pastor did not heed his friend's signal, he did not see it.

Wheelwright, thoroughly enjoying himself, informed the congregation that he and those under the Covenant of Grace were by no means Antinomians or libertines, but that through Grace they had the benefit of holy inspiration. "And," he added, his voice rising to a sonorous shout, "those who deny this are but whited sepulchers, and Anti-Christs, and we must FIGHT them!"

Mr. Wilson sprang to his feet, bellowing, "So it's *fight*, you want, is it! And it's Anti-Christs you call us! I say that Satan himself has got in my pulpit! And I'll get him *out!*" The enraged pastor rushed to the pulpit and swarmed up the steps before Wheelwright understood the meaning of the commotion behind him. Wheelwright found his robes yanked so violently that he overbalanced, and was immediately pounded on the head and shoulders by flailing fists. He stumbled down the steps on top of his assailant, and recovering himself, began to hit back.

Margaret screamed. The meeting exploded into uproar. Another fight broke out amongst the boys in the gallery; there was a scuffle near the door with the bewildered tithing man, and Winthrop standing on his pew, called "Guards! Captain! Captain Underhill! Halt this disgraceful brawl!" before running to help Cotton who was ineffectually trying to separate the two angry ministers.

Captain Underhill had been sitting in the back of the church, and he now moved slowly down the aisle, his black mustache twitching with suppressed laughter. He ignored Winthrop and the struggling parsons, walked instead to Vane, and said, "What are *your* orders, Your Worship?"

"Arrest Wilson!" cried the young governor, excitedly. "He started it."

Underhill shrugged. "I know he did, sir. And I'd like nothing better. But I fear 'twouldn't do. Besides—" He glanced towards the pulpit. Mr. Wilson now sat trembling and vanquished on the step, dizzy from the final blow on the ear dealt him by the much larger and stronger Wheelwright. Nor was the latter unscathed. His nose was bleeding and he looked white and shaken.

"Captain!" called John Winthrop sharply. "What's the matter with you! Where are your guards? There's still fighting in the gallery."

"Only a bit of youthful sport, sir," said Underhill airily, flicking a blob of dust from his shining cuirass. "Taking example from their elders, as you might say."

Winthrop stiffened and turned away. Enemies. The meeting-house was filled with enemies, and this was not the time for routing them. Mrs. Hutchinson, bending over and soothing her brother-in-law, it wasn't only Cotton she had bewitched, but Vane, Underhill and most of Boston. Still she'd not get by with it long. Any more than Roger Williams had been permitted to remain in the colony and promulgate his heresies. I've been accused of laxness and lenity, Winthrop thought. There shall be no grounds for that reproach now. He felt indomitable strength rising in him like a black winter tide. The *other* Bay towns were not beglamoured; when their ministers heard of Wheelwright's sermon they would know how to act, even Dudley would lend his support to the extirpation of this menace. But one must tread with care, with care and due formality, nor ever forget the hostile eyes which watched the colony from across the ocean. "Speak to them—" he murmured to Cotton, and added a suggestion to which the minister replied, shaking his head, "Aye—but this is appalling—appalling, Mr. Winthrop, I beg you to believe I'd no idea that Wheelwright would sermonize like that—the Lord help us all."

Cotton mounted the pulpit, and spreading wide his arms, looked down with deep sorrow at the congregation which gradually stilled. He prayed then, simply and fervently, asking God to heal the breach between them. And he ended by following Winthrop's suggestion, saying that he knew a ship was shortly to set forth for England, and that perhaps some of its passengers were in the meetinghouse today. If so, he commanded that they keep quiet about the lamentable differences that had arisen, and simply say if they were asked about any strife in Massachusetts, that it was not strife; only different ways of magnifying the Grace of God.

"One party," said Mr. Cotton, his beautiful voice ringing to the rafters, "is but seeking to advance the grace of God within us, while the other seeks to advance the grace of God towards us, and so there is no need for conflict."

So great was Mr. Cotton's eloquence that they all filed out quietly, half convinced that the extraordinary scenes they had witnessed never happened, and even Elizabeth was under Cotton's spell until the cold air cleared her wits and she thought with sudden revulsion But what does all that really *mean?* And thought too that the grace of God, whatever that was, either inside or outside, had very little to do with the clashing angers of its proponents.

But metaphysical intricacies could never long hold her interest. As she walked through the snow down the High Street with Margaret who was still near to tears, Elizabeth reviewed the feelings she had had in the meetinghouse. At first when the ministers began to fight she had been as alarmed as Margaret and the other women, but then had come an exhilaration and release, despite the shock of sudden violence. There had been satisfaction too when Uncle John's power had been flouted by Underhill. Power—for a second Elizabeth saw the whole episode as a turbulent struggle for power, regardless of the motives beneath, but then her thoughts dwindled to confusion. There was more than a desire to dominate about Mrs. Hutchinson. As she had tended her brother-in-law after the battle she had appeared distressed, and uncertain. Elizabeth had seen her throw Winthrop a look of pleading contrition which he had ignored. Mrs. Hutchinson's face had grown sorrowful, and yet it kept that luminous conviction. I believe she is a good woman, Elizabeth thought, and echoing Deane's youthful rashness, she added, maybe God does speak to her, how does Uncle John know?

By the time she reached home with Margaret, Elizabeth had determined to meet Mrs. Hutchinson, and talk with her, though unaware that this was the strongest impulse she had felt in a long time, since, indeed she had rushed down Boston Common on Election Day three years ago to greet Will Hallet.

It was the following Tuesday afternoon before Elizabeth found a chance to slip out of the house and go to the Hutchinsons', who lived in a mansion as large as the Winthrops' and only a block or so away on the corner of School Street and the High. John Winthrop did not approve of his womenfolk roaming the wintry streets and would certainly have stopped Elizabeth had he seen her, but he had called a meeting of all the nearby ministers for a council of war and was locked with them in his parlor. Elizabeth from her chamber window had watched them arrive on horseback, except Mr. Wilson who came first on foot from his parsonage. Hugh Peter had come from Salem with John Endecott; old Dudley with his pastor, Thomas Shepard, from Newtown; her own George Phillips from Watertown; the lean rat-faced Thomas Welde from Roxbury with his colleague, John Eliot, the Indian missionary; and others whom she didn't know. Mr. Cotton, whose true sentiments were doubtful, had not been invited.

Elizabeth bundled herself in her fur-lined cloak and pulled her hood far over her face, then ran lightly down the stairs past the shut parlor door, avoiding the kitchen where the children and servants were gathered. She had her hand on the latch when Deane jumped out from the shadows under the stairs. "And where are you sneaking off to, cousin?" he cried, chuckling.

"Sh-h . . ." she said involuntarily, glancing towards the parlor where there was a clamor of male voices; then she recovered and said haughtily, "What are *you* doing here? You ought to be at school!"

Deane brandished a sackful of books with a very inky hand. "That's where I'm going. What a to-do—" He hunched his shoulder towards the parlor. "All those black crows flapping about Mrs. Hutchinson, they want to jail her, and Wheelwright too."

"Deane—you've been eavesdropping," she said weakly, "and you must show more respect, and they couldn't jail Mrs. Hutchinson, why, she's *gentry* and she hasn't done anything bad."

Deane peered shrewdly at his cousin, whom he admired. "I believe you're sneaking off to one of her conventicles—the Lord save you if Father knew it."

Elizabeth reddened, while Deane's eyes sparkled.

"I won't tell," he said. "But you better hurry, or half Boston'll be there, and you'd be recognized."

She nodded, giving up pretense, and they went cautiously through the front door together. "Put your mask on," said Deane when they were at the garden gate. "Didn't you bring it?"

She nodded again, and pulling a black satin mask from her muff, tied it under the hood. "Everyone wore 'em in London," said Deane. "When it's cold like this, it's odd they don't much here, I guess 'cause there's so few gentlefolk."

"Deane," she said as they neared the Hutchinson doorstep,

"why do you like this lady? You said you did, but you can't know her."

"Don't I though!" said the boy. Suddenly embarrassed, he stopped and began kicking at a snowbank. "Last autumn I was well—downcast—melancholic. I couldn't seem to feel at home here, and Father, he was always, always——" Deane looked up at Elizabeth and feeling sympathy, went on quickly, "Mrs. Hutchinson, she had a fine apple tree in back — don't know why but I—I stole some. She caught me. I thought she'd have me flogged or worse—she could've had me put in stocks. She didn't."

"What did she do?" said Elizabeth.

"She was kind, and said I could have the apples. Then she took me in her house, and she talked. I don't know what she said but I felt different inside. It was about Christ and love, stuff like that, but seemed real——" Dean blushed, gave Elizabeth a funny sideways glance, shouldered his book bag and pelted down the street in confusion.

Elizabeth glanced around and seeing nothing in sight but two dogs and an old scissors grinder, knocked hastily on the Hutchinson door. It was opened by a tiny maidservant who stared at the mask and said. "Be ye come to the meeting, 'cause Mistress she's not holding it today."

"Is she in?" said Elizabeth. "I'd like to see her."

"Wot name, ma'am? And on wot matter?" said the little maid stubbornly barring the door.

Unwilling to answer the first question and unable to answer the second, Elizabeth was struck with the foolishness of her impulse, but it persisted, and she said in tones as imperious as her uncle's, "Tell your mistresss a lady wants to see her. Go!"

The maid scuttled off, and presently Anne Hutchinson herself walked into the hall, glanced without surprise at the crimson-cloaked young woman in the mask—many women of all kinds had come to her for help—and said courteously, "What can I do for you, Mistress?"

Elizabeth looked at the tall, gray-haired woman in the simple dark blue gown and white cap, at the broad forehead slightly lined, the dark compassionate eyes that glowed with fervor, and she answered in a voice that sounded like a stranger's to her, "I don't know, Mrs. Hutchinson, I don't know why I trouble you. I had to come."

Anne listened thoughtfully, hesitated, then smiled, and her plain face became beautiful. "Ah, it happens that way, sometimes," she said softly. "If we listen to the Voice, and seek the Inner Light."

"The Inner Light," repeated Elizabeth. "I fear I've never seen that."

Anne put her hand out, and said, "Come. We can't talk here. Poor child, I feel that you are unhappy." She led Elizabeth into a small chamber where a bright fire glinted on brass andirons, and a huge sheepdog lay stretched on the hearth beside a cradle where a baby slept. She indicated a cushioned chair and sat down near Elizabeth, who obeyed without consciousness of her surroundings.

"I don't think I'm unhappy," Elizabeth said in a wondering voice. "Just empty."

"Then in time," said Anne with certainty, "if you seek you will be filled." She pulled a spinning wheel close to her and began to work the treadle; with deft hands she fed the twisting wool fibers onto the great wheel which hummed quietly. "Forgive me that I work," said Anne. "I have so many children to clothe, and I can hear God's voice as clearly when I labor."

Elizabeth leaned back in her chair. Within her breast there was a quivering, an expectancy, and yet all else around her was still. There was peace in this room, in the sighing of the fire, and the humming of the wheel, above all in the composed figure of the woman who looked at her with wise, tender eyes.

"I've never heard God's voice," said Elizabeth. "Or felt Him near. The ministers say one can't. They say He revealed Himself once and for all in Scriptures, and that is all we can *ever* know of Him."

"They say that—" said Anne, "because they are blind, and still bound by Old Adam's Covenant of Works. They will not listen when The Comforter comes into their hearts."

"I don't understand this . . ." said Elizabeth sadly.

Anne's treadle stopped; she turned from the wheel and bent towards Elizabeth. "But Paul hath said it: *He is the God of all comfort, Who comforteth us in all our tribulation, that we may be able to comfort them which are in any trouble, wherewith we ourselves are comforted of God.*"

"That is beautiful as you speak it," Elizabeth said. "But how if God is wroth and will not *send* comfort?"

Anne put her head on one side, considering, and then she smiled. "*I* do not believe He is ever wroth with those who love enough, for God is Love."

"I've never heard so," cried Elizabeth, startled. "Does it say so in Scriptures? I've heard that He is jealous, and a consuming fire, and almighty, and our salvation, but I never heard of love."

"It *is* in Scripture," said Anne gravely. She closed her eyes, and continued in a low moving voice, "I have tried to love those that hate me like Mr. Wilson and Mr. Winthrop—almost I can, then my unregenerate spirit o'ercomes me—and WHY do they hate me? For that they cruelly twist what I say. I meant no harm in speaking of indwelling Grace and Light, but harm or not, I KNOW that it is true, for I have felt it often, and if *they* come to feel it, they will also be sanctified—but they are not so now."

Elizabeth saw that Mrs. Hutchinson was speaking to herself, and that a troubled look had come into the serene face. There was a silence, then Mrs. Hutchinson went on, "This too they hold against me, that I follow the words of Paul: *Know ye not that your body is the temple of the Holy Ghost which is in you . . . therefore glorify God in your body and in your spirit, which are God's.*"

"The ministers hold that against you," said Elizabeth softly, "I think because they are afraid of you, and of a woman who sees not what they do in the Bible. And they hate this talk of glorifying bodies, or to think that one could listen to God's voice as inspiration. They think it leads to license."

"But it does *not!*" cried Mrs. Hutchinson forcefully. "Has anyone ever known me to be licentious or libertine? When one has Christ's love in the heart one cannot do wrong!"

"No," said Elizabeth on a long sigh of sudden and utter belief. The quivering anticipation in her breast grew keener. It trembled, then seemed to expand like a moonflower until the petals fell wide open, and at their center was a point of golden light which streamed through her body and permeated it with joy. The luminous joy spread until it filled the room with love, glowing on the cradle, the fire, the sleeping dog, the spinning wheel and the quiet woman who sat near it. In all of these Elizabeth saw a meaning she had never guessed, a truth so exquisite that it was near to pain, and she gave a little cry unknowing. At once, the feeling began to fade. Bodily strength drained from her with the ebbing joy, and trembling, she rested her head on her hand.

"My dear," said Anne quietly. "What is it?"

Elizabeth could not speak. Anne rose and put her arm

around Elizabeth's shoulders. In a moment she asked again, "What was it?"

"Something I can't—I don't know. The Light—" The Light was gone, yet still there was a thrilling awe and wonder.

Anne went to the dresser and poured out a glass of wine. She brought it to Elizabeth. "*You* have been blessed with some revelation, I think," she said tenderly. "Perhaps it was The Comforter. There is joy unsurpassed if we be but touched by the hem of His robe. That is Grace."

She looked down a moment at Elizabeth, gave a soft laugh and added, "Will you not take your mask off, Mistress? I should like to see your face."

Elizabeth started. "I'd forgotten it. Forgive me." Since entering the house she had forgotten everything but her strange response to this woman and what had been evoked here. Slowly she took off the little mask and turned her face up to Anne, who stepped back.

"Mistress Feake—!" she cried. "It is indeed Mistress Feake, niece to John Winthrop! I saw you on the Fast Day."

"Aye," said Elizabeth. "But Mistress—" She could not yet go on, dazed by the change.

Anne recoiled further. Her eyes flashed. "You came to spy on me! Fool that I am—indiscreet again—what have I said to you! Beguiled by your voice and manner—O woeful trust!"

"No, no," cried Elizabeth jumping up. "How can you think this of me? Nobody knows I came here, nor will know. I came not as a Winthrop." The other still frowned in disbelief, and Elizabeth caught her hand. "Mistress, you spoke of love, and don't you know I love you and that through you today—I have felt—I have seen—what I never before did guess at. I know now that all you teach is true."

Anne swallowed. The indignation gradually vanished from her gaze. She took Elizabeth's pleading hand and pressed it, then sank down on her chair. "I think I believe you," she said wearily. "But these days I am beset, so harried by doubts and sudden enmities. I have fears that dart like serpents to attack. Ah, but this is weakness."

Elizabeth wanted to cry out in protest. She yearned to speak of her own vision and to give gratitude to the woman who had been the instrument of its coming. But she could not. The time had passed as the vision had, leaving only memory. "I'll go now, Mistress," she said uncertainly. "I've trespassed long enough on your kindness."

Anne turned, and said in a musing voice, "And did I somehow help you, then?" She read the answer, and added, "For that I'm glad. Tell me—is there not a meeting of the ministers at Mr. Winthrop's home today? I have been warned of it."

Elizabeth nodded mutely.

"What are they saying of me, and my brother Wheelwright?"

"I heard nothing," said Elizabeth after a moment, unwilling to add any further burden to this woman whose exaltation had gone, leaving her big-boned face tired and care-worn. "My uncle never speaks to me of such matters."

"My brother Wheelwright is rash, his sermon on the Fast Day was ill-considered but just." She checked herself. "You see I do trust you. Aye, child, you had better go. No, stay— my weakness is passing. God is strengthening me again. And I feel—I hear—something for you." Her drooping body straightened. She clasped her hands and closed her eyes, a faint listening smile came to her lips. "It is this, I think . . ." she said slowly. "You will have much tribulation. Tribulation and shame. You will forget what you have felt this day. Forget that we are all one in Christ. But many years from now, and far from here, It will come again and then—" She drew a quick startled breath, her lids flew open, "Hark! What's that?"

They both heard a commotion in the hall, and the tread of heavy feet. There were loud raps on the door.

"Who's there?" Anne called out sternly.

"Underhill," came the answer, "and Coddington." The door burst open before Anne could speak again, and the Captain, with sword, musket and armor, strode in followed by William Coddington. "Where's Wheelwright, Mistress?" said Underhill urgently to Anne. "And is your husband safe at home?"

"Aye," she said, staring at the two whom she knew to be her friends. "My husband's in his closet casting up accounts, and my brother Wheelwright returned this morn to Mount Wollaston. What's ado, gentlemen?"

Underhill's dark face cleared of apprehension, and resumed its usually ironic cast. "There was some rioting near the dock, drunken brawlers, they set fire to your boat, and burned in it straw effigies of—of your brother and husband and—" He paused and cleared his throat.

"Of me," said Anne.

"There was no harm done, barring the loss of the boat," interposed Coddington quickly in a reassuring voice. "Have no fear. The constable's jailed the knaves, but we wanted to be sure of your safety."

Anne had turned pale, but she spoke with composure. "I know that God will protect us, no matter how evil men try to assault us."

Underhill, who had no such conviction, and whose allegiance to the Covenant of Grace sprang as much from his antipathy towards Winthrop as it did from his liking for the Hutchinsons, suddenly discovered Elizabeth, who had shrunk into her cloak and hood and was fumbling at her mask.

"Why, now, who is this little red bird with the neat pair of ankles!" cried the Captain, leering down at the crimson hood. "One of your disciples, ma'am?"

"Nay," said Anne, frowning at the Captain whose gallantries displeased her. "Leave her alone, pray."

But Underhill was not one to leave any feminine mystery unsolved. His hand shot out and he jerked back Elizabeth's hood. "Why the devil take me, 'tis the fair Bessie Feake!" He slapped his thigh and brayed with laughter.

William Coddington's pursy mouth opened then closed again. A flush ran up his pock-marked skin. Since his return from London with a new wife, he and Elizabeth had caught glimpses of each other, but it has been quite possible to avoid a meeting. Elizabeth had been amazed at the kindness of Coddington's tone towards Mrs. Hutchinson, but she saw that towards herself there would be no tolerance, nor forgiveness of the insults she had given him at Groton.

"Why have you received this shameless female, Madam?" he cried to Anne. "She could only make a mock of you, or worse!"

And Underhill, suddenly sobering, drowned out Elizabeth's unhappy protest, by saying, "Aye, that's true. I hadn't thought. She's a Winthrop." His eyes narrowed, and his voice grew biting. "Perhaps *you* know something about that riot today, eh? Might have picked up a hint or two at Winthrop's table?"

Elizabeth stood up and faced the Captain squarely. "John Underhill, that is outrageous," she said. "Whatever you may think of my uncle, whatever enmity he may have towards some people, you know that he is not a petty plotter, nor would ever demean himself to incite rogues to crime!"

"Well said, Mistress Feake," said Anne, "and truly, I think."

Underhill looked discomfited, but he shrugged and laughed. "My apologies, dear Mistress Bess, I'd not cross swords with so pretty a woman."

Coddington was not softened. "The Devil has given her her tongue," he said. "You need put no faith in it. *What* is she doing here? I see I'll have yet one more matter of debate to bring before Mr. Winthrop when I see him tomorrow."

"Oh no, I beg!" cried Elizabeth. "Don't tell him I was here!"

Anne, convinced by this unmistakable note of fear, said, "Nay, dear—he won't," but Coddington settled his double chins into his ruff and folded his arms. "I shall do as conscience bids me," he said. "This woman, with or without her uncle's knowledge, means you no good, 'twere best to cut her claws in any case. You must rely on me, Madam—" He turned to Anne with the look of genuine warmth that again startled Elizabeth even in the midst of her discomfort. "Rely on me to do what is best for you and those of us under Grace," Coddington finished.

Anne accompanied Elizabeth into the hall. She gave her almost the same lovely smile that she had in greeting, but now there was sadness in it and preoccupation. "You had better not come to me again," she said. "Not until God has quieted our troubles. But I do believe you love me, no matter what they say. And I shall pray for you."

Elizabeth went out of the door into the winter darkness, longing for solitude in which to think, but no sooner had she stepped into the snowy street than she felt her arm caught and an angry frightened voice said, "Bess!" in her ear. She jerked her arm away, uncertain for a moment in the darkness, and the shaking voice whispered, "Before God, wife, how *could* you go there! I couldn't believe, but I've been waiting this hour!"

"Robert?" she faltered, as she recognized the voice and caught the whiff of lavender he always used, though his black beaver hat was pulled low over his ears, his face muffled by his cloak. "You're back from Dedham?" she said foolishly, trying to meet this new dismay. "How did you know where I was?"

"Deane told me, when I came to the house. He stopped me from questioning our aunt and uncle, and before the ministers too. Yet Aunt Margaret had missed you. I lied as

best I could—I said that in a message you had told me you
thought to visit Jack's wife."

Elizabeth gave a curt laugh. "A likely tale! You might
have told a better lie than that."

"What could I do? Dear God, if Uncle John should find
out—what wicked folly made you go to that virago, that she-
Beelzebub!"

"She's none of that," said Elizabeth, beginning to walk.
"You do but ape what you have heard my uncle say. Must
you *always* think as he does? Tell me, Robert, would you
have been so hot to wed me had I not been a Winthrop?"

She felt him wince and knew that she had hurt and vanquished him, as she always could, except in the rare times
when the "strangeness" was on him. "Bess, you speak so
cruel," he said faintly. "So hard and cruel. Is this what you
learned from Mrs. Hutchinson?"

"No," she answered, stopping dead by the Winthrop gate.
"No." She bowed her head. "Already I've forgotten what I've
learned. It doesn't stay." She drew a long sobbing breath.

A pine knot torch flared on the corner of the house, and
by its light he peered into her averted face. "You weep,
Bess?" he whispered unbelieving. He bent nearer, anxious
and uncertain. She did not draw away. He put his arms
around her, and she laid her cheek against his cloak. "Ah,
husband—" she said. "Forgive me that I do not—" she could
not finish aloud. But her whole thought echoed in her heart.
Forgive me that I do not love enough.

12

THAT WHOLE YEAR of 1637 was the most troubled that the Bay Colony had known. By March Winthrop had consolidated all the ministers but Cotton with the two powerful magistrates, Thomas Dudley and John Endecott. They were ready for attack and they moved. They haled Wheelwright before the General Court, accusing him of contempt and sedition, as evidenced by his Fast Day speech. The Hutchinson party was thunderstruck and then rallied to the defense, violently protesting the allegation, and its methods, and averring that these hearings behind closed doors remarkably resembled the tyrannies of the detested Star Chamber in England. Fifty-eight of Boston's most prominent citizens signed a remonstrance demanding proper procedure and indicating sympathy for Wheelwright. John Underhill's name headed this petition, which had Governor Harry Vane's and William Coddington's passionate approval. Vane and Winthrop thereupon held stormy private sessions, from which the young governor and his deputy emerged each angrier and more obdurate than ever.

Winthrop's party was, however, compelled by Boston's outcry and the Governor's authority to temporize until the May elections. Moreover as the spring advanced they were all forced into a brief truce by the recognition of acute danger on their western borders. The Pequots were on the rampage.

Plymouth had for some time been writing anxious letters to the Bay. Roger Williams had been sending warning messages from Providence, where he had carved himself a little settlement in the wilderness after banishment from Massachusetts. Boston paid scant attention until Haynes and Hooker both wrote from Connecticut describing the horrors of a Pequot massacre at Wethersfield. Nine of its inhabitants had been scalped and roasted alive; two girls had been captured.

That was different. These were people whom the Bay Colony knew, for they had come from Watertown. The menace became real. The Bay hastily prepared for war.

Elizabeth was at Watertown as she had been since the day after her January visit to Mrs. Hutchinson. Robert had been in a fever to leave Boston before Winthrop should hear of Elizabeth's disgraceful behavior, and she, a little frightened herself, had obeyed his pleadings. She was all the more willing because, as a climax to the strange experience at Mrs. Hutchinson's and Elizabeth's consequent remorseful softening towards Robert, they had come together again as man and wife. He had lain in her arms that night, and she had known bodily release, and some contentment. The contentment deepened when she shortly afterwards found that she was with child. Depressions and doubts vanished; in a state of calm well-being she ceased to think much of Mrs. Hutchinson, especially as reports from Boston indicated that after the inconclusive hullabaloo over Wheelwright, the conflict had quietened. Nor obviously had Coddington reported Elizabeth's visit after all.

Margaret's occasional letters were as affectionate as usual, and ended as usual with "Your uncle sends his love, and prayers for your favor in Christ." So Elizabeth was able to reassure Robert.

One morning during the second week of May, Elizabeth was in her garden, sitting on a bench under the maple tree and trying to teach five children—her own and three of the Patricks'—their letters from a hornbook. Discipline was difficult. Elizabeth herself was almost as distracted as the children by the perfume of her growing herbs and flowers, the twittering of the birds in a white-spangled cherry tree and the antics of the Feakes' new puppy which imagined it had cornered some sort of enemy in the lush grass.

"Now children, again," said Elizabeth tapping her straw pointer on the hornbook. "What is this?"

"M?" said Lisbet, tugging at one of her flaxen curls. "M for mouse."

"Not *M*—you silly," cried Joan shaking her brown head importantly. "That's W. Isn't it, Mama?"

"Which is it, Dan?" Elizabeth asked of Patrick's young son, who was lying on his stomach teasing an earthworm. "Sit up and pay attention!"

He glanced at the hornbook, said, "I dunno, ma'am," and yawned.

"Well, you've got to learn," cried Elizabeth, "or I'll tell your father to switch you. Stand up! All of you!"

They straggled to their feet and reluctantly recited in chorus as her straw moved up and down along the first two rows of the hornbook. "Big A, little a, Big B, little b—" They had reached R when the youngest Patrick gave a delighted squeal and ran to the corner of the house to greet Daniel Patrick who was dismounting from his horse.

"Faith, Bessie—" he said, patting his offspring and advancing to the group, " 'Tis a pleasant schoolroom ye've found for yourself. How's Danny at his letters?"

"Laggard," said Elizabeth severely. "But I think he knows his catechism." She turned to the boy. "Dan, what is the chief end of man?"

"Man's-chief-end-is-t'-glorify-God-'n-enjoy-Him-forever," said Danny glibly.

"What rule hath God given to direct us how we may glorify and enjoy Him?"

"Word-O'-God-contained-in-Scriptures-Old-n'-New-Testament's-only-rule-t'-direct-us-how-we-may-glor'fy-n'-enjoy-Him," said Danny on one breath.

"Good. Good lad—" interrupted Patrick hastily, before Elizabeth could continue. "I see we'll not have that blasted tithing man on our necks again, thanks to you, Bess. 'Ods body but I'd like to slice off his prying ferret nose fur him."

Elizabeth made a warning gesture because of the listening children, but she thoroughly agreed. Job Blunt, the tithing man, had several duties beyond keeping order on the Sabbath, and had recently made the scandalized discovery that the Patrick children had not been taught their catechism, an offense punishable by fines and public humiliation.

"Be off wi' ye—childer," said Patrick to the group. "School's out fur the nonce!"

They obeyed with alacrity, scampering from the garden towards the river, except Lisbet whose tastes never ran to wild games.

"I want to talk to ye, Bess," said Patrick sitting down on the bench beside Elizabeth. "There's news from Connecticut. From Underhill. The Pequots're massing, they even dared attack Saybrook Fort, though little came of it. They've killed more settlers at Hartford this time. We've not enough soldiers there. I've been summoned."

"Well, that's what you want, isn't it?" asked Elizabeth, knowing how the big redheaded captain had chafed at being ordered to remain home on guard while Underhill sailed off with his force of twenty men to join Captain John Mason in Connecticut.

"Aye," said Patrick grinning at her. "I've no fancy to be left out when there's a spot o' fighting, though I've no special stomach fur shooting Indians as a rule. And if that damned old fool, Endecott, hadn't stirred up all the Pequots last summer wi' that hapless raid on Block Island, we wouldn't have this wasps' nest buzzing about our ears. Still and all, they *are* buzzing, and must be quelled."

Elizabeth nodded and waited.

"They won't let me leave for Connecticut till after the election, next Wednesday," Patrick went on, frowning. "Expect trouble, they do, and want me and my men to stand by."

"Trouble here?" said Elizabeth. "Over the election? Won't Governor Vane be returned again?"

"Ha!" said Patrick. "Not if your uncle can stop it, and he's taken mighty good care to stop it. Election's to be at Newtown so Vane and Mrs. Hutchinson's Boston friends'll have less chance. I tell ye, Bess, this squabble at the Bay'd make a cat die laughing! Folk going about hissing that they're Works or Grace like in the old country they'd be Papist or Protestant. Only *that* made sense and I can't make head or tail o' this."

"Nor I," said Elizabeth. "Except—" But even to Patrick, of whose understanding she was sure, she didn't wish to speak of Anne Hutchinson.

"That's not what I came to say," said Patrick, pulling a dirty clay pipe from his leather pocket, stuffing it with tobacco, and lighting it after some difficulty with his flint and steel. " 'Tis Robert," he said puffing out a long trail of smoke.

"I wonder should I order him to go along wi' me to Connecticut."

Elizabeth swallowed, astonished that she had not thought of this. "Why, yes, I suppose so," she said uncertainly. "He's your lieutenant, I know he'd want to go with *you*."

Patrick glanced at her, his vivid Irish eyes clouded, and he stared at the cherry tree. Innocent Bess was, and unperceptive when it came to Robert of whose peculiarities Patrick was well aware, and yet he had sympathy for the man quite aside from his admiring fondness for Bess. Back in the monastery near Armagh there had been one of the monks a bit like Robert, a quiet meek man called Brother Edan who was forever telling his beads and at his devotions, gentle too with the younger brothers, who were all fond of him. And then one terrible night the Abbot found out something. Daniel, though he hadn't understood much then, remembered yet the shocked horror that had swept the monastery, the hushed conferences in the chapter house, the special masses, the whisperings, and then the end—a week later—when Brother Edan had been found dangling in his cell, hanged by his own knotted scourge. God save his poor soul somehow, for it was madness did it—all of it—Daniel thought, and turned to see that Elizabeth was watching him uneasily. "Ye see, m'dear," he said quickly, "I was just considering, would ye be content without your husband now, seeing that you're breeding and all—and," he added gently, "I'm not sure Robert's what ye might call a fighting man."

"No," she agreed after a pause. "But I think he'd like to be." Always Robert was happy for a while when starting a new venture, and when he felt himself accepted in a world of men. But it didn't seem to last. She sighed, and Patrick, who had been watching her, followed her thoughts enough to ask, "The settlement at Dedham's come to naught for ye, hasn't it? What happened?"

"In truth, I don't know," said Elizabeth. "Though he said he had a dream warning him not to settle there. I was dismayed at first, but then I thought it might be better if my babe were born here at Watertown, and Anneke to help me again." She looked at him with her quick pretty smile that brought soft lights to her hazel eyes. "For both Robert and me, you Patricks seem our only true friends."

"I' faith!" he cried. "We feel so too!" He gave her a bear hug, kissed her on the cheek, and got up. "Where's Robert now, in the fields with the men?"

She frowned, turning the hornbook over and over on her lap. "Nay," she said at last, "I fear he's gone to the burying ground. Somedays he goes there and sits amongst the gravestones, reading his Bible!"

"A pious pastime," said Patrick with a grimace. "Doubtless edifies the godly, but not me. Aye, Bess, I'll take him off to Connecticut, willy-nilly, at least knock some morbid dithers out o' him."

On the following Wednesday, May 17, the General Election was held at Newtown; an occasion fully as disturbed as had been expected. Governor Vane and those who had signed the remonstrance wished it publicly read, Winthrop did not. Mr. Wilson clambered up the oak tree, and perching on a lower limb like a stout angry crow, vehemently harangued the meeting. There were furious shouts. There were fist fights. There was tumult; which Winthrop overriding Vane's shrill protests, managed to quiet by a direct command that they ignore the petition which had nothing to do with the election, and proceed at once to vote. He was greeted with cheers and hisses, but the cheers predominated. Winthrop had planned shrewdly when he had got the election moved to Newtown, which was far more accessible to the freemen of Watertown, Roxbury, Charlestown and the towns on the North Shore than Boston. These other towns had not been impressed by Vance or influenced by Mrs. Hutchinson; they had been during the last weeks continually exhorted by their ministers.

John Winthrop was returned to office by a huge majority, Vane and his party suffered crushing defeat.

Late that night Elizabeth heard of the election from Robert, who was jubilant. "A great day it was, wife," he said happily, as he helped himself to an unaccustomed drink of sack. "So now after three years our uncle is Governor again, and we may all rejoice."

"Except Mrs. Hutchinson and her family," said Elizabeth on a dry note.

"Oh, they'll see the error of their ways," said Robert without interest. "They'll have to. Wife, where's my leather jerkin, and my sword belt? Daniel says we'll be off tomorrow."

She looked at him with attention. His fair skin was flushed from the sack and from excitement, his thin silver-gold hair was almost tousled, his long white fingers were restlessly tripping the hammer on his musket; while so often he was gray and wan, now he looked younger than his thirty-five years. "You're not afraid, Robert dear?" she said. "And be careful of yourself, won't you?" Suddenly she had realized he was going into danger and she felt compunction that she had not thought of this before. The inadequacy of her question and the tardiness of the emotion prompting it made her go to him and kiss him.

He responded with grateful surprise, as he always did to any overture from her. "Will you miss me, Bess?" he asked humbly. "I'd not leave you except Daniel says we'll be back long before the babe comes."

Daniel says, she thought, aye that was why she had had no fear for Robert; of course, they both leaned on the huge captain, as trustingly as did his own children. "To be sure I'll miss you," she said, "but I'm proud to have you go, and I shall be quite safe."

During the next two months she was indeed safe enough at Watertown, which was now thickly populated, and there was nothing to fear from the local Indians of whom only a dozen or so had survived the smallpox three years ago. The days were hot, and Elizabeth's pregnancy made her indolent, so that she skimped all but the most necessary chores, and wished fervently for a maid, even so inefficient a one as Sally had been. The little girls reluctantly helped with the dishwashing and bedmaking, and from time to time Elizabeth was able to hire the twelve-year-old daughter of her immediate neighbor to the east, Goodman William Bridges, but Dolly Bridges was a flighty child. If not constantly watched she incited Joan to naughtiness, and terrified little Lisbet with tales of ghosts, and a black man who hid under the stairs. Elizabeth preferred to do without her when she could. Besides herself and the children she had the two menservants to feed, her garden to tend, baking, brewing, rush peeling for candlewicks, malt and corn grinding, the stilling of necessary simples, and the constant mending of clothes and linen. There were now a few shops in Watertown, and Robert had left her supplied with several pounds, so that she could buy soap, sugar, and even wheat flour ground at the Watertown mill, but there was still so much to do that she fell exhausted into bed at night and after a vague prayer for Robert, slept without dreaming.

A letter from Margaret received on the fourth of July was exceedingly welcome. Elizabeth received it from a Winthrop servant and hurried along the river path to Anneke Patrick's.

Anneke was shelling peas on the Dutch stoop Daniel had made for her, and she greeted Elizabeth with her usual dimpling smile. "Velcome, Bess! Vat makes you hasten so this hot day? Nothing bad, I hope?"

"No," said Elizabeth sitting down beside her friend, and waving the letter. "Good news! From my Aunt Margaret. She confirms what we heard. The Perquots are wiped out. There was a battle at a place down there called Mystic, an Indian town. Daniel was there with Robert, and Captain Underhill, and Captain John Mason that used to be in Dorchester, remember?"

Anneke nodded, her plump rosy face earnest between the white lace wings of her Dutch cap. "So Daniel is unharmed —and Robert? Good, I have been so anxious, so anxious." She drew a deep breath. "Vat else does the letter say?"

"They killed almost all the Pequots but the chief, Sassacus. Daniel is going to stay down there and chase him a bit longer, with Underhill, but we're not to worry, my aunt says. None of our men were lost."

"Och, I am happy," said Anneke. She put down the pan of peas and called into the house, "Danny, Danny! Tell your sisters vader is vell, and the bad Indians are beaten!" There was a joyous whoop, and Danny rushed out.

"There's more," said Elizabeth. "My aunt summons me at once to Boston, because forty-eight Pequot women and children are to be landed tomorrow. Captives sent up by boat. They're to be parceled out on the Common, and though some have been bespoke already, Aunt Margaret says she and Uncle John will see that I get a squaw."

"Vat for?" asked Anneke puzzled. "Vat do you vant of a squaw?"

"Why, for a maidservant. Maybe I could get you one, too."

Anneke chuckled. "I vouldn't have those filthy creatures in my nice clean house. No, Bess, lieveling, I'm used to vork hard always, you are not. I hope you get a good squaw."

She put her arm around Elizabeth and said happily, "Ve must drink a little something for gladness that our men are vell. My good genever from The Hague I've been saving, and my special cheese I made from the nanny-goat's milk!"

Anneke's kitchen, like Anneke's person, exuded a sparkling cleanliness which always shamed Elizabeth. Anneke's aprons were as spotless as her brick hearth. Her copper kettles and pewter dishes twinkled like stars; from her coils of yellow hair, smooth as butter, no strand ever was misplaced. Placid and practical, she understood the effortless management of domesticity, and loved her work, never suffering from the rebellions and spasmodic yearnings which afflicted Elizabeth, who was always calmed by Anneke, and returned from each visit determined to cope better with her own housekeeping problems.

Today, as usual, Elizabeth was defeated. She arrived home hot and tired from her walk, wishing only to sit and contemplate her flowers while indulging in delightful plans for their future as medicines and pot pourris and perfumes. She was greeted by little Dolly Bridges with a gloomily triumphant list of emergencies. The cornbread in the bake oven had burned to a crisp. The water bucket had developed a leak, making it impossible to haul water from the well, and consequently the huge stack of trenchers, pots and mugs was still unwashed. Worst of all, one of the last precious linen sheets brought from England had torn right down the middle while Joan was making the bed. Elizabeth, who loathed sewing as much as she had at seven, glared at the sheet, lost her temper, boxed Joan on the ear, and set grimly to the unsuccessful conquering of muddle, which like a jellyfish oozed up in a new place as soon as one side was flattened.

Boston Common on the sixth of July presented an extraordinary appearance. A hundred square feet had been fenced off near the ducking pond, and the Pequot captives put in the enclosure, loosely roped together at the waist. There were about forty young squaws; the older captives had not been sent—and a handful of children, well grown enough to be of service. Though some of the women were taller and some fatter than others, at first they looked much alike. They were all naked from the middle up, and all wore short doeskin skirts. Their coarse black hair flowed loose. What ornaments or wampum necklaces they might once have had were long since removed. Within the barricade they stood motionless and soundless, staring at the ground, ignoring the milling crowd which surrounded them and avidly discussed their physical points.

All the more prosperous Boston housewives had come, and a sprinkling of men. Governor Winthrop was there too, standing on a little platform near the enclosure, while Elizabeth and Margaret were near him. Behind the platform on which Winthrop stood, a plank had been upended and down its length were nailed the severed hands of dead Pequot warriors, sent from Connecticut.

Winthrop was dressed in his most ceremonious suit of rich black satin, topped by the old fashioned lace-edged ruff he still wore. His broad black beaver hat was garnished with silver braid and a glittering buckle—the sumptuary laws naturally did not apply to the Governor. His tricolored baldric supported the great sword of state. He was flanked by his new halberdiers, Vane's guard having proved insolent and been dismissed; and his expression was definitely complacent. It was apparent to Elizabeth that Uncle John was very glad to be back in office.

He raised his arm, and his watchful drummer beat a tattoo, thus silencing the throng. Winthrop then said, "Before proceeding with this afternoon's business, I shall offer a prayer to the Almighty that He may continue to shed blessings on us." He went on to thank God, for having exterminated the Pequots, and for having sent them these captives. It was God's manifest purpose that the captive Indians should now labor for their new owners, and be Christianized as well. He trusted that they would profit by sight of the row of mangled hands to realize the wickedness of their warlike folly and that the Christian God alone could save them. It was a joyous day for the captives, did they but realize it.

They obviously did not realize it. Elizabeth looked at the dark sullen faces, some tattooed, some scarred, and felt from them an actual wave of hatred, which dismayed her. She began to wonder if, after all, a Pequot squaw would make a good maidservant.

The other ladies of Boston apparently had no misgivings. The instant Winthrop stepped off the platform, indicating that the constable should take charge, there was a bedlam of greedy cries, while the would-be owners nearly stampeded the barricade. Some grabbed at the hair of the squaw of their choice, some called frenziedly, "That big one. That one, I want that one!" There was also shrill dissension when two ladies picked on the same squaw.

"Gentlewomen and goodwives!" shouted the constable over the hub-bub. "Ye can't have 'em like *that!* Some is bespoke. The large one over there," he gestured to his guard who hauled the squaw in question to one side, "she goes to Mr. Stoughton. That little one with the three marks on her belly goes to Lieutenant Davenport. Mrs. Calacott has been allotted that one; them two heathen boys and girl're going to Salem."

As he eliminated several more and tied around their necks red strings with labels of ownership, there were groans from the disappointed housewives. "Now fur the rest," said the constable pompously, squinting at a list. "I'll call off the names in order o' consequence to take their pick. First, Mistress Winthrop, our Governor's lady!"

Margaret, who did not need a squaw herself but had promised to get one for Mary Dudley in Ipswich, said, "Oh dear, they all seem so fierce. That one, I guess—" She pointed nervously to one of the youngest. The Indian girl was duly tagged.

The constable continued reading from his list: Mrs. Cotton, Mrs. Wilson, Mrs. Dudley the elder, Mrs. Endecott, Mrs. Saltonstall, all of whom made a choice. He had finished with the gentry on his list and was moving down into the goodwives when Winthrop, who had been watching benevolently, suddenly turned to Elizabeth and said, "Why, the constable's left you out! The best ones are nearly gone. Halt!" he cried.

The constable stopped anxiously. "Aye, Your Worship?"

"Where's Mistress Feake's name?" said Winthrop. "She ranks long before those you're reading."

"I—I didn't know, sir—" stammered the constable, who was newly appointed. "Her being of Watertown, n' wi'out special word I was told to take them from t'other towns last."

"Never mind," said Elizabeth hastily. "I don't think I want any of them."

"Nonsense," said Winthrop, stepping forward. "Your aunt says you need a servant, and I shall certainly not have my niece slighted. I'll pick one for you." He stepped up to the barricade, and pinched a fat brown arm. "This one seems solid, and healthy, you shall have her, my dear."

"No!" cried Elizabeth. Not again should her uncle foist his own choice on her. She ran up to the fence and grabbed a handful of hair at random. "Her, I'll take her."

There was a ripple of astonished laughter from the other waiting owners and Elizabeth saw the reason for it as her squaw turned around. The Indian had but one eye. In place of the right one there was a red pulpy socket. The right side of her face was hacked with hideous purplish scars which ran down her neck and ended in a crisscross pattern on the distorted right breast.

"Oh, Bess!" Margaret cried. "She's the worst of the lot. She'll frighten the children."

Herself, appalled, Elizabeth hesitated, though noting that the squaw was quite young, and lithely muscled, her skin smooth and golden brown away from the mutilations. Then the squaw made a curious motion with her hands like an unconscious plea, the left eye looked steadily at Elizabeth, and though it seemed expressionless, some dilation of the pupil conveyed suffering and intelligence. Why, it's a human being! Elizabeth thought. She, like all the others, had viewed these mute dark-skinned bodies as cattle, to be selected on the grounds of use. "I'll *take* her," she repeated more firmly.

"An unfortunate selection," said her uncle, but not even Elizabeth's customary headstrongness could annoy him today. He walked back to Margaret, and began to chat with young Mrs. Saltonstall. Elizabeth remained uncomfortably beside her squaw, wondering what to do with her. While she stood there the interpreter came up to them. He was a Narragansett, and had been shipped north from that tribe which had been allied with the English in the Pequot war. He had been taught English by Roger Williams and spoke it well.

"Missis—" he said. "You want know your squaw's name, or other matter?"

"Oh, yes," said Elizabeth. "I want to know all about her."

The Narragansett spoke for some time, while the squaw listened motionless. There was a pause, and Elizabeth with dismay thought she had got herself a maid not only repulsive but mute. Then the squaw spoke in a rush.

The Narragansett turned to Elizabeth. "She say her name Telaka, which mean, before night—not day."

"Twilight?" suggested Elizabeth, and the Indian grunted acquiescence. "She speak strange—not Pequot." He stopped because Telaka burst out with vehemence at the word "Pequot." The Narragansett held up a hand to stop her, and she became silent, the one shiny black eye looking anxiously at Elizabeth while the Indian translated. "Now I know," said the interpreter. "She NOT a Pequot. She hate them. They capture her from a tribe far far to the setting sun, where no white men live. Siwanoy tribe was hers, Sagamore Mianos, her father."

"Was she a chief's daughter?" asked Elizabeth astonished.

The Narragansett shrugged. "She *say* so. Pequots very bad to her. Burn her, cut her because she run away. Pequots do this." He swept up and down Telaka's ravaged face, neck, and breast with an indifferent hand.

"Ask her," said Elizabeth, "how old she is, if she's married and has children."

Telaka answered this more quietly, and Elizabeth realized that the guttural voice was musical and rather pleasant.

"She say," said the interpreter, "She not know age, but has seen many winters, mebbe like you, Missis. She was married in her tribe, but her man was killed by Pequots."

Yes, thought Elizabeth, faintly amused at the "many winters," I suppose she is about my age, poor thing. "Ask her," she said finally to the Narragansett, seeing that many other owners were awaiting his help in questioning their new acquisitions, "if she is willing to work for me, and will try hard to be a good servant."

When Telaka answered this she turned her head away, and Elizabeth saw the thin brown hands clench.

The Narragansett's mouth twitched in a grim smile as he translated. "She say you look kinder than Pequots, but she no like to be *anyone's* slave. She say she never lie, she won't answer more. She say too that she very homesick."

So, thought Elizabeth wryly. I suppose that means she'll run away, and I doubt that I care.

The constable put Telaka's rope in Elizabeth's hand, saying, "Here y'are, Mistress Feake. D'ye want a guard to help get her home?"

Elizabeth shook her head. "Take the rope off her, constable. I can't lead her about like a cow."

The constable obeyed but protested. "I fear ye've got a bad 'un, ma'am, have a care she don't murder you in your bed, I don't like the look in that eye."

Elizabeth was not sure that she did either, but the squaw, who had stiffened and sucked in her breath as the constable untied her bonds, watched the rope fall to the dust, then turned in obvious astonishment towards Elizabeth, who put out her hand and said, "Come, Telaka." Telaka seized the hand and held it between both of hers, a warm, and surely not unfriendly, grip. When Elizabeth began to walk towards the Charles landing where the Feake boat and one of the men-servants waited, Telaka followed quietly one pace behind her new owner.

During the weeks before Robert's return with Daniel Patrick, Elizabeth got used to her squaw, though she never had any certainty as to what Telaka was thinking. Elizabeth made her a black eye patch, and gave her an old dress of her own to wear. This covered much of her mutilation, so her appearance though grotesque was no longer repulsive. The children after their first startled curiosity accepted her without question, and indeed in her own expressionless way she was good to them. She made Lisbet a corn-husk doll, and sometimes when nobody was around Elizabeth heard her singing to the girls, strange monotone little songs that sounded like wind in the pine trees. Moreover, she was a good worker. Elizabeth had only to show her once, and thereafter she could perform any task, even the detested sewing. She spoke seldom, but listened much with a sort of concentrated purpose, and at the end of August, Elizabeth realized that Telaka was learning English exceptionally fast, and understood almost everything she heard.

Elizabeth preened herself on her choice, and the intelligence of her squaw, nor would she listen to the neighbors' warnings that there was something sinister about Telaka. Goodwife Bridges was particularly caustic now that Elizabeth no longer hired Dolly to work. She and Goody Warren and Goody Knapp talked a good deal about Mrs. Feake and the ugly heathen she'd got, and for all anybody could see on neighborly calls didn't seem to be converting at all.

"Last Wednesday," said Goody Bridges to her cronies one day, "I ran in for the loan of a smidgin o' yeast, and finding that squaw alone, and polishing the coppers which they surely needed, I must say, I asked her right out, Did she know God and did Mrs. Feake teach her the catechism?"

"What'd she answer?" asked Peg Warren, her mouse face eager.

"She said, 'My missis, *she* mind her own business.' That's what she said, and in as good English as you or me, a'most. I was skeered I can tell ye, wi' that one toad eye a-gleaming at me. She's uncanny, that's what that savage is."

The three women looked at each other with meaning. Peg Warren said, "Depend on it, the Devil's helped her learn English so as to run away better, like all them squaws in Boston, allus taking off for Connecticut. I hear Mrs. Wilson's was brought back from Narragansett and branded on the forehead, but now she's gone again. I wouldn't trust that Telaka far as you can throw a barrel."

The goodwives Warren and Knapp nodded solemnly. "Is that blue jay still there i' the kitchen?" asked Goody Warren after a pause.

"Aye," whispered Goody Bridges. "Tame as you please,

hopping about on the table and squawking and eating from that Indian's hand. 'Tisn't natural."

Again they met each other's eyes, but said nothing more. Elizabeth was now again the Governor's niece, walls had ears sometimes, as all had discovered in the old country as well as here, indiscreet speech was dangerous, and authority could hale anyone up before the court for slander at the slightest complaint. They dropped Mrs. Feake and her uncanny squaw in favor of a topic quite safe in Watertown and scarcely less interesting; the inexorable progress of the chastisement of the infamous Mrs. Hutchinson and her brother-in-law Wheelwright.

Elizabeth was scarcely aware of what was going on. First in early September there was the excitement of Robert's and Daniel's return from Connecticut. They were full of the Pequot war and its successful conclusion; except that Sassacus, the Great Pequot Sachem, had escaped and fled to the Mohawks, though that, said Daniel, was of no consequence. The Pequot wasps' nest had been destroyed, all the other Connecticut Indians were jubilant. Uncas, in particular, the Mohican chief, was now violently pro-English, and the settlers' lives were at last safe.

"Was there danger? Were you nearly wounded?" asked Elizabeth tremulously, feeling the ancient female thrill of awe for the returning warriors, and glad that Robert looked well, and had actually gained weight.

"Why, o' course there was danger, silly lass!" laughed Patrick, not adding that he had protected Robert from it very skillfully. "We're a couple o' heroes, aren't we, Rob?"

Robert had seen some fighting, and been anxious to do his part, but it had developed that he was most useful at the Fort, acting as scribe and accountant. Neither he nor Daniel mentioned this to Elizabeth, and Robert basked in her admiration.

Then in September Elizabeth was brought to bed of another girl. The birth was easy, there was no time to summon Anneke, and Telaka quietly did what was necessary. Elizabeth was bitterly disappointed that she had not borne a son; for some days in the weakness of lying-in she was depressed and tearful, until the healthy pleasure of suckling the infant and delight in its sturdiness and crop of red-gold curls brought acceptance and soon she realized that she loved it very much. That, tiny as it was, she had a special feeling for it, different and more intense than for the other two at that age. For some reason, as the baby lay in her arms and nuzzled her breast she thought again of the strange beautiful experience in Mrs. Hutchinson's parlor, and she told Robert that she wished to call the baby Anne.

"If you like, dear wife," he said tenderly. "It was your mother's name, was it not?"

"Aye," she said. She had almost forgotten that. "But wait—" She raised herself on her elbow, looking up at Robert with sudden dismay. "Now I remember that Uncle Winthrop once said the name was hapless in our family. Three babes he has had named Anne, and all died so soon." She kissed her baby and hugged it against her breast.

"Well," said Robert who had much knowledge of the Scriptures, though he seldom showed it, "call her Hannah then. 'Tis the same in Hebrew, and both Anne and Hannah mean Grace."

"Do they?" Elizabeth said smiling dreamily. "How strange." She lay back on the pillows and said, "Have you heard aught of Mrs. Hutchinson? How she does?"

"How she does?" repeated Robert astonished. "Why, she goes on trial soon, and Wheelwright is banished."

"Dear Lord!" cried Elizabeth starting up again. "What do you mean?"

"Why, I mean just that," said Robert a trifle sharply. "You must know that the synod of all the colony ministers at Newtown found that woman and her brother guilty on eighty-two points of heresy."

"No," said Elizabeth. "I didn't." She added through tight lips, "And I presume my Uncle and Mr. Wilson ably found eighty of the points themselves."

"Bess! It frets me when you speak in that tone of your Uncle Winthrop. I cannot understand you."

"Don't try," she said. "But tell me what has become of Mrs. Hutchinson's powerful friends? Of Harry Vane, and Mr. Cotton, of Captain Underhill and Mr. Coddington; do they not help her?"

"Vane has sailed back to England," said Robert slowly, unwilling to go on, but also anxious not to cross her who was still in childbed. "Mr. Cotton, when the ministers all exhorted and prayed with him at the synod, confessed at last that he had been in error to support that she-Satan in her wicked heresies. He was penitent."

"Oh, was he indeed!" she said. "So Mr. Cotton is now safely enfolded with all his godly colleagues, and need no longer be embarrassed by Mrs. Hutchinson's long trust and affection."

"Wife!" cried Robert suddenly anxious. "You're not yourself. You speak unreasonable." He came close to the bedside and took her hand. "Pray forget all this, it has naught to do with you."

She withdrew her hand. "What of the other two, Underhill and Coddington, and the many more who believed in her?"

"In truth," said Robert, "I do not know." His lids blinked and the stubborn shut look stiffened his face.

She did not mention the subject again to Robert, but she thought of it much, and relied on Daniel Patrick's visits to keep her informed.

The Captain attended Anne Hutchinson's trial in his official capacity, and came back each evening from Newtown increasingly disgusted with what he had heard. "She's a fine, spirited gentlewoman," he said one day when Robert was out, and they could talk freely. "Holds her head high and answers 'em with so much pith, they get dumbfoundered. They quote Scriptures, she quotes back at 'em, and I'd a laughed except there's something goes against me grain to see thirty men badgering one lone woman. She doesn't look well either, and they say she's with child, poor soul."

"Who's hottest against her?" said Elizabeth quietly. "My Uncle Winthrop, I presume."

"Aye," said Patrick with a rueful laugh. "He acts as judge and prosecutor both, and a sharp sarcastic tongue he has, trying to trip her up. That long-nose pastor from Roxbury, Thomas Welde, he and Hugh Peter're the nastiest, but there's not one of 'em decent to her, far as I can see, now Mr. Cotton's slid t'other side o' the fence."

"She has no friends at all left?" whispered Elizabeth.

"Oh, I wouldn't say that." Patrick rubbed his nose and frowned. "But they're not let in the courtroom, 'cept Mr. John Coggeshall, and *him* the Reverend Peter muzzled at once. Mr. Coddington too, he spoke up for Mrs. Hutchinson right smartly. 'Here is no law of God that she hath broken,' he said, 'nor any law of the country that she hath broken. Therefore she deserves no censure.' But they wouldn't listen."

"What law can they pretend she has broken?" said Elizabeth. "How can they do this to her!"

"Well, Bess—" said Patrick fumbling for his pipe, and shrugging. "The way I see it, His Worship and the magistrates and reverends have somehow turned a woman's liking for one kind of preaching above another kind o' preaching into a hideous crime against the Commonwealth, 'n that's the nubbin o' it."

Elizabeth fretted that night about what she had heard. Had she been quite recovered she would have braved any consequences to get to Newtown to try to see Mrs. Hutchinson, though she knew very well the lady was under guard, and no woman would be allowed in the courtroom. As it was she prayed for her friend, and sent her uncle thoughts of intense dislike.

The next evening, long after supper, Daniel came again to the Feakes'. Elizabeth had gone downstairs for the first time, and was sitting in their best chair by the fire. Robert was hunched over the table writing a letter to his nephew, Toby Feake, who was still in Germany with Robert's sister but intended to come to New England. This prospect pleased Robert, who explained to Elizabeth, "A likely lad. Sister Alice says he's handy with boats and shipping, is very fond of the water. He'll be useful to us, especially since Hugh's bond is nearly up and we'll be short a man."

Elizabeth cared little whether Robert's nephew came to live with them or not, but she agreed with the practicality of replacing one of their servants, and thought it might be pleasant to have a kind of son in the house. "You're sending him the passage?" she asked idly, watching the flames dancing between the big black andirons. Robert grunted, and Telaka came in from the kitchen with a tankard of hot spiced beer. "Drink," she said, thrusting the tankard at Elizabeth. "Make milk."

"Why, thank you, Telaka—" said Elizabeth smiling. "How well you've mulled it, but I'm not thirsty."

"Drink!" said the squaw, her one eye growing stern. "Baby cry too much." She stalked out, her blue cotton skirts swishing.

It was true, Elizabeth thought, sipping at the beer; her milk had diminished during these days of worrying about Anne Hutchinson. She must fetch dried dill and fennel from the garret tomorrow, make a decoction of them. They always made the milk come. I should be spinning, she thought, not sitting idle, then raised her head gladly as they heard Patrick's knock.

The Captain strode in puffing and beating his hands. " 'Tis cold out. Snow in the air. 'Twill be a hard winter if November starts like this." He tossed his mantle on the chest, drew a chair up to the fire and toasted his steaming leather boots. He glanced at Robert, who had smiled a welcome before returning to his letter. "It's all over, Bess—" he said to her, quite low.

She stiffened, looking her question.

"Banished," said Patrick. "Banished as soon as the trails're fit to travel, imprisoned now in Welde's brother's home in Roxbury."

"It's monstrous!" Elizabeth cried, no longer caring whether Robert heard or not. "Where can she go?"

"Nowhere in Massachusetts, or Connecticut, *that's* certain," said Patrick. "Perhaps Roger Williams'll take her, being open-hearted and having suffered himself."

"But that's wilderness—" said Elizabeth, thinking of the charming comfortable home she had visited in Boston. "What has she done to be cast away like that?"

Patrick pulled a scrap of paper from his doublet. "I wrote down the verdict for ye. These are the very words. Governor Winthrop he said:

Mrs Hutchinson, you hear the sentence of the court. It is that you are banished from out our jurisdiction as being a woman not fit for our society. And you are to be imprisoned until the Court send you away.

Then Mrs. Hutchinson said:

I desire to know wherefore I am banished.

Governor Winthrop answered, as haughty as a Duke:

Say no more! The court knows wherefore, and is satisfied.

And that was the end of it."

"So my wise charitable uncle has won again," said Elizabeth, after a long pause.

"Now, now wife—" interposed Robert hastily, putting down his pen, "you must get this maggot from your head, my dear. Uncle Winthrop knows what's best, and this shameless woman has been traducing the ministers, she has pretended to direct revelations from heaven, and Dan hasn't told you that she flew into a passion crying that *she* should be delivered from the lion's den, and your uncle and the whole colony ruined."

Patrick cried with sudden anger. "The gentlewoman was

ill and so weary she could hardly speak. Beset by all those
yapping curs continually, is it wonder she talked a little
wild? 'Tis a shocking business and no fit work for *men*. I
marvel, Robert, that you seem to back it."

Robert's pale eyes widened, his face fell to dismay. Was it
contempt they both had in their eyes? Or simply anger, which
was bad enough. He looked from his wife to his best friend,
and the formless fear, which was never long defeated, oozed
out again from hiding. His lids fluttered, and his hands
trembled as he said anxiously, "I'll say no more. It is only
that Uncle Winthrop and all the ministers, they are our
leaders."

"I'faith they are," said Patrick more quietly. "And I like
it not. There's many more don't like it, either, as you'll soon
be seeing—Well," he suddenly gave them his wide blunt-
toothed grin, "I've had me bellyful o' squabbles. Bess, if ye're
not drinking that fine tankard o' beer, I'll relieve ye of it."

Anne Hutchinson was duly imprisoned at Roxbury, and
her husband went south to find some place in Rhode Island
where they might be sheltered. Her brother-in-law, John
Wheelwright, was cast from the colony immediately, despite
the bitter weather. He fled farther north to Piscataqua.

Winthrop, however, was by no means finished with his
measures for subduing what he had come to look upon as
a probable insurrection. Having punished the principals to
the utmost limit that he dared, he now turned his implacable
gaze on all Anne Hutchinson's sympathizers.

He began by disenfranchising Captain Underhill, and removing him from office. Even Margaret was appalled when
she learned of this, and seizing a bedtime moment, when
John was usually more tender and open, dared to question.

"These are matters you cannot comprehend, dear wife,"
Winthrop said, settling comfortably in his half of the big
bed. "Underhill's name headed that Remonstrance to the
Court last May and he defended Wheelwright."

"But, dearest," said Margaret. "To dismiss Captain Underhill like that, and disarm him, and take away his franchise!
Why, he fought nobly in the Pequot war, and he has been
your captain since you landed."

"He is a wicked and lecherous man," said Winthrop, blowing out the candle. "I like not speaking of these things to you,
but several women have made complaint of his lewdness,
and when caught the other day behind locked doors with

the cooper's wife, he impudently said he was praying with her, and in any case, he had the effrontery to say that since he was sealed by the Covenant of Grace, it was impossible for him to do wrong. You see, how libertine and Antinomian he is."

"I see," she said unhappily, and did not speak again, but her heart was heavy, and she knew that her beloved husband was not as he used to be. Harsh he had always been at times, though not to her, but now the justice and mercy he had used to show seemed to have faded away, leaving only self-righteousness. Margaret's sad thoughts drifted back to the golden days at Groton, as they often did.

Underhill's humiliation was only the first of many, and a cataclysmic edict in late November rocked the Bay. *All* the signers of the Remonstrance, also seventeen alleged Antinomians from other towns, were to be disarmed. Seventy-five men were thus ordered to bring in their muskets, their fowling pieces, their swords and their carbines and surrender these to the sergeant. They were not only treated as naughty children, but they felt themselves emasculated by the loss of their weapons, and their rage was such that it nearly touched off the insurrection Winthrop had thought to subdue. He doubled the guards, alerted all those whom he knew to be loyal, and enforced his law.

A few of these disgruntled men, like the Reverend Mr. Cotton before them, suddenly saw the errors they had committed and the invidious heresies they had been beguiled into. They wrote abject letters of apology and were forgiven. The rest, including Mr. Coggeshall, Mr. Aspinwall, and eventually Mr. Coddington, decided that they had had enough of Bay tyranny forever. They departed for Rhode Island, and exile. The Governor was triumphant, and the ministers saw therein God's cherishing providence for His elected saints.

There remained but one anticlimactic detail, which was duly scheduled for the following March of 1638—Anne Hutchinson's formal excommunication from the Church and her actual departure from the colony. Nobody had much doubt as to what the result of Anne's church trial would be, though the ministers had been laboring with her, and some said she showed signs of repentance. "She may repent till she's blue i' the face, poor mortal—" said Patrick, "and who could blame her, imprisoned and bedeviled like that all winter, deserted by Cotton, and seeing everything she worked so hard for in Boston taken from her. But they'll boot her out on some flummery no matter what she says."

"I don't believe she repents her teachings," said Elizabeth. "I pray she does not, for I think them to be true. And I'm going to Boston to see her."

Patrick looked at her with sympathy, but he shook his head. "Keep out of it, Bess. Ye'll do no good and get yourself and Robert into trouble."

Elizabeth longed to cry out that she didn't care, that loyalty and indignant pity for a friend outweighed the thought of any personal dangers, but she could not honestly do so. Robert's spirits had lately been good, he was happily anticipating the arrival of his nephew, Toby Feake, and Toby's sister Judith was coming too. Robert had enlarged his house in Watertown, so as to accommodate his nephew and niece, and was moreover very much pleased that he had again been elected a Watertown deputy to the General Court. Then there was their children's welfare to consider, the three little girls, and a new one, for Elizabeth had just discovered herself to be pregnant again.

"I shall be most discreet—" she said at last and with some shame to Patrick. "Nor let my uncle guess my true feelings, but I pray for a chance to say some word to Mrs. Hutchinson before she is banished."

"Your heart does ye credit, lovey," said Patrick gloomily. "If ye *are* going to Boston, an' ye see a ripe moment, put in a word for me wi' your uncle. I've not had me bounty money that was promised for the Pequot war, nor the grants o' lands neither. If 'twasn't for this money owing me, and that Anneke's so content here, I'd show a pair o' heels to this wretched colony meself. I vow I envy Underhill despite the shocking treatment he got!"

Elizabeth nodded. "Aye," she said with a tremble in her voice. "Soon he'll be in England."

Her friend put his arm around her shoulders, and gave her one of his quick hugs. "Would ye like to be, Bess?"

"Nay," she said, thinking of Martha. "There's naught to go back to. And yet—'tis not this kind of life I had in mind when I came over. I was a foolish, green girl then, no doubt, but I thought I'd find freedom—and true love," she added in a whisper to herself. She thought of Jack, whom she has not seen in months, his residence was still mostly at Ipswich; but she knew that he traveled all over the New England coast promoting various enterprises and investigating mineral deposits.

"Aye—" said Patrick who had also been thinking. "We all have many a dream that doesn't come true. But there's something about ye, Bess—something smothered an' held in. Ye got fire an' ye got beauty, seems wrong to me to see you pressed down into a little Watertown housewife, but that's the way it is."

"That's the way it is," she said turning away.

On the day before Anne Hutchinson's trial ended, Elizabeth took one of the men and the saddle horse and rode to Boston, knowing that Margaret would welcome her for any reason, but nevertheless furnished with an excuse for the visit, as a large shipment of silks and linens had just arrived from England and were for sale at Mr. Coggin's warehouse. Robert had given Elizabeth three pounds to outlay on dress materials for herself and the older girls.

Margaret welcomed her warmly, and the two ladies spent a pleasant afternoon at the warehouse handling the rich velvets and taffetas, which were more costly than Elizabeth expected, but Margaret helped out with a generous gift, and ther returned to the Winthrop mansion, followed by a servant bearing lengths of yellow and rose and blue.

Margaret was full of joy over the birth of a son to Jack a fortnight ago, and insisted that they stop by the younger Winthrops' to admire the baby who was called Fitz-John. Elizabeth concealed her usual reluctance to see Jack's wife, who was extremely pleased with herself and her son. She admired the baby, learned that Jack had been there for the birth but had now gone into Connecticut, and finished the entirely feminine afternoon by sitting in the Winthrop parlor with Margaret sipping raspberry cordial and eating honey cakes. It was only then that Elizabeth brought up the subject which was on her mind.

"Aunt Margaret," she said casually, "Mrs. Hutchinson is on trial in the meetinghouse tomorrow, isn't she?"

"Oh, *don't* mention that dreadful woman!" cried Margaret. "The whole matter is so distressing. I vow your uncle's not had a moment's peace in months. Tell me instead how little Joan is doing with her letters, and the precious Lisbet; that child looks so delicate, and yet I know, dear, that you tend and physic her skillfully, you have so much knowledge of those things." She gave Elizabeth a loving smile, "And how does baby Hannah do? I see you must have weaned her, or you could not leave like this; does that horrid-looking squaw of yours take good care of the children?"

"Aye," said Elizabeth. "Very good, and I had to wean Hannah, because—" She shrugged, smiling at Margaret and wondering how to turn the topic back to Anne Hutchinson.

"You mean another babe?" cried Margaret, delighted. "This time for sure 'twill be a son."

"I hope so," said Elizabeth, and plunged in. "Could I go to the trial tomorrow? I mean, I have curiosity about that woman, even in Watertown we've heard so much about her."

"Why, I suppose so," said Margaret frowning, "though you're not a Boston Church member; still your uncle wants me to go, and the boys. If you've a desire to see that Jezebel overthrown, I presume he'll make no objection."

"Aunt Margaret—" said Elizabeth after a moment. "Aren't you at all sorry for her? 'Tis unlike you to speak so stern."

"No, dear. I'm not sorry for her," said Margaret. "She is an instrument of Satan, sent by him to ruin our colony. I didn't understand at first, but your uncle very tenderly exhorted me until I did." Her brown eyes widened and she leaned forward, whispering, "And you don't know, Bess, what is being said about her—what Mr. Welde thinks—"

"Nothing good, I'm sure," said Elizabeth, startled to see that Margaret's gentle face suddenly showed actual fear, that she moistened her lips and looked over her shoulder before going on in a nervous little whisper. "He thinks she has commerce with the Devil, carnal—you know what I mean—and that the child she carries—is—" Margaret stopped; she shut her eyes and her lips moved in prayer.

"No," said Elizabeth, after an appalled moment. "Not witchcraft! That's a cruel lie, and what possible reason has he!"

"Not only he," whispered Margaret. "There've been rumors, I don't like to think on them, but Mrs. Hutchinson's friend Mary Dyer, the milliner's wife—they say that she last fall brought forth a—monstrous birth, and that the midwife— Goody Hawkins—the very one I had for my poor Sarah— God help us and forfend it had naught to do with my babe's death—this Goody Hawkins, my John thinks she may be a witch."

"And if she is!" cried Elizabeth. "What has this folderol to do with Mrs. Hutchinson?"

Margaret drew herself up and said with more reproof than Elizabeth had ever heard from her, "Mrs. Dyer and Goody Hawkins have both been infected with Mrs. Hutchinson's fiendish heresies, and I marvel at the lax way *you* speak, Bess!"

Even Aunt Margaret! Bess thought with dismay and some fear. Can I be wrong about Anne Hutchinson? Did I imagine the beauty of those moments with her, could I have been beglamoured by evil unbeknownst?

"I'm sorry," she said slowly, coloring a little. "I didn't mean to speak lax."

"I know, dear," Margaret patted her niece's hand. "Now let's forget the whole shocking topic."

The next day Elizabeth accompanied Margaret to the meetinghouse for the trial, and sat as before in the left front pew. John Winthrop and his elder boys were in the Governor's pew across the aisle. No longer was the congregation pro-Hutchinson; her party had long ago fled, been banished, or recanted. Two guards led the accused down the aisle where Wilson and Cotton together sternly received her by the pulpit.

Elizabeth could not forbear a gasp when she saw Anne, standing there, her head drooping, swaying a little and reaching back against the pulpit for support. Anne's hair was now as white as the cap which partly covered it, her rough brown prisoner's robe hung loose over a wasted body that yet showed the clumsy thickening at the middle which confirmed her condition. She looked old and when the trial began she seemed confused. She kept putting her hand to her forehead and shaking her head as though to clear it, while Wilson, his face aglow with the long-postponed revenge and triumph, thundered out yet once more the articles of her indictment. Once or twice she tried to speak, but Wilson drowned her out, until at the end he cried, "*Now*, Mrs. Hutchinson, what say you?"

Cotton stepped forward, and looking coldly on his former pupil, said, "I have labored much with her, I think she is subdued, and will acknowledge that she hath greatly erred. Tell us, Madam!"

Anne swayed again, her skin turned a sickly green, she looked up at the pastor she had followed here from Lincolnshire, and faltered, "I feel ill, forgive me. May I have a seat?"

"See how she doth pretend a bodily infirmity!" said Winthrop audibly, but Cotton brought her a stool. She sat on it, and drawing a paper from her bosom began to read in a low choked voice an apology and statement of repentance, confessing that she had often spoken rashly, unadvisedly, and out of heat of spirit, and had cause to be sorry for anything she might have said to slight the magistrates or the ministers.

"And what do you confess to be the root of all your gross and fundamental errors?" asked Cotton as she stopped speaking and stared at the floor.

She lifted her head and gazing towards the window said in a dead voice, "The root of all was the height and pride of my spirit."

Ah, she is truly abased, Elizabeth thought, in poignant sorrow. Yet with Anne thus humiliated, and beaten, at least now they must be satisfied, and desist from further harrying of this obviously sick woman.

But they did not. The ministers closed around her, Shepard, Wilson, Cotton, Welde and Eliot; they shouted accusations which were not intelligible to Elizabeth, except that she saw that they were trapping Anne into contradictions, into, as Shepard cried out, "gross and monstrous lies." He accused her again of "traducing the ministers, of slighting the Scriptures, of teaching devilish falsehood."

Whereupon Anne stood up, and with a remnant of her old force, said to Mr. Shepard in a measured and dignified voice:

"I do NOT *allow the slighting of ministers, or the scriptures, nor anything that is set up, by God; and if Mr. Shepard doth conceive that I had any of these things in my mind then he is deceived; and my judgment is not altered though my expression alters."*

A long sigh of relief came from her pursuers, Elizabeth with a shudder saw the gloating in their faces, for Anne had again condemned herself.

"You hear!" cried Shepard. "She accuses *me* of deceit, she casts shame on others! And in the same breath she confesses that her repentance was false, her pretended judgment is unchanged!"

Wilson mounted his pulpit and cried, "We should sin against God if we should not put away so evil a woman, this notorious imposter!"

There was an exultant chorus of agreement, of invective, of denunciation, all aimed at the woman who stood with clasped hands while the waves of shrill anger beat on her. Wilson quickly put the matter to the vote, which was received by the silence that meant consent. He smiled and drew a deep breath, then turning in his pulpit, pointed a stubby forefinger down at her who stood alone on the floor near the Communion Table, and he cried out with ringing relish the sentence of excommunication:

> *"Therefore in the name of the Lord Jesus Christ and in the name of the church I do not only pronounce you worthy to be cast out, but I do cast you out! In the name of Christ I deliver you up to Satan. . . !"*

As Wilson pronounced those words, Elizabeth saw Anne's rigid face quiver, the dark sunken eyes opened wide, and terror came into them. They turned towards Cotton who stood with head averted, they came back and met by chance Elizabeth's anguished gaze. For a moment the two women looked into each other eyes, and the terror left Anne's. Strength flowed back into her and she seemed transfigured, a luminousness enfolded her as Elizabeth watched, and at the same time Elizabeth felt an echo of the comfort she had known before in Anne's parlor; an awareness of peace far above this murk of hatred.

Wilson finished the excommunication:

> *"Therefore I command you in the name of Christ Jesus . . . as a leper to withdraw yourself out of the congregation!"*

There was a hushed silence. In the back of the church someone was weeping. Margaret whispered involuntarily, "Oh, how terrible," but Anne, still with that shining secret look on her face, smiled a little. She bowed her head as though courteously to them all, and said, "The Lord judgeth not as man judgeth. Better be cast out of the church than to deny Christ." And she began to walk slowly down the aisle.

Elizabeth, without thought or reasoning, stood up in the pew, pushed past Margaret and followed Anne. The congregation swiveled as one head and watched in stupefaction. Winthrop jumped up with an inarticulate sound. The crowd standing in back of the church parted silently, and the two women walked out, when Anne paused on the step. "Ah no!" she cried seeing Elizabeth. "What madness, child! Go back! Did you not hear that I am a leper and delivered up to Satan?"

"Then I am too," Elizabeth whispered. "For I love you, and I know that God does."

Anne drew in her breath, her shining eyes filled with tears. She bent and kissed Elizabeth. "Christ will bless you for that," she said, "but go—See, I'm not friendless quite—" She pointed to a tall young woman who hovered near. "Mary Dyer has not deserted me!"

Elizabeth would have protested but she had not time. John Winthrop strode out of the church, and seizing her arm swept her down the steps. "Come!" he said in a voice more appalled than angry. "Come back with me at once!" She did not speak as he hustled her along the street to their house. Inside the parlor, he turned on her. "Have you gone mad, Elizabeth? 'Tis all that I can think! Of mine own family— and such monstrous behavior—Wilson is to follow, he will pray with you!"

"I am not mad," she said over a pounding heart. "I want none of Mr. Wilson. You have cast out as a leper one who is truly a saint."

The dark blood surged up into his face, he raised his hand as though to strike her, then checked himself, looking at her with disgust and something that was almost fear. "Go to your room," he said. "Stay there, until I decide what is to be done!"

She wanted to cry out against him, saying that she was not a child, and had no longer need to obey. But she could not, her courage had gone.

She spent many hours in her room, wondering as to her punishment, knowing that there was nothing in reason that her uncle could do to her, and yet—had he not continually shown himself invincible against those who defied him? The daylight faded and night drew on, and still nobody came to her. Hunger and thirst began to fret her, and increasingly dire forebodings. At last her anxiety was lightened by a muffled rap on the door, and Deane's strident whisper, "Let me in!"

She did so, and the boy hastily shut the door behind him. "B'yr lakin, cousin—" he whispered, "that was a brave thing you did, in the meeting! I was watching from the gallery and near fell over the rail."

"It did no good," she said. "No good. Only to bring trouble on me and Robert and the children, just as Daniel said."

"It *did* do good," cried the boy passionately. "All brave things do good, even if we don't see it."

"Well, I'm not brave now," she said, sinking down on the bed. "What's he going to do with me?"

"Nothing—I don't think," said Deane. "He and my

mother've been talking a long time with Mr. Wilson. They all think you were bewitched by Mrs. Hutchinson. She overlooked you, and made you do her will. My mother says she saw Mrs. Hutchinson witching you during the excommunication."

"She's not a witch," said Elizabeth, letting her head fall to the pillow. "She's good."

"I know," said the boy, "and you don't have to say she isn't. Just keep quiet and let 'em pray over you. Then say you don't remember very well *what* happened in the meeting-house."

"I don't—" said Elizabeth from a great fog of weariness and physical discomfort, "but I'll not lie, and add one more burden to Mrs. Hutchinson."

"They can't do anything more to her," said Deane. "They've done it all. And you can't help her either."

"No," said Elizabeth, and buried her face in her hands.

13

Though the troubles which afflicted the Feake and Patrick families became acute in 1639, yet the remainder of 1638 did not pass without uncomfortable events.

Winthrop forebore to punish Elizabeth for her outrageous act at Mrs. Hutchinson's trial, partly because of Margaret's insistence that Elizabeth's state of health and the she-Satan's influence had caused a monetary aberration, and also because he instinctively protected his own family from public censure. Elizabeth did not however get off scot-free. In late September she was commanded to appear in Boston with Robert, and attend a special Lecture Day.

Elizabeth had assumed, with no enthusiasm, that this was a family summons for the purpose of greeting the Downings, who had at long last made the break with Old England and were arriving in the New. She would be pleased enough to see her Uncle Emmanuel again, and her reputedly wild young cousin George Downing, but renewal of contact with Aunt Lucy was not attractive.

The Feakes however obediently set off down the Charles, in their own tiny sailing shallop, which was efficiently skippered by young Tobias Feake. Toby had arrived last month from Germany via England, and proved to be a hobble-de-

352

hoy lad, lumpish, freckled, and possessed of an enormous appetite. Elizabeth found him stolid, and rather stupid. He did, however, justify his Aunt Dixon's boasts as to his seamanship, though he was a great disappointment at farming. His sister Judith had accompanied him, but being a pretty lass of seventeen, she had been snapped up by a young man called William Palmer. She married and departed at once for the new settlement at Yarmouth in Plymouth Colony, so that Eizabeth had not had the companionship from Judith she had hoped for.

As the little Feake boat skimmed down the Charles, Elizabeth turned towards the North Bank. "Why, see, the college at Newtown is all built!" she said looking at a small brick building. "And full of scholars, isn't it, Robert?"

"Cambridge, wife—" said Robert absently. "We must call Newtown 'Cambridge' now, the court so ordered in May."

"Aye, I forgot," she said. "Didn't some minister lately die and leave the college a vast endowment?"

Robert nodded. "One called John Harvard," he answered and dropped the subject, which did not interest him. He was miserably wondering what really lay behind this summons by Uncle Winthrop, for he did not think that the Downings' ship had been sighted yet, nor did he know anything about Elizabeth's behavior at the trial last March. His apprehensions were about himself. Was the Governor displeased with the voting at the last court? Or could there have been any complaint from Watertown secretly sent to Winthrop? Robert's flesh chilled and a hollowness came in his stomach. He thought of that night a week ago when something had happened—or had it? He remembered a barn, and a face looking up at him like that other face in London—could anyone have seen what happened in the barn—or had it *all* been a nightmare? He had not dared ask Elizabeth if he had left his bed that night, and she had said nothing one way or the other. Robert dug his nails into his palms. The sparkling river and the turquoise sky went black, while a voice in his head began to drone the Eighteenth Chapter of Leviticus, as it sometimes did though never past the first five verses. After those verses it always stopped as at a wall, then started over in the buzzing whine that could not be stilled.

"What is it, Robert?" asked Elizabeth gently. "You look very odd."

"Nothing," he said starting and blinking fast. "The sun is strong. Aye, you were speaking of the college . . . Toby would you like to attend it?" He turned quickly to his nephew who sat at the tiller.

"Naw," said Toby. "I've enough learning." He resumed chewing on a piece of spruce gum.

Elizabeth gave Robert an anxious look. There had been signs of "the strangeness" again lately, after a long period of quiet. Nightmares and tossing sleep, and a disquieting moment last week when he had risen from their bed and with eyes fast shut begun to make marks on the wall with his finger, marks that looked like pairs of S's or possibly numerals like 22 over and over. She had got him back to bed without waking him, but then he had begun to whimper like a child, while muttering a name in tones of utmost horror mingled with pleading. The name sounded like "Ralph" but she could not be sure, nor knew anyone called that. Since then she had been heaping marjoram on his stewed meat, for it was known to ease melancholies.

Toby, steering skillfully through the river traffic of canoes, rowboats, and shallops like their own, skimmed up to the Charlestown landing, and Elizabeth clambered to the dock and walked with Robert past Windmill Hill and around the millpond and through twisting lanes of gabled houses towards the market.

"How the town has changed since we first came," she remarked, looking at the crowded stalls where not only local foodstuffs were now sold, but imports from Virginia, the West Indies and England. "But the people look drearier than they used," she added. "Their clothes so drab and plain."

"Aye," said Robert, squinting towards the great King Street wharf. "There's no English ship in. The Downings aren't here. That's not why he summoned us."

"In truth—" she agreed, also perturbed but not as Robert was. "Surely it isn't only to hear Mr. Cotton's lecture that he wished us here today!"

But it was. Winthrop received them at his home with his usual chilly courtesy, and hardly noticed Robert who was at once relieved. Then Winthrop said to his niece, "I trust you have quite recovered your senses since I saw you last in March."

"I don't know what you mean, sir," said Elizabeth, as bravely as she could.

"That may be true," said Winthrop judicially. "Your aunt thinks you were beglamoured, yet in case some of those devilish doctrines still linger with you, I desire you to hear what punishment God has sent to the woman you imprudently averred to be a saint."

Elizabeth started and her face grew hot; neither fear nor Robert's look of anxious warning could silence her. "And what misery for Mrs. Hutchinson are we to gloat over *now?*" she cried. "Is she not safe at least in Rhode Island?"

"Bess!" whispered Robert, and to Winthrop he said quickly, "She is not herself, sir, forgive her—"

Winthrop inclined his head. "Since her earliest years it has often been necessary to forgive Elizabeth. And attempt her correction. I shall leave the latter now to Mr. Cotton. She shall hear that God's just vengeance cannot be deflected by escape to Rhode Island or any other place."

Thus it was that Elizabeth was conveyed to the packed meetinghouse and forced to listen to the Reverend Mr. Cotton's announcement from the pulpit that Mrs. Hutchinson as a manifest result of her heresies had last month given birth to a monster. There had been an earlier rumor of this, but it was now confirmed by letter from the attending physician, Doctor Clarke. And as an object lesson to anyone in Boston who might still be affected by the woman, Cotton proceeded to describe the monster minutely. It had been composed of twenty-seven gelatinous lumps of different sizes held together by fleshy strings . . .

Mr. Cotton's organ-toned voice continued for an hour, dwelling on each disgusting detail, and ingeniously deducing parallels between the embryo's physical malformities and Mrs. Hutchinson's spiritual ones. The congregation listened in fascinated horror; Winthrop, who knew all this and had himself written a letter to Dr. Clarke, requesting the monster's exact description, nodded gravely as the minister made his points.

Elizabeth sat motionless, sickened and full of loathing for these men with their pitiless exposure of a woman's suffering, yet unable to withstand a fearing doubt. Why *had* God let this hideous thing happen to Anne? She tried to shut her ears to the minister's voice and recapture the moment of sureness she had felt in this very meetinghouse last spring, but there was no glimpse of light vouchsafed.

When the meeting was over, she filed heavily out with the others. As she came to the spot on the step where Anne had last spoken to her, Elizabeth turned giddy and swayed. She nearly fell. Robert caught her, while her uncle hurried up behind them. "She swoons?" Winthrop asked Robert with satisfaction, and hastened to support Elizabeth. "It is as I hoped. The Lord has struck His Truth into her heart, she will come now to repentance."

"No—" whispered Elizabeth. "Not repentance, only blackness and hate—" But they did not hear her. The men helped her back to the house and her uncle, pleased with her for once, himself poured her a medicinal nogginful of brandy.

Two days before Christmas, Elizabeth bore the long-awaited son. There was of course no Christmas celebration in the Bay Colony; tithing men, deacons and constables all were vigilant to see that the day was marked by no secret observance either. But Elizabeth was so excited and happy that she ordered Telaka to use all of their flour and raisins for a Christmas pie, and recklessly invited the Patricks over for a wassail bowl on Christmas night.

There was a roaring fire in the bedchamber, where Elizabeth lay with the dark-haired infant snuggled against her. The wassail of hard cider and rum steamed on the hearth in an iron pot. There were pine boughs in the corners of the room, cut for Elizabeth by Toby in bland disregard of Robert's remonstrance. It seemed that in Germany one always brought pine boughs into the house at Christmas, and even little fir trees studded with candles. Elizabeth thought it a charming idea but unfeasible. She did, however, instruct Telaka to light a dozen bayberry candles and place them around the room, where they trembled like stars and gave forth a pungent smoke to mingle with the scent of pine.

When the Patricks stamped in on a blast of cold air, both laughed with pleasure. "I'faith, Bess, ye've got it snug in here, smells good too!" cried Daniel, dropping a tiny pewter porringer on the bed. "Here's for the heir! God bless him!" He inspected the crumpled face on Elizabeth's arm, and said, " 'Od's Body,' but 'tis a *Winthrop* ye've hatched this time, lass!"

"Aye," said Robert proudly, standing at the foot of the bed. "There's a resemblance. We shall call him John for the Governor."

NOT for the Governor, Eliabeth thought—for Jack if you like—but she was too happy to upset Robert who had emerged again from his melancholy.

"I bring you 'speculaas,' Dutch cakes—special," said Anneke, smiling and kissing first Elizabeth then the baby. "From little vood shapes ve use for children." She presented a basketful of cookies molded into stars, windmills and tiny soldiers.

Toby was invited up, and attacked the wassail and cookies with vim. Soon Daniel started a song, and gulping from the ladle began to toast everyone's health. Robert's demur that drinking healths was illegal, Daniel greeted with a roar. "Don't ye be a long-faced spoilsport—Robbie, me lad! By the Mass, if a man can't enjoy himself when he's got him a son 'tis a sorry world indeed!" Daniel quaffed another ladleful, and began to bellow, "Wassailing, wassailing, kiss me, m'dear! I wish ye a Merry Christmas and a Happy New Year, a pocket full o' silver money and a cellar full o' nappy beer!"

Elizabeth giggled, slightly tipsy herself. Anneke sang in Dutch, Toby in German, and Daniel flinging off his sword and mantle danced an Irish jig.

Elizabeth clapped and laughed, crying, "Now I'll sing, and you all join in!" She raised herself on the pillows and sang a song from Groton days when her grandfather had made Christmas a feast of hospitality:

> *"Come bring with a noise, My merrie boys,*
> *The Christmas log to the firing;*
> *While my good dame she, bids ye all be free,*
> *And drink to your heart's desiring!"*

"Aye—drink! Drink!" shouted Daniel, lurching about the room, and "Dance!" He caught Anneke around her plump waist and began whirling and twirling his wife, who shrieked and protested but could not get away from him, while Toby and Elizabeth sang the song over and over and louder and louder.

They did not hear the knock on the door below, nor steps on the narrow stairs, and Daniel was exuberantly kissing and spanking Anneke when the chamber door was flung open and Job Blunt, the tithing man, stood on the threshold, staring at them with a blend of disgust and malice. "Aha!" he cried. "I thought as much from the noise, *which* Goodman Bridges he heard all the way over to his place! Drunk, roistering, and—" he glanced at the pine boughs, the many candles, the wassail pot, "keeping Christmas too. I heard what you sang!"

Robert cleared his throat and drew himself up. "I have a new son," he began. " 'Tis no sin to be glad of it—" But Patrick, who had taken a moment to recover, drowned him out in a great roar, "God damn ye, Job Blunt, ye prick-arsed knave, what d'ye mean by bursting in here?"

The tithing man stiffened, but stood his ground. *"You'll* find out what I mean when this ribaldry is reported to the court, and your lewd speech to me, too, Captain Patrick!"

Daniel thrust Anneke aside, he hunched his red head between his shoulders, his great hairy hands clenched into fists.

"Ye can report this to the court too, then—" he said softly. His right fist shot out and landed on Job Blunt's long chin. The tithing man crumpled like a straw man on the threshold.

Elizabeth gave a cry, then they were all silent looking at the quiet huddled figure. Suddenly Toby laughed, his oxlike face grown animated. "What'll we do with him?" he said. "Is he dead, Captain?"

Anneke whispered, "God allemachtig!" She and Robert both moved at once and rushed to the tithing man. Job Blunt was not dead. They turned him over, and he breathed and moaned. "Give him to drink!" said Anneke. Robert obeyed, and ladled some of the fiery wassail into the tithing man's mouth. Job spluttered and feebly moved his hands.

"Here—" said Patrick who had quite sobered. "I'll dump him downstairs. When he comes to, mayhap he'll not remember, and we'll deny everything."

" 'Tvill do no good, Danny," said Anneke sadly. "So many complaints there've been of us lately. So many fines. And you wrote that foolish angry letter to the Governor."

Elizabeth knew of the letter, but Robert had not been told and he looked his dismayed question from Anneke to Daniel who said roughly, "I lost me temper! I've not had me bounty money *yet* fur the Pequot war, nor the lands that were promised. I know his Worship's got scant use fur me, and would treat me like Underhill if he had cause, but I want justice."

"You'll not get it with angry demands—nor probably at all," said Elizabeth, falling wearily back on the pillows. Her head was spinning and the merry Christmas had broken into jagged pieces.

"How I detest this God-blasted Bay," said Daniel through his teeth. He picked up the inert Job, flung the man over his shoulder and carried him downstairs, where Telaka was waiting with obvious anxiety in her eye.

"Missis all right?" she asked. "Much noise, much loud talk not good for her or babe."

"She's all right," said Daniel. "Now. But I doubt she or any of us'll take our ease for long. Tend this carrion, Telaka, till he comes to his senses, then I suppose ye'd better boot him out, though I'd like to wring his neck."

"E-ne-my?" said Telaka carefully, watching Patrick. "He is bad man?"

Patrick gave a snort of disgust. "Enemy forsooth! Worse'n a Pequot. At least the Indians don't go sneaking and tattling, whatever else they do." He went back upstairs.

Telaka repeated the word "Pequot" under her breath. She turned the tithing man over with her bare foot. Then she knelt down beside him, and extracted a small deerskin pouch from the bosom of her blue cotton dress. She poured some powder from the pouch into her brown palm, spat on it, and rolled the mixture into a ball. She was trying to insert this ball between Job Blunt's flaccid lips when he raised his lids, gazed up at the glittering black eye and the mutilated face, gave a wild shriek and shoved the squaw violently.

When Daniel, Toby and Robert ran down to see what the new commotion was, the tithing man had fled stumbling into the night, and Telaka stood with her arms folded by the kitchen fireplace.

To their agitated questions, she gave only one answer. "Bad man gone." The left side of her mouth lifted, but whether it was a smile or not there was never any way of knowing.

On the following day, Job Blunt took his complaints to Watertown's minister, the Reverend George Phillips, and Mr. Phillips listened in silence to all the heated accusations —drunkenness, lewd singing and dancing, keeping Christmas, bodily assault, cursing and obscene language. The minister was a quiet man of decided opinions which frequently did not agree with those of his fellow ministers at the Bay. When he thought it right he had defied Winthrop and the Boston clergy, as in the matter of Elder Browne's Anglican views some years ago, and of Watertown's due representation in the government. He owned a large library and was a man of learning which in him had instilled perspective. He would brook no disorder in his town, but disliked fanatical methods of subduing it; he also disliked Job Blunt, though he concealed this.

At the end of the tirade he said, "Yes, Goodman, these are regrettable charges. I observe that by and large they concern Captain Patrick rather than the Feakes. We've been having trouble with the Captain of late. Perhaps I've been lax in my pastoral duty. I shall visit the Patricks, exhort them and pray with them."

"But, sir—" objected Job, frowning. "He's got to be punished! The court should give him the whipping post for hitting me, and the language he used!"

"Quite so," Phillips agreed. "Though neither the Captain nor the Feakes are of the class one associates with the whipping post, are they? I shall investigate the matter, and you may be sure of admonishment and fines." The minister's lean terrier face indicated dismissal; he glanced longingly at the Ovid he had been reading before Job's interruption, but the tithing man was thoroughly dissatisfied.

"Sir," he said, lowering his voice and leaning over the minister's table, "I haven't told you the worst, I was a'most afeared to—"

Phillips sighed, "Well . . . ?"

"That squaw the Feakes got. The heathen wi' half a face—she tried to murder me! I caught her stuffing something bitter in my mouth, it burned my lips, and the look in her eye—I tell you, sir, it was devilish."

Phillips leaned back in his chair. "This, ah—incident took place after the blow on your chin, when you were still addled?"

"I see what you're getting at, sir," cried Job in angry excitement. "You think I fancied it, but I didn't. And what's more the whole town's talking about that savage—they know she's a *witch*."

The minister contemplated his tithing man steadily. "Now, Goodman, you have made a very grave accusation indeed. On what evidence is the '*whole town*' saying this?"

"Well," said Job, sulkily after a moment, "Goody Knapp and Goody Warren, Goody Bridges too, they all think so. They saw that squaw overlooking a cow in the Bridges pasture and next day it died, and she has a familiar too."

"Ah . . . " said the minister, raising his eyebrows. "So she had a familiar. A black cat perhaps? Or a toad?"

"No, sir," said Job. " 'Tis a blue jay. It stays in her kitchen, she talks with it."

"Indeed," said the minister. "An unusual familiar. Is Mistress Feake aware of these suspicions about her servant?"

"I doubt that," said Job, hunching his skinny shoulders. "She's a bad un herself, by all accounts—no better'n a trollop."

Phillips stared, his eyes narrowed, and he said with icy

quiet, "What do you mean by *that?*"

Job looked a little frightened; he licked his lips and his eyes slid from the minister's stern face to the floor. Phillips waited, and Job finally burst out defiantly, "You must know there's long been talk about her and that knave Patrick, in and out of her house at all hours, hugging and kissing too, little Dolly Bridges says, n' then when that last lass o' Mistress Feake's was born—that Hannah wi' *red* hair—"

"Goodman Blunt!" said the minister rising. "You have certain specified duties to me and the town. These duties do not include the spreading of malicious slander, which I may remind you is punishable by the court. You are dismissed from your office!"

Job gasped, he mumbled apology, he demeaned himself to beg for the continuance of his position which had brought him many sly perquisites, but his pastor was adamant. Job finally went off in a fury which he solaced at the ordinary across the meetinghouse green.

Phillips sat down again and shook his head, knowing very well that this move would not control the slanders he had heard, but would only send them underground. Twinges of pain in his stomach became insistent as they often did when discouragement followed his efforts at the wise handling of his flock. He pushed the Ovid aside and opened his Bible at the New Testament, which unlike his colleagues at the Bay he greatly preferred to the Old.

In his journal for that year, John Winthrop wrote:

> *The devil would never cease to disturb our peace, and raise up instruments one after another.*

And he retailed "the plots the old serpent had against us."

These included the hanging of a mad woman at Boston, continuing Baptist and Antinomian heresies, the disgraceful behavior of Captain John Underhill who, having returned from England and professing repentance, yet proceeded to commit adultery; whereupon being banished again from the colony he went to the Piscataqua region and got himself appointed Governor of Dover, to Winthrop's great annoyance. There were also misunderstandings and high words about boundaries with both Plymouth Colony and Connecticut. Indeed all the offspring colonies instead of honoring the supremacy of their parent at the Bay were showing themselves undutiful. Worse than that was a sudden wave of migration from Massachusetts to Virginia and Barbadoes. Winthrop struggled to restrain these renegades but the Devil continued his subversive machinations. There was a fearful threat from England. After five years Matthew Cradock wrote again for the Charter, saying that news of the colony's dissensions and jealousies was causing grave worry about the Bay's welfare, that the banishment of Mrs. Hutchinson and so many other people was a source of marvel, and that there was a strong possibility that a governor-general would be sent out from England to regulate matters. As they had five years ago, Winthrop and his assistants decided to ignore the letters and foster assumption that they had never been received. King Charles had been so much occupied with his own troubled affairs after the last summons for the Charter that the demand had been dropped; perhaps it might be so again.

The Bay kept Fast Days, Days of Humiliation, in the endeavor to find out how they had offended God, and lost His cherishing care.

Yet the disasters continued. There was an epidemic of smallpox, there were earthquakes and hurricanes. There was drought. There was an eclipse of the sun. All these were recorded in Winthrop's journal, which was designed for public consumption and seldom indicated any viewpoint but the Governor's. At the May Elections of 1639 he was very nearly defeated, and was sufficiently stung to write more personally.

> *Mr. Winthrop was chosen governor again, though some laboring had been, by some of the elders and others to have changed, but not out of dislike of him, (for they all loved and esteemed him) but out of their fear lest it might make way for having a governor for life, which some* had propounded as most agreeable to God's institution and the practice of well ordered states.

Despite the "love and esteem" of all, Winthrop's worries continued, but he never chronicled the family ones, and in the summer of 1639 these had to do with his ever unregenerate niece, Elizabeth. She came to him in Boston, one July day, disheveled, having dressed hurriedly, and more distraught than he had ever seen her.

"My uncle, I must speak with you," she said, pushing past

the servant with scant ceremony, upon seeing Winthrop alone in his study writing letters.

"Well, well, niece," he said, rising politely. "What is it? You seem very agitated. There's no ill stroke on your family I trust?"

"In a way—" she said. "Nay, 'tis not the children—Robert though." She paused, unwilling to explain how much Robert was upset. " 'Tis Captain Daniel Patrick and his wife—they're leaving Watertown! You've driven them away!"

"My dear daughter," said Winthrop exasperated. "That is not a sensible speech. Captain Patrick is neither a godly man, nor suitable friend for you or your husband. I did not in fact know that you were intimate. He has been formally accused of lewd attempts on the virtue of a young wench called Sturgis; she has written an affidavit to that effect."

"But he *didn't!*" Elizabeth interrupted. "He barely knew her—it's a conspiracy. He has enemies in Watertown—it's that tithing man put the Sturgis girl up to it. Daniel wrote you it wasn't true."

Winthrop folded his hands behind his back, walked to the cold fireplace, and turning regarded his niece. "Patrick has written me several rash letters," he said in measured tones, "and I have been very patient. My patience is at an end. I have permitted Captain Patrick to leave the colony, which I believe he will do tomorrow."

"This is the way you requite him for his services!" she cried. "Treating him just like Underhill, like everyone who doesn't go about whining psalms and doting on the ministers. And he's not had the lands or bounty he was promised; if it wasn't that Anneke has a nest egg he'd be destitute unless he can sell his land at Watertown!"

The dark flush ran up under Winthrop's skin. His nostrils flared and he drew a harsh breath. "You speak remarkably warm about this—this Patrick, Elizabeth," he said watching her narrowly.

"He's my friend!" she said, not in the least understanding him and the anger in her eyes matching his. "And he's Robert's. Robert is very fond of him."

"I cannot believe that your husband shows such ill judgment," said Winthrop. "And I do not *wish* to believe an inference I might draw from your behavior. Patrick and his family are sailing tomorrow; they may go wherever they please so long as they leave this colony."

"Then we'll go too!" she cried wildly.

"No, Elizabeth," said Winthrop. He walked over and stood beside her. He was not a tall man and yet to her he seemed to tower as high as the beams. "*You will go nowhere.*" Each word dropped like stone on stone. She drew back slowly until she leaned against the table.

Her uncle saw the defiance drain out of her and smiled coldly. He went to the door and called, "Wife, come here!"

Margaret came running in from the kitchen, and Winthrop cut across her greetings to Elizabeth. "Here is our niece, my dear, who has been indulging in one of her peculiar fits of passion. I suggest that you pray with her, and ask God to calm her wayward heart."

The Patrick family left Watertown the next day. All their goods were piled on a flatboat to be poled down the Charles and then transferred to a ship bound for New Amsterdam. Robert and Elizabeth stood on the little river landing to say farewell, and only Anneke wept. Robert was mute, though his eyes were very bright and his skin unnaturally reddened. He looked at Daniel, clasped his hand and then stood staring into the water. Elizabeth had cried during the night but now she was as silent as Robert.

"I'll write ye, Bess," said Daniel as he kissed her forehead. "If it wasn't fur you two, I'd be GLAD to go, I've told ye before. I'll find a place far from here as I can, New Netherlands or Virginia, and write ye of it. Then you and Rob can come too."

"He'd never let us," she said in a wooden voice. "I can never get away." And Daniel had no doubt whom she meant.

"There, lovey—" he said, much distressed. "You mustn't lose heart. Maybe ye'll settle down better in Watertown wi' us gone, can't tell. I only hope *he*—" he gestured towards Robert and did not finish. "By God," he burst out, "I hate to leave ye like this, I'll pray fur ye. Haven't tried it in a dog's age, but a Pater Noster or Ave might work. I'll even make me a rosary outa corn or huckleberries!" he said chuckling anxiously, but Elizabeth did not smile.

She and Anneke kissed each other, the Patrick children waved, the flatboat started downriver, and the Feakes turned back to their home.

Robert spoke not at all the rest of that day, until as they entered their bedchamber he suddenly said, "Bess, I feel very ill. It is a judgment for my great wickedness, as losing my friend is a judgment on me."

She thought it was "the strangeness" coming on, but it was not. By midnight, Robert had a raging fever, and was vomiting, also he was seized with cramps and bloody flux. There was now a physician at Watertown, Mr. Simon Eire, and Elizabeth hastily summoning him found that the physician confirmed her own fear—Robert had contracted a cholera.

For the next weeks while she nursed him, there was scarcely time to regret the Patricks or realize how lonely she was.

Robert recovered very slowly; by the end of October he was still weak and could leave his bed but an hour a day. Elizabeth at Doctor Eire's direction fed her husband laudanum and elixir of vitriol, and her own decoctions, supplemented by a sassafras broth Telaka made and said was used in her tribe to bind the bowels. Yet still, though the violent symptoms had long stopped, Robert gained little ground, and Elizabeth suspected that he had not the heart to do so. He was docile and quiet, he often spoke to her with tender gratitude, there was no hint of the real "strangeness," but he would lie for hours staring at the rafters and when she tried to rouse him by bringing in the children, he would respond with a feeble smile, then slip back at once into the hinterland where he preferred to dwell.

During the worst of Robert's illness the neighbors had been kind. A new one, Mistress Stone, whose husband Simon had bought land adjacent to the Feakes', helped tend Elizabeth's children. Goody Bridges helped with the constant laundering of fouled sheets; even the goodwives Knapp and Warren had come to the house bearing possets.

Elizabeth suspected more of avid curiosity than genuine warmth in these attentions and declined them courteously as soon as she could. Besides, Telaka continued to show an extraordinary efficiency. By this time Elizabeth had noted the fear with which the neighbors regarded her Indian, and had even been warned of Telaka by Goodwife Bridges. "I know ye won't hold wi' what I say, Mistress," said Sarah Bridges one day when they met on Bank Lane, "but 'twouldn't be my Christian duty not to point out that yon scar-face squaw o' yours is monstrous weird."

"Just her looks," said Elizabeth quickly, hurrying on. "She's very good to us."

"How d'ye *know?*" persisted Sarah, panting along, her fat earnest face turned up to Elizabeth. "How d'ye know what she does i' the dark o' night? I mean it kindly, Mistress, you being a young gentlewoman as hasn't seen the Devil's works as clear as I have."

Elizabeth gave an impatient smile. She liked Sarah Bridges better than the other goodwives, but she was tired of discussing Telaka, and anxious to get back to Robert. "Telaka's a fine woman," she said. "We understand each other."

This speech was later reported to Goody Bridges's gossips, and served in due time to light the powder keg which finally exploded under the Feakes.

Elizabeth arrived at home at dusk, and for several dismayed moments wondered if she would have to eat her confident words to the goodwife. As she entered the garden Elizabeth saw her squaw standing under the great maple tree; from an Indian pipe in her hand the blue smoke curled upward. Telaka had made the pipe herself from a hollow stick and a pierced stone, and she sometimes smoked a few puffs, an indulgence permitted by Elizabeth; indeed several of the old women in town had their corncob pipes. But Elizabeth had never seen Telaka standing in such a peculiar stiff position, with face upraised towards the sky, nor heard her give forth such strange low noises. Elizabeth ran to the squaw crying sharply, "What *are* you doing? Why aren't you in the house?"

Telaka raised one arm to hush her mistress, then putting the pipe to her mouth inhaled a deep breath and bowing to the west chanted, "Chekefuana, Chekefuana, Chekefuana!" while the smoke drifted from her nostrils. Telaka held her hand to her ear and appeared to listen until a look of what seemed to be triumph illumined the mobile side of her face. She sighed deeply and clasped the pipe to her breast. "It is good—" she said to Elizabeth in a voice of joy. "Chekefuana and Manitoo they have answered. Long have I asked them at this time of Telaka, when they must hear me, but till now they would not speak."

"What nonsense!" said Elizabeth crossly. "What do you mean by this gibberish—those Indian words?" she amended seeing that the squaw did not understand.

"Chekefuana is the—god of the west wind," said Telaka with reverence. "And Manitoo is over all like your English God. They hear me best at Telaka for it is my—my totem."

"At twilight?" asked Elizabeth, "That's what your name means, isn't it? What have they told you, these gods?" she added curiously, despite herself.

"They tell me a happy thing," said Telaka. "For me, for you. Look!" she cried, kneeling suddenly on the path. She picked up a stick and began to draw on the dirt. She drew a rough indented line, and then a projecting shape like a large thick axehead. "This," she said, "is my country, land of Siwanoys. Here," she pointed to the underside of the axehead shape, "are many bright sands. My people camp there. White men have come. The red-haired captain is there now!"

"What!" cried Elizabeth. "You can't mean Captain *Patrick?*"

"It is so," said Telaka rising. "I saw it in sky, I hear it from Chekefuana. Patrick is there and *we* will be. I shall go back to my people."

Elizabeth was touched by the thrill in the usually expressionless voice, and she shook her head saying gently, "Ah, Telaka, I understand your longing, it's natural. But your wishes've deceived you. Captain Patrick is at Fort Amsterdam or mayhap Virginia by now. He would never stop in your land, wherever it is, nor—" she added, "have we heard from him as he promised. I pray that they are well."

The Indian did not listen. She said something in her own language, and walked into the kitchen, clutching her pipe against her breast.

Elizabeth soon forgot Telaka's odd behavior in a succession of domestic incidents. The three little girls took the measles, and Lisbet was very ill for some time. When she recovered, Toby announced that he did not like Watertown, felt that his uncle was sufficiently well to be left alone, and wished some London property he owned on Lombard Street to be sold, so that with the money realized he could buy a large decked-over shallop he had seen building in the Boston yards.

Robert made not the slightest objection; he showed no more interest in his nephew than he did in anything else, and though up and about most of each day now, wandered through the necessary acts of living like an automaton. Accordingly, as Toby's guardian, he signed the necessary papers, and Toby, who was enterprising enough in all nautical matters, bought his boat and hired as crew a Norfolk lad, Ben Palmer, who was kin to Toby's brother-in-law. Toby then set off to be a modest coastwise trader. The Feakes heard nothing from him for months.

The winter passed in snow and bitter cold—so much dirty

weather that folk were forced to stay at home, huddling by their fires and praying that there was sufficient wood stacked in the shed to last them. By February the wolves were howling nightly in the forests near Beaver Brook, and everyone's fare was reduced to moldy powdered beef and the last scrapings of the corn bins. The Feakes fed better than most, since until April when his bond terminated and he left for Wethersfield, they still had their manservant who could be sent with a sledge along the frozen Charles to Boston for provisions. But by March all the family suffered from colds, and even Elizabeth's excellent health was affected. She had frequent headaches and her spirits had grown nearly as despondent as Robert's. In March the snow at last began to melt, the wild geese flew honking towards the north, the sap rose in the awakening trees, and Telaka, knowing what their bodies so urgently needed, made expeditions into the forests where she gathered the inner bark of spruce and slippery elm to infuse with the first birch sprouts.

These expeditions and their results were known. The goodwives of Watertown kept watch on Telaka, and it was seen that though there was scurvy in almost every house, the Feakes escaped.

"And ye needn't tell me that munching *bark's* what keeps 'em hale," whispered Goody Warren one afternoon when she and Goody Knapp were settled in the Bridges' kitchen, where young Dolly Bridges, now a lass of thirteen, was shucking corn by the fading daylight at the west window. The three older women were haggard; Sarah Bridges had lost her four front teeth during the winter. Peg Warren's mouse face had sharpened, and her skin erupted into tiny sores, while Goody Knapp had a constant pain in her belly and her gums. The two visitors had brought their knitting, and Sarah Bridges sat at her spinning wheel, but the work went on languidly. It was the first time they had gathered since the thaws set in, and their apprehensions, released from daily struggle for survival, turned with renewed interest to the fearsome topic which their minister had quelled last year. Besides there were alarming developments.

" 'Tis against nature," continued Peg Warren, glancing at the others. "That SHE has gone unscathed through her husband's illness, an' this terrible winter. I saw her yester e'en, red cheeks—those green eyes long like a cat's, treading light as a girl to the well, an' that Indian stalking behind her."

Goody Knapp laid down her knitting, and leaning forward, said in her strong Suffolk burr, "Oi was on the ship wi' her when we come over. There was a fearful tempest, an' St. Elmo's foire—I didn't think at the toime—but if the Reverend Eliot he hadn't prayed the tempest away we'd a drownded, each mortal o' us, 'cepting *her*. Oi vow."

"Whist—whist, Goody—" said Sarah Bridges, shaking her head. "Where are ye leading? 'Tis not Mistress Feake we've had suspicion of—'tis not right to talk so loose, 'tis perilous."

"Peril is for us to be winking at what goes on, and holding back and ne'er daring to speak out what we think!" cried Peg Warren in a rush. "What o' Goodman Griggs who fell from the barn roof last week? Think on Tom Flagg's three sows 'at died, and Jack Doggett's house 'at burned?"

"Why, but she can hold no grudge 'gainst *them*—she nor the squaw—" said Sarah Bridges uncertainly.

"Did ye not say yourself she told you she had an *understanding* with that squaw?" cried Peg Warren, "And are ye so knowing o' the Devil's way, Sarah Bridges? An' what about Job Blunt then? Have ye forgot Job? There's grudge enough there!"

Sarah was silenced. The tithing man had had a run of disasters since the minister had dismissed him from office. One of his children had drowned in the Charles, his wife had got consumption, and a putrid abscess had developed in his buttocks.

"The spectral loight's been seen again," whispered Goody Knapp in a frightened tone "Loike last Halloween. My goodman saw it hisself, 'twas flaming up o'er the river then smallened and grew pig-shaped like a swoine, it ran swift as an arrow on the water towards—" She pointed with a shaking finger in the direction of the Feake house.

"I didn't know that," murmured Sarah, turning pale. They were all silent, when Sarah looked around to see that her daughter had crept up to them and was listening avidly. "Get thee back to thy shucking, Doll!" snapped the mother. "This talk's not for thy ears!"

Dolly made no motion to obey. Her heavy child's face and her dull eyes were lit by sudden excitement. "I' the night —" she said, "Ye heard me cry out, Ma? Something pinched me. 'Twas fiery black an' had one eye. Pinched me here." She raised her linsey-woolsey skirts, and exhibited a bruise on her stout little thigh.

"Lord a' mercy!" cried Goody Knapp touching the bruise and shuddering. "Forfend 'twill not be a case like that lass

Oi knew in Suffolk. She was afflicted by an ould witch in Bures, the poor girl took fits, an' was pinched black an' blue by the foul fiends, afore we caught the witch."

"How did they catch her?" asked Sarah Bridges, staring with horror at her daughter's bruise.

"Forsooth the lass accused the witch each toime she took a fit, she'd thrash and quiver on the ground and cry out, 'Help, help! The ould woman o' Bures is tormenting me. Ow! Ow! The Davel is after me!' There was a great to-do all o'er the town, an' they sent judges from London to question the lass."

"What happened to the witch?" asked Dolly, letting her skirts fall and staring hard at Goody Knapp.

"Why, they burned her. 'Twas a rare edifying soight we all turned out to see. We treated the poor wee lass like a countess too, and gave her shillings for having suffered an' saved us from witchcraft."

Dolly heaved a long pent-up sigh, glanced at her mother, then walked back to her corn-shucking.

The three women looked at each other. "Ye see?" breathed Peg Warren. "We dare not shilly-shally longer."

"What can we do—?" whispered Sarah.

"Speak to our goodmen," said Peg rising with decision. "John Warren's working the home lot today. I'm off to him now, an' this time he'll *have* to heed!"

The goodmen heard their wives' suspicions with varying degrees of masculine indifference, all of them far too busy with the spring planting to give much credence to accusations involving the Governor's relatives. But on the last Sabbath day of April two things happened.

Elizabeth was awakened at dawn by hallooings and commotion on the river by their landing. She jumped from bed and throwing wide the casement saw a large sailing shallop dropping anchor, and on the deck saw Toby Feake's broad body and red Monmouth cap. She leaned out to shout greeting. Toby waved and she ran back into the room crying, "Robert, wake up! Here's Toby back at last!"

Robert started up from sleep, seeming frightened; he murmured in confusion, "What is it? What happened? Is it the constables?"

"Nay, dear," she said laughing. "Why should it be the constable? Have you had another of those sorry dreams?"

He leaned his head on his hands, his frail shoulders hunched under the linen night shirt. "Bess," he said so low she barely heard, "did I leave my bed last night?"

"Why, I don't know," she said, dashing water on her face and seizing a comb. "I was dead for sleep. Perhaps you went to the privy—but, Rob, here's Toby back. Aren't you glad to see your nephew?"

"Aye, I suppose so," said Robert after a moment, his pinched white face drooping. He climed slowly out of bed, and clutched at the post.

"Another giddy spell?" she said with a twinge of impatience. "Here, take some of the elixir."

Robert obediently swallowed from the pewter mug she tendered him, then straightened up. "That helps," he said apologetically, "In my skull the thoughts're foggy and seem to swirl."

"A pity," she said briskly, so used had she become to Robert's ailments.

Toby met them in the parlor, his freckled face burned darker, his legs akimbo, his leather jacket stained with sea water and rum, the very picture of a competent young mariner.

He barely greeted his uncle and aunt before saying, "D'ye see the *Dolphin*? That's my ship. Isn't she trig and saucy? Since I left I've plied the coast with her from Piscataqua to New Amsterdam. Look, my uncle!" He dragged Robert to the open door and pointed out the beauties of his shallop.

"Very fine, nephew, very fine," said Robert vaguely, turning back into the parlor.

Then Toby recollected something. "Oh, and I've news. I've been with Captain Patrick. I left him not five days agone!"

"With Daniel!" Elizabeth cried whirling around. "Oh, Toby, why didn't you tell us first thing! How are they? Where are they? Why didn't he write?" She looked at Robert, who had made an odd noise in his throat and who had started to tremble. "Sit down, Rob," she said. "I know this is a shock to you, albeit so joyous."

Robert sank down on the settle. "I thought he was dead," he said, looking up at Toby. "I thought my friend was dead."

"Pah!" said Toby spitting into the fireplace. "Not dead at all. Sound as a nut. He was buying lands from the Indians at a place the savages call Norwalk when I left him; that is to say—" added Toby with a chuckle, "he was promising 'em a mort o' goods he hasn't got, like hatchets n' hoes n' drills, but he said they'd get all that someday, and they drew their marks on the deed. I witnessed it meself."

"Where is this place?" asked Elizabeth eagerly. "Does he mean to settle there?"

"Naw," said Toby. "Just took a fancy to it. Aunt, I'm famished, can't we breakfast?"

"To be sure," she said, calling for Telaka to bring beer and bread. "But, Toby, tell! Where are they? What are their plans?"

Toby would not be hurried. He downed a tankard of beer, and stuffed a quarter loaf of wheat bread in his mouth before answering. "He's settled himself further west, near a sheltered cove," Toby said thickly through his munchings, "and a neck o' land with a great beach on it, 'bout ten leagues by sea this side o' Amsterdam, I judge."

"Dutch then?" said Elizabeth, shaking his arm impatiently as he bit off another hunk of bread.

Toby shrugged. "Might be Dutch, might be English, 'tis so far away it's no matter. The Indians own it but're willing to sell."

Telaka had not left the parlor; now she glided up to Toby and said, "Siwanoy Indians, and place called Monakewaygo."

Toby's stolid face showed faint surprise. "Aye, some such uncouth name." He turned to Elizabeth. "How does *she* know? Did Patrick write that in his letter?"

"We've had no letter," said Elizabeth, looking uneasily at her squaw. The bright black eye met hers triumphantly. "It is as Chekefuana said," murmured Telaka.

"We got no letter," repeated Robert, who had not been attending to Telaka. "Did he send a letter?"

Toby nodded. "By a pinnace, but we heard 'twas lost off Cape Cod. I've brought another." He fumbled within his leather jacket, while Elizabeth cried out, "Oh, Toby!" and grabbed a sweaty crumpled piece of paper from his hand. She ran with it to Robert, and they deciphered the few lines together.

Daniel wrote that he, Anneke and the family were well, had found a place to their liking and wintered in a sod hut. There were a couple of Englishmen living within a mile or two, and one of these called Jeffrey Ferris had named the place Greenwich, which, said Daniel, was a jest since no place could be less like the magnificent royal palace on the Thames. It was rough wilderness, too rough for the Feakes, he said, but suited him because you could be your own master. He ended with love from them both.

"How can we write back to them?" said Elizabeth, disappointed in the letter, which sounded as though the Patricks had nearly forgotten them.

"I doubt that you can," said Toby shrugging. "Until I sail that way again, which I've no mind to this year, I've a fancy for running up to Casco Bay and get me a cargo o' their beaver pelts."

"I'd like to see him," said Robert turning the letter over in his thin white fingers. "I'd like to see Daniel, but I suppose 'tis impossible."

"Aye," said Toby, wiping his mouth on his sleeve. "Patrick dassn't come back here, and *you*—" he gave his uncle a look of good-natured contempt, " 'd hardly eke out *there*. Aunt, have you a bit o' beeswax? I've need of it on the boat, there's a sail to thread."

Elizabeth started. "Lack-a-day, Toby—'tis the Sabbath! I'd forgot. You shouldn't have been sailing. We'll have to say you came yesterday. And we must all go to meeting, or the new tithing man'll be after us!"

Toby made a grimace, but accepted the inevitable. An hour later all the Feake family but the baby John, and Telaka, trudged up Bank Lane to the meetinghouse. Mr. Phillips's sermons were never unduly long, and their content Elizabeth found of some interest when he told dry little anecdotes to illustrate a point. After the service, the Feakes lingered on the green a few moments, while the minister greeted Toby and asked about his travels. The Bridges family and other neighbors stood a short way off and watched, when suddenly the quiet Sabbath air was rent by a piercing scream.

Everyone jumped. Elizabeth instinctively gathered up her little girls and stared around, as they all did. The scream shrilled out again, and a small figure in gray linsey-woolsey hurtled around the corner of the meetinghouse and, to Elizabeth's stupefaction, flung itself down on the grass at her feet and began to thrash, with violent motions of the arms and legs, and continuing screams.

"Dear Lord—" cried Elizabeth. " 'Tis Dolly Bridges in a fit!" She bent over the girl, and at once Dolly cried, "Help! Help! She's tormenting me. She's pinching me!"

"Who is? What is? Oh, God save us!" cried Goody Bridges, rushing up to her squirming daughter. "What ails you, Dolly love? Oh, this is fearful."

" 'Tis SHE!" sobbed the girl pointing at Elizabeth. "The *witch!*"

A low gasping sound ran like a breaking wave around the meetinghouse green. The people drew back inch by inch, staring at Elizabeth, who stood dumbfounded, while little Hannah clung to her skirts and wept.

The Reverend Mr. Phillips recovered quickly. He strode to Dolly, leaned down and shook her shoulders. "Stop this at once!" he said. "Stand up and behave yourself!"

"I can't. I can't!" howled Dolly, writhing. "They won't *let* me! Ow, ow—how they hurt me!"

"Nobody's hurting you, you little fool!" cried the minister. "This is Mistress Feake whom you know well, as we all do. You've lost your reason, lass!" He spoke with such angry force that Dolly opened her eyes and stole a look at him. She screwed them quickly shut again and began to writhe, screeching. "Then if 'tis not her, 'tis t'other one. The Indian wi' one eye. *She's* witching me, she's sent the Devil to torment me wi' his pitchfork. Help! Help!"

Again the sighing gasp ran through the bystanders, and Peg Warren's high excited voice rang out, "I *told* ye, John Warren! Ye wouldn't listen."

A male voice cried from near the stocks, "So 'tis the Indian— the Indian squaw. Job Blunt spoke truth."

"Job Blunt did NOT speak truth," shouted the minister, "nor does Dolly Bridges!" He stiffened his slight body and glared at each member of his muttering, huddled congregation. "Men," he said, using the strong pulpit voice which had always ruled them. "Surely you've too much sense to credit these fantastical slanders!"

There was a stir, and murmurings amongst the crowd, until Simon Stone, a large serious man, walked forward into the circle where the Feakes stood alone by the minister.

"Well, it's this way, Parson," Stone said respectfully, but firmly, as befitted a deacon, prosperous landholder, and person of authority in Watertown. "Ye can't deny there's been devil's work o' late. I heard the rumors but thought 'twas mostly a maggot the women'd got hold on, but when it comes to our children being afflicted—" He glanced down at Dolly who had stopped squirming to listen, then turned to his ten-year-old son whom he had dragged along by the hand. "Tell the parson what you saw, Sim."

The lad wriggled, dug his finger sheepishly into his ear, and blushed scarlet. "The black man," he stammered at length when his father had prodded him. "Black man in a cloak, behind our barn, he jumped at me, and held me in his great skinny arms, like he was hugging me."

The minister's heart sank. More wild accusations, more sinister hints which were obviously going to involve the Feakes. And yet this one could not be checked by a bald denial. Simon Stone was a man of consequence and little Simon was known to be truthful.

"Did this black man speak to you?" said the minister sighing.

Simon grew redder, and kicked his toe into a grass tuft. "He kept whispering to me, like he was begging me to do—do something. He called me a name like 'Ralph.' I was afeared n' struck him, I felt his fingers pressing, burning on my windpipe. I cried out n' he let me go, he ran—"

"Or did he fly, son?" interrupted Simon Stone gravely. "Did the black man fly through the air?"

"I dunno, sir," said the boy. "Mayhap he did. He went towards Mr. Feake's and—melted away."

"Did he go in the Feake house?" said his father. "You can see their house from our barn, and there was moon enough last night."

The little boy swallowed, and began to weep. "I—I think so, sir. He might've gone in a window, I couldn't see much n' I was skeered."

There was a heavy hushed silence, broken by a startled sound from Elizabeth, who like the rest of them had been staring at little Simon. "Robert's swooned," she said in a dazed voice. They all turned to see that Robert Feake had quietly fallen and, half hidden behind Toby and the minister, lay prone on the grass.

"Oh, poor gentleman," said Mr. Stone. "Him so sickly, these shocking signs of the Devil's presence have o'ercome him!"

"Aye. Aye!" cried a dozen voices. "In his own house too! The Devil's loose in Watertown."

"An' we know why!" shrilled Goody Knapp. "Witchcraft!" she screamed hysterically. "Witchcraft, witchcraft!" The confused cries and murmurings became a roar, though still the crowd kept back uncertainly, held by their minister's will.

"Won't someone bring water?" Elizabeth pled, while she knelt by Robert and chafed his clammy wrists. "Fetch me water to revive him."

No one heeded her and Phillips with a foreboding glance at the crowd, which he saw would soon be out of control, said under his breath to Toby, "Take the horse from my stable, hasten to Boston. Fetch the Governor. Hurry! There's sorry work brewing."

Toby, who had been standing slack-jawed watching this scene, shut his mouth with a snap. His slow wits cleared at the prospect of action. He nodded and ran off behind the meetinghouse towards the parson's stable. His going was not noticed because Dolly who had lain quiet for some time was suddenly taken with another fit, and though the minister jerked her to her feet and slapped her face, the moment of abeyance was broken.

"Dolly Bridges is tormented again. Get the Indian! Get the witch! Hang her! Burn her!" yelled a voice and the crowd surging forward began to move in a body down the Meetinghouse Lane, some running, some like Mr. Stone and John Warren treading heavily, but all with implacable purpose.

"I must be with them," said the Reverend Mr. Phillips, bending over Elizabeth and the still unconscious Robert. "I can't stop them taking your squaw but I'll keep them in hand as best I can."

"I don't understand," said Elizabeth, looking up at him with wide frightened eyes. "I don't understand what's happening."

The minister shook his head. He looked down at Robert. "Get him somehow to my parsonage, fast. You'll be safer there." For he knew that the seizure of Telaka might only increase the mob's hysteria, which would then seek the other accused.

"But my baby——" whispered Elizabeth. "Little John's at the house. I must get my baby."

"I'll see to the babe. Go to the parsonage!" Phillips hastened off after the roaring mob.

"Robert—Robert!" Elizabeth moaned, gazing distractedly around the deserted green. "The well!" she said. "Joan, stay with him. Rub his wrists, his temples, till I come back!"

Her eldest nodded, her brown eyes awe-struck, while Lisbet and Hannah, both sobbing, ran after their mother to the town well. Elizabeth drew water up in the bucket, and staggering back to Robert, dashed the whole bucketful in his face. He whimpered and opened his eyes.

"Get up! Walk!" she cried, propping her shoulder under his armpit. Joan held him on the other side. He swayed but began to walk. In ten minutes they got him to the parsonage where a maidservant let them in. Elizabeth bolted the door and eased Robert down on the big bed in the parlor.

"Why are we here?" he whispered, the pupils blackening his pale eyes. "What has happened?"

"Don't you remember?" she said, pushing her disordered hair from her face and trying to quiet the little ones. "You swooned, and no wonder—it's terrible—fantastical—"

"Don't remember," he said thickly. "I don't remember. That Stone lad was—what was he saying?" He held up his hands before his face and squinted at them. "I'm frightened," he said. "I don't want to stay here. I want to go far away . . ."

"Hark!" she whispered. "They're coming back!" Outside there was a deep animal sound like the bellowing of bulls. She shivered and dragged to the window. Dimly through the little diamond panes she could see the crowd as it surged across the green to the gaol house next the ordinary. They had bound Telaka with ropes and two men were carrying her like a log between them.

"Oh God—" Elizabeth whispered. "What are they going to do to her?" She slumped to a chair, and stared down at the floorboards. Hannah climbed into her lap and fell asleep exhausted. The two other girls curled up near Robert, who did not move.

Elizabeth tried to think, but found that she could not. Her ears rang incessantly with Dolly's screams, and she could see only the faces of her neighbors—glowering, accusing, full of fear and hate.

An hour and a half ticked by on the parson's wall clock before the Reverend Mr. Phillips came back. Elizabeth ran to unbolt the door and he rushed in, bolting it again behind him "They've gone mad," he said. His black robes were torn, his falling-bands askew on his shoulders. "Most of the men are getting drunk in the ordinary. Some are for taking your squaw to Great Pond and ducking her now, some for hanging her tomorrow. I told them they can't without a trial, but they swear no trial is needed for an Indian."

"Have they hurt her?" whispered Elizabeth.

"Not much, not yet. They spat on her and hit her but we got her locked in the gaol and I've got the key. They're wild—Some led by Goody Knapp and Job Blunt're coming after *you*, Mistress—I feared it. Mr. Stone's trying to reason with them. I've done what I could."

"My baby," Elizabeth cried. "Where is he?"

"Mrs. Stone took him. She's a good woman and gentle-hearted." The minister wiped his face on a napkin. "I must pray . . ." he said brokenly. "Must quiet myself with God's word. I think the Devil *is* loose amongst us!"

As Elizabeth made a horrified sound, he said "Nay, nay—I mean not I'm convinced of witchcraft, nor think that poor squaw or you—but evil's come here, and I must have God's strength to fight it." He went to his Bible stand, and opening the Book leaned over it, his lips moving.

He had begun to pray aloud when there was a banging on his front door. He opened it a crack and saw Simon Stone on the doorstep.

"I can't hold 'em back much longer, Parson," said Mr. Stone, pushing into the house. "They know you've got Mistress Feake here. They want her too, in gaol at least, and to search her body for witch teats. Though they know they must try HER. But those women, Warren and Knapp, are both ranting. Now they have it that all Mr. Feake's illness and his swoon today is witchcraft, Mistress Feake's doing. They say she and the squaw've been feeding him bark, so as to—" The deacon stopped as Robert suddenly sat up.

"My wife is good to me," he said, looking at the deacon. "She does not know of my terrible sins."

Stone shrugged and shook his head. "Poor gentleman," he said of Robert in a low voice to the minister. "What a coil this is, and I don't see where truth lies myself, but—" He stopped abruptly, turning towards the window. "They're massing on the Common," he said. "D'you hear 'em? They'll be here directly."

Elizabeth turned gray as the plastered wall she backed against. Her heart thundered on her ribs. "They can't take me," she said. "I've done nothing." She shut her eyes and saw against her lids the image of the hunted terrified gypsy Peyto. Oh, Jack, Jack—she thought—you helped Peyto—

Stone gave her a long appraising look as she stood there. Suddenly convinced, his eyes softened and met those of the minister. "Have you firearms, Parson?" he said. The Reverend Mr. Phillips bowed his head, and gestured towards the kitchen. Both men went in and came back with a loaded carbine and two muskets. "Here," said Stone to Robert. "Can ye stand up and protect your wife?"

Robert gasped. He got off the bed and took the musket Simon Stone tendered him. "Bess?" he said in a wondering voice. "You need protection?" She could not speak, and he put his arm around her. "Why, wife," he said, "this is very strange."

"They come now," observed Stone, pulling back the match-lock and sprinkling powder in the flashpan of his gun.

"Don't shoot unless we must," said Phillips. "And aim at nobody."

The indistinct roar and shouts came nearer, and now words were distinguishable. "Bess Feake! Bess Feake! Come out, Mistress Feake, to your just reckoning!"

"They've rounded the meetinghouse," said the minister who was watching at the window. "Yes something's stopping them—ah—" he breathed. "Praise our dear merciful God."

Stone crowded to the window beside Phillips. "Horsemen?" he cried. "Several horsemen? What can that be?"

"The Governor and his guard," said Phillips, propping his musket against the chimney. "Toby Feake's done well."

And now ringing out above the suddenly hushed crowd Elizabeth heard her uncle's angry voice. "What is the meaning of this riot? Disband at once!"

"They obey," said Phillips grimly. "I doubt there's one of them has the courage to tell the Governor whom they were after." He walked to the door and unbolting it, threw it wide open.

"Here, Your Worship, if you please—" he called. "Will you come in?"

John Winthrop dismounted, while his halberdiers and Toby Feake scattered the mob. Winthrop entered the parsonage, and stared from Elizabeth's chalk-white glistening face to that of the minister. "What broil is this!" he said. "Can you not better rule your congregation, Mr. Phillips?"

"Not when there are charges of witchcraft, Your Worship," said the minister evenly. "And you have come but just in time to save your niece from gaol."

Winthrop flinched and stiffened. "An outrageous statement," he said, drawing off his gloves, and placing his hat on the table. "Which I wish to consider in detail, and in privacy, Deacon—" He bowed coldly towards Simon Stone who bowed back and went out the door.

"Now," said Winthrop, seating himself in the minister's armchair. "Kindly explain to me what has happened."

Mr. Phillips complied, speaking in carefully unemotional statements, aware that the Governor himself was not devoid of bigotry and superstition, nor unduly fond of his niece. Those things were true enough, and such accusations would usually have swayed Winthrop to anxious investigation, but now Winthrop was shocked and furious.

"Those yokels!" he cried at the end of the account. "Those ribauds, some of them my own Groton Manor tenants, that they should DARE so to affront a Winthrop! For that they must be punished, though doubtless it is that Pequot squaw's doing! Verily she must be a witch. You remember, Elizabeth, I warned you not to take her but you persisted as always—see how your folly—" He checked himself on this well-worn path, and said, "But no matter. We must think what's best to do."

"I know what to do," said Elizabeth quietly. Her color had returned, her knees had stopped trembling, and at the sound of her uncle's voice she had seen the answer. She spoke with such calm assurance that the men gazed at her, waiting.

"We will leave Watertown," she said. "We will leave the Bay. We will sail west, Robert and I, to join Captain Patrick."

"I forbid it!" Winthrop cried. "This is shameless, witless—" but his words lacked their usual force. The hasty ride here had tired him. The Feake predicament, beyond its immediate urgency, daunted him as evidence of another straw in the mounting wind of his unpopularity with the people, and he knew he would not be re-elected in May. But even this blow was not as great as one he had suffered yesterday and which would soon be public. His trusted steward, James Luxford, had been exposed by Stephen, who had long suspected something dishonest in the man's financial jugglings at Ten Acres and other of John Winthrop's estates. The exact sums were still in question but it was certain that the Winthrops had been mulcted of over a thousand pounds. Which meant near ruin.

Oh, why does God thus afflict me from all sides? Winthrop thought. What have I done to merit these chastisements? Anger and despair washed through him, and he could scarcely bring his mind back to the Feakes.

"Shameless and witless my resolve may be, Uncle," said Elizabeth. "Nonetheless it is what we shall do. Toby'll take us on his boat."

She looked at Winthrop with sudden pity, knowing that for once she was not afraid of him, and seeing that he was old and weakened. "Do not think me ungrateful, sir," she said. "I've always been a trouble to you, and now it's best that we go."

"Aye—" echoed Robert. "It is best that we should go, before my wickedness is known."

Winthrop fixed his hollow eyes on Elizabeth's husband and was stricken by compunction. The man was ill, his pale wambling looks were as silly as his speech. A frail reed, a slimsy half-man—that was what he had married his niece to. He clasped his hands tight and turned his head from Robert. "Go then, Elizabeth," he said very low. "It may be best. God gives me no direction."

"Yes, Your Worship," said the minister. "They had better leave tonight. Even your presence will not long quiet the town, but if the Feakes are gone I can handle my folk who are sick from the hard winter and even the soberest of them unclear of judgment."

Winthrop nodded. "And they'll have the Indian witch to occupy them."

Elizabeth drew a sharp breath of protest, but the minister met her eyes and gave her a private warning headshake, while his lips formed the word "Wait!" To Winthrop he said, "Will you refresh yourself, sir, and stay at my house till morning? While you're here they'll not dare pry. I'll conduct the Feakes to their home."

Winthrop rose. "I will stay," he said. "I am a-weary. Take my halberdiers with you to keep order."

Elizabeth rounded up her little girls, and came to stand before her uncle. "So this is farewell? she said. "I—I can scarce believe it. Will you give love to my Aunt Margaret? I shall think of her so often, and oh, Uncle—where is Jack?"

"I know not," said Winthrop dully. "I've need of my son John now. I've sent to Ipswich for him, but I doubt he's there."

John alone, the beloved son, would know how to cope with the financial disaster and make plans for its alleviation. Winthrop pulled his attention back and kissed Elizabeth on the forehead. "God be with you," he said. "I can do naught to help you, except—except hush this matter up, and remember you in my prayers." He looked at the bed Robert had quitted. "I'm a-weary," he said again. "A touch of ague. Farewell, niece. Farewell."

Before dawn while most of the town slept at last, and those who might have interfered were guarded by the halberdiers, the Feakes sailed from Watertown on Toby's *Dolphin*. Telaka went with them. Mr. Phillips had so contrived it, after commanding one of the Governor's guard to make the gaoler drunk. The minister had himself unlocked the prison's iron gate and helped Telaka down the lanes and secreted her on the shallop. "May God forgive me for this and the lies I shall perforce tell," said the minister to Elizabeth as they hurriedly piled into the boat such of the goods and chests as they could take. "But they will kill the Indian if she stays behind, and I cannot have that murder on my soul."

"Oh, sir—" Elizabeth whispered. "All these years here I never knew how kind you were!" She caught his hand and kissed it.

"There, there, child," said the minister sadly. "May our Blessed Lord protect you, and lead you to a land where you may find contentment."

PART THREE

Connecticut and
New Netherland

1640–1655

14

A FAIR NORTHWEST WIND blew all the night that the Feake family escaped from Watertown. And the next day it blew Toby Feake's little *Dolphin* past the islands of the harbor and down the ocean side of Nantasket and the South Shore, until twilight, when Toby steered his shallop into Plymouth Bay.

"Why do we stop here, Toby?" Elizabeth cried anxiously. "Oh, don't put in to Plymouth!" She was sitting on the half-opened hatch with the wriggling seventeen-month-old baby John in her lap, while keeping a watchful eye on her two youngest daughters who had been roped together for safety, then attached to the mast where they squatted happily on the deck playing tick-tack-toe with some beans. Joan, who was seasick like her father and Telaka, was lying with them below in the cabin. The *Dolphin* was large for a shallop, near forty feet long, and stumpily built with a broad beam, but she was excessively crowded by five adults, the children, and the household gear the Feakes had managed to stuff in her before the flight. Toby was out of humor, had barely spoken to Elizabeth all day, and now ignored her question while he shouted over her head to the bow, "Ready wi' the boathook, Ben! I'm straight for the pier. Mind that pinnace, you dunce!"

"Aye, sir," called the Norfolk lad who acted as crew.

"Toby!" cried Elizabeth sharply. "Answer me! Isn't this Plymouth? Why do you stop here?" She had not recovered from the terror of the night before. Still she felt hunted and threatened by the strange evil which had leapt at her without warning. Plymouth Colony she knew could be as harsh as the Bay, and it was much too near Watertown. Suppose that her uncle and the Reverend Mr. Phillips couldn't hold them, and the enemies had hurtled off from Watertown to stop the Feakes. She pictured them galloping towards Plymouth— Job Blunt, the Warrens, the Knapps, Dolly Bridges—a horrible cavalcade streaming through the forests, yelling of witchcraft and vengeance.

"We stop here because we must," said Toby sourly, watching Ben make the line fast to the iron ring on the pier. "We're outa water and provisions, nor is there beer enough. D'ye expect me to sail dry all the way to Greenwich? There's naught to be afraid of," he added. "Watertown folk'll not flout the Governor, and'll have sobered today."

Elizabeth knew the truth of this, but could not feel it, though the landing was quiet and their arrival excited no interest amongst a sprinkling of sailors and loungers.

"I'm sorry, Toby," she said at length. "We were so hurried —I know you didn't want to take us—but is there no other place to get supplies?"

"Naw," said Toby. "Without I sail into Narragansett some days hence, if we've the winds, which I've no mind to. Quickest done soonest over for *this* voyage." He jumped from the deck to the landing. "You've money, I trust, Aunt; Plymouth shops'll not fit us out for charity."

She nodded. Even in the panic of departure last night she had not forgotten to scoop up the contents of her heavy bride's chest. Clothes, linens, Jack's glove, Harry's pin, Robert's gold chain had all been flung into a sack, and the ninety pounds of her jointure she had hung from her belt in a leather pouch. She drew out two sovereigns. "Will this do?—and Toby—"

"Aye?" he said more amiably, pleased by the sight of gold.

"If we should buy lands down there, how do we pay the Indians?"

Toby knitted his scraggy brows and scratched his nose while he ruminated. "Aye," he said. "They want English coats an' hardware. I'd best lay some in, though you've left me precious little room for cargo. Still, gi' me two more sovereigns. I'll see what I can do."

"Be careful, Toby! Tell nobody who we are, and hasten I beg of you. I'll hide down in the cabin with the others."

Toby, who shared none of her apprehensions, and whose gallantry and family loyalty had ebbed with the day, merely shrugged; telling Ben to watch the boat, he shambled along Water Street towards a cluster of clapboarded buildings which looked far humbler than those of Boston.

While Elizabeth watched Toby, Robert stuck his head up through the hatch and said, "What is it, wife? Where are we?" His blinking gaze scanned the flat sandy shores, the huddled little town. "Surely 'tis not Boston!"

"No, no—" she said. "Plymouth. Boston's far behind. Stay below, Rob, out of sight. I'm coming down."

"Why?" he said leaning on the hatch and retching a little. " 'Tis foul in the cabin. I want air. Joan and the Indian too, they've been seasick."

"I know," she said relieved that he spoke sensibly, and that though his face was green and he looked ill, the confused wild light had gone from his eyes. "But there might still be danger. The less we're noticed the better. I'll clean up the cabin." She descended the ladder and he followed her. Danger? he thought. Aye, there had been some sort of danger; folk shouting, accusing and threatening, but what about he did not know, nor how long ago—except it seemed far past. No use thinking of it, and Bess knew what to do, if aught must be done. His stomach qualms were ceasing, he felt hungry and confident, for they were off to join Daniel. That he knew clearly. He ate bread and some pickled beef, then set about cleaning the reeking cabin. Joan, quickly recovering, helped too, but Telaka whose legs were purple and swollen from the bonds they had put on her last night, could not yet move. She lay on a straw pallet with her face turned towards the bulkhead.

Night came on, the cabin freshened. Elizabeth fed the little girls. And still Toby did not return.

It was a soft spring evening; through the open hatch they could see the stars quiver out like new shillings against the thin black sky. The water lapped softly against the *Dolphin*'s hull. There were voices and lanterns on other boats at anchor in the harbor, but except for Ben's tuneless whistling as he patiently awaited Toby's return, there was quiet on the *Dolphin*.

Robert wished for sleep, the children were yawning, so Elizabeth bedded the little girls in the two narrow bunks and spread out on the planking the great feather bed they had brought. She tucked the baby beside his father on the feather bed, and was glad to see Robert's arm circle his son, and that he kissed the dark fuzzy little head. It was long since Robert had noticed his children and yet at times he could be the fondest of fathers. He's better, she thought. The strangeness had again passed, had in some way been frightened out of him last night. But the memory of last night, which domestic efforts had held off, now wrenched her anew. Her fears swooped back. Why was Toby so long in coming? Could it be that he was in some sinister way detained?

She climbed the little ladder and peered cautiously over the hatch. The immediate short front loomed dark and still, except down by the corner of the First Street where swung the sign of an ordinary. Candlelight flickered from its windows, and through the half-opened door came occasional bursts of male laughter.

Restless and uneasy, Elizabeth went up on deck to inhale the salty air which smelled of clams and seaweed. Ben, who was curled up dozing on the bow, raised his head, and said, "What's ado, Mistress?"

"Nothing," she said. "Why, *why* doesn't Master Toby come back?"

"Master's not one to hurry hisself," said the lad sleepily. "Wind's died. Can't sail till morn nohow. Don't ye fret, mum—" he added. Benjamin Palmer was only fourteen, but nimble and sharp-witted. He thought Elizabeth very pretty, also he had a good heart which had been moved by her ordeal in Watertown.

"I know it's silly," she said, impelled to speech with anyone who did not have to be protected from worry like Robert and the children. "But I feel eerie—a foreboding. Can't stop it. Yet I had none before—before the trouble yesterday."

Ben sat up and asked anxiously, "Has yer left eye bin itching ye? Or ha' ye seen a spider ternight?"

"No," said Elizabeth, half laughing. "I just feel something's going to happen."

"Naught bad, then," said Ben with confidence, and curled up again with his head on a coil of rope.

Elizabeth sat down on the gunwale and stared out to sea, trying to quiet her unease with a dozen different musings. She thought of Jack, and wondered what he would say when he heard of the flight, but the thought of Jack always now brought an accompanying image of the other Elizabeth—fair, complacent, genteel, an Elizabeth who could never conceivably get herself involved with hideous accusations and the threat of prison. There was no escape from pain in these thoughts, so she tried to envision the future—the axe-shaped Neck with the white sands, the reunion with the Patricks, but these speculations were misty and juiceless. And all the time her ears were alert for any unusual noise on the shore.

At midnight she heard it, jumped, then felt ashamed as she discovered it was but the tavern door opening wide to let out a crowd of men who came stumbling and raucous into the street.

Some of the men had lanterns. She saw several lights lurch around the corner and disappear, but two figures with a lantern detached themselves from the others and came towards the waterfront. Elizabeth soon recognized the stocky leader as Toby. Giddy with relief she jumped from the boat to the pier, and waited there.

Toby's gait was unsteady. As he neared her she heard the guttural chuckles he emitted when drunk. The other man hung back behind a great pile of dried fish nets.

"Well, Aunt . . . well . . . " cried Toby as he came up to her. "All ready and waiting to be taken?" He chuckled again, swinging his arms.

"I'm so glad you've come," she said quickly. "Get on the boat and to sleep, you're cup-shot. Where're our goods?"

"Not so fast . . . " mumbled Toby swaying. "Oh-ho! Oh-ho! Didn't ye hear what I said? Ye're summoned! Governor Bradford wants you. They've sent from Watertown."

Her stomach lurched. "What do you mean—" she whispered staring past him at the empty pier. "Toby, for God's sake—"

"Come wi' me, Aunt!" said Toby putting a thick hand on her arm. "They're waiting at the Governor's, they've readied the gaol here."

"No," she whispered. "Toby, I don't believe you. I'll get Robert—"

But Toby grabbed her other arm and turning propelled her forcibly ahead of him down the dock, where the man with the lantern suddenly stepped out from behind the nets.

"Here she is, constable!" cried Toby in a great voice. "Here's the witch."

"Shhh-h," said the other man sharply, and put his lantern on the planks. "You're frightening her."

Elizabeth stared through a blur of panic. The light wavered

upward over a very tall man in a leather jerkin. He had a shock of lanky brown hair that swung to his huge shoulders, and he looked down at her with a peculiar intensity.

"Will Hallet—?" she cried in utter disbelief. "Is it you, Will?" Her knees gave way and she stumbled forward. He caught her against him, and held her tight against a broad hard chest where even in her daze she could feel a strong heart beating.

Toby gave a guffaw. "Fair diddled, wasn't ye!" he cried, slapping his thigh. "Swallowed it whole, she did, Hallet! Thought ye was the guard come to gaol her! Ye shoulda seen her shaking."

"Hold your tongue, you dolt," said Will over Elizabeth's head. " 'Twas a sorry jest. Come, Mistress, no need to fear. I'd not hurt you for the world." He said the last words into Elizabeth's hair, and she became aware that she was still clinging to him, that his arms supported her, that she was savoring a strong masculine smell of sweat, leather and tobacco, and that her panic had given way to a delicious feeling of shelter.

"Sho-ho!" said Toby gaping at them. "I didn't know you were on hugging terms, but hug away. I mind me there's a leetle jug o' rum I hid 'neath the stern sheets, I'll hug *that*—" He made a smacking noise with his lips, zigzagged carefully down the dock, and disappeared into his boat.

Elizabeth straightened up, pulling herself from Hallet. His arms fell instantly and they confronted each other. He was in full manhood now, she saw, with a stubble of dark beard and a powerful long jaw. His blunt nose had lengthened too; there were furrows beside it. His cheeks had lost all boyish roundness. "How does this come about, Will?" she asked hurriedly to keep herself from staring at him. "How did you meet Toby?"

"In the ordinary," he said with the gently bred intonation which startled her anew. "I've been at Yarmouth with my cousins a week or so, and saw his sister, Judith Palmer, there. Besides, when I heard some fellow in the tavern call him Feake, I asked if he was kin to you."

"You still remember me?" she said, trying to laugh. "It's been six years since that Election Day on the Common when you bested the blacksmith."

"Aye—" he said. "I still remember you. And still find you beautiful."

She could not help a gasp of pleasure, at the same time

wishing passionately that she had combed her hair and changed this rumpled olive wool dress, worn since setting off for the meetinghouse yesterday. "The lantern light is kind," she said, looking up at him through her lashes as she had almost ceased to do with men. "Tell me of yourself, where have you been these years?"

"If you like," he said. "But shall we sit?" He motioned to the pile of nets, and taking her hand, drew her down beside him. His touch befuddled her, and the nearness of his big body. He doused the lantern and began to talk, but at first she could scarcely listen to him. She watched the starlight on his face, and knew that never even in those first days with Harry had she felt quite like this. How was it that again she became timid, dithering, virginal as she had been so long ago on the *Lyon*. And yet Hallet was twenty-four and she thirty. Soon she forgot even that as she listened to him, and she forgot the sleeping Robert on the boat, and the children.

He had been in Virginia for two years, and then run a trading post for a wealthy Connecticut gentleman called William Whiting. This trading post was on the Delaware River where the Swedes were trying to establish a colony. Their advent had ruined the English traders, who moreover had been harassed by the Dutch who also claimed the territory.

" 'Twas a failure, my trading post," said Will with his usual wry candor. "I owe Mr. Whiting money, which galls me. I'll not rest till I pay it back, but I find I've not the kind of wits for merchanting and trading. 'Tis the land I like. And making something from it with my own two yeoman hands."

He fell silent while she found the courage to ask a question. "You've a wife now, for certain?" she said, winding and unwinding a loose piece of fish net. "And babes?"

"Why, no," he said, laughing a little. "There was a wench in Virginia I was fond of. She lived with me at the trading post, without benefit of magistrate or minister. When I came north we parted pleasantly. Fortunately she was barren, so I've no bastards about that I know of."

"Ah—" said Elizabeth on a long breath.

He turned suddenly and stared at her hard. "Why are you glad I'm not wed? What does it matter to you, Bess Feake?"

"I don't know—" she stammered. "It doesn't. How could it? You mistook me. Dear Lord, I've been so frightened and turmoiled these last two days, I scarce know what I'm doing."

"To be sure," he said, in a different voice. "Toby told me
something of your trouble in Watertown, but jestingly. Will
you speak of it to me, would it ease you?"

"Oh, yes," she cried. "It would. You see yester morn, after
the meeting, Dolly Bridges took a fit . . . "

She poured it all out to him in a tumbling flood, saying
more than she knew when it came to Robert's behavior. Will
listened intently, trying his best to follow this tale of a mutilated Indian, witchcraft, pain, fear, howling mobs, the
minister and the governor. And escape at midnight.

At the end, she could not stop herself from weeping.
"They hated me," she sobbed. "They wanted to kill me, and
kill poor Telaka. What happened that they hated so? What
did we do?"

"Hush—" he said. "It's over. You'll be gone in the morning. You'll be safe. Hush, sweetheart," he said and took her
in his arms.

She quietened, lying soft against him. Like honey and fire,
she felt throughout her body the endearment he had called
her. The stars danced and sparkled over their heads. She
shut her eyes and her thoughts stopped while she raised her
face to his, her mouth eager, beseeching, under his hot firm
lips.

He crushed her to him with a force that gave her blissful
pain. He kissed her mouth, her lids, her neck, she felt his
hand burning on her naked breast, and melted closer to him
murmuring she knew not what.

"By God!" he said, suddenly holding her off, and looking
at her with what seemed like anger. "I never thought 'twould
be like this. Bess, I want thee—I must have thee. Come!"
He pulled her to her feet. "Over there," he said hoarsely.
"The beach—by the marsh grass."

She stood panting, so weakened that he lifted her in his
arms. "No!" she cried. "No! Put me down!" For as he lifted
her she had seen to the end of the dock. The dark line of
the *Dolphin*'s mast. "Let me go—Will—" she cried with
anguish. "I cannot."

He set her slowly on her feet, and stood apart from her.
"You cannot?" he repeated. "And why not, since you want
it, as I do?"

She bowed her head, looking down at the black water
lapping against the piles. "Adultery," she whispered.

He made a rough sound in his throat, and folded his
arms across his chest. "An ugly word, Bess. And one not

used in the noble household I once knew. There, as I observed it, it was called 'chivalric love.'"

"Perhaps," she said still staring at the water. "But I was not raised in a noble household, and between us there's been no mention of love."

"And what is love?" His voice now held sharpness. "'A torment of the mind, a tempest everlasting; and Jove hath made it of a kind, not well, nor full nor fasting.' So says the poet."

"It pleases you to mock," she said dully.

There was silence between them, while the first dawn breeze fluttered the ripples, and a pearly light shone on Plymouth Bay's horizon. Then Will spoke. "No, Bess, I do not mock. It is that I know not what to say. Nor why it is that we should both throb and quicken so for each other. But you were right to stop us. Will you sit down near me again? I would look long at you, and keep your lovely face in my memory."

She started and turned, crying in fear, "You're not going? Where are you going?" She ran to him and took his hand.

He did not smile at this unreason; he sighed and said, "Yes, my dear, I am going to England. I've been waiting a ship at Plymouth, but now I hear of one that's soon to sail from Boston, and shall sign on as carpenter."

"England," she whispered. "Not so far . . ."

"But I must. There were letters for me at Yarmouth. One from my brother who says my mother is very feeble and yearns to see me again before she dies. The other—" he frowned and added with reluctance, "from Lord George Digby, the Earl of Bristol's heir."

"What does HE want of you now?" she cried. "You said you were quit of them all at Sherborne Castle, that you despised them! Do you then go creeping back like a spaniel if one of those lords beckons?"

He flushed, but answered soon. "The times are wretched over there, Bess. The King's march to Scotland came to naught. The people cry out against him. He will not call a Parliament. There's grave fear of civil war."

"Let them fight then!" she cried. "What's it to you?"

He raised her work-roughened hand to his lips and kissed the palm. But he continued inexorably. "No matter Lady Bristol's conduct to me I cannot forget my duty to the Earl, nor my affection for his son. Lord George writes he must see me, he is in trouble from a duel, confined to his castle.

He writes he has need of a man such as he believes I may now be to help him in certain matters—confidential missions."

"But you *said*—" she burst out, "that all you cared for was the land, and yeomanry!"

"I also said that I must earn money to pay back Mr. Whiting, which I can quickest do by working for the Digbys. Furthermore, I cannot ignore Lord George's plea, nor my mother's."

She snatched her hand from his. She turned her head and spoke carefully. "Then you'll never come back. I'll never see you more."

In the growing dawn light he had caught the look of her eyes, before she turned away and made her shoulders stiff and proud. Unwilling, he felt a shock of pain.

"It's *not* farewell, Bess," he said. "I'll return. I swear it."

"What good is that?" she said, holding herself tight. "We can be nothing to each other, and you do not even know where I'm going."

"I know where you're going. Toby told me. And do you think I couldn't find you anywhere?"

"Aye, when I am old and wrinkled and forspent."

By this bitterness he was troubled. He had much experience of light love, but until tonight had never guessed the pangs, nor found a woman who could turn him from any purpose he had set himself. Yet it was not only in Elizabeth that strange new feelings had awakened. A longing to protect and cherish her had subdued his passion despite his first quick male fury at being thwarted. Now he finally spoke uncertainly. "What would you have me do, Bess? Stay near you always, yet gazing from afar? Shall I give up my voyage to England?"

"Ah, no," she cried piteously, the false anger draining from her. "Forgive me. I spoke like a child. Go, go quickly. Forget me, Will. Forget this night as I shall try to."

He turned her by the shoulders, lifted her head and pushing back the tumbled black curls, looked into her face. With his great brown forefinger he touched the rose of her cheeks, the dark arch of her brows, the cleft in her chin, the full white curve of her throat. "I'll not forget thee, Bess," he whispered against her mouth as he kissed it. "I'll not forget thee."

He was gone before she could speak, or cry out to stop him. She heard his quick footsteps on the wooden planks of the pier and then no more as he went up the sandy street.

She did not turn to look after him; she sat as he had left her on the dried fish nets, gazing out past the swaying mast of the *Dolphin*, to the sea where red streaks flamed on the dark distant water to the east.

The *Dolphin* sailed at eight that morning, moderately provisioned and with a bundle of trading goods lashed to the deck. Toby had arisen sober enough, and surly. He said nothing of Hallet, and Elizabeth soon saw that he did not clearly remember the night before. She escaped all questioning since none of the sleepers on the shallop had awakened. For this she was grateful, though during the long days and nights of sailing she found no other cause for gratitude. Often enough in her life she had thought herself miserable, but it was never like this. She moved through the necessary duties in a haze, tending the children, emptying the slop buckets, boiling as best she could succotash and salt beef over the tiny fire which was laid on an iron slab in the cookpit. Beneath these surface actions was a gnawing ache that sharpened at night to pain, while she relived those hours on the dock at Plymouth. Lovesickness, she thought at times, taunting herself in an effort to reduce the pain by ridicule. Or lust, what more than that? The lewd wantonness of a gentlewoman; mature wife, and four times mother, flinging herself like a tap wench into the sweaty arms of a common carpenter, then panting, pleading, clinging in a shameless bawdry to this fellow who had not even spoken of love. Thank God sanity and decency had rescued her in time. But no sooner had she thought thus than all her sour triumph fell apart, the pain returned a hundredfold, and burying her face in the pillow so the sleeping Robert might hear nothing, she would weep because she had not yielded. Why *had* she not gone with him to the beach by the marsh grass and known at least the piercing sweetness of the flesh and its desire assuaged. Surely he could not have left her then, or if he had, she would have known he would return, for the seal would have been on them. These thoughts at night, but in the morning others.

After Robert arose she would lie on, staring at the deck above and telling herself cold reason. Will Hallet would never return, nor would he had she yielded. For certain at Sherborne Castle there were elegant ladies, very young ones, perfumed and painted, with soft white beringed hands, ladies versed in the arts of "chivalric love." And he, no longer a

common carpenter but a lord's intimate, seeing these ladies—
who could not help desiring his strength and careless manhood—what memory then would he retain of a tousled plain-
garbed woman who had found no better love words than a
mealy-mouthed prating of adultery. "I'll not think of him
again," she said each morning to herself. "I swear it." And
each hour broke her vow.

Robert, dimly aware of her silence, and that she hardly
ate, ascribed this to yearning for the Winthrops or to the
hardships of the voyage. He treated her with kindness which
she scarcely noted, and helped her with her duties. He was
no longer seasick, and indeed felt better than he had in years.
As each day brought them further west, he took more interest in their journey and the coastline that they glimpsed
at intervals. They rounded Cape Cod without mishap, sailed
between Martha's Vineyard and the Elizabeth Islands, then
passed Narragansett and the Isle of Aquidneck or Rhode
Island so far out to sea that they could barely distinguish
the shore.

Once Elizabeth had thought of begging Toby to stop at
Aquidneck so that she might visit Anne Hutchinson, and see
how she fared. When she heard Toby tell Robert their position on the third day after rounding the Cape, Elizabeth
roused herself and asked how far it was to Portsmouth on
the Island.

"Ye mean where lives that Hutchinson woman now?" said
Toby. " 'Tis yonder many leagues to the north. Newport's
the nearest settlement, but I'd not put in there even if the
wind wasn't contrary."

"William Coddington's settled himself at Newport with
others who grew weary of Mrs. Hutchinson ere long," said
Robert glancing at his wife. But it seemed that Elizabeth
was entirely cured of her perverted interest in the false
prophetess, for she asked no more questions and went below
to the cabin with a bowl of food for Telaka. The squaw's
injured legs were better, she never complained, but she continued intermittently seasick, and still lay on the pallet.

As the shallop entered the Sound past Fisher's Island they
were becalmed for two days. The lug sail hung inert across
the mast, or slatted feebly, while the *Dolphin* wallowed in
great oily ground swells. The hot May sun beat down on
them, and Toby, frowning, worried about their provisions
and said if this kept up they'd have to row; he and Ben on
one of the great oars, Robert and Elizabeth on the other,

and they needn't think it would be easy. A breeze sprang up next morning, but it blew strongly from the west and the shallop had no means of sailing into the wind. Toby, muttering several robust curses, maneuvered his boat southward until he touched bottom near some oyster beds at the tip of Long Island. He dropped anchor, pulled up the little skiff they had been towing, and jumped in it. "Ben, stay on board wi' the boat," he commanded. "You others, 'cept the squaw and the babies, 'll come ashore and gather shellfish. Uncle, bring your fowling piece."

Robert stared at him in astonishment. "We're going ashore? Where are we?"

"I don't rightly know where we are," said Toby gruffly. "I've never been to Long Island, but 'less you don't mind starving, ye best do what I say."

Elizabeth welcomed this distraction, which interrupted her ceaseless churning. Joan and Lisbet, wild with delight at being on shore, rolled on the shingle like puppies and plunged in and out of the eelgrass before Elizabeth could make them help her gather mussels and clams. At this task she was none too expert herself, and the disgusted Toby had to show her the good mussels from the poisonous, and the bubbly spots in the mud which marked a buried quahog. And as the tide came in, the lobsters crawled up on the beach and Lisbet got her toe painfully pinched by one. Over the child's shrieks, Toby said to Elizabeth, "Fine family for the wilderness *you* are. Lotta dunderheads. N' there's Uncle can't even hit a nesting mallard!"

It was true that Robert's gun had banged out twice and missed. Elizabeth said with apology, "I know, Toby. But we'll learn. Don't be so cross. Shall we make a fire and boil these things?" She indicated the pile of shellfish they had gathered.

He nodded. "Save all those quahog clamshells."

"Why?" she asked, amazed that he should burden his boat with such truck.

"Because ye can make the purple wampum out o' them, something to do of a winter evening, and these are specially fine ones."

"Wampum beads—like the *Indians?*"

"Aye, like the Indians and the Dutch who call it seawant. 'T passes for money down here, ye'll find. Now, Aunt, stop blabbing and hasten. Cook up this stuff whilst I fill the water barrel at the creek."

She opened her mouth to rebuke his speech. Toby was never overcourteous, yet it was unlike him to be quite so rude, unless he had been drinking rum, which she knew to be exhausted. Nor was it like Toby to hurry. Her rebuke was never spoken, for from the corner of her eye she saw stealthy movement amongst the scrub pines on the shore behind them. A singing swish zoomed by her ear and a turkey-feathered arrow splattered the sand near Joan.

"The devil help us," said Toby. "I feared it. Get to that rock!"

Elizabeth scooped up the children and obeyed without knowing that she moved. Behind a great upended boulder Toby squeezed next to her. "Netop! Friend! Netop!" he shouted over the rock, while keeping his loaded musket ready but out of sight.

Two grotesque painted faces peered through the pine branches. From one issued a furious harangue, completely unintelligible. Another arrow whizzed out and struck the sheltering rock.

Toby yelled in a mixture of Dutch and German, "We are friends, we mean no harm!"

The Indians shouted back in their own tongue, and one of them glided nearer.

"I'll have to shoot," muttered Toby. "Though I can't hit both."

Lisbet began to cry, a feeble wail. The nearest Indian jerked his head up, listened and laughed. He emerged onto the strip of beach, a young buck with feathered scalplock, naked except for a breechclout. He sidled down the sand, seeking a better aim, fitted an arrow and drew his bow, while Elizabeth, Toby and the little girls crept around the rock to keep it between them and the Indian.

"Toby," Elizabeth whispered, crouching over her children. "Look *that* way!"

They had now exposed themselves to the other Indian who was also taking aim. It can't end like this, Elizabeth thought. She wasn't frightened, she was astonished. Surely death didn't arrive on a sunny May morning, while one was clamming on a pretty beach. It was incongruous, funny— as a two-headed calf is funny. I wonder where Robert is, she thought, if he's watching.

Robert was not watching. He was a quarter of a mile away in a salt marsh where he had finally shot a duck. But on the *Dolphin* they were watching, and as the second Indian pulled back his bowstring, a clear voice rang out from the boat. "*Michashong anum dabanda!*"

The startled Indian's hand dropped from the bow. He stared first at his companion who was obviously also startled, then they both located the voice which continued a flow of indignant command.

" 'Tis your squaw," whispered Toby exhaling sharply, his musket still poised. "They seem to understand her."

Telaka stood on the deck, clinging to the mast and to Ben who had summoned her. Her scars and her empty eye-socket showed clear in the sunlight, her blue cotton dress was stained and torn, her long black hair was matted, her arms were like trembling brown sticks, but she spoke with a power that daunted the hostile Indians. Careless now of the party hiding behind the rock, they moved to the water-line and shouted back at Telaka, who answered, then presently called to Elizabeth, "Missis—fetch me in boat! Fear not!"

Toby, his musket under his arm, warily set off in the skiff and rowed to the *Dolphin*.

When Telaka came ashore, she disdained Elizabeth's support, and stood proudly alone on the beach. She spoke again to the two Indians, and Elizabeth distinguished the words "Mayn Mianos" and "Siwanoy." The Indians grunted, and bowed slightly. Telaka turned to her mistress. "They are Corchaugs," she said. "Hate white man. This their land. They say you steal their wampum. I say you hungry. Only want food. They know my father, Sachem Mianos. Corchaugs have peace with my Siwanoy tribe."

"Tell 'em," cut in Toby, "if they'll let us take food and water we'll give 'em white man's knives, or a hoe. As they like."

Telaka interpreted this, turned back to Toby. "They want to see first. Don't know white man's things."

When Toby again returned from the *Dolphin*, Robert walked onto the beach carrying a mallard. He stopped dead at the sight of the Indians.

"It's all right now, I think," said Elizabeth quickly. "There *was* danger but Telaka stopped them. Don't say anything. Put the gun down."

The Corchaug braves pointed at the duck, which was certainly very small, pointed at Robert's fowling piece and shook with laughter. They spoke to Telaka, who translated.

"They say white man's fire-rod go bang, bang but get nothing. White man stupid."

Robert flushed, but Elizabeth said, "Well, at least they won't want our guns."

Telaka nodded. "They not sure what guns can do. Very simple tribe."

They did, however, appreciate the knives Toby brought, fine sharp English steel with heavy wooden hilts. The hoes, which they had never seen, they disdained. They squatted down, testing and fondling their knives.

"They say you may eat and get water, but leave quahog shells alone," said Telaka. "They wait till you go."

It was an uneasy meal, and would have been inadequate for the remaining journey, except that while the mess of shellfish—clams, mussels and lobsters—was boiling in the iron pot from the *Dolphin*, one of the braves suddenly disappeared. He came back soon with a large wild hen turkey slung over his shoulder. He threw the turkey contemptuously down at Robert's feet, and removed the arrow from its breast. "He says you can take this," said Telaka.

The Corchaugs watched each passage of the skiff, until the Feakes were again stowed on board the *Dolphin*. They frowned, murmuring to each other as Toby unfurled the sail and the shallop moved sluggishly away from shore. The wind was still in the west, but Toby dared not stay within bow shot too long. Telaka advised against it. The Corchaugs were unpredictable. They might decide they wanted more knives, or with renewed hostility might summon the rest of the tribe. There was nothing for it but to get away and hope the wind would change before the boat was driven back east too far.

At least they had the turkey to supplement the scanty remains of beans and salt beef. As Elizabeth started plucking the bird, she said to Telaka, "Rest now, my dear. I need not tell you of our gratitude."

"Aye—" said Toby gruffly from the tiller. " 'Twas a bad spot ye saved us from. Have some beer." He offered the squaw a pull from his own tin mug, a sacrifice, since the beer keg was near empty. Telaka accepted, then licking a finger, held it up to the wind. "Chekefuana blow too much," she said. "I will tell him to stop, we need Wompanand to take us to Monakewaygo." She crept unsteadily to the bow, crouched there and began a low chanting.

"What's all that mean?" said Toby, staring at the squaw.

"The winds, I think—" said Elizabeth. "Chekefuana is the god of the west."

"Pah!" said Toby spitting scornfully over the gunwale.

Nevertheless in an hour the wind veered. Dark clouds formed, raindrops spattered on the deck, and by nightfall the *Dolphin* was skimming down the Sound before a moderate nor'easter. By then Telaka had ceased chanting and gone below to lie on her pallet and retch with seasickness.

The next day, although it cleared, the east wind held. Toby kept close to shore as they skimmed past tiny new settlements. Relieved at the prospect of soon getting rid of his unwieldy boatload, Toby amiably named these villages as they glided by. That red mountain near the mouth of the Quinnipiac River sheltered a few houses called Roodberg by the Dutch, New Haven by the English, who were establishing themselves there under a minister named Davenport, and a merchant, Mr. Theophilus Eaton. A few thatched roofs further west along the coast Toby could not name, but he recognized Norfolk where he had been with Daniel Patrick, because though there were no English houses, there was an Indian village on one of the little islands.

The next morning everyone was up at dawn. " 'Twill not be long now," said Toby to the excited hovering Feakes. He ran his stumpy finger over a tattered chart he had made. "See that spit o' land ahead?" he said, pointing towards a heavily wooded promontory and glancing down at his chart. "That's called Shippan by the Rippowam Indians, their Sagamore Wascussue lives there, or maybe 'tis Ponus, a great chief in these parts. Don't remember. But there was a couple o' Englishmen from Wethersfield chaffering for land thereabouts when I came by last month."

"I hope," said Robert anxiously, "the savages down here aren't like those Corchaugs on Long Island. You don't think there's been any danger for the Patricks, do you?"

Toby shrugged. "Far as I can see an Indian's a varmint, an' I wouldn't trust any of 'em."

"*My* tribe is friendly," said Telaka, suddenly appearing in the hatch, her eye darting disapproval at Toby. "Siwanoys friends with Patrick who is good man. Will be friends with Feakes, but not like bad things said of them." She glared again at Toby.

Toby did not even listen to this speech, for he was busy trimming his sail and steering his clumsy boat as far south as he could get her, to avoid a cluster of humpbacked rocks which showed above the water. They continued down the middle of the Sound, far out because the tide was low, the shadows of rocks and shoals visible. The coastline showed no distinguishing features to Elizabeth, but she was conscious of her squaw's tenseness. Telaka gripped the corner of the hatch and muttered to herself in Indian, obviously naming landmarks. Suddenly she straightened and put her hand on Elizabeth's shoulder, an astonishing intimacy. "Look!" she cried, pointing far to the right of the bow. "Look, Missis! Monakewaygo—the white sands!"

Telaka's thrill communicated itself to Elizabeth. They peered ahead towards a long white strip gilded by the rising sun. Never before except that night at Sandwich before they sailed on the *Lyon*, had Elizabeth seen a real beach, and then the sands had been brown, not of this shining purity. There were canoes drawn up in a tiny cove and several curls of smoke rose above the trees.

"My people," said Telaka below her breath. "They camp there now near the sand gods for fishing."

"I wonder where the Patricks may be lodged," said Robert eagerly. "Is this where they'd be, Toby? Where's his hut?"

"Down there a piece—" said Toby. "D'you see that wet stony bit 'tween the neck and the mainland? 'Tis a deep passage at high water. Patricks're not far from it on t'other or *cove* side. I'll wait here to get through wi' the tide."

He steered inland and they saw movement on shore. Indians running back and forth, pointing to the *Dolphin*, and gathering near the narrow pebbly isthmus.

As the *Dolphin* dropped anchor a hundred yards from shore, Telaka stood up. She waved to the curious crowd of Indians, making signs with her fingers. For a moment they gaped at her, then an old woman screamed out "Telaka!" and ran to the water's edge, her arms outstretched. "It is my mother," said Telaka. "Those sachems behind are my brothers, Amogerone and Keofferam." For the first time since Elizabeth had known her the squaw seemed conscious of her horrible appearance. She loosened her right braid, pulling the black hair forward so that it covered the scarred half of her face. The Feakes embarked in the skiff. Elizabeth forgot Telaka and the Indians as a big man with red hair came running from the forest to the isthmus.

"By God, it *can't* be!" he cried as the skiff touched shore. "Damme if I believe me eyes! Rob! Bess! and the children. Damme, but 'tis good to see ye. I can't believe it!"

He whanged Robert across the shoulders, pumping his hand, and he engulfed Bess in a great hug. "Ha' ye come on a jaunt?" he cried. "Are ye junketing about? Holy Mary, I'm glad to see ye!"

"We've come to stay, Dan," said Robert, looking up at his friend with trustful joy. "We've come to settle here."

Patrick instinctively looked towards Elizabeth for confirmation of this astonishing news. She nodded slowly. " 'Tis true. We've fled from Watertown—from the Bay. We'll plant ourselves here with you—if you want us."

Moisture sprang to Patrick's blue eyes. "If we *want* ye! Anneke'll be—be—" He stopped, unable to express what this would mean to Anneke. "She's the only white woman," he went on. " 'Tis lonesome—no mincing that. A hard life— we'd a'most lost heart. But wi' you folks here—" He broke off, blew his nose between his fingers, wiped it on his buckskin sleeve. "I'faith I'm blubbering like a baby. Now then up to our hut wi' ye. I can't wait to see Anneke's face!"

That night the Feakes laid pine boughs on the ground and slept outside the Patrick cabin on pallets and the feather bed. The cabin was not large enough to accommodate all the newcomers, even though Toby and Ben stayed on the boat. Telaka had announced that she would return to her tribe that night. She had done this courteously, and also said that she would be back soon to help Elizabeth with the settling. But there was a difference in her manner. It was plain that she no longer considered herself bound. This was her country, and she was a chief's daughter; only friendship and inclination could command her services now.

Elizabeth awoke before the others and lay gazing up through oak leaves at a fleecy blue morning sky. She felt a curious pleasure, and surprise that the night air had not been harmful. For the first time since Plymouth the anguish of longing was muted. She thought of Will Hallet, but not with immediacy. He had withdrawn to some secret chamber in the center of her being. It was possible to bolt the door and look outward.

Robert stirred as she left the feather bed. "Nay, dear—" she said. "No need to waken yet. The sun's scarce up. Sleep more. There's a stressful day ahead. I'm going to cleanse myself."

Robert grunted and turned over. Baby John who had slept between them made a whimpering sound but did not wake.

Elizabeth glanced at her three little girls, snug on two joined pallets, their arms sprawling, their faces rosy and sweet as gillyflowers topped with brown and flaxen and red hair. My pretty babes, she thought, over a pang of fear. Anneke and Daniel had lost their youngest last month. The child had ailed, Anneke said, ever since they had come to Greenwich. Nor were young Danny and his sister quite well. Anna had some bowel complaint, Danny had cut his foot on a clam-shell, and the wound kept festering. Elizabeth thought of the herbs she would have used to help these children, and of other medications she relied on to keep her own brood healthy. But the garden was a hundred leagues away in Watertown, and of her dried or bottled supplies she had brought nothing on the night of the flight.

But the morning was too beautiful for gloomy thoughts. Elizabeth tucked up her woolen skirts and leaving the little clearing around the Patrick cabin, followed a trail towards the waters of the cove. Again the tide was out, and she was not attracted by mud flats or matted tussocks of eelgrass. She pushed south along the cove and came to the isthmus, which connected the mainland with the axe-shaped neck called Monakewaygo. It was a narrow bridge of drying pebbles scarce fifty feet across and she ran over it lightly, drawn by the dazzling white sands ahead. The sands were deserted. The beach lay like a silver crescent tinged with pink by the early sun. Seven miles to the east she saw the dim streak of Long Island, but between that and the beach there was only heaving burnished water, small waves that gurgled and plashed on the sand. She kicked off her shoes and kilting her skirts higher, plunged into the ripples, laugh-ing at the shock of cold and the soft tickle of running sand beneath her toes. Soon she flung off her dress and shift and splashed herself all over, rinsing away the staleness of the voyage. The sparkling glow intoxicated her, who had never yet bathed in the sea. At last a little chilled she rubbed herself dry with her shift. She lay down between two mounds of sand and let the sunlight beat on her body. The gulls wheeled lazily over the whispering water. Elizabeth sniffed the salt and fragrance from a clump of wild roses that grew close to the beach.

The sun grew warmer, her well-being mounted but changed gradually from pure sensuous basking to curiosity, and a zest for adventure. She pulled her gown on, and her thin soft shoes, then buoyed by a delicate excitement, set out to explore further. She had eaten but scanty food the night before, yet she felt no hunger. She walked further south along the beach and saw the smoke of a fire amongst a stand of sumac and locusts. Faintly she heard a woman's voice singing. The Indians, she thought—perhaps Telaka. She turned inland at once, unwishful of seeing any human. The singing died away. She mounted to higher ground and entered a virgin forest of huge oaks, pines and maples where the warblers and the thrushes trilled. In the center of the forest there was a marshy fresh pool. It glimmered with an iridescent light. Blue herons streaked upward as she approached, and a white-tailed doe, her dappled fawn beside her, raised a startled head and gazed at Elizabeth with gentle eyes.

This neck of land that Elizabeth explored that morning was but a mile long, and half as broad. Seldom did she lose sight of the sea. There were boisterous waves and flying spray at the far southwestern point where the wind blew unchecked for many leagues, there was rippling dark water amongst the grassy islands of the sheltered cove which stretched up to the north, past the spot where she had set out from the Patricks' and where the *Dolphin* now lay at anchor. For Elizabeth every view was magic. Her steps never flagged unless she paused to watch a chipmunk nickering to its mate, or to pluck the flowers which grew thick as a carpet near the pool; lady's slippers and blue flags—the strangely petaled rose and green of the pitcher plant. In one warm sheltered spot she found wild strawberries and crammed herself with them until the rosy juice stained her face and fingers. Thirsty then, she went back to the pool where the doe had been drinking, and gulped up handfuls of the sweet water.

She had never dreamed that it was possible to fall in love with a place, nor quite realized now what caused her exaltation. It was not until she again went back to the white sands and stood with the breeze blowing through her hair that her trance was penetrated. It came to her as a shock—the yearning for possession. "I want this," she said aloud to the wind and the water, "for my own."

During a moment of hopeless yearning, she sank sadly down on the sand, until with wonder a new idea came to her. She walked back briskly along the beach until she came to the isthmus, and stopped in astonishment. The bridge was gone. Monakewaygo had become an island, separated from the mainland by many rods of water, how deep she did not know.

She was daunted only for a second, then she laughed. All the better, she thought. It is thus *more* my kingdom. And she sat down on a rock to wait for ebb tide.

She had not waited long before she heard the plash of oars and the squeaking of tholepins from the cove side of the neck. It was Daniel in a clumsy little rowboat he had made himself.

"Ahoy there, mermaid!" he called as she ran to meet him. "Marooned, are ye? Ye've given us all a turn, but I guessed this might be the way o' it."

He beached the boat as she came to him and stood beside the gunwale, her hazel eyes shining. "Dan," she cried. "I want to buy this—" She waved her hand over Monakewaygo. "All of it, for my own. D'you think I could?"

Patrick laughed. She looked like a happy child with her skirts kilted up, her black hair all tangled on her shoulders and her mouth berry-stained. "I'm certain ye could. The Indians'll sell anything if ye have aught ter gi' 'em. I haven't had. Been squatting and making promises I've not been able to fulfill. But wot would ye *want* wi' that old neck? Naught but sand and trees."

"It's beautiful," she said. "It's enchanted, I think. It belongs to me, and I to it."

"I'faith, lass—ye're daft," Daniel snorted. "Ye need good meadow land to support a family, rich soil what'll grow corn and crops."

"I know," she said. "We'll get that too, on the mainland somewhere."

He sighed, and stretched out his big paw to help her in the boat. Full of joyous vim Bess looked this morning. No longer taut and weary-faced as she had so often been in Watertown. She'd no idea of true hardship yet, of the back-breaking work it was to subdue the wilderness. But he would not dampen her spirits now. And he understood that she who had never known freedom, nor done as she pleased without accounting for it, in particular to that long-nosed prig of a Winthrop, would naturally yearn for a place entirely her own.

"Aye"—he said, hunching over the oars. "The lust for land runs thick and strong i' the blood. We all feel it. I do meself. Bought those islands at Norwalk, but I've not been back 'cause I've naught to gi' the Indians fur 'em. Bess— had they sold my home lot at Watertown? Toby doesn't know."

"Oh, yes," she said. "I'm sure it's sold. Mr. Phillips has the money for you. We left so fast that—"

"Don't ye try to tell of it, lovey," Daniel cut in. "I understand the black fiendish way they acted. But what of your own property there, and furnishings—ye've brought so little. There's nothing to buy *here*, ye know . . . and Robert—" He shook his head. Daniel was very glad to see the Feakes and relieved that Robert's spirits seemed good, his mind clear and confident like the best times at Watertown. Still his body was delicate, the slender white hands were unfitted for rough work, and by temperament he was hardly a promising pioneer.

"I'm going to send Toby back to the Bay," said Elizabeth with sudden decision. "We've gold and he'll be willing. He can bring your money and ours when Mr. Phillips has arranged the sale of our place at Watertown. Also bring some of our possessions that we couldn't take. You'll see, Dan. All will go well with us here. We shall be manor lords. And I, myself—" she added, half smiling at her excitement, "shall own Monakewaygo and the white sands."

Two months later on July 18 of that year 1640, the Feakes and Daniel Patrick bought from the Indians all the land that the English called "Greenwich." A tract running north without limit between the great cove and Asamuck brook on the west; and the little stream to the east called Totomack which marked the boundary line of Stamford.

It was a broiling hot afternoon when the deed was signed, but the usual south breeze blew at Monakewaygo, where Elizabeth had insisted that the momentous transaction should take place. Moreover Telaka had reinforced this notion which the white men all thought foolish. It seemed that between the sands and the Indian fishing camp there was a huge rock which the Siwanoys considered sacred. The rock was used for powwows and councils; its spirit or Manitoo might be annoyed if the white men ignored its power.

When on the morning of the purchase Elizabeth explained this to Daniel, he laughed, saying, "So be it then! We'll sign this *on* the confounded rock, if you an' your squaw're so set on it. I'm not the rascal to gainsay two determined women. What do ye say, men?" He turned to the five other Englishmen who stood by his hut door and were to act as witnesses. These were Jeffrey Ferris, a lean taciturn farmer of thirty, with a crest of auburn hair, near as red as Patrick's. Ferris had decided to establish himself in Rippowam, or Stamford, five miles away since that tract had just been bought by the New Haven Colony, but Ferris had already wintered on land west of Totomack cove and wished also to retain this small portion of Greenwich.

There were present today besides Jeffrey Ferris a Robert Husted and his son, Angell, who intended to settle in Stamford and were already living in wigwams by the Rippowam River while their own negotiations pended. The other two, Andrew Messenger and Richard Williams, were enterprising lads exploring the coast, whose boat had only yesterday put into the Rippowam.

Daniel, through Jeffrey Ferris, whom he knew better than the Husteds, had summoned these Stamford men so that there might be as many English witnesses to the deed as possible. They all waited near the Patrick cabin, while Daniel laboriously finished the document. Anneke bustled around deploring the lack of beer or rum to signalize the occasion, and wishing plaintively that Toby had returned. It was now six weeks since the *Dolphin* had sailed back to the Bay, and they had decided not to wait for Toby any longer. The Siwanoys were on the move, and would spend the rest of the summer far less accessibly in one of their northern villages. Besides, thanks to Telaka's good offices, the Indians were selling cheap. Eleven English coats would satisfy them as down payment, fourteen more to be handed over later when Toby came back. This was far less than the New Haven Colony—in the person of Captain Nathaniel Turner—had paid the Rippowam tribe a few weeks ago and the Stamford pioneers were envious and astonished.

"Still and all—" said the elder Husted, while the entire party walked along the trail to Monakewaygo, "Ye're taking a chance o' trouble wi' the Dutch. Going it on your own like this. I'd ruther be fair n' square under New Haven Colony, and know where I stand."

"*We* wouldn't!" Elizabeth flashed. "We want to be our own masters."

Goodman Husted laughed, thinking this handsome wench must be a handful to manage, and from all appearances that ninny-hammer husband wasn't the one to do it. But it was none of his business, and a good thing to have white folk living west of Stamford, whatever they were. His goodwife would be relieved when she heard, and less unwilling to follow to the wilds.

Jeffrey Ferris said nothing, because he never spoke idly and was in a hurry to finish these negotiations and get back to his patch of corn which was ready for picking.

The Indians awaited them behind the great rock. Not the whole tribe, but only the sachems concerned in this sale, and Mayn Mianos, the chief, who had walked here from his main village of Petuquapan which lay some miles to the west across the great river which the English called Mianus in his honor. Mianos, overlord of a large territory, would not ordinarily have concerned himself with such an insignificant sale, nor did he like white men. It was Telaka who had brought him, and gained his consent to the transaction. Though he bowed gravely once as the English party approached he spoke not a word, while the deed was spread out on the rock. He stood with arms folded under his turkey-feather mantle, a wolf's tail—his totem—dangling from his roach of scarlet-dyed deer hair which held six heron feathers tipped with copper—the sign of sovereignty. He and the lesser sachems wore wampum earrings and necklaces. On their foreheads were painted the yellow stripes of peace. But Mayn Mianos did not look particularly peace-inclined. His fierce old eyes moved slowly over the eager faces of the three purchasers—Daniel, Robert and Elizabeth. He did not smile when they did. He raised his hand in a sharp impatient gesture.

"My father wishes you to read the paper," said Telaka. "I will tell him what it says." She spoke pleasantly but looked very strange to Elizabeth in a doeskin mantle embroidered with shells. The ravaged side of her face had been painted white, there was a white star on her good cheek, and into her long braids, glistening with bear grease, the ceremonial scarlet deer hair had been woven.

They all crowded near—the ten lesser sachems, two of whom were sons of Mianos, two sons of Ponus, the powerful neighboring chieftain. And they listened solemnly while Daniel read the deed and Telaka translated.

> *"We Amogerone and Owenoke, Sachems of Asamuck; and Ramatthone, Nawthorne, Sachems of Totomack have sould unto Robert Feaks and Daniell Patricke all their rights and interests in all ye several lands between Asamuck river and Totomack . . . except ye neck by ye indians called Monakewaygo, by us Elizabeth Neck, which neck is ye peticaler perchace of Elizabeth Feaks,*

*ye said Robert Feake his wife to be hers and her heaires
or assigns forever . . . "*

Elizabeth sighed deeply, and listened no more while Daniel
continued to read. She rubbed her foot secretly along the
ground. It's mine—she thought. I can do as I like here. She
looked with passionate gratitude across the rock at the Indians who were giving her this joy. None of them looked
back except Keofferam, Telaka's brother, who noted Elizabeth's expression with astonishment. He was a short squatty
young brave, lavishly tattooed with black and red dots as
befitted a great chief's son. His intelligent gaze was puzzled
as he inspected Elizabeth's glowing face, then his lips lifted
in a faint smile, as though he had understood. Certainly the
other Indians did not. They had no passion for land ownership, nor clear recognition of what they were selling, except
that they agreed not to fish within a mile of any white man's
weir. What of that? There were innumerable rivers and
plenty of fish. If the white men wanted to bestow the warm
gaudy English coats for the privilege of building huts and
planting corn, why, let them. There was room enough for all.

And so they signed their marks in squiggles and whorls,
the four sachems who were selling, and the others as witnesses, using Robert's quill pen and some excellent ink made
from sumac berries.

Robert Husted and Andrew Messenger were the English
witnesses. When they had all signed, Jeffrey Ferris gravely
requested the addition of a paragrah.

*"Keofferam hath sould all his right in ye above sd. to
Jeffere Ferris," witnessed by* "Richard Williams" *and*
"Angell Heusted."

Jeffrey nodded and stepped back satisfied. He had no certainty, at present, of remaining on his little Greenwich plot,
but still it was well to have his ownership attested.

Mianos had not moved during these proceedings; he now
spoke to Telaka, who turned to the English. "My father say
put the coats on the rock, and we hold powwow."

"Holy Mary," said Daniel. "Ha' we got ter watch 'em sing,
an' smoke that vile pipe wi' 'em? Well, can't be helped."

He and Robert heaved the bundle of scarlet and blue coats
onto the rock. Mianos counted them carefully and stepped
aside, beckoning to his shaman. The priest walked forward,

raised his arms in invocation, and began to chant. He wore a bear's head over his own and anklets of wooden rattles which he shook rhythmically. The Indians chanted with him. The ceremonial pipe was brought, and passed from mouth to mouth, first to the Indians, then to the white men. "*Werritige*," said the Indians as they exhaled, which meant, said Telaka, "The bargain is sealed." So the white men said it too—"*Werritige*." Only Mayn Mianos did not smoke the pipe with them, and when the white folk finally left Elizabeth's Neck bearing their precious deed, Daniel said a trifle anxiously, "I marvel that Chief Mianos held off so. There was something in his eye I didn't care for."

Elizabeth was walking beside Daniel and she laughed gaily. "Why, you sound fretty as Robert!—Mianos's *sons* signed, and it's all done, and oh, Dan, think of it! We've bought miles and miles. We own land bigger than the whole of London, as big as all West Suffolk, I believe! We've got meadows and hills and valleys and forests and rivers all our own!"

"Aye," said Daniel. He gave her a glance of rueful amusement. "And you've got that queer-looking axe-shaped neck ye hankered after, may you enjoy it, me poor lass." And may it, he thought, make up for all else you've missed.

15

NEARLY TWO YEARS after the purchase of Greenwich, on the eighth day of April, 1642, Elizabeth was again aboard the *Dolphin,* Toby at the tiller, and Daniel Patrick beside her in the cockpit. They were bound for New Amsterdam on a momentous mission, and had embarked in a mood of stiff determination which followed weeks of anxiety. While the shallop bobbed down the Sound towards the Dutch capital, nobody spoke for a long time.

Patrick sat frowning at the bilges, his plumed helmet on his knee. Anneke had polished his captain's helmet and cuirass as best she could and patched his old camlet breeches; nonetheless, his armor shone but dully, the helmet's white ostrich plumes hung bedraggled with age. Elizabeth too had tried to appear elegant for the occasion, and was wrapped in the venerable squirrel-lined velvet mantle she had bought in London, but her best taffeta gown, when unpacked from the chest where it had lain for two years, was cracked along the folds. Moreover, it did not fit, since Elizabeth was seven months pregnant. She wore perforce a loose homespun, which she had dyed a soft orange with sassafras bark. However, her wide lace collar was fastened with Harry's brooch, Robert's gold chain circled her neck. Greenwich should not be entirely shamed by its representatives.

"Flushing over there—" said Toby, breaking the silence and indicating the Long Island shore with his chin. "One or two English. *They* get along under the Dutch."

"Oh, and so will we," cried Elizabeth quickly. "We must. I'm sick of quarreling and uncertainty."

"Aye," said Daniel. "This is the only thing for us to do. Better be chivvied by Governor Kieft, pigheaded windbag that he is, than by those ferrety Stamford saints. An' Kieft's a whole lot further away from us."

Elizabeth nodded. They had been over all this many times. "Yet why can't we just be let alone?" she said with a wry little laugh. "It's our land. We bought it. I never thought New Haven Colony and the Dutch'd each claim us, fighting over us like a couple of hounds with a knucklebone."

"Well—" said Daniel. "Per'aps we shoulda guessed we'd have to pay allegiance somewhere. 'Twon't really make much difference. Besides, Bess—we may need protection."

"I can't believe it!" she cried, looking at Patrick with a mixture of fear and indignation. "Our Siwanoys would never harm *us*, even if they had aught to do with those wretched Laddins but they didn't. I'm sure of it. Besides, don't you believe Mianos? He denied it. And Telaka came to me as she always did, you know that, I trust her. The children love her and her brothers are such good Indians, how would we ever've got our house built without Keofferam and Amogerone? Or lived through last winter—all the game they brought us—you too."

"I'faith," agreed Daniel gravely. "Just the same, who *was* it murdered the Laddins?"

Elizabeth was silent, though she would not be convinced. Because the new-come Captain Underhill, knowing nothing about it, insisted that the ghastly deed had been done by the Siwanoys, and because the Siwanoy brave Powiatah's mangled body had been found with Laddin in the ravine at the bottom of the great cliff was no proof that Mianos was in any way concerned. She shrank from reviewing the tragedy, but having started, could not stop.

Cornelis Labden—or Laddin as the English called him— had been an old Dutch rascal, foul-mouthed and steeped in rum, which there was every reason to suppose he sold to the Indians for beaver pelts and wampum. He and a disreputable young woman he called his daughter had wandered to Greenwich last fall and set up a cabin in the uninhabited northern part of the town, near the inland Indian trail which connected the fords on the Mianus and Rippowam Rivers. Labden paid the Feakes a string of wampum for his homestall, and after that they saw no more of him, nor wished to. Robert had been dubious about selling to an unsavory Dutchman, but Elizabeth backed by Daniel had overruled Robert. Their community would exclude nobody on a morals charge, as did the sanctimonious New England towns, as Stamford now with fifty-nine godly settlers was already doing. There should be freedom for all in Greenwich. Besides, Labden's little property was hidden in deep forest, miles from the Feake and Patrick homes on the Great Cove.

Labden's fate, and that of his woman, might never have been known, except that Robert and Daniel set out for Stamford one day last month to see John Underhill, of whose arrival there they had just heard. The mercurial Captain had led a checkered life since Elizabeth had last seen him in Anne Hutchinson's parlor in Boston. He had been Governor of Dover on the Piscataqua until Dover residents, incited by John Winthrop, had ousted him. Underhill had returned to Boston and appealed against his banishment. Beating his breast and quoting Scripture, he vowed repentance for his early sins. He sprayed the meetinghouse with tears of contrition, and was finally forgiven by the Church. But this availed him little. Winthrop's power had returned; he was about to be re-elected Governor in place of Richard Bellingham, and his distaste for Underhill continued. The Captain, finding after all no employment in Boston, began to make new plans, when an opportune letter arrived from some old friends of his, Andrew Ward and Matthew Mitchell, now at Stamford. They wrote that being fretted by the Indians, and threatened by the Dutch, they would deem it an honor if so doughty a soldier would settle with them, and become their military leader. Underhill, leaving his Dutch wife, Helena, in Boston, had sailed to Stamford for a quick reconnoitering trip, and was pleased by his reception and the handsome recompense the Stamfordians promised him. He accepted their offer. This news reached the Feake house in Greenwich one morning by means of Toby, who now confined his coasting trade to the nearby Connecticut and Dutch towns, while using Greenwich Cove as a home port.

Robert and Daniel started off at once on foot to greet their old acquaintance, and garner news about the Bay. Last summer a Boston pinnace bound for New Amsterdam had brought Elizabeth an affectionate letter from Margaret saying that all was well and that Jack was on an extended voyage to England. But since then they had heard nothing.

The muddy March thaws and consequent floods had rendered impassable the shore trail along the Sound to Stamford, so Robert and Daniel took the drier northern path. As they turned east through dense forest they smelled smoke, and heard groans and agonized Dutch cries for help. They traced the sounds to the foot of a tremendous granite cliff, and there saw old Labden lying by a brook, his back broken and blood running from his mouth. A Siwanoy brave, Powiatah, reeking of rum, lay crushed and dead beside him. Labden died too in a few minutes, while Daniel bent over him trying to understand the bubbling gasps which indicated that several Indians with tomahawks had pursued the Dutchman who had fled to the concealed top of the thirty-foot cliff, and dodged, so that the Indians, unaware, might plunge over. Only Powiatah had done so, but he had dragged Labden with him as he fell.

This disaster, though certainly distressing, was not as horrifying to the two Englishmen as the sequel. Labden's last words were of his woman, Gretje. And his fears were justified.

Leaving the two corpses in the ravine, the men skirted the cliff and on the top saw that Labden's hut was burning. The flames, impeded by the dampness of the wood, had consumed only the back corner of the hut and the men rushed in. Gretje lay on the earth floor near the door, her headless body bound by buckskin thongs. Her head was on the table propped against an iron skillet. Her hands had been cut off, and had vanished. Around each wrist stump had been tied a painted snakeskin such as the Indians used for girdles.

They had fled from that charnel hut, Daniel as shaken as Robert was, and run the rest of the way to Stamford village. There they had found Underhill inspecting the new house by the Rippowam which the Stamford men had started building for him.

And Underhill, thought Elizabeth, brash and cock-sure as always, had immediately given it as his opinion that Mianos and all the Siwanoys were on the rampage. He had with great difficulty been prevented by Patrick from a headlong attack on Mianos.

There had been high words between the two old comrades-at-arms; Daniel, losing his temper completely, had told Underhill to mind his own business, and ascertain a few facts before meddling in other folks' territory, and upsetting relationships precariously established while Underhill was still smugly repenting in Boston.

John Underhill, secure of backing from the admiring Stamford settlers who resented Greenwich's independence, retorted that Patrick had always been a contentious fool, and a sly Indian-lover to boot, and that it was a good thing that these far-off isolated English towns had now acquired a strong military leader to protect them.

"And that did it!" Daniel told Elizabeth when he recounted the day's events. " 'Oh no, Johnny, me lad—' I cried to him. 'Ye'll not captain it over me an' *my* lands, nor Robert Feake's neither!' Then an' there I made up me mind we'd go to the Dutch! An' told him so. Mad as a bull he was, and the Stamford men too. Ha!"

Elizabeth had ultimately agreed with Daniel, though Robert for some time had not. He had shown one of his mulish streaks, and for days kept repeating obstinately, "I am English. Bess is English, we cannot turn Dutch. It won't do. I'm going to put us under New Haven Colony."

"And answer to Stamford and Underhill for every breath we draw!" shouted Daniel. "Let alone those Puritans at New Haven! By God, Robert, ha'nt ye got your bellyful o' fines and restrictions, an' tithing men an' meetinghouses, an' sour slandering neighbors? Why else did ye come here? The Dutch leave a man be. I've lived wi' 'em, and I know."

"It's different for you, Dan," said Robert, shrinking from his friend ger but still persistent. "You're not really English, and Anneke's Dutch. But Bess and I aren't. Imagine what the Winthrops would say if we betook ourselves under the Dutch flag."

"A pox on the Winthrops!" Daniel roared. "And a pox on you for a faint lily-livered numbskull!" He had been swilling rum steadily since the day they found the Labdens, and his temper—never placid—was dangerous. His fist clenched, his red beard quivered, and Elizabeth, fearing he might hit Robert, had intervened hastily.

"The Dutch have the best claim to our land, husband. You *know* that. Remember Governor Kieft's stern letter! If we persist in denying them, it'll be worse for the English, might even start a war."

It was this argument which eventually wore down Robert's resistance, joined to his innate dependence on Elizabeth's judgment and his fear of Daniel's disapproval. Moreover, at this time he developed blinding headaches, and his night-mares returned. They did not seem to be based on the horror he had seen in the Labden hut, as might be supposed, but from his muttered cries at night, Elizabeth deduced that he was again bedeviled by the old mysterious trouble in London. During the last week she unwillingly recognized some signs of the "strangeness" which had been absent for two years, but ascribed this to the headaches for which she dosed him unavailingly with witch-hazel. When Toby's *Dolphin* yesterday entered the cove, and the expedition today had been decided, it was clear that Robert, though no longer opposed, was not well enough to go. He had been wan and moaning with headache at dawn today when they sailed off towards New Amsterdam. Anneke and Joan were tending him, and caring for the younger children.

"Sit down i' the bilges! Hold fast, and keep outa my way!" suddenly commanded Toby, tightening sail and pushing the tiller hard over. "Ben, watch it!" he called to the bow. Elizabeth crouched, holding on to the combing, but Daniel said sharply, "What for?"

"Hell Gate," said Toby. "Fall overboard then, if you wish."

Daniel looked ahead at a narrow stretch of boiling waters, where a small Dutch sloop was pitching and churning violently, while the skipper with a steering oar tried to free his craft from a whirlpool. Daniel sat down in the bilges. "Do we have to go through *that?*" he called to Toby, who did not bother to answer but plunged into the roaring rapids cannily steering close to a large rounded point on the Long Island shore, where the current ran freer. The *Dolphin* grazed a hidden rock, then shot through the tide-rip like an arrow, and settled down in quieter waters near a long splinter of an island where swine were grazing.

"Good for you, Toby!" cried Elizabeth, exhilarated. "No wonder 'tis called Hell Gate. And what a fine sailor you are!"

"Chancy run-through at this tide, couldn't a done it later—" said Toby, his heavy freckled face indicating recognition of Elizabeth's compliment. "Now we'll soon be to the Fort," he added with satisfaction. Toby approved of this mission. He liked the Dutch and enjoyed himself at New

Amsterdam. They had a dozen taprooms, overflowing with rich food and a variety of potent liquors. Also most of the mynheers were easygoing and liberal with their guilders. They'd buy all the beaver and otter pelts Toby could pick up, and pay well besides for messenger service between the Long Island settlements and Manhattan. There had, however, been some recent awkwardness since Director General Kieft had demanded the submission of the Feakes, and had his request ignored. Toby had found his New Netherland markets shutting against him. On his last visit the schout, or sheriff, had rescinded his trader's license and warned him away from the Fort until the matter of his uncle's allegiance should be settled. So Toby had needed no inducement to make this trip.

As they skimmed down the East River and neared Manhattan's tip, the water traffic thickened. They passed Indian dugouts with pointed stern and bow, heavier built than the New England canoes. The paddling Indians, clothed in wildcat and wolfskins, with lopsided hair arrangements, also looked different. "Hackensacks, Raritans, or mebbe Mohawks from way up the North River," said Toby indifferently in answer to Elizabeth's question. "There's a ship in from Holland!" he added pointing. "My pelts'll fetch a good price soon as you and Patrick've cleared us."

So filled was the harbor with shipping—sloops, yachts, canoes, shallops and barges—that at first Elizabeth did not see the great high-pooped West Indiaman, riding at anchor near the Breucklen shore. When she did, she looked from its ensign to the larger counterpart on the Fort's flagstaff, a piece of cloth with horizontal red, white and blue stripes fluttering in the breeze.

Elizabeth, accustomed to the English cross of St. George, thought that this neat tricolor did not look like a flag at all, and was dismayed. Oh, what are we doing! she thought. And to Daniel she cried sharply, "I think we must be mad! We can't give Greenwich to Holland. Robert was right. Let's go back!"

The two men stared at her in astonishment. Toby shrugged and steered for the landing. Daniel said soothingly, "Me dear girl, ye're talking nonsense. 'Tis late days fur patriotic qualms. What's more, we can't help ourselves. Can't go it alone in case o' trouble."

The Indians again, Elizabeth thought, annoyed. Daniel had changed, grown jumpy and crotchety as an old woman. It was the drink perhaps. She knew Anneke was worried.

"Bess," said Daniel, watching her. "Stop sitting there all broody. We'll have no chopping an' changing now. Ye're a smart woman, and used to your own way, but ye ha'nt allus got good sense and ye'll take orders for once."

Elizabeth's rebellion was soon quenched by self-doubt, and the realization that even did she change her mind, there was little she could do. Daniel had Robert's signed authorization in his knapsack.

"Aye, perhaps you're right," she said at last.

New Amsterdam was a quaint colorful town dominated by the peculiar many-angled earthen fort and a windmill. Strung along the shore, outside the fort, were fifty little bouweries, plots of land each with a house, topped by a steep-pitched roof sparkling with red tiles. The houses were enclosed by picket fences and gardens already bright with daffodils and early tulips. In every window there were starched white curtains. Despite the noisy chickens and pigs rooting in the swill which had been dumped in the dusty streets, the little town gave an impression of cleanliness and gaiety. Elizabeth's spirits rose, for there was much to look at.

On their walk from the landing place to the new City Tavern, which Kieft had erected for the reception of strangers, they met a motley assortment—working folk bunchily clad in vivid linsey-woolseys clomped along in wooden shoes, and a fat mounted burgomaster rode by in a richness of fur, plumed hat and big lace ruff such as she hadn't seen since London. His wife ambled beside him looking placid and prosperous in an otter-trimmed gown and velvet cap edged with tiny pearls. But New Amsterdam was a cosmopolitan town and transiently contained many nationalities.

They met two Spanish sailors with scarlet bandannas and gold earrings, and an Angol slave, his sleek black body barely covered by a white cotton shift, and then they saw a Jesuit priest solemnly walking from the Tavern, his missal open in his hand, a brass crucifix around his neck.

"Will ye look at that!" Patrick cried, pointing to the priest. "Free as air, an' nobody hindering him."

"What *is* he?" asked Elizabeth, staring at the long black robes and the tonsure.

"What I ha'nt seen in donkey's years," said Daniel, rushing up to the priest, while Elizabeth stopped in surprise, though Toby walked on. "Father, Father—will ye gi' me a blessing?"

cried Daniel to the priest, sweeping off his helmet and looking humble for the first time in Elizabeth's knowledge.

The Jesuit raised his head and smiled. "You are Catholique?" he said gently in a strong French accent, and at
Daniel's somewhat shamefaced nod the priest raised two
fingers and made the sign of the cross. "Que Dieu vous
bénisse," he said, and bending his head continued to read his
missal.

"Where do ye lodge, Father——" said Daniel, urgently
following the priest. "Might it be that you'd hear me confession?"

The Jesuit looked up again, his wise eyes searching the
rugged red-bearded face. "If you wish, my son," he said. "I
lodge at the Tavern, until I go to my mission with the
Iroquois."

"*Mass,* Father?" asked Daniel below his breath.

The priest inclined his head. "Each morning in my attic
chamber."

Freethinker though she felt herself to be, Elizabeth was
shocked, while the horrified epithets, "Anti-Christ," "Roman
lewdness," "Scarlet idolatry" echoed through her mind in
Winthrop's voice.

Daniel, still looking humble, shamefaced, and yet happy,
gave her a keen look as he returned to her. "Well, ye knew
I'd been a Papist, me dear——" he said with a lopsided smile.

"But not for many years," she answered uncertainly. "And
confession; Mass; a priest, all that—why I never thought it
of you, Dan."

"Nor I," he agreed. "It come over me, when I saw the
good Father. I don't know the state o' me soul, except 'tis
bad. Should I die sudden, at least I'll be shriven once again,
and had the sacrament."

Elizabeth shook her head. "'Tis my turn to say *you're*
talking nonsense. You won't die. And all that claptrap surely
wouldn't help you!"

Patrick stopped dead on the street. "Bess, you're a fool!"
he exploded. "A meddlesome stiff-necked Puritan fool!" He
cried so loud that a white-capped woman leaned out of a
nearby window, and a small boy in sabots turned and
giggled. Elizabeth caught her breath and walked on quickly.
Never before had Daniel glared at her with resentment.

"Don't let's quarrel, Dan," she said at length, trying to
steady her voice. "I'm sorry I said anything."

The throbbing in Patrick's head subsided. He walked beside her in silence until they came to the new stone building which was called the City Tavern.

"I need another drink," he said in semi-apology. "Some o' the fair an' fiery white genever I used to relish in Holland."

Daniel did not however get drunk that night. He sought out the priest, made his confession and received absolution. At dawn he attended Mass with the Spanish sailors and a trader from New France. Elizabeth went to bed early, in a room she shared with two other women, a mevrouw from up the Great North River at Rennselaerswyck, and a Bermudian gentlewoman en route to Virginia.

The next morning, which was Saturday, an ensign called Gysbert deLeeuw summoned the Greenwich proprietors and escorted them to the Director General of the New Netherlands. Kieft lived in an imposing brick mansion inside the Fort, next to the new church which was but half built. The pounding of sledgehammers and the shouts of workmen in both Dutch and English came through the open windows and accompanied the ceremony in which Greenwich was transferred.

William Kieft was a small fat man like a skittle ball. In a carved thronelike chair, he perched upon two red velvet cushions so that his head might be higher than his associates who were ranged on either side of a long table. Ensign deLeeuw ushered Daniel and Elizabeth into the wainscoted room. Elizabeth who was very nervous stumbled over the edge of the Turkey carpet and, clumsy with pregnancy, would have fallen—except that a tall thin young man jumped up from the end of the table and caught her. "Careful there!" he said smiling. "Can't have you plunging headlong into patroonship!" He looked down admiringly at her embarrassed face.

"You speak English!" she cried in relief, trying to hide her swollen body under her cloak, for she saw all the Dutch eyes fixed on her.

"I *am* English," replied the tall man. "George Baxter, English secretary to the Director General. You're Mrs. Feake?" As she nodded, he continued, "This is Mr. Feake?"

"No. My husband is ill. This is Captain Patrick . . . I came in my husband's stead."

George Baxter turning to Kieft translated this. The Governor frowned. He smoothed the gilded plumes on his beaver hat. He drummed his fingers on his neat little paunch. He made small explosive remarks to a grave Frenchman who sat beside him.

"I've brought Mr. Feake's authorization, Your High Mightiness," said Daniel, and as Baxter started to translate, Daniel interrupted. "Don't bother, thankye, I can do it meself." And he began to address the Governor in halting but obvious persuasive Dutch.

Baxter motioned Elizabeth to a chair beside his own. "Do sit down, Madam," he said low behind his hand. "This'll take a while. Kieft's a fusser. Doesn't think fast. He expected Mr. Feake."

"They won't refuse us now?" she whispered, suddenly anxious.

"Oh no," said the secretary. "And 'tis not a matter of 'they' anyhow."

Baxter glanced at the faces around the council table. Van der Huyskens the Fiscal, Cornelis van Tienhoven the secretary, Dominie Everard Bogardus the pastor, Ensign Van Dyke the incompetent head of the militia, Doctor de la Montagne the councilor. Not one of them save de la Montagne could influence Kieft, and he seldom. The pompous little ass'll ruin us with his stupidities, Baxter thought, but he pays me well. The secretary, seeing that Elizabeth was looking at him expectantly, went on with a smile.

"Kieft does as he pleases, only other person with a vote is his councilor there, Jan de la Montagne, French Huguenot he is, able man—physician and soldier both. But even *he* can't stop Kieft, once he's made up his mind."

"Stop him from what?" she asked, feeling more at ease, and glad to find so nice an Englishman in this alien place.

"From anything. But it's the Indians that concern us right now. Kieft's heading for trouble. Bullying and oppressing our Manhattans, other tribes too. He'll get us massacred yet." He checked himself, aware that the pastor, Bogardus, was staring at him and that he was talking too freely to this pretty woman. "Ah," he said—"see, the Director General is nodding. Your business is settled!"

"Baxter! Winkelman!" called out Kieft in his guttural, rasping voice. The English secretary and Dutch clerk both sprang to their feet. Kieft waved his pudgy hand towards paper, inkhorns and pens which were set out in readiness. The two men sat down again and began to write at the Governor's dictation.

Daniel came over and stood by Elizabeth. "All done," he said putting his hand on her shoulder.

"What does the document say?" she asked in a low voice. "What's all that Dutch mean?"

"Here, Madam," said Baxter, sliding the English translation over to her. "'Tis fairly put and you'll not regret it."

Elizabeth glanced down and read:

> *Whereas we, Captain Daniel Patterick and Elizabeth Feac, duly authorized by her husband Robert Feac, now sick, have resided two years about five or six leagues east of the Netherlanders, subjects of the Lords States-General who have protested against us declaring that the said lands lay within their limits . . . and whereas we understand nothing about the matter and can not any longer presume to remain thus on account both of the strifes of the English and these treacherous and villainous Indians, of whom we have seen horrible examples enough . . .*

Elizabeth paused and raised her eyes to Daniel, and he interpreting her look, said, "I know, me dear. Ye still don't think us in any danger from the Indians, mebbe we're not, but ye didn't hear what His High Mightiness's been saying. There's been murder down here too—an old cartwright chopped to bits, and other outrages in Haverstraw."

"At least you can't blame our Siwanoys for those," said Elizabeth, and returned to the document.

> *We therefore betake ourselves under the protection of the noble Lords, the States, his Highness the Prince of Orange, and the West India Company or their Governor General of New Netherland, promising for the future to be faithful to them as all honest subjects are bound to be, whereunto we bind ourselves by oath and by signature, provided we be protected against our enemies as much as possible and enjoy henceforth the same privileges that all Patroons of New Netherland have obtained . . . This done and signed in the presence of the underwritten witnesses, the lxth of April, 1642.*

Even while she finished the English translation Daniel signed his name to the Dutch paper, and the witnesses—being the two men nearest at hand—were the purple-nosed

Dominie, Everard Bogardus, and the little Dutch clerk, Johannes Winkelman.

"I needn't sign?" asked Elizabeth slowly.

Baxter translated this to the Governor, who shrugged, waggled his fingers jocularly at Elizabeth, winked, and said "Kus! Kus!" amongst other sallies which provoked van Tienhoven to a lewd guffaw. Daniel and Baxter chuckled too, and the latter said, "You don't sign, you're only a woman. But the Director says you must now kiss the flag for yourself and husband and then you may kiss him!"

"Indeed," said Elizabeth after a moment. She lifted her chin and watched while Daniel performed the ceremony of allegiance. And what is it to him? she thought. A rough soldier, a Papist who's served under the Dutch flag before, and to begin with was an Irishman. She saw Patrick suddenly through Winthrop's eyes, and shame flooded her at this association.

"Now you, Bess," Daniel said coming back to her. " 'Tis just a matter o' form."

As she did not move, he cried, "Holy Mary! Ye can't back out now! Think o' Robert and the children. Think of Anneke. And ye've given your *word* on the document."

She bit her lips, hesitating. All the men were staring at her, Kieft's piggy eyes glared down the table, hard, unwinking.

"It would not be wise to anger the Director General, Madam—" said Baxter softly, and sympathetically. His quiet English voice pierced her defiance.

"No—" she whispered. "And I've given my word."

She rose and walked down the room towards the flag which was displayed on the wall behind the Governor's chair. She bent near it, but did not touch it with her lips. She then went towards Kieft and made to kiss his hand as Daniel had done, but the Governor, chuckling, grabbed the neck of her gown and jerking her head down, gave her a great smack on the mouth. "Kus! Kus!" he cried, and pinched her on the buttock, while the men all roared.

Foul little dandiprat, Elizabeth thought, but she managed to smile. Kieft burst into a torrent of Dutch, and stood up; his hat barely clearing the table.

"He's pleased wi' ye, lovey—" said Daniel, much relieved. "Thinks ye're a beauty, and wants us to dine with him. Come along!"

The newly made Dutch subjects spent the afternoon in

feasting. Elizabeth ate what she could of the "Hutsepot" or stew, the capons, oysters, freshly caught shad, crullers, waffles and gingerbread. She drank strong Rhine wine from the ritual "clover-leaf" goblets, toasting at the Governor's command all the good things that come in threes. The Trinity, the Three Graces, the Three riddles, the Three betrothal kisses. She listened to innumerable Dutch oaths of which "Verdomme!" soon became familiar. When the Director roared for his gaming cup, she obediently cast the dice for him, and herself befuddled with excitement, and wine, watched uncaring while the men gambled with stivers, or the white and purple wampum beads they called "seawant."

It was the Sabbath Eve before Kieft rose from his table and she assumed that, especially since Dominie Bogardus was present, decorum would now return, and the Sabbath quiet begin. She was quite wrong. Kieft, being unable to get an arm around her thickened waist, hung on to her elbow and tottered with her out of his house into the Fort. The other men followed, and as soon as they reached the village street a group of giggling girls erupted from a taproom and joined them.

"Where are we going?" said Elizabeth crossly to Daniel who didn't hear her, for he was singing, "Titty cum tawty the duck's in the water, Titty cum tawty the geese follow a'ter," at the top of his lungs.

George Baxter answered her somewhat thickly. "Why, to play skittles at the Tavern, His Excellency always does on Saturday night!"

"Does he so?" said Elizabeth. "And what does he do on the Sabbath?"

"Why, he plays skittles," said the young man, surprised. "Or no, I think tomorrow there's a cockfight."

Elizabeth looked behind her at the pastor. One of the girls had hold of his white Geneva bands and was playfully tugging at them while Bogardus smirked down at her amorously.

"Oh Lud," said Elizabeth, and suddenly burst into hysterical laughter.

"Vat ist? Mevrouw. Vat ist?" said Kieft peering up at her. Baxter too stared at her in astonishment. Elizabeth could not stop laughing, until Daniel noting the commotion ran up. "Bess, what ails ye? Too much wine?"

"Nay—" she said between gasps. "I was thinking of Boston. I was thinking of my Uncle John's face if he could see us now!"

"Oh-ho!" said Daniel kindly enough though his wits were slowed by drink. "Your High Mightiness, she thinks of her uncle, Mr. Winthrop, that was Governor of Massachusetts," he explained to Kieft, who was pleased. One of the English governors was naturally not nearly so important a man as the Netherland's Director General; still it was agreeable to have lured away a lady of high birth from the arrogant English. The High and Mighty Lords of the States General at home would be delighted when they heard. Nor, thought Kieft, was this the only Jonkvrouw to repudiate the English in favor of the felicities bestowed by New Netherlands. "Baxter!" he called suddenly, releasing Elizabeth's elbow. The young secretary hurried up to him.

"Aye, Your Excellency?" Baxter listened to the Governor and translated to Elizabeth. "Two other English ladies have written for permission to settle on Dutch land. He asks if you know them. One is the Lady Deborah Moody from Salem. She is an Anabaptist, I believe—been banished from the Bay."

"Why, no—" said Elizabeth, mildly interested. "At least, in London years ago she bought physic at our apothecary shop, but I never met her. Who's the other one?"

"Mistress Anne Hutchinson," said Baxter a trifle ruefully. "Quite notorious, I gather, also a religious fanatic. But I will say for the Governor he accepts any creed here, so long as they make responsible settlers."

Elizabeth had not heard the last of his remarks. "Mrs. Hutchinson," she repeated with wonder. "Aye, I know her. Is she leaving Rhode Island? I'd dearly love to see her again."

"Well, you may, no doubt," said Baxter. "Her husband's died and she plans to move all her family to a bouwery called Vredeland. 'Tis on the mainland about twenty miles from Greenwich."

Kieft interrupted impatiently, wanting to know what Elizabeth was saying. Baxter explained that Mrs. Feake knew both the English ladies, and tactfully added that she said they would be a great credit to the Dutch. Elizabeth was deeply comforted. All her remaining doubts were laid by the knowledge that Anne Hutchinson herself was not scrupling to change allegiance. Elizabeth gave the Director General her most beautiful and dazzling smile.

After that, he redoubled his attentions, commandeered the whole taproom at the City Tavern, and invited most of the

Tavern's heterogeneous guests to an open house in honor of Greenwich's new patroons.

Elizabeth did not escape until midnight, and by that time jollity had given away to snores and stupor. There had been trouble earlier when a fight arose between Daniel and a Dutch soldier named Jan Blauvelt. Elizabeth, half dead from weariness, did not see what was happening until she heard Daniel roaring out Gaelic battle cries, and saw him pitching and weaving, his great fists thudding against Blauvelt's portly person. The Dutchman's nose was dripping blood all over the sanded floor, but he seemed to be giving as good as he got.

"Oh, stop them—" cried Elizabeth. Nobody paid attention until the Director aroused himself, stared at the two battling men, and called out, "Halt!" The officers Van Dyke and deLeeuw obeyed their Governor's command, and separated the combatants.

"Let me at him!" Daniel panted, striving to free himself. "Lemme at that bastard! I'll teach him a lesson *this* time!" He gave the officers a mighty shove, and plunged towards his opponent.

"My son! My son!" said a clear voice from the doorway. "Is this the way you show penitence? Encore des péchés?"

The Jesuit priest walked slowly through the crowd, and laid his hand on Daniel's shoulder. To Elizabeth's amazement the big Irishman heeded the touch. He stepped back, while Blauvelt collapsed on a bench, spitting out a tooth and holding a wadded napkin to his streaming nose. Blauvelt seemed utterly defeated but Elizabeth happened to see the look he sent Daniel through puffy, discolored lids. It was a glare of purest hatred, malignant as a serpent's. Shocked, she turned quickly towards Daniel and the priest.

"He's an old enemy, Father," mumbled Daniel, staring at the floor. "Did me dirty at The Hague once, long ago. Told lies about me to me general, was jealous o' me advancement."

"That makes no difference, my son," said the priest with a faint compassionate smile. "Now go to your bed. You are very drunk."

The Hollanders intently watched this scene, disappointed that the fight had not been resolved. Elizabeth and Kieft alone were relieved, though the Governor's intervention had sprung from no objection to anything so natural as fighting, but from a point of etiquette. A patroon of New Netherlands must not demean himself by fisticuffs with a common soldier. His Excellency gulped down a few more swallows of wine, stroked Elizabeth's cheek, then put his head down on his arms and went back to sleep.

On Tuesday morning, Toby, Daniel and Elizabeth finally sailed home to Greenwich. Toby had refused to leave until he had sold his pelts and taken aboard a cargo of spirits, spices and squealing piglets, the latter having been specially commissioned by New Haven.

Daniel was in a fine contented mood. He had drunk very little since Saturday night and was pleased with all that had happened on the expedition to New Amsterdam; especially by his encounter with the priest. Daniel had been to Mass again each morning and held long converse with the Jesuit. Besides that he had won six fathoms of seawant in an archery contest Sunday.

"Ye know—Bess," he said as the shallop again sailed past Flushing, "those Nederlanders're a fine merry lot. I'm glad we joined 'em. Only thing I regret is not having knocked that ugly Blauvelt's face in fur him afore the Father stopped me. But now I've vowed not to."

"Promised the priest?" she said slowly, remembering the vicious look in Blauvelt's eyes. "And you'll keep it?"

"To be sure—" said Daniel. "Wi' the Blessed Virgin's help. I'll try to love me enemies." He gave her a quick, boyish grin.

Elizabeth was touched and puzzled. No longer vexed with Daniel, or shocked by the Romanism which had caught her unawares, she was able to appreciate this new facet of his nature which she had always thought as fundamentally irreligious as her own. She could not conceive of finding comfort in papacy herself, but she now had a moment of wistful recognition that it would be sustaining to believe in *something*, and she thought with far-off poignancy of Anne Hutchinson.

"D'you know where Vredeland is?" she asked Toby. "Mr. Baxter said the Hutchinsons would settle there soon."

"Somewhere up yonder," said Toby waving towards the Mainland, north of them. "Nobody there yet but the Weck-quasageek tribe."

"Vrede means 'Peace,'" said Daniel thoughtfully. "Hope the poor woman finds it at last, she's been hunted plenty from pillar to post."

"Aye," said Elizabeth. "Peace for her and for us, I believe. Don't you feel it, Dan?" She thought of Monakewaygo, her beloved island of retreat. Tomorrow I'll go there, she thought, just for a little while. I'll take the children. We can eat on the sands. We'll be happy.

Daniel crossed his legs, and the wind having died, pulled pipe, tobacco and tinderbox from his pouch. He lit his pipe and answered Elizabeth. "I believe ye're right, me dear. Till now I've been overfull o' frettings and foreboding. 'Tis gone. D'ye know—" He leaned nearer so that Toby wouldn't hear. "Ever sense finding those wretched Laddins, God rest their souls, I've had a kind a feeling. Shivers down me backbone, as though 'twas waiting for an Indian tomahawk . . . Death—" he said, beneath his breath. "I could smell it, as me old grannie used ter say in Armagh . . . " He smoked hard for a moment while she looked at him with sympathy. "Well, i'faith!" he said, straightening up. " 'Tis not like Danny Patrick to be skeered o' Indians, an' me ditherings're over!"

"I'm glad," she said softly.

" 'Twill be good to be home," said Daniel. "Can't wait to see Anneke's face when she sees the lace coif I've brought her. 'Twas the costliest in New Amsterdam."

"I've a box o' ginger for her," announced Toby suddenly from the stern sheets. Daniel and Elizabeth turned and gaped at him. Toby had never been known to offer gifts. "Said she hankered for ginger," said Toby, with what would have seemed like confusion in a less stolid face, and he cut short Daniel's amused thanks by shouting to Ben, "Look sharp there, dunderhead! Can't ye see that clew's a-loosening?" The lad jumped, and Elizabeth laughed, wondering if Anneke was aware of her admirer, and reminding herself that though Toby often acted like a man of fifty, he was in fact scarce twenty-one.

In July, Elizabeth's fifth baby was born. It was a big boy, yet the birthing was so fast that Elizabeth barely got home from Monakewaygo, where she had gone to gather wild beach plums with the children. By the time Joan had fetched Anneke from the Patrick house, Elizabeth was lying on a hay-filled pallet in the kitchen, laughing, and with the baby beside her.

"Oh! Hemel, Bess," cried Anneke rushing over to the pallet. "You do not vait at all any more? You do all yourself like a squaw?" She picked up the baby in her plump cleanly hands, gave a cluck of approval, and said to Joan, "Soap and hot vater."

Joan, now a big girl of twelve, went to the kettle which hung from the lug pole, poured water into a pewter basin, and came back to Anneke. "Soap's all gone," she said help-lessly. "We've not tallow to make it. Perhaps Toby'll bring some from New Amsterdam."

"Och!" said Anneke laughing. "Vat sad huisvrouws you are here! Vell, then run back to my house and fetch some, Joan. And keep the other children out of here, until I clean Mama and the little brother."

Joan nodded docilely, but she did not go. She was a plain, brown child, and no longer bore the slightest resemblance to Harry. In fact, her lack of enterprise and general timidity reminded Elizabeth sometimes of Martha, but she had not Martha's flashes of winsome intuition.

"Shoo! Scat! Vy don't you go?" said Anneke in some surprise while straightening Elizabeth's coverlet.

"I don't know where to find the soap," said Joan, her stocky legs spread. "And Johnnie's naughty, jumping tussocks in the cove, getting all wet and splashing Lisbet who's crying. They won't mind me." The child waited again passively.

"Hemel!" cried Anneke in rare exasperation. "My soap is where it always is. In the vat in the lean-to. As for the children let them jump! Go!"

Joan obeyed with deliberation.

"Where's Hannah?" said Elizabeth faintly. The elation of birthing was leaving her, she felt weak and tired. "Call Hannah, Anneke. *She* can manage Johnnie. I don't want Lisbet to get wet, she takes cold so fast."

Anneke bent and kissed Elizabeth, pushing the sweaty hair off her forehead. "Ja," she said smiling. "Little Hannah is your right hand, isn't she? A good girl. Rest now, Bess. Go to sleep. I'll find Hannah."

Robert came back that evening to a tidy, contented house-hold. He greeted his new son with quiet pleasure so as not to disturb the drowsing Elizabeth. "Ah—Anneke—" he said, sitting down at the kitchen table and accepting a trencherful of the rabbit stew she had made. "What would we do with-out you? It was dreadful that year in Watertown, when you and Daniel were gone."

Anneke gave him a thoughtful look, while she scoured Elizabeth's pewter. "No headaches of late?" she asked.

"Bess's medicine helped? Now you will be able to see to the mowing of the south pasture yourself. The corn too must soon be brought in."

"I know," said Robert humbly. "So much to do, and in my bad times I can't seem to. But today—" he brightened. "I talked with Angell Husted, he wants to leave Stamford and come to us. I'm going to sell him land over on the sea. He has nobody but himself to look out for yet, and he said he'd help us with our crops."

"Good," said Anneke. "Since Jeffrey Ferris is gone, ve are so few here."

Ferris had protested the shift to Dutch allegiance, said he'd named the town "Greenwich" because he liked to be reminded of England, but that since his tiny holding obviously gave him no say against the main proprietors, he would withdraw before Greenwich was called by some outlandish Netherlands name. This view was expressed with a certain grim humor. Nevertheless he had barred the door of his little house on Totomack Creek, and gone back to Stamford where he owned ten acres.

"Richard Crab may come over to us too," said Robert eagerly. "I was talking to him outside Stamford Meetinghouse today. Crab, he wants more freedom than he gets in Stamford, doesn't like the minister either. I said we had good meadow lands to the west, we might sell to him."

"Och!" said Anneke smiling. "That Crab and his wife! Always quarreling. Daniel said he saw her throw a skillet at her goodman last month."

"Where is Dan?" asked Robert. "Has he seen my new son?"

"Nay. He and Danny are in the fields yet. It looks like rain tomorrow, they must hurry. You too, Robert," she said, thinking that a day in Stamford was all very well, and she was glad to see him take an interest in new settlers, but if the field work was not done soon, the Feakes would face another difficult winter in which they must depend on buying supplies in Stamford or New Amsterdam with their cash which she knew to be dwindling. "Dan cannot help you this year," she said. "Ve have so much to do on our own place. Before Angell Husted comes, maybe you should try to hire some of the Indians."

"Aye," said Robert, slowly. "I thought of that. I talked to the Tomacs on my way to Stamford. To Nawthorne."

He pushed back his trencher. His pale eyebrows knitted in their anxious frown.

The nearest Indian village, a collection of bark huts, lay at the head of Totomack Cove on the shore road to Stamford. It was a subdivision of the Siwanoy tribe and ruled by a chieftain called Nawthorne, who was answerable of course to Mianos. Last summer the Tomacs had been helpful to the Feakes and gathered most of their corn crop in exchange for a bushel of ears. Today, when Robert had entered the village, he had been received in silence. The squaws had not looked up from the deer hides they were tanning, Nawthorne had continued to chip at a flint arrowhead. It was hard to be sure that this discourtesy was intentional, because as soon as Robert had addressed the sachem, Nawthorne put down his arrowhead and said, "Good day, Mister," quite pleasantly.

The conversation, which proceeded by means of signs, Nawthorne's meager English, and Robert's four words of Algonkian, resulted in a bland refusal. Nawthorne stated that all his braves had gone out on a fishing expedition. They were unavailable. Neither could any squaw be spared. But, said Nawthorne, they could have Wasobibbi if they wanted, and the sachem burst into sly chuckles. Wasobibbi was Nawthorne's son and a half-wit. He was quiet and biddable but far less intelligent than one of the Indian's yellow curs—at last year's planting the Feakes had hired him unknowing and found that he dug up and ate the precious seed corn as fast as he planted it. Robert refused the offer of Wasobibbi.

"Something's changed them," said Robert, reporting this to Anneke. "I don't like the way Nawthorne acted, yet I'm not sure."

"The Tomacs vere never much good," said Anneke soothingly. "Do not fret. Ve vill ask Telaka ven she comes here again. She can get her father to send you some boys."

"Aye," said Robert, his face clearing. "I hadn't thought of that." He walked over to the pallet and looked down at his sleeping wife and baby with proud tenderness. Then he went into the other room where the children were sleeping. Through the open door Anneke could see him bend over and kiss them. He came back into the kitchen and opened his carved oak Bible box. He took out his Bible and began to read. Anneke, briskly scrubbing the trenchers with sand, glanced at Robert tolerantly. What if he were inept at chores, and of a womanish delicacy, what if he were sick and melancholy a great deal, still he was not a bad husband, and she could not believe the dark allusions Daniel sometimes made about him, even once a warning to Anneke, "There's a deal ye don't know about Robert, he's like a man groping blindfold on a stone wall. If anything should push him over, there'd be danger." All this the practical Anneke considered nonsense, just another of Daniel's wild fancies when he drank too much.

Little Robert Feake's birth was duly recorded by Toby on July 17 at New Amsterdam in the Book of Baptisms, though no official baptism had been performed yet. This might wait until the child was old enough to be taken to the capital, or until Bogardus or some other minister of the Reformed Church should happen through Greenwich. The permission had been accorded Elizabeth by Kieft during her visit to New Amsterdam, and was customarily given to settlers in far-flung parts of New Netherlands. The important thing was that the new subject should be registered as Dutch. Elizabeth thought this funny. "My little Dutchman," she called the baby. "Gobbles like one, anyway," and she amused herself by learning a Dutch lullaby to sing to him. The Feakes and Patricks seemed to have found the peace so confidently prophesied by Elizabeth. The harvest was excellent. And Telaka had duly brought some Indian boys to help the Englishmen in garnering it. These boys spoke no English, and as Telaka did not mention it, nobody knew that they were not Siwanoys but Rowaytons under the overlordship of Ponus. The Indians worked well, and soon the Feake shed was overflowing with corn and beans and the great round golden pompions. They had no apples yet, but there were plenty of wild grapes on Monakewaygo. During many of the crisp blue-and-gold autumn days, Elizabeth's conscience permitted her to escape from the house and ramble over her own beautiful property gathering grapes and the odd little grayish bayberries which they would melt down into fragrant candle wax during the winter nights ahead.

Robert remained well, the children throve and the two families enjoyed several festivities together. Anneke celebrated St. Nicholas' Eve, and baked "Sinter Klaas" cakes. She told the children the legend of the saint and how he would come down the chimney in the night, then she secretly filled all the little shoes with raisins and tiny whittled puppets. In return Elizabeth celebrated Christmas with a wassail bowl, carol-singing and a great feast gratefully provided by Telaka's brother Keofferam.

They had seen nothing of Keofferam that autumn, until one day in November he had come limping through the snow to the Feake house with Telaka. Elizabeth who was husking corn by her kitchen window had seen the two Indians approach. They seemed to be arguing, Keofferam shaking his head and his sister clutching at his arm as though to force him on.

Elizabeth opened her door and called a welcome. "Come in. Come in. 'Tis long since I've seen you both." She noted that Keofferam who was short and had been stoutish for an Indian had lost much weight. That his eyes glittered as though with fever, and that his cinnamon-colored skin was flushed, though it was hard to tell beneath the tattooings.

"He is sick," said Telaka, pushing her brother into the house. "Powwows not cure. Shaman not cure. Plants I give not cure. Chekafuana tell me to bring him to you. He not want to."

"But, of course," said Elizabeth, smiling reassurance to the Indians. "You knew I'd help if I could, Keofferam. We're friends, aren't we? Netops?"

The young Indian gnawed his lip, then looked away. "Netop," he finally agreed, very low. He dropped his turkey-feather mantle on the floor and stood naked but for his breechclout. On Keofferam's right thigh was an enormous fiery purple abscess, big as a porringer, and under the dark skin red streaks ran up into the groin. Elizabeth was dismayed. Once or twice she had treated cankers, but nothing like this. She saw Telaka's eye fixed on her trustfully, and she tried to look confident. "Wait," she said, and went to her bride chest which Toby had brought on his last trip back to Watertown. She got out her Father's old Apothecary Book and the chirurgery box with its lancets and nearly empty salve pots.

She read the section of the book which treated of "Cancers, cankers, Chancres." She felt the abscess gingerly while Keofferam stood unwincing. The top yielded a trifle though the rest of the huge hot scarlet cone was hard as wood. "Tell him I shall cut it," she said to Telaka, her heart beating fast. She seized a lancet but it was thick with rust. Keofferam, watching, silently, proffered his hunting knife, and giving herself no time to think, Elizabeth jabbed the point deep into the abscess. Yellow pus spurted out a foot and spattered on the floor planks. "Aieyeh!" said Keofferam in amazement. He looked down at his thigh. "He says feels better," said Telaka.

"Well," answered Elizabeth with a shaky laugh. "You must pray to your Manitoo it stays better, because I'm not at all sure."

Keofferam however gradually healed. He lay at the Feakes' several days while Elizabeth poulticed the wound with red couperus and marigold salve. As she nursed him she grew quite fond of him. And for the Christmas feast he repaid her care with the gift of a whole deer, already dressed and cut into venison as he knew the English liked it. He also brought them two great turkeys and a wild swan, drank beer with them and, smiling, said "Merry Christmas" when little Hannah asked him to. Elizabeth was certain of his good will. Yet as the winter months went by they did not see him or Telaka again.

The snows fell thick that February, the wolves howled in the forest near the ruins of Labden's hut, and everyone must stay in after dark for fear of them. But it was snug enough at home. Driftwood and hickory fires roared up the great chimney, while ice cracked in the cove and the sullen gray winter breakers beat on the snow-blanketed sands of Monakewaygo.

In the first week of March there was a thaw and Daniel set out for Stamford to buy gunpowder. He had shot so many wolves, foxes and an occasional bear during the winter that his stock was low.

He came back the next day and rushed to the Feake house where the entire family was dipping candles.

"Harkye, Rob and Bess—" he said plunging in his haste through the dripping wicks and nearly upsetting the dipping pot. "What d'ye think I heard in Stamford? That damn fool Kieft, that wicked puddingheaded bastard—what d'ye think he's done!"

"What, Dan?" said Robert carefully picking up the wet half-formed candles.

"He's murdered near two hundred Indians in cold blood. That's what he's done. Let 'em all run to him for protection from the Mohawks, waited till they slept, then turned out his soldiery and butchered all the poor devils."

"Dreadful," said Robert whose apprehensions were seldom

roused by occurrences which shocked others, but only by secret workings in his own mind. "Why did he do that? Must've had a reason. They were his own Manhattan and North River tribes, I suppose."

"Aye," said Daniel angrily, sitting down on the settle. "Does that make it better? His reason was revenge, 'cause the Hackensacks wouldn't give up the young buck who revenged his father's death by murdering Claes the wheelwright last year. So Kieft massacres a whole lot a innocents who never heard o' Claes. I think he's gone mad."

"Mr. Baxter seemed to fear something like this last spring," said Elizabeth slowly. "What does it mean, Dan? What will happen?"

"Indian war's what'll happen," said Patrick, scowling at the hearth. "No human being, white or red-skinned, is going to lie tame and quiet under a slaughter like that. We can only hope the trouble stays within the tribes that were outraged."

"Oh, no doubt it will," said Robert. "We're in no danger anyway. I thought Nawthorne was acting peculiar last summer, but I met him over by the South Rig yesterday and he was all smiles. Forced a present on me. I have it someplace." He walked to his knapsack which hung on a peg near the oak dresser and extracted a circlet made of small bones pierced and strung up a buckskin thong. " 'Tis a necklace, perhaps," he said. "Lisbet, would you like it?"

"Aye indeed, Papa—" cried the child, running to her father, her silvery hair flying, her pale little face that was so like Robert's eager for his recognition. As he tied the circlet around her neck, Elizabeth suddenly cried, "Don't! Don't! Don't let her wear it!"

"Why ever not, wife?" said Robert. "She has few toys."

"I don't know why not," answered Elizabeth after a moment. "I had a sudden queasiness, Dan—" she said, turning to him. "From whom did you hear all this shocking news?"

"From Underhill," he said bitterly. "He hopes there'll *be* Indian fighting—gi' him a chance for glory, no doubt. He'll not stay quiet at Stamford long, no matter what, ye can be sure of that."

16

THAT YEAR of 1643 was known thereafter in New Netherlands as the "Year of Blood." The fears of all those who had tried to dissuade Kieft from his insane Indian policy were immediately realized. All the tribes around Manhattan went on the warpath, and avenged Kieft's slaughter of the harmless Indians who had fled to his protection in Pavonia and at Corlear's Hook. By April, thirty of the Dutch had been tomahawked, and terror stalked New Amsterdam. Kieft hastily strengthened the Fort. He sent for soldiers from Curaçao to reinforce his militia. He ordered detachments to make raids in all directions—on Long Island, along the North River, and even into Siwanoy country. Most of these raids were futile. A few Indians killed, a few captured. And the war went on.

Then Roger Williams arrived in New Amsterdam to embark for Old England on Rhode Island affairs. Williams summoned the nearby sachems to a parley, and such was his reputation amongst all the tribes, and so great were his powers of persuasion, that he effected a truce. He sailed for England with a calm heart. But his influence soon faded as the Director General's stupidities continued.

In Greenwich, until August, there was quiet. News of the

dire happenings around Manhattan was incomplete and late
in coming. Toby was away on an extended trading trip up
the Connecticut River, so Greenwich had no direct contact
with New Amsterdam. They depended on what filtered
through Stamford, and eventually heard about the truce,
which much relieved the Feakes and Patricks. There had
been some disquieting little changes in the Siwanoy routine.
The main tribe had not gone to the fishing camp on Monakewaygo this spring as it always did. But Telaka who reappeared one day in May explained this, and also explained
her long absence. She said that Mayn Mianos had decided
to fish on a neck called Byram this year, that the Siwanoys
had been over there some time, and the distance was so
great that it had been hard to come and see Elizabeth. Telaka
brought some fine moccasins as gifts for the children, but
she seemed hurried and nervous. She stayed but a few
minutes, refused food, and while taking her leave, acted very
strange.

Lisbet was playing as she often did with the bone circlet
Nawthorne had given Robert, and Telaka, suddenly seeing
it, recoiled, then snatched it from the girl's hand.

"Where you get this?" she cried to Elizabeth, who explained.

"Hobbomock, Hobbomock," whispered the squaw flinging
the circlet on the floor. Elizabeth's heart thumped. She knew
that Hobbomock was the evil spirit all the Indians dreaded,
but it was the shaking of Telaka's hands and the anguished
tone of her voice that shocked Elizabeth.

"What do you mean, Telaka?" she cried.

The squaw recovered herself. She picked up the bones.
"I take and throw in sea," she sighed. "No good for you."

And to all Elizabeth's questions she would answer nothing
more. Her eye had become veiled and impassive. She
hastened away.

By the first of August, Toby returned to the cove with
the *Dolphin* and young Ben Palmer. The shallop had sprung
a leak on the trip down from Connecticut, and Toby laid
her up in the cove for repairs. While he was about it he
decided to get himself a new mast. He had seen, to the north,
trees of just the proper straight white pine growing near the
western bank of the Mianus, some two miles across the
river from the Siwanoy fort, Petuquapan. Toby and Ben
several times explored the pine forest hunting for the best
mast tree. On one of these trips, as the young men beat

their way through underbrush back to the trail, Toby tripped over a rotting stag's head. Cursing, he looked down and saw that the stag's head was propped by stones on a mound and that some very fine beaver pelts hung from its antlers. Next to the stag's head was a clay pot full of red and blue corn. "Indian claptrap," said Toby, but the pelts were exceptionally lustrous, and doing nobody any good. He gathered them up and hung them on his belt, kicked the stag's head which rolled off the mound upsetting the pot of corn, and went back to the trail unaware that somber eyes were watching him, as they had been for days.

The next morning, by arrangement, Daniel joined Toby and Ben, and they all set out for the pine forest where Toby had blazed the tree he wanted. Daniel took his loaded carbine with a view to supplementing Anneke's larder, the two younger men carried axes.

It was a soft gray foggy day, a welcome break after a hot spell, and Elizabeth profited by the coolness to work in her garden, while the baby crawled on the grass beside her. Robert had taken Johnny with him and gone to join Angell Husted in the mowing of the east pasture. Joan and Lisbet were leading the Feake cow to good grazing near Asamuck brook. Hannah was her mother's helper in the garden. The only one of the children who showed an instinctive love of flowers and herbs, thought Elizabeth fondly, watching the little red-gold head bend over the sage plot, and the chubby fingers loosen and pat the earth as deftly as she could have done herself.

"Thou'rt a sweet poppet—" Elizabeth said, giving Hannah a hug. "And a hard worker. Rest a moment, and I'll show thee a game I used to play in Suffolk."

The child laughed, nestling against her mother. She loved the rare times when Elizabeth would talk about the far-away country across the sea which to Hannah sounded all flowery-golden and full of magic. "Tell about the day you met the King and Queen, Mama!" said the child eagerly. "Or the day you were wicked and danced around the Maypole!"

"Not now, pet." Elizabeth scooped up the baby who was trying to cram a large dirty stone in his mouth. "Here, look!" She picked a fox-glove, and pulling off the crimson bells, put one on each of the delighted Hannah's fingers as a cap. "Now you've ten little elves, and they talk to each other like this. Right thumb speaks first, bowing—'Innikin, Minnikin, where's my wand?'"

"Innikin, Minnikin—" began Hannah, when they were interrupted by the barks of their sheepdog.

"Now who could that be?" said Elizabeth. Evidently not a stranger since the dog stopped barking. In a moment Telaka came around the corner of the house. Her entire face, both the whole and the ravaged side, was painted with long black stripes. Black was for mourning, Elizabeth knew, and she hurried up to the squaw anxiously. "Oh, Telaka, what's happened?"

"Send inside," said Telaka indicating the children. "Speak alone."

Elizabeth saw both great urgency and fear in Telaka's manner. The squaw kept glancing back over her shoulder. Elizabeth sent the children to the house and said, "What is it? What's wrong?"

Telaka took her by the arm and pulled her down the rise to the edge of the cove; again she peered this way and that way through the mists. "Missis—where Toby Feake and Ben?" she asked in a harsh whisper.

"Why, they went with Captain Patrick long ago up north into the forest for a mast."

"Gone," said Telaka in a heavy hopeless voice. "Then they are dead."

Elizabeth stared through the drifting mist, uncertain what she heard.

"Mayn Mianos, my father—" said Telaka. "He wait for them. Now too late."

"What do you mean?" whispered Elizabeth, sweat breaking out on her scalp. "I don't—why—we must *run! Warn* them . . . !"

Telaka shook her head. "No good." She grasped Elizabeth's wrist, holding her forcibly. "I will tell—Listen. Always my father hate you white men—"

The squaw spoke in a desperate rush, forgetting her English sometimes, but as Elizabeth listened the danger came clear.

Mianos had never wished to sell his lands, but had yielded to Telaka's pleadings and the greed of his sachems who wanted the English coats. But since then the Indians had discovered how paltry a price that was. The coats were already torn and faded, but the English remained on the land ever encroaching and scattering the tribes' game with their banging guns. Still Mianos was just, he had no intention of repudiating his bargain. But then the Labdens came and

settled, though Mianos had thought there would never be
but the two English families to endure. Labden robbed the
Siwanoys of wampum when he had given them firewater
which drove the young braves crazy. Mianos saw the morale
of his tribes disintegrating, but still he did nothing, held by
his pact. It was Nawthorne and the Tomacs who had murdered the Labdens. Nawthorne who served Hobbomock—
the Devil.

"The bones . . . " whispered Elizabeth. "An evil spell
to hurt us?"

"Bones—" said Telaka, "were fingers of Labden woman."

Elizabeth gave a choked cry, but Telaka went on. Greenwich had turned Dutch, and Mianos heard constantly of
Dutch atrocities committed against other tribes. Telaka had
reasoned with her father, saying that the Feakes and Patricks
were not responsible, were not really Dutch. The old chief
had listened angrily, but he had listened, and then issued
orders. There must be no more contact with the white men.
Henceforth the Siwanoys would live unto themselves, guarding their ancient rights and the integrity of their tribe. Soon
afterwards the two hundred Indians had been slaughtered
at Manhattan and Pavonia, and Miantonomo, the Great
Sagamore of the Narragansetts, had secretly come to the
Siwanoys urging them to wipe out the white man—while
they still could. Many of Mianos's own sachems had begged
him for revenge. And the chief had wavered, had begun to
plan attack. Then Elizabeth had cured Keofferam's leg.
Mianos acceded to the urgings of his favorite son, and re-
considered. But he had forbidden either Keofferam or Telaka
ever to see the white folk again, on pain of death.

Even now, he had not ordered his warriors to join in a
general attack. He had gone on the warpath alone, today,
to avenge his wife.

"But why—" Elizabeth cried. "What have we done!"

"Toby Feake and Ben," said Telaka. "Each day they go
to our Manitoo forest. A spy of my father watch. Yesterday
Toby Feake, he—" Her voice dropped into a low moan. She
put her arms around her head and swayed, moaning. She
raised her face and tears ran from her left eye down through
the black paint. It was the new grave of her mother Toby
had desecrated. He had kicked the protective stag's head
away, he had spilled the corn which would feed the old
woman on her last journey. He had stolen the beaver with
which she would have paid her way into the happy land of

Manitoo. Her spirit was lost forever, damned by the white man.

Elizabeth stood appalled beside the weeping squaw while wave after wave of fear swept over her, and her mind darted in frantic spurts seeking a plan of action. Only one came. She must summon Robert and Angell from the fields. There might yet be time. She ran into the house for guns and powder horns—the men were unarmed—and staggering under their weight, she reached the path when she saw figures coming through the trees from the north. She stopped, clutching the guns against her chest, squinting ahead, and released a long sigh. Toby's square-set figure was in the lead, and behind she saw Daniel's unmistakable red hair. They seemed to be carrying something between them, doubtless the mast. Oh, wicked squaw, she thought with the sharp anger of relief. Mistaken in the whole story, or trying to frighten—or just the incomprehensible Indian mind?

Elizabeth rested the guns and powder horns against a maple and went to meet the men. Her relief vanished when she saw Toby's face. It was oyster-white and glistening, his eyes stared ahead, fixed, unseeing. He wavered like a man drunk. She looked down at what they were carrying. It was Ben Palmer, a long arrow protruding from his left breast, and a foolish surprised grin on his blue lips.

"Bess," said Daniel in a high-pitched voice. "Help us carry him!" She silently put her arms around the boy's sagging hips and they continued into the house. They eased him down on the trundle.

"D'ye dare take the arrow out, Bess?" said Daniel in the same voice.

"'Twould do no good," she said. "He's dead, Dan." She went and shut the door to the other room where Hannah was playing with the baby.

Toby turned and looked at her. "Dead," he repeated. "So would I a been 'cept for Patrick." He wandered over to the dresser, knocking against the table and stools. He pulled down the rum jug, and tilted it into his mouth.

"It was Mianos," said Elizabeth quietly to Daniel.

"Aye," he said, not questioning how she knew. "I got him afore he got Toby. Mianos was hiding behind a tree. He shot Ben around the tree. Then he stepped out and aimed at Toby, a-jabbering an' yelling, an' pointing to some old antlers. That's how I had time to shoot him."

"We have his head," said Toby, with a chuckle that turned

Elizabeth's stomach. "We have his head, in return for Ben."

Elizabeth did not understand, but Toby walked to a sack he had dumped on the floor when they carried Ben in. This morning it had held a jug of beer and their nooning meat. Toby kicked the sack and it rolled over, opening a little. Elizabeth saw a bloody mass, and heron feathers tipped with copper strands, and long black hair.

"My God," she whispered. "Take it away, Toby . . . If poor Telaka should see—" She grabbed a dishcloth and threw it over the sack.

"Telaka!" Toby spat out the name. He took another pull from the rum jug.

"She came to warn us," said Elizabeth. "She tried to save you!"

"And will come no more," said a voice from the doorway. The Indian squaw stood there, stiff and proud as she had stood on the beach the day she daunted the Corchaugs. There were no tears now on her cheek. "You kill Mianos," she said pointing her long finger at Toby.

"*I* shot him," said Patrick, lifting his great hands and letting them fall helplessly. "What could I do, Telaka? He shot Ben, he would have killed us."

"Aye," agreed the squaw slowly, turning to Daniel. "So Mianos's blood curse is on *you* then. Must be paid."

"No!" Elizabeth cried, running to the Indian. She seized the squaw's hands and held them tight against her breast. "Telaka, listen—we've been through much together, you feel something for me, I know you do—for us all or you wouldn't have come today. This murder and revenge must stop. For God's sake, I beg you, don't inflame your tribe. Daniel couldn't help doing what he did. You know that—" Her voice broke, she squeezed the quiet brown hands tighter. "Look!" Elizabeth cried, pointing to the boy on the trundle, with the arrow still upright in his breast. "Look at poor Ben. Isn't that enough?"

Telaka's hands quivered, she removed them gently from Elizabeth's grasp. She closed her eye and lifted her head, seeming to listen. At last she spoke in the chanting voice, and she looked at Elizabeth.

"Because you brought me back to my people," she said. "And because you own Monakewaygo and its Manitoo, I will not tell the tribe. I will lie for you white men. But Patrick pay blood curse even so. Chekefuana tell me— *Noonway wayasama,*" she added solemnly touching Elizabeth's forehead. "*Noonway wayasama*—Missis—It is farewell."

They buried Ben beside the trail to the north, on a pleasant hill overlooking the Great Cove. Robert read from the Bible while they stood around the grave, the Patricks, the Feakes and Angell Husted. They sang a psalm together, and then Daniel suddenly raised his head and recited what he could remember of the Latin Prayers for the Dead. Toby stood motionless, staring down at the grave while they placed a great flat stone over it for fear of wolves.

They went back to the Feake house and ate in silence. As they rose Toby said, "I'm going to New Amsterdam for protection. Ye were promised it and ye shall have it. Mianos's head goes with me."

"What good is that?" said Elizabeth dully. "Bury it, Toby, bury it at sea."

Toby did not answer. Elizabeth's senseless trust in Telaka's promise did not affect him. He would demand a force sent from New Amsterdam, and in case Kieft would not heed him, exhibit the great chief's head, painted as it was with the red stripes of war. "Better ye keep all together here," Toby continued. "Guns loaded. Or better yet go to Stamford, let Underhill guard you."

"Nay, Toby——" said Patrick quickly. "There's no need o' that. Keofferam's chief o' the Siwanoys now, and even if Telaka breaks her word, which she won't, they'd never attack until their month o' mourning for Mianos is up."

"True," said Angell Husted, nodding. "Ye can count on that wi' the Indians. I'm not going back to Stamford and leave my crops, after all the bother o' settling here, and I agree wi' Patrick we've no need to call in Underhill. He can stir up trouble, fast as quiet it."

Robert murmured agreement, whereupon Toby said, "Ye're a pack of fools, you men! Aunt Bess too, but I'd think Mistress Patrick had more sense." He glanced at Anneke who was knitting hose for Daniel, her apple cheeks very pale, her delft-blue eyes red from weeping at Ben's graveside. Elizabeth, startled, wondered if it were possible that Anneke was Toby's sole concern.

If so, Anneke was quite unaware of it. She gave Toby a faint motherly smile. "I think as Daniel does, Toby. Ve vill be all right."

Toby wasted no more words on them. He set off for New Amsterdam.

The August days slipped by in the usual summer routine. They saw nothing whatever of the Indians, even the nearby Tomacs, who had temporarily deserted their village and gone to the tribe's main town at Petuquapan to participate in the elaborate mourning rites for Mianos. The Tomacs left behind only Wasobibbi, the half-wit, and an old squaw to care for him. What fears the Greenwich community might still have had were finally laid by young Danny Patrick. He set off alone one day in his father's rowboat to catch lobsters at the tip of Elizabeth's Neck. A sudden squall had blown up from the south. The twelve-year-old Danny battled the waves as best he could until he lost an oar, then he tossed helplessly in the half-swamped boat, rigid with fear since he could not swim. The squall died as quickly as it came, but Danny had no means of reaching shore. He had already drifted past the mouth of the Mianus River when he was discovered and rescued by two Siwanoy braves in a canoe. Danny had never seen these Siwanoys before but they treated the boy with great kindness, retrieved his oar, rowed his boat and took him up a brook to Petuquapan, where Keofferam met him sympathetically, and fed him. Danny had seen Telaka in the distance and she had raised an arm in greeting before disappearing into one of the long bark houses. Later Keofferam had sent the two braves in the canoe to escort Danny and his boat until he entered Greenwich Cove safely.

"They were good to me," said Danny. "Keofferam called me 'son.' They're not angry wi' us."

"No," said his father quietly. "Telaka kept her word, or they'd a skinned ye alive, lad. They're decent folk, and I'll not forget they saved ye neither. Only that Mianos was dangerous an' it's not hard to see why he felt as he did, poor devil."

Elizabeth, who had listened to this account, wondered if Daniel ever thought of Telaka's "blood curse" prophecy, and hoped he didn't. She herself had tried to dismiss it as a natural vindictiveness under the circumstances, and told herself that the accuracy of Telaka's other visions from Chekefuana had been coincidence. At any rate Patrick seemed cheerful, and was not drinking nearly as much as he used to. The two families were content, they went often to Elizabeth's white sands, even Anneke would leave the housework occasionally during the hottest days. As for Angell Husted, he had got his farm in fine shape, built him a good one-room house with a view of the Sound, and told Elizabeth that he was off to Wethersfield to wed a lass named Rebecca he'd taken a fancy to. Soon there would be another woman in Greenwich.

On Saturday, September 14, Elizabeth went to Monakewaygo with her little girls to gather bayberries and grapes. She had borrowed Daniel's rowboat as a vehicle, and pulled it up on shore at the north side of her Neck where the best bayberries grew and where it was easy to fill the boat. The girls were skilled at stripping the gray berries from the prickly bushes, and soon dumped many basketfuls into the boat. Elizabeth picked the wild purple grapes which were too high for the children, occasionally stooping to examine the ground for herbs. It was a pleasant task and a beautiful sparkling day. A crisp southern breeze ruffled the long reaches of the Sound, the air was hazed blue over the mainland from countless small fires where the Siwanoy were burning off their land to prepare for new crops. As Elizabeth pulled the fragrant grapes she thought suddenly of Anne Hutchinson, who must be in Vredeland by now, and wondered how soon they might see each other. I think she'll be glad to know I'm so near, Elizabeth thought, smiling. Anneke was a dear friend, but sometimes one longed for an Englishwoman of one's own breeding. How happily she and Anne might talk together now, in freedom.

By noon the boat was full and Elizabeth, proffering the usual reward, said, "Shall we go to the pond and see if our fawn's still there?" Some time ago they had discovered a wounded fawn, lying by the green pool, its hind leg broken. Elizabeth had made a splint for the leg, which healed, though the little creature hobbled pathetically. Since then it had become very tame, and the children loved it.

"There's ships, Mama—" said Hannah, pointing west. "Are they coming to us?"

"Of course not," said Joan with elder-sister scorn. "Three big ships wouldn't come *here*. They'll be going to the Connecticut or Boston, won't they, Mother?"

Elizabeth started to agree with Joan, but she paused, frowning, and shaded her eyes. The ships were very near. They were unmistakable Dutch yachts, large ones—two-masted, gaff-rigged, and flying the tricolor flag at bow and stern. From the high ornamented poop to the squat stubby bow, the ships were black with men. With soldiers, she saw, as the three yachts veered towards the cove, and she distinguished the glint of helmets and cuirasses and halberds, the slender muzzles of guns.

"They *are* coming in," she said, astonished and uneasy. "We'd better get back quickly."

She bundled the children into the boat amongst the grapes and bayberries, and began to row. She had barely reached their landing when the first ship dropped anchor off Green Island and lowered her longboat. Elizabeth stood and waited on the shore until the longboat slithered up her muddy beach amongst the tussocks.

"Good day, Madam!" said a tall man jumping to land. "I hope we're not too late? Is all still safe?"

He wore the armor of a Dutch officer and it took her an instant to recognize him as Kieft's English secretary.

"Good day," she said, smiling uncertainly. "We're in no trouble, Mr. Baxter." She looked at the longboat crammed with men, the other boats putting out from the ships. "We're not in need of soldiers. Did Toby Feake send you?" she added, shaking her head.

"In a way," said Baxter. "But there's more than that." He did not smile, he looked very grave. "With your permission I'll land my men. I've been appointed lieutenant of this force."

"Certainly," she said. "But I don't understand."

"Where is Mr. Feake, Madam?" said Baxter firmly. "I would speak to him. Also, of course, to Captain Patrick. Be good enough to summon them."

Elizabeth hurried up to the Feake barn where she thought Robert might be restacking the corn. He was not there but she found him at the Patrick house chatting with Daniel.

"We've got the Dutch army landing on our place!" cried Elizabeth with a rueful laugh. "Mr. Baxter seems to be in command, and he wishes to see you two at once."

"Holy Mary!" said Daniel. "I was wondering if Toby'd given up his project and rejoicing that he had."

"The Dutch army?" said Robert, staring at Elizabeth. "Why, there wouldn't be room for them in the cove, wife!"

"Well, 'tis a lot of soldiers, anyway," said Elizabeth impatiently.

It was actually a hundred and twenty men. When Elizabeth and Anneke got back the soldiers were scattered all over the Feake waterfront and garden, trampling Elizabeth's precious flowers, and terrifying the children by their raucous foreign voices.

In the parlor Elizabeth discovered that Baxter was not the only officer. There was a sergeant called Pieter Cock, and a captain, Jochem Kuyter.

Anneke and Elizabeth set about opening a keg of beer to serve the officers and were stopped by Baxter. " 'Tis kind of you ladies," he said bowing. "But we've no time, and 'twould be wiser to leave us alone."

Elizabeth's color rose. She had as much right to knowledge of anything concerning Greenwich as did Robert or Daniel, and she was not used to being excluded. "I hardly see—" she began stiffly, when Daniel interrupted her.

"Let us be, Bess," he said. "There's a reason." He closed the kitchen door, shutting out the women.

What reason? she thought suddenly frightened. The look in Daniel's eyes had been disquieting.

"Can it be something has happened to Toby?" said Anneke in a low voice. "He isn't here, is he?"

The women stared at each other. The children sat in a row on the trundle gazing anxiously at their mother.

Elizabeth went to the kitchen door and looked out. The men were sprawled in all directions, some throwing dice, some drinking from canteens. She said to the nearest one, "Do you speak English?"

"Nee," he said, eying her lewdly, from her bare ankles to her lovely sunburned face.

"Anneke—" said Elizabeth. "Ask him!"

The soldier transferred his appreciative stare to Anneke, and grinned when she spoke to him in Dutch. He replied at some length.

"He says Toby is vell," Anneke reported with relief. "He is coming, but had trouble vith his boat, cannot be here so soon."

Elizabeth scarcely heard. While Anneke and the soldier had been speaking, she had seen the face under another helmet farther off. Blauvelt, she thought in dismay. Daniel's enemy, the man he had fought in the City Tavern. She started to tell Anneke, but stopped. What use was there in distressing her? Amongst so many soldiers Patrick might not see this man, and as for Blauvelt, while under orders he could hardly pursue a private feud.

"We won't have to put up with this long," she said to Anneke. "Since we don't need protection, they can sail right off again." But she was not as sure as she sounded. Daniel's look of shocked pity had still to be explained.

It was half an hour before the door opened and Daniel came out. "Bess," he said. "I want to talk wi' ye. Anneke—get her a swig o' rum."

"I don't want any rum," said Elizabeth. "Whatever it is, tell me at once."

"I'faith, lovey, then I will," Daniel said gravely. He turned away, fixing his eyes on the hearthstone. " 'Tis bad for us all but 'tis worse for you, knowing how ye felt about her."

"About WHO?" cried Elizabeth sharply.

"Mistress Anne Hutchinson, Bess. She was massacred last week at Vredeland and sixteen of her family with her."

Anneke gave a low cry. Elizabeth said nothing. She stared at Daniel. He went on, "They'd only just come, were settling in to their new home. Mrs. Hutchinson, she didn't believe in violence, or bearing arms. There wasn't a gun on the place when the Indians attacked. 'Twas the Weckquasageeks did it, Bess. Murdered all the Hutchinsons except a little lass they captured. Murdered and burned."

"Why?" she whispered. "Why did they do it?" She sank down on a stool and buried her face in her hands. Daniel put his arm around her and she shook him off with sudden fury. "Why didn't God protect her? She was good. Why did the Comforter not save her? Why was she hounded, persecuted, always driven from the peace and beauty that she yearned for, that she could bring to others? Hounded on to *this!*"

"I don't know, Bess. But there've been Holy Martyrs before now. Mebbe she was one . . . " Daniel poured himself a noggin of rum. "That's why these fellows came today," Daniel went on heavily. "Oh, Toby tried to stir 'em up, but they were busy chasing Indians on Staten Island. And now this happened to the Hutchinsons. The Weckquasageeks're known to be friendly to the Siwanoys. Kieft has commanded an attack, tonight."

"Attack?" repeated Elizabeth, staring at the floor. "Attack on whom?"

"Why, our Siwanoys at Petaquapan. They want me to lead 'em."

Anneke made a sharp motion. "Not ven they saved Danny! No, Dan, you vouldn't do that! And Telaka forgive you for killing her vader!"

Daniel banged his great fist on the table. "By the Mass,

Anneke! What can I do? We're Dutch subjects, these are orders from our Governor!"

Anneke frowned, twisting her head from side to side, then she stooped and kissed him on the cheek. "You vill think of something, Daniel, I know. More and more wrongs do not make right."

Lieutenant Baxter came into the kitchen with Robert, leaving the two Dutch officers in the other room.

"Well, Captain Patrick," Baxter said. " 'Tis getting dusk and time we started." He glanced at Elizabeth's white, strained face. "You've told her? A horrifying thing, brings the danger home when one knows the people involved. Good thing you sent for us, Captain."

"I didn't," said Daniel. " 'Twas Toby Feake."

"But you killed the chief, Mianos," said Baxter, mildly surprised.

Drunk, he thought. The big Irish captain's face was flushed and sweating. He looked confused. Understandable perhaps. The Hutchinson massacre was enough to addle anybody. "You'll guide us to the Siwanoy Fort, now!" said Baxter in a voice of clear command, designed to penetrate Patrick's daze.

"Not sure of the way—" said Daniel slowly. "Specially at night. 'Tis a long march through forest."

Robert stared at his friend. "But, Dan, surely you—"

Anneke interrupted. "Ve never go to Petuquapan. It is far across a river. Daniel vould get lost."

They saw Baxter's face darken with puzzled suspicion. Daniel's wits cleared, and he saw a way out. He straightened and spoke with decision. "There's an Indian at Tomac village'd guide us, 'd do anything for wampum and is no friend to the Siwanoy. I'll go get him. 'Twon't take long."

Baxter was relieved. "Aye, fetch him quickly then."

Robert looked from Baxter to Daniel. "You can't mean Wasobibbi, Dan?"

"Aye," said Patrick. And the glare he sent Robert quelled further questions. Baxter paid no attention to Robert's interruption. During the previous conversation in the other room, Baxter had taken Robert's measure. An ineffectual man, obviously guided by Patrick. Baxter returned to the Dutch officers, while Daniel walked off towards Totomack Cove.

"Why is Dan getting Wasobibbi, wife?" said Robert querulously, sitting down by Elizabeth. "I don't understand him.

Why doesn't he guide the troops himself?"

"Sh-h-h—" whispered Anneke, glancing towards the half-opened door through which they could hear Baxter's voice explaining the plan in Dutch. "Trust Daniel, Robert. Say nothing no matter vat you think. You vouldn't have us betray our friends, vould you, Robert?"

"Our friends!" he repeated. "You mean the Siwanoy? Lieutenant Baxter says they'll murder us if we don't get them first."

"Baxter doesn't know them," said Elizabeth with difficulty. Horror and grief for Anne Hutchinson were pressed down by a leaden apathy, while far detached and void of feeling her thoughts made fumbling attempts at reason. Baxter might be right. Daniel and Anneke might both be dangerously blind and mistaken. Anne must have trusted the Weck-quasageeks as they were trusting the Siwanoys. Anne Hutchinson who had refused to have guns in her home would never wish revenge, or would she? Had all her teachings been mistaken? And at the end, had she repudiated them? Still, it was not the Siwanoys who had massacred her. Yet even if it were—

Elizabeth made a weary motion. "Let Daniel do as he wishes, Rob—" she said in wooden voice.

Robert jerked his head up, his eyelids blinked fast. The stubborn look hardened his mouth. "I don't need you and Dan to tell me always what I should do," he cried. "I'll make up my own mind. Maybe I'll lead the troops myself. Waso-bibbi certainly can't."

Anneke looked frightened. Elizabeth did not speak. Robert's defiance did not touch her. Suddenly she saw Anne Hutchinson's face as it had been once or twice, luminous, exalted. She heard the tender serenity with which Anne had said, "I do not believe God is ever wroth with those who love enough. For God is love." And where was that face now? Crushed, mangled, burned. The voice silenced forever. And Anne the helpless victim of implacable cruelty which had begun in Boston Meetinghouse. Cast out as a leper she had been, delivered up to Satan, by the ministers, by John Winthrop. She had dared to disbelieve the curse, and had been wrong. The God of Love had not saved her after all.

Robert tried to voice his protest when Daniel came back with Wasobibbi, but he had no chance at Baxter, who left the house at once to call orders and inspect the men's arms. Robert tried to make his wishes clear to the two Dutch

officers, who stared at him blankly and shoved him away.
He went outside with his gun and Baxter, seeing him, called,
"You stay home, Mr. Feake. Guard the women and children.
Now then, Patrick, tell your Indian to get going."

Daniel nodded solemnly and took Wasobibbi's arm. The
Indian giggled and muttered, "Wampum, wampum."

"Wampum—there . . . " said Daniel pointing to the
east—the opposite direction from Petuquapan. "Go find
wampum," he said in Siwanoy.

The Indian giggled again, stroked Daniel's hand like a
pleased child and started up the trail, Daniel immediately
behind him, followed by the Dutch officers, the hundred and
twenty men in single file, and Lieutenant Baxter to bring
up the rear.

Anneke watched them go, though Elizabeth did not. "Almost
I could laugh—" said Anneke. She glanced quickly at Robert
whom she had forgotten. "Sit down, Rob," she said in a
coaxing voice. "I fix you a nice little supper."

Robert sat down angrily. " 'Tis not right. Dan treating
me like this. He should tell me what he's doing. I own more
land than he does here. He treats me like a fool, and so the
officers thought I was. I'm not. I know he's diddling them.
Bess, why don't you say something? Baxter's an *Englishman*,
and you put us under the Dutch. Yet all you think of is
those Indians."

"That's not true," she said. "I'm not thinking at all. I
don't know what's right. 'Tis cold in here. Shut the door,
Rob. I'm very cold."

Her peculiar tone disturbed him from his grievance. He
closed the door, and looked at her anxiously. " 'Tis the
Hutchinson massacre's upset you so, wife?" he said, patting
her shoulder. "A terrible thing. That's why we must wipe the
Indians out, don't you see that, my dear?"

"Don't talk," she said. "Leave me alone."

"Come—" said Anneke again. "Here is baked pumpkin
and oysters for you. Come and eat."

The night went by. Elizabeth and Anneke put the children
to bed. Robert read in his Bible, then slept on the truckle.
The women lay down but did not sleep. It was noon that
Sunday before they heard male voices and the clink of armor
coming down the path.

Elizabeth opened the door, saw Baxter and Patrick in the
lead and all the soldiers straggling haphazardly down through
the trees.

"We didn't find the Siwanoy fort!" Baxter cried sharply when he saw Elizabeth. "All night long we've wandered through the forest. The Indian was a fool, or a knave. He ran away at the end, when Captain Kuyter started to beat him."

"Aye," said Daniel walking up to the house. "We've had a grievous night, couldn't find Petuquapan at all. Lieutenant Baxter has had to come back to the ships for supplies. Bring me rum, Bess!"

She silently complied. Daniel swallowed the entire mugful. Baxter and the Dutch officers drank a little beer.

The sullen hungry troops gathered in the yard again, resting their loaded muskets on the ground, grumbling and cursing. Elizabeth saw Blauvelt, leaning his backside against the well, his fat malignant face watching Daniel from under the helmet.

"Dan," said Robert stiffly, walking up to his friend. "If you really had forgotten the way, why did you get Wasobibbi? Everyone knows he's a natural."

"What's that?" said Baxter who had been conferring with Sergeant Cock as to the next procedure. "What's that you said, Mr. Feake?"

"Why—" said Robert with defiance, despite the look that Daniel gave him, "Wasobibbi could never make an able guide, he's little better than an idiot. You should have taken *me* with you, Lieutenant, I told you—"

"What does this mean, Captain Patrick?" cut in Baxter, turning on Daniel.

"Naught," said Daniel. "Feake often gets confused. Isn't it so, Bess?"

Before she could answer, she was roughly shoved aside. Blauvelt strode up to Daniel. "Vot it mean?" he shouted. "I tell you!" He thrust his vicious face within an inch of Daniel's. "Ha, Patrick!" he cried. "At last the High Command they vill know vat you are. *Verrader! Verrader!*"

Daniel turned white, gaping at his enemy, whom he had not known was there. All the night long Blauvelt had stayed far back in the file, watching and waiting for opportunity, but daring to make no move.

"This fellow calls you a traitor," said Baxter, while the Dutch officers stiffened, murmuring to each other, looking sideways at Daniel.

"Ja, verrader, traitor!" shouted Blauvelt, and he went on in a torrent of Dutch. "He was thus in Holland, as I know well. Bribes, corruption. He led us astray tonight, because the Indians paid him to. He betrayed the Prince of Orange the same way, taking money from the Spanish."

"You lie," said Daniel softly. "You know you lie, Blauvelt." His fists doubled, his head lowered, he began to weave it to and fro. Blauvelt stepped back, and Baxter said sternly, "These are grave charges, Captain Patrick. Isn't this the man you fought with at the City Tavern in New Amsterdam?"

"Aye," said Daniel. "Aye, and was stopped by the priest." His hands fell slack, a look of confused bewilderment came into his eyes.

"You see?" cried Blauvelt, slipping his pistol from his belt. "What a coward he is, Mijnheeren, this knave that you trusted and exalted! He finds no words to defend himself. He cannot! Coward and traitor that he is!"

Daniel trembled. He made a sound like a sob. "You whoreson bastard—" he whispered, and spat full into the fat taunting face. "God forgive me," he whispered. "God forgive me that I near broke my vow to the Blessed Virgin." He turned blindly, making for the door where Anneke stood shocked and not understanding.

Blauvelt raised his pistol, took quick aim and shot Daniel in the back of the head. Daniel staggered two paces and fell. His legs twitched convulsively and were quiet. He lay with his shattered head on the doorstep, while Anneke screamed.

Nobody moved. There was no sound but Anneke's screams, until Baxter said, "Jesus, what a coil! Here, seize that fellow!"

Sergeant Cock already had pinioned Blauvelt's arms and knocked his pistol from his hands. Captain Kuyter said in Dutch, "Och, this is bad. Bad. Poor woman. Can nobody stop her screaming?"

Elizabeth moved mechanically towards Anneke, but she could not pass what lay on the doorstep. She stopped by her herb bed, turned a little and vomited.

Blauvelt, looking at the officers, whined, "He was a traitor. 'Tis no sin to kill a traitor. You should let me go, Mijnheeren."

"What will we do with him?" said Kuyter contemptuously, indicating Blauvelt.

"Take him to Stamford, put him under guard with Captain Underhill," said Baxter after a moment. "We can't leave here now, until this—" he looked at Daniel's body, at Anneke, at Elizabeth retching in the herb bed, "this is all cleared up. Kieft'll be furious."

Then he noticed Robert. "Oh, My God—" Baxter whispered. "What is Mr. Feake doing . . . "

Robert was edging up very slowly to Daniel's body. When he came to the doorstep he knelt beside it, staring down with a puzzled frown, until suddenly he smiled, a sad secret smile, as though he had received some private revelation. Still smiling, he began to wash his hands, carefully, in Daniel's blood.

17

IT WAS SOME TIME before the news of Daniel Patrick's death reached Boston, via somewhat inaccurate letters from Captain John Mason at Windsor and Edward Winslow of Plymouth.

John Winthrop, Governor once again, and immersed in Bay matters, was thus reminded of Elizabeth, and uttered a fervent prayer that this distressing event would be salutary for her. Winthrop had been disgusted when he heard of Greenwich's transferal to Dutch sovereignty, and angered by the occasional rumors which continued to couple her name with Patrick's. But on the whole, except for Margaret's sadly affectionate remarks at times, he had managed to forget his niece. That last incredible night in Watertown when Elizabeth had in some extraordinary way got herself in danger of gaol—if not worse—and he had felt sick and old too—that night he preferred never to dwell on.

He did however record the Patrick death in his journal, with his own characteristic emendations:

> *Captain Patrick was killed at Stamford by a Dutchman, who shot him dead with a pistol. This captain was entertained by us out of Holland (where he was a com-*

mon soldier of the Prince's guard) to exercise our men. We made him a captain and maintained him . . . But he grew very proud and vicious, for though he had a wife of his own, a good Dutch woman and comely, yet he despised her and followed after other women; and perceiving that he was discovered, and that such evil courses would not be endured here, and being withal of a vain and unsettled disposition, he went from us, and sat down within twenty miles of the Dutch, and put himself under their protection, and joined to their church without being dismissed from Watertown; but when the Indians arose in those parts he fled to Stamford and there was slain. The Dutchman who killed him was apprehended but made an escape. And this was the fruit of his wicked course and breach of covenant with his wife, with the church and with that state who had called him and maintained him, and he found his death from that hand where he sought protection.

It is observable that he was killed upon the Lord's Day in the time of afternoon exercise . . .

Margaret, who prayed often for Elizabeth, worried about conditions down there in Dutch country where the Indians were doing such fearful things, like massacring the Hutchinson family. John saw that particular tragedy as the natural end result of Mrs. Hutchinson's heresies and her excommunication. Margaret never doubted that he was right, yet she could not exclude pity, nor anxiety for Elizabeth no matter how many of her niece's afflictions were also sent by a just God as chastisement.

Even Lucy Downing, when she heard of Daniel's death, wrote John Winthrop a letter about Elizabeth saying:

I have not had opertunity to writ to her since she leeft the Bay, nor have I heard of her but by others, and that only which was not like to be for her good, or our comfort. And now I hear Patricke is cut off, which makes me hope that by the use of some good means theer might be more hopes to reduce her . . . every one is not hir mother's childe, theerfore I am thus bould . . .

This last sentence with its nostalgic reference to Elizabeth's mother—Lucy, and John's sister Anne—disquieted the Governor, and it did, with Margaret's urgings, incite him to write the Feakes a letter tepidly suggesting that in view of the Indian menace and obvious Dutch dangers, they might come to Boston if they wished. He added that if Elizabeth came he would endeavor to pardon her many follies, find her a home in Boston, and supervise the godly rearing of the children.

He consigned the letter amongst others to the master of a Virginia-bound sloop, then turned to write a far more congenial letter to Jack, who was endeavoring to establish an ironworks at Saugus with workmen he had just brought back from England.

Elizabeth did not receive her letter until April, since contrary winds had prevented the master of the sloop from putting into Greenwich Cove, and he left the letter with Captain Underhill in Stamford to be delivered. Underhill was extremely occupied that spring of 1644 and knew nothing of the letter for many weeks. Had Elizabeth received it in March, she might have gone back to Boston, for the children's sake, and because her spirit had been crushed. By April however her thoughts ran differently.

The time following Daniel's death passed in misery so acute and constant that she was spared full realization. No glossing or uncertainty about the "strangeness" availed her now in regard to her husband. Whatever precarious hold he had had on reality broke off sharp when his friend was killed. Robert was mad.

He had not been violent when the horrified Dutch officers removed him from Daniel's corpse, nor needed the bonds they put on him. He had not seemed to notice when they lashed him to a chair in the kitchen, but sat there docilely, murmuring senseless words in a faint babbling voice, rubbing his hands together in a ceaseless washing motion, even after they were cleansed of Daniel's blood.

When Captain Kuyter took the murderer Blauvelt to Stamford and put him in Underhill's custody, Mr. Baxter had remained at Greenwich Cove out of pity and concern, doing what he could to help the two stricken women. Three of his soldiers dug Patrick's grave and buried him next to Ben Palmer, while Baxter read the Church of England burial service. This gave Anneke comfort, and she regained control in a few days. She was strained and woeful, often taken with paroxysms of sobs, but she performed her housewifery with her usual effortless skill and therein found some solace. The arrival of Toby Feake also contributed to her recovery, though she felt for him no romantic attraction. He was simply an older son like Danny, on whom she could depend and who helped both unhappy manless households with the heavy work.

Toby's presence, and the return of Angell Husted with his bride, reassured Baxter, and he came to Elizabeth one morning saying gently, "We shall sail for New Amsterdam today, Madam. I needn't tell you how—how deeply I regret all that's happened. Terrible—" The young man shook his head. "Have you thought what you'll do with him?" He indicated Robert who sat on a stool by the fireplace, crooning to himself while he wound and unwound a ball of yarn. Elizabeth had managed to substitute this activity for the hideous hand-washing.

"What *is* there to do with him?" she said calmly.

Too calmly, Baxter thought. He had daily expected her to break down, sobbing and bewailing like Mrs. Patrick. But she had not. A woman of great strength, Mrs. Feake was, and showing a stony endurance he respected though it made him uncomfortable.

"Will you and the children be safe?" he asked in a low voice. "Suppose he turns violent?"

"I'm not afraid of Robert," she said. "More beer, Mr. Baxter?"

He saw that she could not bear discussion of her tragedies, and had withdrawn into a proud aloofness, but he persisted. "Couldn't you go back to your Winthrop relations? I could arrange passage for you."

"No," she said starkly. "They don't want us. I never hear from them. My uncle was very angry when he heard we'd gone to the Dutch, nor—" she added, "have I been a favorite of his."

"Captain Underhill then," said Baxter after a moment. "Oh, I know what you think of him, and I'm privately inclined to agree. That was a shabby trick, his letting Blauvelt escape or at least not guarding him properly. You'd think that whatever his doubts about Patrick, Underhill'd want to see the murderer punished."

"What good would that do?" said Elizabeth. "There was a blood curse on Daniel, it had to happen one way or another. Daniel killed Mianos."

Baxter did not follow this logic, so he reverted to his previous thought. "You had better go to Stamford, to Underhill's protection—in a large community with plenty of men should there be trouble."

"Trouble?" she said, her beautiful eyes green and hard as beryls. "Can there be more trouble than there has been?"

"Of course there can," he said sharply. "The Indian matter's not settled at all. The danger continues, is greater even—from what Underhill tells me. He's an experienced Indian fighter and has offered us his services. I've no doubt Director General Kieft'll accept them. We MUST end this constant warfare; secure the lasting safety of all our settlers."

"No doubt," she said. "Mr. Baxter, you've been very kind, and mean well. I know you can't help obeying Kieft's orders. But I wish you'd leave us alone here. And leave our Siwanoys alone too. Their chief, Keofferam, is our friend, and Anneke told you what they did for Danny Patrick."

"But, Mrs. Feake—" he cried. "They're very artful, I regret to remind you of the Hutchinson massacre, and Underhill says—"

" 'Underhill says—'!" she interrupted acidly; turning her back on him she walked into the great fireplace, and opening the oven where pumpkin bread was baking, inspected the loaves.

A haughty woman, Baxter thought, somewhat vexed. Handsome though, very—even though she seemed much older than the time he had seen her in New Amsterdam. Then, despite her pregnancy, there had been a girlish merriment, a most appealing prettiness about her. The charm that had so pleased Kieft. Baxter had thought her very young, the mid-twenties perhaps, but now, lacking all smiles and sparkle, her abundant curly black hair drawn severely into a knot, her full lips compressed, and the red of her cheeks gone pale beneath the fine white skin, she seemed ten years older than he had first thought her. Still young enough for a better fate than this, however, Baxter thought, admiring her slender back and graceful movements as she scooped the loaves from the oven with the heavy iron peel. He determined to urge Kieft to help her if Mr. Feake continued to be deranged.

The three Dutch yachts sailed out of Greenwich Cove that afternoon and Elizabeth did not bother to watch them go, though the children did.

Lisbet and Johnny wept at seeing the departure. The soldiers had made great pets of them, playing games with them, letting them ride out to the ships and teaching them Dutch words.

"Oh, dear, I wish they wouldn't leave," said Joan as the last sail disappeared down the Sound past Great Captain's Island which Daniel had bought and named for himself.

"Well, you needn't weep after them," said Elizabeth dryly. "Very likely they'll be back."

"You're glad they're gone, aren't you, Mama?" said little Hannah, looking up into her mother's stern face. "They made bad things happen. They made Uncle Dan be dead, and made Father be so silly."

Elizabeth put her hand on Hannah's curly red hair, but did not answer.

"Shall I feed him tonight, Mama?" went on the child. "He lets me."

Her mother nodded. "Thank you, poppet, it would help." She gave Hannah a bowl of cornmeal mush and stewed rabbit. The child seated herself beside Robert, who did not cease winding the yarn, but he ate when Hannah put the wooden spoon to his lips.

The only one of the children who showed fear or revulsion towards Robert was Lisbet, who kept away from him as much as she could. Joan took the change passively, and helped with Robert's care when told. The little boys were too young for wonder, and with the acceptance of childhood soon forgot that Father had ever been any different.

At times however Robert grew agitated, sang or laughed incessantly and tried to get out of the house. Toby Feake and Angell Husted therefore built for Elizabeth a lean-to on the north side of her house, and opened the great chimney so that there might be another fireplace. In this third downstairs room they installed Robert, where during the worst periods he could be locked up. Toby slept in the loft, Elizabeth and the children in the two upstairs chambers.

Anneke and her household, a few hundred yards up the cove, managed well enough. Young Danny was strong. Also Toby was there a great deal in the daytime, taciturn and stolid as ever, avidly consuming Anneke's good food, forsaking his shallop which he had raised on stays for the winter.

The months passed. There was much snow. Game grew very scarce, and the families relied on their powdered meat and corn. At Christmas time Keofferam and three of his Siwanoy braves suddenly appeared down the northern trail, bearing gifts as he had the year before—a whole frozen venison and three turkeys.

"Mer-ry Christ-mas," he said carefully to Hannah, proud of remembering the phrase she had taught him last year. The young chief knew almost no English, but by means of signs he managed to convey to Elizabeth his regret for Daniel's death and his shock at seeing Robert's condition, neither of which he had known. He was following Mianos's orders in keeping his tribe segregated from the white men. But his code of honor, and gratitude for the cure Elizabeth had wrought a year ago, prompted him to this commemorative visit.

Elizabeth received the offerings with fervent thanks, gave the Indians beer and a few of the precious marchpane sweets Anneke had made. She asked after Telaka, and understood from Keofferam's nod and smile that the squaw was well. Nor was she surprised that the squaw had not come with her brother. It was a final farewell Telaka had made when she gave her promise on the day of Mianos's death. And she had kept her word in all things.

The Indians did not stay long. They padded back through the snow on their swift moccasined feet; Keofferam's short, squatty figure was invested with new dignity by his father's magnificent turkey-feather mantle, by the red deer hair and the copper-tipped heron feathers in his roach.

"Whew—" said Lisbet, fastidiously wrinkling her delicate little nose. "They smell, and're always so bear-greasy. I don't like Indians. Look, Mama, here's a louse I saw jump off Keofferam."

"Aye—" said Elizabeth, squashing the louse. "But you must take the fat with the lean in this world and the gifts they brought are very welcome." Her heavy heart was lightened by the visit. For a while it seemed to restore some order of balance and decency. It conveyed meaning, where all else in her life was compounded of monotonous, blind struggle.

Then Joan, having reached the age for it, developed weeping spells and painful cramps in her little belly, and finally a mysterious fever which required constant nursing. Elizabeth endured through each day as it came.

By February Joan had recovered, but blizzards set in. The north wind whistled down the cove, snow piled in drifts up to the lean-to eaves. The cow died of cold, and the howling wolves came nearer than they ever had. Anneke's spaniel, having ventured too far one evening, was devoured by a wolf. They found the tracks around the house next morning.

In the third week of February the cold let up. Ice floes melted in the cove. Muddy brown patches showed through the snow, and the wind veered to the south. Early one morning Elizabeth awoke to an authoritative banging on her front door. Shivering, she got out of the great feather bed which she now shared with Joan. She dressed and wrapped herself in her fur-lined cloak. She opened the upper half of the door and peered through the crack. Captain John Underhill stood on her stone step, shining in new Dutch armor, a sword dangling from his belt, a musket on his shoulder.

"Hola! Mistress Feake—" he said. "Pray let me in."

She opened the door, courteous but unsmiling. "How in the world did you get here, Captain?" she said. "Is the trail clear from Stamford now?"

"Didn't come from Stamford," said Underhill, poking at the kitchen fire and turning to warm his buttocks. "From New Amsterdam. I just landed. My ship's in the cove, two more'll soon be here."

Elizabeth walked to her one glazed window, rubbed off the hoar frost and saw a large Dutch yacht at anchor by Green Island. There were a dozen soldiers on her icy little beach, pulling up a longboat.

"What is this about, Captain?" she said, going back to the hearth and swinging the crane with its iron pot full of snow water over the fire.

"We're massing here for the attack, Mistress," Underhill said, watching her closely. "General de la Montagne and I are in command of a fair-sized force. Larger than last September. The job'll get done this time."

Elizabeth turned and examined him. A thick-set dark man of forty-six, new wrinkles on the weathered cheeks, a touch of gray in the mustache, but the same rather sardonic smile on the sensual mouth, and in the black eyes the same mixture of malice, boldness and determination.

"Surely," she said, "you are not still meaning to attack the Siwanoys?"

"Indeed we are," he answered.

She raised her square cleft chin and stared coldly into his startled eyes. "I forbid it," she said.

For an instant of dismay he was reminded of her uncle, Governor Winthrop. Then he burst into sharp laughter. "Oh, my fair Bess, ye've not changed as much as I first thought. The same fiery spirit. But 'twon't do. Ye can neither forbid nor permit."

"This is my house, Captain Underhill, and these are my lands. I forbid you to use this as a base, and as the—only surviving and competent patroon of Greenwich, I forbid you to attack the Siwanoys who have naught to do with you at Stamford."

Underhill laughed again, more kindly. "Brave words, Mistress. I admire your courage, though I don't admire an Indian-lover. But I tell ye, you can't help yourself, whatever maggot ye've got in your pretty little head. 'Tis from here we march for the attack." Indeed the Feake house had been specially chosen for this purpose after long debate at Fort Amsterdam. Chosen for its isolation, which made premature discovery by the Siwanoys unlikely, and also for its comparative nearness to Petuquapan. The rough location of the latter Siwanoy Fort Underhill had now ascertained. He was an experienced tactician, and a canny Indian fighter. Since selling his services to the Dutch last autumn, he had been successful in several minor skirmishes with the Long Island Indians. The time had come for a major victory.

"Where is your General de la Montagne?" said Elizabeth. "I shall appeal to him. As I remember him at Kieft's Council Table he looked a sensible man."

"He is, my dear," said Underhill. "And therefore he agrees with me. Come, come, Mistress, this is very—" He broke off, twisting his head towards the lean-to door. "By God, what's that? You've got some beast closed in there? Yet it sounds like laughter."

She did not answer, but he saw her face before she turned abruptly. With an indrawn breath, he said, "Forgive me. I didn't guess. Baxter told me what had happened to Mr. Feake, but I didn't know 'twas like that. Poor lass—" he said, and he put his hand on her shoulder.

Elizabeth moved away. How can I stop them? she thought. How can I warn the Siwanoys? Later when the other soldiers have come. They won't be watching me. But could she get through the snow and across the Mianus by herself on a trail she'd never followed? Angell Husted then——but he was ill with an inflammation on his lungs, and were he well, she wasn't sure how he'd act. If I went by boat? she thought. Daniel's rowboat, take young Danny with me, he knows where it is. Yet how to get down the cove past the Dutch ships, and through all the floating ice. I must try it on foot, she decided, her heart beating fast. There was nobody else who would go. Certainly not Toby, who came downstairs from the loft and was pleased to see Underhill.

"'Twas about time you came," he said gruffly. "I hear a man was tomahawked over to Norwalk last week."

"Aye," said Underhill. "Nawthorne says 'twas done by a Siwanoy."

"Nawthorne!" cried Elizabeth involuntarily. "What do you know of Nawthorne?"

"A great deal," said Underhill, and hesitated wondering in view of her evident feelings how much it was wise to tell. All these Greenwich folk were daft apparently when it came to the Indians. "Nawthorne came to me from Tomac village some time ago," he said quickly. "I was going to make him suffer for the diddling that half-wit son o' his gave Baxter, and—" he paused, went on with an ironic shrug, "—and Patrick. But Nawthorne offered to spy for us. I took him to New Amsterdam. He's on the ship now. He hates that new Siwanoy chief they've got. Keoff—something. Nawthorne'll be our guide to the Fort tonight."

"He's a devilish Indian," Elizabeth said. "He murdered the Labdens."

"Maybe he did," said Underhill. "But he'll guide us to the Fort because he knows he'll be well paid if he does and shot if he doesn't."

"I—I must go to Anneke," murmured Elizabeth faintly. "Must tell her the soldiers are here. She'll help me ready things for you; we have little beer but we have some cider, we could make you some journey cakes—" She moved towards the door, and Underhill stopped her.

"Oh no, my dear. We've brought our own provisions, thank ye, and you will stay right here, and so will your children. Toby Feake may go and tell Mrs. Patrick if he pleases." He made Elizabeth a small malicious bow.

Later, she thought, surely I can slip out somehow.

But later it began to snow, a dense swirling whiteness that hid every landmark. The soldiers stayed on board the anchored ships. General de la Montagne came ashore and with him Ensign Van Dyke. The Huguenot councilor was pleasant and grave, but he spoke no English. Neither did Ensign Van Dyke. Underhill watched Elizabeth constantly. She had no chance even for a private word with Anneke. The snow continued all night. Nobody slept but the children, and Robert. He had seen armored soldiers through his little barred window and become very disturbed. He had begun to shriek something about a pistol and blood. Elizabeth finally gave him laudanum.

By noon next next day the dazzling sun came out and the snowfall proved to have been only four inches. All the soldiers landed and were ready for the march. Toby was going with them. Elizabeth profited by a moment when Underhill was conferring with General de la Montagne on the doorsteps. And to Toby she made one last despairing plea.

"Toby, can't you stop them? You know this is a wicked, horrible thing to do. Stop them somehow."

"An' get shot in the head for a traitor like Patrick!" he said roughly. "What's more I don't want to. High time Ben's death was paid off. Leave be, Aunt, ye're acting silly as my uncle. This is not woman's business."

"Ready, Feake?" asked Underhill sticking his head in the door. "Nawthorne says this night'll be even better than last. They've got some kind o' religious powwow going on. Feasting. And all the nearby tribes've come into the fort with the Siwanoys. Might be seven hundred o' them, maybe more."

"Seven hundred!" repeated Elizabeth. "And you've not a quarter of that. This is rash and useless, Captain Underhill. Surely the General doesn't mean to attack when he's so outnumbered!"

"Ye've forgot what we did at Mystic in the Pequot war," said Underhill. "We got 'em then and we'll get 'em now— by surprise. BY SURPRISE," he repeated, looking at Elizabeth with the sardonic twist to his brows. " 'Tis too late for any misguided person to give warning, let alone that any such'd perish in the snow or get eaten by wolves! Come, Feake!"

Again as she had in September, Elizabeth watched them march off. Underhill and de la Montagne tramped in the lead with the Tomac sachem, Nawthorne, between them. A long rope around Nawthorne's waist was attached to Underhill's sword belt. Behind went Toby and the armored soldiers with their muskets and pistols and bandoliers, single file, plodding through the snow. Ensign Van Dyke marched in the rear. She waited until they disappeared amongst the black tree trunks to the north. Then she floundered up the snowy path to Anneke's. "Oh, what'll we do?" she cried bursting into the kitchen.

Anneke was polishing her Dutch hearth tiles. She looked

up sadly. "Ve can do nothing, Bess. And perhaps Toby is right. Ve are not safe vith all those Indians so near us." She sighed. "My Daniel vouldn't have died had I not urged him to folly. That hurts me here—" She put her hand to her breast. "And now I must pray for Toby, that he comes back."

"So it is only Toby you think of!" Elizabeth cried. "His opinions, his safety. How you've changed!"

Anneke bent over her tiles, rubbing at a speck on the blue and white Noah's Ark. "Ve have all changed, Bess," she said very low. "Needs must."

Elizabeth returned to her own house, where the children were in high spirits, delighted at this break in the monotonous winter days, eager to talk about the soldiers, and Captain Underhill.

"I like him!" said Lisbet. "He told me I was fair as a lily. He gave me a ribbon off his doublet. Look!" She held out a fragment of yellow silk. "He said 'twas 'like my hair.' " She tossed her silver-gold curls and simpered a little.

Elizabeth did not glance at the ribbon. She went into Robert's room and found him still asleep. She walked to the lean-to's cove window and gazed out towards the ragged line of bare snowy trees on the Mianus Neck shore. Somewhere, many miles past that to the west, lay Petuquapan.

Telaka, she thought. "Telaka!" With a desperate concentration she tried to call the squaw, to project summons through the thin bright winter air. "Danger, Telaka!" Over and over she said it in her mind. "Danger, Telaka! Warn Keofferam!" She stood by the window until the lowering sun turned red.

At last Robert whimpered and sat up on his bed. "Ralph! Listen to me!" he said clearly in the high babbling voice. "I'd not hurt you if you'd answer. Then it wouldn't happen, though the silver cream jug's not been delivered to Milady Brooke yet. Near Ludgate, Ralph, that's where she lives. Mind there's no blood on the cream jug. Always wash it off, Ralph, blood makes clean."

Elizabeth walked over to the bed. "Hush," she said. "Get up, Rob. I'll get you some food."

He glanced at her sideways. His hands slowly began their rubbing motion, but he got out of bed and sat down in his chair while she covered his frail skinny body with a blanket.

It was the greatest victory against the Indians there had

ever been in the whole New World. Greater even than the
Battle of Mystic. Captain Underhill said so the next evening
in his Stamford home as he recounted the triumph to leading
Stamford settlers—Andrew Ward, Matthew Mitchell, Richard
Lawe. After the battle General de la Montagne and Underhill had marched their men straight back to Stamford, where
the fifteen wounded could be properly nursed.

"Only fifteen sick, what a marvel, and most of those just
frostbite!" cried Underhill, his eyes shining. "Only one dead
too! What good fortune we had!"

" 'Tis not fortune, except as God was on the Christian
side," said Andrew Ward. " 'Twas your military prowess.
Your great leadership."

"Well—" said Underhill with a glance at de la Montagne
who sat quietly sipping beer, and trying to understand the
English talk. "Of course, the General was there too. I can't
take all the credit."

De la Montagne bowed as he saw the men looking at him,
then he turned away. He was neither as young nor exuberant
as Underhill. The last twenty-four hours had exhausted him,
nor was he elated by the outcome.

Massacre! he thought to himself. Meurtre. Near a thousand unsuspecting Indian men, women and children roasted
alive. Le Directeur Générale would be enchanted. There was
no doubt that Indian resistance had been entirely shattered
here. There could be no Indians left in these parts to resist.
As for the eastern tribes towards the Connecticut they would
be terrified. Une belle victoire, thought de la Montagne,
wryly. He wrapped his cloak about his ears to shut out the
sound of Underhill's strident voice, eagerly describing the
battle.

"We got to the Mianus River about eight o'clock, and had
to ford it. 'Twas fearful cold, and bright moonlight. That
bugger Nawthorne guided us all right, but once we crossed
the river we didn't need him. You could hear the Indians,
they were singing and howling and dancing in their bark
huts, and when we got over a steep hill 'twas easy to see
their town in the moonlight. Built under the brow of a long
cliff it was. A good thing for us. They couldn't escape at
the rear, because of the cliff."

"Didn't they hear you coming?" asked Mr. Lawe.

"Not for a bit, they were making so much noise at their
feasting. We'd time to surround the town and build a bonfire in readiness before they heard us. They ran out then—

some of the young bucks—but we shot 'em down before they'd time to aim properly. Our armor mostly turns the arrows anyhow. Well, we forced 'em all back into their wigwams, like at Mystic, then we flung fire-brands over the bark roofs, and retreated beyond arrow's length to watch. We'd not long to wait until the whole town was in flames."

"Aye," said Andrew Ward nodding. "By God's Providence a brisk wind was blowing last night. Did any escape?"

"I doubt it," said Underhill. "We shot down the few that ran out. The rest stayed in. Odd thing, you know—they didn't make a sound, not a cry, not a scream while they burned up."

There was a brief silence before Mr. Mitchell said slowly, "No one has ever denied their courage. Pity they've no knowledge of *other* Christian virtues as well."

Helena, Underhill's fat gloomy Dutch wife, came in with a fresh tankard of beer, poured into all the mugs and went back to the kitchen.

"We are very grateful to you, Captain," said Andrew Ward. "And Governor Kieft'll certainly be when he hears of last night's work. I trust he won't reward you with Dutch land so tempting that you won't come back to us in Stamford."

"Why—" said Underhill genially, for he intended to move on to most desirable Manhattan land Kieft had hinted would be granted him, "that's very flattering, but you'll have no need o' me now, will you? There'll be no more danger from the Siwanoys."

The next afternoon, the three officers and the troops reappeared at the Feake house on Greenwich Cove, for the embarkation.

Toby Feake, who had come home instead of continuing to Stamford with the others last night, had already told Anneke and Elizabeth the outcome of the attack on the Siwanoy Fort.

And Elizabeth had at last broken down. All night she had lain sobbing beside Joan who had been frightened at first, then plaintive.

"Mama, Mama, don't cry so," the girl implored. "I can't sleep and you're shaking the bed. Mother, pray stop!"

But Elizabeth could not stop, though Joan finally went to sleep.

In the morning when Elizabeth dragged herself up, her

face wan and ravaged, her head throbbing, all feeling was blunted. Nor did she think of anything at all, except that as usual the hasty pudding must be made, the trenchers washed, snow water brought in, Robert fed, also the baby, while the girls were allotted their customary tasks: spinning for Joan, knitting for Lisbet, corn-pounding in a mortar for little Hannah.

While the soldiers clambered into the long boats, Underhill came in to say goodbye, still in an exultant mood, still wishful of discussing his great victory. But he was not devoid of sensitivity, and was shocked by Elizabeth's appearance.

"Farewell, Mistress," he said, courteously holding his plumed helmet in his hand. "I see I'm most unwelcome, and I'll not harrow ye with account of what happened, except to say you'll be grateful some day." He hesitated. Most women cheered up if you gave them a bit of flattery, even a kiss, but Bess Feake was different. Had always been, even in Boston, when he had considered her the fairest woman at the Bay.

Suddenly he slapped his thigh. "Damme if I haven't just remembered to tell ye something. Nay, don't shrink like that. 'Tis something to please you, I'll warrant."

Elizabeth continued to stir the boiling cornmeal.

"Saw a friend of yours in New Amsterdam t'other day," he went on brightly. "Young man by the name o' William Hallet. Was asking for you."

"In truth?" she said. Will Hallet and the night at Plymouth seemed as remote and unreal as her agonies last night over the Siwanoy. And yet, unexpected and causeless as an adder's sting, came a dart of pain. "So he's come back from England," she said.

"Aye, but he's off for the Indies. Was awaiting a ship. Said he had to go, but to tell ye he hadn't forgot."

"Forgot what?" she said, ladling the mush into a trencher.

"Why, I don't know," Underhill chuckled. "He seemed to think you would. He wanted to write a letter for me to bring ye, but I hadn't time to wait for it. But if he's still there when I get back to New Amsterdam, what shall I tell him?"

"Tell him," said Elizabeth, "that *I* have forgot." She put the filled trenchers on the table, and began to cut snippets from a block of maple sugar.

"Cold message, my dear, for a man who seems to have your welfare at heart," said Underhill shrugging. "Spoke very earnest about you, he did. I almost thought—" He looked at Elizabeth's shut, pale face. Underhill had almost thought there'd been some love passage between them, from the way Hallet spoke. Now it didn't seem possible. "Well, I'm off," he said. He glanced at the lean-to door. Robert could be heard babbling softly inside. "I wish ye luck and a better future, my dear. At least you've many fine children to comfort you. Ye can be glad of that."

"Aye," she said, pulling the crane off the fire. " 'Tis true, Captain Underhill, I can be glad of that."

In March, Toby put his shallop in the water again, and sailed to Stamford where he signed one of the Finch boys as crew before setting out for New Amsterdam and the resumption of his coastal trading.

When he returned to Greenwich Cove he carried to Elizabeth a letter from George Baxter.

"Ye've been given all the land here to administer as you see fit, haven't you?" said Toby watching Elizabeth read the letter. " 'Twas what Baxter told me."

"Yes," she said slowly. "That's what he writes—that Governor Kieft agrees too, in view of Robert's complete incompetence and as long as he shall remain distracted. I'm to do as I think best with the land, for our greatest benefit, and the children."

"Makes ye a rich woman in your own right, Aunt," said Toby with respect. "In a manner o' speaking. Land-rich. And ye can sell off parcels. Several Stamford men're ready to buy."

Elizabeth turned somber eyes to the window where she could glimpse the tree line of Monakewaygo, her own particular purchase four years ago. And now she had a hundred times that acreage to do with as she pleased, to dower the girls, to educate the little boys, to buy what she liked. Power. *Everything else has failed me*, she thought. *But there is this.*

"I'll be careful how I sell," she said. "Land values are going up fast, I've been talking with Angell Husted. He wants more good pasturage. But I'll wait until I get four shillings an acre for my best. Now that the Indians are—are gone, the back country'll open up, settlers will be clamoring from all over. Dutchmen too. I shall be canny."

Toby's little eyes opened wide. He had never heard her speak like this, nor, he thought, actually looking at her with attention, had she ever seemed hard and purposeful before.

"That's sense you're talking, Aunt, at last," he said. "Anneke too, though she's not got as much as you, still'll realize a tidy sum, in time. We'll start by selling some o' the salt marsh."

" 'We'?" said Elizabeth, raising her eyebrows.

"To be sure," said Toby in an offhand way, his stout freckled face reddening slightly. "When the year o' mourning for Patrick's up, Anneke and me'll run down to New Amsterdam and get wed. She's a mite old for me," said Toby, "but she suits me. Besides her cooking and her goodly property offset the age."

"I see," said Elizabeth. "And can't say I'm surprised. No doubt you'll content each other very well."

Oh Dan, Dan—she thought with a twisting sorrow. But she would not allow herself to continue into memory.

She sat down and read Baxter's letter again, turned the paper over, and fetching her quill and sumac ink, began to draw as best she could a map of all the Feake lands.

That night she had a strange dream about William Hallet. In the dream she was furiously angry with him, she hated him. Hated him so that she struck at him with Baxter's rolled up letter, which had grown hard like a club. She hit Hallet in the face with it, but it did not injure him, for he laughed and jeered at her. And then in the dream she wept, pleading his forgiveness, but the face was no longer his. It was Jack's, it was Harry's, it was at last John Winthrop's.

She awoke to a bleak and steely determination.

18

ON AN EXTREMELY hot Saturday in June of 1646, the six Greenwich families performed an unprecedented act. They trudged along the four miles of shore trail to Stamford with a view to attending Sabbath services at the Stamford Meetinghouse. And this they did in honor of little Joan Winthrop who was to be married today. Joan's betrothed, Thomas Lyon, had asked that the Greenwich residents with whom he was allying himself should show due decorum and godliness as an accompaniment to his marriage. And Elizabeth had agreed. It was a reasonable request, and she had sometimes felt guilt about her family's lack of religious observance.

She did not however much like her prospective son-in-law. He was pleasant enough, even ingratiating, big and handsome with fresh cheeks and curly hair, but she thought his close-set eyes had a calculating look, and she knew him to be conventional and very much impressed with the Winthrop name, since he had recently come from Boston. Still the sixteen-year-old Joan was in love with him in her own passive way. And being a plain-featured brown little thing with no hint of coquetry, Elizabeth recognized that they might have to wait a long time for another good offer. Thomas Lyon was twenty-six, well enough educated by a

Suffolk grammar school, and was also connected with the Winthrops' distant English kin—Sir Henry Mildmay. Thomas had little cash and was sparing with that, but he was very strong and seemed ambitious.

So there was no valid objection to the marriage. Indeed, as Thomas frequently pointed out, it should greatly increase Elizabeth's comfort, since the young couple were to live with the Feakes at Greenwich Cove.

"You have room in that fine house of yours and 'twill save me building my own," said Thomas in proposing this. "And you need a man to help with your affairs, and with Mr. Feake's care."

Which was true enough perhaps—and yet, thought Elizabeth proudly as she walked on the shore path towards Totomack Creek, I've done quite well alone these two years. She had made a few judicious sales, and had invested in pigs which needed little tending; by thrift she had managed not to encroach on the few remaining pounds of her jointure.

Also Robert was better. He stumbled along beside her now, clutching a fold of her violet tiffany skirt. His head was bowed, he stared at the ground, occasionally murmuring to himself, but he was not utterly lost to his surroundings any more. He knew that Joan was to be married today, and had wanted to be part of the occasion. Or at least he had not wanted to be left alone without Elizabeth.

Their children were, of course, part of the expedition. The fastidious Lisbet, thirteen now and very conscious of her flowerlike prettiness; Hannah, a sweet and chubby red-head, who kept near her parents; the little boys, Johnny and Robin, scampering on and off the path.

As they all passed the Husted homestall near the Sound, Angell and his wife came out to join them. "Why, good day, Mr. Feake!" said the young farmer, trying to hide his astonishment. "I didn't think you could—that is—how well you look—doesn't he?" he finished awkwardly to Elizabeth as Robert made a vague motion with his free hand, and did not look up.

"Aye," she said, smiling faintly. Robert had put on weight in his years of inactivity. His delicate bones had vanished into plump flesh which was suitably garbed today in a new fawn-colored doublet and breeches trimmed with silk braid and made in New Amsterdam. Elizabeth had provided new clothes for all her family, who were dressed in the latest Dutch fashions.

Bright spots of color they made along the leafy path; not only the Feakes, but their new neighbors, the Richard Crabs, John Coes, the Sherwoods, and Robert Husted—Angell's father—who had moved his homestall across the boundary from Stamford to Greenwich, preferring the latter's independence and lack of restriction, as had all these new settlers.

"Och—" said Anneke suddenly, mopping her flushed face with a small lawn kerchief. " 'Tis varm. Ve'll be melted ven ve get to Stamford. I hope if Toby makes a good price on this voyage of his, he can buy a horse. I cannot valk as I used to."

"Well," said Elizabeth. " 'Tis in a good cause. The child didn't want a Dutch marriage, even if we could have found a minister. And Thomas is a thorough-going Puritan." She sighed and Anneke glanced ahead at the young couple who headed the procession. Joan's short figure was dressed in dark green sarcenet, Thomas Lyon wore a sober gray suit and black hat. His curly hair was cut very short in the manner of the Roundheads, which seemed to be a name given to the Parliamentary forces in England who were commanded by a man called Oliver Cromwell. This Cromwell was fighting King Charles in a civil war which had arisen in the homeland. Thomas Lyon had brought the tidings from Boston. In Greenwich they had heard rumors before about the war, but dismissed them as negligible, the sort of unrest and rebellion they had all grown up with in the old country, nor wholly escaped in the new.

But now Thomas brought the incredible news that the King was losing—that his Queen and children had fled abroad—that Charles himself had surrendered to the Scots. Elizabeth and her neighbors had been astonished and concerned for a day or two, until they had decided it must be only a temporary defeat. It was impossible for the throne of England to be overturned by a commoner. Moreover it was all happening so far away, and the news six months stale, and doubtless exaggerated. When a violent northeaster blew off most of Angell Husted's roof shingles and flattened all the tender new greens in Elizabeth's garden, English affairs dropped from interest.

The Stamford-bound procession reached Totomack Creek where there was a rough footbridge, the boundary between Dutch and English territory. Elizabeth looked to the right, down the little cove towards the ruins of the Indian village which had been deserted immediately after the destruction of the Siwanoys.

"I wonder where that foul Nawthorne went after Underhill paid him off," she said to Anneke in a bitter tone. "Thank God we're quit of him and his half-wit clan."

"Ja," said Anneke, without interest. "They say all the Indians who vere frightened from here fled across the Sound. You should use this land, Bess, 'tis yours. Good fishing place. Or sell it." They both gazed at the small sheltered cove, which had once held canoes and chattering Indians. The cove, rock-bordered, was shaded by lofty elms and maples, its dark-green waters were steaming in the heat above rich oyster beds.

Robert raised his head. "Where're the Tomacs?" he said. "Where are their wigwams?"

Elizabeth and Anneke both started. They turned and gaped at Robert.

"Do you *remember* the Indian village, Rob?" Elizabeth said, as calmly as she could. "Do you really remember it?"

Robert blinked rapidly and let go of Elizabeth's skirt. "To be sure I do," he said with impatience. "Why shouldn't I? And Nawthorne who gave me the bone necklet I gave Lisbet."

"Hemel!" whispered Anneke. "So now vat comes! Vill it last?"

It appeared that it would. They reached the Rippowam, a tidal river, in spate so that they could not ford it. They hailed a man to ferry them over in his flatboat and as they walked up the river path on the eastern bank, Robert made several puzzled comments. "The gristmill's running," he said, looking at the great waterwheel below the millpond and dam. "I thought it burned down."

"They rebuilt it," said Elizabeth gently.

Soon, from his other remarks, about the size of the town which now had a hundred homes clustered around the green and meetinghouse, she realized that Robert remembered nothing since the day Daniel was killed nearly three years ago.

She did not enlighten him, because he seemed to accept the discrepancies. When they all trooped to Mr. Richard Lawe's house for the marriage, he greeted the men he had known before at Stamford quite naturally—nor seemed to note their astonishment.

Richard Lawe was chief magistrate, and had after some persuasion agreed to perform the ceremony. It was irregular, since Joan was a Dutch subject but her betrothed was not, and in any case, Mr. Lawe, in common with the other leading Stamford citizens, and the strict new minister, the Reverend John Bishop, felt that any hold which they could get on their unpatriotic, irreligious neighbors was eminently desirable. Greenwich with its rich arable lands, its splendid home sites should belong to New Haven Colony. How infuriating that because of Mrs. Feake's headstrong folly it did not.

The Lawes had a big house, almost a mansion, since they had taken over and enlarged Captain Underhill's after his departure for Manhattan and subsequently Long Island. And the Lawes had invited all Stamford gentry to be present at this function today. Many of the Stamford guests had never seen the Feakes, either Anneke who had been wife to the traitorous rogue Patrick and was now wed to a godless mariner, or Mrs. Elizabeth Feake who was reputed handsome, had been a Winthrop, and lived in mysterious seclusion with a mad husband. But the town fathers had a reason more devious than curiosity for entertaining not only the Feakes, but rebellious ex-Stamfordians like the Crabs and Husteds who had dared to cross the border. Objurgation having failed, persuasion might succeed in extending Stamford rule and Church membership.

The Lawes' Great Hall was filled as the Greenwich party entered. The Stamford ladies were all dressed in sad colors and wore plain fichus, aprons and caps. The Reverend John Bishop was very severe about such things. Elizabeth curtseyed and murmured politely, deciding that the group was very much like Watertown. Some of the women such as Mrs. Andrew Ward were pleasant and seemed to wish her well, the men on the whole were admiring, and it was agreeable to see again the look of startled interest in male eyes.

Her hostess, however, gave her the same resentful stare that Peg Warren used to in Watertown.

"This is a rare pleasure, Mistress Feake," said Mrs. Lawe as she offered Elizabeth a mug of small beer. "Stamford is indeed honored." Almost the lady kept sarcasm from her voice, but not quite. She glanced meaningfully towards Mrs. Bishop, the minister's wife, then at Elizabeth's gown of violet tiffany, the gold chain above a very low-cut bodice edged with heirloom lace, the puffed, slashed sleeves which exposed bare rounded forearms, at the many small dark curls which framed Elizabeth's rosy face beneath the becoming wisp of winged cap.

" 'Tis a pleasure to be here, Mistress Lawe," said Elizabeth blandly. "There are so many of us, I fear that after all we may discommode you if we spend the night in Stamford, or is there room at the ordinary?"

"Oh, Madam," cried Mrs. Bishop. "You couldn't stay *there!* We have place in our homes for you. I beg you and Mr. Feake will come to the parsonage." Rebecca Bishop was an anxious, gentle little woman. She was often forced to regret impulsive cordiality and she glanced nervously at her husband who deplored the heathenish Feakes.

"Nay, Rebecca," said Mrs. Lawe with hauteur. "It is arranged that the Feakes should stay here. 'Tis more fitting, though I fear my poor house isn't fine enough for Dutch patroons, so elegantly clothed. Are those the fashions in Amsterdam, Mistress?"

"I hope so," said Elizabeth sweetly. "And they are not unlike what I used to wear in England and the Bay."

"Oh, yes," chimed in Mrs. Ward. "We always used to dress according to our station. But Mr. Bishop doesn't wish us to. I think you look very charming, Mrs. Feake."

Elizabeth smiled at Mrs. Ward, while Mrs. Lawe tightened her lips and walked away.

The company regrouped themselves. The young people stood up before Mr. Lawe's table. The magistrate pushed his spectacles down his nose and the sparse civil service commenced.

When Elizabeth heard the words, "Martha Johanna, do you take this man—" she came to attention, and tears stung her eyes. Martha Johanna, aye—that was Joan's real name, and years since she had remembered it. "Martha" for the little sister whom Joan somewhat resembled, and "Johanna" for Jack. So long ago at Groton, in the beautiful bedroom where she had birthed this baby in agony, where she had known hot reckless love with Harry, and the pain of parting, and where she had known bitter jealousy of this same Martha and Jack. Where had all these feelings gone? Drowned in Salem's river with Harry, buried with Martha in a sad little grave in the wilderness. And Jack, even remoter than the other two. Though she had heard that he was nearer geographically now. That he had moved his family into Connecticut, and meant to settle there. And was he happy with the other Elizabeth, the "intruder"? Aye, to be sure he was, though no wife and family could capture all of him. And herself so much like Jack in many deep ways, Elizabeth understood that once they had finally parted, he no more than she would wish to look back, or renew the discomfort of their relation.

Yet, as she watched Joan being married, she felt a formless yearning, and a bleak emptiness.

Then she heard Robert breathing hard beside her, and turned with quick apprehension. "A wedding," he said in a hurried shrill voice. "A wedding, Bess, do you remember ours? In the Governor's house in Boston? The night that I first called thee wife?"

"Sh-h—" she said, for those nearby looked at them. This was not the babbling of madness, and yet his pale blue eyes were very bright, he spoke in haste as though some force propelled the words. He quietened for a moment, but as Mr. Lawe closed his book, Robert said even louder, "Let the husband render unto the wife due benevolence, and likewise also the wife unto the husband. The wife hath not power of her own body, but the husband, and likewise also the husband hath not power of his own body but the wife."

There was a startled silence before Mr. Bishop stepped forward. "True, Mr. Feake," said the minister, nodding approval. "I see that you can quote appropriate scripture. It is well for the young couple to hear that, and I'll use it as one of my texts in the sermons tomorrow."

"Aye, thank you, sir," said Robert, "and is my wife not fair? And he that is married careth for the things of the world how he may please his wife, but still it is better to marry than to burn."

"True. True," said Mr. Bishop hastily, embarrassed yet thinking that Mr. Feake was not nearly so unsettled in his wits as rumor had it. Obviously a pious man who might be induced to join the Stamford Church, whereupon all these other unregenerate Greenwich folk should follow suit.

Robert did nothing else untoward for the rest of the day, but Elizabeth sensed his inner agitation while he kept close to her, not in the clinging childish way, but in a way she had seldom seen in him. He touched her often, her bosom, her neck. When they sat down to eat, he put his arm around her and whispered in her ear, "Wife, wife—when shall we be alone?"

When they finally went up to their bedchamber at the Lawes', she watched with a trembling heart as he bolted the

door. All during the worst of his madness she had never
been afraid of him, but she was afraid that night. His eyes
glittered black from the dilated pupils. He flung his clothes
upon the floor, his pallid face ran with sweat. He shoved
her onto the bed and his hands clasped around her throat
lightly, but she felt the pressure of his fingers like a burn.

"This is a strange house, a strange house. And I have
strange feelings," he said in the jerky rushing voice. "You
aren't you and yet I know you are my wife. Come, come,
don't shrink from me like that. You know what my hands
can do to those that shrink and cry out. Nay, you don't
know. I forgot. And 'twas but a dream. A dream."

He took his hands from her throat and blew out the candle.
But then panting like a dog he seized her violently by the
shoulders. She dared not speak or move. When it was finished,
he fell slack on the bed beside her. "Oh God," he whispered.
"Oh God, I cannot stand it. Vile. Vile—"

She lay shivering, struggling for breath. She felt him raise
himself as though to look at her through the darkness, and
she inched away trying to make no sound. If she jumped
from the bed and ran for the door, would he be quick
enough to stop her? She had slid one foot over the edge
when he spoke suddenly. "Bess—" he said quietly. "Forgive
me. I shall go. I know I must leave you. God wishes it."

Her terror ebbed, she exhaled a long sobbing sigh. Through
the darkness his voice came as it used to be in the first days
of their marriage.

"I've a devil in me, Bess," he said. "I hurt what I love.
I know now what happened to Dan. I killed him."

"No, no!" she cried, pity mastering the fear. "You didn't
do that. 'Twas not your fault. The soldier Blauvelt shot Dan."

There was silence as though he were unsure, and weighing
the truth.

"Then 'twas because of what I said, the soldier shot him. I
hated Dan that day. 'Tis all the same."

"It is *not!*" she cried. "It wasn't as you fancy. Blauvelt
but waited his chance."

"Stop, Bess," he said. "Don't confuse me whilst I can
still see clear. God calls me back to face my just tribunal
from which I fled. I must go. How else will I be cured of
my sickness?"

"But you were better," she whispered. "Much better,
Rob. You will be cured." She stretched out her hand towards
him, groping until she touched his bare arm. She felt him

shudder and shrink away from her in the bed. She drew back her hand.

Many moments passed, then Robert spoke again, "No," he said. "I'll never heal because I've sinned too much."

Robert did not relapse into the witlessness of the past years, nor did he maintain the lucidity of that day in Stamford either. After the Feakes returned to their house on the cove, he entered a silent halfway state wherein he cared for himself, ate with the others, and even performed simple chores when Elizabeth asked him to, though these he often did not finish but went instead to his room and sat staring out the window with a dark brooding look, or turned the pages of his Bible, muttering verses to himself. Otherwise he seldom spoke, and when he did sometimes the words were apt, sometimes they sprang from his secret preoccupations. He made no attempt to approach Elizabeth again as a husband, for which she was deeply grateful.

Revulsion and the memory of fear now tinged her pity for him. And she suffered a miserable shock when she realized at the end of July that she was with child. After the conceptions of the four other little Feakes she had welcomed the signs, and been consoled for the varying disappointments in Robert by the bearing of his children. She had felt strong and happy throughout each pregnancy. This one, from the beginning, was different.

She suffered from morning sickness and malaise. The summer heat oppressed her, where formerly she had thought it exhilarating. Of nights she tossed sleepless beside Hannah.

Robert did not notice her discomforts, but one day she snapped at him with so much irritation that he stared at her in dim astonishment.

"Go fetch me *water* in the *pail* from the *well*," she cried furiously. "Always you must be told! *I* cannot do it and 'tis your fault I am breeding."

"Breeding?" he repeated uncertainly. "How can that be, since I've not lain with you in years? How can the babe be mine?"

"Oh my God, Robert!" she said in disgust. "Of course it's yours. The night of Joan's wedding in Stamford."

He shook his head indifferently—"I don't believe it," and he shambled out with the water pail.

Of what use? she thought. Why be angry? Yet she continued to feel anger and disgust. Nor was the presence in her house of Thomas Lyon and Joan a comfort. Thomas was lazy, his mother-in-law soon discovered. He, as well as Robert, had to be reminded of chores, which he performed reluctantly. The only occupation he enjoyed was figuring out various schemes by which the three hundred acres she had given Joan as dowry might be best exploited, or interfering with the management of her own property, even to selling her best sow to Robert Husted without consulting her.

There was a painful scene about the sow. Thomas protested that he knew more about swine than she did, that the sow was too old to farrow again, and that he had made a sharp bargain with Husted, for which she should be grateful and give him a commission.

The younger children, particularly Hannah, were upset by this scene when they saw their mother's rare anger flash out. Joan wept and backed her new husband. Elizabeth ended by giving Thomas two shillings, and went off alone to Monakewaygo as she had taken to doing whenever she could.

The children wanted to come with her, and she denied them sharply, telling them to go to Anneke's or do their tasks, or anything they wished, but to leave her alone. She knew that Hannah looked after her, watching from the garden, the chubby little face forlorn, but Elizabeth did not relent.

The tide was halfway in as she walked across the strip of shingle which connected her Neck with the mainland. Good, she thought. For six hours she would be totally cut off from all that troubled her. And have no means of getting back herself. No claims, or quarrels, or duties to harass her—safe on her island for a little while.

She walked to the white sands and stood at the water's edge, staring out at the rhythmic blue billows which gurgled and lapped on the hot sand. The metallic August sun shimmered in a sky filled with woolly cloud-puffs. She squinted her eyes against the glare and walked farther down the beach until it curved into a tangle of sumac and goldenrod. In there amongst the little pines had been the Siwanoys' great fishing camp. Now there was nothing left but the grassy walls of the earth fort that had stood there for four hundred years, since the Siwanoys' first ancestors came here out of the west. And the midden—a field of huge oyster and clam shells, discarded through the centuries and bleached whiter than the sands. She looked at the great flat rock where they had signed the purchase. The Manitoo Rock. Because she owned that rock, Telaka had spared them the Siwanoy revenge.

Elizabeth touched the rock and sighed. She wandered back to the beach, and slipped off her clothes. She lay naked on the sands in the shade of the sumac, until she grew too warm. Then she plunged into the water, splashing herself and lying where the gentle waves could bathe her. Cool at last, she went back up the beach to the sumacs and lay down on her green dimity dress. She wrung the water from her hair and spread the long black curling strands on either side of her to dry. As she lay with her head raised a little by the bank she could see far out over the Sound, and farther to the northeast horizon, as Martha once had. She thought of the day on Heartbreak Hill, and of what Martha had said: "I am made of cobweb that tears at a touch, but you, Bess, have fiber like the great seines that seldom break, yet if they do they can be mended again and again."

Mended again and again. For what?

"Aye, I know," she said aloud in answer to a monitory voice. Because of the children—but they would soon be grown, except—this one. She looked down with repugnance at her belly, still flat and taut, at her slender flanks. Because of Robert then—but he no longer cared, or needed her as he had even in his worst madness. Because of property perhaps—the tiny power it had brought, the game of acquisition and increase. But that now was thin and disappointing, tarnished too by her grasping son-in-law. Because of Monakewaygo then—and here like the chiming of a muted bell there seemed to be an affirmation. Yet she could not quite hear its sound, and when she tried to listen more intently there was nothing but the coo-roo-roo of the mourning doves in the rustling trees, and the lap and swish of water.

She lay so still that a sandpiper hopped by her foot and the little hermit crabs scuttled in and out of the seaweed near her elbow. Half drowsing and wholly secure on her island she paid no heed to small noises in the brush behind her, nor the cracking of twigs. Nor saw the shadow of a man fall across the sands.

It was William Hallet who stood rooted on the bank above Elizabeth, gazing down at her.

He had watched her from a distance as she splashed in the water, and been amused by the wantonness of her tanned body and the rich darkness of her floating hair. Always she had had this wanton quality, and he knew that in the past he had aroused desire in her, as he had in many women. True she had checked him at Plymouth, and thereby made it harder to dismiss her from his mind. That, and the promise of return he had incontinently made. These past years in England, at the mercy of Lord Digby's weathercock whims, had increased his innate reverence for a promise, which like all debts must be paid.

He still believed himself untouched by her except as any pretty, voluptuous, slightly older woman could arouse a man.

In his eyes, as he came through the bushes to the bank and looked down at her, there had been an amorous challenge, and the light touch of mockery with which he would explain his presence here.

But she lay there on her green gown, naked, beautiful, and defenseless as a child; the long lashes shadowing her sun-reddened cheeks, her soft lips curved down forlornly, her whole quiet face molded in bitter sadness.

The tenderness which he had repeatedly denied in these years welled up like a spring and dismayed him. He looked away, ashamed. He tried to back off noiselessly before she should be hurt or frightened by his intrusion. His foot twisted on a stone and he stumbled.

She jumped, grabbing her shift from a bush, clutching it to her body. "What is it?" she whispered, staring behind her with huge fearing eyes.

Hallet ran down the bank and knelt beside her on the sand. "Forgive me," he cried. "I didn't mean to startle you. Forgive me."

Her amazement at seeing him in Plymouth was nothing to this, yet now she felt no impulse of unconsidered joy, as she had then. She clutched tighter at her shift. Her eyes turned green, her nostrils flared.

"How dare you come here on my land? How dare you spy on me!"

"I know," he said, agreeing with her resentment. "I didn't mean to. I'll try to explain." He drew away a few paces and turned his back. "Dress yourself, if you wish," he said gently over his shoulder. "But you've no need to be abashed, your body is very fair, I've seen none more lovely."

"My humble thanks," she said through her teeth. "And for giving me permission to dress." She pulled her shift over her head and fastened herself into the green dimity gown.

"Now, William Hallet," she said standing. "What are you doing here, and how did you come, since the tide is up."

"Well, I swam," he said apologetically. "The distance so short, and the day so hot."

She raised her head and examined him with anger. Aye, his white shirt was clinging wet, so were his brown breeches and dark hose. The wetness revealed the thick muscles of his big body. His lank colorless hair was darkened by sea water. His brown face was longer-chinned than she remembered, and bonier. A common rustic's face, rough-hewn, uncouth, except the gray eyes which responded to her scrutiny with a faint smile.

"I'm waiting," she said coldly. "For what reason did you suddenly feel the need to track me down, even to my private island? Or was it not to find me you came here?"

"Aye, of course it was. I've come on horseback from New Amsterdam, where I landed some days ago. I had converse with George Baxter, Kieft's secretary. I inquired for you, as I did from Captain Underhill once before when I sent a message saying I hadn't forgot, Bess. Nor had I."

"And I sent one back, saying that I *had* forgot, if you mean our foolish dalliance in Plymouth. Also it seems that years at a time go by between whiles that you remember."

"And yet—" he said slowly, "I missed my ship in New Amsterdam waiting until Underhill returned with your message."

She glanced at him quickly, then down at the sand. What other message could I send?" she said. "And why are you here today?"

"Because my association with Lord Digby is now finished for aye, and my debt to Mr. William Whiting of Hartford is finally paid off. I've thirty pounds in my purse, a horse, and a provisional land grant from Governor Kieft for a farm on Long Island. I told him however that I wished a look at Greenwich before I decided where to settle. Baxter says that Kieft thinks it a good idea. He wishes this border town strengthened by more settlers, since most of its territory is owned by two weak women, Elizabeth and Anneke Feake." He paused, with a half-smile, "So I came to see one of them today."

"I see," she said evenly. "You think to buy some of my land."

"It might be. That's what I told the young man whom I found at your house a while ago. He seemed very eager to discuss the matter, and disinclined to tell me where you were."

"My son-in-law, Thomas Lyon," she said through tight lips. "How then did you find me?"

"I was well directed by a fiery-topped moppet, who has a smile as enchanting as I remember that her mother had, though today I've no way of judging. Your daughter pointed out the white sands and said that's where you'd be."

"Could this business of yours not have waited until I came back?"

"It could, to be sure, but having started any enterprise I like to see it through."

There was a silence. She felt his gaze as she stood rigidly on the sand, her head turned towards the sea. I must not be a fool again, she thought, nor let that gentleman's voice and the strength of that big body bewitch me as they have before. I shall be chill and stern, bid him swim back as he came, leave me in peace. But the words of dismissal could not quite be commanded.

"What did you really come for—" she said. "To see me or to buy fine cleared land?"

"Both," he answered promptly with his usual frankness. "But now that I *have* seen you, 'tis more one than t'other."

She was reminded of the nakedness he had seen, and that her hair was flowing down her back like a goose girl's and that her feet were bare. She blushed.

"Sit down, Bess," he said. "I assume you don't swim, since earlier I confess I watched you romping in the water, like a sea nymph. So we must wait until the tide runs down again. Let's chat in comfort."

"I came here for solitude," she said. "There's nothing to stop *your* going back to the mainland."

"No. And I will if you really wish it. I want only your good." The bantering note had left his voice, and its sincerity startled her. It was long since anyone had thought particularly of her welfare—not since Daniel died.

She sat down on the bank in a tentative way, slipped her feet into her shoes and began to braid her hair. He did not encroach on her, he sat on a driftwood log, breathed deeply of the salt air and sighed with the same sensuous pleasure she often felt herself. "There's content in this place," he said. "I do not marvel that you come here." He picked up two yellow jingle shells and frowning down at them chipped them idly together. "Bess, you've had heavy troubles since

I saw you last. Baxter told me and today—I saw your husband."

"Robert's somewhat better," she said quickly. "And for the rest I don't want to think of them, not here on Monakewaygo. 'Tis not fitting."

He smiled, touched by the youthfulness of this, yet himself aware of a mystic charm here, an other-worldliness and peace. She looked very young, sitting so primly, her hands tight-clasped together, and the long loose braid hanging down to her lap.

What man has ever looked at me like that? Elizabeth thought, seeing in his eyes amused tenderness and understanding. A thickness came into her throat, and she said very fast, "I know nothing of *your* life in these years, have you—?" she stopped short as he burst into laughter.

"Oh hinnie, hinnie-sweet!" he said. "I know what you will ask since you do each time we meet."

"Hinnie?" said Elizabeth puzzled and trying to smile. "Do you call me 'hinnie,' for you think I'm a horse?"

He shook his head. "Though there's few things sweeter than a saucy little mare. 'Hinnie' is 'honey' in the North Country, where by the way I've spent some time with Digby—fighting."

"Fighting?" she said slowly. "How so?"

"For the King. Until Digby changed his mind and we changed sides for the nonce, and back again. I found it confusing." He spoke with curtness, for these memories displeased him. "Wouldn't you like me to answer what you were going to ask me? I can do it in a border ballad, having learned several to while away cold winter nights of deferred battle."

"Can you indeed?" she said with dignity, but the corners of her mouth flickered.

"It is called 'The Faire Flower of Northumberland,' and some of the verses go rather like this." William tilted his head, and watched her as he sang in a rough baritone:

" '*Hinnie-sweet, I am no foe,*' *he said*
(*Follow my love, come over the strand*)
'*By thy bonny face here was I stayed*
For thee, faire flower of Northumberland.'

" '*Sir, why dost come here for sake of me,*
(*Follow my love, come over the strand*)

Having wife and children in thy countrie?
—And I the faire flower of Northumberland.'

" 'I swear by the blessed Trinitie,
(Follow my love, come over the strand)
I have no wife nor children, I,
So be my ladye in this islande.

" 'I swear by Him that was crowned with thorn
(Follow my love, come over the strand)
That I never had wife since the day I was born,
And I live a free lord on my own free land.' "

He got up and made her a courtly bow. "Have I answered
your question, hinnie?"

He had, though she was unwilling to admit it. When of a
sudden her pride dissolved, and she too began to laugh, her
eyes crinkling and an unexpected dimple showing in her
cheek to match the cleft in her strong chin. "It seems I do
repeat myself," she said. "For I must cry again as I did on
Boston Common, 'Will Hallet, you're fantastical!' And you
read me all too well."

He glanced at her quickly and sobered. There was greater
danger in shared mirth than in shared tears, especially for
her who must have been long without gaiety, or her face
could not have held the look he had surprised on it when
he stood on the bank. Take care, he chided himself, this
woman is nothing to you, and you'll merit hell fire if you
increase the hardness of her lot.

He picked up the jingle shells, dangled them in his big
callused palm. "Shall I tell you something of my travels,
Bess?" he said in a courteous formal tone. "Would you hear
of England, or the Indies—Nevis, Christopher, Antigua
where I finished business for my Lord Digby and from
whence I've just returned?"

"All of it," she said. "You can't doubt it, but first would
you like to see more of Monakewaygo? The secret pool
which no one knows of, except me—and the children. 'Tis
very lovely in this westering light."

She spoke shyly, wondering at herself that she wanted
so much to show him the heart of her treasured domain,
aware that in this desire there were elements both of testing
and of fate.

He rose at once, glad of action, "Aye, let us to the pool."

She led him inland through underbrush and thick-set trees, fine hardwoods, he thought seeing the trees with the yeoman's eye, straight hefty oaks, chestnuts and elms. Mighty little stuff like this left in Old England. It was hot in the forest, gnats and mosquitoes swarmed about his head, he saw and avoided clumps of the glistening poisonous three-leaved ivy, having been well blistered by this plant in his first years on these shores.

Elizabeth flitted on ahead, a green figure amongst the green leaves. When he could glimpse her face, he was puzzled by its expectancy, a hint of devotional exaltation, such a look as he had seen on the faces of communicants during Mass at Notre-Dame in Paris, where he had accompanied Digby, during one of that volatile lord's Papist veerings.

She led him over a brown carpet beneath a stand of hemlocks, and stopped at the edge of a dark still pond which the hemlocks partly shadowed. "Look!" she whispered. "Hush—"

A white-tailed doe stood at the edge of the pond drinking. The doe raised her head and stared at them with thoughtful eyes, then she hobbled over to Elizabeth and nuzzled her shoulder.

" 'Tis Sprite," said Elizabeth softly, scratching the furry ears. "The children named her. I've not seen her for long. I was afraid she—"

She stopped, unable to explain how dismayed she had been of late when the doe had disappeared.

"She's hurt her hind leg?" asked Will, slightly embarrassed, conscious of intensity in Elizabeth, and the fringe of some secret meaning he no longer shared. It was a pretty woodland pool, set in gray rocks and ferns, but he had seen a hundred others much like it on his travels.

"Aye, she broke her leg when she was a fawn," said Elizabeth watching the doe limp off to a sassafras tree and begin to browse. "I tried to heal it but I couldn't quite. So she must endure to hobble."

"Poor beast," said Will politely. "I'm thirsty, Bess. Is this lake water sweet?"

"Aye, indeed," she said, as to a foolish question. "Come drink." They knelt together on the mossy margin, and cupping their hands drank of the clear cool water. "Are you anhungered too?" she asked smiling. "There's a blueberry patch t'other side of the great rock."

"Not hungry," he said. She nodded, and sat down on a

bed of fern and moss, laced her fingers around her knees and seemed to be smiling now at the pool and waiting. She had lost all self-consciousness, and, he thought, lost awareness of him too, which piqued him.

He had a strong desire to kiss her, to reawaken the sensual response she had always showed, but her attitude confused him. More than her attitude, some subtle emanation from the place itself as it touched her, though he felt it only by indirection.

He sat down beside her on the ferns, and started to speak.

"Hush—" she said again, taking his hand. A friendly little gesture like a child's.

He stared at the pool, trying to see what she did. The tranquil dark green water was nearly black in the shadows. Now he noted two snowy herons, preening their feathers in the marshy brink at the far side, also the purple of loosestrife and red-berried trillium in the woods near them, but surely nothing to explain her expectancy.

"What are you looking for?" he whispered, closing his fingers around her hand.

She started a little, realizing that she had expected him to know. "It's the way the light comes through the trees, just at sunset; once I almost caught it, when it turns the pond to gold, but I was too late. I saw only the shimmer as it passed. Just there between the hemlocks."

All this for a sunset, he thought. What a strange little pagan she was, burning with some crystal flame he did not understand. But he kept very still, conscious of her hand so trustingly clasped in his.

He saw the sun rays slant through the hemlocks and then vanish into darkness. She sighed, her hand fell from his. "It won't come today," she said. "There are too many clouds."

She looked around at him, and he met her gaze with a question.

"You don't feel what I feel, do you, Will?" she said, with a rueful smile. "No matter, at least you've been with me here, perhaps it is something one can only feel alone." She was quiet a moment and with a sudden change of mood, she jumped up.

"Let's go back to the beach," she cried. " 'Follow my love, come over the strand!' "

He was bewildered by her and the tender teasing with which she quoted his own ballad to him.

"Can we not stay here?" he asked humbly. "The tide won't be down enough yet."

"We can't stay here," she said. "One shouldn't stay here long."

She ran back through the trees, and he lumbered after her, feeling awkward and uncertain, yet more charmed by her than he had ever been. They reached the beach where they had sat before. "The tide *is* down," she said. "See, how far out on the sands the water's gone." As she spoke the glow in her eyes darkened as the pool had done. Her features grew sharper, her mouth tight. She had been ageless, shining with a fey, mysterious beauty. She became in an instant a woman, still fair but mature. It hurt him to see the change.

He caught her around the waist, and pulling her roughly against him, kissed her on the mouth. She did not resist. Her warm lips opened under his. Her breath was sweet as milk. Desire rushed through his body. "Christ—" he whispered against her lips. "It begins again, dear heart, as it was in Plymouth."

"And will end as it did then," she said, looking up at him steadily, her eyes so near that he could see their gold flecks and each separate eyelash.

"No!" he cried. "It cannot end so. This time is different. Bess—I fear that I love thee."

They stood silent, their bodies pressed close, while the gray gulls circled lazily above their heads.

"Aye," she said at last. "I think you do. 'Tis strange."

Strange indeed, he thought, since he had lusted for many women, but never yet spoken of love.

"I see you do not want me," he said very low, turning from her.

"If you see that, your sight is gravely amiss." She gave a little laugh that caught in her throat. "I want you as you want me. And Will, I love thee too. I believe it's love. I felt it strongest at the pool. It pierced my heart though you were unaware."

"Then come to me, darling. It's no sin. 'Tis not like last time. Now your husband is—" He jerked his head as though to rid it of a burden.

"My husband is mad, yes," she said still looking at him steadily. "But yet I am with child by him."

He stiffened and made a harsh sound. She thought he would harden into the cold fury that he had before when she denied him. But he did not.

He took her in his arms again and smoothed her hair. "Oh hinnie, hinnie-sweet," he said. "What a coil we have got into. What a miserable coil."

"So now," she whispered, "you will go again, dear love. Where shall it be this time? Virginia or the Indies?"

He sighed, still gently smoothing her hair. "I cannot go, Bess," he said in a tone of wonder. "I cannot leave thee. It shall be in any wise you wish it, but I will stay near thee, and help."

19

WITH ONE EXCEPTION all the Greenwich settlers liked William
Hallet from the first. "An able stalwart man," said Richard
Crab to Robert Husted, summing up the general opinion.
"He's seen a lot o' the world, is not afraid o' work, and has
much skill at husbandry."

"In truth," agreed Husted, "and having no family yet,
Hallet can give his mind to town affairs, knows summat o'
soldiering too, though he won't talk of it. I've been thinking
we should get us a train band here. He could drill us now
and then. Every proper town has a train band, and no reason
why we should depend on Stamford come any trouble."

So they chose Will for their captain. And they respected
his opinion in matters of fencing certain fields, and of
alloting common land and fishing rights. He told little about
his earlier life, made no reference to the Digbys and Sherborne Castle. He was accepted as a Dorset yeoman who had
been trained for a joiner, and the excellencies of his speech
were put down to Dorsetshire peculiarities.

Will established his homesall on Totomack Cove, near
the spot where Nawthorne's clan had lived. He bought six
acres there from Elizabeth, after refusing her impetuous
offer to give him the land. His pride forbade a gift, but also
they must, for her sake, be careful to conceal their love for

each other, or any signs of intimacy. He particularly wished
to protect her from the growing animosity of her son-in-law.

Thomas Lyon had been annoyed when the Greenwich
men elected Hallet to leadership. He felt that as new son
to the largest landholder the position should have been his.
And he resented Hallet's frequent presence at the Feake
home, where everyone welcomed the fellow with excessive
cordiality. Mother Feake never said much to Hallet, but she
seemed to change when he was around, looking softer,
smiling more and acting as though that common carpenter
was an equal and a friend. As for the children, they followed
Hallet about, obviously admiring while he quietly performed
many neglected tasks. For months there had been a leak in
the lean-to roof. Hallet repaired it. He also fixed the pigsty,
and made Elizabeth a brand new chopping board of hard
maple to replace the old splintery pine one.

The fellow Hallet also had a curious effect on Father
Feake, who often left off reading the Bible or staring into
space to ask him sensible questions—about the best storage
for the salt hay, or the possibilities of marketing their excess
corn crop.

Before many weeks passed, it seemed that Hallet was
looked to in all matters as though he were the man of the
house. Thomas felt himself supplanted, and was all the
angrier since he could find no real cause for complaint.
Hallet was very helpful, not only at odd jobs, but with crop-
tending. He was generous with the loan of his horse, and
he shared with the Feakes the game he shot in the forests.

There could be no doubt that Will Hallet's advent had
eased all their lives, and Thomas, who was as shrewd as
the next man, very soon began to ask himself why.

It did not occur to him that Elizabeth had anything to do
with all this—a middle-aged woman of thirty-six, swollen
with pregnancy—nor had he any illusion about his Joan's
attractions either. And Lisbet was too young, surely, to be
the magnet. Though Thomas retained this as a possibility.
Perhaps the fellow had an eye to the future, and the securing
of a fine dowry, but in the meantime what more likely than
some plot to alienate the Feake property? To so worm his
way into Mother Feake's gratitude that he could gain control of their affairs, buy land for a song, even set himself
up as *the* Greenwich patroon.

Thomas at last sought for sympathy from Toby Feake.
This was during the winter. Toby had now bought himself
a sixty-foot sloop and had been at sea some months, but

returned to Greenwich in January to await better weather. Thomas left Joan at home, because though she obeyed him very well, and always thought as he did, she nonetheless showed a tiresome lack of concern about her own interests, and seemed to share the family besottedness over William Hallet.

Toby Feake was dozing in a large armchair by a roaring fire. He was smoking a clay pipe, a tankard of strong ale stood on a stool at his elbow, the buttons of his velvet doublet had been opened for greater ease in the digestion of Anneke's fine cooking. Toby's heavy thighs were comfortably crossed, his shoes twinkled with silver buckles. He was the very picture of a prospering burgher, and he was disinclined to think about anything, except the best market for the next cargo of beaver pelts with which he would embark in the spring.

"I don't see what you're complaining of," Toby said after listening to his new kinsman. "Naught wrong wi' Hallet that *I* can see."

"You should be glad he helps poor Bess, and Robert is brighter too," said Anneke, taking a fragrant loaf of ginger-bread from her oven. "Your Mother Feake has had a very hard time. Young folk like you don't alvays notice."

"That's just it!" cried Thomas. "Why does he do all he does? 'Tisn't natural!"

"Quite natural," said Anneke, so sharply that Toby opened his eyes. "Villiam Hallet has a good heart, also he's known Bess since he vas a lad, crossed on the *Lyon* ven she came over." Anneke spoke sharply because secretly she did think there was something odd about the relationship. Once or twice she had caught a glance exchanged between Hallet and Bess, and been struck with a disquieting speculation. Which she had no intention of letting Thomas know, or anyone. Bess had misery enough to contend with.

"It is often unvise," said Anneke, "for a young couple to live vith the parents. Flyspecks then grow big as toadstools."

Thomas, who disliked the implied advice, hastily dropped Hallet in favor of another topic he had spent much thought on.

"Cousin Toby," he said. "Did you ever hear of aught coming to Joan through her father's property on Barbadoes?"

"Why ask me?" said Toby yawning. "I know nothing of Winthrop affairs. Ask my aunt."

"She denies it. But says the Governor handled all that."

"Governor Winthrop has no head for money," said Toby.

"You got a good jointure wi' Joan, yet if you think more's coming to her, why don't ye write to Winthrop himself? The *Victory*'ll likely touch at Stamford in a week or two. Could take the letter to Boston." He yawned again. "Anneke, bring me more ale, but first mull it a bit wi' cinnamon." He closed his eyes and clasped his hands over his rounding belly.

Thomas went back home disappointed. But he wrote a letter to John Winthrop, a politic humble letter, expressing his great joy at becoming the Governor's grandson, unworthy as he was, reminding him that Joan was not living in the manner appropriate to a Winthrop, and wondering if there might be some property due her. He made vague allusions to unsettled affairs prejudicial to Joan's interests, and the ungodly behavior of certain parties, and closed with a plea for advice. He did not mention the elder Feakes to Winthrop, nor mention his letter to Elizabeth. He settled back to keep matters under close observation, and bide his time until a reply might come, and show which way the wind blew.

He was not however destined to need patience for long. Matters reached a head before his letter arrived in Boston.

The thaws came early that year, and on a bright warmish morning at the end of February little Johnny rushed in to Elizabeth, crying that the sap was running in the maples, Danny had cut one and found it so. It was time for the sugaring-off. Could they start at once? There'd be a full moon too, for the next nights.

Elizabeth tried to smile. The sugaring-off was always a happy frolic for the children, and a pleasant gathering of neighbors, but it also meant hard labor, not only the gashing of the trees as the Siwanoys had taught them, and affixing of spouts and buckets, but the tending of many fires to boil the sugar.

Moreover as the best stand of sugar maples belonged to her and grew north of her home, those who helped would expect not only a share of the product, but food and drink for several days as well.

And she was weary to the bones. She had now carried the babe through the eighth month, and it weighed her down like a great sluggish lump. She had a steady pain through her groins, other pains which she had never felt before. Her spirits were as heavy as her body, except when Will came, and then she suffered that he should see her like this distorted and clumsy, trying always to keep back weakly tears.

"*Please*, Mama—" said Hannah eagerly from behind the spinning wheel. "Lisbet and I'll help you. 'Twon't be much work."

Joan had gone off to Stamford with Thomas to attend Sabbath services, and would not be home for several days. Thomas also wished opportunity to discuss his father-in-law's return to sanity with the Reverend Bishop. If Robert were adjudged sane, Mother Feake would no longer have control of the property.

While Hannah was speaking, Robert came into the kitchen with an empty bucket, which had contained swill for the pigs. He put the bucket down and looked at Elizabeth. "What do the children want?" he said. "What are they begging you for?" His pale eyes had their new cold hardness, as they had since the night of the baby's conception, and particularly when they were turned on her. He never called her wife any more or even "Bess." Sometimes it seemed to her that there was a wary, hostile animal hiding behind his eyes, and then she would chide herself for distraught fancies, because to others he seemed nearly normal; everyone had remarked on it—particularly Thomas.

"Why, it's time to begin the sugaring-off," she answered with effort. "Johnny says the sap's running."

"What does Will Hallet say? Does he think it's time?"

Robert did not look at her, he looked at Hannah, who said, "I don't know, Papa. Shall I run over to his house and ask him?"

"Aye," said Robert with relief. "He'll know." He walked into his lean-to room, came back with his Bible and pulling a stool near the window began to read.

It was a strange thing, thought Elizabeth, stirring the everlasting cornmeal mush. Some of the dependence, the blind trust Robert had used to have for Daniel, seemed to have transferred itself to Will.

Oh, what are we going to do after the babe is born? she thought. How can it go on and on like this? Yet she shrank from trying to look ahead. Will and she had been in a state of tacit abeyance since the afternoon on Monakewaygo. They had never dared meet alone, a few snatched private words were all they had, but her love had grown a thousand-fold, nourished by the quiet, sensitive protection that he gave her.

She heard his step at the door, and his voice saying something to Hannah. Her heart quivered and paused when she heard him. She bent over the stew pot as he came in scraping snow off his boots on the threshold. She turned her head a little, and their eyes met for that precious instant of private signal. In his look there was a steady reassurance, in hers she hoped there was no pleading or pain.

"Good day, Feake—" Will said. "Hannah tells me you're thinking of sugaring-off. I don't know much about it, but seems a good idea. Why don't we go out and test the trees?"

Robert looked up. Something like a smile lightened his face, which had subtly coarsened as it had grown plump. He put his long finger on the open Bible page. "I was just reading that," he said in a tone of triumph. " 'And Jonathan said unto David, Come and let us go out into the field. And they went out both of them into the field.' 'Tis a sign! The woman would not understand that, would she?" He glanced sideways at Elizabeth. "She that is filled with sinful fruit."

Will felt a shock, though he showed nothing. I must watch over her more carefully, he thought. Watch this man, who is not perhaps as harmless as Bess and the others through custom have always thought, nor do I think he is truly better.

They started the sugaring-off that afternoon and continued by the brilliant moonlight. The next night the fires burned red across the snow patches, while the delectable fragrance of the syrup intoxicated the happy children who candied driblets on the snow.

Elizabeth too knew a moment of happiness. Both she and Will, freed from Thomas's vigilant eye, felt greater freedom to talk with each other. As she ran the sap from a filled bucket into a kettle it was natural that he should help her. His hand closed over hers, and he whispered, "Hinnie-sweet, we will think of a way. Be staunch and have faith. I love thee."

"Still . . . ?" she whispered. "And I grown so ugly and so mopish."

"I see thee always as on the day at Monakewaygo, and as you will soon be again, God willing." He said the latter below his breath, for he was afraid of the childbirth, and afraid for her with Robert, who had now gone off by himself to a hillock and was staring up at the moon.

"Hallet! Hallet!" called Richard Crab. "Gi' me a hand wi' this kettle, I vow ye're the only man here can lift it!"

"Tom Lyon could," called Angell Husted, laughing. "We must set a wrassling match atween those two bully boys come spring. A bit o' sport. Are ye for it, Hallet?"

"Aye, forsooth," agreed Will amiably. "I can beat Tom with one hand tied."

There was a chorus of good-natured jeers. John Coe cried, "Hark at the braggart!"

They don't know, Elizabeth thought. They knew nothing of the strains in the Feake home, nor guessed how true a battle they were jestingly urging. They knew nothing of the turmoils of her inner life. She lived amongst her neighbors in a spirit of isolation. And yet these were good neighbors, not basically censorious like those of Watertown or Stamford.

She leaned against a tree trunk and watched with sad detachment the good-fellowship of sugaring. Rebecca Husted laughing at some clumsiness of her young husband, Angell; Goody Crab stout and quick-tempered giving the rough side of her tongue to one of her young; the Coes and the Sherwoods working together on a clump of maples nearer the cove, and everywhere running and shouting were the children, her own and a dozen others. Scarlet-hooded they were, most of them, little redheaded woodpeckers, tapping at the trees, flitting across the snow in the light of fire and moon. But always her eyes went back to the tallest male figure in the leather jerkin, as he helped stoke the fires and handle the great kettles.

While she leaned against the tree, a violent pain knifed up her flanks. It can't be, she thought, frightened. 'Tis too soon by a month. And Anneke ill! Anneke had recently suffered a violent attack of sciatica, for which Elizabeth had given her a decoction of minced bay-leaves, but she was not yet able to move about.

Elizabeth's pain came again, so agonizing that she fell to her knees, and called out in a muffled voice to the nearest woman, "Goody Crab!"

The goodwife dropped her ladle and hurried over. "What is't, Mistress? Oh, I see—Lord, Lord—poor wight, an' so far from home. Can ye walk?"

Elizabeth shook her head, clinging to the tree trunk. "No—" she gasped. " 'Tis worse than I ever remember it." She clamped her mouth against a shriek.

"Here, Angell," said Will's quiet voice. "Take her legs, I'll take the shoulders, mind now, don't double her up! Steady, Bess!"

She felt Will's arms around her, and the support of his hands. Through the fear, pain and humiliation she knew a flash of joy. But the next pain was worse, though she tried with all her force to hold it back. As she screamed, she felt a gushing of water and blood.

"We'll take her back by the fire, Angell—" said Will, his voice unsteady. "She can't go on."

They laid their cloaks on the snow and put her down. Rebecca Husted and Goody Crab bent over her holding her hands. Goodwife Coe shooed the children off to a safe distance and kept them there. The men drew away behind the trees frowning and sheepishly uncomfortable.

"It don't look good—" said Crab, shaking his head. "I lost me first wife like that. Birthing should be easy after so many, but 'tisn't allus. Matters go amiss."

"Hold your tongue, Goodman!" Will cried, sweat breaking out on his forehead. "There's naught amiss."

Crab smiled at him in mild surprise, which was checked by Robert's sudden appearance. Robert clutched at Will's arm.

"Why does the woman cry out like that?" he asked in a high excited voice. "For what is she being punished?"

" 'Tis your wife Elizabeth, you crazed fool!" Will shouted in anguished fury, as he heard her give another gasping scream. "And she is being punished for your foul lust!"

Robert staggered back as though Hallet had hit him. He made an odd bubbling sound in his throat. He turned from the group of silent men. He covered his face with his hands, walked a little way, stopped on a patch of snow and stood there, his shoulders shaking.

Will did not watch Robert. He strode to the frightened murmuring women. "Why can't you help her?" he cried to Goody Crab who was kneeling by the heaving body on the cloaks.

"I don't know what else to do," snapped the goodwife. "I might if she could be still a moment, poor lass, she thrashes so."

Will knelt down on Elizabeth's other side and took her hands in his. "Quiet, Bess," he said sternly. "You must keep quiet, hinnie. Do you hear me?"

She gave a low animal moan, clutching at his hands until his knuckles cracked, but she tried to obey. Goody Crab profited at once by the lull. "Hold the lantern nigh—" she said to Rebecca. "I'll see what I can do."

With the next pain Elizabeth was delivered, and she swooned. Will bent down and kissed her clammy forehead. The women did not notice. "I'faith," whispered Rebecca. " 'Tis a puny mite to cause such trouble. Does it live?"

The goodwife did not answer; she cut the cord with the scissors which hung from her girdle and slapped vigorously. There was a thin mew like a kitten's. They examined the baby quickly and wrapped it in a corner of the cloaks. "It looks horrid," whispered Rebecca. "What's wrong wi' its face?"

"Sh-h—" said Goody Crab with a glance at Elizabeth.

"What is it?" Will asked in a tone of authority, to which the goodwife responded, never thinking it strange until later.

" 'Tis a girl," she said very low. "But has been cursed somehow by an evil goblin. 'T has a hare lip."

Will shook his head. "Don't let Mrs. Feake know until you have to. We must get her to the house."

He put Elizabeth's inert hands softly on her breast, and went towards the men. " 'Tis born," he said. "We'll make a litter from poles and cloaks for her."

The men sprang to work. But Angell said, "You spoke dreadful harsh to poor Mr. Feake, Will. I hope ye've not sent him daft again."

Will looked around and saw Robert wandering slowly towards the place where Elizabeth lay. Will grabbed a pole and ran back, ready for trouble.

But Robert·did nothing. He stood staring down at the blood on the snow. He bent closer and examined the baby's face. "Aye," he said to Will. "You were right. I see now it is mine, since the Devil has put the mark of his cloven hoof here. I'm going, Hallet. I cannot stay. I mustn't stay near her. She that was my wife."

"Where are you going?" said Will, amazed that there seemed to be a thread of reason in this, and even a sane kind of sorrow.

"Tonight I go to Stamford," said Robert. "To Mr. Bishop. I have need of a minister, you see, a man of God to help me in my thinking. I cannot think here—with *her* whom I have blasted."

"Why, you mustn't go tonight, Mr. Feake," said Goody Crab. " 'Tis no time to be journeying," she added soothingly.

"I must," said Robert. "I hear God's voice, it tells me what to do." He walked rapidly away through the trees towards the trail to Stamford.

"Let him go," said Will. "We can look for him later. We must get Mrs. Feake to shelter."

For five days Elizabeth was desperately ill, nor conscious of what went on around her. Anneke limped over from her home to help Goody Crab and Rebecca Husted who took turns at the constant nursing of both mother and baby. They relegated the frightened girls, Lisbet and Hannah, to the kitchen and its now strenuous duties. The Coes took the little boys home with them. Nobody sent for Joan and Thomas. "Ve manage better vithout them," said Anneke curtly.

Elizabeth had a raging childbed fever, her breasts caked, and she had no milk, but the baby could not suck in any case. Its upper lip was cleft in two, as was the palate inside its mouth. Rebecca brought her nanny-goat from her home to the Feakes', and the women trickled goat's milk down the infant's throat but it could hardly swallow. They used what medical lore they had on Elizabeth but as Anneke constantly wailed, "*she* vould know vat to do, my lieveling Bess. Alvays she has been the vun to go to in sickness! God allemachtig, I pray for her, and pray."

Will also prayed with a vehemence he had never before known the need of. Words came in the simple little prayers his mother had taught him, and which he had thought forgotten. He searched for faith in a benevolent God who would not let her die, nor could find that faith for more than an instant. He tried then by force of willing to keep her here, and cursed aloud that he could not stay with her, holding her in his arms, giving her of his strength. He did the heavy chores mechanically, he lay down on Robert's bed in the lean-to at night but could not sleep. He paced the Feakes' kitchen floor, listening always for sounds from upstairs and awaiting Anneke's appearance with bulletins, which for days were nothing but a sad shake of the head.

Lisbet's volatile nature soon adjusted to the crisis, and she enjoyed being in charge of the kitchen. The nine-year-old Hannah was Will's only solace. They did not speak of the love they shared, but Hannah understood, and would sometimes slip her hand into his and look up to him for comfort.

The women wondered, of course. One day Goody Crab said crossly to Anneke, "What ails that man? Why doesn't he go home? You'd think *he* was the father, though I vow my goodman ne'er took on so when I near died birthing Jemmie."

"Can you begrudge her anyvun's concern?" asked Anneke quietly. "And her husband is gone too." She piled more blankets over Elizabeth who from burning heat had plunged into a chill, and her shivering shook the bed.

"Aye," said the goodwife grimly. "Her husband's gone, if

that's an affliction, but I'll keep my thoughts to m'self." She bent over and examined the baby. "This miserable worm's not long for this world. We'd best christen it."

Anneke nodded, averting her eyes from the baby's face.

"I've got the old prayer book at home," said Goody Cràb. "But no time to fetch it. I think I remember the words. What'll we use for holy water, and what name?"

"Use snow," said Anneke. " 'Tis pure enough. And the name—" she glanced at Elizabeth's closed eyes, her fever-red cheeks, her chattering teeth. "Ve can't ask her—so any name, Sarah vill do."

Between them the two women baptized the baby, said the Lord's Prayer over it—Goody Crab in English, Anneke in Dutch, and were relieved when it was done. Especially as the baby died that night. While she led her nanny-goat home again, Rebecca Husted wept bitterly, for she was young and frightened, and with child herself; but the older women thought the baby's death a blessing, as did Will Hallet. He set at once to making a pine box for the tiny body, grateful that this last repugnant link with hideous memories should be broken for Elizabeth.

And the next day she was much better. The fever had gone; she lay spent, too weak to move, but conscious.

Anneke waited until the other women went home for a bit, then called Will upstairs. "You may see her," she said, "but don't speak."

Anneke remained in the corner of the room, as Will went to the bed. She saw him gather Elizabeth very gently into his arms, and that she turned her head against his chest with a long sigh, and the pale lips curved in a faint, happy smile.

Tears came into Anneke's delft-blue eyes as she nodded to herself. It was then as she had guessed. But others must not guess. She shook her head while her practical mind outlined all the difficulties and could see no solution. Hallet must go away, she thought, as soon as Bess was strong enough to bear it, nor did she doubt that Elizabeth would agree. After so many years of friendship, Anneke well knew the Winthrop pride and sense of duty which underlay Elizabeth's rebellions. Now too there were the children to consider, and Thomas Lyon, and Elizabeth's standing in the community. Greenwich folk were tolerant in most ways, but they were not libertines. And there was Robert, still in Stamford, staying with the Reverend Mr. Bishop. Angell Husted had seen Robert at a distance on market day, and said that Thomas Lyon and Joan had been talking to him. Robert would be back and need his wife as always, poor man, when his present aberration was over.

Anneke determined to bid Will Hallet begone—it was hard, dreary hard, but it must be. There was no other way.

Anneke's common sense did not, however, reckon either with Robert's unpredictable behavior or with the strength of William and Elizabeth's love.

Elizabeth improved with amazing rapidity, and Anneke delayed her serious talk with Hallet, because she saw that his visits were contributing to Elizabeth's recovery. Once the danger was passed he returned to his home, but he came each day at dusk to sit by Elizabeth's bed for a while.

She was still in the peaceful detachment of convalescence, while her healthy body poured all its forces into recuperation, and Anneke with the girls protected her from any worrisome intrusion. She accepted the baby's death without comment, and asked no questions either about it, or Robert. During this period—alone in the big bed while she savored privacy she had never known before—Elizabeth was able to believe that life was as she wanted it to be, and would continue so.

Also Will brought her books, the four that he had with him. These books were to her a revelation. Her father had owned a few volumes of sermons, but his reading, except for the Bible, had consisted of Gerard's *Herbal.* The Winthrops had a library at Groton which had never attracted her, for the books were in Latin and had unappealing titles. Mary Winthrop, to be sure, had been a great reader of religious works and occasional histories, but Elizabeth's active mind and body had never been subdued to the state of contemplation necessary for the enjoyment of these. Nor had she guessed that there might be reading which would yield pure enjoyment.

Will Hallet's four books represented the crystallization of his own taste insensibly formed by the Digbys, but now entirely individual. He brought Elizabeth therefore Florio's translation of Montaigne's *Essais,* which he appreciated for their cool sensible astringencies. His humor was gratified by the Reverend Thomas Fuller's *Holy and Profane State,* a collection of "Characters" wittily presented, and unlike anything Elizabeth had ever imagined.

"Can this author be a *clergyman?*" she asked in amazement one day after reading in the "Good Schoolmaster" that "the schoolmaster deserves to be beaten himself, who beats nature in a boy for a fault,—And I question whether all the whipping in the world can make their parts which are naturally sluggish, rise one minute before the hour nature has appointed."

"Aye," said Will smiling. "Fuller was rector of Broad-windsor in Dorset, when I got home this time. I met him often at Sherborne Castle, and admired the man. He is like John Donne who said, 'Religion is not a melancholy, the spirit of God is not a dampe!' "

"Did he?" said Elizabeth wondering. She lay back on her pillows, remembering what she knew of St. Paul's famous Dean, whom even John Winthrop had not—in those days—disapproved of. Yet how incredible a concept, confusing, topsy-turvy. Neither by precept nor example had she ever found reason to believe that religion was not a melancholy, that the Spirit of God was not a damp. Except with Anne Hutchinson, who had perhaps believed something like this, and yet in that tragic life there had been no touch of levity.

Elizabeth sighed, and then smiled at Will. "My wits are woolly," she said. "I can't seem to think. I can't quite follow your Montaigne either, though he and this—" she touched the Fuller, "are precious to me for your markings. And when you're away from me, they bring me close to you."

"You like *this* better?" he said, picking a small vellum-bound book from beside her pillow, "and *The Temple?*"

"Both," she said with dreamy content. "I ne'er knew poetry before, except my lute songs. Now I lie here with these two books, and they picture England, as I think she never really was, except in my brightest fancies. They help me see all beauty, the springtime and the sorrow, and the yearning which is part of something I have never known except with my gardens or at Monakewaygo—and now in your love."

"Oh, Bess," he said gruffly. "Fair words you speak yourself."

Inviolate she was, imbued with a transparent simplicity which could not long endure. Far more than Anneke he dreaded the day when she would no longer be sheltered in this quiet bedroom, and the period of serene drifting must end.

"Read to me, Will," said Elizabeth, languidly crossing her thin white arms behind her head. Looking from his face to the crackling fire, she snuggled deeper into her feather bed and gave a contented sigh.

Will laughed. "Indeed, Madam, I am yours to command.

The poetry, I suppose . . . which shall it be?"

He had brought her two books of poetry, one a collection of John Milton, which Digby had given him on the day they parted, and had suitably inscribed. Except for the inscription, Will would not have carried it across the ocean since it had not the appeal for him of his other books, especially *The Temple* by the Reverend George Herbert. Herbert's spiritual poems epitomised for Will all the religious wisdom for which he occasionally strove. They combined with Montaigne's Essays to voice his own philosophy. But he was not surprised that Elizabeth, more sensuously aware of image than he, preferred Milton.

"Start, 'To hear the lark begin his flight,' prithee," she said smiling.

"What, *again?*" he cried in mock dismay. "Let's try 'Lycidas' for a change. For sure you like the flowers in it!"

"Aye," she said acquiescing. "I see them all as they were on a May Day morning in Groton."

"And think how to turn them into simples for the cure of sickly folk . . . I hope," he said teasing her and as a criticism of Milton's floral catalogue, which he considered somewhat sugary, and was unable to visualize except as a pasture in great need of mowing.

"Nay," she said seriously. "I see all the flowers glistening like jewels in a golden light, they remind me of something in my childhood, I can't quite remember, a tinted glass window, I think. Read please—Will."

He pulled the candle closer, and began—

"Bring the rathe primrose that forsaken dies,
The tufted crow-toe, and pale jessamine
The white pink, and the pansy freaked with jet
The glowing violet,
The musk-rose, and the well attired woodbine,
With cowslips wan that hang the pensive head. . . ."

"Hist!" she said suddenly putting her hand on his arm. "What's ado downstairs?" She sat up clutching her chamber robe around her.

He closed the book and they listened, hearing light footsteps hurrying up the stairs. Lisbet burst in, her flaxen hair flying, her blue eyes wide with dismay. "Father's back!" she cried, twisting her hands. "He's fled from someone, he's been running. He wants to see you. But he's pulling stuff out of his chest in the lean-to, packing a sack. I don't know what to do with him!"

Will put the book on the table by the candle and stood up. Elizabeth pushed hard against the pillows, and waited until the sickly hammering of her heart eased. "Well, tell Father to come up here then, dear," she said as quietly as she could. "How does he seem?"

"I don't know," said the girl. "I was afraid when he ran in. Hannah's with him, and the boys."

As Lisbet went out, Will bent over Elizabeth. "I'm going to stay here," he said. "Don't be afraid, hinnie, there's no need." He glanced at the poker by the hearth, and slid near it, his wary gaze on the door.

He relaxed as Robert rushed into the chamber carrying a knapsack and looking both frightened and triumphant. He was breathing hard, his shirt was torn, and he was sweating, but no stranger would have thought him mad. He stood on the threshold looking at Hallet.

"Thanks be to Almighty God that I find you here!" said Robert. " 'Tis what I wanted before I leave. They're after me to stop me. They had me locked in Mr. Bishop's house. I got out the window. 'Twas not truly Christian of them, when I had told them what God said."

Could this be her husband, Elizabeth thought—husband for sixteen years, father of her children? This little middle-aged man, stout, bald, disheveled, gazing up at Will with an intense and pathetic determination. This man whom she had pitied and feared and despised. Her head swam and her lids drooped. It was Will who questioned in a steady voice.

"Who's after you, Feake?"

"Why, Thomas Lyon, to be sure, and others. You see they don't want me to give you the property. The Reverend Bishop doesn't either. For days they've argued with me. They treat me like a child. Which I am not." Robert looked up into Will's face with a certain dignity. "I know what is right to do now, though I have done so much terrible wrong. And I shall do it, no matter what they say."

Will swallowed, startled like Elizabeth into a new recognition of Robert, wondering if they had really locked him up, or was this a delusion. "You're safe enough now, Feake," he said gently. "And you can talk to me, but not in here. Bess isn't strong enough, she's been very ill."

"Has she?" said Robert not looking at her. "Aye, she suffered on my account, did she not? And would again if I stayed. I had begun to hate her, but God says I must not hate her. You don't hate her, do you, Will, *you* wouldn't harm her?"

"No," said Will, color rushing up his face. "Come downstairs, Robert. You can't talk like this here."

"But, they may be coming and you've not got the paper!" Robert cried. "Here, wait—'tis here." He fumbled in his torn shirt and brought out a scrap of paper, heavily inked with muddy cramped writing. "The maidservant brought me the materials, while I was locked in Bishop's house." He tendered the paper to Hallet who glanced down expecting to see some raving written there.

But there was not. It was a simple document giving to Elizabeth Feake the ownership of all Robert's landed property and half his cash which was hid in a chest by the lean-to fireplace; moreover, William Hallet was to be co-administrator of this property, and dispose of it as he thought best for the benefit of Elizabeth Feake, her children and himself. The paper was signed "Robert Feake, Stamford, March 1647."

Will read it twice with stupefaction. "But great God, Robert," he said finally, speaking without restraint and as to a man in full possession of his wits. "This is fair enough to Bess if you mean to go away—in fact, generous, but there's no reason to include me in there, let's strike that out."

"Nay," Robert shook his head in the stubborn mulish way of his saner years. "'Tis the way I want it. I know what's right to do. Farewell—my friend," he said hurriedly to Will. "I've taken my share o' the money from the lean-to chest, and I'll be off. You'll see to the rest for me, won't you?"

"Rob—!" cried Elizabeth, who had been watching in an anguish of indecision. She did not know what was in the paper, but she saw by a dozen signs that Robert was nearer to his normal self than he had been in years. "Rob, you can't be off like that! Where are you going?"

At last he looked at her. Into his pale blinking eyes there came a mist, as though she were someone long dead whose memory brought dim sorrow. "Why, I'm going back to England to see how God will deal with me there!" he said. "'According to this judgment shall it be done unto him,' saith the Lord."

"What judgment?" she whispered. "Rob, what is it that has darkened all your life, has driven you even to distraction, whatever it is, poor Rob, there's no need to go. You're not well enough for that hard journey."

The poignancy of her voice struck to Will's heart, and even penetrated Robert's obsession.

"For sure I'm well enough," he said slowly. "God gives me strength to suffer what I must. It was Ralph you know, Bess, that I must suffer for. I've not forgot you and the children, I showed that on the paper, but that's over, don't you see? I've nothing left for you or them, 'tis only with effort I can believe you exist."

"You feel so now," she said very low, "but perhaps it will change again. Robert—what is it that happened with Ralph?"

For a moment Will thought Feake would answer her, and he knew that she from decency was making a last effort to help her husband, despite all she had suffered, careless even of himself and their love.

Robert hesitated; he raised his hands, still long and thin, though the rest of his body had thickened. He glanced down at them quickly, staring at them in a puzzled way. Then he put them beneath the folds of his doublet. "Nay, woman," he said with sudden anger. "You ask too much. Always now you obscure the Voice of God. Let me be! You're naught to me!—Hark!" he cried whirling towards the window. "There are voices outside!"

"Aye—" said Will who could see through the shutters a streak of lantern light. "There's no need to fear, Robert. They can't harm you."

But Robert had gone, running down the stairs and out the door to the cove, while the front passage door opened below and they heard Thomas Lyon's voice.

"I'll fetch him back, Bess," said Will. "He can't get far."

"No," she said with a weary motion of her hand. "Of what use? Let him go. I believe he has sane plans. And he must follow whatever fate it is he thinks is calling him. He can find no rest here."

She closed her eyes and tears slipped down her cheeks.

The weighty footsteps of her son-in-law stamped up the stairs and an angry voice called out, "Father Feake, Father Feake, what a chase you've led us!" Thomas walked into the room, and scanning it quickly, said, "Lisbet *said* he was up here!"

"He is not," said Will, standing in the center of the floor.

Thomas, who had been certain of locating Feake at last, rearranged his thoughts with difficulty. He stared at Elizabeth in the bed, and back to Hallet, whereupon he started, and scowled. "What the devil are *you* doing in here?" Thomas shouted.

Elizabeth's days of sheltered peace were over.

The next month was one of constant discord. Thomas
spared no opportunity to upbraid Elizabeth, especially after
they heard that Robert had indeed been sane enough to lay
sensible plans for his escape. The servant in the Bishop
house had helped him. Robert, having taken nearly a hundred pounds from the lean-to chest, had bribed the maid
with a few shillings and she in turn had hired her sweetheart
and his rowboat to convey Robert along the coast to Fair-
field, where a Boston-bound ship had given him passage.
And he had reached Boston. The master of the ship touched
at Stamford upon his return, and the story all came out.
The Bishop's maidservant was hauled before the Stamford
court, questioned, and severely rebuked. She was also put
in the stocks for an hour, but there was nothing else that
the Reverend Mr. Bishop, or Thomas Lyon could do about
it.

The servant, weeping, averred that poor Mr. Feake's wits
were as clear as anybody's, and it was a mortal shame to
lock him up as her master had done. The ship's captain
agreed, saying the gentleman was quiet and gave no trouble,
and had gone straight to Governor Winthrop upon arrival
in Boston. This last news incensed Thomas more than anything else, since he had not yet had a reply from Winthrop,
and now had little hope of controlling the situation except
by reversing himself on the subject of Robert's sanity,
especially in view of the signed transfer of property Will
showed him during the violent quarrel which took place
in Elizabeth's bedroom on the evening Robert escaped.

The quarrel would have come to blows had it not been
for Elizabeth, and the frightened Joan who clutched at her
husband's arm, and went into a kind of hysteria as she
wavered between her mother's and her husband's claims.

Will refused to give up the paper, and Thomas finally
had to content himself with forbidding him ever to enter
the Feake house again.

This order Will obeyed out of consideration for Elizabeth.
He stayed on his place at Totomack, keeping himself doggedly
occupied with the spring sowing and improvements on his
one-room cabin. His only news of Elizabeth during that
period came from a visit he made to Anneke, who received
him kindly, told him that Elizabeth was nearly well, and
had resumed most of her household duties; but Anneke was
otherwise starkly discouraging.

"You do her no good here, Villiam," said Anneke. "You must sell and go avay. You vill forget each other in time."

"Has Bess said that?" Will asked, his jaw tightening.

Anneke shook her head. "Ve do not speak alone. Thomas, Joan or the children are alvays there, but believe me it is best. She and Thomas vill manage better together some day, if you are not here."

"Anneke!" said Will violently. "Have you ever really loved anyone? Loved so much that it's a desperate hunger night and day, and calm, sensible advice about forgetting and managing better are as meaningless as the droning of a fly? Have you loved like that with your whole body, heart, and mind?"

Anneke looked a little frightened. "But, vat could you *do*?" she said. "You vould not make a whore of my Bess, surely?"

"No," said Will, his eyes hardening. "But I'll not give her up either, unless she wishes it. I've got to see her. Anneke, will you give her this note?"

She showed distress. Under the snowy fichu Anneke's bosom heaved, but she backed off, leaving his hand extended in mid-air with the note. "I cannot," Anneke said. "Leave her alone! Go avay! She has had enough vithout you bothering her—And don't go to the house either!" she added sternly. "It only makes trouble for her."

Will went home, sunk in despondency. Anneke's certainty had shaken him, and surely Bess might somehow have sent word to him in these weeks. Could it be that her love had after all been a transient thing, born of her miserable relationship with Robert and her physical weaknesses? Freed of both now, was she also freed of her need for him? Will reached his home, fed the horse and started sharpening poles for a fence to enclose the barnyard. But his hatchet slipped repeatedly, he swore and gave it up. He began to pace up and down along the path he had made to the water, his unheeding steps crunched on broken oyster shells the Indians had left. He did not feel the soft April sunlight, or notice the first green tips of the early wheat he had experimentally sown on the Tomac camp site. As he paced he tried to reason with himself, forcing himself backward in memory to the attitude he had had towards Elizabeth before the day he found her on Monakewaygo. He rehearsed all the drawbacks she presented. She was older, six, seven years—he wasn't sure how much. She had a husband, five children and a son-in-law. True she had a fair body, charm, and strength of character, but plenty of unencumbered women possessed these. And more. He thought of Lady Alice, Digby's sister, who had looked very sweetly on him, and made it clear that she might talk her father into a marriage if Will should ask her. Lord Bristol himself had hinted that the times were so troubled, and the leveling forces typified by Cromwell were so much in the ascendancy, that a match with fine yeoman stock, with a man, moreover, who had proved himself of such loyal worth to the Bristols, would not be inconceivable.

I might have had Alice, Will thought. A handsome virgin, an Earl's daughter, why didn't I take her? Why not go back now, and see if she is still unwed?

He turned on his heel, angrily kicking a stone out of the way. These were futile questions since his inherent honesty answered them as soon as he asked. He hadn't wanted Lady Alice, and he hadn't wanted to continue at the beck and call of the Digbys. He did want Elizabeth, without discovering any logic in it. More remarkably, however, he also wanted her happiness above his own, which seemed to produce a painful state of deadlock quite contrary to all pious teaching.

Montaigne might have helped, or George Herbert, but Elizabeth still had his books, unless indeed Thomas Lyon had thrown them into the cove. God blast and damn it all! Will thought, and striding into his house, drank a tankard of beer and flung logs on the fire with which to roast a wild duck for his supper.

Will had slept an hour that night, twisting and tossing on his hay mattress, when he was awakened by a knock on his door. He jumped from bed, naked except for his breeches, and called out, "Who's there?"

There was a murmur and another knock. He lifted the wooden latch and peered out, expecting to hear that Angell's cow had jumped the fence again and must be found.

The night was dark and he did not at first recognize the hooded and cloaked figure on his doorstep.

"Can I not come in, Will . . . " whispered Elizabeth. "Don't you want me?"

"Aye—" he said on a long breath. "I want thee."

He pulled her into his room, shut and bolted the door. He took her in his arms and kissed her with such violence that he hurt her, and she gasped, though not in protest.

He released her and poked at the fire until it gave light enough to see by. "You've made me glad, Bess," he said coming back to her and taking off her cloak. "In these weeks of waiting I began to doubt—"

"Nay, love—" she said. "How could you doubt? I didn't. But Thomas has kept constant watch on me, and until the last few days I've not had strength to walk so far."

"Could you not have sent me some message, hinnie-sweet?" He smoothed back her hair and looked down into her face, which was yet thin and pale from her illness, but seemed to him lovelier than he had remembered.

"I nearly did by Hannah, and then I thought it was not right to make her keep a secret. And too, I had many things to think out myself."

"And having thought?" he asked, sitting on his bench and pulling her down to his knees, where she rested her cheek against his bare shoulder.

"Why, I came to you," she said shyly, smiling up at him. "And will stay the night if you wish it. Thomas is in bed with an attack of dysentery, too weak to move. I locked my chamber door, and can slip in again without their knowing."

"Oh Bess—Bess—" he said, half laughing, yet with roughness in his throat. "You offer yourself to me like this, so simply, so quietly—"

"But I love thee," she said in surprise. "And I need no longer think of Robert."

He set her on her feet and stood up, walking towards the fire. "Then I must," he said. "Of Robert and many other factors. You cannot sneak back and forth like this, nor start a shoddy intrigue. Our love is no longer like that, whatever I may once have thought. And *you* are not like that. Soon you would hate yourself and me."

She flushed, looking down at the floor and twisting her hands. "I should not have come. Your heart has changed. I've been a fool."

"No, Bess," he said. "Foolish only in one thing. Don't you see what we must do?"

She shook her head. "Unless you mean to go away." She lifted her chin and tried to speak without faltering, but the choked-down sob cut her breath.

"You precious little ninny!" he cried. "Have you not thought of divorce—that we may marry?"

"Divorce . . . ?" she repeated in amazement. "I never heard of anyone having a divorce, except King Harry of England, and some duke, I think."

"Yet now and then, for good and sufficient cause, there *are* divorces granted, particularly in Dutch countries," Will said. "Your husband's madness and desertion should certainly be cause."

"Divorce Robert . . . " she whispered, her mind still caught on this incredible concept. "Aye—he wouldn't care, would he? He said he wished no more to do with me, or the children."

"He also handed you over to me, if you remember," said Will with a dry laugh. "A complaisant husband, but as it happens I ask nothing better."

She stared at him, her heart began to beat thick and heavy in her chest. "We could marry, you said. You would *wed* me, after?"

"Aye, Bess." He gave her a rueful smile. "It seems that I've on a sudden developed a desire for respectability. I don't wonder that you gape. It happens that I love thee too much for a hole-and-corner tumbling, and I want thee for my wife."

She sank down on the bench, still staring at him—his head and big naked shoulders dark against the flickering fire. "Thy wife . . . " she whispered. "Oh, Will, it couldn't be. I scarce can think, I'm afraid to think—God wouldn't let us, would He?"

"I don't see why God should have any objection," said Will. "I fear I think it more important to find out what Governor Kieft's opinion will be. Go home now, hinnie. Tomorrow leave the house at seven. Tell any lie you wish. But they can't forbid you to go out. Walk to the burying ground where I'll meet you on horseback. Take money in your purse, as I shall. Leave a note for Joan, so that the children may not be upset. We may be gone a day or two."

"Gone where?" For still she could not believe the possibility of what he proposed.

"To New Amsterdam, you'll ride pillion with me—ah, don't weep, my foolish Bess—I never thought you a watery woman. 'Tis no time to undeceive me now."

20

WILL HAD HOPED to cover in one day the forty miles of trail between Greenwich and New Amsterdam which was on the southern tip of Manhattan Island; but they had to ford many rivers swollen with spring rains, and the horse, unused to double weight, tired easily.

Nightfall found them still at some distance from Manhattan, and though Will trusted his memory of the old Indian trail by day, he felt it wiser to stop in darkness.

So they finished the loaves of cornbread Elizabeth had smuggled from home under her cloak and slept for a few hours under a great sheltering pine. They slept in each other's arms, passionless as children, and as content. At dawn Will awoke her by kissing her nose and shifting the arm which had encircled her all night. "Come, slug-a-bed," he said. "We've much to do!" He yawned and stretched as she sat up. "I'faith," he said. " 'Tis the first time I've slept chaste as a stone with a woman. I find it rather sweet, but not something I'd make a practice of."

"Nor I," she said laughing joyously. "Can it be that by tomorrow we'll be wed—d'you think, Will?"

"Why not!" he answered exultantly. "You'll beguile Kieft as you did before, and 'tis easy for him to sign the decree, his Council'll do as he tells them."

"Ah—" she breathed, in utter happiness, which made her

515

want to dance, and sing, to embrace the trees, the rocks, the awakening birds, even the horse which was a singularly ugly roan with a long bony head.

Her joy was dampened a little later as they crossed another river and came upon the charred ruins of several buildings scattered through a field of rank new grass.

"What's that?" Elizabeth asked astonished, for they had seen no white man's habitations save two empty trading huts since leaving Greenwich. "Vredeland," said Will briefly. George Baxter in giving him directions for following the trail last summer had named this site, and told him of the Hutchinson massacre.

"So it was here . . . " Elizabeth whispered, shuddering. "God forfend 'tis not an evil omen—" she added to herself. But he heard her.

"Nonsense, hinnie!" he cried. "What omen can there be in those old stones? 'Tis of the past, and naught to do with us!"

Of the past, she thought, pray God that all my past is dead and peaceful as this green field that covers a day of horror.

"The child, Susannah Hutchinson, who was captured has been returned, you know," Will said, seeking to lighten her mood. "They say she did not want to leave the Indians, had become fond of them."

"Not surprising," said Elizabeth in a muffled voice. "They're no more cruel than we are. No apter at evil. You didn't know our Siwanoy—but I assure you the Hutchinsons were well avenged."

He glanced at her with slightly puzzled sympathy. He knew little of her experiences with the Indians, though he knew that these were linked in pain with other tragic phases of her life.

They rode several miles before she regained her happy expectancy.

At the Haarlem River they found a ferry and crossed to Manhattan Island and from then on they passed isolated bouweries, Dutch farms with high-stepped roofs, neat picket fences and an air of snug opulence.

"Good land," said Will, admiring the rich brown earth. "Bess, d'you see that round point over there, across the East River?"

"Below Hell Gate?" she asked looking at the turbulent, swirling waters. "I remember it from last time when I came by boat with Toby."

"That was where my land grant was," said Will. "On that point—had I not settled in Greenwich, and *bought* land instead!"

"You regret it?" she said pouting prettily. "You would have preferred over there on Long Island where presumably no tiresome woman would have confused your life?"

"Nay, I don't regret it," he said more seriously than she expected. "Though there's a kind of thin soil near the point that puts me in mind of certain Dorset earth. I think 'twould grow the rye they've no success with in Greenwich."

"Ah, Will, darling—" she said laughing. "So I shall have a husbandman for husband at last! I've much to learn, and hope you'll bear with me."

"I'll bear with you," he said, and turning in the saddle kissed her, much to the amusement of a group of fishermen who were angling along the riverbank.

They reached New Amsterdam by ten, and went directly to the City Tavern, where they breakfasted, and Elizabeth made herself presentable. She had worn the violet tiffany, which was somewhat wrinkled but otherwise as elegant as any gown she saw on the wealthy mevrouws. She had also worn her jewelry, Robert's gold chain and Harry's brooch, and she had brought the little lace cap. When she had carefully recombed and dressed her hair, at the tavern's parlor mirror, she knew that she looked charming. The vivid color had returned to her cheekbones; she had the glow of a woman in love, who sees consummation within reach.

Will also looked proud and glad. Several people stared admiringly at the couple as they walked along the street towards the Fort, where George Baxter lived in a small house near the Governor's.

Baxter was at home too, and though he had many private troubles just now, he greeted Elizabeth and Will with cordiality when the manservant showed them into his parlor. The atmosphere changed however when Elizabeth haltingly and ingenuously made known her errand.

"What's that you say, Mistress Feake?" said Baxter, his jaw dropping. "You want a *divorce!* But, my dear lady, this is preposterous!"

"Not at all, Baxter!" said Will sharply. "You know very well what Mrs. Feake has suffered with Feake's madness, and now he has deserted her."

The dismayed English secretary stared from one eager hopeful face to the other. They're in love, he thought, poor fools, and as addlepated as lovers always seem to get. And what a time to choose to come here with impossible requests!

"I do know some of the tragedies of Mrs. Feake's life," he said, shaking his head. "I was present at them, and have every sympathy—but divorce, my dear Madam, you don't understand the law."

"Show him Robert's paper, Will!" Elizabeth cried. "He'll see for himself."

Will hesitated, but he drew from his purse Robert's document. Baxter perused it carefully, and handed it back. "Am I to understand that you wish the Director-General to issue a divorce on the grounds of your husband's madness and desertion?" he asked carefully with a rueful smile.

They both nodded, and Baxter said, "Then you had best not show this paper as evidence, for it seems to disprove both. This is a lucid statement from a man who is about to take a journey—no more; the unusual feature is your inclusion, Mr. Hallet."

"I know," said Will. "I begged him not to, but Mr. Feake isn't sane. My God, Baxter—you know that. He said he was through with Bess and the children forever, and he meant it. He knew I'd protect her, and I will."

"Aye—" whispered Elizabeth, and the soft adoring look she gave Hallet touched Baxter in spite of himself. He heaved an exasperated sigh.

"Don't you know this is a poor moment to approach Kieft?" he said. "He's been recalled to The Hague for investigation—leaves very soon. We've a new governor coming from Curaçao, Petrus Stuyvesant."

"Indeed," said Will frowning. "We hadn't heard. What's the trouble?"

Baxter shrugged. "Complaints of Kieft—his maladministration, of his inciting the Indian Wars, of lax personal conduct, of constant quarrels with our Dominie Bogardus who is also recalled for questioning. Kieft hasn't been inside the church for three years and amuses himself firing off cannon during Divine Service. To put it frankly, New Netherland affairs are in a muddle. I don't know whether I shall keep *my* position, and all in all, I doubt that Kieft'll bother with you. He's drunk most the time anyway." From the stricken look in Elizabeth's beautiful eyes, he turned away. He had seen something like that expression in the eyes of condemned prisoners who were denied reprieve. And he tightened his lips, and rose.

"Well, well—I'll see what I can do," he said brusquely. "It'll take a while. Wait in the courtyard by the church."

Elizabeth and Will wandered outside. He took her arm and squeezed it but they did not speak until they came to the huge new church with the curious peaked roof, topped with a weathercock.

Elizabeth walked under the church porch and Will said without emphasis, "You going to pray, Bess?"

She started. "I suppose I might, but I wanted to find someone who'd record the baby's baptism." She did not explain a superstitious feeling that heaven might be more propitious if she made this last gesture for Robert.

She had never mentioned the baby, and Will was astonished, but he said nothing. He followed her into the church where they found the baptismal book chained to a lectern near the font. They also found the sexton, who did not at first understand Elizabeth's request, grumbled and backed off, until she offered him two guilders. Whereupon he shrugged, and wrote "Sarah" at her direction under the present date of April 14.

"Vader?" said the sexton, looking at Will.

"Robert Feake," said Elizabeth sternly and watched while the sexton scrawled an approximation. "But the baby isn't living any more." she said.

"Watblief?" asked the sexton, bored and edging away.

"Oh, never mind," she said. "I don't know why I wanted to do this. Will, darling—wait outside, please, in case Baxter comes back. I want to be alone."

When he had gone she crept into one of the great box pews and tried to pray, but no prayer came. Her mind was a chaos of hopes and fears. She could not quiet herself. She left the church in discouragement, which she tried to hide from Will who had his own black thoughts.

Thus they were not unprepared for difficulties, but neither of them suspected the outcome of their interview with Kieft.

It took place in the same Council Room where Elizabeth had sworn her Dutch allegiance. Though today there were present besides the Governor only the new Fiscal, Ensign Van Dyke, who had participated in the destruction of the Siwanoys, a Dutch secretary, and Baxter. All of them were smoking.

Kieft's recent troubles and imminent disgrace had aged him. His fat cheeks were pendulous, his scraggly locks were gray beneath the imposing red-plumed hat. A silver mug stood at his elbow. He was half drunk and had been as annoyed at this interruption as Baxter had expected. The English secretary first tried to gain the interview for Elizabeth by insistence on her connection with Governor Winthrop, and her own importance as Greenwich patroon. Neither of these pleas any longer influenced Kieft, who snapped that she might as well put her case before Stuyvesant then. Let the incoming governor deal with it.

Baxter had heard enough of Stuyvesant's strictness and puritanical morality to know this was impractical, so he tried a different tack, reminding Kieft with adroit flattery of Elizabeth's personal loyalty to him. He then gave a dramatic account of her ordeals through the years, and said she was counting on the Director-General's well-known goodness of heart, and that she remembered him with great affection. Kieft snorted, but he said, "Let her come in, and be quick about it!"

When Elizabeth and Will entered the smoke-hazed Council Room, Kieft examined them both with a leer. He licked his shining purple lips and chuckled, saying something to Baxter.

"What does he say?" asked Elizabeth, standing straight and stiff at the end of the table and trying not to look frightened.

"He says," answered Baxter reluctantly, "that you are still a beautiful woman, and he doesn't wonder you like a little bit of fun."

She flushed. "Have you presented my plea for divorce, Mr. Baxter?"

He nodded, and spoke at some length to Kieft who listened impatiently, drumming his fat fingers on the table. "Bah!" cried the Governor, interrupting. "Overspel! Overspel!"— and he added a brief angry speech.

Baxter spoke again, and Kieft banged his hand on the table. "Overspel!" he shouted staring straight at Elizabeth, before turning with a contemptuous shrug towards Will who had sat down in the back of the room.

"What is 'overspel'?" Elizabeth asked swallowing.

Baxter left the Governor's side and walked to Elizabeth. " 'Overspel' means adultery, Mrs. Feake. I'm sorry to tell you that the Director-General will grant a divorce on no other terms, indeed those *are* the only terms which are legal."

"That's not true!" Will cried, jumping up. "I know of a case last year which he granted for desertion alone."

"Aye—" said Baxter in a low voice. "That was before he was accused of taking the law into his own hands. He dare not be lax now."

"Robert has not committed adultery," said Elizabeth,

leaning her weight on the table.

"No, no, Madam," said Baxter with pity. "You don't understand. The divorce would be granted to Mr. Feake in absentia, because of *your* adultery; it is the only way you can get it."

"That's monstrous!" cried Will, rushing forward. "And a foul lie. You can't do it, Bess!"

Baxter was startled. There was the ring of truth in this, though he and Kieft had naturally thought otherwise. He went back to the Governor and spoke again.

Kieft's bloodshot little eyes sparked, his underlip thrust out. "Nee! Nee!" she shouted, glaring at Elizabeth. "Neen! Nee!"

She did not need Baxter's unhappy murmur of explanation. "He says 'no,' to any but the terms I told you, and I'm afraid he may soon change his mind on those."

"Then I accept," she said quickly. "Make the decree as he says. Hush, Will—what difference, if I get it?"

"It can be kept private, Mr. Hallet," said Baxter uncomfortably, wishing that he had never let his sympathies lead him on, and yet increasingly sorry for both of them as he foresaw what the next move would be. "It'll be buried in the files here and your English neighbors won't be able to read your copy. You can tell them what you like."

Kieft saw submission in Elizabeth's face, and was seized with obscene laughter. It tickled him that the proud English "dame" should humble herself like this and into his genever-soaked brain there came a glimmer of what use might be made of this incident in Holland, when they dared to question his own conduct. It had been the bawdy English who made the administration here so difficult. "Look what they're like!" he would tell their High Mightinesses. "Even in the Winthrop family they confess to adultery!" He turned to his Dutch secretary and began to dictate rapidly, while the Fiscal Van Dyke yawned and stared at the wainscoted ceiling.

Nobody spoke or moved, while Kieft affixed his signature and seal to the decree, which he sent flying down the table towards Elizabeth. She bit her lips, and picked it up, her cheeks flaming. "So I am divorced?" she said to Baxter. "Mr. Hallet and I can be married at once?"

"I am afraid not, Madam," said the English secretary sighing. "Permission to remarry requires a separate document and a full meeting of the Council and there is customarily some delay. Also I wouldn't ask Kieft for it now, he wouldn't give it."

Elizabeth gasped. The color drained from her face, leaving it as white as the parchment in her hands. "Then we're no better off than we were!" she whispered.

"Oh yes, you are—" said Baxter. "This decree is necessary first."

She did not listen to him; she ran to the end of the table and seized the Governor's pudgy beringed hand; kneeling beside his chair she spoke wildly, pleading, the words of entreaty stumbling over each other.

"What does she want *now?*" asked the Governor, delighted and rubbing his thick finger along her neck.

Baxter explained, and Kieft chuckled. "So hot?" he said in Dutch. "The pretty little bitch. What does she need marriage lines for? Hasn't she enjoyed her bed-sport well enough without?"

Elizabeth caught the sense of this, and her eyes filled with anguished tears. "No!" she cried. "You don't understand! 'Tis not true. Your Excellency, I beg you—"

Kieft hesitated, slightly moved by her distress, then he grunted and snatched his hand from hers. "Let her cool off a while," he said. "I'll think about it. She makes my head ache—Go avay!" he added in English, giving her a little shove.

"Come, Bess," said Will, raising her from her knees. "Don't abase yourself further."

"Yes—better go," said Baxter. He walked with them through the Council Room door, and out into the Fort. "I'm sure I can get it for you," he said. "Very soon perhaps, but any persistence makes him more stubborn. Can you wait here in New Amsterdam?"

"I can," said Will. "It wouldn't be wise for Mrs. Feake to, under the circumstances. Nobody would believe that we weren't—" he stopped.

"Aye," said Baxter understanding and agreeing. "There's one of our ships New Haven-bound—to leave this afternoon. I can get her aboard that; the Master'll drop her off at Greenwich. When you get the marriage permission you can go and fetch her, Mr. Hallet."

"Will—" Elizabeth cried. "How can I go back home like that, what'll I tell them? Why can't I stay here with you?"

Baxter shook his head, and walked to the Fort entrance to wait. He now saw clearly that these two were innocent of the divorce charge and that Hallet was trying desperately to protect her from scandal. They've got "the name and not the game," he thought wryly—'tis a sorry coil. And he determined to wrest the marriage permission from Kieft somehow.

"You must go back, dear heart," said Will to Elizabeth. "Tell them nothing—or what did you say in your note to Joan?"

"That I had business in New Amsterdam and wanted to register the baby's birth. I didn't mention you."

"Well, they'll buzz, of course, and guess. But they won't *know*. Bess, you're a grown woman and the head of a family, you don't have to account for all your actions; but if you stayed here with me, there'd be no glossing matters, and besides, do you think we could keep apart much longer? We've gone this far, hinnie—so terribly far—I never should have let you get that filthy sham of a divorce, but it seemed the only way, and now we must be patient yet for a little while."

"Aye," she said, bowing her head.

"It won't be long," he said with genuine optimism. "That old swine has no reason to withhold consent. The instant I get the permission I'll gallop back for you, darling. Why, I may be there almost as soon as you are."

But it was a month before William Hallet returned to Greenwich. During that time Elizabeth summoned all her courage, and encased herself in a haughty aloofness, which even Thomas Lyon could not penetrate, though he did his best. To the natural spate of questions as to why she had gone off to New Amsterdam—and how—she replied that she had business to transact with the Governor, and had accepted William Hallet's courteous offer of an escort, since he also had business in New Amsterdam. She offered no other explanations, and the angry Thomas was completely baffled, especially by her return alone on an official government pinnace.

Thomas finally expressed his resentment by not speaking to his mother-in-law at all, which eased matters. The children, of course, were quickly satisfied and very glad to have her home again. She had bought them each gilded gingerbread toys before sailing.

The Greenwich neighbors thought Hallet's sudden disappearance strange when they discovered it, but they were on the whole an incurious lot, very busy with their planting, and inclined to agree with Richard Crab's jest, that it wasn't very astonishing for a lusty young man like William to take a sudden fancy for city life in the springtime. "Plenty o' luscious Dutch harlots at Amsterdam, I hear," said Crab with a wink, which elicited a resounding slap from his peppery goodwife.

Elizabeth waited, and suffered in secret. Her only comfort was the reading of Will's books. Even the children were not in focus for her, though she gave them a great deal of her time, and was very gentle with them as some sort of guilty compensation.

With Anneke, and Toby who had just returned from Nova Scotia, a coolness had arisen. Toby remarked that there was something odd about his aunt's behavior, and if there were any more of it he would feel it his duty to speak out, much as he disliked giving Thomas any satisfaction. Anneke held her peace, though she had more reason than anyone to suspect the true state of affairs. She had great hopes that Hallet had finally taken her advice and gone for good, and waited, sadly, for Bess to regain her normal affectionate frankness.

On a late afternoon of a clear May day, Will came down the northern trail and pulled up his horse before Elizabeth's gate. She was upstairs in the bedroom when she heard the clop-clop of hoofs, and Will's admonishing voice as the tired horse stumbled. She ran to the window and gazed out with poignant joy, savoring relief so keen that it was almost painful. The horse and Will were both mud-spattered, for it had rained earlier, his lank brown hair was matted, there was a stubble of beard on his chin, but she saw him through a radiance, no longer remembering when she had thought him rustic and uncouth. Then as he dismounted she saw bleakness in his unguarded face, and a weary set to his big shoulders beneath the leather doublet. She drew a hard breath and walked downstairs.

Thomas had gone to the Sherwoods for the loan of a sickle as his own was always breaking. The little boys had taken the cows to pasture. There was nobody in the kitchen but the three girls: Joan and Lisbet mending, Hannah cleaning alewives they had seined from the Asamuck River.

As Elizabeth opened the door to Will, Hannah jumped up with a glad cry. "Why, 'tis Mr. Hallet back again!"

Joan bit her lips and said nothing, being aware of her husband's feelings. What does this mean? she thought, and hoped vaguely that her mother would give the fellow short shrift.

"Good day, Mrs. Feake—" said Will in a level voice,

sending the girls a courteous smile. His eyes met Elizabeth's with a dark intent look.

"Oh, Mr. Hallet," said Hannah rushing to him. "Have you been to New Amsterdam? Pray tell us of it! Mama says 'tis a fine city now where they sing and dance and play skittles all day long!" The child grabbed his hand, her rosy face beaming up at him.

"Well, moppet," Will said, tousling her auburn curls. " 'Tis not as gay as that, except one day of celebration I did see when the new governor Petrus Stuyvesant landed. Perhaps I'll tell you about it. But now I wish to talk alone with your mother."

"Aye," said Elizabeth quickly. "We can walk outside, I'll get my cloak."

Joan put down the shift she was mending. "Thomas wouldn't think that seemly, my mother," she said nervously. "Mr. Hallet can have nothing private to say to you."

"Tom thought you'd gone for good," put in Lisbet, not quite understanding all this, but anxious to be included. She gave her tinkling little laugh. "Tom won't speak to Mama any more, 'tis like a game. I keep waiting to see if he'll forget, and he almost does."

"Hold thy tongue, stupid—" cried Joan with unusual heat. "Must you be forever gabbling everything to strangers!"

Lisbet tossed her head, her pale blue eyes sparkled.

"Mr. Hallet is not a stranger, Joan," said Elizabeth, glancing sadly at her eldest daughter. This situation was hard for the girl, and would soon be harder, but the time for temporizing had passed.

"I am going out with Mr. Hallet," she said. "I don't know just when I'll be back. But when I am, I solemnly promise you a full and satisfactory explanation."

Joan licked her lips unhappily and subsided. She could no more combat her mother's firmness than her husband's.

Elizabeth fetched her crimson cloak and her purse. Each day she had been ready, her under linen fresh and scented, her hair carefully coiffed, and wearing either of her two best gowns, despite the girls' wondering questions. Today it was a soft golden wool, lace-trimmed, not as elegant as the violet tiffany, but more serviceable and fully as becoming.

"By God, I'm glad to see you, hinnie-love," said Will softly as they went through the gate together. "But I've much to say, and want no interruption. Where shall we go?" He picked up the horse's bridle and they all began to walk.

"Monakewaygo," Elizabeth said automatically, and indeed

she had already started down the path that led to it. But when they reached the isthmus it was covered by the tide. She stared at the strip of water in dismay.

"Aye—there's a barrier, isn't there?" Will said quietly, with a meaning deeper than the words. "Perhaps it's as well, Bess. We'll go to *my* lands, not yours. I like it better so."

The wind blew fresh, and ruffled the water with white flecks. She started out towards her beach and the line of shining sands, then turning looked up into his face.

"You didn't get it, did you, Will?"

"No," he said. "I didn't get it."

He yanked the horse's bridle and led it towards the fork and the Sound path to his house. Elizabeth followed. Neither of them spoke. Presently they passed Angell Husted's farmstead. Angell was working in his south lot. Elizabeth saw his blue smock, and her instinct was to shrink behind the horse and hide herself, though she resisted it. But Angell was too busy heaving stones to notice them. The trees grew denser as they approached Totomack Cove, then opened out around Will's clearing.

They entered his yard. Will hauled up water from the well, gave the horse a pailful before leading it into the shed and forking it some hay. Will sluiced his head with water, came back to her where she stood by the gate and said, "Would you come in, hinnie, or stay outside?—Nay, I needn't ask—" he added with a faint smile. "Nature ever sustains you in some mystical way I envy, but don't quite fathom. I made a bench for you," he said, "while you were ill, hoping you'd use it someday."

He led her along a path to a ledge of rugged pink and gray rocks which jutted out into the little cove. Against a huge waterside elm he had placed a bench with arms and back and feet, all whittled into graceful curves. Along the back he had carved a long panel of hearts and square-petaled roses interspersed with E's.

"It's lovely, Will!" she cried, stroking the carvings.

"A sentimental tribute of the joiner's craft," he said bitterly. "I had hoped, however, to be able to offer you more than sentiment."

She sat down on the bench, and clasped her hands. "Tell me. What happened?"

He folded his arms, standing beside the bench and scowling at the brown waters of the cove. "Nothing happened. Kieft refused to gather his Council for *any* purpose, let alone to issue a marriage license, which Baxter finally dis-

covered he had some daft notion against giving anyway.
Finally I got desperate and forced my way into his home.
His three guards threw me out, and I spent the night in gaol.
The next day Stuyvesant landed, and Kieft's power ceased.
Baxter hastily had me released."

She gave a choked cry. "You weren't hurt, were you?"

He made a disdainful sound. "After that I waited until
Baxter'd had a day or two to feel out the new governor."
He paused remembering his own sight of Stuyvesant—the
gaunt eagle-beaked face with thin pressed-in lips, the peg-
leg with its silver collar, the harsh strident voice of command designed to bring immediate discipline into the unruly
colony.

"Stuyvesant is a staunch Calvinist," said Will, "the son
of a clergyman. He is tolerant neither in religious nor civil
matters. He flew into a passion when Baxter even mentioned
some other divorce case, and of course he doesn't know
our story or the extenuating circumstances. In fact, Bess,
there is no hope at all."

She leaned her head against the elm trunk, and watched
the quivering of the leaves in the maples across the cove.
"I see," she said. "I see. What simpletons we were to think
God would grant our wish. I think He takes pleasure in
mockery."

Will turned and stared at her. He sat down on the bench
and took her hand in his. "Hinnie—that isn't God. One
mustn't blame God for all human miseries. Oh, I know
your Uncle Winthrop and his ilk think so, but I do not. A
peevish Jehovah with a long beard isn't what I call God."

"What is, then . . . ?" she said, her hand lying limp in
his.

"I can't say it," said Will frowning. "I can't find words,
though perhaps Herbert did—

"Love bade me welcome, yet my soul drew back
    Guilty of dust and sin
  But quick-eyed Love, observing me grow slack . . .
    Drew nearer to me, sweetly questioning
      if I lacked anything."

"They are fine words," she said, "but they weren't meant
for our kind of love."

"Perhaps they were, Bess, that too. 'Tis part of the whole.
Look at me!"

She raised her head slowly. Her shadowed somber eyes

met his earnest gaze. "Shall I leave you?" he said evenly. "Sell this land, and go far off, perhaps to the Indies?"

"No, no!" she cried in sudden terror, flinging her arms around his neck. "No!"

He pulled her hands from his neck, and held them tight. "Then—" he said. "We must be practical, we must be worldly, and we must be brave."

"How?" she said.

"I shall become your husband in the sight of God—the God *I* mean, and in the sight of man, if we have luck," he added with a grim laugh.

"We will pretend we're married?" she asked faintly after a moment. "Oh, dear love, how can we?"

He saw a wincing pass over her mobile face, a recoil. He loosed her hands. "I've thought and thought about this, Bess," he said. "I cannot believe that the mumblings of some magistrate or preacher matter to our inner selves, but we must live an outer life as well—the world's opinions can't be flouted—and either we part or it must be this way."

Why must it be? she thought. Why are my wishes never granted? Why is there always fear and tarnishing?

She drew a long sigh. "Yes," she said. "I suppose so." They neither of them spoke for some minutes, until she straightened and gave him a little sideways smile. "Are we married now then, Will?" she asked, a feeble spark of humor in her eyes.

"No," he said rising. "You shall have more ceremony than that, my poor little bride. Yesterday I bought rings in Amsterdam, and wine too, the best canary. Come into the house love. I'm conventional and feel a wedding should be dignified by four walls."

She nodded and tried to laugh, but could not forbear a quick glance down the path, knowing that beneath his attempt at lightness there was the fear of discovery by a neighbor—or by Thomas.

Once in his little house he shot the great iron bolt. He built the fire up, and she with uncertain nervous gestures tried to fill the pot with cornmeal and salt meat for their supper. They drank quickly of the strong canary, until the trembling of her knees passed. Then he stood beside her on the hearth, and held out two thick golden rings.

"I've never had a wedding band before!" she said, her voice shaking. "How shocked my Uncle Winthrop would be—Oh Lud!" she added on a note of hysteria. "Why did I speak of him?"

"Hush, Bess," he said. "Hold out thy hand!"

She did so, sobering at once. This isn't play-acting, she thought. Dear Lord, forgive us, what else can we do!

He took her hand. "I, William, take thee, Elizabeth, for my wife, and swear to love, honor and cherish thee until death do us part." He put the ring on her finger. And she with a steady voice repeated her own vow and placed his ring.

They looked at each other shyly, as their hands dropped. "I think you should kiss me, now," she said.

He bent and kissed her awkwardly, hurriedly, as he never had before. "Oh, Bess—" he whispered. "Bess, it *is* real enough isn't it?"

"Aye, my darling." She felt a sharp stinging in her eyes, and said briskly, "Now, my husband, I shall start our married life by proving me a shrew. Comb your hair, and shave your chin and take off that old leather doublet. Forsooth what sort of groom are you to grace the marriage bed!"

"A hobbledehoy," he said with a lopsided grin. "A rustic clown—or what was it you called me on the *Lyon* the day of the fishing at the Banks?"

"I don't remember, Will Hallet," she said. "But I think I already loved you then, and what a strange toilsome journey we've come since."

Nor is that journey ended yet, he thought. By God that we should get in such a fix.

The rising sun made golden cracks between the shutters, when the intrusion came which they had been expecting. Will's sharp ears heard distant voices, and the horse whinnied in the shed.

He turned on his elbow and looked down at her, at the fair body which had responded so rapturously to his. Her long eyes, languid now and very soft, met his gaze with confidence, her red lips smiled a little.

"They're coming, dear heart," he said. "Are you ready? 'Twill be nasty."

"I'm not afraid," she whispered. She raised her head and kissed him. "Indeed I had not known there could be such content."

"Nor had I," he said in a voice of wonder.

His horse neighed again. Will jumped from the bed, and pulled on his breeches. "Hasten, hinnie," he said. "Dress thyself."

She had not fastened the buttons of her yellow gown

before there was a thunderous banging on the door. And Thomas Lyon's voice shouting, "Open up, William Hallet, open up at once or we shoot!"

"What the devil ails you!" Will cried back with anger. "What's the meaning of this?" He threw the bolt, and flung wide the door so suddenly that Thomas stumbled through and nearly fell. Behind him were Angell Husted and Toby Feake. All three men were armed.

"I *knew* she was here!" Thomas shouted, pointing at Elizabeth. "Oh, strumpet! Oh, shameless whore!"

Toby's face turned red beneath his freckles. He gaped at Elizabeth. "I couldn't a believed it," he mumbled. "I couldn't."

"Believed what?" said Will, stepping in front of Elizabeth. "Is it so strange that my wife should spend the night with me?"

"WIFE, forsooth!" cried Thomas, shaking. "Ye must think we're crazed. She *has* a husband, you foul knave."

"She has," said Will. " 'Tis I. As I shall shortly prove to you, if you'll stop bellowing."

The two big yeomen glared at each other and Angell said uneasily, "Best listen to him, Tom. There's summat strange here."

"Aunt, Aunt—" said Toby still gaping at Elizabeth. "How could ye so disgrace the Feakes!"

"I haven't, Toby," she said lifting her chin, and staring back at him. "I am divorced from Robert. 'Twas why I went to New Amsterdam."

"Divorced," repeated Thomas whirling on her. "You lie. You cannot be divorced!"

"I've the paper to prove it," she said after the flicker of a glance at Will, who signalled back a "yes."

She took the folded parchment from her pocket and spread it silently out on the table.

Thomas, Toby and Angell crowded round, staring down at the red New Netherlands seal, at Wilhelm Kieft's unmistakable signature, and the date April 14, 1647, which was clear enough.

"Ye know we can't read that!" Thomas blurted, but his eyes shifted. "They're diddling us! It might say anything there."

"It was for that reason," said Will, "that I've brought you an English confirmation." He went to his saddlebag and took out a statement signed by George Baxter which said tersely that Elizabeth Feake's divorce from Robert Feake was quite in order. Further than this slight ambiguity Baxter had not dared go in giving Will the statement. But as Will had hoped, it so startled the three men that they were silent. Toby and Angell would have been satisfied, but Thomas's wits were quicker and his interest stronger.

"So maybe she's divorced," he said jerking his head. "Though I never heard the like for a sly sneaking bit o' skullduggery. But that's no proof of your marriage. When was *that* supposed to be?"

"After the divorce," said Will with cold finality. "You see our wedding bands, and there's an end to it!"

"Why, so it is," said Angell smiling suddenly. He had always admired Mrs. Feake, and he liked Will Hallet. Nor had he stomach for the violent scene Thomas Lyon had urged on him as his duty.

"'Tis an upset," said Toby slowly, mulling it over. "Ye might've told us sooner, Aunt, and spared us this morning's jaunt. I've not even had my ale yet. Hallet, where's your keg?"

"Oh, I'll get you something, Toby," cried Elizabeth, exhaling her breath. "And there's enough for all!"

"Not so fast, my dear mother—" said Thomas, catching her roughly by the arm. "I'M no fool. This is some trick o' Hallet's to get possession o' the property. Where're your marriage lines?"

Elizabeth's mind swam, but before she could think of an answer, Will jumped over and struck Thomas's hand off her arm. "There'll be no more of your bullying!" he cried furiously. "And no more of your questions either! And also, Thomas, I feel that you've lived long enough at my wife's house. I suggest you move to Stamford and those friends there you're so fond of. You might spend your own money for a change!"

Thomas flinched, confused by this sudden attack, and switch of topic. His great fists doubled uncertainly. Will lowered his chin and stood ready. Angell hastily ran between them. "Now, now—men—" he said. "I allus wanted to see ye wrassle but not like this, not in bad blood. Ye best give in, Tom. Will Hallet's got the right of it."

Thomas's eyes darted to Angell's face and then to Toby's, then returned to Will's icy watchful gaze. Thomas mastered his rage. Fighting the fellow would butter no parsnips now, and they were all against him at the moment. Also these startling developments wanted thinking out, and investigating.

There was evasion somewhere, something fishy. He was sure of it.

"The matter'll not end here, Hallet," he said, picking up his musket. "But out of *respect* for my mother," he made Elizabeth an ironic bow, "I'll say no more at present. Are ye coming, men?"

"Aye," said Angell. "My stock's not been watered. I give you good day, Will, and—Mrs. Hallet, I suppose I should say now! Rebecca'll be in a rare taking when she hears this!" He grinned and followed Thomas out the door.

Toby remained, noisily guzzling the ale Elizabeth brought him. "That Thomas is a rare one for stirring up trouble," he said meditatively. "Says he's had a letter from Governor Winthrop."

"What!" gasped Elizabeth, putting down her mug. "From my Uncle John? Thomas hasn't been writing to *him!*"

"Oh aye," said Toby calmly. "About the property and what's due Joan, which he thinks not enough, and about that paper my Uncle Feake gave you an' Hallet afore he went to Boston."

Panic struck Elizabeth as it had not during all Thomas's rantings. "What has Thomas been telling them in Boston?" she whispered half to herself.

"I dunno," said Toby, belching pleasurably. "But Anneke thinks he's working on the Governor to get Uncle Feake to repudiate that paper. But now——" said Toby shrugging, "that you've divorced my uncle, I expect there'll be more confusion. 'Tis a good thing you've married Hallet, Aunt, or you might be in danger o' losing everything you own."

21

ELIZABETH and Will in her house on Greenwich Cove had some months of uneasy peace. It was the happiest time they had ever known, perhaps because they felt an urgency to savor each moment, and a lurking threat, though they never spoke of this. In their big bed upstairs at night they both learned the unguessed delights of passion when it was also mingled with tenderness and humor. By days they worked at their separate tasks—and though often apart from sunrise to sundown, they were always conscious of each other.

Thomas and Joan had duly moved to Stamford. Elizabeth was saddened at parting with her daughter, and by the sullen look in Joan's brown eyes, but once the Lyons were gone the house took on a lightness and gaiety it had never known through the long years.

The children blossomed. They accepted without question the news of their mother's marriage and Will Hallet's installation in their home. The girls were delighted, Lisbet in her own frivolous way, Hannah with a loving welcome for a normal and responsive father at last.

As for the little boys, Will gave them companionship and some much needed discipline, and he taught them to whittle and chop and make good tools.

During the short time that they were left in peace, Will

enormously improved Elizabeth's estate, which had never
been well managed. He sold some of her most northern acres
to a Dutch settler, and bought livestock with the proceeds;
two more cows, and a bull to service all the township. He
bought five ewes and a ram. He changed the feed for Elizabeth's puny swine, and they began to thrive. He burned down
trees, as the Indians did, to clear many acres which he
cannily planted for the highest yield in barley, wheat and
corn.

He farmed his own Totomack lands too; and as all this
industry taxed even his great strength, he hired one of the
new Dutch lads and young Danny Patrick to help him.

Since Toby did no farming, Anneke could well spare
Danny, who was now a big hearty youth, and she had
forgiven Elizabeth and Will.

"Och Bess—" she said one day. "I vas so upset about you,
I thought you vere turning light and vicked. Divorce is bad,
ja—but I can't blame you, lieveling. And you have got a
good husband at last."

"I have, I have," said Elizabeth, her eyes shining as they
always did when she thought of Will. She no longer felt
guilty when anyone referred to their marriage. Surely there
was no real deception, and they had harmed nobody. With
each evidence of their increased prosperity, she felt more
secure. Even Thomas seemed no menace now. They never
saw him and though Elizabeth sometimes missed Joan, the
affection of the other children amply made up for it. She
was so happy that summer and so busy that she scarcely
visited Monakewaygo, and then only the beach. The secret
pool no longer called her. In fact the memory of her former
feelings for the pool made her uncomfortable. Her garden
and her children—and Will's arms at night—sufficed. She
wanted to think of nothing else.

The first blow fell at their Harvest Festival, a day of
Thanksgiving and feasting observed at different times throughout all the colonies. Elizabeth and Will, as Greenwich's
undisputed leaders, and the owners of the largest house,
invited the whole community, and selected the date—the
thirty-first of October.

"Halloween it'll be too," said Elizabeth gaily to the children. "We'll have the games and sport we used to have at
Groton when I was little, and jack-o'-lanterns! We used to
make them from turnips, but our pumpkins'll do better, and

bobbing for apples, fortune-telling with chestnuts, and a bon-fire!"

"Couldn't you manage a husking bee as well, Bess?" said Will with a twinkle. " 'Twould be a pity to miss anything, and I'd like a chance at finding a red ear of corn."

"Oh, you would, would you?" she said tossing her head. "And pray whom would you kiss?"

"Goody Crab," said Will solemnly. "I've got a hankering for her."

The children burst into delighted squeals, and Elizabeth gave her rare joyous laugh.

"Nay—but make it a real gaudy night," Will said, squeezing her waist. "We've all had a fine harvest and much to be thankful for."

"So much," she said, looking up into his eyes.

The neighbors were excited at the preparations, all the housewives baked and brewed for days, and the men boasted about it in Stamford, when they went there on market day. Thomas Lyon heard of Greenwich's festival, and delayed by a little certain plans. The results would be far more rewarding if all Greenwich was there to witness.

He went off to confer again with the Reverend Mr. Bishop and Mr. Richard Lawe.

All Hallows Eve was a hazy autumn day, with enough chill in the air to make very welcome the huge bonfire, and later the four hearth fires Elizabeth extravagantly lighted in her house. By midafternoon the neighbors began to straggle in, shuffling through the fallen leaves, each bearing some donation for the feast. They laughed when they saw the pumpkin jack-o'-lanterns the children had carved into grinning faces, and lit by candles from inside; they jested with each other, and told tales of goblins and spectral lights seen in Old England on this night.

Goody Crab after several noggins of rum—and she could hold her drink as well as any man—was reminded of a tale she'd heard in her Yorkshire girlhood, something about a witch's coven flying through the black sky on broomsticks, but Elizabeth checked her. Witchcraft was no jesting matter; some of the guests looked uneasy, and Elizabeth herself preferred not to be reminded.

They gorged on wild turkeys stuffed with sage and chestnuts, and on the great roasted oysters from Totomack Cove. They had pumpkin pies sweetened with maple sugar, and boiled "plum" puddings made with huckleberries. Each woman had brought her specialty. Anneke, her famous gingerbread, Rebecca Husted some loaves of the precious wheat bread, Elizabeth offered a fragrant conserve of rose petals and wild strawberries. There were apple dowdies and pressed cheeses, there were even sugared raisins which the elder Mrs. Husted had been saving against a great occasion. The housewives had with much ingenuity avoided using Indian corn—the all too familiar staple of everyday meals.

The men brought hard cider, rum and ale, but Will had provided lavishly. He was a genial host, happy in the new pleasure of dispensing hospitality, after the bachelor years of wandering, of solitude in trading posts, or of subservience in Sherborne Castle.

By eight o'clock, there was a pause. Some of the older guests began to think reluctantly of bedtime, the Husted and Sherwood babies, with other children, were already asleep in an upstairs chamber. But nobody wanted the holiday to end.

Richard Crab sprang up and waved his mug. " 'Tis like old times in Essex at Squire's manor house when I was a lad!" he cried exuberantly, his gnarled weatherbeaten face beaming. "Now we got Will Hallet for squire, him and his good lady! Drink to 'em, cronies! Gi' a rousing huzzah for the Hallets!"

They all cheered and huzzahed and cried, "God bless you!"

Elizabeth caught Will's arm and held it tight, while she curtseyed and he bowed.

"I've got me old jew's-harp," cried Crab. "Let the youngsters have a romp!" And he began to play, twanging away at some unrecognizable but spirited tune.

Lisbet who had been roasting chestnuts in the fire seized young Danny Patrick; they sprang up and whirled together, not quite in time. Hannah with other children joined hands and scampered uncertainly around in a ring.

Angell Husted grabbed his young wife's waist, and tried to lead her in a country hay, which they neither of them remembered.

"Well, hinnie—" said Will gaily in Elizabeth's ear as they stood near the passage together watching. "Shall we tread a measure too? For sure we could show them a galliard, couldn't we? What's the matter—" he added in consternation, for Elizabeth's eyes were full of tears.

"They don't know HOW to dance . . . " she said, in a choked voice. "The young ones don't. They don't know how it used to be, and they can't learn here in this harsh land. There's a shadow."

He stared at her. "What melancholy vapors, Bess! Have you drunk too much, or not enough? You *were* enjoying yourself mightily."

" 'Tis Halloween," she said, trying to laugh. "I'm afflicted with ghosts, and the sense of doom."

"Then stop it, hinnie. There's no doom but what we make. I ne'er heard you superstitious."

"I would be merry," she said, "but I dare not, when always something punishes my merriment—Aye—I thought so," she said turning towards the window. "Don't you hear horses?"

Will listened, and he did. "Bess, what on earth—have you gone fey, has some wizard given you the 'sight'?"

"Perhaps," she said wearily. "I had a dream last night; but also there was something Angell told me all unknowing. He saw Thomas in Stamford two days agone. Will, I *know* Thomas has been biding his time and now found out something. I feel it."

The muscles knotted in Will's jaw. "Stand firm then, Bess," he said. "Admit nothing."

He strode into the passage and opened the door. "Come in, friends!" he cried, still uncertain whether Bess were right or not, though as three figures moved into the light he saw that she was.

"Good evening, Thomas," he called out smoothly. "Ever you come unexpected to my door accompanied by two other gentlemen. I find this a trifle monotonous, yet perchance you've come to help Greenwich celebrate its excellent harvest? If so, you are most courteously welcome."

Will spoke deliberately in slight exaggeration of the speech learned in his aristocratic years. Thomas's companions—the Reverend Mr. Bishop and Mr. Lawe, who barely knew Hallet by sight—were startled. Both were men of education, and did not ascribe Will's way of speaking to Dorset accent as the simpler folk had done. Here was certainly not the low common fellow Thomas Lyon had represented, and they changed their attitudes.

"We regret to intrude, sir," said Mr. Bishop. "But Goodman Lyon has, er—troublesome matters to divulge."

"They must be of paramount importance, good sirs, if they have excited the attention of two such eminent gentlemen as—?" Will paused, cool and supercilious as ever Lord Digby had been when confronted by vulgarity.

"I am John Bishop, Stamford's pastor," said the minister, uncomfortably. "And this is Mr. Richard Lawe, our magistrate."

"Precisely," said Will, bowing and concealing dismay though he had been almost sure of their identity. "Two such *eminent* gentlemen." He turned his back on Thomas who had been trying to speak, and walking into the parlor, cried, "Neighbors, we have guests! Stamford guests! We must make them welcome! Wife, pour out the ale, unless you would prefer rum," he said with anxious courtesy to the two Stamford leaders, who looked nonplused.

"We didn't come here for drink!" cried Thomas belligerently, trying to regain his confidence. Richard Crab put down his jew's-harp; all the Greenwich folk had drawn to the end of the room, and were watching with astonishment and hostility.

"True—" said Mr. Lawe, who wished he had not come. "However, a small tot of ale, perhaps." He sat down in Elizabeth's carved court chair. Why didn't Lyon tell us Hallet was a gentleman? he thought. The matter shouldn't be handled roughly like this. He drummed his fingers on his knee.

The minister also appeared uncertain, but a glance at the renegade Greenwich folk, who had once been his parishioners, decided him. Reveling they had obviously been, celebrating a Thanksgiving as they pleased, without benefit of clerical decree, prayer, or blessing. He folded his arms behind his back and standing by the fireplace, spoke in his pulpit voice.

"We regret to cause you embarrassment, Madam." He bowed to Elizabeth who was busily pouring ale.

She looked up smiling. "But indeed you don't. We are delighted to see you, sir." Her heart was pounding against her ribs.

"Not the embarrassment of our presence, the embarrassment of our coming disclosure," said the minister quickly, and hurried on. "I have received a letter from Mr. Robert Feake. Written the day before he finally sailed for England."

"Ah!" said Elizabeth, with a glimmer of relief. This was not what she had feared. "Poor Robert. How is he?"

"Quite, quite sane now," said Mr. Bishop sternly. "As evidenced by his letter to me. H suggests that undue influence was used on him here—" Bishop glanced at Hallet. "The day he ran away from my home, being distracted of wits. He rejects the paper he incontinently signed, and asks that I, and Thomas Lyon, shall reserve the whole of his property until he sees how God will deal with him in England. He says that he now sees he and his children would be wronged by the terms he had given, and regrets his folly."

There was a blank silence. Elizabeth did not understand, Will was too stunned to speak. It was Richard Crab who sprang out from the gaping crowd, and cried, "Now then, parson, what the devil d'ye mean by that folderol? The Hallets own the land fair and square, and the rest o' the estate too. Feake he took his share when he run away, and can go signing papers till the last trump, 'twouldn't change things. He's not got his wits, as all of us know who've lived here."

Mr. Bishop flushed and said stiffly, "You're scarcely a judge of the legal aspects, Goodman Crab. Mr. Feake has written me to conserve his property, and Governor Winthrop of Massachusetts has sent Goodman Lyon a corroborating letter."

Elizabeth drew a harsh breath, her dilated eyes fixed on Thomas. "Where is that letter?" she said. "The letter from my Uncle Winthrop."

Thomas bit his lips, there were certain aspects of Winthrop's letter he preferred not to disclose, since he had written indiscreetly, voicing suspicions as facts, nor was Winthrop's reply quite in the tone Thomas had indicated to the Reverend Mr. Bishop and Mr. Lawe.

The latter now leaned forward. "Goodman," the magistrate said coldly, "I know you have Governor Winthrop's letter with you. It must be produced."

Everyone stared at Lyon. Will stepped back, beside Elizabeth. "You shouldn't have insisted, hinnie," he said in her ear.

She did not hear him, she cried again according to a deep compulsion. "I wish to know what my uncle has written— if indeed he *has* written!"

"Very well! Damme!" cried Thomas. He yanked the letter from under his shirt. "I'll read it to you!"

"*I* will read it, Goodman," said Mr. Lawe, holding out his hand. Thomas surrendered his letter with ill grace.

The magistrate glanced at the signature, and nodded. " 'Tis Winthrop's indeed, and 'tis dated from Boston three weeks ago. It says 'Dear grandson Lyon. Your letters went unanswered because of the severe affliction God has sent me in the loss of my beloved helpmeet . . .' "

Elizabeth gave a strangled gasp. "It can't be," she cried

wildly. "He can't mean my Aunt Margaret!"

Mr. Lawe glanced up at her. "I'm afraid that's the meaning, Mrs. Hallet, 'the loss—of my beloved helpmeet, in the summer sickness we had here . . .'"

Elizabeth turned blindly and sank to the settle by the fire; she held her hand against her face to shield it from the curious observers. Margaret is dead, she thought, my dearest mother, the only person who truly loved me in all those years. She knew now that she had thought Margaret would be always waiting, and that someday they would meet again, and she would tell Margaret everything, and bring Will to her for blessing. Mr. Lawe's voice went on, but Elizabeth did not listen.

" 'I myself,' " read Mr. Lawe, " 'have been disabled with much bodily weakness, and the feebleness of my head and hand deny me liberty to write as I do desire. Lieutenant Baxter coming here to me with salutations from the new Dutch governor has told me somewhat of my daughter Feake's concern. Your letters also raise grave doubts that I know not at present how to answer. I send you what I can for the necessities of my granddaughter Martha Johanna and am sorry to hear there is such need. Mr. Feake has I believe written as you so desired, and is sailing for Old England, being much afflicted. You may tell your mother Feake that her aunt had prayers for her in her last moments . . .' "—That," said Mr. Lawe looking up with a frown, "is the letter, nor do I find it quite as I expected."

Nor did Will, who let out a long sigh of relief. It was clear enough to him that Thomas had written his doubts of the marriage to Winthrop, but the old Governor either because of his illness, or because of family loyalty, or possibly from distaste for his importunate grandson-in-law had maintained an admirable discretion. Bess was right to have made them read the letter, Will thought, looking at her averted face with sympathy, knowing how much Margaret Winthrop had meant to her.

"I can't see what that there letter proves, Thomas!" said Goodman Crab with a disgusted shrug, "except you've been plaguing Mr. Winthrop to give you something and made yourself out to be in desperate straits, as I've never seen signs of meself. And it's brought bad news to Mrs. Hallet, and I say we'd all best go and leave her to her grief."

The Greenwich folk murmured agreement, and Mr. Lawe stood up nodding.

"Hold on, sir—" said Thomas to him sharply. "The case

isn't altered. However come by, my father Feake's wishes are plain put in writing, which our minister has got. You and me and Mr. Bishop came here tonight to restrain Hallet from further use of the property, and to take it into our hands. There's the money in the lean-to chest we must have too, or if that fellow's spent it he must make restitution Over eighty pounds it was my father left behind."

"That's true," said Mr. Bishop, recapturing his earlier certainty. "Give them the injunction, Lawe, as you had it ready!"

Will would have spoken then, but Crab saved him the trouble. "Bah!" said the Goodman spitting into the fire. "Ye Stamford men can yammer injunctions and restraints an' what ye will, but your wits have gone as addled as Mr. Feake's if ye think it'll profit ye any! Have ye forgot this is New Netherland? Ye've no more say this side o' Totomack Creek than ye have in Spain, and we'll all thank ye very kindly to go home again!"

"Bravo!" cried Will, laughing outright at the minister's expression, while Thomas Lyon sent Will a look of hatred.

Mr. Lawe walked over to his colleague, and spoke to him in a low tone. "I'm afraid that what the goodman says is true, Bishop. I always knew there was a flaw in this procedure, if it occurred to them to find it. There's nothing we can do at present."

"Aha!" cried Crab, who had cupped his ear to listen. He winked jubilantly at Will, then grinned at the Greenwich folk who had all begun to chuckle and murmur amongst themselves.

The Stamford men grimly went away. As Thomas slammed the door behind him he called out in a voice trembling with fury, "You needn't think this is the end, William Hallet! I know a thing or two will make you sing a different tune, and I know how to go about it *now!*"

Except for Will, the company all jeered, and Crab cried, "Hark at him squealing like a snared coney, and just about as fearsome!"

But Will was not so sure this was an empty threat, though he said nothing disturbing to Elizabeth, and comforted her while she grieved bitterly that night for Margaret.

The snows fell thick and heavy that winter, and it was early March before Thomas could put his new scheme into action.

Will and Elizabeth enjoyed the quiet shut-in months,

wherein they felt increasingly secure. Nobody molested them, they had no news from the world beyond their coves. From time to time they saw a neighbor when the trails were passable, and they made one or two land sales—of a salt meadow to John Coe; of an upland strip which Angell wanted to round out his holdings. Will made enjoyable plans for investing the proceeds in more livestock and in tools and household goods to be bought at New Amsterdam in the spring.

In January, Elizabeth discovered that she was with child, and was delighted. Will could not at first prevent dismay. Deeply as he had buried the consciousness of it, he was not always able to forget their ambiguous position, also he had horrified memories of her last agonizing childbirth. She however had neither fear nor misgivings, she welcomed this natural proof of their love, and bloomed at once—as she had in every pregnancy but the last—into heightened well-being and increased beauty.

"It will be a boy," she said confidently. "Another William Hallet, and you will dote on him, my darling, so much that I'll be jealous."

"*I* shall be jealous of the little knave," said Will laughing. "And it's you who dotes on babies—they frighten me." But he found that the thought of fatherhood grew deeply pleasing to him, and he secretly made plans, and worked harder than ever so that his child might not be ashamed by small-ness of estate compared to the Feake children.

Their peaceful lives were shattered without the slightest warning, on a particularly beautiful early April day, when clouds were scudding across a brilliant blue sky, and the daffodils and English violets were blooming in Elizabeth's garden.

Anneke had strolled down the muddy path to visit with Elizabeth, who was working at herb-planting with the two girls. Will was repairing his plough in the barnyard, and could be heard whistling. A cheerful sound which contributed to Elizabeth's content. She loved to know that he was near.

"When's Toby going to sail again?" asked Elizabeth of Anneke, who settled herself with a comfortable sigh on the bench Will had carved, and which he had moved from his own property to Elizabeth's garden.

Anneke started her knitting, and said, "In a few days, not a long voyage this time. Only to Virginia for tobacco."

They both glanced down the cove towards Toby's sloop which rode at anchor near Green Island. He had with unexpected sentiment named his new vessel the *Ben Palmer* in memory of the lad Mianos had killed. Toby had a crew of three now, and the women could see him standing on the cargo hatch and directing the placing of the ballast.

"There's another ship, behind," said Anneke in surprise. "She's coming in the cove, vat could she vant?"

Elizabeth and the girls stood up, staring curiously. " 'Tis a Government pinnace," said Elizabeth, seeing below the Dutch flag the fluttering colors of the West India Company. "Thank God," she added, " 'tis not yachts full of soldiers come to massacre our Indians! That cannot happen again."

"Nay," said Anneke, ceasing to knit as she was also caught by bitter memory. "Those bad times are gone. 'Tis some new shipping rule, perhaps?" she added as the Dutch pinnace dropped anchor near the *Ben Palmer* and the captain waved over the water to Toby.

"But there *are* soldiers," said Elizabeth with a puzzled frown, seeing the sickeningly familiar glint of helmets and cuirasses as a dozen men climbed down the ladder into the pinnace's longboat. She went to the corner of the house. "Will!" she called. "Come here, dear!" But though disquieted, she had no premonition of disaster.

Will, however, did have—when he had come running from the barnyard. As he walked down to their little landing and waited for the longboat to arrive, he thought, This is it. It has come. He stood stiffly waiting, while Sergeant Pieter Cock jumped ashore. "Mistress Feake here?" he asked of Will, whom he had never seen before.

Elizabeth came forward walking slowly. "Good day," she said, staring at the stolid bearded Dutch face beneath the helmet. "Aren't you the officer who came here with Lieutenant Baxter four years ago?"

"Ja," said Sergeant Cock, unsmiling. "My English not good. I have letter from Mynheer Baxter, also proclamation from the Director-General."

"Will!" Elizabeth cried. "Will, 'tis the permit, at last. Baxter's got it!"

"Hush, hinnie," he said. "I'm afraid not." He put his arm around her. "You must be brave." He knew that it did not take a force of soldiers to deliver a marriage license.

"We go into house," stated the Sergeant. And led the way, after motioning his soldiers to follow behind Elizabeth and Will.

"What is the meaning of this, Vandrager Cock!" cried Anneke in Dutch, seeing with stupefaction that the marching procession looked very much as though the Hallets were being arrested.

"You will soon know, Mevrouw," said the Sergeant. "Since you are Dutch, you can translate the document for them better than I."

"Best stay outside, lasses," said Will quietly to the two girls, who were staring with round frightened eyes.

Cock motioned again to his soldiers who encircled the house, standing on guard, their muskets resting on the ground.

"Mynheer Baxter's letter," said the Sergeant when they were in the parlor.

It was not a letter but a hurried note. Elizabeth and Will bent over it together. "I regret this profoundly, and have done what I could to alleviate it. But Gov. S. could do no less in view of Thos. Lyon's and the pastor's representations here. 'Tis very serious. You must obey.—G.B."

Elizabeth licked her lips, and grabbed Will's hand which was cold and wet. The Sergeant glanced at them both indifferently.

"You will translate, Mevrouw," he said to Anneke, handing her a parchment adorned with a huge red seal. Anneke bent her head and glanced at the document. She stared, her jaw dropped. "God allemachtig!" she cried, staring at Elizabeth. "O hemel! Vat is *this!* I can't say these things."

"Read it, Mevrouw," said the Sergeant sternly. "I command you to."

Anneke bent her head again and haltingly, her lips trembling, she translated the document.

"*Whereas Elizabeth Feake has for adultery been legally separated from her former husband, Robert Feake, before our arrival, by the preceding Director General and Council, and since that time continued to . . . cohabit and keep company with her cope-mate and adulterer in a carnal manner as the witnesses declare, contrary to all good laws and our published order . . .*"

Anneke's voice broke. "Bess, Bess—" she said. "But you are *married* to Villiam, here is some fearful error."

"Not precisely married," said Will with stony calm. "They wouldn't suffer us to be. We made our private vows."

"Continue, Mevrouw," said the Sergeant stridently.

Anneke obeyed in a thickening voice.

"*And endeavored with him to . . sell . . . the lands,*

*. cattle, furniture and other property of her former hus-
band Robert Feake . . . whereby the children finally
impoverished would become a charge either of the
Company, or on this Commonalty. This can not be
suffered or tolerated in a good well regulated government. Therefore we do hereby, as well for the mainte-
nance of justice as protection of still minor children,
fatherless orphans, declare the above named Elizabeth
Feake unqualified and incapable of disposing, or . . .
selling any property whether of her former husband or
belonging to the children."*

"But this is nonsense!" snapped Anneke in Dutch, her
sense of justice overcoming the shock of the Hallets' deception. "The children never *had* a true father until Mr.
Hallet came, and he has much improved their property."

Cock shrugged. "That paper has nothing to do with me,
except to enforce it."

"Go on, Anneke," said Will. "Let's get it over."

*"And though deserving of much severer castigation
and punishment, yet through special favor & for private
reasons . . . we consent to her . . . residing at Greenwich, within our government with the children, under
such Curators as . . . we have appointed . . . or may
appoint, to be supported out of funds that have been
left—but this, on the condition that she remain herself
apart from him on pain of bodily punishment . . ."*

"By God!" cried Will, the blood rushing into his head.
"What does the scoundrel mean by that!"

"Flogging. Branding. Gaol. No doubt the ears cut off—"
answered Cock with a certain relish. "Since ve have the
new governor, ve do like English colonies. The rest—" he
added, pointing to the document, "is for *you*, Hallet."

Anneke's voice was hardly audible as she read the last
portion of the document.

*"We do hereby sentence and condemn William Hallet,
the adulterer to remain banished out of this our jurisdiction . . . and government and to depart therefrom
within one month from date, nor molest or trouble
anyone within our government on pain of corporal
punishment; furthermore condemning his pretended
property to be forfeit . . . Thus done in Council, in*

Fort Amsterdam in New Netherland, the 9th of March, 1648."

Anneke put the parchment on the table. The Sergeant sat down—now that the official aspect had been discharged—crossed his legs and fumbled in his pouch for his pipe.

"Banished," said Will in what might have been a calmly amused manner except for the look in his gray eyes. "Banished from Bess, on pain of bodily punishment. My property all forfeit, hers given to curators. I should say that Thomas Lyon and the Reverend Mr. Bishop had had excellent success at last."

"It can't really be like that," said Elizabeth in a puzzled voice. Her mind seemed to have detached itself while Anneke was reading. The words conveyed very little, and seemed to refer to other people. The faces of Will, Anneke and the Sergeant swelled and shimmered as though she looked at them through water.

Cock spoke in Dutch to Anneke, who raised her head and said woodenly, "He says to start making your plans, Villiam. There's not much time, and the soldiers stay here until you go."

"It said a month!" he cried. "You read a month!"

"Month from this—" said the Sergeant putting his dirty forefinger on the date, " 'March 9,' there vere delays, you have six days now."

"Bess," cried Will, sweat breaking out on his forehead. "Come upstairs, I've got to speak to you alone. My God, I don't know what we're going to do."

"You cannot speak with her alone, no more," said the Sergeant calmly, sucking on his pipe. "There must be no more 'overspel'—adultery, if she remains in Greenwich."

Elizabeth's daze shattered as she saw the terrible look on Will's face. She felt his muscles tense and knew that he was about to spring at the Sergeant, who was also watching, and raised his voice sharply. "Cornelis!" he called.

The guard at the door rushed in, his pistol cocked.

"But I'm not going to remain in Greenwich," Elizabeth said quite gently. "Do you think I would let Will go away from me?"

"Vere could you go, Bess?" said Anneke. "Vere *could* you go, vith nothing. They vill not let you take anything. O hemel!" she raised the half-knitted sock which had lain in her lap, and wiped her eyes.

"I don't know where we'll go," said Elizabeth. "I can't

think yet. But wait—aye—perhaps I can."

Will stared at her without hope. He thought her distracted with the shock and himself saw nothing but ruin and despair ahead.

The Sergeant too stared at Elizabeth, a slight smile on his bearded lips. The Director-General would not be displeased if the foolish woman decided to follow her paramour out of New Netherland, thus leaving all her estate under the Dutch government's jurisdiction. This is a fine place, the Sergeant thought, big house and barns, in good condition. It occurred to him that it would make a splendid bouwerie for himself, he might get it as a grant, since the Director-General had indicated that he wished there were loyal Dutch patriots living on this troublesome frontier instead of the disorderly English.

"Tell her if she goes," Cock said in Dutch to Anneke, "that she may take some household goods and a cow or two, this I say on my own authority, I would not seem too severe."

A cow or two, thought Will. He stared at the floor that he might not look towards the barns and granary, the cow byre, bull pen, and the sheepfold where all the ewes would soon be lambing. He thought of the south field where he had meant to plow this afternoon. Of the fields already planted, and awash with green. Of the plans he had made for the buying trip to New Amsterdam.

"Bess, you can't leave all this," he said hoarsely. "You can hire Danny or someone to help you. I can't have you destitute because of me."

She shook her head. "What good is anything without you? —Anneke, we must get Toby at once. Signal him to come in."

"Ja, but vat can Toby do, my poor Bess?" said Anneke.

"He must go to Pequot—and to Jack," she added in a whisper.

"To your cousin John Winthrop?" said Will appalled.

"To my *brother* John," she said, her eyes wide and strained, seeing backwards through the years to a scene in the Governor's house in Boston, and beyond to a brown beach at Sandwich, and a London garden.

She walked rapidly from the parlor, and went upstairs to their bedchamber. She opened her bride chest and pushed back the laces and the piles of linen until on the bottom she found Jack's glove. She stared at it, and rubbed off a spot of mildew on the embroidered running hare. Then she sat down and wrote a note. She put the glove and the note in a little canvas bag and came downstairs again.

"Toby is rowing in," said Anneke.

"But, Bess," Will cried. "What good to send Toby on a wild-goose chase! No Winthrop could condone us. Dear Lord, don't you see our position, hinnie?"

"Aye," she said. "I see it and 'tis desperate, nor do I know for sure what Jack may do. But I think he will not break a vow. There was much love between us once."

Will flinched, and turned away.

"I have no solution to offer," he said walking to the window, where he looked out at the soldiers standing at attention around the yard. "I must abide by whatever you decide."

Six days later the unhappy couple were in Stamford under the dubious protection of the New Haven Colony. The Dutch soldiers had marched with Will, Elizabeth, the four children and the two cows. They marched to the boundary bridge on Totomack Creek. The Greenwich neighbors followed, angry and muttering. Goodman Crab indeed had tried to foment an insurrection, but Will had stopped him, wearily. "Even if you could best these soldiers, my good friend," he said, "you can't fight the whole Dutch government."

Robert Husted had made a practical offer of the little cabin he still owned down the Rippowam River in Stamford. "Ye can stay there till your affairs straighten out," he cried heartily, with an optimism none of them felt. They had all bought their land from Elizabeth, at one time or another, and it was impossible not to see in these developments a threat to their own titles.

Anneke and Rebecca Husted also came to the boundary with the banished family—the other goodwives stayed at home, uncertain and distressed. Nobody knew precisely what the charges were, Anneke would say nothing, and nobody would speak to the Sergeant, but the rumors flew all the same. There had been adultery, there had not been a marriage, there was disgrace. And the Hallets explained nothing.

They crossed the creek into English territory. They crowded into Robert Husted's cabin on the Rippowam and waited, praying that some answer would soon come from Jack. Toby had sailed three days ago, bearing Elizabeth's canvas bag with the glove and the note.

Now Stamford hummed with excitement. And its court took immediate provisional action—on "behalf of Mr. Feake and the children." A party of armed Stamford men came to the cabin and searched it. They impounded all the money which Elizabeth and Will had managed to bring with them—a few pounds of his own, and the ten pounds remaining of her jointure. Cock had prevented them from touching the lean-to chest. Mr. Lawe took charge of the money.

Thomas did not go near the cabin. Joan was in a nervous weakly state, terrified of her husband, for she dimly knew what he had done, longing for her mother and yet not daring to let Elizabeth into the house, the once she came.

Thomas was dismayed at the way matters had worked out. He had not foreseen precisely how Stuyvesant would act, and it was all very well to strip Elizabeth and Hallet of everything they owned, but the Greenwich property, now confiscated, was benefiting no one at all except the West India Company. Nor had Thomas profited by Stamford's action either.

The angry and baffled Thomas decided that another letter to Winthrop was expedient. He therefore wrote on April 14—

> *Loving Grandfather, my Humble Duty remembered unto you. This is to acquaint you that I have received your kind Token you sent to my wife . . . which I humbly Thank you for . . . but my trust is in the Lord . . . Although I am base in degree to you, and poor yet, that you should look upon me to help me the goodness of god is great.*

Thomas continued in this sanctimonious vein for some time, then he proceeded to franker speech and filled pages with his explanation.

> *Concerning my wife's Mother, she has dealt very harsh with me, withholding my right from me in several cases, the reason as I conceive and no other I shall tell you. When I married first I lived in the house with her, because my Father being distracted I might be a help to her, whereupon seeing several carriages between the fellow she hath to be her husband and she . . . which was to her disgrace which grieved me very much, and I can say the Lord knows her fall hath been the greatest grief and trouble to me . . . and I desire myself and others may take notice of her fall and be warned . . .*

Thomas wrote on far into the night, repeating the sad charges about "My Mother and William the fellow," until he at last finished and reached the pitch of his intention in the postscript.

> *The occasion of my writing is to inform you of the truth lest you might be Informed otherwise . . . I entreat you to write to the Dutch Governor who has taken the Land Away that so I may not lose my right, If you please. Thus not to be over-tedious I leave you to the Protection of the All mighty.*
>   *Your dutiful and Obedient Grandson.*
>   THOMAS LION.

He dispatched his letter by Goodman Lockwood, who had business in Boston, and settled down to await developments as anxiously as did Elizabeth and Will, whose discomforts and privations went from bad to worse. After a few further days of hesitation the Stamford Court issued an injunction distraining Elizabeth and Will from making any disposition whatsoever of the household goods, the scanty store of provisions and the two cows, and threatening them with trial before the General Court in New Haven.

Whereupon, there being no sign of Toby and no word of hope from any place, they went to New Haven themselves and had a thoroughly unsatisfactory interview with Governor Theophilus Eaton. Eaton who had already had letters from Bishop and Lawe at Stamford was at a loss. These two were undesirable members of the colony according to Stamford report, they were almost certainly not married, though on this there was confusion and their own replies were evasive. The disposition of their property appeared to be entangled in such an international muddle that Eaton could not make head or tail of it. He demanded time to consider, ordered Hallet to appear before the next Magistrate's Court, reaffirmed the seizure of what estate they had with them in Stamford, and decreed that Elizabeth's two middle children, Hannah and Johnny, should be taken from her at once and boarded at some godly house in Stamford, nor must she try to see them again. This he did to protect the children's morals from contamination, humanely leaving Elizabeth the baby Robert, and Lisbet who presumably was already corrupted, and too set in vice for continuance in the dissolute household to matter.

Will and Elizabeth came back to Stamford, both haggard and silent. They barricaded the door and sat down to eat the dried corn pone and watered cider to which they were reduced. And they owed the cider to the secret kindness of Mrs. Andrew Ward, who slipped out at night and ran down the river to the isolated cabin with donations. The rest of Stamford shunned them, at the behest of the minister who preached several telling sermons on God's punishment for lewd wickedness.

"Well—" said Will on the night of their return from New Haven. "What do we do now, Bess? I should think they'd take the children from you by tomorrow or next day at latest!"

"They can't!" she cried. "I won't let them! Even they can't be so cruel!" But she looked with fear at the flock mattress where Hannah slept with her little brothers in the corner of the cabin.

"Mama," said Lisbet, earnestly. "Why haven't you heard from Uncle Jack? I hate this place. I haven't anything nice to wear, and this morning when I walked along the river-bank some girls threw mud at me and cried 'There goes the strumpet's daughter!' Is our life going on and on like this?"

"No—" said Will. "There is a way in which you'd all have considerably more comfort." He got up and began to throw into his saddlebag his knife and spoon, a mug, a shirt, an extra pair of breeches. They had not been allowed to bring the horse. It had remained in Greenwich.

"What are you doing, Will?" cried Elizabeth sharply.

"What do you think?" he answered with anger. "Fool that I was not to do it earlier. Fool that I was ever to come near you in the first place!"

Lisbet stared at them both. She had never seen anger between them.

"Go then!" Elizabeth cried. "Leave me to bear all this alone. Leave me to bear your child alone!"

He flung the saddlebag on the floor and stalked out of the house.

"Oh God . . . " she whispered. "Oh God." She crouched down beside the saddlebag. She flung her arms out and buried her face on them.

Lisbet stared at her mother's shaking shoulders, and tried to go on eating but she could not swallow. She pushed the plate away.

Hannah woke up, and ran to Elizabeth who gathered the child against her breast, and sat on, there on the floor, leaning against the saddlebag.

Their meager fire went out. The spring night grew chill. An owl hooted in a nearby tree. Hannah went to sleep again in Elizabeth's lap. Lisbet lay down on the flock mattress with the boys. Elizabeth did not move.

At midnight she heard a footstep on the path outside and raised her heavy head. The door opened. Will came in, and stood by the door in the darkness. He had been pacing the river path for hours, cursing a malign fate, bludgeoning it or a possible deity for a solution to their miseries.

"Bess!" he whispered in sharp fear. "Darling, aren't you here?"

She moved a little without answering, but he heard and groped his way towards her. "He's come, Bess—" Will whispered. "Toby's come. Your cousin John has sent for you. Toby's bringing the sloop up as far as he can. We'll go down the riverbank, rouse the children. I'll lead the cows. You can get your stuff aboard."

He lit a candle, and they both silently and swiftly gathered together their few belongings. The children were very quiet.

The tide was high and Toby had come quite near the house. It took them very little time to get their goods and the children on board. The cows were pushed and hauled along the little gangplank.

"Farewell, hinnie-love," said Will, as Toby began to hoist sail. "You're safe now. Your cousin John didn't forget his vow. And forgive me for all I've done to you. I didn't mean it so." His voice broke, and he turned from her.

She had put her foot on the gangplank and now she drew it back. "Will Hallet!" she said. "Have you forgot *your* vow? Does your promise you made me, in the sight of God, mean as little to you as these people here all think?"

"It is for you—" he said roughly. "You know I love you, but you're shamed and disgraced enough. Do you forget I am an adulterer? I cannot come with you to your family."

"And I cannot live without you," she said. "Don't you know that, Will?"

"God-damn it!" Toby called out from the deck, but cautiously. "What's the matter with you two? You want to chatter there until all Stamford comes to help you flee?"

Will made a long harsh sound in his throat. He took Elizabeth's hand. "We're ready, Toby," he said. They walked silently up the gangplank onto the sloop.

22

A MONTH after the Hallets' frantic midnight flight from Stamford, John Winthrop, Jr., sat in his large study at Pequot, frowning at a lump of graphite which had been sent him from his Tantiusque lead mine in Western Massachusetts. He was not thinking of the graphite, he was thinking of Elizabeth—thinking of her with perplexity, dismay and a yearning tenderness not unmixed with anger, because his usual self-discipline and detachment seemed to have deserted him. But he again forced their return by picking up his magnifying glass and making a dogged examination of the graphite. There were also ranged before him on his table some samples of ore, possibly gold-bearing, which Roger Williams had sent from Providence for assay. And on a stone slab at the back of the room, a retort bubbled slowly. Jack was brewing his all-purpose remedy, the "Rubila" with which he successfully dosed his family, half his town, and a great many acquaintances throughout the colonies who wrote to him for medical advice.

The soft June air blew through the open window, and brought a faint musical sound. It was Bess's voice, she must be out in the courtyard. Jack went to the window and saw her dark bent head. She was sitting on a bench packing rose petals into a pomander and singing a sad little tune. "If my

553

complaints could passions move, or make love see wherein
I suffer wrong—"

It was a song that Bess used to sing, accompanied by her
lute, at Groton. One summer night that he especially remembered, she had sat under the mulberry tree, Martha
had been there too. The sisters had sung in harmony. And
behind them had towered the great cream and brick sheltering walls of the Great Manor House. What summer was
that? Anyway, long before he had ever thought to leave the
beautiful home behind forever.

Jack shut the window with a bang, latched it and sat down
again at the table. What ails me? he thought with disgust.
Regrets, nostalgia—futile morbidities—And right here at
Pequot he had now built for himself as fine a clapboard and
gabled mansion as any in the New England. Why hark back
to old outworn places . . . and feelings? He shoved his
minerals aside, and picking up his quill pen began the determined writing of a business letter.

After a disappointing winter at nearby Fishers Island, Jack
was at last really established at Pequot, or "Nameag" as
the Indians called this lovely hillside on the west bank of
the deep blue river harbor.

Convinced of his little settlement's eventual pre-eminence,
Jack had asked the Hartford authorities for permission to
christen the place New London. The Governor of Connecticut—Edward Hopkins—was sympathetic, the Deputy
Governor John Haynes was not, and had conveyed a message of reproof, saying that other settlements throughout
New England had considered this grandiose name for themselves and eschewed it as being too presumptuous.

Jack, whose enthusiasms were not easily daunted, and
who had a concealed antipathy towards Haynes, determined
to persist, and in fact already called Pequot's river The
Thames. Though he had small hope of official sanction, since
Hopkins and Haynes alternated the governorship each year,
and Haynes would soon be in again. It was John Haynes
who back in 1634 had ousted Jack's father from the Bay
control, it was Haynes who had accused the elder Winthrop
of "too much lenity" and who had pronounced the actual
banishment on Roger Williams. A narrow, rigorous man was
John Haynes, the type of Puritan, Jack well knew, who was
responsible for some of the odium the colonies had incurred
in England.

It was unfortunate that Massachusetts had relinquished
Jack's huge Pequot domain, and he had been forced to put

it under Connecticut Colony, but geography and common sense made the move inevitable.

Jack had need of his large mansion, and the almost manorial outbuildings he had erected at Pequot. He was one of the most influential men in the four—now confederated—colonies, of the Bay, Plymouth, New Haven and Connecticut. Some thought him the most important settler between Boston and New Amsterdam. At any rate he was the most popular, and he received many visitors.

Also his family was large. He and Betty Winthrop had six children, and she was expecting another in August; moreover, her widowed sister, Mrs. Lake, lived with them, and there were five servants to be housed.

Mrs. Winthrop, an accustomed hostess, usually took chance-comers in her stride, but it was on a question of hospitality that she had decided to invade her husband's private sanctum this Saturday morning in June. She had been a large, handsome, fair-haired girl, with the assured manner of one who was well born and well dowered. At thirty-three she was unchanged. She had no whims, no melancholies, and no humor. She made John an excellent wife, and had punctually produced all the children he had so desired with Martha. Jack was fond of her, and his manifold projects and frequent travels prevented an occasional hint of boredom from growing to uncomfortable proportions.

He had built himself this study, which was semi-detached from the main house with its constant bustle of shrieking children and barking dogs. The room—a combination office, library and surgery—reflected his interests, the interests on which of late he found it so hard to concentrate.

"Come in, my dear," said Jack looking up from the table in answer to his wife's firm knock. "And good morning sister Peggy," he greeted Mrs. Lake, a small, fluffy-headed woman who followed her sister about, rather like a spaniel after a large setter. Both ladies were elegantly dressed in striped dimities.

"I regret to disturb you, John," Betty said, seating herself in the armchair across from her husband, "but there are several matters to take up. First, the servants. Kaboonder has got into the rum again, and I think he should be thoroughly flogged."

Jack inclined his head. "Very well." He knew that he was too lax with his big black slave, who was an engaging rascal, reputed to have been a king in Angola before he had been captured and sold at Boston by a West Indian trader.

"Also," said Betty, "do you think it wise to trust Robino as you do? I don't pretend to understand all this new turmoil between the Narragansetts, and the Pequots, and that Mohican sachem—Uncas—and I don't wish to interfere, husband, but I doubt if Robino always delivers your messages aright."

Jack frowned, for he had some doubts himself. Robino was a Pequot; he lived with the scattered remnants of the tribe, only a few miles from here. Robino spoke English and was an excellent runner. Jack constantly used him to carry letters to Hartford, or Providence, or even Boston.

"What makes you suddenly distrust my Indian?" asked Jack anxiously, knowing that Betty always had sound reasons.

"Something my sister heard," she said nodding towards Mrs. Lake.

Peggy Lake fluttered and blushed at the sudden notice. " 'Twas while I was in the dairy, helping Nannie skim the cream," she said. "Robino was boasting to Kaboonder directly outside the window; he said he knew how to get wampum out of Ninnigret with one hand while he took it from Uncas with the other. He said the white men were such fools."

Jack sighed and shook his head. "I see. I think these are vain boasts designed only to amaze poor Kaboonder, but the Pequots are certainly subtle, and I'll endeavor to investigate this." He glanced at letters he had recently received from Roger Williams, and from Captain Mason at Hartford. They both treated uneasily of Indian affairs. Williams, the peace-maker, as usual favored his Narragansetts, but was aware of Pequot and Mohican unrest which must be soothed. Captain Mason was keeping an eye on Uncas, the great Mohican chief, who professed undying devotion for the English, but also seemed to be toying with a Mohawk alliance, one moreover that Governor Stuyvesant was rumored to be promoting for his own wicked anti-English ends. But there were always rumors. Jack had seen too many of them flare up and die to be upset.

He saw that Betty had not finished and smiled at her. "What else, my dear?"

Her level blue-gray Saxon eyes met his squarely. "John—how long are the Hallets to remain here?"

Aha! Jack thought. He had been expecting this for some time. "Why, I don't know," he said. "It's a most awkward situation as you know. They've no other place to go. You find the house too crowded?"

"Somewhat," he said. "But 'tis not that. I've been patient, I believe, and not inhospitable since the day last month when the six of them appeared at our doorstep. I've held my peace. I know my duty towards you and your relations. I am aware that through circumstance as well as kinship, you once took a particular interest in Elizabeth." Betty said this seriously without a trace of sarcasm.

Jack could not help a chuckle, nor asking, "Surely you're not jealous, my dear?"

She considered a moment and shook her head. "Not at all. I simply don't understand her, nor is she the type of woman I can like. Really, John, the extraordinary things she's done! She favored that dreadful Hutchinson female. She set Watertown by the ears, and was forced to leave. She bought land, then abjured her nationality and turned it over to the Dutch. I pass by the scandal one could not help hearing which coupled her name with that Irish Captain's. But then the Captain gets murdered, and her husband goes mad."

"Some of these tragic facts my sister Bess could hardly prevent," said Jack.

"Possibly," said Betty without conviction. "But you must admit her responsibility for her recent conduct. After all, John, a *divorce* on whatever grounds! I never met a divorced woman before in my life!"

"Indeed we haven't," put in Mrs. Lake, her eyes widening with dismay as she considered her sister's résumé. "Papa— Mr. Reade that was—would have been scandalized, and our present father, Mr. Peter, his wife is quite mad, but nobody would ever *dream* of divorcing the poor thing."

"And that's not all—" went on Betty, ignoring her sister's interruption. "I don't understand why she is now penniless, unless it is from the folly of marrying Mr. Hallet who is NOT a gentleman, it seems, however he may sound like one."

Jack bit his lips. Betty in her calm incisive voice had indeed piled up many awkward facts about Elizabeth. It was a mercy that there was one of which she was ignorant.

"Don't you like Hallet?" he said quickly. "I do, in spite of—" he checked himself from saying "Bess's indecent passion for him" and substituted—"his humble birth." Yes, oddly enough he liked Will Hallet though he had been prepared to detest him.

"He's well enough," said Betty. "And I'm sorry for the

children, but I do not think that their peculiar rearing fits them as constant companions for ours."

"As usual," said Jack after a slight pause, "you speak very sensibly, wife, and I agree with you. I shall give the Hallets a grant in town, build them a house at once, and you shall be relieved of their company."

"Thank you," said Betty rising. "Though I still don't understand why they've no place to go but here, and I believe you haven't even heard from her in years?"

"No," said Jack and attempted an explanation which was truthful as far as it went. "The Dutch have some singular laws, wife. I wouldn't expect you to understand them. You know that Governor Stuyvesant has been acting in a gravely inflammatory way; he claims all our Connecticut land for Holland, and indeed he claims everything as far as Cape Cod. I believe that to some degree Bess is being used as a pawn, her personal dilemma is a reflection of the international one."

"It may be so," said Betty with a vague smile, thinking of all the baking which must be done today before the Sabbath began at sundown.

It was one of her virtues that she never hammered on a point once it was made. She gave her husband a courteous bow and departed with Mrs. Lake.

Jack was left to indulge in some more uncomfortable reflections.

The Hallets were a problem, how serious a one neither Betty nor anybody at Pequot knew—so far.

The reception of his own glove, accompanied by Elizabeth's desperate little note, had been acutely embarrassing. At forty-two one did not expect to redeem an impulsive romantic promise made in youth, nor did he at all understand the urgency, though after questioning the laconic Toby Feake, the Hallet predicament became clearer. It was not until Jack had reluctantly sent Toby back to fetch the beleaguered family, and had a private talk with Elizabeth, that he discovered the full extent of her plight.

The interview had taken place in this room on the night of the arrival. Elizabeth had concealed nothing from him. She had told the whole story of her love for Hallet, of Robert's irrational acts, of Thomas Lyon's vindictiveness, of the Dutch governors' behavior—both of them; of the banishment, and of Stamford and New Haven Colony's relentless persecution.

Jack at first found it incredible that a Winthrop should

be seething in such an unsavory stew and thrust there apparently solely by reason of a reckless passionate love, but as he listened his initial shock of distaste gradually faded.

Bess was still, at thirty-eight, a beautiful woman, her curly dark hair showed no gray, her lips were red, her cheeks rose and white. He discovered that her long voluptuous eyes still had disturbing power to move him, especially when they shone with unshed tears. When she had finished, he spoke, however, somewhat dryly.

"This is a most distressing story, Bess. I confess I'm appalled though also sympathetic. But there is, I perceive, one stark circumstance which makes resolution of your problem quite impossible. You are not legally married to William Hallet."

"But we *are* married!" she cried. "The best they'll let us. We tried, I told you how we tried. We feel married. You see my ring!"

"Unfortunately, little coz," he said, "the law is not sentimental, and takes no account of good intentions."

"Then *you* marry us, Jack darling!" she cried, seizing his hand and holding it against her cheek. "It's just a few empty words. You can do it. 'Tis this hope I've been living on. Jack—you see, I'm with child by Will. You'll not deny me this!"

His heart gave an uncomfortable thump, a long-vanquished desire sprang up at the touch of her hand and cheek. But he saw that this was no longer true for her; that kinship, confidence and the desperate need for help were all that she still felt of the old bond, which had been at last replaced by a stronger love. He looked away from her imploring eyes and sighed heavily. "I *must* deny you, Bess. Alas, I have no choice. I've not been sworn in as magistrate for Connecticut Colony, since we've just come under its rule here. And even if I were, my poor girl, I couldn't marry you. You're not divorced by English law, only by Dutch."

She dropped his hand and turning from him stared down at the table. "Then what can we do?" she whispered. "Where can we go now—and we have nothing to live on."

"You can stay here," he said slowly. "The question of your marriage need never be raised, it'll be assumed. In the meantime, I'll write letters for you. To Eaton and Stuyvesant—to my father."

A gleam of hope had come into her face, but at his last words she stiffened. "To your father? Then we're lost. He'll send after me himself. Have me flogged and branded, banish

Will from New England too as he has so many. He has no heart."

Jack's eyes hardened, he spoke with sharpness. "You misjudge my father as usual. You see but one side of him!"

"Ha!" she said bitterly. "You think he has a heart? How then could he take another wife, six months after my Aunt Margaret died, and after all the protestations that he made of loving her? 'Tis sickening."

"Bess, you forget yourself!"

His annoyance was the greater because he had been as startled as anyone by his father's precipitate remarriage with a wealthy Boston widow called Martha Coytmore.

"He's sixty," said Elizabeth angrily. "And I think might have contained himself at least the customary year out of respect for my dead aunt, but no—it seems the new wife is already breeding. What he calls lechery in others no doubts wears some sweeter name when he applies it to himself."

Jack's chair scraped on the floorboards. "You are outrageous! How dare you speak so of my father!"

They confronted each other across the table, both cleft chins squared, the eyes unlike in shape but alike in glittering indignation.

The anger ebbed first from his, for he knew that she was thinking of her sister as well as of Margaret, and he dimly understood how painful it would be for a woman to see how quickly consolable most widowers were.

"We'll not quarrel, Bess," he said, sitting down again. "In fact, how foolish of you to quarrel with me now. But you've never had discretion even for your own good. Nor can you scheme and play the hypocrite to gain your ends. So you've the virtues of your rashness, and we'll let this matter drop."

"Aye," she said after a moment. "I'm sorry, Jack. But please, please don't write your father about our concerns. He'd be pitiless."

He had not argued with her, nor been quite sure himself what his father would do if all the circumstances were presented to him. But he had written at once, and told the truth, adding some recommendations of his own which he knew would carry weight. The reply had not yet come.

The Hallets were as glad to leave the Winthrop home as Betty Winthrop was relieved at their departure. For Will especially there had been weeks of humiliation, in the repetition of circumstances he had once endured at Sherborne Castle. He had sworn never to live again on someone's bounty, nor eat the bread of patronage, yet now by reason of the trap of love, he found himself forced to do so, and he suffered.

Elizabeth seeing this was frightened, and tried in all ways to save his pride; she clung to him, she enlarged upon the liking Jack felt for him, she poured her own love out to him, yet was ever watchful not to cloy or surfeit him, and she knew that Will's deep feeling for her had not changed.

But still there was a difference. He grew silent, the humor that she loved flashed seldom, he did not read his books, or talk at all about the future.

Once established in their own cabin on Meeting-House Hill life was a trifle easier. Will gradually took an interest in the six acres Jack had granted him. He started planting anew as best he could, but it was necessary to borrow tools from the Winthrops, also household equipment, and to accept the neighbors' help which they gladly gave, for they liked Will at once and made him part of the community. But the fact remained that the Hallets were as poor as the humblest cotter in Pequot, and that they were beholden to others for almost everything they did have.

At the beginning of August, Jack received two letters in answer to those he had written. One was from Governor Theophilus Eaton of New Haven Colony and it was exclusively and unpleasantly concerned with the Hallets.

Mr. Eaton began sternly:

Sir, Yours of the 17th present, I have received, by which I understand, William Hallet etc. are come to your plantation at Nameag. their grievous miscarriage hath certainly given great offense to many ...

With mounting indignation, Governor Eaton noted the shocking manner in which his injunctions and decrees about the Hallets and Mrs. Feake's children had been flouted until finally, "in a secret underhand way they had taken the children, two cows, the household goods" from Stamford and stolen off into the night. Mr. Eaton's respect for young Mr. Winthrop barely checked the angriest expression of his righteous indignation.

So all that Elizabeth had told Jack was confirmed. Nowhere in New Haven Colony might she be safe. Jack heaved a sigh of worried exasperation, then opened his other letter, which was from his father. When he had read it he mounted his horse immediately and rode to the Hallet cottage.

He found Elizabeth in her yard hanging out the wash with the help of Lisbet, Hannah, and his own twelve-year-old

Betty. Jack was further amused to see that his little sons,
Fitz-John and Wait-Still were playing a rough game of handy-
dandy with Elizabeth's boys. And he thought that his wife's
plan for keeping the cousins separated was not entirely
successful. He paused a moment to watch, remembering
another set of cousins who had played together long ago in
a different land, but with the same exuberance, and the same
unconscious yet deep recognition of kinship. And of that
older set of cousins, not one was living now, save himself
and Bess, he thought with shock. Harry, Forth, Mary, Martha
—all of them gone. "Eheu! fugaces . . ." he murmured and
walked towards Elizabeth with so serious a face that she
dropped a wet sheet, and cried, "Oh, Jack, what is it?"

"A letter from my father," he said smiling. "Aye, Bess—I
know you think that must be bad, but you're quite wrong!"

She picked up the coarse darned sheet, flung it over the
line; and wiping her hands on her apron walked with him
to a secluded corner of the yard.

"He writes me news that wouldn't interest you," said
Jack, "Until the postscript. And this you may read for yourself." He tendered the letter to Elizabeth. She looked down
with a fearing pang at the well-remembered writing.

*Commend me to my daughter Feake and tell her I have
written to the Dutch Governor about her business already
as much as I can. Desire her also if she have any writings etc; to shew for her land in Barbado that she send it
to me with speed and a letter of Attorney to Mr. Turner
to recover it and I shall help her to somewhat for it,
perchance a good sum of money; my wife salutes you
all: the Lord bless you all: your loving father*

JO: WINTHROP

26 (5) 48.

"It has a kindly tone," said Elizabeth dubiously. "For sure
he cannot know the worst about me!"

"He does," said Jack. "Though in my letter I admit I
stressed certain aspects more than others. Bess, could you
really think he'd let so close a member of our family suffer
gravely without trying to help?"

"Perhaps," she said frowning. "But have you forgot how
terrible he is in persecution? Subtle even, and devious, as he
was against Anne Hutchinson and others—Ah, you may be
angry with me again, Jack, but what cause have I to trust
him? You don't know *what* he's written to Stuyvesant. And

what is this tarradiddle about land in Barbadoes? He knows I've none, and that what little Harry left me—melted unaccountably."

Jack kept his temper with an effort. "You're determined in your hatred. I'm disappointed in you."

"Call it distrust and fear if you like," she said coldly. "I've never dared to hate him—ah, now I see. This mention of Barbadoes is one of Thomas Lyon's concoctions, ever wishful of getting something more with Joan. *There* is one I hate! and I'd like to injure him as he has us!" Her eyes narrowed and glinted green as she cried passionately, "Would I *were* the witch that Watertown once thought me, and I'd blast Thomas Lyon into perdition, but I'm helpless, helpless!"

"Hush, Bess—Hush!" he cried for the children had all turned to stare at her. "Don't talk so wild."

" 'Tis not for what he's done to me, nor yet the children," she said lower but with the same venom, " 'Tis for what he's done to my Will!"

The fury changed to pain in her strained eyes and Jack was touched. He felt again sharp though fleeting envy for a love so powerful, and which had now forever passed him by.

"Yes, I know," he said. "But 'tisn't only Lyon. For there are many reasonable men who think as he does, Bess." He hesitated, then decided not to tell her of Governor Eaton's tirade. He continued quietly, "The rights of your case are clear to me, and clear now to my father, whatever you believe, but for the others we must be patient. I too have written Governor Stuyvesant, and will again."

"He hasn't answered," she said bleakly, the fire gone from her.

"No—and it's awkward, since he blusters and threatens, claiming all these colonies for the Dutch. I fear he's not inclined to do a favor for any English person."

She made a bitter sound and turned away.

He took her arm and led her farther from the children to the tangle of underbrush next their clearing. "Bess, have you heard aught of Robert since he sailed to England?"

She shook her head, astonished. "Have you?"

"Aye," he said, and paused, uncertain what to tell her, while fervently wishing that the news had been of Robert's death. How simple then would have been Elizabeth's solution.

"Do you have any feeling left for Robert Feake?" he asked slowly. "I know you never loved him, and yet did your duty kindly. I saw Robert in Boston, you know, and realized better than Father ever has, what you must have endured."

"Yet—" she said with difficulty, "when you saw Robert he had near recovered. Perhaps in England he'll lay the ghost that troubled him so sorely."

Jack looked at her with keen attention, and saw that he might speak without distressing her too much.

"He's in gaol, Bess. In the Fleet. And you spoke more truly than you knew, when you said he went to lay a ghost."

"In gaol . . ." she whispered, her cheeks whitening. She glanced over towards her children. "Oh, Jack, this is worse disgrace than anything has happened, always I fear so for them."

He shook his head. "You needn't. They're nothing like him, and remember—for that one weak broken mind they have thousands of strong and healthy ancestors. His is not a hereditary taint."

"Why is he gaoled?" she said, wincing. "From whom did you hear?"

"From Edward Howes, our old friend, whom we can trust. I wrote him to keep an eye on Robert. It seems the piteous man, on the day he landed, went to a London magistrate and confessed to a terrible crime committed over seventeen years ago. He said that he had strangled his apprentice, Ralph, and wished to suffer for it."

She stiffened with an inward gasp; then she shuddered and drew back. "You tell me this, and that it's no disgrace! How can you be so cruel!"

"Because, Bess—there's much perplexity. The other goldsmiths on Lombard Street, when questioned, said that a Ralph Barton had some years ago gone off to New York to set up for goldsmith on his own. That they were nearly sure it was the same as had been 'prenticed once to Robert Feake. Still all England is at war, and inquiries most difficult. They put Robert in the Fleet for safekeeping until some trace of this Ralph Barton could be found. Edward had a hand in this, and arranged that Robert be imprisoned under an assumed name. It's also by Edward's humane efforts that Robert was not sent to Bedlam. At the Fleet he has his own apartment and a servant to care for him. He is much distraught again, and nobody believes his story, though they can't free him until they're sure." He put his hand gently on her shoulder. "Did you ever guess what it was Robert wished to go to England for?"

She was silent a long time. At last she answered very low,

"It may be. At least now I see many things I wouldn't look at before." She stopped because an eerie memory displaced the memories of Robert's "strangeness." Against the sultry blue New England sky she saw herself and Edward Howes pausing on Fleet Bridge in the snow, and she saw again the prisoner's hand clenched on the bar of a window in the Fleet. Only a vague pathos had she felt then, and some recognition of the loss of freedom foisted on herself as she reluctantly became Edward's betrothed. Now it might be Robert's hand that clenched at that same bar. She turned and spoke with conviction. "Jack, I believe he did *not* do it. 'Twas one of his hideous fancies sent, I verily believe, by the Devil. Robert has always had a demon fighting in him. He was at times possessed as truly by an unclean spirit as ever was the Gadarene whom Christ delivered."

"Aye," said Jack solemnly after a moment. "And may Christ deliver Robert. Do you pray for him, Bess?"

"I can't pray," she said. "My prayers were never answered when I did. There's naught to be done with a God of Wrath but creep away and hide from His notice. I will not seek afflictions, and deem them joyous marks of Divine Favor. I don't think pain and cruelty ennobling."

Jack was troubled, and her speech dismayed him. He had never questioned such things, but accepted the teaching he had been reared with, and he thought it needful to say reprovingly, "You speak like a heathen, Bess. I grieve to hear it. You must think of your immortal soul, and bear your cross for His sake and for your own salvation."

She looked at him with a sad smile. " 'Tis no use, Jack. I'm in the darkness, and there is but one thing I desire of life."

His grave brown eyes looked their question.

"To hold my William's love, and to be his true wife," she said.

"Poor Bess," he murmured. "Poor little coz. It would be much, but I'm sure—not enough." He sighed and walked over to his children.

Later that week, Betty Winthrop was delivered of a daughter who was named Martha in a compliment to Governor Winthrop's new wife, and with apparently no recollection on Betty's part that the name might commemorate a different Martha. Elizabeth's skilled midwifery was not requested, nor for some time were there any but most formal relations between the great mansion and the little Hallet cottage.

When Elizabeth's own delivery took place in October, her

neighbor Goody Langdon did what was needful, but the birth was as easy as the last had been hard.

It was a boy, as Elizabeth had prophesied, and when she saw Will bend over the red-faced mite, and saw the leap of excited pride in his eyes, she knew a moment of rapture.

"Your son, my dear love," she whispered. "Isn't he big and strong and lusty—like his father?"

"In truth—" said Will gazing down with wonder as the baby's fist closed around his finger. "I think he does look like me, has the same great ape jaw."

"For shame!" she said. "Little William Hallet's a beautiful baby!" She raised her arms and pulled Will's face down to hers. "Does he make you happier? Aren't you glad now, darling?"

"Of course, hinnie," he said kissing her and trying to keep all hesitation from his voice. "I am well content. I love thee and this little poppet." He smoothed her hair back and kissed her again. But she knew that he was thinking of all that he had meant to do for this son, and that in strict legal terms it did not even bear his name.

"Can't you forget that?" she cried as though he had spoken. "Must you keep fretting over what we can't help? Jack understands, and nobody else here suspects."

For how long? he thought. And does she think I can be happy when I am here on sufferance and she under the protection of another man? But he said nothing. He went out to hammer on the shed where the roof was not yet finished, noting grimly that the cow whose leg had been injured upon landing from the boat seemed no better. The other cow had died, soon they would have to borrow milk.

The winter dragged by. A hard winter of ice and blizzards. The Hallets would have suffered without Jack's watchful kindness, also Betty Winthrop who had a perfect sense of what was fitting stifled her disinclination and extended hospitality. Will and Elizabeth accepted it for the children's sake. And their visits to the mansion provided each of them with distraction. Elizabeth often worked on Jack's medical formulas for him; she learned to mix—as well as he could himself—the secret ingredients of his "Rubila" which were antimony, niter and salts of tin, colored red.

Will, glad of providing some return, helped Jack with his voluminous correspondence, and particularly by classifying notes on his development projects; the ironworks at Saugus which were at last turning out eight tons a week, the con-

templated saltworks at Pequot, though so far no saltworks
had prospered; the Pequot gristmill; and continual mining
ventures. Will utilized his clerical training under the Digbys,
and Jack was pleased by the results.

During the winter Jack also wrote two letters to Governor
Stuyvesant on the Hallets' behalf. The first one, to have
gone by a ship's captain, Thomas Alcott, was not delivered,
and when Jack discovered this, he wrote another.

> *Noble Sir, I wrote to you in the winter . . . to know your
> pleasure concerning the estate of mrs. Feake . . .*
>   *I am bold . . . to request your favour concerning her
> . . . that whereas there was an agreement made with
> William Hallet for the managing of the estate (which Mr.
> Feake before his going to England told me at Boston that
> he fully consented to, knowing Hallet to be industrious
> and careful, which I find since his being here to be very
> true) that you will be pleased to let the estate be again
> returned into his hands, not knowing any other way how
> it can be improved to the comfortable maintenance of
> her and the children, who . . . for want of it are in a
> necessitous condition:*
>   *. . . as also that you will be pleased to grant him
> liberty to return again within your jurisdiction . . .
> which license under your hand I beseech you to send by
> this bearer . . .*

Your Humble servant
JOHN WINTHROP.

Will and Elizabeth read the letters before they were sent,
and were hopeful, being sure that this time Stuyvesant must
answer, at least enough to clarify his own position. But still
no answer came. And meanwhile two deaths occurred which
powerfully affected their future.

On the twenty-sixth of March, Elizabeth and the girls were
at the Winthrop mansion. They had spent the day there to
help with the annual soapmaking, an operation requiring the
labor of as many women as possible, so that the confusion
might be finished off quickly. The household tallow and
drippings had been hoarded for months, and stank abominably
when they were thrown into the great kettles full of lye and
boiled outdoors in the barnyard. There were always anxious
moments while waiting for the soap to come, and recrimina-
tions if the lye had not been strong enough. Betty Winthrop
walked amongst the kettles, adjudging the condition of the
boiling noisome messes, reproving firmly, sometimes adminis-

tering praise; an efficient commander of her forces.

And when two dozen barrels had been successfully filled with the soft clear jelly, she presented Elizabeth with one as recompense, and invited her to stay for supper.

Elizabeth was reluctant, being anxious to get back to Will and the boys who were corn-planting, but Lisbet and Hannah looked so disappointed that she agreed. She nursed the baby, put him at Betty's direction in the cradle with the infant Martha, and gathered with the others in the Great Hall, where Jack joined them.

Jack had a visitor with him. This was Captain John Mason, the commanding officer of the Pequot war in 1637, and the present military leader of Connecticut. He was a small, serious man, with bright darting lizard eyes; a strict Puritan and fervent church member; a magistrate at Hartford and much approved by Haynes and Hopkins. He was utterly unlike the other two captains Elizabeth had known so well—Underhill and Patrick.

Mason had arrived at Pequot to investigate at first hand the behavior of certain Indians who lived on Jack's lands, particularly Robino. He had spent the afternoon rehearsing complaints which had been brought to him, of canoe-stealing, of depredations made by swine, and a graver one that the troublesome Ninnigret, chief of the Niantics, claimed he had received permission from Jack to hunt "all over Pequot Country." Which seemed to have been an invention of Robino's.

Jack appreciated the Captain's meticulous attention to possibly threatening Indian affairs, and gave Mason his usual courteous attention, but he found the exacting little man dull company, and was relieved when they joined the ladies for supper in the Great Hall. The unexpected sight of Elizabeth dismayed Jack. He had so far kept her out of sight whenever there were Hartford visitors or any visitors who might be inclined to pry or know more than he wished them to.

But there was no help for it, and he introduced her rapidly as "Mrs. Hallet," then went on to a topic he hoped would fix Mason's attention.

"The phantom ship!" he said. "Have you heard the latest news of that weird phenomenon, Captain Mason?"

"Aye," said Mason, "since I've recently been to New Haven. They talk of nothing else. Some gaffer's seen it again, afloat in the air, and all the doomed passengers wailing ghostly on the decks." He spoke somewhat absently, for he was looking at Elizabeth, and wondering if it were possible that she was the woman he had heard of in New Haven. Governor

Eaton had said little, and that little with constraint, but there had been a hint of scandal. It had passed from Mason's mind, but now on seeing this handsome woman, who had a warm challenging quality, the Captain felt his interest piqued. He glanced at her wedding band—startled at seeing so non-Puritan a symbol in this household—and having a neat mind averse to puzzles, determined to solve this one.

He waited until Mrs. Winthrop and Mrs. Lake had stopped exclaiming on the phantom ship, then said to Elizabeth, "You've recently come to Pequot, Madam? You have some interest in our Connecticut country?"

"Why, to be sure!" said Peggy Lake brightly, breaking the small ensuing silence. "Mrs. Hallet's a cousin of my brother John's and was a Winthrop once herself!"

"Indeed?" said Captain Mason bowing. "Ah, to be sure, I remember from our Boston days. You were then Mistress Feake?"

Jack and Elizabeth both stiffened, but she smiled briefly and said, "Aye." Betty Winthrop, who was not interested in these inquiries, nor ever anxious to notice Elizabeth any more than courtesy demanded, said incisively, "I hope the phantom ship will not come here. They say it's been seen along the coast and always betides evil."

"Oh, I think not, my dear," said Jack. "I've made some study of these things, and believe 'tis only an optical trick joined to superstitious fancy. I've not yet in all my travels seen a chimera which couldn't be explained away and—" He would have continued because he hoped to thoroughly divert Mason's attention from Elizabeth, but they were interrupted.

The slave Kaboonder came lumbering in, his eyes rolling, his black features twisted with alarm. "Master!" he cried kneeling by Jack's chair. "Master! Messenger come. Terrible news!"

Jack stood up and looked towards the door where a Massachusetts Indian stood panting, a small scroll of paper in his hand. Jack beckoned to the Indian who came forward and held out the scroll.

Jack broke the seal, unrolled the paper and looked down. He lifted his head and gazed blindly at the window shutter.

"What is it, John?" whispered Betty.

He moistened his lips, still staring at the shutter.

"My father's dead," he said.

His mouth contorted in a grimace. He turned and hurried out of the room.

Betty Winthrop gave a cry and rushed after him. The

others made pitying murmurs. Mrs. Lake grabbed the un-comprehending little Fitz-John and burst into tears.

Elizabeth felt the blood drain from her head, she saw the walls begin to spin and darken. The sickening emptiness in her head surged down and engulfed her whole body. She slipped sideways off the chair and onto the floor so quietly that it was a moment before the others saw, and ran to help. She lay for many minutes in the only swoon of her mature life.

Jack left that night for Boston on his fastest mount. He covered the hundred miles of trail by the morning of March 31 and reached Boston with a foundered horse.

Adam and Deane were alone in the parlor by the closed coffin when Jack came. The widow, and her six-months-old Joshua, lay in the bedchamber, prostrated with shock and grief. Stephen was in England fighting for Cromwell, Samuel was in the West Indies at Antigua.

Boston had been waiting for Jack to come, had postponed the funeral so that he might have ample time.

Before the official condolences began—the visits of the ministers, Mr. Wilson and Mr. Cotton, and of Thomas Dudley, the Deputy Governor; of old John Endecott, Richard Belling-ham; all the elite of Boston—Jack had an hour with his half-brothers.

"Oh, brother John, why didn't you come earlier?" Adam cried. "I wrote you how ill he was, and sorely longing to see you. His last words were of you."

Jack stared at the coffin, so small and mute beneath its black velvet pall. "I didn't get the letter, Adam," he said hoarsely. "When did you send it?"

"A fortnight ago, by Clark's pinnace, when Father's cough and fever had brought him very low."

"I had no news of him," said Jack, turning away; he slumped in his father's great high-backed chair, his shoulders shaking.

"He asked, as though it were his last request, that you 'strive no more about the Pequot Indians,' " said Adam, "that you 'leave them to the Commissioners' order.' He shrank from all thoughts of conflict, and grew mild."

"Aye . . ." said Deane sighing. "He changed much at the end. Seemed to regret many harshnesses. He refused to sign a court order of banishment saying that he had 'done too much of that work already.' He blessed each of us and asked

our forgiveness for any wrong he might have done us.—
And every day he looked for you."

Jack made a violent motion with his hand, and Deane went
on quickly, "Oh, he knew 'twas not lack of love that caused
your delay, and he drew great comfort from Mr. Cotton's
prayers . . . Brother John, the day before he died he spoke
about Harry's drowning—and of our cousin Bess. We thought
him wandering because he said a strange thing about her."

Jack raised his head to look at Deane. "What strange
thing?"

"He said, 'I should *not* have made her kiss the rod, there
mercy should have tempered justice.' He said it several times,
as though the thought tormented him, though we didn't
understand."

Nor did Jack for a moment, then to his grief-dulled mind
there came a memory—the Hall at Groton, a terrified swoon-
ing little girl, a bloodstained hazel switch. "Aye," he said. "I
think I know. 'Twas long before you were born." He looked
at the coffin. "Leave me alone with him, brothers, I would be
alone."

They buried Governor John Winthrop on the third of April
of that year 1649. The funeral procession wound throughout
all the Boston streets, and the mourners were all its citizens
and many from the other towns. Prolonged salutes were fired
by the Ancient and Honorable Artillery Company, Mr. Cotton
preached the funeral sermon, and the new meetinghouse bell
tolled at intervals all day long—sixty-one times for the years
of his life.

They entombed him next to Margaret in the burying ground
on Trimount Street, they read elegies at his graveside. And
even his enemies wept, acknowledging the courage and single-
minded purpose which had led the Great Migration, and
established in the wilderness a new nation which would endure.

Some days later Jack thankfully left the Bay which now
held little to interest him. Aside from his sorrow, he had an
added depression in that he saw clearly that Endecott was to
be the next governor, thus making some futile sort of full
circle, since it was Endecott who had been Governor at Salem
nineteen years ago, when John Winthrop came sailing into
its harbor on the *Arbella* with the new charter and his own
appointment.

Endecott—the narrowest bigot of them all! And notorious
in England for his ill judgments, as when he had publicly

cut the Cross of St. George from the English flag, averring that he could not bear to see that Papist symbol. Jack's appreciation of the Bay had been waning for years, and now the last strong tie was cut. From now on his home and affections should be engaged by Connecticut.

On his way back Jack briefly visited Roger Williams at Providence, and there heard an extraordinary rumor which was confirmed some days after the return to Pequot.

Elizabeth learned this news from Will, who had gone up to the mansion to see Jack on an errand he had not discussed with her.

Since the night when the message arrived announcing John Winthrop's death, and Elizabeth had fainted, she had been ailing. She had no pain, but slept badly, her breath was short, and she could not hurry up the hill to their home as she used to. Her usual brisk vigor seemed to have drained out of her, and Will watched her anxiously. She was not pregnant. There was no reason for her sudden debility except prolonged strain, and the news of Winthrop's death. She seemed not to realize herself how deeply this news had affected her, but to Will it seemed that some mainspring of her life had broken. She was for the first time in his knowledge of her lost and groping, unable to think for herself.

He had several uneasy conferences with Jack which he did not mention to Elizabeth, since their upshot was uniformly worrisome.

On this May evening he walked back to his little cottage, and found Elizabeth lying on the pallet in the kitchen, languidly directing Hannah's efforts to concoct a makeshift mithridate, for which many ingredients were unobtainable. But Elizabeth knew that something must be tried to strengthen her, and Jack's "Rubila" had not helped.

Her eyes brightened as Will came in, and she tried to get up, then sank back on the massed pillows. "You've been long with Jack, love," she said. "Whatever were you talking about?"

He inspected her quickly, dismayed at her continuing pallor, and the dark patches beneath her heavy eyes. He sat down beside her on a stool and told her a part of the discussion.

"There's high news, Bess! From England. I still can't credit it, but 'tis confirmed. Myself—I don't know whether to weep or rejoice!"

"Oh, Will!" As he had hoped, she looked more eager, and

with something of her old impatience, she cried, "Tell! Don't tease me!"

"Here it is then," he said. "King Charles has been beheaded, and we have no more a monarchy."

"Beheaded—" she repeated. "Why, that couldn't *be!* Who would do such a thing! Kings aren't beheaded."

Will laughed curtly. "This one has been, on the thirtieth day of last January in the courtyard outside Whitehall. And now, hinnie, my dear, we have a Puritan Commonwealth under the leadership of Oliver Cromwell—that doughty general. Kings have been abolished, the House of Lords has been abolished. I too find it amazing—and—" he added frowning, "I wonder what's happened to the Digbys, since many Royalist Lords were executed. I believe however that Lord George at least will ever be able to run with the hares *or* the hounds."

"I saw the King once . . ." said Elizabeth slowly. "He seemed so small, and yet royal. What's happened to the little Queen?"

She found the news of interest, but it did not move her deeply.

"The Queen's fled to France, I believe," said Will. "The Royalists have proclaimed Prince Charles the new king at Edinburgh but I doubt he ever reigns. The Commons and Old Noll are firm entrenched—'tis what most the people wanted."

" 'Tis what most want here, of course," she said. "Jack must be pleased?"

Will laughed. "Aye, since we'll have no more interference. Besides your cousin Betty's stepfather—Hugh Peter—preached a terrible denunciation sermon to the King before the execution. The colonies'll have strong friends in England now."

"Puritan friends," she whispered. The sudden weariness returned and her lids drooped. "Will—" she said, with pauses for breath between the phrases. "How marvelous are the— tangles of destiny. Had the King not ousted my Uncle John from his position—at the Court of Wards and Liveries— twenty years ago—I wouldn't be here now, nor any of us." Her own words astounded her and she looked up at Will with sudden fright. "And had I not talked too rash to the Countess of Carlisle one Christmas morning, would Uncle John have kept his office? Ah, I *have* been truly wicked all my life, and he was right to detest me!"

"Nonsense!" said Will sharply. "Your cousin Jack told you how soft his father spoke of you at the end. Nor are those murky delvings of the slightest use. What's done is done."

"I said I didn't hate him, but I did," she said faintly. "And yet now he's gone—I'm empty and forlorn. It was as though I drowned, when he died."

Will pressed his lips and walked over to Hannah who stopped stirring the mithridate and looked at him sadly with an understanding far beyond her twelve years. Will started to speak of what was in both their minds, then he checked himself for Elizabeth might hear, and said, "Well, poppet, what do *you* think of the news about the King?"

"It seems odd," answered the child politely. "I suppose he was a very bad man?"

Will started and laughed. "Upon my word, Hannah, I don't know! These happenings so far away now seem as pithless and fantastical to me as they do to you. And—" he added bitterly to himself, "they don't serve to displace more personal concerns."

For some days the execution of King Charles and establishment of the Puritan's Commonwealth was a matter for wonder and rejoicing throughout New England, and then, as for William Hallet, the great news was forgotten in the press of immediate affairs. And yet, though they little dreamed of it, this regicide had a direct bearing on the lives of Elizabeth and Will.

It was also in May that Governor Stuyvesant received at Fort Amsterdam the official communication from the States General at The Hague. It told him that their High Mightinesses and the Prince of Orange had consented to King Charles's execution, that they had recognized the Puritan Commonwealth. The West India Company therefore wrote instructing Stuyvesant "To live with his neighboring colonies on the best terms possible."

The Governor withdrew into his private study, rested his peg-leg on a stool, and meditated long on the various aspects of this startling development. Then he summoned George Baxter. At the end of their interview, Stuyvesant shoved aside a pile of communications—most of them aggrieved—from the various English colonies, and his fierce eagle-eyes lighted on a letter which had been buried. "And this too—" he cried in Dutch to Baxter. "Again that *verdomde* Winthrop woman! She's a nuisance. Can they write of nothing else?"

Baxter hid a smile while he bowed in agreement with the Governor's annoyance. "Yet now, Your Excellency, in view of this communication from The Hague—" And he went on to suggest certain politic considerations.

Stuyvesant listened intently, scowling beneath his bushy

gray brows, nor did he say anything when Baxter had finished. He stood up and stumped rapidly out of the room, as was his custom when displeased. But George Baxter sat down and wrote a note to John Winthrop, Jr., at Pequot. And he dispatched the note by Toby Feake who had been a week in port at New Amsterdam, and was about to leave for Providence with a cargo of tobacco and potash. Toby had no reason for putting in to Pequot, and was unmoved by Baxter's query as to whether he didn't wish to see his aunt and cousins.

"What for?" said Toby shrugging. "I suppose they're safe enough where they are, and I've no mind to get in that broil again."

"No doubt you'd be well paid for making the stop," said Baxter, "and it may be of great importance."

"Not to me," said Toby. "My aunt and Hallet have no money, that's one certainty in all the pother."

"Mr. Winthrop'll surely pay you, and you might pick up some beaver," said Baxter patiently.

"Naw," said Toby. "I'd not chance it."

Baxter swallowed his exasperation, and finally advanced Toby some guilders from his own pocket, at the same time chiding himself for a soft fool, but Elizabeth's tragedies had always disturbed him, and the various influential letters received at Fort Amsterdam had made it impossible to forget her.

Toby accepted the guilders and sailed off up the coast in his own good time.

On May 23 Captain Mason rode into Pequot from Hartford bearing with him a letter from the newly elected Governor Haynes which fulfilled all the worst expectations that Will and Jack had been enduring since the Connecticut elections.

Jack summoned Will, and awaited him in the study at the mansion. As Will came in, the two men exchanged a long silent look, and Jack nodded grimly.

"So it's come," stated Will, his gray eyes hardening. He had passed Captain Mason in the Hall, and noted that the little Captain hastily turned his back as Will walked through. "Mason brought it, no doubt," continued Will. "Is it bad?"

"Aye," said Jack scowling down at the letter. "As bad as can be—arrest and trial." He gave a mirthless laugh. "I've been appointed magistrate. Mason's to administer the oath at once, and for the express purpose of Bess's arrest. Neatly arranged."

The muscles knotted in Will's long jaw. "I should like to see the warrant."

"Certainly," said Jack. "'Tis here in Governor Haynes's letter." He held the paper out to Will who read in stony silence.

There is cognizance taken by our Court, of some parties resident with you, that are of ill fame, as one that was the wife sometime of Mr. Feake, and who it seems did confess herself an Adulteress (which is upon record at the Dutch) and now pretends marriage with another man . . .

I am therefore to acquaint you that she . . . is sent for by warrant to appear at the Court here . . . we could do no other but seek to do Justice in such horrid facts . . .

Will threw the letter down. "So Bess now bears the whole brunt," he cried.

"Yes, since you have no wife, and therefore yours is a lesser crime, but they'll find counts against you too."

"The scurvy stinking ferrets," Will said. "Would to God that I could kill them wih my bare hands. What do they mean to do? Drag her off to trial at Hartford like a common whore? Flog her unto death? Or hang her!"

"Surely they couldn't," said Jack, but his voice trembled. The Mosaic law and the Body of Liberties both ordered capital punishment for adultery, rare as its fulfillment was in the observance. And Haynes knew no mercy. It might be that he would consider it his duty to make a terrible example of a gentlewoman.

"There's naught for it but to flee," said Jack, "as we suspected. Though this danger is far worse than I feared. Try Rhode Island next, though I doubt even Roger Williams'll give you asylum if he knows the circumstances—and no use for you to leave Bess—the warrant is for *her* arrest and Mason would march her off whether you were here or not."

"I'll not leave her," said Will. "The time for that's past. Now she's weak and helpless, and if she can't stay near you, she must have me to fend for her."

Jack's unhappy eyes softened, he looked up at the big yeoman with a sad smile. "Aye . . . Hallet," he said. "You love that troublesome wench, and so do I. I think you'll risk your neck to prove it."

"And you—" said Will quietly. "Your lifework and your reputation."

The brown and gray eyes met in a brief wry glance.

Then Jack sat down. "We must plan quickly. The General Court'll not meet till next week at Hartford. I can hold Mason off a day or two while you ready Bess. Does she know aught about this new fear that we had?"

Will shook his head. "She's not been well enough. Though lately she's stronger since you gave her that powder."

Jack nodded. "The leaves of fox-glove. Digitalis. It often cures weakness and want of breath if Rubila won't—Hallet, can you manage a shallop?"

"I can row. I can't sail. 'Twere better that we go by land into the Narragansett country, if that's where we must go."

"I can think of no other place," said Jack grimly. "Except Virginia, but there's no boat to take you. And anywhere you go now you must assume an alias, and live in hiding—poor souls."

For some time, while Mason fumed outside, Jack and Will tried to make plans, each concealing from the other how impractical these plans were. The Hallets must leave the Feake children in Jack's care until it was possible to send for them. Jack would provide two horses, and a guide, and the escape might be easy, since they could go by night and Mason would be at the mansion, surely never doubting Jack's obedience to the Governor's warrant. But both men knew the dangers of the wilderness between Pequot and Providence, where the Indians were increasingly restive. And both knew that there was scant hope of permanent safety anywhere.

They agreed despondently to wait a day or two for Elizabeth's strength to increase. Then Will strode off, and returned to the cottage.

And the next day Toby sailed the *Ben Palmer* to the Pequot River landing. He disembarked and made his way directly to the Winthrop home, having no sentimental desire to see his aunt, nor knowledge as to where she lived in town. Jack was closeted with Mason in the study when Toby shambled up to the door and asked to see him.

Betty Winthrop was sewing in her parlor with her sister and she heard their slave, Kaboonder, questioning some caller. She went out into the passage, and asked, "What is it, sir? You have some message for Mr. Winthrop?"

"Aye, ma'am," said Toby, holding out a letter. "From New Amsterdam."

Betty nodded, seeing that he was a sea captain, and many such came through with letters. "Thank you. I'll give it to Mr. Winthrop," she said. "He can't be disturbed at present."

Toby hesitated, torn between the wish to wait and see if

Winthrop would pay him for his service, and the need to
sail off before the wind changed. He decided for the latter,
touched his hat and departed for his ship.

It was thus an hour later before Jack received Baxter's
letter, and when he had read it he rushed to the stable, and
demanded that his horse be saddled fast. He went back into
the house, and pulled Betty to one side. "Bring me a tablecloth," he said. "Quickly! And, my dear—I've no time to
explain, but you must keep Captain Mason inside with you,
I don't wish him to go near the harbor."

"Why, John—" said Betty, her blue eyes startled and
affronted. "What do you want of a tablecloth, and how can
I keep the Captain here? What is this about?"

"Talk to him, read to him, sing to him—I care not. But in
this you will obey me! Hasten, Betty!"

She swallowed and stiffened. Then she bowed her fair head.
"Very well, husband." She took a white cloth from the
linen press and gave it to him. She watched with dismay as
Jack lifted his musket from the wall pegs, and poured powder
into the flash pan, but she asked no more questions. When
Jack had gone she walked to the study where stood the
annoyed and baffled Captain who had been unceremoniously
deserted by Jack. She smiled and said, "Oh, Captain Mason,
will you come to the parlor, my sister Lake and I find it so
dull sitting alone, and we want to ask you about Hartford."

Neither Mason's murmured protests, nor endeavors to find
out where Mr. Winthrop had rushed to, were of any avail
against her calm, well-bred assurance.

Jack mounted his horse and set off at a gallop. As he had
hoped—knowing that the tide was coming in, and seeing
that the wind was veering to the south—Toby's sloop had
not progressed far down the river. Jack galloped to a little
point of land ahead of the boat, stood on a rock by the
water and waved the tablecloth frantically, then he fired his
musket into the air. He waved and fired again, until they
finally saw him, and lowered the longboat. One of Toby's
crew rowed over, until he was near enough to hear Jack's
shout. "Turn back! Go back to the landing! I'm Mr. Winthrop."

The lad waved in reply. Jack waited until he saw the vessel
lose steerageway, the sails slat, and the boom swing over as
she came about, then he galloped back to the Hallet cottage.

Will was on the lane side of his lot staring at the ripening
pea pods and wondering who would gather them. But they
belonged to Winthrop now. In anticipation of trouble, Jack

had for ten pounds bought back the land from Will. A maneuver Will considered only slightly better than charity, though Jack truly affirmed the land had been improved to that extent, and more, during Will's tenure.

Jack reined the horse in, and called, "Hist! Come here, Hallet!"

Will vaulted the fence and strode to Jack in surprise.

"Where's Bess?" said Jack.

"Inside, cooking supper. What's happened?"

"Toby Feake has come from New Amsterdam—with a letter from Baxter. Here it is, Hallet, there's some hope, I think. But don't tell her yet, lest she be cruelly disappointed again. Tell her only you must flee for a time, until an awkwardness blows over. Don't mention me at present. I can't see her. Mason has made me magistrate, I took the oath, and conniving though I've been to this extent, I can't see her whom I'm bound to arrest. I'll speak to Captain Feake and explain that you must sail with him at once. Then I must get back to Mason—keep him in the house until you sail. Send the children up to me as we arranged. God bless you and her. I'll pray for you!"

He slapped his horse's rump and galloped off towards the landing where the sloop was once more anchored, and a sulky Toby awaited explanation of the summons to return.

Will broke the news to Elizabeth as gently as he could, but she was confused and frightened. He told her nothing but that it was necessary for them to leave Connecticut for a while, and they would go on Toby's boat which had fortunately appeared.

"But where to?" she asked. "Where can we go?"

And he, mindful of Winthrop's warning, said "Virginia" at random. And he hurried her sternly, seeing that she wished to refuse. "You must believe me, hinnie—gather your things."

"But the children?" she cried. "Will, I don't understand—there must be far worse happened than you've told me. And where's Jack?"

"He'll take the children," Will said. "We can't drag them off on Toby's boat. 'Tis all arranged."

"Jack wishes to be rid of me like this without a word."

"No, Bess," said Will. "He meant to say farewell I'm sure. No doubt he thought you'd leave on Toby's voyage back from Providence, but I think it better to go now. Come, hurry! There's not time for all these doubts."

Will gathered up the Feake children and put them in Lisbet's care to be conveyed later to the Winthrops. Lisbet was delighted at the thought of staying at the mansion. So were the boys. Only Hannah wept a little, but she kissed Elizabeth cheerfully when Will explained that this trip was for her mother's health.

Elizabeth was dazed, but her heart was very sore, and she could not help feeling that Jack's affection for her had at last been sundered.

Toby did nothing to dispel her confusion, having received instructions from Jack and money as well.

The minute Elizabeth set foot on deck, one certainty pierced her bewilderment. She cried, "But I can't leave like this. What'll Jack think of me, after all he's done for us. Toby, you've got pen and ink in the cabin. I must write a note! I want to thank him—even if he doesn't wish to see me anymore!"

Toby growled. Will tried to stop her, while he cast nervous glances at the creek that led to the Winthrop house. But she would not be stopped, and she wrote stiffly, and with pride, wishing Jack not to think that she was bitterly hurt by his mysterious arrangements for shunting her off to Providence and then Virginia.

"Sir," she began, having stopped herself from writing the usual "Dear Brother":

> *My cousin being put back by weather desireth us to go with him now; for if the wind be fair as he cometh back he shall be loath to put in; also I am willing to see that place, being moved thereto by something which I heard from a woman in this town. I entreat you to pardon me that I—"*

Her hand shook suddenly, she made a blot and an erasure, then went on hurriedly:

> *have not come to you to manifest my thankfulness and tender my service to yourself and my sister; the speedy going of my cousin prevented me therein; yet I shall ever remain yours in all unfeigned love and service.*
>
> ELIZABETH HALLET.
>
> *From aboard the vessel.*

"Hurry!" cried Will holding out his hand for the note. "It really doesn't matter, Bess, this isn't necessary."

"It *is*! It *is*!" she cried. "How can you not see it?—Oh and all the things we borrowed from them, some in the house, but

I put others in the yard—would you have Betty Winthrop think we're stealing them?"

Hastily she wrote a postscript.

I pray you remember my best respects to Mrs. Lake. We have left your table board and frame, and bellows boards upon the cow-house and the rake in the yard.

At last Will got the note away from her, and gave it with threepence to a lounger on the landing for delivery.

Toby hoisted anchor, the sails slowly filled; on an ebb tide now the *Ben Palmer* moved down the harbor mouth. And just in time. As the landing glided into distance, Will saw a stir on the waterfront, and the gleam of metal that must be Captain Mason's helmet.

Poor Winthrop, he thought, wondering how Jack would deal with Mason's anger, and with Governor Haynes. He turned to tell Elizabeth a more connected story of the day's happenings, but saw that she was lying half asleep on Toby's bunk, with the baby Willie, and in her face was a bewildered and pathetic resignation.

23

A WEEK after leaving Pequot, Toby again entered Long Island Sound and skimmed down the coast, passing the familiar settlements at some distance.

Elizabeth, no longer in ignorance of their true goal and feeling much stronger, sat on the forward hatch and watched the little towns slip by. They had passed New Haven and were nearing Stamford when she spoke to Will, who was whittling new tholepins for Toby's longboat. "I find it curious," she said, raising her eyebrows, "that at none of these places could we land in safety. And that there seems to be no place in the world where we'd be welcome."

Will glanced at her, relieved at this ironic tone which he knew showed improved health.

"We might try New France," he said, jesting, yet half in earnest. "If—" He did not finish and she said nothing.

While they were at Providence, waiting for Toby to exchange cargoes, Will had told her about the Hartford warrant for her arrest, since he did not want her to go ashore. There was no use risking new complications or making themselves known to Roger Williams, whose attitude was unpredictable. Williams gave asylum to religious exiles, but he did not shelter felons, and it was also possible that Captain Mason, guessing their destination, would send a messenger by land with extradition papers.

Even Toby had been sufficiently impressed with their danger to hurry out of port.

And Will, feeling that Elizabeth should now know the whole truth, had shown her Baxter's letter. It was brief and guarded.

It said that if certain parties now residing with Mr. Winthrop, and who had vital interest in New Netherland, came at once to the Dutch capital, they might there find something to their benefit.

Jack's fear of raising excessive hopes in Elizabeth were unfounded. She had no hope. " 'Tis doubtless a trick," she said. "Oh, not of Baxter's probably, though I trust nobody anymore, but of Stuyvesant's. We'll no sooner land than we'll be arrested."

"Not you," said Will. "They won't harm you *there* or Baxter wouldn't have written. It'll be I that's gaoled in New Netherland since my banishment is still in force." And he laughed.

"Will!" she cried, staring at him. "But we can't go then! This is desperate folly. Make Toby take us to Virginia, as I thought—or the Indies."

"No, hinnie," said Will. "We're going to New Amsterdam. We should have done it long ago. I no longer wish to live in pretense. You know what my admired Herbert says:

> *"Dare to be true; nothing can need a lie;*
> *a fault which needs it most grows two thereby."*

It's time we heeded the old parson."

"Even if it means imprisonment and torture?" she whispered.

"Even so."

Beneath her fears she felt a shock of relief, a clean and free sensation which she had not known since the day they had fled to Stamford over a year ago. It did not last. Her fears continued, but she hid them, and when they spoke of their situation now it was often with a sardonic humor which Toby thought demented.

That afternoon, they passed Monakewaygo—Elizabeth's Neck. There was haze, and she could see little but the outline of the trees. She turned quickly and went down into the cabin, where she occupied herself with the baby.

They anchored off Long Island shore that night, since

Toby would not run Hell Gate in darkness. When, at sunrise, they had shot through the rapids and the eddies, Will gazed long up at the eastern shore, and the round point of land for which he once had owned a grant. The point was pink beneath the huge sun that hung like a scarlet plate over the gray horizon.

" 'Twill be a dirty day," said Toby also looking at the sun. "Good thing we're near to port."

Neither Will nor Elizabeth said anything. They sailed on down the East River. As they passed Corlear's Hook, some recognition of the anxiety his passengers might be feeling penetrated Toby's stolidity. "Ye better have a good swig o' rum," he said, and he yelled to the Finch lad who acted as cabin boy. "Isaac, fetch the keg!"

Will and Elizabeth each drank some of the fiery "kill devil," Will a watered mugful, Elizabeth only a swallow, for it seemed rather to increase than quell the sickly feeling in her stomach.

Soon they saw the silhouette of the Fort, the windmill and the weathervane on the high-peaked church.

"Fewer ships in than when we were last here," observed Will casually.

"Aye," said Toby. "Stuyvesant's ruining foreign trade with his fierce customs duties and confiscations. There's a mort o' complaints. Very high-handed he is."

Elizabeth moistened her dry lips. Will put his hand over hers and gave it a hard clasp.

"He can't be worse than Kieft," she said faintly.

"Harsher," said Toby. "And a shocking temper—lays about him with his stick and screams and stamps that pegleg when angered. He thought Kieft too easygoing, lax—him and the Pastor Bogardus. They say Stuyvesant believes that's why they were drowned on the *Princess* those two. Judgment of the Lord."

"Aye," said Will quickly to divert Toby from Stuyvesant's character. "It was a strange thing that Kieft and his mortal enemy, Borgardus, should both be drowned on the way home for questioning. But life is unpredictable—and not *all* its surprises are bad, hinnie."

"To be sure," she said as steadily as she could.

There was a clear berth by the great wooden dock Stuyvesant had recently erected. Toby made fast alongside of it. "Ye can sleep aboard if you like," he said gruffly, as Elizabeth started down the gangplank with the baby in her arms. "Save you money at the Tavern."

If we don't sleep in gaol, she thought.

It began to rain as Will and Elizabeth walked down the wooden wharf, then past the crane and the gibbet to the customhouse. Under Kieft's regime they had never been questioned upon arrival in New Amsterdam, but now an armed guard dashed out of the customhouse and stopped them with a flow of Dutch.

Will repeated Baxter's name several times, and said, "He expects us."

The guard hesitated. He understood what Will meant, but thought it unlikely that so shabbily dressed a pair really had an appointment with the Governor's secretary. Also he sensed something queer about these two and his suspicions were aroused. Finally he motioned them on and stalked behind through the little streets, his musket on his shoulder. The people stopped and stared, one little boy cocked a snoot at Will, threw a pebble at Elizabeth, and ran off jeering.

As they approached the Fort it rained harder. Elizabeth covered the baby with a fold of her worn cloak, and he began to whimper.

They were challenged by a sentry at the entrance to the Fort, but their guard said something and they passed through, heading at once for Baxter's house.

Baxter's door was opened by a liveried slave, who gaped at the trio—the tall man, the woman in rumpled homespun clothing, and the guard frowning behind them.

"Mr. Baxter," said Will. "We wish to see him at once."

The slave shook his head. "Master gone. Not here. Gone to Bruecklin."

The customs guard made a sharp derisive sound. "Kom!" he said laying his hand roughly on Will's shoulder.

"Are we already arrested?" said Elizabeth. " 'Tis sooner than I thought for."

"No, by God!" Will cried, shaking off the guard's hand. "We're going to Stuyvesant. *'Directeur-Generaal'!*" he shouted into the guard's startled, resistant face. Will took Elizabeth's arm and they sloshed through the increasing rain across the Fort towards the Governor's mansion. The guard followed angrily, his musket ready cocked.

It was while they were crossing the slippery paving stones that Elizabeth plummeted, between one step and the next, into despair. The thunder and pound of effort ceased, she was alone in a silent black cell—in a dungeon, where shadow upon shadow wavered around the implacable stones. No one to call to, no one to help. "From the ends of the earth will

I cry unto thee when my heart is overwhelmed—for thou hast been a shelter for me. I will trust in the covert of thy wings." What shelter? What wings? Pious lies to be finally surrendered along with these puny strivings—along with pitiable hope.

They reached the Governor's house. Will mounted the stoop, and banged the great bronze door knocker, while the guard protested angrily, but after a stare at Will's expression did not interfere. Elizabeth looked at Will's back—a stranger —as alien to her as all the people she had once loved, love slain by the God of Wrath who neither solaced nor forgave.

She stood on the paving stones, the rain dripping off her hood, and running down onto the baby who began to wail with the full strength of his healthy lungs.

A woman appeared at an upstairs window and looked down at the group in the courtyard. She noted the scowling guard, and a big man whose attitude showed strain and fierce determination; puzzled, she looked at Elizabeth who was mechanically trying to soothe the howling squirming baby and protect it from the rain, and she had a glimpse of Elizabeth's face. A face like marble; mute, white; a mask of desolation.

The woman left the window and ran downstairs.

The Governor's servant had already opened the door a crack, and begun to deny entrance in a blustering voice. Judith Stuyvesant pushed him aside and flung wide her door. "Kom in!" she said to the bedraggled couple.

The guard rushed forward and spoke to her in rapid but respectful Dutch, telling her that these were but disreputable English folk, unworthy of her attention, that they had no credentials, and had asserted Mr. Baxter expected them— which was not true.

Mrs. Stuyvesant, whose warm heart sometimes led her into difficulties, paused, and inspected again the two who now stood on her threshold. Elizabeth's somber eyes gazed back, seeing as through fog a pretty woman of her own age, exquisitely gowned in rose taffeta with a huge fluted ruff, and with pearl earrings dangling beneath elaborate puffs of honey-colored hair. A woman of fashion, she thought vaguely, from the world that I once knew. She turned to leave, anticipating the dismissal which would soon come.

"We would like to explain ourselves, Madam," said Will harshly, "but we speak no Dutch."

"I can some English," said Mrs. Stuyvesant. Abruptly she

waved her hand at the guard. "Ga weg!" He bowed and went off muttering.

"Rest, Mevrouw," she said to Elizabeth, and led her into a small salon, elaborately furnished. Will followed uncomfortably.

Elizabeth sat down on a carved stool by the fire, while Mrs. Stuyvesant put her hand on the baby's head. "How old?" she asked.

"Eight months," said Elizabeth, in a dragging voice.

"The same as my Nicholaes!" cried Mrs. Stuyvesant. "I thought so when I saw you stand so sad, in the rain." She bent down over the baby, "Zuigeling, zuigeling—" she crooned to him. "Thou shalt be dry and warm now, and Mama feed thee . . ." The baby quietened. Elizabeth looked up into the lady's compassionate eyes, and her own were lightened by a faint wonder.

Mrs. Stuyvesant rushed out, and came back with an armful of infant clothes and diapers. She tidied and warmed the baby, dressing him in the elaborate robes of the Governor's own son. Then Mrs. Stuyvesant motioned briskly, and Elizabeth obeyed the gesture, unfastening her bodice and giving suck. "Now—" said Judith in gentle command. "Speak slow, and tell me why you are so sad—and your man so—so wild."

Haltingly, a few words at a time, and in a voice which seemed not to be her own, Elizabeth complied.

Will stood by the window, staring out at the blinding rain, with thoughts as miserable as Elizabeth's had been. He was glad of respite for her, and that his son was warmed and fed, but he thought of these feminine rites as only that—respite or delay, and of no consequence to their black situation. In this he was mistaken.

Judith Stuyvesant had been born a Bayard, of French extraction, and of a gallantry like the famous Chevalier. She had charm, learning and quick sympathy. She loved her own two baby boys better than anything in the world, but she had managed to find something lovable in the irascible, autocratic, one-legged old General whom she had wed. Of all the people who surrounded him, she was the only one who never feared him, though she could not always sway him.

Elizabeth had not spoken much before Judith arose with decision. "You stay here," she said. "I find my husband. If he's in Council with his Nine Men, I don't disturb him, for then he always bad-humor. I find out."

As she left the room Will walked over and stood by Elizabeth. " 'Tis the Governor's lady . . ." he said.

"It would seem so," Elizabeth answered in the dragging faraway voice. "Strange that she did not shrink from me, when I told her, yet perhaps she didn't understand."

Will said nothing. They waited, while the baby went to sleep, and the rain slashed like knives at the glistening diamond panes.

The Governor was not in Council, he was in his office dictating to his Dutch secretary. He looked up in surprise, but not annoyance as his wife entered. She explained her errand, and Stuyvesant began to laugh—dry grating chuckles, so unusual that the secretary looked alarmed, and Judith astonished.

"Och, Juutje!" the Governor said suddenly sobering. "So the Winthrop woman has now turned up here in your own salon, and has got *you* for advocate!"

"She is terribly unhappy, Petrus," said his wife softly. "They seem good people to me. And the baby—the same age as our little Claes."

"The baby!" said the Governor sharply. "One born in sin, of adultery. Do you forget that?"

"No, dear husband, I don't," said Judith, laying her hand on his arm. "Yet as she is divorced, it would be so easy for you to make this little one legitimate. Mr. Baxter already once told me something of their story, these two."

"Oh, he did, did he!" growled the Governor. "Baxter talks too much. Cackle, cackle, cackle like an old hen." But there was a veiled twinkle beneath the heavy hooded lids. "This woman—Winthrop, Feake, Hallet, whatever she's called. I'm sick of her. So many letters from her family, and now they begin from Greenwich too. The inhabitants, my own subjects, write in her favor, and the property, her lands they say are going to ruin. I think—" said the Governor, rubbing his beaked nose and slyly watching Judith, "I'll give the Feake-Hallet land to Pieter Cock, who pesters me for it. This Greenwich is the most troublesome town in New Netherlands—No, no, wife—" he added as he saw she was about to speak, "Enough of this wicked pair! They have broken the law, they were warned what would happen if they came back here. They must be imprisoned . . . eh?"

"Petrus!" she cried, shaking his arm. "You will not be so cruel, not when *I* beg you!" She stopped, uncertainly, for the little grating chuckles had begun again.

"Bring me the Winthrop file," said the Governor to his secretary.

The man walked to a huge Dutch kas, filled with shelves and stacks of paper. He brought out a small packet tied together with a red thread. The Governor picked the top sheet off the pile and held it out to his wife. "You see, my dear, all your pretty begging is quite wasted breath."

Judith looked down at the document in her hand, and saw her husband's official seal at the bottom, and she read the opening " 'Whereas, Elizabeth Feake erstwhile of Greenwich in our jurisdiction, has been legally separated from her husband, Robert Feake—' " Judith skipped several lines, then with a gasp of pleasure, she read out loud " 'therefore, for particular reasons known to us, they are both reinstated in full possession of their lands, and Elizabeth Feake is given permission to remarry, provided that she wed the above-named William Hallet'—Oh, Petrus, you had already written it!"

"A week ago," said the Governor dryly. "And not for the sweetly sentimental reasons you give, but because England now has a Puritan Commonwealth, I am directed to placate the Puritan colonies as much as I can with honor, and I think it expedient to confer a favor on a woman connected with so influential a family as the Winthrops. This John Winthrop, Jr., I've heard much about him, and think his friendship of greater value than his enmity. Now take this paper to your protégés, and I trust I'll not be bothered with them any more."

The Governor's hope was not quite fulfilled since Elizabeth and Will lay that night at his house in two separate guest bedrooms. This was Judith's doing.

When she returned to her salon with the marriage license, she had been deeply moved by their reception of her news. The numbness of shock, the sudden blaze of joy in William Hallet's eyes, the way he kissed his woman, and looked down at his baby. While she—Mrs. Feake—had continued for some time dazed and incredulous, fearing a malicious jest, asking tremulous questions, and upon having the document translated for her the third time, suddenly bursting into sobs and laughter so heartrending that Judith had wept with her, and presently dared intrude again upon her husband.

"Petrus—" she said, still wiping her eyes on a lace kerchief. "You have bestowed such happiness today." She kissed his thin furrowed cheek, while the Dutch secretary discreetly went and stood by the window. "Now there's one thing more. They must have a church wedding. Please order Dominie Backerus to perform it tomorrow."

Stuyvesant frowned, though he did not draw away from her, as he did when he was angered. "This is not the sort of marriage for church record," he said. "She is neither maid or widow. Hemel! Is she not satisfied with marriage by magistrate? She would have to be in one of her own Puritan colonies."

"No doubt she would be," said Judith quietly. "She was so wed by magistrate to Robert Feake, which never seems like real marriage to me. But I feel there is that in her which wants God's ceremony and His blessing on her union with Hallet—she should have it."

"You and your whimsies . . ." said Stuyvesant, tapping his peg-leg on the floor. "This woman has bewitched you. There, there—Juutje, I'll speak to the Dominie. Be off with you!"

So it was that William and Elizabeth Hallet were quietly married in the Church-in-the-Fort next day at noon, by the pastor, Johannes Backerus, who was about to sail for home, being displeased with affairs in Manhattan and critical of the Governor, though the Hallets did not know this, nor would have cared.

The Governor was not present in the church, but his lady was, and George Baxter, and Toby Feake. Toby, stuffed into his best bottle-green doublet, and full of celebration rum, was as astonished and pleased at this development as he was capable of being. It even occurred to him as he watched his aunt and Hallet kneeling by the rail that they were a handsome couple. Will still wore, perforce, his brown homespun suit, but it had been pressed by the Stuyvesant servants, and he had bought himself a new linen collar and cuffs. Elizabeth, however, had been dressed by Judith, in one of that lady's best gowns of yellow satin with an upstanding wired frill of finest Mechlin lace. Judith had also lent a short veil of golden gauze, and supervised her maid at the hair-curling, the powdering, the judicious application of fragrant Hungary Water.

Will was thunderstruck when Judith led Elizabeth towards him in the church. She had never been more beautiful, and he had forgotten that she could look like this after seeing her for months pale, tired, and clothed in drab, increasingly shabby garments.

They did not understand the Dutch service, but as the Dominie gave to Will and Elizabeth the rings they had taken off, and while they replaced them on each other's fingers, they both thought of the cabin on Totomack Creek, and Will whispered to her, "The pretense came true, hinnie."

"It was no pretense," she whispered back, looking up into his eyes.

Suddenly Elizabeth began to tremble. She was thrilled with awe as she stood beside Will at the church rail. How strange it was that at that moment of her utter despair on the threshold of the Governor's mansion after she had abandoned strivings or any hope—the release had come. The wings, and the shelter, were they perhaps not lies after all? Could it be that joy was permitted as well as suffering which most certainly was not only permitted, but ordained? Joy. Gratitude. Thanksgiving. Did one dare surrender to these? She felt that her cheeks were wet, and quickly wiped them on a corner of Judith's little golden veil.

The Dominie went on, unheeding. They stood and knelt and stood again in answer to his gestures, and knew that it was finished when he turned away, and George Baxter cried out fervently but with an edge of laughter, "Thank the Lord! I feared never to see this day!"

Nor would they see it now, if Stuyvesant had known the whole tale, Baxter thought with wry amusement as he walked up to congratulate the bride and groom. Will and Baxter had had a long conversation that morning, during which Baxter had been appalled to hear of the persecutions in Stamford, the Winthrop woman has now turned up here in your own New Haven and finally Hartford—none of which had filtered through to New Amsterdam. And so the Hallets had been at long last favored with a stroke of luck. Stuyvesant assumed that because Massachusetts Colony in the person of the late Governor Winthrop, and Connecticut, represented by John, Jr., were Hallet partisans, that all the Puritan colonies must be. He would have thought twice before reinstating a couple in disgrace with Governor Eaton and Governor Haynes.

But it was done now, and the Hallets were safe.

"Respectability," said Will, grinning, as Baxter pumped his hand. "A novel, and delightful sensation, isn't it, Bess?" He put his arm around her and kissed her. She laughed, a laugh with a quaver in it. *"Happiness* is a novel and delightful sensation, I don't know what to do with it."

"Come back with me," said Judith, radiant with sympathy. "We have a little wedding feast. His High Mightiness said he would be there too."

The Hallets lingered a while in New Amsterdam at the City Tavern, enjoying with sharpest pleasure the change in their fortunes. They were no longer poor, nor dependent on anyone's charity. Pieter Cock had dutifully brought to Stuyvesant the money and valuables the Hallets had been forced to leave behind in Greenwich fifteen months ago. Their property had been locked in the Munitions room at the Fort. The Governor now issued an order for its restitution, and the Hallets were enabled to make necessary purchases before their return to Greenwich.

They talked much and gratefully of Jack, whose extensive help in solving her troubles Elizabeth now understood. They all, Stuyvesant, Baxter, and the Hallets, hoped that Jack might come and settle in Dutch territory. Stuyvesant particularly wished this because he had not enough Dutch emigrants to populate the lands he claimed, and therefore must rely on English settlers. And to capture one as prominent as Mr. Winthrop would certainly improve inter-colonial relations.

On July 15, George Baxter wrote Jack a letter warmly inviting him to visit New Netherland, and incorporating in the letter the cryptic and discreet statement which he knew would be understood. "Mr. Hallet hath graunted him what he required." Under separate cover there were official instructions for the return of the Feake children to Greenwich, and these Jack immediately carried out.

Jack also received a letter from Elizabeth who was back in Greenwich and hers he held in his hand and read with a medley of strong emotions. He read and reread the first sentence.

Deare Brother, All the love and service and thankfulness I am able to express is next unto god due unto yourself as the instrument of my present well being . . .

It had pained him to receive her incoherent little note from Toby's ship knowing that she had misunderstood him when he sent her away, and he had been extremely anxious over the outcome in New Amsterdam. His relief now was poignant.

At last he put Elizabeth's letter down and went in search of his wife, whom he found in the dairy. "Will you step outside a moment?" he said to Betty. "I want to talk to you."

They went into the barnyard amongst the pigs and clucking chickens. Jack drew his wife down beside him on the bench near the stable, and said, "I've just received a letter from Bess, a most happy one. It confirms that all her troubles are over, she sends you her respect and gratitude."

Betty compressed her mouth. "I should think so," she said. "The embarrassment she has caused us—and the deceit! John, that *you* should have been party to that monstrous deception they foisted on us here, harboring those two shameless—"

"Hush my dear," he interrupted. "It's over, and I want you to forget. Bess, by temperament or fate, has incurred discredits which could never afflict you, I know that, and admire you for it. But I must remind you that there are many societies and periods of history when the Hallets' conduct would not be shameful, when indeed their fretted love and loyalty to each other might rather be thought brave and praiseworthy."

Betty looked at him blankly, apprehension gathering in her startled blue eyes. "You worry me when you speak like that, John. I simply don't know what you mean, except that your poor father would have been much grieved. As for Governor Haynes—I shudder to guess what he thinks of you."

"I know very well what he thinks of me," said John dryly, having received several secret and outraged missives, "but 'twill blow over now. All the same, I confess I'm restless, the climate of the Bay under Endecott, and of Connecticut under Haynes, I find both harsh and stifling. I'm strongly urged by Stuyvesant and Baxter to join with them . . . and I wonder—"

Betty rose abruptly, and her well-bred voice had lost control as she cried, "John! You are mad! I never gainsay your moves and sojourns. I have gone with you to Ipswich, to Salem, and Ten Hills! I uttered no complaint when we moved to Fishers Island and then to here. But I will not tolerate your going to the Dutch, not for any reason you could give. And in my turn I wonder—"

She stopped and laced her large white hands tightly together. "Is it possible that the strength of your attachment to your *'sister'* Elizabeth is more binding than I suspected, or than you are willing to admit?"

Jack's mouth tightened as he looked up at his indignant wife. Aye, he thought, it is possible, and also very undesirable. How useless and cumbersome were trailing emotional attachments, once the main trunk had been cleanly cut. This past year he had certainly given too much thought to Bess, and Betty, though mostly unaware of this, had real basis for her anger. More than anger, he saw now, for proudly as she was trying to conceal it, there was hurt in the quivering of her lips and the moisture in her eyes.

"Then stop wondering, my dear," he said rising and kissing her on the forehead. "You're an excellent wife to me, and I wish you to be content. We'll not refer to this again and I'll make my peace with Haynes."

Betty's face softened and her fair skin flushed. "John—" she whispered and leaned near as though to kiss him too, but she saw Kaboonder shuffling through the courtyard towards the stable, and she drew back.

"Are the Plymouth commissioners to arrive tonight?" she asked, smiling and in her usual calm voice. "Do you wish to do them special honor, and if so, I had better direct the maids to bake your favorite blueberry pie?"

"That'll be splendid," said her husband. "You make me very comfortable, Betty."

He went back into his study, laid Elizabeth's letter in a chest with other family papers, locked the chest, and walked out to the creek to see how the building of the gristmill was progressing. He ignored a sense of blankness and loss, and gradually as the days went by it receded, so that he could put his whole heart into family and business matters again.

In Greenwich, Elizabeth thought herself settled at last. Their house welcomed them, it was a joy to be surrounded with their own furnishings. The great silver salt, and ladle, the pewter dishes, all twinked once more on the dresser. The Turkey carpet glowed upon the newly polished parlor floor. They replaced items which had been left behind at Stamford and at Pequot. Will rounded up the livestock, which neighbors had been tending. Several had died but he started again. He mended the outhouses and fences, and in the spring ploughed the neglected fields, and planted crops. Anneke and the other Greenwich folk had fervently greeted the Hallets. No awkward questions were raised, only Anneke knew the exact date of the marriage, the others did not care to know. The Hallet reinstatement at New Amsterdam confirmed their land titles, and that was enough.

One day shortly after Elizabeth's return she set out for Stamford to see Joan, whom Anneke told her had been delivered of a daughter named Mary. Elizabeth, anxious to see her grandchild, and though still detesting Thomas, never dreaming that he might still be dangerous, asked Will to saddle the horse, and she set out along the shore trail towards Stamford.

She had not reached the boundary creek near Will's old cabin when she heard him shouting for her. He came running through the trees. Richard Crab stumbling after him.

"Halt, Bess!" Will called. "You mustn't cross the frontier! Fool that I was not to think of it!"

Astonished she reined the horse in, and waited until the men came up to her. "I mayn't see Joan?" she asked half-laughing. "Why, that's ridiculous now."

"Nay—Mrs. Hallet," said Richard Crab, his weatherbeaten face all twisted with concern. "They'd grab ye fast's a cat can wink his eye if ye go into Stamford. Haul ye to New Haven, very like."

"They couldn't!" she cried. "That's all finished."

"Not in New England, Bess," said Will. "There you're not divorced, nor are we married. Crab tells me Thomas hasn't given up at all, still claims your property."

"The whole of Stamford thirsts for Greenwich land," said Crab. "The bastards. That's what we wrote to Governor Stuyvesant—Husted, Sherwood, John Coe and me. We're clear for the nonce, but I sometimes fear they'll be too strong for us yet."

Elizabeth angrily turned the horse around, and as it walked back home, her resentment against Thomas Lyon revived with added strength and now included Joan.

The awed joy and gratitude of Elizabeth's marriage day had inevitably faded, as indeed had the corroding memories of shame and persecution which preceded it. Both the anguish and the ecstasy now seemed to her hysterically exeggerated and even embarrassing. Her one desire was to wipe out all the past and live in secure wedded love with Will. That there should be any continuing frustrations or thwartings infuriated her.

She sent her daughter a curt message by Angell Husted, and one day the girl came to see her with the baby. It was a miserable meeting. Joan looked wan and peevish. She had a sore on her breast which Elizabeth silently poulticed for her, but there was no warmth between them. The baby resembled Thomas, and Elizabeth scarce looked at it. Joan whined a good deal complaining of poverty and a dismal lot. Once she picked up the great silver salt cellar, and said, "This'll be mine when you die, won't it, Mother? Since you got it from my great-grandfather, Adam Winthrop. My Feake sisters and brothers have no right to it."

"I see that you've acquired your husband's greed," said Elizabeth, "And I regret to tell you that I'll never give you anything that he may enjoy. You had your jointure, and not one farthing, not one tin spoon of my property shall Thomas Lyon inherit!"

"You're hard, Mother," said the young woman gulping. "You usen't to be hard. It isn't fair. I'm not getting my rights. And I'm not well, you see that I'm not well. Now that you're rich again, I thought you'd do something for me."

"What?" said Elizabeth. "And why?—If your husband had

had his way I'd have been hanged, 'tis true you might thus have got my property, which would, I gather, have been so sweet that you could ignore any foulness in the manner that you came by it."

"Mother!" Joan cried. "Don't look at me like that! You frighten me! I've never meant you harm. Nor has Thomas exactly. You've never understood him."

"Bah!" said Elizabeth. "Go back to him then. You've made your bed. So lie in it!"

This was the beginning of a series of vexations. Another one came from Lisbet. Pequot and the Winthrop mansion had provided the girl with a life she much preferred to Greenwich. She yearned for it and was discontented. Having met many more sophisticated lads, she no longer thought Danny Patrick attractive, and there was no one else in Greenwich of her age.

Elizabeth's sons, Johnny and Robin, were not discontented, they were always pleased to be near Will, but they were growing into noisy, dirty, quarrelsome boyhood, impatient of her mother, scornful of their sisters—a natural state, but Elizabeth found it trying. Even Hannah was not as sunny-tempered as she had been. She took to going off by herself, and reading Will's books. She learned many of George Herbert's poems by heart, and thought about them. She read the Bible too, steadfastly, from cover to cover, propping it up against the wall as she did her tasks, poring over it at night by candlelight.

That this worried Elizabeth, Will found amusing, and one night in bed when he spoke of it, he said, "Good Lord, hinnie, you pick strange things to fret about, most mothers'd be delighted at a daughter's piety."

"I mistrust piety," she said. "And I can't help remembering how Robert—" She stopped, never wishing the thought of Robert to intrude on them.

To her surprise, Will spoke seriously into the darkness. "Hannah has true sane knowledge of the spirit. Leave her alone, Bess. It would be better if *we* had the enlightenment that child has got."

"Why, darling—" she said twisting around, and trying to see his face, "I didn't know you thought of such things."

"I think of them," he said. "I feel a lack."

This frightened her. Always she tried to believe that there could be no lack in their private life anymore.

She put her hands on either side of Will's face, and kissed him. "We have each other now for aye," she whispered, "and so *I* feel no lack. It saddens me that you do."

His arms closed about her, and he held her tight, while her head found its accustomed place on his shoulder and her long soft hair spread over his chest. But he did not speak for a time, and she was nearly asleep when she heard him say in the quiet cold tone with which he met difficulties, "Robert is back, Bess. He's in Watertown."

She started, and raised her head. "What!"

"Robert is back from England," he repeated in a level voice. "I've not wanted to worry you, but now I must. Thomas has been to Watertown. He has somehow inveigled Robert into writing yet another document invalidating all our claims here."

"My God—" she cried sitting up. "It can't be—how can this—coil start up again!"

"It has, hinnie," said Will quietly. "And must be dealt with. 'Twas Angell told me of this. He says all Stamford's buzzing. They say Robert's destitute, and very wild against us. That he swears we've stolen all his property, and I have stolen his wife."

"But he was in London, in the Fleet, and quite distracted. I told you what Jack said. Oh, I can't understand this—" Her voice cracked, she turned her face into the pillow with a short dry sob.

Will stared up at the great tester. "I'm going to Watertown, Bess. Tomorrow. We must find out the truth. From now on we'll never again hide our heads in the sand, and live with deceit and evasion. And if injustice has been done to Robert, we must rectify it."

"Oh, don't go—" she cried. "Will, don't leave me here, wondering and fearing, how do you know you'll be safe up there?—or what Thomas has done now! God, how I loathe that man! I hope you kill him, if you meet him—nay, I don't mean that but I hope God strikes him dead, or the Devil who is certainly his master—and as for Robert— oh WHY did he come back!"

"Hush, hinnie!" said Will sharply. "You've more sense than this. Hatred of Thomas Lyon'll do no good. Nor yet a wish that Robert should disappear forever. He hasn't. You must pray as I have that the right course will be shown us. Have faith."

"Faith in what?" she said, turning away from him on the bed.

"In decency and kindness, then," he said with a curt laugh.

"If you can think of no loftier objects. Nor am I sure that I can."

Her passionate tears and turmoil checked themselves. She sighed hard, then she lay back quietly on the pillow. "The old fairy tales—" she said at length in a controlled voice, "I remember those my nurse would tell—'and so then, Miss Bessie, the prince married the princess, wi' the castle bells a ding-donging fur joy—'n they lived happy ever arter'— she believed it and I believed it, yet we'd only to look about us to see differently."

When Will left next day by horse for Watertown, he carried with him all the cash they had on hand, also the silver ladle and the gold chain Robert had given Elizabeth as bridal gifts.

The journey took a week, and presented no dangers, beyond the routine ones of swollen fords, drenching rains, and a temporary lameness of the horse. The long trail was well worn now, and easy to follow.

Will avoided Boston and rode directly to Watertown. He crossed the Charles by the Mill Bridge, and after inquiries, went to the parsonage, as being always a font of information.

The Reverend George Phillips had long since died, and the Reverend John Sherman had succeeded him. Mr. Sherman was at home, working on a sermon. He received Will cordially, and with no recognition of his name.

"Sit down, sir, sit down," said Mr. Sherman who was square, bristle-haired and bright-eyed, rather like a benevolent woodchuck. "What can I do for you, you've traveled from New Netherland, you say? My, my—a long journey."

"And a worrisome one," said Will. "I've come to see Mr. Feake, Robert Feake. He's here, isn't he?"

The minister's smile faded. "Oh dear, yes—he's here, poor creature. 'Tis very sad. Silly, you know—mad as a March hare, though harmless. Are you a relation?"

"In a manner of speaking," said Will. "I'd like to see him, and also to be sure that he wants for nothing."

"Excellent," said the minister, looking relieved. "There's been another kin of Mr. Feake's here recently, a boisterous man called Goodman Lyon, had some long-winded tale of rights and property of Feake's, and a wicked wife—a Winthrop she was once, and lived here too before my time. Left in a hurry ten years ago, the Feakes did. But Simon Stone, our head selectman, he doesn't want that talked about. Thinks the town did very wrong by the Feakes, that's why he's arranged to keep poor Mr. Feake now—since he wants to stay here. At least he seems to from his babblings. But I fear he'll be a town charge."

"That he won't, sir," said Will. "That's why I've come."

The minister rose with a kindly smile. "I'll direct you to Mr. Stone, he knows far more about this matter than I."

Will made his errand known to Simon Stone, who examined him gravely for some minutes, and being a man quite capable of making up his own mind and a shrewd judge of character, Stone thereupon discounted all that Thomas Lyon had told him. His decision was strengthened when it appeared that Mr. Hallet was determined to see that Feake had immediate support, especially as Lyon had done nothing for Feake except badger him and force him to write letters.

"Come with me, now—" said Stone, "and we'll see Mr. Feake. We've put him temporarily in the home of Samuel Thatcher, who has an extra room, and will doubtless continue to take charge of him if adequately paid."

They walked down Bank Lane and passed a handsome house upon the riverfront. "That's where the Feakes lived when they were here," said Stone, "belongs to the Rainsboroughs now. Samuel Thatcher's place is the next beyond."

Will glanced up at the house which had sheltered Elizabeth so long, seeing with a pang that it was a much finer place than the one they had at Greenwich. "Mr. Feake lives next door to his old home?" he asked.

"Aye," said Stone with pity. "That's why we put him there. He's quieter when he can see his former house. Thinks he's living in it. He seems to have no memory for anything that's happened in his life except at Watertown, but'll say anything you tell him to."

Will was silent until they reached the Thatchers', and saw Robert sitting on the grass, with a musket in his lap.

"Good Lord!" cried Will involuntarily. "Is that safe, and shouldn't he be confined?"

Mrs. Thatcher came down the steps and heard this, she bowed to Stone and answered Will. "Oh, he's quite safe, poor gentleman. He's very good when he can see his house and the river. And the musket isn't loaded. He likes to think he's cleaning it, in readiness for drilling on the Common. A lieutenant he was, it seems, with a Captain Patrick years ago . . . Come now, Mr. Feake!" she said to Robert. "Here's visitors for you."

Robert looked up. He had gone completely bald and very fat. His pink scalp and pink beardless skin gave him the look of an old baby. He smiled politely, the pale watery eyes resting on Hallet without surprise.

"So you came to see us, after all," Robert said. "Bess'll be so pleased that you didn't sail before you visited us. She's in the house, but she's going to Ipswich tomorrow to see her sister, Martha Winthrop, but you must spend the night with us. Sally—!" he said to Mrs. Thatcher. "Run down the lane and see if Captain Patrick and his wife'll sup here. They're very agreeable folk," he said, turning back to Will. "Our closest friends. I'm sure you'd like to meet them."

"Aye, I would, thank you," said Will hoarsely. His throat tightened, and he looked away.

Robert resumed polishing his musket, and Mr. Stone said in a low voice to Mrs. Thatcher, "Bring us that paper—maybe Mr. Hallet can understand it."

Mrs. Thatcher brought a folded parchment and gave it to Will. It was an affidavit signed in England by the House of Commons. It stated that Robert Feake had been granted full pardon for an unnamed offense.

"I think I know what it means," murmured Will. "He had delusions. Thought he'd committed a crime that he hadn't."

"'Twas all we found in his pocket when he got here," said Mr. Stone. "Not a farthing besides. 'Tis a miracle how he ever got back to Watertown."

"I never *left* Watertown," said Robert suddenly, with faint reproof. "Why should I leave Watertown?"

"Mr. Feake," said Will abruptly. "Do you know aught about your property in Greenwich?"

"Oh no," said Robert. "A stranger asked me that some—some days past. He wanted me to say 'yes' so I did. One must always be courteous to strangers. Governor Winthrop, my Uncle Winthrop that is, he says so, and 'tis true. A most courteous man, and has taken *much* notice of me. He comes to visit us often—Bess being his niece." Robert gave a pleased little laugh.

"I'll get him to his dinner now, sirs," said Mrs. Thatcher. "He's very biddable, but in truth, I don't see how we can keep him longer, he has such a good appetite, and I've barely enough to make do with as it is."

"You shall have enough from now on, Mistress," said Will. "And may God bless you for your kindness."

When he left Watertown he had deposited thirty pounds with Simon Stone in full payment for all Robert's erstwhile lands in Greenwich, and in case that should not be enough he left the gold chain and the silver ladle. The town was to administer these funds and pay the Thatchers from them. In return Will got a deed and quitclaim from the selectman who shook his hand warmly and thanked him several times, having learned enough about the case to know that Feake had no legal right to further funds.

Will left the Bay with a far lighter heart, and rode whistling through the splendor of the autumn leaves. Feeling now greater security than when he had journeyed up, he did not avoid the settlements. Ten miles below Hartford he ferried across the Connecticut to Wethersfield, to spend the night there in an ordinary.

Here in the taproom he heard some startling news as he sat on a corner bench, drinking a pint of ale and thinking with pity of Robert, and yet relief that the madnes had taken so benign a form, and the man escaped into a span of memory where he was content to be.

Will was jerked to awareness, by a voice saying "Greenwich," then he heard "Stuyvesant" and jumbled exclamations of astonishment and laughter.

What NOW! Will thought, stiffening.

He pulled his wide hat lower over his face, and looked carefully around the smoky low-beamed taproom. There were a dozen men sprawling on the benches, and near the fire, but all of them were strangers.

Will got up and joined three men who sat at a corner of the trestle table. "Your pardon," he said, "but having just come from the Bay, I'm fair bewildered by the things you're saying. Did I understand aright that the Dutch Governor is at Hartford?"

"Oh, indeed," and "To be sure," chorused the men, nodding and chuckling. "A week he's been there."

"What for?" said Will, instinctively addressing a lean man with a crest of sandy red hair, who had an air of quiet authority.

"Why, for the boundary dispute—settle old Peg-Leg's fantastical notion that Holland owns half New England," answered the sandy-haired man.

"And is it settled?"

"Settled indeed, since we're in possession. 'Twas bluster anyway. And a good diddling we gave him! We agreed to call Dutch his moldering old fort on the Connecticut, and in return he moves the boundary west and gives us Greenwich. That's a wee settlement t'other side of Stamford. Has fine lands."

"*You* ought to know, Jeff!" cried one of the other men,

chortling. He turned to Will. "Jeffrey Ferris here, he was first settler in that Greenwich. Named the town, didn't ye, Jeff?"

"Aye," said Ferris. "Still got a plot there. But I left when the largest landholders went to the Dutch and turned patroon. Now I've a mind to go back again since it's English."

"Where is the boundary now?" said Will in a voice he strove to make casual.

"Four miles further west, at a river ye wouldn't know—called Mianus."

So! Will thought, one negligent pen stroke in Hartford, and they lost their home again. His stomach knotted in a spasm of rage. His eyes stung. He clamped his teeth on his lip, and the mug of ale wavered in his hand. The inner shaking ceased gradually at the men went on talking, and he heard Ferris say, in answer to a question, "I don't know what the Greenwich settlers'll do, they've leave to stay o' course if they want to, being Englishmen, but I'd like to pick up some acreage if I can."

Will bided his time until the curfew horn blew at nine, and the barmaid yelled out the sums that were owing. Then as the other men rose, Will said to Ferris, "I'd like a word with you in private."

Ferris grunted, and they moved behind the settle.

"D'you want to buy most of Greenwich?" said Will in a voice so sharp with irony that Ferris stared and backed away. "No, I'm not drunk, nor jesting either," said Will. "I'm William Hallet, my wife Elizabeth and I are those largest landholders you spoke about. It seems that we will have to sell."

Ferris tilted his head and frowned. "Not a likely tale," he said. "Where's Robert Feake and Daniel Patrick?"

"Feake is mad, and I have bought his interest. Patrick is dead. You've heard nothing of this?"

"Nay. I've not been in Stamford for some time." Ferris scratched his chin, watching Will thoughtfully. At length he spoke. "Are you off to Greenwich in the morning?"

Will nodded.

"We'll travel together and discuss the matter," said Ferris.

Will arrived home three days later, and he broke this latest development to Elizabeth as well as he could, hiding with brave words, his own discouragement. "And so we're on the move again, hinnie," he said. "I think we must be born beneath the sign of Mercury, naught else would make it so hard to keep a home."

"I never have kept anything for my own," she said, turning her back on him and staring out the window towards the cove. "And, I'll *not* give up Monakewaygo!"

"You must, darling," he said. "Ferris is willing to buy *all* our holdings, and we'll need every penny we can get. And what use is that Neck to you? God knows when it'll be safe for you to enter English territory."

She pressed her face against the pane, looking at the dim white line of sands far beyond the mud flats and the shingly isthmus. "Monakewaygo was always mine," she said, "even if I didn't go there. I knew it was waiting."

"There are other places you can buy, be hopeful."

"So Thomas Lyon has won," she said in a strangled voice.

"No, Bess, he hasn't. You're thinking's muddled. He'll get no profit out of this, nor has he actually from any of his efforts. And what is he really, but a meddlesome, greedy, stupid young man? And not all bad either, nobody is. Remember he felt himself defrauded, and that moreover our behavior offended his religious principles, as it did those of many other people."

"I hate him," she said not heeding. "He's stolen my Joan from me, he tried to destroy us."

Will swallowed, looking at her set white face. His Bess was as staunch a hater as she was a lover; dimly he recognized that this one blind unreasoning streak in her might come from long-past injuries as well as more recent ones, and that perhaps something never quite expressed in her relationship to John Winthrop the elder had openly transferred itself to Thomas Lyon. She had cause certainly for both antipathies, but in respect to her son-in-law, she had created an invincible image of shrewd jeering malevolence which did not exist. Will could face it fairly now. His and Elizabeth's past troubles had come largely from their own flouting of the conventions, while this present setback, though it sprang partly from that too, insofar as Bess was forbidden residence in New England, was largely chance— Governor Stuyvesant's impulsive acceptance of an international bargain. Would these reasonings solace her? He glanced at her anxiously and saw that they would not.

"Don't look like that!" he said. "I understand how you feel at giving up everything here that we've struggled so hard to keep. I too was filled with helpless rage when I first heard of this in Wethersfield, but we must be the 'seasoned timber that never gives,' as my old parson advises. There's naught else to do."

She turned and looked at him somberly. "Where are we going this time?"

Will laughed wryly. "To Hell Gate, hinnie! To Hell Gate!"

The hardness and the green glint left her eyes, her hands unclenched. "Ah, that was what you always wanted, wasn't it, Will? For that at least I can be glad."

He sighed. " 'Tis not the way I wanted it, and not at all for you, knowing how you love this place."

A wincing and renewed shadow passed across her face. "I doubt that I've the courage to start over again," she said.

"Oh yes, you have." He took her by the shoulders and looked down at her searchingly. "You've endurance and courage beyond the reach of most, as who knows better than I."

She stood stiff and quiet under his hands, gazing past him to the window.

" 'Follow my love, come over the strand . . .' " he said softly.

She turned slowly back to him, and in a moment she met his intent searching look with a shrug and a faint smile. "Aye, my love—needs must," she said bitterly, "over and over again."

24

By MIDMORNING of September 14, 1655, Elizabeth began to watch for guests to appear on the lane which led to Hallet's Point above the Hell Gate whirlpools. The guests had been invited for a fête to celebrate Hannah Feake's eighteenth birthday.

In the roomy Hallet farmhouse there had been days of preparations, and Elizabeth on this bright morning was tired, but full of satisfaction. Ready-dressed in a gown of soft blue taffeta she sat on the sunny bench Will had carved for her long ago in Greenwich. It had been painted white, and placed near the stoop where it overlooked the garden and the lawn. Elizabeth had a proper English lawn now, Will had made it for her, and the boys tended it with enthusiasm because one part was a bowling green, where they were allowed to play skittles whenever the chores were finished. The garden was decorated today in Hannah's honor; there were garlands of pink daisies nailed to the surrounding locust trees, there was a target set up for archery, and since there was to be a special ceremony a little platform had been built, and two chairs, wound with scarlet streamers, placed upon it.

What wonders they had achieved here in the five years since leaving Greenwich behind, thought Elizabeth, admiring the garden. Her complacent eyes went to a trestle table which was set up in the shade of an elm near the well, and covered with a fine new linen cloth. Lisbet and Hannah ran gaily to and fro the kitchen laying the table for the feast later.

Elizabeth watched them, then turned with a smile as Anneke plumped down beside her on the bench. "Oof—" said Anneke, fanning herself with her apron and loosening the laces of her puce silk bodice. " 'Tis good to sit." She had grown very stout of late years, beneath the white cap her neat hair had lost its gold, but her face was still like a rosy apple.

She had driven over in an oxcart from Flushing the day before so as to help with the party. The Toby Feakes had moved to Flushing when the Hallets left Greenwich, and though both were on Long Island and in Dutch territory, six miles separated the families and they did not meet as often as they used to.

"Pretty girls—" Anneke said following Elizabeth's glance. "And your sons handsome too. They take after you!"

"Oh, Anneke," said Elizabeth laughing. "Such flattery, and so early in the day."

"How is it vith Robert?" said Anneke, after a moment. "Do you ever hear?"

"Aye," said Elizabeth. "Now and then we hear from Watertown. He's just the same—eats well and lives entirely in the past, poor soul. Yet they say he's quite content."

Her eyes returned to her daughters, to Hannah first, because she had always been first, but also because this was the child's great day. Elizabeth saw Hannah through a tender mist—the auburn curls tied up with a green ribbon to match her petticoat, the little freckled nose, the wide leaf-brown eyes that met all glances with warm interest and serenity. Lisbet had more regularity of feature, and her flaxen hair, silky as milkweed down, always caught the eye, but there was something brittle and elusive about her.

"Vy doesn't Lisbet marry?" said Anneke, pursuing the same thoughts. "She's twenty-two, and has offers a-plenty."

"She won't," said Elizabeth, and shrugged. "She gives no reason."

Anneke clicked her tongue, and said with meaning, "Is Captain Underhill invited today?"

"Not invited. He's at Southwold, and I wish he'd stay there, but he doesn't."

"Oh," said Anneke. "Bess—that girl *can't* be in love vith him, he could almost be her grandfather!"

"I've no idea what Lisbet feels," said Elizabeth. "Yet distressing as it is, they seem to have an attraction for each other—even when she was a child. They correspond now. Fortunately he has a wife, though I hear she's bed-ridden."

"Underhill has a bad reputation vith vomen," said Anneke. "Is Lisbet safe?"

"Aye, I think so. There's no hot blood in her, she knows what she's doing, and if there were, how could we stop her? We can't lock her up."

"Oh vell," said Anneke philosophically pulling her knitting from her pocket. "You're pleased with *Hannah's* choice."

"So very much," Elizabeth's voice quivered. "Though I'll miss her terribly, even though she moves only as far as Flushing."

"But not till next year." Anneke paused and thinking of another son-in-law, asked with hesitation, "Bess, do you ever hear of Joan and—and Thomas Lyon?"

Elizabeth winced. She drew a rough breath and her mouth went harsh.

"Joan is dead," she said. "We heard it from Jack a month ago. Thomas never even let me know she was ill. When I begged her to come and say goodbye before we left Green-wich, Joan sent back word that she preferred to forget I was her mother."

Anneke made a shocked sound. "Dreadful . . ." she murmured. "That vas never a good marriage."

"It was a damnable marriage!" said Elizabeth with such venom that Anneke started.

"Och, I don't blame you that you hate him, Bess," said Anneke. "Vat he did to you and Vill, and maybe poor Joan, but still there is your grandchild. Vat about her?"

"She's *Thomas's* child," said Elizabeth. "Can we talk of something else?"

Anneke stared down at her knitting. The days of Thomas's persecution were long past as were the days of the Hallets' disgrace, one might think that Joan's death and the plight of the motherless child would move Bess, despite every-thing. Still it was none of her business, thought Anneke, and she loved her friend too much for criticism.

Anneke reached over and patted Elizabeth's arm. "Aye, ve talk of something else." She was suddenly struck by the arm's thinness, and looked up quickly. Elizabeth had stayed slim, and though there was a little gray at her temples she seemed younger than her forty-five years. The long hazel eyes were still beautiful, and she had kept all her visible teeth, which Anneke had not, but Elizabeth's fine skin was drawn tight over the delicate bones, and there were dark smudges beneath her lower lids. "You feel vell, Bess?" said Anneke casually. "You look a little tired."

"I'm all right," said Elizabeth. "Only sometimes limp and short of breath, then I take fox-glove leaves as Jack taught me to. It helps."

"Good," said Anneke. "Don't let all those noisy boys of yours vear you out. Hemel! You have four and my little Jemmy keeps *my* hands full." Anneke had finally in 1650 borne a son to Toby, while Elizabeth had two Hallet babies now. Sammy had been born three years ago, at the same time that Will's first famous crop of rye finally matured on the very field here that he had hoped it would. He had been delighted with both events.

"There's Will now," Elizabeth cried, suddenly catching sight of his tall figure standing at the gate and talking to someone. "Isn't he splendid in that new scarlet coat? I had a time getting the everlasting leather jerkin off him."

Anneke laughed. "Bess, you look at your husband, eager as a girl vith her first sveetheart. And at your age, lieveling!"

"Aye—" said Elizabeth breathing deep. Then she added slowly, "Why, he's talking to the young widow Thorne, she seems to be the first arrival."

Anneke glanced sideways at her friend, and knowing Elizabeth as she did, sensed a withdrawal, though Elizabeth's face showed nothing. Anneke examined the widow Thorne who was very pretty, had dark curly hair, and a roguish smile. She was demurely dressed in black, with a plain white collar. She looked about twenty-five. Anneke had never seen the young woman before and was struck by a resemblance to someone. In a moment she realized to whom. In coloring, and height, in the tilt of the head while laughing up at Will, there was a suggestion of Elizabeth as she had been when Anneke first met her in Watertown over twenty years ago.

"Do you see much of this widow Thorne?" asked Anneke, carefully counting the stitches on her needle.

"From time to time," said Elizabeth, and went on with some incoherence. "Susannah Thorne lives over in Maspeth with her father Mr. Booth, rather lonely for her, and she comes to visit the girls. The Thornes were Dorset folk so Will and Susannah often reminisce too. I expect she'll marry soon again."

"No doubt," said Anneke, knitting fast while she had an uneasy thought. Will Hallet was only thirty-nine, and men of about that age were susceptible. Her Toby was much younger than she, but it did not matter, since romantic passion had never been their bond, and she neither inquired nor cared what he did on his voyages. When Will and Susannah Thorne walked over to them, Anneke favored the pair with a sharp stare. But Will gave his wife his usual warm attentive look, while Susannah cried in sincere pleasure, "Oh, Mrs. Hallet, I'm so *glad* to see you! What a wonderful day for Hannah's fête!"

Elizabeth smiled, and pressed Susannah's hand with extreme cordiality because the thoughts which had just occurred to Anneke, she had already suffered many times; ever since she had first seen the pretty young widow, and the resemblance to her younger self, and Will's unconscious response to it. She was miserably ashamed of these thoughts, but they fretted her at night, and added to the sleeplessness which had been growing of late.

"Have you seen Mr. Wickenden, Bess?" asked Will as Susannah ran off to greet the girls. "I want to talk to him about his sermon."

"He's in the barn—cobbling," said Elizabeth with a rueful laugh. "On a pair of Johnny's boots. He says he's as near to God when he's working as he is when he prays, and that he wants to mend Johnny's boots because he can thus best show his love for us."

Will answered seriously, "And so he can. He's a strange little man but he really seems to follow Christ's teachings and I find the things he says about God more convincing than any I've ever heard."

"I know you do," said Elizabeth bleakly. "I only wish he weren't a *Baptist!*" She spoke with such emphasis that Will laughed outright.

"Oh, hinnie,' he said. "Your Puritan blood cries out in you, even though you don't know it. A Baptist is a 'heretic,' isn't it—that's what your Uncle Winthrop thought when he repeatedly banished them from the Bay."

She looked at him in dismayed astonishment. "You think I'm like my Uncle Winthrop?"

"At times," said Will, chuckling.

"But I'm not godly or pious, and I never go to meeting, or quote scriptures," she cried indignantly, while Anneke whom they had both forgotten, stared at them.

"In those ways you're not like him," Will said. "I didn't mean to vex you. But I wish you wouldn't close your mind to what Wickenden says. It brings comfort to think that Christ may speak directly to one's heart, without benefit of minister or priest. I'd like to believe it."

"Arminianism—" she said involuntarily, and Will laughed again. "Is it not also what Anne Hutchinson taught?" he asked.

She raised her head, startled. "In a way, I suppose, but she was deluded. If there is a God, He proved His wrath at her, just as the ministers foretold in that excommunication."

"I wonder," said Will, and there was a moment's pause before he added, "But in any case, of this I'm certain, Bess: Every human being should have the liberty to worship—or not—exactly how he pleases, which has always been the virtue of the Dutch, though Stuyvesant, the old fool, seems to be forsaking his homeland's tolerance—Ah," he said in a different tone, "Here come the Bownes, now Hannah will be joyous."

He walked towards the gate, and as Elizabeth rose to greet the newcomers, Anneke said, "This is a surprise! Vat's got into Villiam?"

"A little cobbler from Providence called Wickenden, a friend of Roger Williams, I think," said Elizabeth with hesitation. "Turned up last month, asking if we'd any shoes to cobble and is still here. He's beglamoured Will, somehow. I don't like it."

"Vy not?" said Anneke. "If it makes Vill happy?"

Elizabeth walked towards the guests and did not answer. There was the old confused rebellion in her heart, and mingled with it the fear that Will was escaping from her into a realm where she could not follow. Jealousy. This new and bitter feeling she had discovered in regard to Susannah Thorne, but surely it was not the same feeling when directed at the little cobbler? Resentment then, annoyance at the hours Will spent shut up with Wickenden, talking, talking. Hours which used to be sacred to her, in the evenings when they sat together, when their day's work was done. The hours that she lived for, when he became hers alone. I'll not stand for it, she thought, as soon as Hannah's fête is over, I'll get rid of that cobbler. And Susannah too. It should not be difficult to limit the young woman's visits to the times when Will was in the fields.

"Good day, ma'am—" said a pleasant voice in her ear, and she started and turned to see Hannah's young man smiling diffidently at her. "I'm sorry, John!" she cried. "I was woolgathering, my dear son."

" 'Tis kind of you to call me that," he said. "There's been a lack since I lost my own mother, and now 'tis filled. Is Hannah inside?" he added eagerly.

Elizabeth laughed. "In the kitchen, counting minutes till you come."

As John Bowne hurried to find his sweetheart, Elizabeth watched him with affection. He was dark and slight, and he had charm. The charm of competence, good will, and integrity. There was a fresh strength about him too as though he had imbibed it from the mountain air of the Derbyshire Peak district where he was born, at Matlock, twenty-six years ago. His father, old Thomas, and his sister Dorothy with her husband, Edward Farrington, had come with him from Flushing today and Elizabeth saw them all laughing at the betrothal chairs on the platform, and teasing Hannah and John who were standing with locked hands smiling into each other's eyes.

By noon when the guests had all arrived, Will mounted the platform and stood by the two chairs; looking down earnestly at the forty upturned faces, he made a speech.

"Good folks, we welcome you all, and hope you'll make merry and have sport and feasting later. You were invited to celebrate our little Hannah's eighteenth birthday, there is another occasion which we will also solemnize—it may," said Will smiling, "be no surprise to most of you. Hannah Feake and John Bowne are to be formally betrothed today, but before that ceremony, and with their most earnest agreement, I've invited someone to ask God's blessing on this event, and to talk with us. Are you minded to hear him?"

There was a stir and polite murmurings of assent. How I wish Will wouldn't do this, Elizabeth thought. It'll spoil the day. I never expected *he'd* take to sermonizing or holding prayer meets, and while the little cobbler climbed up on the platform, she set herself to endure boredom and annoyance. The ministers had been bad enough, but at least they were men of education. Wickenden was not, and he spoke with the raw thick accent of the Midland Counties.

He was a small shrunken man, beside Will on the platform he looked dwarfed, he wore a patched homespun suit, his graying hair and beard were both ill-kempt, his hands were densely callused from his trade. Elizabeth sighed with exasperation as he began to speak, solemnly—"I greet 'ee terday, bretheren an' sistern i' the Fellowship o' Christ."

He went on to tell them that he had once been a "Seeker," never easy in his spirit with the strict Presbyterian ways, the ways that said a man was damned or saved forever by God's original decree, and had no way of knowing Truth for himself. Nor, said Wickenden, could he find rest in the Old Established Church, for there again there were priests and Bishops, and they made such a din with their prayer books that he for one could never hear the voice of Christ strike through the tumult. But then in Old England he had met two men, who showed him the way out from the sorrowful seeking.

The first man he had met long ago, and what the man said was sensible. He said that Baptism was the symbol of the Christian life commenced, and so it was useless to give it to weak silly infants, "An' this, friends, I still believe on!" cried Wickenden, his voice suddenly rising in power. "But 'ee needna, if ye wish not—fur the very nub o' all I'm a-telling ye is that ye must listen to wot the sperit says to ye *direct*, ye shouldna take a creed from *any* man. Ye mun listen fur The Voice! Wait fur The Voice!"

Elizabeth's wandering thoughts came back. She stared at the little cobbler, and something in her moved feebly, like a ripple on a still black pond, then it was gone. But she heeded as Wickenden went on. He had been back to England two years ago, back to Nottingham, his old home. And there he had heard another man speak—outside it was, on the edge of Sherwood Forest. George Fox was this man's name and he didn't think that God preferred steeple-houses to any other place when He came into one's heart. George Fox didn't talk of baptism, or of communion, he spoke only of Christ's own words. He said that Christ was not far off in the sky, that He was not even in some heavenly place with the angels, He was here and now and every day. You'd but to reach your hand out and He'd take it. He'd come inside you and you'd know it, from the filling of you up with love and peace and light.

"An', He does!" cried the little cobbler, "if'n ye'll wait quiet an' let Him. Will ye try it, friends?—Aye, that's wot George Fox calls those who've found the Christ inside their own selves. The *Friends* o' Truth, he calls them, the Children o' Light!"

He talked on, he talked of love in a gentle childlike way, but Elizabeth's mind had paused on the phrase the

"Children of Light"; again she heard a whisper, felt a quivering, but then it stopped when she saw that Wickenden with closed eyes and clasped hands was offering some kind of silent prayer. Many of the company were restless, she noted, doubtless thinking this an odd kind of entertainment. Her embarassment returned. In the silence she heard the bull-like roaring of the whirlpools below their Point.

Wickenden finished, and stepped down from the platform. Some of the company crowded round to speak to him, she saw that John Bowne and Hannah did. Others held back. Thomas Bowne, John's old father, looked angrily disapproving. He shook his head and tapped his cane impatiently.

It was time for the betrothal. Will led Hannah to the platform. She blushed and grew very serious as John joined her there and they sat down in the two chairs. It was the Dutch form of betrothal they were using, plighting their troth before the guests, exchanging confirmatory little gifts, and after the young couple were plighted they reigned as King and Queen while the dancing and the games commenced.

Elizabeth looked to her duties as a hostess. She joined in the chat of the older guests, wondering with them how Governor Stuyvesant was faring in his attack upon the Swedes along the Delaware. The Governor had sailed off ten days ago with all his army, determined to establish New Netherlands once and for all in the South, since the English had been too strong for him in the North.

Will talked farm prices with the men, and could not hide his pride when they congratulated him on his successes at husbandry. Later there was dancing, and skittles and archery. Only Anneke noticed how weary Elizabeth looked, and how much of an effort she was making to be gay.

The afternoon was fading into dusk when Johnny Feake who had run to the Point after an errant skittle ball, ran back crying, "There's a whole lot o' Indian canoes just shot through Hell Gate. Look, you can see 'em on the river!"

Everyone got up and looked. An occasional canoe was usual. The nearby Long Island Indians—Canarsies and Matinecocks—often went to New Amsterdam for trading. But now they saw at least thirty canoes, skimming down the East River, and though too far off to see the Indians clearly, there seemed a great many of them jammed into the heavy dugouts. The white folk could not see far, but the hawk-eyed Indians could, and several feathered heads turned to stare at the people gathered on the Point.

Eleven years had passed since the destruction of the Siwanoys, and the end of the Indian Wars, since that time all the Indians had been friendly—those whom the white men met. Fat Matinecock squaws wandered into Flushing daily, bearing baskets full of shellfish, or moccasins for barter. In New Amsterdam there were always some Indians, lounging in the streets, wheedling for the rum or gunpowder, which Stuyvesant's decree forbade them to be given.

That afternoon on Hallet's Point, nobody thought of danger. Least of all Elizabeth. And she agreed with Will when he said casually, squinting at the swiftly passing canoes, "They're off to some junket, no doubt, maybe up the North River where the Hackensacks are forever holding powwows."

"That's true," said Edward Farrington. They all trooped back upon the lawn. The fête merrily continued for some time.

The Bownes left last, as was fitting, being now part of the Hallet family, and it was for this reason that old man Bowne allowed himself a lapse of courtesy.

"Whatever do you see in that pawky little cobbler?" said Mr. Bowne peevishly to Will as they exchanged farewells by the stoop. Wickenden had gone back to the barn to finish Johnny's shoes by candlelight. "Lot o' wicked balderdash he talked, shocked me it did." The old man waggled his head.

"Now, Father—" said John Bowne. "You've no need to think as Wickenden does. He said so. He was but giving us his own faith. Hannah and I we liked it." He turned to Will with an apologetic smile. "Father—he's an Anglican."

"I believe in the established church of my own country," said the old man querulously, "and so were you raised, son John. I'll thank ye to remember it."

"I do, Father," said John Bowne gently. "But I remember too that our Flushing Patent gives every mother's son the right to worship as he pleases—unmolested. 'Tis a wondrous thing, and rare enough in this world."

"Aye—" said Will. "Liberty of creed and conscience. What marvel if it could be had in all the colonies!"

"You'll not wallow in such laxness long under Stuyvesant," grumbled the old man unconvinced. "He's getting stricter every year, and a good thing too, *I* think. New Netherland is becoming a worse sink-hole than Rhode Island. Why, they've got Jews now in New Amsterdam, I saw some t'other day. Jews, Baptists, Catholics, Lutherans, Mennonites,

Separatists—even a heathen Turk I saw, and I call it disgusting!"

Will and John Bowne exchanged a glance of sympathy and agreement but they said no more. Elizabeth was too weary to follow this discussion, she uttered the last goodbye, and turned back into her kitchen where Anneke and Lisbet were cleaning up. Hannah had gone back to Flushing with the Bownes, to spend a few days with her John's family.

"Rest!" said Anneke firmly, as Elizabeth picked up a dish towel. "Ve finish here. It was a lovely fête, only I vonder vy Toby hasn't come. Must have been delayed in Amsterdam. I asked him not to go to town today—but you know Toby! There vas a shipment of sugar in from Jamaica, and he afraid of losing his share."

"I think he's coming now," said Will, walking into the kitchen. "I hear a horse on the lane. You look spent, hinnie," he said. "Go to bed." She frowned a little and said "Presently." I look spent, she thought. And haggard and old, no doubt. Susannah Thorne had not been spent, she had danced all afternoon, odd conduct for a widow. She had danced with Will, too, a lively hay. He had looked as young as she did, as they twirled and capered.

"It *is* Cousin Toby," said Lisbet, looking out the window. "I see the silver buckle on his hat."

Will opened the door, and Toby lumbered in. "Folks all gone?" he said. "I hope you've plenty food left. Fetch me a drink, Anneke—couldn't get here sooner. Those stupid niggers took an age t' unload the ship."

"Any news in the city?" Will asked, stretching out his long legs, and smoking placidly. "Have they heard how Stuyvesant's campaign against the Swedes is doing?"

"No news yet," said Toby. "But it should be easy to mop 'em outa the Delaware, there's only a few Swedes and Stuyvesant's taken seven hundred men. Nay, the town was quiet today, barring some talk about that blackguard Van Dyke."

Elizabeth looked up. Hendrik Van Dyke had been the third officer with Underhill and de la Montagne in the long ago attack upon the Siwanoys. Since then he had risen to be Schout-Fiscal, and fallen again, having quarreled with Stuyvesant as everybody seemed to.

"What's Van Dyke done now?" asked Will with mild interest.

"Oh, last week he shot dead an Indian squaw who was

stealing his peaches," said Toby. "The Manhattans are sulking, want some kind of reparation made, but there's nobody much left at the Fort to deal with 'em."

"Van Dyke should be severely punished!" said Elizabeth with sudden energy.

"Aye, in truth," said Will. "And the Governor doubtless will, when he returns. Toby, a lot of canoes went by at dusk this afternoon. Did you see more Indians than usual on the river or at Amsterdam?"

Toby shook his head. "Didn't see any at all." He took a laden plate from Anneke and began to eat. "Is that cobbler Wickenden still with you here? M'boots need stitching."

Will nodded. "But he's leaving in the morning. To stay in Flushing for a while. Some men that were here today asked him—and I think Bess has had enough of him." He quirked his mouth in her direction, and she felt a prick of compunction, mixed with relief.

"We've had so much company," she said defensively. " 'Twould be pleasing to be alone a while. No visitors at all," she added thinking of Susannah.

Will sighed. He loved her and was slightly concerned about her health. But recently he had for the first time felt her to be demanding and unsympathetic. Not so much her lack of interest in Wickenden's religion—though to himself the little cobbler had brought much illumination—nor her increased dependence either exactly, he had always responded to her need for cherishing. But she showed a new suspicion and restlessness when he was away, there were questions as to what he did each minute of the day—a subtle feeling of confinement or restriction, which their relationship had never had before. He could not understand it and it made him uncomfortable.

He would have liked to stay up a little longer, chat with Toby, visit Wickenden again in his bedroom in the stable loft, but he knew that Elizabeth would not go to bed until he did, exhausted though she looked.

"Come on—" he said to her. "Time for sleep."

She heard the faint undertone of exasperation, and was hurt. She spent another night of tossing and dozing fitfully, while Will slept the heavy sleep of a hard-working healthy man.

Eight miles down the East River from the Hallets' isolated farmhouse the dawn of September 15 brought dismay to New Amsterdam. One by one as the citizens awoke they were perplexed to find that the streets were crowded with prowling Indians. Indians from many tribes, all men, able-bodied, armed with spears, tomahawks, and some of them with muskets. They were stripped to the breechclouts. Their faces and chests were gaudy with red paint, but the burghers were not at first alarmed, because the Indians were quiet and seemed to have no special purpose. They milled through the streets, and occasionally knocked upon some door to inquire from the startled householder whether any Mohawks had been seen. There was, said the Indians, a rumor that a Mohawk band had stolen into Amsterdam, and was concealed about the town.

The story did not seem so thin at first, since all the New Netherland tribes were allied with the Dutch against the terrible Mohawks, and many of these Indians who were slipping through the silent streets were familiar to the burghers—Manhattans, and Hackensacks who came often to the city with their trading goods.

It was the physician and one-time General, Jean de la Montagne, who first discovered the Indians' true designs. He was still one of Stuyvesant's Councilors but he had been appointed Schoolmaster and lived quietly with his daughter next to the schoolhouse. No Indian rapped on his door, but he heard the unusual bustle outside and investigated. He had not covered many blocks before realizing that an alarming number of Indians were deployed through the town. At least eighteen hundred of them; far more than the adult male population remaining in New Amsterdam since Stuyvesant had withdrawn all troops to the Delaware.

The Indians did nothing, they drew silently aside as he passed, he received the impression that they were awaiting some signal. He hurried to the entrance of the Fort, and saw there an old sachem whom he knew well—Minettah, chief of the Sapokanicans, one of the local Manhattan tribes. "Good day, Minnetah," said de la Montagne, bowing gravely. "What is the meaning of this invasion? So many Indians!" He spoke in Dutch and Minettah answered him fluently in the same language.

"We search for Mohawks, we are protecting you."

"Absurd!" said the Councilor sternly. "Tell me the real reason; we've always been friends, I thought."

The old sachem hesitated. Between wrinkled lids he gazed steadily at de la Montagne. "Where is Van Dyke?" he said at length. "Give us Van Dyke."

Nom de dieu! de la Montagne thought. That sacré Van

Dyke! I *told* them he should make instant reparation. "I
don't know where he is," the Councilor said. "He much
regrets that anger made him shoot the squaw, yet she had
no right to steal his peaches. Was she of your Sapokanicans?
He'll pay you much seewant." Which was unfortunately
incorrect. Van Dyke had several days ago refused any discussion of the squaw's murder—let alone compensation.

"Seewant no good now," said Minettah. "We want Van
Dyke. All these tribes want revenge, they have been waiting a long time for it."

"What do you mean by that?" de la Montagne said
sharply. "You've no grievances except against Van Dyke."

"Many grievances," said the sachem. "Through the years.
Many. Not forgotten."

De la Montagne felt fear. While he talked with the sachem
the Indians had been silently gathering. Three-deep now,
they were quietly ringing the Fort; more of them had
muskets than the Councilor had first realized, and his backbone prickled.

"Wait!" he cried to Minettah. "Tell them we'll parley!
You know you've been fairly treated by this governor. As
soon as he returns, you'll have your rights."

The old sachem gnawed on his lip, and finally nodded.
He raised his voice and spoke to the encircling, wary Indians. De la Montagne entered the Fort.

All day the hordes of Indians stood quietly outside the
Fort, while their sachems parleyed with the Councilors and
Burgomasters, hastily summoned by de la Montagne. He
posted guards around the Governor's mansion—where
Judith and her boys were sent to the cellar for safety—
praying that the Indians were not fully aware of how weak
the Dutch forces were. They primed in readiness the cannon
on the Fort.

In the Council Room, the dissolute Fiscal van Tienhoven
and de la Montagne led the conference with the sachems.
The white men were secretly appalled to find how many of
the Indian tribes were represented. Even though not all the
sachems identified themselves, there were certainly Mohicans,
Wappingers and Tappans, and even Montauks from Long
Island.

These chiefs were glum and uncommunicative. They
would not smoke, they would not sit, they demanded Van
Dyke, and for some hours resisted all the frantic white men's
offers of seewant, of tobacco, and even—at last in despera-
tion—of rum and ammunition.

It was then, with this last offer, that a gaunt, hideously tattooed sachem spoke up in passable Dutch, and said, "How much rum, and how many pounds of musket balls and powder, General?"

De la Montagne, who was addressed, started and stared hard at the Indian. " 'Tis Nawthorne . . ." he murmured to Van Tienhoven. "The Siwanoy who led us to the Massacre in Greenwich, betrayed his people."

"He might again," whispered back the Fiscal. "Draw him off, and let's talk to him alone."

Nawthorne was willing. The other sachems murmured and watched while the erstwhile Tomac chieftain palavered, making exorbitant demands. He readily explained that since leaving Greenwich he had been living with the Corchaugs on Long Island's far eastern tip. He further said that this situation was very grave, the tribes' long smoldering sense of wrong had burst to flame, but that he—Nawthorne—always the Dutchmen's friend—*he* would save New Amsterdam. While Nawthorne and the Councilors conferred, a short stocky Indian watched impassively from a corner of the room. He had a face tattooed with black and red dots, and he wore heron feathers tipped with copper in his roach of greasy hair.

Nawthorne came back to the other sachems. He was grinning slyly. He grinned all the time he spoke to them in Mohican language which the Dutchmen could not understand at all. When he had finished, the listening Indians grunted and a few of them laughed.

Nawhorne explained then to the Councilors that the Indians were ready to come to terms. The casks of rum and barrels of ammunition should be heaped for them in the courtyard, and in the meantime the various chiefs would go outside and pass the result of the parley on to their tribes.

"I wonder if we should let them go—" said de la Montagne uneasily. "This seems too simple."

"Bah!" said Van Tienhoven. "They're fools. We'll water the rum kegs, and put sand halfway up the powder barrels. They'll not find out until they've all dispersed. There'll be no more trouble."

But Van Tienhoven was wrong. After the chiefs had left the Fort, not twenty minutes passed before the Councilors heard agonizing shrieks splitting the twilight air. And a terrified lad came running to the Fort. "They've got Van Dyke!" he screamed. "They chopped his hands off, and then they bashed in his head! They're killing some other man now!"

The burghers and what guards there were grabbed up their guns. They ran and shot and ran, in panic, but the Indians were scattered through the streets and far too numerous.

Then the Dutch fired the cannon of the Fort—a rusty disused cannon, but the Indians were frightened by the noise, and a few of them were felled by the cannon balls. So they took to their canoes, and paddled swiftly out of range. Some went down the Bay to Staten Island, where there were ninety colonists. The Indians killed them all, and burned their bouweries. They laid waste Hoboken and Pavonia, killing or capturing the inhabitants. And two war canoes sped up the East River, back towards Hell Gate.

The Hallet family supped on the lawn that evening, since the air was summery, and Elizabeth ever preferred to be outdoors when she could.

She was not so tired today, even though she had slept badly. She was rested by the absence of all guests. Little Wickenden had driven off to Flushing with Toby and Anneke. There had been no sign of Susannah Thorne.

Elizabeth had Will to herself, and her family around her. The big boys, Johnny and Robin, were whittling horn spoons, which were to be a wedding present for Hannah when the Dominie Polhemus married her to John Bowne in the spring. Willie lay on his stomach and tickled Don the watchdog's nose to make him sneeze. Lisbet sat a little apart from the group netting a purse with nimble fingers and humming softly.

Sammy lay on his mother's lap, drowsily watching the fireflies light their tiny sparks in the syringa bushes.

Will was finishing his last nightly mug of ale, and admiring the trim lines of his house. He had built it all himself, with the boys' help. And it was as much like his old Dorset homestead as he could manage when the only easily available material was wood. Later, he thought, I'll build a solid brick one here—like the Dutch. If the crops continued as good as they had been, he would not need to wait long. Or—he thought with pleased excitement—I might build me a kiln. I'm sure the venture'd be profitable. Folk'd drive from Maspeth and even Flushing for the bricks. Be much cheaper than hauling them from Amsterdam.

As he started to tell Elizabeth of this idea, they heard the distant booming from the Fort. "Now what's that for?" said Will, sitting up and listening. "Sounds like cannon, but I didn't think those moldering old relics at the Fort could possibly be fired."

She listened too, vaguely perturbed. The cannon boomed again.

"Oh, I know what it is," said Will. "Stuyvesant's returned. He's trampled down the Swedes, and is master of the Delaware. New Amsterdam greets its conquering hero."

Elizabeth smiled, and Lisbet said primly, "Stuyvesant is a rogue and scoundrel, no matter how many Swedes he's vanquished."

"Oh, come now, Lis," said Will, eyeing his stepdaughter with amusement. "I hear through your silvern tones the strident voice of Captain Underhill. And perhaps he's right in part. But you must give your mother and me leave to think more kindly of the Governor, at least in one respect."

"Aye—" said Elizabeth on a long fervent note. "And of his sweet lady, Judith."

They were silent, each with private thoughts. Lisbet resumed her humming. The big boys sheathed their whittling knives and stood up.

" 'Tis getting dark," said Will smothering a yawn. "We'd best go in, and you to bed, Bess. I want you to be sensible until you're quite rested up."

"I'm not weary," she said. "Let's sit inside a while and talk, when I've put Sam and Willie to bed. Or read to me, Will, please, the way you used to? 'Tis long since you've read to me. I'd like to hear 'L'Allegro' again."

He repressed impatience. He wanted to cast up his accounts, see if this year's profit could possibly justify the brickyard, as well as the purchase of another seven acres that he meant to add to the eastern field. "Oh, Bess, I can't read tonight," he said. "I'm busy."

The quick hurt tears stung her eyes. She bit her lips, and when they went into their kitchen, she walked in stricken silence, which made him feel guilty and consequently cross. He spread his papers out on the table, sharpened his goose-quill pen, and began his figuring.

She put the little boys to bed upstairs in the room they shared with their half-brothers. Robin and John presently went up also. Lisbet retired to the parlor where she slept.

Elizabeth came back and sat down between the kitchen fire and the light of the one candle which Will was using. She riffled idly through the calfbound volume of Mr. Mil-

ton's poems, but none of them caught her interest. She
looked at Will with longing which very soon would change
to anger, or any weapon which might shatter his imper-
viousness. He continued to write with his head bent, making
neat figures on the paper. Amongst his calculations was one
for the procuring of a bondservant for Bess who would
need more help when Hannah left. But this Elizabeth did
not know. Feeling excluded, unconsidered—she sat staring
at his back.

She had cleared her throat for the saying of something
sharp when the watchdog lifted his head and began to
growl.

Will put down his pen and turned. They both looked at
the dog, who growled again and got up, the hairs rising
along his backbone.

"Can't be wolves," said Will. "There aren't any this part
of the island. Some prowler, maybe." He rose and started
for the pegs where his guns and powder horns were hung.

The dog whined, growled again, then precipitated himself against the outside door.

"Steady, Don. Steady, old fellow. We'll see what it is," said
Will. "Sure the back door's bolted, Bess?" She nodded. He
poured powder in the flash pan of his musket, pulled the
hammer back in readiness, and opening the front door
said, "Shan't be a movement. I expect it's only a fox."

She nodded again, not frightened. Her under thoughts
were still churning with the angry longing and the need to
force him to respond to her.

He opened the door and stepped out. The instant he
was off the stoop she heard a sound like the hooting of
an owl, then a short high bark like a fox, mixed with the
growling of their dog. She got up, still more puzzled than
alarmed, and froze with her hand on the chair arm as she
heard Will's voice raised in a wordless shout, as of surprise. Then there was silence for an instant, before the
night exploded into pandemonium. Sobbing yells, howls,
ululating and inhuman. A lion, she thought, like in Ipswich—
there's panthers out there; her hand clenched tighter on
the chair arm, while the uproar outside swelled into hoots
and caterwaulings in which she now distinguished spurts
of devilish laughter.

"God—" she whispered. Her numbness broke, she ran to
the wall pegs and jerked at the big carbine. It caught on
the pegs, nor was it loaded. As she stood there tugging

futilely at the carbine, Lisbet rushed in wearing her night shift. "Mother, Mother, what's ado?"

"Take the fire shovel!" cried Elizabeth. She rushed to the hearth and grabbed the long iron peel. She had no sooner grasped the peel than the front door burst open. Jumping and leaping in orgiastic triumph, a dozen Indians hurtled through the door and filled the kitchen. One knocked the fire shovel out of Lisbet's hands, and hooting crazily grabbed her by her long flowing flaxen hair. He jerked her to her knees, and yanked her head back and forth by her hair. Lisbet screamed, then fell to sobbing.

Elizabeth raised the peel to strike down the Indian who was tormenting Lisbet. Another Indian by the door took aim and shot at Elizabeth. His shot went slightly wild, for he was drunk with brandy he had stolen in the city. Elizameth felt a dull, thudding pain in her upper left arm. The heavy peel clattered on the floor. It was Nawthorne who had shot her, but she did not know it. She heard stamping feet and cries and shouts upstairs where several of the Indians had swarmed when they came in. Upstairs where the boys were bedded. "Sammy!" she cried. "Let me have my baby!" and she stumbled towards the stairs.

Nawthorne gave a whinny of laughter. "Let me have my baby—" he mimicked, in a high squealing voice, and he rushed for Elizabeth with his musket butt upraised. She ran—the Indian who was now binding Lisbet with buckskin thongs stuck his foot out, and Elizabeth fell.

She saw an Indian bending over her, and thought it was the man who shot her. But this Indian had an English hatchet in his hand, she saw the edge of gleaming steel. The Indian grabbed her hair and jerked her head up, so that he might see her face. It was not Nawthorne but another— who had knocked Nawthorne to one side.

Elizabeth stared up from glazed eyes at the face above her; tattooed and painted with the red of war, a mask of furious vengeance, but she recognized it.

"Keofferam . . ." she whispered. "Keofferam . . ."

The Siwanoy chief stood rigid, poised, his left hand gripping her hair, his right drawn back with the gleaming English hatchet. The other Indians all turned to watch, knowing how long Keofferam had waited for this revenge on the white woman who had betrayed the Siwanoy, from whose home the soldiers had marched that day for the destruction of Petuquapan.

"Keofferam . . . have mercy!" she cried as though he could

understand her. "I didn't do it—Telaka knew I didn't do it . . .'"

He heard his sister's name and his eyelids flickered, while still he gazed down into her hopeless eyes. He gave a sudden shiver, and his hatchet arm went slack. He released her hair.

Nawthorne protested violently. Keofferam answered in tones of sharp command. The Tomac chieftain's eyes began to glint, seeing the moment come at last when he could rid him of his Siwanoy overlord. An apt moment since the other Indians would not think of this as treachery. "Look how soft and womanlike the once great Siwanoy has grown!" he cried to the Corchaugs. "Look how he weakly spares the life of her who killed his people. Did I not tell you that he has a rabbit heart?" The Corchaugs moved uneasily, watching, uncertain.

"Now!" cried Nawthorne with exultance. "Let him now join the dead white men he so loves!" He lurched around with his long hunting knife and leaped at Keofferam. Keofferam stepped sideways, and as Nawthorne stumbled past him, brought the English hatchet down across the Tomac's head.

Nawthorne's brains spurted on Elizabeth's gown and on the polished floorboards. Keofferam picked up one of her dishcloths and wiped his hatchet. He spoke to the other Indians, giving orders which they obeyed at once. If Nawthorne were dead, Keofferam's authority over this particular band was undisputed. The expedition had been undertaken at Keofferam's request.

The Indian who had gone upstairs had rounded up Elizabeth's sons, and bound their wrists for captives—as Lisbet was bound. Gray-faced and trembling the boys stood in the passage. One Indian had the shrieking baby slung across his shoulders.

Keofferam nudged Elizabeth with his foot. "Go!" he said and pointed to the door. She tried to rise and fell back, panting. Keofferam looked at the blood which was soaking down her arm from Nawthorne's bullet hole. Keofferam picked her up and carried her outside, where he dumped her on the far side of the lawn near Will who lay bound and gagged in the tall grass, and near the dead watchdog who was transfixed by an arrow. The Indians herded out Lisbet and the boys, they put the unhurt Sammy down carefully by his mother's skirts. Then they went into the house and lit faggots at the fire. They ran quickly through the rooms touching their flaming brands to the curtains and the furniture, they threw firesticks upon the roof shingles.

They set the barn alight, the pigsty, dairy and the henhouses. They tossed a burning brand into the rye field. But they set no fires near the Hallet family, and they cut the bonds on Lisbet and the boys before they left.

High flames were bursting from the house and barn when the Indians filed down the path that led off the cliff to Hallet's Cove. They boarded the two war canoes and paddled up the river towards Hell Gate. In three days they would be back in the wild Corchaug country.

Elizabeth lay on the lawn where Keofferam had dumped her. She saw the red reflection on the sky, and saw the quiet stars glimmer in the arc of sky that was still black and deep. She had no thoughts. She felt a dreamy peace. The grass was cool and moist against her cheek.

The boys recovered first. Will made a convulsive motion, and they saw it by the flames' light. They both rushed to him, and cut his bonds with their knives. They pulled the gag of bearskin from his mouth. "Are ye hurt, sir?" cried Johnny. "Did they hurt you?"

Will shook his head, flexing his cramped muscles, chafing his swollen hands which throbbed and tingled as the blood flowed back in them.

"Where's Bess?" he said. "Where's my wife?"

"There—" said Robin in a stifled voice.

Will staggered to his feet, and went over to her. He crouched down and his hand slipped in the dark clotted blood on her sleeve.

"Hinnie love—" he whispered in anguish. "*Hinnie*—!"

She turned her head towards him. "I'm all right," she said faintly.

He did not dare to touch her. He looked down from her dim white face to the burning house and barns and the rye field. A great sob clotted in his chest and burst out through his lips. He had laid his head down beside hers on the grass.

"There's someone coming!" Johnny cried. "Men with lanterns on the lane!"

In Maspeth they had seen the flames. At Johnny's guiding shout a score of men came running over the lawn with cries of pity, and horror.

From New Amsterdam they sent a desperate summons to Stuyvesant, and he returned at once. He found the Fort jammed with terrified citizens. They had built a wooden curtain wall around the Fort, and at long last repaired the bastions which had always been neglected.

The Indian fury by now was spent. Many of the tribes had vanished into the wilderness they had come from. Those remaining near Manhattan, once Stuyvesant was back with all his army, were willing to negotiate for ransom of the captives they had taken.

But in those three mid-September days of the attack, a hundred Dutch folk had been slaughtered, twice that taken prisoner, and countless bouweries and crops destroyed.

The Director-General found that his rapid bloodless victory over the Swedes scarcely won him the acclaim he had expected and he set angrily but conscientiously to the handling of home affairs. The panic passed. New Netherland began to breathe again.

On October 17 when the sachem of the Hackensacks came sheepishly to New Amsterdam to return the first white captives, Elizabeth set out from Flushing with Will in a small sailing shallop. They had hired it in Flushing Harbor. Toby, at his grumpiest, was handling the tiller. Of all the voyages Elizabeth had persuaded or bribed him to undertake in her behalf, he thought this one the silliest. So, to some extent, did Will. But he could deny her nothing now.

After the Indian raid they had taken her to the Bownes at Flushing, where Hannah's devoted nursing pulled her mother through the festering and fever from the bullet wound in her arm. The wound healed well, it had not involved the bone, and Elizabeth had shown amazing fortitude; far more, Will knew, than he had shown himself.

For days he had not been able to throw off a sullen silence, while in his locked inner self he raved and stormed. It was Elizabeth this time who tried to comfort, as he had in Greenwich five years ago. "We can buy again," she said gently. "And build again."

"I've not the heart for it," he said, and would not answer otherwise to her efforts at encouragement. The buildings were destroyed, and all the beasts, the rye field was blackened to a crisp, and much of the corn as well. But they still had some money. Their cash had been hidden deep in a brick-lined cubbyhole in the great chimney, and was untouched by the fire.

"You must start again, dear love," she said at another time. "What else is there to do? We can buy here in Flushing near the Bownes. Hannah tells me that Edward Griffin has a small house and barn he'll sell. 'Twould be a place for us to live, until you can build as you like somewhere."

"I'm sick of starting over. I've not the heart for it," he repeated angrily, and stalked out of the bedroom where she lay convalescing. The Bownes tried to rally his spirits but to no avail. So did little Wickenden.

"Naow then, Mr. Hallet," said the cobbler, giving Will a compassionate smile. "Rouse tha'self, 'twas a fearful happening, but the Sweet Lord sent protection too—the children come through unscathed an' tha poor missis almost well . . . Christ gives thee comfort."

"Aye—?" said Will grim-faced, and he continued to brood, thinking of life's injustices. The mistaken hanging of his father, the arbitrary rulings of the Digbys, while they blew hot and cold; the miseries of the persecution he and Bess had suffered; and of how each time he'd thought to get ahead on his own land—in Virginia, in Greenwich, in Pequot, and finally achieved it all as he wished, at Hallet's Point—only to have his every work destroyed again.

Two things finally forced him from the black and bitter mood.

One was a talk with Hannah about Elizabeth, a scolding it was, which was so startling from Hannah, and what she said so disquieting, that Will was upset afterwards and remorseful. Though he did not let himself believe what she had said about her mother's health.

The second spur to prick his lagging courage came from Elizabeth herself. She told him one day with diffidence, transparently afraid he might be angry, that she had bought the Griffin house and land. "It need only be for a little while, if you don't like it," she said anxiously. "But we mustn't trespass on the Bownes much longer and they all say this is a fine bargain."

For a moment he was very angry, until he saw how dark her eyes were with pleading and the wish to help. Shamefaced, he muttered something noncommittal, and went to inspect her purchase. It was indeed a bargain—fine soil, good meadows both sweet and salt, the homestall already fenced, and a tight snug little house which might be easily enlarged. And there was an apple orchard, well grown and bearing. He had never been settled long enough for his own apple seedlings to mature. Tears came to his eyes as he stared at the apple trees.

He went back to Elizabeth, and kneeling by the bed, gathered her in his arms, gently so as not to hurt her wound.

He kissed her as he always used to do. She kissed him warmly in return, but there was no demand or clinging about her now. He realized as he held her now thin and frail she was, but he refused to recognize anxiety. The wound had healed, the memories of terror would recede, and she'd be well and strong again.

In a few days she was much stronger, and she awakened him one morning, and spoke with her old intensity.

"Will, listen—I have had a dream. There's something that I want to do. I must."

"What, Bess?" he said sleepily.

"In my dream I heard a voice," she said in a breathless wondering tone. "It was in the wind, a chant, a song, I hear it yet—it went like this—" She raised her head and gazed into the distance: " '*Mo-na-ke-way-y-y-go*,' it called me like that, beautiful it was. '*Mo-na-ke-way-y-y-go*,' " she sang again, three soft plaintive notes, rising on the fourth, then dropping in a sigh.

He swallowed, disturbed by the haunting sound, and more so by her intent listening look.

"Just a dream, Bess," he said. "One hears and sees strange things in dreams."

She did not heed him. "I've got to go back there. Go back today."

"Go back? You don't mean to that neck of land you used to own in Greenwich? Why, 'tis sold long ago to Jeffrey Ferris, don't you remember?" He spoke with patient calmness, for he thought the fever had returned.

"Of course I remember," she said, looking down at him with a smile. "My wits aren't wandering. 'Tis just to see it once again, that I must go. We'll hire a boat, make Toby take me since he's ashore. Tell him. Tell him I'll pay him what he asks."

"You're not strong enough yet. Wait, dear—if indeed you wish so much to go."

"*Today!*" she said. "I'll find the strength."

He started to protest again but something stopped him. He jumped out of bed to pull on his clothes. "Be ready then when I come back,' he said. "We must sail at once to get there before dark for sure."

"We?" she said. "I didn't mean to trouble *you*, Will."

"Do you think I'd let you go alone, hinnie?" he said.

It was foggy as they started out of Flushing harbor, but soon the west wind blew the mists away. Gold sparkled on the white-flecked water and stained the sharp blue October sky, where the long white mare's-tails were streaming.

Elizabeth lay in the cockpit, propped on the cushions Will had brought. She was snugly wrapped in a brown cloak of Dorothy Farrington's. Her clothes were burned, all her personal possessions gone. And she seemed not to mind. He had known her in many moods—in apathy, despair, and anger, he had known her spirit crushed as it had been at Pequot, and seen her mute with bewildered resignation. Yet now the night of terror, her injury and losses seemed not to touch her. In her eyes there was quiet expectancy. He couldn't understand it, and he asked her what she was thinking.

"I was thinking of Mrs. Hutchinson," she said. "And that the horror of her death is gone. I was spared and she was not, but I came to the brink in the same way, and it is not as one imagines."

"Don't talk about it!" he said sharply.

She smiled a little and was silent, still thinking of Anne Hutchinson. Of words Anne had spoken in her parlor that day nearly twenty years ago. The personal words that Elizabeth had long put from her mind, repudiating them with all the other teachings which had seemed to be Anne's pitiful delusion. She could not quite recapture them, those words, and yet surely they had begun. "You will have much shame—much shame and tribulation, you will forget what you have felt this day . . ." and then what . . . ?

There had been more. And another prophecy about her life, long long ago, at the beginning—who had made it?

"There's Byram Neck," said Toby brusquely. "Never did the trip so fast. Soon be at Greenwich and that blasted neck you used to own, Aunt, and which was never any good that I could see." Toby fished a fat sausage from his pocket and munched on it."

Will glanced at Elizabeth and saw that she had not heard. Her eyes were closed and against the lids she saw a cluttered attic, and the little shivering gypsy peering at her hand. Beneath them in the attic there had been the muffled noises of the great Manor House, the sound of voices long since mute. John Winthrop—the harsh stern voice of disapproval, but had it really always been that way? Had it not held many softer notes to which she would not listen? And he had suffered often, she knew that now. She sighed and thought again of all the silenced voices. Harry's laugh as he stumbled up the chimney stairs that night. Martha and Margaret, Mary too—below in the Manor House. And Jack.

Jack for whom she'd eaten her heart out. Dear brother . . . she thought tenderly, and then came remembrance of what Peyto had said as he huddled over her palm.

She opened her eyes, and gazed down at her palm. The veins showed through now, the mesh of lines had deepened in the pinkish skin, yet she could hear Peyto's whisper: "Striving ever striving for what ye can't have—hankering after freedom—ye'll get what ye want in the end, but ye won't know it at first, for it'll not be what ye thought to be seeking all the long years . . ."

What had it meant? Or nothing. Hankering, yearning— ever striving. And what was this trip today? What was the dream last night? What drove her on to this, and bore two reluctant men along with her?

Her tranquillity was shattered. She looked up at Will, and dared not say "Ah—let's turn back. I was mistaken." But he turned and met her eyes, and read what she was thinking.

"Cold feet, Bess?" he said.

"I think I've been a fool again," she answered, very low. "An obstinate fool."

He reached over and squeezed her knee. "I don't believe so." He had been thinking of the day he had discovered her here, and of the strange effect the place had on her. "A pleasant sail it is, anyway," he said lightly. "Put in there to the cove side, Toby, we'll beach her there. Not over by the sands." For Will knew that the spot he suggested was the nearest by land to the pool where he was certain Elizabeth wished to go.

"To be sure," said Toby crossly. "Ye didn't think I was going to sail all the way t'other side o' the neck, did ye?"

They all three glanced up the Great Cove, and saw the rooftops of the houses where they had lived. There was smoke coming from the chimneys. Nobody said anything. Toby ran the little shallop onto the shingle. Will helped Elizabeth out. "Can you walk so far?" he asked. "I think you want to be alone."

"Aye," she said. She looked at him with swift gratitude. At last again there was no barrier between their thoughts.

"Hurry up!" said Toby. " 'Tis midafternoon. I've no mind to dawdle here for long.'

"Leave Bess be," said Will. "Why don't you sail up the cove and see what changes have been made? I'm content here with my book and pipe."

"I might," said Toby more graciously. "We left an iron

kettle behind. Anneke's always fretting for it. I'll see if it's still there.'

Elizabeth stood a moment by the water's edge. She saw the bayberry bushes and smelled the wild grapes that were tangled amongst the saplings in the thicket. To the right, there was a giant tulip tree, and then a stand of locusts. She began to walk, and plunged into the forest through the red leaves and the flaunting ruby spears of sumac. The birds had not all left for the South. As always in this forest they swooped from branch to branch, and cawed or warbled or chirped without restraint, almost heedless of her passage.

Her feet crunched on fallen leaves, lemon-yellow or brown, except where one of the maples had released a drift of crimson through the glades.

The way was longer than she remembered, but she felt no weariness, nor was troubled with a want of breath. Her heart beat slow and strong. The earlier misgivings had vanished. A delicate excitement tingled through her body. She scrambled on through brambles, the dying meshes of jewelweed and the red-tinged creepers. She saw the three hemlocks first, towering black-green against the sky. She pushed through the last of the underbrush, and came suddenly upon the pool beneath the hemlocks and the one gray overhanging rock. The pool was smaller than she had remembered, but in the mysterious brown waters she saw the same tranquillity.

Her feet sank into the cool moss amongst the autumn-browned ferns. She leaned against the rock, waiting, watching for Sprite, the crippled white-tailed doe.

But there was no motion near the pool, except the birds. A flock of wild pigeons flew overhead while she stood there, momentarily darkening the sky. The doe was gone, was dead of course, by this time.

Bewilderment washed over her, was it the doe that she had come to find? What had compelled her against all reason, and drawn her back to this long-forgotten solitary place? She felt something brush her hand as a woolly caterpillar inched along the rock. She snatched her hand away.

There's nothing here for me, she thought, I must go back to the men, not keep them waiting. Yet still expectancy entwined with disappointment.

A chilly little wind stirred the hemlock needles and rustled the dead leaves. She could not see the sun, was was screened by the hemlock boughs.

She wrapped the cloak around her and sat down on a

rotting tree stump. Suddenly she caught the sound of movement in the bushes. She turned quickly, hopeful, relieved. Was it the doe come after all?

The bushes parted and a woman glided out and stopped beside the rock.

A woman with an empty eye socket, purple scars and long black hair. "Greeting, Missis," she said in a calm passionless voice. Her left eye narrowed and the left corner of her mouth lifted in a smile.

"Telaka . . . ?" whispered Elizabeth. A ghost—a vision, bringing little fear, but rather release and a fulfillment.

"I wait for you," said Telaka complacently. "Today you come." She had a basket of nuts in one hand, a clay pot in the other. She walked to the pool, dipped up water in the pot and drank thirstily.

Elizabeth rose and moved forward. She touched the brown arm. It was warm, not very clean, there was a mosquito bite on it. Elizabeth drew a deep breath. "Telaka—what are you doing here? I thought you were slaughtered with the rest."

"No," said Telaka. "Six escape. Keofferam and I—four others. They go to Corchaugs, I come here—to Monakewaygo."

"*Here?* You've been here, all these years, alone. I never saw you.

"Saw *you*," said Telaka. "I keep away. Manitoo not want we meet, till now."

Elizabeth sat down again upon the stump. Telaka put her pot and basket on the moss, squatted down beside them companionably.

"Keofferam wanted to kill me—did you know?" said Elizabeth after a moment. "Instead he killed Nawthorne."

"Ah—" said the squaw "Keofferam stupid. Not listen when I say Nawthorne is with Hobbomock, Nawthorne betray our people. Keofferam think always that you did it."

"Then—" said Elizabeth, "Why *didn't* he kill me? He stopped."

Telaka's eye conveyed surprise. In the slightly impatient tone which explains the obvious, she said, "Keofferam not kill because you heal his leg that time."

Elizabeth stared at the squaw. "One small unconsidered act of kindness . . . !"

Telaka shrugged. "Was enough." She pulled her basket onto her lap. Her long brown fingers sifted through the nuts, hickory and sweet chestnut. She pinched and weighed them, discarding some which rolled into the leaves. Suddenly she looked up at Elizabeth, examined her, appraising, thoughtful.

"You die pretty soon, Missis," Telaka said judicially. "Few months maybe."

Elizabeth winced and stiffened. The instinctive human panic gripped her, and then it passed. "Aye, I believe I knew it," she said. "I'm not afraid."

"I die soon too," said Telaka returning to her basket. "Will be glad."

"Glad—" Elizabeth repeated. "Ah, yes, for you, perhaps, you've nobody to leave behind, and it must be lonely here—"

Telaka put down the basket and raised her head, she turned and looked toward the west where the sunlight had begun to gild the green leaves.

"You have children," said Telaka. "They will have children, soon all this land will be theirs—no more Indians. Here on Monakewaygo will be many many white men—run all over."

"Oh no!" Elizabeth cried. "Not here, Telaka! This belonged to your people and to you—and it was mine for a little time—but—"

The squaw shook her head and interrupted sternly. "Can't keep it! Nobody can keep things long. Chekefuana tell me so."

A faint amusement rippled over Elizabeth's surface mind. But from the deeper part she spoke without volition. "And what of love, Telaka, can one keep that . . . ?"

The squaw did not answer. It was as though she did not hear. She rose slowly and walked over to Elizabeth. She took her hand. "Look—" she said, "and be quiet."

At the touch of the slim brown hand, a thrill ran up Elizabeth's arm. The pool, the rock, the hemlock trees shifted and changed focus. Each one stood out distinct and seemed to shimmer. The wind blew stronger, she heard it whispering and rushing by. A ray of sunlight slanted down between the tree trunks, it touched the pool with liquid gold.

The pool became transparent to its golden depths, and her self was plunging in those depths and yet upraised with joy upon the rushing wind. The light grew stronger and turned white. In this crystal whiteness there was ecstasy. Against the light she saw a wren fly by; the wren was made of rhythm, it flew with meaning, with a radiant meaning. There was the same meaning in the caterpillar as it inched along the rock, and the moss, and the little nuts which had rolled across the leaves.

And still the apperception grew, and the significance. The significance was bliss, it made a created whole of everything she watched and touched and heard—and the essence of this created whole was love. She felt love pouring from the light, it bathed her with music and with perfume, the love was far off at the source of light, and yet it drenched her through. And the source and she were one.

The minutes passed. The light moved softly down, and faded from the pool. The ecstasy diminished, it quietened, but in its stead came a serenity and sureness she had never known.

She felt again Telaka's hand. It was trembling. She looked at the squaw's face and no longer saw the mutilation. She saw it whole, and still touched by the afterglow.

"It's come before but not like this . . ." Elizabeth whispered. "Glimpses through a tinted Papist window, when I was a child—with Anne Hutchinson—perhaps even with a little Baptist cobbler—in my gardens—and now with Telaka . . ."

She was not talking to the squaw, but Telaka listened and nodded solemnly. "All same light," she said. "Come different ways, but from same place."

"Ah, Telaka—" Elizabeth cried. She took the squaw into her arms and kissed her twisted mouth. "Come home with me, let me take care of you for the time that's left to us. Don't stay here alone!"

There was an instant when Telaka's body softened, and she leaned against Elizabeth, but then she drew away. "I stay here, Missis," she said. "Better so." She reached down quickly for the basket of nuts and put it in Elizabeth's hand. "For the children—" she said. And she was gone, gliding off into the forest as she had come.

Elizabeth turned and left the pool. She walked back through the tangled underbrush, and when she reached the little beach, Will came running to her. "Hinnie, hinnie—I was worried. I tried to find you—" He checked himself, staring at the face she turned up to him. Radiance. A transfiguration the like of which he'd never seen.

"What's happened to you?" he whispered, staring. "My God, you're beautiful! What happened in there?"

She tried to answer but she could not. She put the basket of nuts down and held her hands out to him, smiling. "I would tell you, Will darling, but I can't, except—except that all is changed and now I *know*."

"Changed . . ." he repeated, very nearly dismayed. She seemed far from him, untouchable, shining with a young and mysterious loveliness. Was that a trick of the gathering twilight? But he knew it was not, and her voice had altered too, it held the startling lilt of joy.

"But you must be able to tell me *something!*" he said, taking her hands in his. "I'm at a loss. You look as though a candle had been lighted inside you."

She understood his urgency and she clasped his hands tight, and searched for words. Then she said, "Perhaps I can put it this way, as you did once. I've found at last that 'Religion is not a melancholy. The Spirit of God is not a dampe.' "

He swallowed. "Have you, Bess?" he said humbly. "Have you?"

"Aye." She sat down on the bank, and after a moment he sat down beside her.

"How else have you changed?" he asked anxiously. "Not towards me, I hope, not your love?"

"Aye," she said again, looking at him with a tender smile. "For now there is nothing *but* love for you. The jealousies and the fears are gone. I am in you and you in me. We are *all* one."

He did not understand, but far below reason he felt a melting and an awareness. He put his arm around her, and she rested against his shoulder, quickly responsive as she had always been. As their bodies had always been to each other. He felt a stirring of passion, and the desire to kiss her, but he did not. The closeness between them was too sweet for interruption.

They sat for some time looking at the waters of the Cove. Then Elizabeth said, "Will, where's Toby?"

"Why, down there . . ." he said rousing himself and pointing. "Do you see his riding lights? He's sailing back there. He'll be in a hurry to get home."

"Poor Toby," she said laughing. "And yet I think we cannot permit him to sail home tonight."

"Whyever not?" Will asked astonished. "Is there some other place you want to go, hinnie?"

"Aye," she said. "Where I should have gone long ago. To see Thomas and my grandchild."

He made a sharp sound. "Not *Thomas Lyon!* Why, Bess, you vowed to hate him unto death."

"I know," she said. "It was a stupid vow. I no longer feel the hurtful thing that prompted it. It's vanished in the light. And I do feel that my Joan's little girl has need of me; at least I must find out." He looked so stunned that she laughed again softly. "If Keofferam showed mercy, do you not think that I might?"

Will was silent, awed by the change in her, almost envious of whatever it was that had happened to her back there by the pool, yet deriving from it and from her love his own renewal of courage and acceptance.

She shivered in the increasingly cold wind, and he drew his arm tighter around her. They sat quietly on the bank watching the lanterns bob on the shallop as Toby steered it down the cove towards Monakewaygo.

HISTORICAL AFTERWORD

THE LAST direct documentary reference to Elizabeth is her purchase of land in Flushing and Newtown, Long Island, from Edward Griffin, October first, 1655, though there is an interesting item in the Journal of Captain Brian Newton of New Amsterdam in which he tells of a trip through Hell Gate, "Where William Hallet's house and plantation formerly stood, which was laid waste by the Indians, about September of the year 1655."

William Hallet became "Schout" or chief official of Flushing in 1656, and was shortly thereafter temporarily imprisoned and banished by Stuyvesant for allowing William Wickenden to hold Baptist conventicles in Hallet's house. Hallet was released but deprived of office. Toby (Tobias) Feake replaced him as Schout. William eventually married again, and he died, prosperous, at the age of ninety-four.

Lisbet (Elizabeth Feake) married Captain John Underhill after his wife's death, in 1659. Hannah Feake and her John Bowne were duly married in 1656, and both became famous and persecuted Quakers. Their biographies are readily accessible, but a reminder should be given here about the "Flushing Remonstrance" of 1657, which demanded tolerance for all the sects gathered at Flushing. This Remonstrance played a considerable part in the eventual establishment of religious freedom in this country.

Elizabeth's daughters had many estimable descendants; so did young John Feake (including Robert Feke the painter) and her two Hallet sons, William, Jr., and Samuel.

Robert Feake, the elder, died, unimproved, at Watertown, Mass., in Samuel Thatcher's home, 1661.

John Winthrop, Jr., became Governor of Connecticut Colony, and, at the English Restoration, personally procured a charter from Charles II, returned home with it, and thereafter governed the entire state of Connecticut until his death in 1676.

Anya Seton

Tempestuous Novels of Passion and Violence

☐	AVALON	23308-1	1.95
☐	DEVIL WATER	22888-6	1.95
☐	FOXFIRE	X2916	1.75
☐	GREEN DARKNESS	C2728	1.95
☐	KATHERINE	23497-5	2.25
☐	MY THEODOSIA	23034-1	1.95
☐	THE TURQUOISE	23088-0	1.95

A-25

PRIZE-WINNING NOVELS

- ☐ THEM—Oates   23467-3   2.25
- ☐ THE CENTAUR—Updike   22922-X   1.75
- ☐ TALES OF THE SOUTH   23669-2   1.95
      PACIFIC—Michener
- ☐ THE KEEPERS OF THE HOUSE—Grau   23031-7   1.50
- ☐ ANGLE OF REPOSE—Stegner   C2717   1.95
- ☐ CHIMERA—Barth   23152-6   1.95

Buy them at your local bookstores or use this handy coupon for ordering:

Please allow 4 to 5 weeks for delivery. This offer expires 1/79.